Praise for

The Decameron

"Celebrated in the Renaissance as the foremost stylist of Italian prose, Boccaccio has seldom met his match in English translation. Giving us a fresh new translation of the author's masterpiece, Wayne Rebhorn captures the vibrancy, vitality, and variety of its many distinctive styles. His fluid and dynamic rendition hits the mark on every page."

—William J. Kennedy, Cornell University

"The *Decameron*, an inexhaustibly rich late medieval feast of narrative cunning, bawdy humor, and sly wit, is a celebration of the sheer pleasure of being alive.... With gusto and energy, Wayne Rebhorn has risen to the daunting task of translating this great work into lively, contemporary, American-inflected English."

—Stephen Greenblatt, Harvard University

"A lively, readable translation of the greatest short story collection of all time. It manages to be a twenty-first-century American rendering without losing the flavor of fourteenth-century Tuscany. The laugh-out-loud quality of Boccaccio's delicious vernacular is admirably preserved."

—Leonard Barkan, Princeton University

"A strikingly modern translation of Boccaccio's medieval Italian classic.... Rebhorn's translation is eminently readable and devoid of the stilted, antiquated speech associated with the classics. His translation's accessibility allows for the timeless humanity of the work to shine through."

—*Publishers Weekly*

"This translation rediscovers for the reader the authentic qualities of the original: the inventiveness, rhythm, tonalities, oscillations, and disguises—the endlessly fresh, fascinating play of language through which Boccaccio retrieves the values, passions, imagination, and eccentricities that make livable the human world."

—Giuseppe Mazzotta, Yale University

"Rebhorn's translation skillfully reflects the facets of Boccaccio's style, by turns comic, low-down and dirty, pathos-ridden, ironic and mocking, surprisingly delicate, always charming."

—David Quint, Yale University

"Rebhorn's vibrant translation makes Boccaccio's scoundrels and victims alike come back to life."

—Jane Tylus, New York University

"Rebhorn's translation of The *Decameron* is a thoughtful piece of work, with populist intentions. With a concern for the common reader, he has tried to make the slang sound natural, and he succeeds. If you want the true, mixed, fourteenth-century book that Boccaccio wrote, choose Rebhorn."

—Joan Acocella, *The New Yorker*

"This superb, powerful, beautifully crafted, and indeed definitive, translation of the *Decameron* introduces readers anew to the sparkling and colorful writing of a pre-Renaissance Italian master."

—Valeria Finucci, Duke University

THE NORTON LIBRARY

The Decameron

WAYNE A. REBHORN is the Mildred Hajek Vacek and John Roman Vacek Chair in English at the University of Texas, where he teaches English, Italian, and comparative literature. His translation of Boccaccio's *Decameron* won the 2014 PEN Center USA's Literary Award for Translation.

THE NORTON LIBRARY

2020–2021

For a complete list of titles in the Norton Library, visit
wwnorton.com/norton-library

THE NORTON LIBRARY

Boccaccio
The Decameron

Translated and Abridged by

Wayne A. Rebhorn

W. W. NORTON & COMPANY
Independent Publishers Since 1923

W. W. Norton & Company has been independent since its founding in 1923, when William Warder Norton and Mary D. Herter Norton first published lectures delivered at the People's Institute, the adult education division of New York City's Cooper Union. The firm soon expanded its program beyond the Institute, publishing books by celebrated academics from America and abroad. By midcentury, the two major pillars of Norton's publishing program—trade books and college texts—were firmly established. In the 1950s, the Norton family transferred control of the company to its employees, and today—with a staff of five hundred and hundreds of trade, college, and professional titles published each year—W. W. Norton & Company stands as the largest and oldest publishing house owned wholly by its employees.

Editor: Pete Simon
Associate Editor: Katie Pak
Project Editor: Maura Gaughan
Manufacturing by LSC Communications
Book design by Westchester Publishing Services
Production Manager: Jeremy Burton

Library of Congress Cataloging-in-Publication Data

Names: Boccaccio, Giovanni, 1313–1375, author. | Rebhorn, Wayne A.,
    1943–, translator.
Title: The decameron / Boccaccio; translated by Wayne A. Rebhorn.
Other titles: Decamerone. English
Description: New York, N.Y. : W. W. Norton & Company, [2021] |
    Series: The Norton library
Identifiers: LCCN 2020023315 | **ISBN 9780393427882 (paperback)**
Subjects: LCSH: Plague—Europe—History—Fiction. | Storytelling—Fiction.
Classification: LCC PQ4272.E5 A3613 2021 | DDC 853/.1—dc23
LC record available at https://lccn.loc.gov/2020023315

ISBN: 978-0-393-42788-2 (pbk.)

W. W. Norton & Company, Inc., 500 Fifth Avenue, New York, N.Y. 10110
    www.wwnorton.com

W. W. Norton & Company Ltd., 15 Carlisle Street, London W1D 3BS

1 2 3 4 5 6 7 8 9 0

Contents

DAY 8

night to a certain spot, where he is thrown into a
ditch by Buffalmacco and left to wallow in filth.

Torello is transported by magic in a single night to
Pavia, where his wife's second marriage is about to
be celebrated. She recognizes him, and he then
returns with her to his house.

Induced by the entreaties of his vassals to take a
wife, the Marquis of Saluzzo, wanting to choose
one his own way, selects the daughter of a peasant.
After he has had two children with her, he makes it
look to her as though they have been put to death.
Later on, pretending to have grown weary of her,
he claims he has married another woman and
arranges to have his own daughter brought home
as though she were his bride, meanwhile having
turned his wife out of doors wearing nothing but
her shift. On finding that she has borne everything
with patience, however, he takes her back home
again, dearer to him than ever, shows her their
grown-up children, and honors her as Marchioness
and causes everyone else to do so as well.

Introduction

The *Decameron*'s status as a classic is demonstrated, albeit indirectly, by the fact that it has been repeatedly translated into English (and many other languages) over the centuries, including some half dozen times in the last sixty years. And yet, if readers in the English-speaking world today know anything at all about Giovanni Boccaccio's vast collection of one hundred stories told by ten narrators over the course of ten days (*Decameron* comes from the Greek *deca*, meaning "ten," and *hemeron*, meaning "days"), they usually think of it as a collection of salacious, ribald, even "dirty" stories. This is true enough, even though it contains many tales that do not fit into that category. In most people's minds, the typical tale that defines the collection chronicles the ways in which clever people—mostly men, but often women—deceive others, who almost always come off as gullible, naive, and linguistically challenged. We are invited to identify with the former, and to enjoy a vicarious, triumphant pleasure as we watch them dupe their victims. For the most part, Boccaccio wants us to laugh, or at least smile, as we read his stories, and to forget, for the time being, the harsh realities of the world. This is, of course, a worthy end, but it only begins to explain why we should treasure the *Decameron* as a classic.

In his native Italy, Boccaccio is considered one of *le Tre Corone* (the three crowns) of Italian literature, along with Dante Alighieri, the creator in Italian of the long epic poem, *The Divine Comedy*; and Petrarch, whose *Canzoniere* (*Song Book*), the first long sequence of lyric poems about love, defined both the lyric and the lyric sequence for subsequent generations of Italian and European poets. Boccaccio is in their company because he is credited with inventing in his *Decameron* a rich and sophisticated prose style in Italian that rivals the artistry of these exemplary poets. Moreover, it was the first "framed" collection of stories in Europe. Although there had been framed collections in the East before then, the Arabian *Thousand and One Nights* being the best known today, and they may have influenced Boccaccio's work by way of various intermediaries, his *Decameron* established the genre for the West, influencing collections in Italian as well as in other languages, including Chaucer's *Canterbury Tales*, the most famous framed collection of tales in English. But the *Decameron*'s historical importance does not necessarily make it a "classic," and translations, such as this one, can only suggest the stylistic richness that made the work the model for Italian prose style in the years after its appearance. As a result, the *Decameron* has seemed destined to remain something of a stealth classic, at least in the English-speaking world. But in this introduction, I hope to show why it is—or should be—a genuine classic, for it is a book that still speaks to us, no matter what language we are reading it in, and it deserves to have its own distinctive place as a masterpiece alongside the works of Homer, Shakespeare, Cervantes, and Tolstoy.

To understand the *Decameron*, we need to place it (and its author) in historical context, in the period of the Black Death, the great plague that swept through Europe in 1348 and killed off approximately 60 percent of the population of Florence. Boccaccio uses the devastation wrought by the plague as the frame, or setting, for his work, and it becomes the motive that prompts his narrators to flee the city into beautiful palaces in an idyllic countryside where they decide to pass the time by telling stories. In the simplest sense, the stories of the *Decameron* can thus be read as a kind of "escapist literature." After all, when living through a horrific calamity that has devastated the society and culture of Florence as well as most of the rest of Europe, where can one find something like a normal world—and in Boccaccio's text, often a happy one—except by escaping into the imaginary realms we create in the stories we tell? These stories have been offering a similar escape for readers ever since.

But the *Decameron* offers us much more than the temporary pleasures of escapism. In fact, it may be misleading to talk about escapism at all. The *Decameron* is, to be sure, about the joy human beings can have, however temporary, by immersing themselves in the fictional worlds of stories. Those worlds are not, however, so much an escape from reality as a re-creation or reimagining of it. In essence, the group's leaving Florence behind is a step toward freedom—artistic, social, cultural, even political. As they depart from the disorder of their city, they enter a space that offers them an opportunity to reflect on, indeed to rethink, the basic nature of their society and to reconsider some of its rules and laws and limitations. Although they may not expressly say so, through their stories they imagine a society that is focused on the basic need human beings have for happiness in *this* world. Consequently, among other things, their stories celebrate the body and its pleasures—including some illicit ones—that offer an alternative or a correction to their "normal" social order that defined itself through many kinds of rules and restrictions that meant an inevitable repression of people's needs and desires.

Boccaccio's Life

Giovanni Boccaccio was born during the summer of 1313 most likely in or near the Tuscan town of Certaldo, roughly twenty-five miles southwest of Florence. A bastard, he was quickly legitimized by his father, a man from Certaldo named Boccaccino di Chellino, who had relocated to Florence around 1300 where he worked for the powerful banking firm owned by the Bardi family. Growing up in Florence, Boccaccio was encouraged to study Dante's poetry by the father of one of his closest friends, and he would be deeply influenced by Dante's works throughout his life. When Boccaccio's father went to Naples in 1326 to assume a position in the Bardi bank there, his son accompanied him. After spending six unproductive years working in his father's bank, Boccaccio was allowed to enter the Neapolitan *Studium*, essentially the university, where he fitfully studied canon (that is, Church) law, but never took a degree. Instead, he had an opportunity to deepen his knowledge of a variety of fields, especially literature, which was his real passion. The Kingdom of Naples, which included all of southern Italy, was ruled by Robert the Wise (born 1277, ruled 1309–43), a member of the Angevin dynasty, which controlled the area from 1266 until the middle of the fifteenth century. Boccaccio gained entrance to Robert's feudal, French-speaking court because of his father's high position in the Bardi bank, and it was here that he formed a largely positive image of aristocratic life in the late Middle Ages. It was here as well that he began writing vernacular works in a medieval vein: long romances, mythological poems, and allegories of various sorts.

When his father left the Bardi bank in 1338 and returned to Florence, having apparently gone bankrupt, Boccaccio reluctantly followed him, most likely in 1340–41. Failing to find a way to return to Naples, he remained in Florence with his father, an elderly widower, as well as with two of the five illegitimate children he would sire during the course of his life. (None of them managed to survive into adulthood.) During this period in Florence, Boccaccio composed more vernacular works in various medieval genres. Because of political chaos in Florence, he moved to Ravenna, where records place him in 1346. Then, in 1348 Florence was struck by the Black Death, the worst plague in European history. No hard evidence exists that Boccaccio was actually in Florence when the plague broke out—indeed, there are records of his having been in the town of Forlí in late 1347 and early 1348—and many elements in his description of the disease come from an eighth-century text. Nevertheless, his father was in charge of organizing relief during the epidemic, and he, as well as many others, may have told Boccaccio many details about the disaster. As a result, most historians consider Boccaccio's description of what happened in Florence relatively reliable.

Boccaccio probably wrote the *Decameron* between 1349 and 1351 or 1352, although he may have been assembling materials he would use in it well before the advent of the plague in 1348. The writing of the *Decameron* came at a turning point in Boccaccio's career. For in 1350 he met Petrarch, who is usually considered the father of the Renaissance, insofar as the Renaissance can be defined as an attempt to revive (*renaissance* means "rebirth") classical Latin and classical culture more generally. Petrarch used his considerable literary prestige to propagandize for that revival, and Boccaccio was persuaded to join him in doing so. What this meant for the latter was that he turned away from the vernacular and began producing works in Latin that were the result of his study of classical materials and that were mainly philological or historical in character. (Indeed, some of his scholarly encyclopedic works about antiquity were still in use as late at the eighteenth century.) And in 1359–60 he persuaded the Florentine government to establish a chair in Greek at the university, for if the revival of antiquity meant the revival of Latin culture, it also meant reviving Greek as well. Ironically, neither Petrarch nor Boccaccio really knew the Greek language they valued so highly.

By 1368, Boccaccio had essentially retired to Certaldo, where he spent time revising his Latin works. In 1370–71 he copied the entire *Decameron* out in his own hand, thus suggesting how deeply he was attached to it. This manuscript, known as the Hamilton codex, is in Berlin and is the basis for all modern editions of the work. In 1373 the Florentine government invited Boccaccio to give a series of public lectures on Dante, which, for the first time in his life, assured him a dependable, steady income, but he had gotten only as far as the seventeenth canto of the *Inferno* before he died. He was preceded in death the year before by Petrarch, whose passing he commemorated in a sonnet, the last poem in his collected *Rime* (Poems). Boccaccio was famously fat and suffered from a variety of illnesses in his last years that finally led to his demise in Certaldo on December 21, 1375.

Boccaccio: Medieval or Renaissance?

Boccaccio's early medieval works still enjoy some limited success today, but primarily with students specializing in medieval literature, and the Latin works he produced after meeting Petrarch are really of interest only to scholars. But the *Decameron*, produced in the middle of Boccaccio's career change from medieval vernacular poet to proto-Renaissance Latin scholar, lives on. It takes a set of medieval genres and fills them with Renaissance themes and characters, creating a masterpiece that is, perhaps confusingly at times, both medieval and Renaissance all at once.

Boccaccio's ten narrators—seven women and three men—tell their tales on ten separate days spread over a period of two weeks. (They take two pairs of Fridays and Saturdays off for personal hygiene and religious observances.) By thus producing one hundred stories, Boccaccio made his text recall Dante's *Divine Comedy* with its one hundred cantos. That resemblance was also enhanced by many textual references within the work to Dante's epic and by Boccaccio's expanding the materials in the frame immediately after Days 3 and 6, thus dividing the work into three large sections that might recall the three divisions of Dante's work. Of course, the *Decameron* is not about the spiritual journey of a pilgrim going to Paradise by way of Hell and Purgatory. Its concern is with earthly matters, and it emphasizes the body and the body's pleasures. The very first sentence of Boccaccio's work does not place its author, like Dante, in a dark and scary wood; instead, the very first word of the *Decameron* is *umana*, an adjective meaning both "human" and "humane," thus underscoring its difference from the work of Boccaccio's great predecessor. Dante taught readers how to gain heavenly salvation; Boccaccio's work is about our life in this very human world and how salvation of sorts could be found there.

Although the *Decameron* doesn't share the classicizing bent that would later define an important aspect of the Renaissance, it does look forward to several aspects of the age to come. For instance, in its emphasis on worldly pleasures, its embrace of sex and the body, and its investment in things material, the *Decameron* anticipates the increasingly worldly and secular side of the Renaissance. In addition, although there is very little in the book to suggest the notion of "self-fashioning" that most modern scholars think of as defining another key aspect of the Renaissance— very little to suggest that Boccaccio imagined human identity as something achieved through one's efforts rather than ascribed to one at birth—he is nevertheless intensely aware of the social mobility that was occurring in his world, and he repeatedly has his characters play roles and adopt different identities, however temporary they may be, creating and re-creating themselves in their clever verbal performances.

This might make the *Decameron* seem a revolutionary work, but the storytellers do not advocate any sort of direct social transformation of Florence. Later in the Renaissance, the humanist Sir Thomas More would imagine a brave new world called "Utopia" as an improvement over the England he lived in—although even then he was careful to make extensive use of irony to qualify his ideal lest he run afoul of the established authorities. After all, the very word *utopia* means "nowhere." While Boccaccio is no revolutionary, let alone a utopian visionary, he does include at least one story in the *Decameron* that shows how the intelligence and linguistic skills of his protagonists can actually lead to social change. That story is the seventh of Day 6, which celebrates the intelligence that is manifested in clever quips and retorts. In this particular story, set in the city of Prato, which was only a few miles from Florence, a certain Madonna Filippa has been caught with her lover by her husband who decides to revenge this insult to his honor by hauling her before a court and accusing her of adultery, which, we are told, was a capital offense. In an unusual move, the lady presents her own defense. After getting her husband to admit that he was never denied her sexual favors, she asks the judge a clever rhetorical question: if her husband was always satisfied with what she gave him, "what was I supposed to do—in fact, what am I to do now—with the leftovers? Should I throw them to the dogs?" (p. 286) Madonna Filippa's clever equation of sex with food moves the courtroom, which is packed with practically everyone living in Prato, to explode in laughter, with the result that not only does the judge declare her innocent but the citizens of Prato actually change their harsh law against adultery. If one wants to think of the *Decameron* as having a revolutionary agenda, this story would certainly support it. To be sure, it is set in Prato, not Florence, but Boccaccio could be suggesting the possibility of new ways of thinking for his fellow citizens: if Prato can make such changes, why can't Florence? But this revolutionary potential is merely implicit in the other stories of the *Decameron*. What is most revealing in this regard is that at the end of the work, the ten young men and women simply return to Florence and resume their normal lives. They certainly do not come back with a political agenda. But that does not prevent the readers of Boccaccio's work from thinking what Florence—or any society—would look like if one could just escape from it long enough to imagine an alternative to the status quo.

Boccaccio's Storytellers and Their Problematic Tales

Boccaccio's storytellers themselves are less fact than fiction, although critics have spent a great deal of effort vainly trying to identify them. Their fictional status is dramatized by such things as the aliases Boccaccio supplies for all of them, supposedly to hide their real identities, although Boccaccio teases us with the aliases he uses because all of them mean something and thus seem to point to the attribute of a real person. The speakers' fictional status is also underscored by the numbers involved: there are ten storytellers, including seven women and three men. All of these numbers had allegorical meanings in the Middle Ages. The number seven, for example, had important associations with such things as the days of the week, the seven (known) planets, the seven virtues, and the seven liberal arts. Like seven, the number three could suggest the Trinity or the three Graces, and it was identified as the male number in some contemporary numerological systems. Finally, the number ten is the result of adding one, the number of unity or perfection or God, to nine, which was considered the "golden number" since, among other things, it was the result of multiplying three, the number of the Trinity, by itself, and thus, in a sense, perfecting it.

This and other examples of number symbolism in the *Decameron* are clearly indebted not just to medieval thought in general, but more specifically to Dante's practices in the *Divine Comedy*. The latter consists of three canticles that, in turn, are composed of thirty-four cantos (an initial threshold canto plus thirty-three others) in *Inferno*, followed by thirty-three cantos each in *Purgatorio* and *Paradiso*, thus making a total of one hundred cantos—or the number ten multiplied by itself and thus perfected. Dante's number symbolism ultimately points to the mysterious, mystical identity of God (one) with the other persons of the Trinity (three). The important point to make here, however, is that although the numbers used in Boccaccio's work may echo Dante's, it would be hard to argue that they aim at such spiritual ends. Rather, they may be seen as Boccaccio's way of presenting his work less as a homage to Dante's than as a challenge, or at least an alternative, to it.

One of the most important things Boccaccio is doing by using fictional names and allegorical numbers for his storytellers is preparing readers to think in allegorical terms about the stories the group will tell. Thinking in allegorical terms was, of course, the default position for Christian readers in the Middle Ages, who had been trained since antiquity to think about the Bible as well as a wide variety of both secular and religious texts, that every narrative—if not everything in the universe—could and should be interpreted allegorically. Like Dante's, those allegories were reassuringly tied to the truths of Christianity. By contrast, the one hundred stories of the *Decameron* are anything but religious in character. Not only do they regularly satirize priests, friars, and nuns but they are often downright irreligious and even parody sacred language by applying it to secular, frequently sexual, activities.

Possibly more important, while the allegorical significance of works like Dante's can usually be figured out, albeit with difficulty, by reference to Christian thought, Boccaccio's stories resist such orthodox interpretations, with the result that they essentially challenge us over and over again to think long and hard about what we have read. Thus, although the *Decameron* may offer us an escape into various fictional worlds, it does not allow us any escape from the difficult, complicated process of interpretation. We may even be left feeling, in the case of some stories, that their meaning is, finally, undecidable, if only because so many meanings are possible. This is not a sign of failure, however. For one of the features of the *Decameron* that justifies its being labeled a classic is the brilliance with which Boccaccio focuses our attention repeatedly on the problematic nature of interpretation. Although interpretation here involves deciding the meaning of stories, we are actually being trained to become better interpreters overall, not just of literary fictions but of the people, issues, and events that constitute the "stories" we live through in what we like to think of as the "real" world.

As an example of the kind of interpretational problems Boccaccio presents us with, let us take the very first story in the collection, that of Ciappelletto. The narrator, Panfilo, attempts to guide—or limit—our interpretation of this character and his story by pronouncing him at the beginning and the end to be the worst human being who has ever lived. The narrative, however, complicates Panfilo's judgment. It begins with Ciappelletto's being sent to Burgundy to collect money owed the French king, a job he actually does quite honestly. But then he succumbs to a fatal illness, and his hosts, two Florentine usurers, worry that if he reveals all his misdeeds in his last confession—or if he refuses to confess at all—he will be seen as the worst of sinners and they, as well as he, will be assaulted by the locals. They are equally worried, however, that if they just chuck Ciappelletto out onto the street, they will be equally exposed to the wrath of the people. Ciappelletto's response is reassuring: find me a simple (that is, simple-minded) holy friar to confess to, he says, and their problem will be solved. Ciappelletto then proceeds to concoct an utterly unbelievable confession for the friar in which he makes himself appear more saintly than the saints. The friar is completely taken in by Ciappelletto's fantastic fiction, and he is indeed made a saint by the story's end. The reader, of course, is not fooled for a minute.

The real problem for the reader here—as with many of Boccaccio's stories—is how to interpret Panfilo's account of what Ciappelletto has done. Although Panfilo tells us Ciappelletto was the worst of men and is very likely spending eternity in Hell, that just intensifies the interpretational problem we are left with: how can we not side with this clever trickster as he pulls the wool over the eyes of the simple friar? In fact, don't we feel a sneaky admiration for him as he fabricates a story—a deathbed confession!—that would make anyone believe him to be a truly holy figure—except, of course, for more sophisticated interpreters, among whose number we count ourselves? Indeed, do we not admire him for facing unfazed the possibility of eternal damnation in order to remain true to the wicked principles by which he has lived his life? Could it be that we are being presented with Ciappelletto as some sort of hero—or perhaps as an anti-hero—rather than simply as a terrible sinner who deserves to suffer in Hell for his crimes? The ten young men and women agreed before they left Florence that they would refrain from telling stories that recalled the misery and death brought about by the plague back in Florence, but Panfilo violates their agreement by speaking of death here in the very first story. In this case, however, Ciappelletto is indeed staring death in the face, but he is laughing at it. At the same time, he is also laughing at God and at a church that uses the fear of eternal damnation to enforce doctrinal obedience. Ciappelletto's laughter allows us—vicariously of course—to escape such a fear. Like so much of the laughter in Boccaccio's book, it is profoundly liberating.

Interpreting the *Decameron*

If deciding on the meaning of individual stories in Boccaccio's work is problematic, that is only one of many interpretational challenges the reader is confronted with. I have already stressed the fact that the *Decameron* is a framed collection of stories, which means that every story is told by *someone*. In other words, we are not dealing with the omniscient narrator one encounters in, say, much of nineteenth-century fiction, but rather with a host of different narrators whose stories necessarily represent their viewpoints, values, and prejudices. Although the stories, when taken together, offer us Boccaccio's distinctive take on the many functions of storytelling—a temporary escape from reality, a challenge to the status quo and especially to religion, a celebration of the human body and its pleasures—the fact that each story is mediated through the personality of its teller means that we cannot simply read it as a full and complete expression of Boccaccio's views. For instance, in the story discussed earlier, the first story of the first day, does the narrator, Panfilo, with his insistence that Ciappelletto will spend eternity in Hell, speak for Boccaccio? Or do the two usurers, who almost admire Ciappelletto's daring mockery of religion? And when the other nine storytellers laugh in response to Panfilo's story, are we to take that as an expression of Boccaccio's meaning—and if so, what can that meaning be?

Furthermore, what do the stories mean when we read them not in isolation, but as responses or rejoinders to *other* stories? This aspect of the *Decameron* is most apparent if we think of Dioneo and the tales he tells. As the bad boy of the group, Dioneo, who is granted the right to tell the last story on every day (starting with Day 2), tells stories that are not only ribald, clever, and extremely irreverent, but that can usually be read as parodies of the stories preceding them and thus of the topic chosen for each day's storytelling. By giving Dioneo the last word each day, is Boccaccio inviting us to see him as his creator's spokesman? If so, how are we then to evaluate the meanings of the nine stories that precede Dioneo's? For example, the topic for Day 5 is comedy, which means the stories in it celebrate marriage—that is, the union of one man and one woman. But Dioneo tells a tale whose protagonist is a married man who is a homosexual, and it ends with the man, his wife, and the man's young lover all spending the night in bed together. Dioneo says several times essentially that homosexuality is wicked, but the story really presents it as just another variant of human sexual relations. So, should the reader adopt this viewpoint and see all the preceding stories as too limited in their view of sex, marriage, and comedy, or is Dioneo just playing with the other storytellers—and us—by extending their notions in an unexpected way?

I have been speaking of the *Decameron* as a framed collection, but it would be more accurate to say that it really has two distinct frames. The first involves the story of the devastation of Florence by the Black Death, the decision of the ten young men and women to leave the city and stay in the countryside for a period of two weeks, and their spending ten days telling stories. But surrounding this frame is another one that presents Boccaccio speaking in his own voice in the Preface, the Introduction to Day 4, and the Author's Conclusion. In the Preface he explains his motive for writing—namely to supply an "escape" through fictions (often involving illicit sex) for love-sick women who are trapped in their homes. He then uses the Introduction to Day 4 to defend his decision from male readers who think his choice of a female audience is beneath him and who criticize the fact that his stories celebrate the human body and its pleasures. Boccaccio defends himself again in the Conclusion, insisting that if readers find sexual meanings in such things as mortars and pestles, this is their problem. There can be no doubt that Boccaccio is mounting a real defense of his work and his choice of an audience—as well as defending the value of literature, however "low" it might be. But can one really square his supposed admiration for women with the way that many of them are presented in his stories, some of whom seem like little more than sex toys for men and who often lack the kind of agency that speech, for example, might grant them? And do any of his readers really fall for his disingenuous claim that they, rather than Boccaccio himself, are to blame for finding sexual meanings in mortars and pestles and the many metaphors he uses for sexual intercourse? Boccaccio's Preface may make him seem some sort of proto-feminist; his defense of the human body and especially of sexual pleasure may make him seem ahead of his time; and his claim that his readers are to blame if they find sexual meanings in his clever euphemisms may make him seem the innocent target of malicious criticism. But does all that really undermine the values he tries so hard to defend? In the Introduction to Day 4, he tells a story about a young man whose father has kept him in a mountain retreat so that he may never see women and lust after them, but the first time he goes to Florence with his father he encounters a bevy of beautiful women and insists that they are the most wonderful things he has ever seen and that he wants to take one home with him. Boccaccio's story is offered as proof that sexual desire is natural and normal and cannot be repressed. Stories are not really proof, of course, but this one does seem consistent with what Boccaccio shows us repeatedly in his stories.

There are two final interpretive challenges facing us as readers. The first is the problem of defining the topics the storytellers choose to talk about. They often seem simple enough at first glance, but they become more complicated, more nuanced, as the ten young men and women tell stories about them. For instance, the power of Fortune is the topic of the second day, and Fortune may seem like a fairly clear concept: it is the name of a goddess who has existed since Roman antiquity and who essentially stands for the uncertainty and unpredictability of worldly events. But how exactly does Fortune work its way in the world, how powerful is it, and does it spell inevitable defeat for human beings who are attempting to control their destinies by using their wits, their verbal skills, and their ability to tell stories? Or take the topic of the very last day, called variously magnanimity, generosity, or liberality. On the surface, this too is simple: it means giving up something one longs for, renouncing one's personal desires, and serving others rather than oneself. But are the protagonists of the stories on Day 10 really all that self-sacrificing and altruistic? Indeed, in the very last story of the collection—about the long-suffering "patient Griselda" whose husband, Gualtieri, subjects his wife to a series of arbitrary, unprovoked tests of her loyalty that become increasingly brutal until he finally feels he has tested her enough and restores everything he has supposedly taken from her—we must wonder who is the exemplar of magnanimity here? If Gualtieri is considered magnanimous, then magnanimity looks like sadism; if Griselda, it looks like masochism. Petrarch, in his own version of the tale, solved the problem the story presents by allegorizing it: Griselda represents the human soul, and Gualtieri is God, who repeatedly tests us to see if we are truly worthy of salvation. But Boccaccio is not Petrarch, just as he is certainly not Dante.

This puzzle about just what each day's topic means in concrete terms applies to all of the topics the storytellers choose throughout the *Decameron*. What is the meaning of *industria*—which I have translated as "resourcefulness," but could also be rendered as persistence or just plain hard work—if we try to define it on the basis of the stories from Day 3 that supposedly illustrate it? The same could be said of tragedy on Day 4, comedy on Day 5, witty quips and repartee on Day 6, and the trickery practiced by the protagonists of Days 7 and 8. The topics chosen for these eight days in the *Decameron*—and the implied topics of Days 1 and 9—provide the storytellers with a shared point of departure for their tales, but the speakers take different routes and reach different destinations. And it is therefore up to us as readers to figure out just where they have gone.

Finally, how can we interpret the evolving structure of the *Decameron* as it moves from one day's topic and the stories it generates to the next? Despite all the allegorical complexities of Dante's *Divine Comedy*, the journey that Dante the pilgrim makes through its one hundred cantos is straightforward. He comes to know the nature of sin by descending through Hell, experiences what penance and repentance require as he climbs the mountain of Purgatory, and achieves salvation as he ascends through the heavens until he comes face to face with God. With his one hundred stories, Boccaccio alludes to Dante's one hundred cantos, just as he alludes to Dante the pilgrim's journey by starting with a story about the worst man who ever lived and is, most likely, rotting in Hell, and by ending with a story about the "patient" Griselda who might be considered, from a certain viewpoint, to be the saintliest of women and who will surely, one day, enjoy the pleasures of Paradise. But the *Decameron* does not take us, in some straightforward manner, along a path that begins in Hell, passes through Purgatory, and finally brings us to Heaven. Considering all the different locations in which Boccaccio sets his tales, one might be tempted to say that like his individual stories, his work as a whole is all over the map, although it is a map that does have a fair number of recognizable landmarks.

Instructively, as Boccaccio's storytellers head back to Florence, they do not return with plans for building some brave new world, even though the social thinking they have done by means of their stories has opened up new ways to conceive of, and thus perhaps to modify, the traditional social order. Instead, the men go off to pursue their different interests, while the ladies assemble briefly once again in Santa Maria Novella before heading home. They all essentially return to the lives they used to lead. But while they were away, they have shown us in their stories many important things: the power of intelligence, wit, and storytelling to shape the world; the necessity of shrewdly interpreting what we see and hear; our need to accept and satisfy our very human desires, including our sexuality; the realization that the vicissitudes of Fortune and the intransigence of others constitute real limits to what even the most intelligent among us may accomplish; the understanding that human desire is not always ennobling and socially productive, but can be destructive and socially disruptive; and finally, the fact that to have a good society, we need a good dose of magnanimity, even if that virtue is problematic because it may well be driven by people's egotism, not altruism or love.

At the most fundamental level, the group's ten days of storytelling have helped them deal with the ruin of the plague by offering them at least a temporary respite from it. Their stories have also provided them with another real pleasure, for the plots of their stories—even the sad ones—all have beginnings, middles, and ends, yielding the kind of satisfying structure and closure that stories can provide in a way that history, especially the seemingly unending sequence of terrifying experiences in plague-stricken Florence, cannot. But when they have told their one hundredth tale, their two-week escape to the country does not leave them or us with some grand conclusion; they simply stop and go back home. What one can say, however, is that their stories have given them—and us as readers—a chance to reflect on what makes for a good society and what does not, what makes for human happiness and how to achieve it, what human intelligence can accomplish and the limits it has to acknowledge. We may never get beyond the feeling that, like the ten young men and women who entertain us while they entertain one another, we are always faced with the challenge of interpretation at every level. We are left in something of a muddle, but in a sense, acknowledging and attempting to deal with the muddle of existence is what classic literary works—including the *Decameron*—are truly all about.

A Note on the Translation

Although most translations of older works necessarily modernize them to make them comprehensible to readers, I have resisted this impulse in specific ways because I want to remind readers that this work comes from another language and from a period that is almost seven hundred years away from the present. These fall into three main categories.

1. Times. Instead of referring to time using the hours and minutes of modern clocks, I have followed Boccaccio's practice and referred instead to the canonical hours, using their English versions. At those hours, church bells would be rung, and the religious would recite prayers. The hours are *matins*, which, followed immediately by *lauds*, was celebrated before daybreak; *prime*, at sunrise; *tierce*, at midmorning; *sext*, at noon; *nones*, at midafternoon; *vespers*, at sunset; and *compline*, after dark. Since days were longer in the summer than the winter and matched nights in length only at the vernal and autumnal equinoxes, the duration of the hours varied throughout the year, being shorter in winter and longer in summer.

2. Meals. Since the plague struck Florence in March 1348 and had been raging for some time before the group of storytellers supposedly departed for the country, their fourteen-day sojourn there probably occurred in April or May, something also reinforced by the fact that the afternoons are said to be hot, so that they begin their storytelling after the heat of the day has passed. We can thus infer that the storytellers rise at 5:00 or 6:00 A.M., occasionally have a little something by way of breakfast (a mealtime never referred to by name in the text), and after that, divert themselves by going for walks and the like. They then eat one of their two principal meals of the day in the midmorning or perhaps a little later. They are said to be dining after tierce, which means they would be going to table between 9:00 and 10:30 A.M. This meal is not given an identifying name, and some translators and critics refer to it as breakfast. However, since medieval and Renaissance Italians—and Europeans in general—ate their main meal of the day in the late morning, dinner seems the much more appropriate label and has been used accordingly. Finally, after taking naps and telling their stories, the group sits down for supper, which seems to occur shortly before vespers, or 7:30 P.M. at this time of the year. Boccaccio actually refers to their having their *cena*, which is still the Italian word for "supper." After singing and dancing, they then go to bed. Since it is dark, one can only speculate that they did so at 9:00 or 10:00.

3. Titles. In many cases, I have retained the Italian word rather than use a modern equivalent, even though occasionally one might have been suitable, since modern versions of those words would be anachronistic. Here are the relevant words:

Frate (or Fra'): The English equivalent for this word when used alone is "friar," and I have translated it accordingly. However, when placed before a name, such as "Frate Rinaldo," I have elected to keep the Italian rather than write "Brother Rinaldo."

Madonna (Monna, Madama): This was the honorific title used for a woman with something like the equivalent of upper- or middle-class status. *Madonna* was sometimes shortened to *monna*, and *madama* was used in certain regions of Italy, such as Sicily, in place of *madonna*. When prefacing a name, I have elected to keep these terms. When used as a form of direct address without the individual's name, I have translated these words as "my lady," which is closer to the original Italian and avoids the anachronistic effect of "madam," which is old-fashioned and speaks to a more modern society with a self-consciously defined middle class or bourgeoisie.

Master: My translation of the Italian *maestro*, itself a version of the Latin *magister*, is a title for someone with a university degree who practiced a profession or was empowered to teach. Since the English term has a long pedigree and is still employed to identify an expert, someone in charge, a teacher, and the like, I felt free to use it for *maestro*, which we use only for symphony conductors nowadays.

Messere (Ser): This was the honorific title used for a man with something like the equivalent of upper- or middle-class status (*ser* is short for *messere*); it was like addressing someone as "sir," but without the necessary implication of aristocratic status. Since there was no concept of a middle class in Boccaccio's time, translating it as "mister" would be anachronistic, and I have accordingly retained the Italian terms. When someone is simply addressed as *messere*, I have translated the word as "sir." In a number of the more satirical stories, *messer* is used before a character's title, as in *messer lo prete* ("Messer Priest"), and I have retained it there where it serves to underscore the satire, since the person in question is hardly deserving of the honor the honorific signifies.

Podestà: This was the title for the chief magistrate and administrative officer in the towns of northern and central Italy during the late Middle Ages. Since those cities were often riven by factions, the *podestà* was inevitably a titled foreigner who was appointed, usually for a short period of six months or so, because he would be impartial, and who theoretically derived his authority from the Holy Roman emperor to whom the towns owed nominal allegiance. The *podestà* held court in his palace and often had judges and magistrates who served under him and whom he brought from elsewhere. In Boccaccio's time, the authority of these figures was on the decline, and they were often intensely disliked by the residents in the cities where they served. Since there is no exact English equivalent for the word, I have retained the Italian form throughout the translation.

Signoria: This was the name for the ruling body of republican city-states in Italy during the Middle Ages and Renaissance. It comes from the word *signore*, which is the equivalent of the English "sir," and which ultimately derives from the Latin *senex* ("elder").

All notes are indicated by the symbol ° and are located at the end of the book.

The Meanings of the Names of Boccaccio's Storytellers

The Women

Pampinea: The Blooming One.

Fiammetta: Little Flame.

Filomena: either The Beloved or The Lover of Song.

Emilia: The Alluring One.

Lauretta: diminutive of Laura, the name of Petrarch's beloved in his *Canzoniere* (*Song Book*), where it also alludes to the laurel tree, whose leaves crowned the poet laureate.

Neifile: The Newly Beloved.

Elissa: another name for Dido, the tragic, love-struck queen of Virgil's *Aeneid*.

The Men

Panfilo: either He Who Is Made Entirely of Love, or He Who Loves All.

Filostrato: thought to mean He Who Is Cast Down or Overcome by Love (the true etymological meaning is "he who loves war").

Dioneo: The Lustful One, derived from Dione, the mother of Venus.

Boccaccio
The Decameron

Preface

It is a matter of humanity to show compassion for those who suffer, and although it is fitting for everyone to do so, it is especially desirable in those who, having had need of comfort, have received it from others—and if anyone ever needed it or appreciated it or derived any pleasure from it, I am one of them.° For, from my earliest youth up to the present, I have been enflamed beyond measure by a most exalted, noble love, which, were I to describe it, might seem greater than what is suitable for one in my low condition. Although I was praised and held in high regard for that love by those discerning individuals to whose attention I had come, it was nevertheless extremely painful to endure, not because of the cruelty of my beloved lady, to be sure, but because of the enormous fire produced within me by my poorly regulated appetite,

3

which never allowed me to rest content or stay within reasonable limits and often made me feel more pain than I should have. While I was suffering, the pleasant conversation and invaluable consolation certain friends provided gave me such relief that I am absolutely convinced they are the reason I did not die. But as it pleased Him who is infinite and who has decreed by immutable law that all earthly things must come to an end, my love abated in the course of time of its own accord, although it had been more fervent than any other and could not be altered or extinguished by the force of reason or counsel or public shame or the harm it might cause. At present, love has left in my mind only the pleasurable feeling that it normally gives to those who refrain from sailing on its deepest seas. Thus, whereas it used to be painful, now that all my suffering has been removed, I feel only the delightful sensation that still remains.

But although my pain has ceased, I have not forgotten the benefits I once received from those who, because of the benevolence they felt toward me, shared my heavy burden, nor will this memory ever fade in me, I truly believe, until I myself am dead. And since, in my opinion, gratitude should be the most highly praised of all the virtues, while its contrary is to be condemned, and since I do not wish to appear ungrateful, I have decided to use what little ability I have, now that I am free of love, to try and provide some relief in exchange for that which I received. And if I cannot provide it for those who aided me, since they, thanks to their intelligence or their good luck, do not require it, I will offer it to those who do. For, however slight my support—or comfort, if you prefer—might be to the needy, I nevertheless feel that it should be directed where it is more in demand, for there it will be more helpful and more appreciated.

Who will deny that it is much more fitting to give this aid, however inadequate, to charming women than to men? Out of fear and shame, women keep the flames of love hidden within their delicate breasts, and as everyone knows who has had this experience, such fires have much greater force than do those that burn out in the open. Restrained by the desires, whims, and commands of their fathers, mothers, brothers, and husbands, most of the time women remain pent up within the narrow confines of their rooms, and as they sit there in apparent idleness, both yearning and not yearning at the same time, the varied thoughts they mull over in their minds cannot always be happy ones. And if, because of those thoughts, a fit of melancholy brought on by their burning desire should take possession of their minds, it will inevitably remain there, causing them great pain, unless it is removed by new interests.° Finally, women's powers of endurance are simply less than those of men.

As we can plainly see, this is not what happens to men who are in love. Should melancholy or burdensome thoughts afflict them, they have many ways to alleviate or remove them, for, if they wish, they never lack opportunities to get out of the house where they can see and hear all sorts of things going on, and where they can hawk, hunt or fish, go riding or gamble, or just attend to their business affairs. Each of these activities has the power to occupy a man's mind either wholly or in part and to free it from painful thoughts, at least for a while, after which, one way or another, either he will find consolation or the pain will subside.

Therefore, I wish, to some extent, to provide a remedy for the sins of Fortune, who has been more niggardly in providing support where there is less strength, as we see in the case of our delicate ladies. And so, I offer here a succor and refuge for those who are in love, whereas for those who are not, they can just make do with their needles, their spindles, and their wool winders. My plan is to recount one hundred stories, or fables, or parables, or histories, or whatever you wish to call them.° They were told over ten days, as will be seen, by an honorable company made up of seven ladies and three young men who came together during the time of the recent plague that was responsible for so many deaths. I will also include some little songs sung for their delight by the ladies I mentioned. In the stories, you will see many cases of love, both pleasing and harsh, as well as other adventures, which took place in both ancient and modern times. In reading them, the ladies of whom I have been speaking will be able to derive not only pleasure from the entertaining material they contain, but useful advice as well, for the stories will teach them how to recognize what they should avoid, and likewise, what they should pursue.° And I believe that as they read them, their suffering would come to an end. Should this occur—and may God grant that it should— let them thank Love who, in freeing me from his bonds, has granted me the ability to attend to their pleasures.

Day 1

Introduction

HERE BEGINS THE FIRST DAY OF THE *DECAMERON*, IN
WHICH THE AUTHOR EXPLAINS HOW IT CAME ABOUT THAT
THE INDIVIDUALS, WHO WILL SOON MAKE THEIR
APPEARANCE, WERE INDUCED TO COME TOGETHER IN
ORDER TO CONVERSE WITH ONE ANOTHER, AND HOW,
UNDER THE RULE OF PAMPINEA, THEY SPEAK ON WHAT-
EVER TOPIC EACH ONE FINDS MOST AGREEABLE.

Most gracious ladies, whenever I contemplate how compassionate
you all are by nature, I recognize that, in your judgment, the present work will seem both somber and painful, for its opening contains the sad record of the recent, deadly plague, which inspired so
much horror and pity in all who actually saw it or otherwise came
to know of it. But I do not want you to be afraid of reading beyond
this introduction, as though you would always be going forward
amid continual sighs and tears. You will be affected by this horrific

beginning no differently than travelers are by a steep and rugged mountain, for beyond it there lies a most beautiful and delightful plain, which will supply them with pleasure that matches the difficulty of both their ascent and their descent.° And thus, just as happiness at its limit turns into sadness, so misery is ended by the joy that follows it.

This brief pain—I call it brief because it is contained in just a few words—will be quickly followed by the sweetness and pleasure that I have just promised you and that such a beginning would not, perhaps, have led you to expect, had I not explained what is about to happen. And truly, if in all honesty I could have led you where I want to go by any route other than by such a difficult path as this one will be, I would have done so gladly. But because, without recalling these events, I could not explain the origins of the things you will read about later on, I have been forced by necessity, as it were, to write it all down.

Let me say, then, that one thousand, three hundred, and forty-eight years had passed since the fruitful Incarnation of the Son of God when the deadly plague arrived in the noble city of Florence, the most beautiful of any in Italy.° Whether it descended on us mortals through the influence of the heavenly bodies or was sent down by God in His righteous anger to chastise us because of our wickedness, it had begun some years before in the East, where it deprived countless beings of their lives before it headed to the West, spreading ever-greater misery as it moved relentlessly from place to place.° Against it all human wisdom and foresight were useless. Vast quantities of refuse were removed from the city by officials charged with this function, the sick were not allowed inside the walls, and numerous instructions were disseminated for the preservation of health—but all to no avail. Nor were the humble supplications made to God by the pious, not just once but many times, whether in organized processions or in other ways, any more effective. For practically from the start of spring in the year we mentioned above, the plague began producing its sad effects in a terrifying and extraordinary manner. It did not operate as it had done in the East, where if anyone bled through the nose, it was a clear sign of inevitable death. Instead, at its onset, in men and women alike, certain swellings would develop in the groin or under the armpits, some of which would grow like an ordinary apple and others like an egg, some larger and some smaller. The common people called them *gavoccioli,* and within a brief space of time, these deadly, so-called *gavoccioli* would begin to spread from the two areas already mentioned and would appear at random over the rest of the body.° Then, the symptoms of the disease began to change, and many people discovered black or livid blotches on their arms, thighs, and every other part of their bodies, sometimes large and widely scattered, at other times tiny and close together. For whoever contracted them, these spots were a most certain sign of impending death, just as the *gavoccioli* had been earlier and still continued to be.

Against these maladies the advice of doctors and the power of medicine appeared useless and unavailing. Perhaps the nature of the disease was such that no remedy was possible, or the problem lay with those who were treating it, for their number, which had become enormous, included not just qualified doctors, but women as well as men who had never had any training in medicine, and since none of them had any idea what was causing the disease, they could hardly prescribe an appropriate remedy for it. Thus, not only were very few people cured, but in almost every case death occurred within three days after the appearance of the signs we have described, sometimes sooner and sometimes later, and usually without fever or any other complication. Moreover, what made this pestilence all the more virulent was that it was spread by the slightest contact between the sick and the healthy just as a fire will catch dry or oily materials when they are placed right beside it. In fact, this evil went even further, for not only did it infect those who merely talked or spent any time with the sick, but it also appeared to transfer the disease to anyone who merely touched the clothes or other objects that had been handled or used by those who were its victims.

What I have to tell is incredible, and if I and many others had not seen these things with our own eyes, I would scarcely dare to believe them, let alone write them down, no matter how trustworthy the person was who told me about them. Let me just say that the plague I have been describing was so contagious as it spread that it did not merely pass from one man to another, but we frequently saw something much more incredible, namely that when an animal of some species other than our own touched something belonging to an individual who had been stricken by the disease or had died of it, that animal not only got infected, but was killed almost instantly. With my own eyes, as I have just said, I witnessed such a thing on many occasions. One day, for example, two pigs came upon the rags of a poor man that had been thrown into the public street after he had died of the disease, and as they usually do, the pigs first poked at them with their snouts, after which they picked them up between their teeth and shook them against their jowls. Thereupon, within a short time, after writhing about as if they had been poisoned, both of them fell down dead on the ground, splayed out upon the rags that had brought about their destruction.

These things and many others like them, or even worse, caused all sorts of fears and fantasies in those who remained alive, almost all of whom took one utterly cruel precaution, namely, to avoid the sick and their belongings, fleeing far away from them, for in doing so they all thought they could preserve their own health.

Some people were of the opinion that living moderately and being abstemious would really help them resist the disease. They, therefore, formed themselves into companies and lived in isolation from everyone else. Having come together, they shut themselves up inside houses where no one was sick and they had ample means to live well, so that, while avoiding overindulgence, they still enjoyed the most delicate foods and the best wines in moderation. They would not speak with anyone from outside, nor did they want to hear any news about the dead and the dying, and instead, they passed their time playing music and enjoying whatever other amusements they could devise.

Others, holding the contrary opinion, maintained that the surest medicine for such an evil disease was to drink heavily, enjoy life's pleasures, and go about singing and having fun, satisfying their appetites by any means available, while laughing at everything and turning whatever happened into a joke. Moreover, they practiced what they preached to the best of their ability, for they went from one tavern to another, drinking to excess both day and night. They did their drinking more freely in private homes, however, provided that they found something there to enjoy or that held out the promise of pleasure. Such places were easy to find, because people, feeling as though their days were numbered, had not just abandoned themselves, but all their possessions, too. Most houses had thus become common property, and any stranger who happened upon them could treat them as if he were their rightful owner. And yet, while these people behaved like wild animals, they always took great care to avoid any contact at all with the sick.

In the midst of so much affliction and misery in our city, the respect for the reverend authority of the laws, both divine and human, had declined just about to the vanishing point, for, like everyone else, their officers and executors, who were not dead or sick themselves, had so few personnel that they could not fulfill their duties. Thus, people felt free to behave however they liked.

There were many others who took a middle course between the two already mentioned, neither restricting their diet so much as the first, nor letting themselves go in drinking and other forms of dissipation so much as the second, but doing just enough to satisfy their appetites. Instead of shutting themselves up, they went about, some carrying flowers in their hands, others with sweet-smelling herbs, and yet others with various kinds of spices. They would repeatedly hold these things up to their noses, for they thought the best course was to fortify the brain with such odors against the stinking air that seemed to be saturated with the stench of dead bodies and disease and medicine. Others, choosing what may have been the safer alternative, cruelly maintained that no medicine was better or more effective against the plague than flight. Convinced by this argument, and caring for nothing but themselves, a large number of both men and women abandoned their own city, their own homes, their relatives, their properties and possessions, and headed for the countryside, either that lying around Florence or, better still, that which was farther away. It was as if they thought that God's wrath, once provoked, did not aim to punish men's iniquities with the plague wherever it might find them, but would strike down only those found inside the walls of their city. Or perhaps they simply concluded that no one in Florence would survive and that the city's last hour had come.

Of the people holding these varied opinions, not all of them died, but, by the same token, not all of them survived. On the contrary, many proponents of each view got sick here, there, and everywhere. Moreover, since they themselves, when they were well, had set the example for those who were not yet infected, they, too, were almost completely abandoned by everyone as they languished away. And leaving aside the fact that the citizens avoided one another, that almost no one took care of his neighbors, and that relatives visited one another infrequently, if ever, and always kept their distance, the tribulation of the plague had put such fear into the hearts of men and women that brothers abandoned their brothers, uncles their nephews, sisters their brothers, and very often wives their husbands. In fact, what is even worse, and almost unbelievable, is that fathers and mothers refused to tend to their children and take care of them, treating them as if they belonged to someone else.

Consequently, the countless numbers of people who got sick, both men and women, had to depend for help either on the charity of the few friends they had who were still around, or on the greed of their servants, who would only work for high salaries out of all proportion to the services they provided. For all that, though, there were few servants to be found, and those few tended to be men and women of limited intelligence, most of whom, not trained for such duties, did little more than hand sick people the few things they asked for or watch over them as they died. And yet, while performing these services, they themselves often lost their lives along with their wages.

As a result of the abandonment of the sick by neighbors, friends, and family, and in light of the scarcity of servants, there arose a practice hardly ever heard of before, whereby when a woman fell

ill, no matter how attractive or beautiful or noble, she did not object
to having a man as one of her attendants, whether he was young or
not. Indeed, if her infirmity made it necessary, she experienced no
more shame in showing him every part of her body than she
would have felt with a woman, which was the reason why those
women who were cured were perhaps less chaste in the period that
followed. Moreover, a great many people chanced to die who
might have survived if they had had any sort of assistance. In general, between the inadequacy of the means to care for the sick and
the virulence of the plague, the number of people dying both day
and night was so great that it astonished those who merely heard
tell of it, let alone those who actually witnessed it.

As a result of the plague, it was almost inevitable that practices
arose among the citizens who survived that went contrary to their
original customs. It used to be the case, as it is again today, that
the female relatives and next-door neighbors of a dead man would
come to his house and mourn there with the women of the household, while his male neighbors and a fair number of other citizens
would assemble in front of the house with his male relatives. After
that, the clergymen would arrive, their number depending on the
social rank of the deceased, who would then be carried on the
shoulders of his peers, amid all the funeral pomp of candles and
chants, to the church he had chosen before his death. As the ferocity
of the plague began to increase, such practices all but disappeared
in their entirety, while other new ones arose to take their place.
For people did not just die without women around them, but many
departed this life without anyone at all as a witness, and very few
of them were accorded the pious lamentations and bitter tears of
their families. On the contrary, in place of all the usual weeping,
mostly there was laughing and joking and festive merrymaking—a
practice that women, having largely suppressed their feminine
piety, had mastered in the interest of preserving their health. Moreover, there were few whose bodies were accompanied to church by
more than ten or twelve of their neighbors, nor were they carried
on the shoulders of their honored and esteemed fellow citizens,
but by a band of gravediggers, come up from the lower classes,

who insisted on being called *sextons* and performed their services for a fee. They would shoulder the bier and quick-march it off, not to the church that the dead man had chosen before his demise, but in most cases, to the one closest by. They would walk behind four or six clergymen who carried just a few candles—and sometimes none at all—and who did not trouble themselves with lengthy, solemn burial services, but instead, with the aid of those *sextons,* dumped the corpse as quickly as they could into whatever empty grave they found.

The common people and most of those of the middling sort presented a much more pathetic sight, for the majority of them were constrained to stay in their houses either by their hope to survive or by their poverty. Confined thus to their own neighborhoods, they got sick every day by the thousands, and having no servants or anyone else to attend to their needs, they almost invariably perished. Many expired out in the public streets both day and night, and although a great many others died inside their houses, the stench of their decaying bodies announced their deaths to their neighbors well before anything else did. And what with these, plus the others who were dying all over the place, the city was overwhelmed with corpses.

For the most part, the neighbors of the dead always observed the same routine, prompted more by a fear of contamination from the decaying bodies than by any charity they might have felt. Either by themselves or with the aid of porters, whenever any could be found, they carried the bodies of the recently deceased out of their houses and put them down by the front doors, where anyone passing by, especially in the morning, could have seen them by the thousands. Then the bodies were taken and placed on biers that had been sent for or, for lack of biers, on wooden planks. Nor was it unusual for two or three bodies to be carried on a single bier, for on more than one occasion, they were seen holding a wife and a husband, two or three brothers, a father and a son, or other groups like that. And countless were the times when a couple of priests bearing a cross would go to fetch someone, and porters carrying three or four biers would fall in behind them, so that whereas the priests thought they had one corpse to bury, they would have six or eight, and sometimes more. Even so, however, there were no tears or candles or mourners to honor the dead; on the contrary, it had reached the point that people who died were treated the same way that goats would be treated nowadays. Thus, it is quite clear that things which the natural course of events, with its small, infrequent blows, could never teach the wise to bear with patience, the immensity of this calamity made even simple people regard with indifference.°

There was not enough consecrated ground to bury the enormous number of corpses that were being brought to every church every day at almost every hour, especially if they were going to continue the ancient custom of giving each one its own plot. So, when all the graves were full, enormous trenches were dug in the cemeteries of the churches, into which the new arrivals were put by the hundreds, stowed layer upon layer like merchandise in ships, each one covered with a little earth, until the top of the trench was reached.

But rather than go on recalling in elaborate detail all the miseries we experienced in the city, let me just add that the baleful wind blowing through it in no way spared the surrounding countryside. The fortified towns there fared just like the city, though on a smaller scale, and in the scattered villages and farms the poor, wretched peasants and their families died at all hours of the day and night. Without the aid of doctors or help from servants, they would expire along the roads and in their tilled fields and in their homes, dying more like animals than human beings. They, too, became as apathetic in their ways as the city dwellers were, neglecting their property and ignoring the work they had to do. Indeed, since they thought every day was going to be their last, they consumed what they already had on hand, neglecting what they might get in the future from their animals and fields and from all their past labors. Thus it came about that oxen, asses, sheep, goats, pigs, chickens, and even dogs, who are so loyal to men, were driven from their homes and left to roam freely through fields in which the wheat had not even been reaped, let alone gathered in. Nevertheless, many of the animals, as if they were rational beings, would eat well there during the day and then return home full at night, needing no shepherd to guide them.

To leave the countryside and return to the city: what more can be said except that the cruelty of the heavens—and perhaps, in some measure, that of men, too—was so great and so malevolent that from March to the following July, between the fury of the pestilence and the fact that many of the sick were poorly cared for or abandoned in their need because of the fears of those who were healthy, it has been reliably calculated that more than one hundred thousand human beings were deprived of their lives within the walls of the city of Florence, although before the outbreak of the plague perhaps no one would have thought it contained so many.°

Oh, how many great palaces, beautiful houses, and noble dwellings, once filled with lords and ladies and their retainers, were emptied of all their inhabitants, down to the last little serving boy! Oh, how many famous families, how many vast estates, how many notable fortunes were left without a legitimate heir! How many valiant men, how many beautiful women, how many lovely youths, whom Galen, Hippocrates, and Aesculapius—not to mention others—would have judged perfectly healthy, dined in the morning with their families, companions, and friends, only to have supper that evening with their ancestors in the next world!°

Since my own grief will be increased if I continue to meditate any longer on so much misery, I want to pass over what I can suitably omit and tell what happened one Tuesday morning while our city was in these straits and had been practically deserted. As I later learned from a trustworthy person, seven young women, who had just attended divine services and who, in keeping with the requirements of the times, were dressed in mourning attire, found themselves in the venerable Church of Santa Maria Novella, which was otherwise almost empty. Each one was the friend, neighbor, or relative of one of the others, none had reached her twenty-eighth year or was under eighteen, and all were intelligent, well-born, attractive, and graced with fine manners and marvelous honesty. I would tell you their real names, but there is a good reason that prevents me from doing so, which is that I do not want any of them to feel shame in the future because of the ensuing stories, which they either listened to or told themselves. For the rules concerning pleasure, which are rather strict today, were then, for the reasons I have already given, very lax, not just for women of their age, but even for those who were much older. Nor do I wish to supply the envious, who are ready to censure the most praiseworthy life, with material that might allow them to denigrate the honesty of these worthy ladies in any way by means of their filthy gossip. However, so that what each one said may be understood without confusion, I intend to identify them by means of names that are either wholly, or partially, adapted to their characters. We shall call the first of them, who was also the oldest, Pampinea, and the second Fiammetta; the third and fourth, Filomena and Emilia; then let us say that the fifth is Lauretta and the sixth Neifile; and to the last, not without reason, we will give the name Elissa.

By chance rather than some prior agreement, they had all come together in one part of the church and were sitting down more or less in a circle. After finishing their prayers, they heaved a deep sigh and began talking among themselves about the terrible times they were going through. After a while, when all the others had fallen silent, Pampinea began to speak as follows:

"My dear ladies, we have all heard many times that there is no harm in exercising our rights in an honest way. Now, every person on earth has a natural right to maintain, preserve, and defend his life to the best of his ability. In fact, the proof that we all take this for granted is that men are judged innocent if they sometimes kill others in self-defense. Thus, if the laws, to which the welfare of every human being has been entrusted, concede such a thing, how can it be wrong, provided no one is harmed, for us or for anyone else to use whatever remedies we can find in order to preserve our lives? When I pause to consider what we have been doing this morning as well as on previous mornings, and when I think about the subjects we have discussed and what we have had to say about them, I realize, just as you must realize, too, that each of us fears for her life. I am not surprised by this, but considering that we all have the natural feelings shared by women, what really does surprise me is why you have not taken any steps to protect yourselves from what each of you has a right to fear.

"Instead, here we sit, in my opinion, as if our sole purpose were to count the number of corpses being carried to their graves; or to hear whether the friars inside the church, whose numbers have practically dwindled away to nothing, are chanting their offices at the specified hours; or to exhibit, by means of our clothing, the quality and quantity of our miseries to anybody who might show up here. And if we go outside, either we see the dead and the sick being carried everywhere about us; or we see people, once condemned and sent into exile for their misdeeds by the authority of the civil law, mocking that law as they rampage through the city committing acts of violence, knowing that those who enforce the law are either sick or dead; or we are tormented by the dregs of our city who, thirsting for our blood, call themselves *sextons* now and go about everywhere, both on horseback and on foot, singing scurrilous songs to add insults to our injuries. And all we ever hear is 'So-and-so is dead' and 'So-and-so is about to die.' If there were anyone left to grieve, we would hear nothing but doleful laments everywhere.

"And when we return home, I do not know whether you have the same experience that I do, but since, out of a large household of servants, there is no one left except my maid, I get so frightened that I feel as if all the hairs on my head were standing on end. And what terrifies me even more is that wherever I go in the house, wherever I pause for a moment, I see the shades of those who have passed away, and their faces are not the ones I was used to, but they have strange, horrible expressions on them that come from who knows where. For these reasons, whether I am here or outside or in my house, I am always anxious, and all the more so, because it seems to me that there is no one possessing sufficient means and having some place to go to, as we do, who is left in the city except us. And as for the few people still around, they make no distinction, as I have often heard and seen for myself, between what is honest and what is not, and prompted only by their appetites, they do what promises them the most pleasure, both day and night, alone and in groups. Moreover, I am not speaking only of laymen but also of those cloistered in monasteries, who have convinced themselves that such wicked behavior is suitable for them and only improper for others. Breaking their vows of obedience, they have given themselves over to carnal pleasures, and in the belief that they will thereby escape death, they have become wanton and degenerate.

"And if this is so—and it most manifestly *is* so—then what are we doing here, what are we waiting for, what are we dreaming about? Why are we lazier and slower than all the other inhabitants of this city in providing for our safety? Do we consider ourselves less valuable than they are? Or do we believe that our lives, unlike those of others, are tied to our bodies by chains so strong that we need not worry about all these things that have the power to harm them? We are mistaken, we are deceived, what bestial stupidity for us to think this way! The clearest argument against us is the frequency with which we are forced to recall the names and conditions of the young men and women who have been struck down by this cruel pestilence.

"Although I do not know if things appear to you the way they do to me, for my part I have come to the conclusion that the best thing for us to do in our present situation would be to leave the city, just as many have done before us and many are still doing, lest we fall prey through timidity or complacency to what we might possibly avoid if we desired to do so. We should go and stay on one of our various country estates, shunning the wicked practices of others like death itself, but having as much fun as possible, feasting and making merry, without ever overstepping the bounds of reason in any way.

"There we will hear the little birds sing and see the hills and plains turning green, the fields full of wheat undulating like the sea, and thousands of kinds of trees. There we will have a clearer view of the heavens, for, even if they are sullen, they do not for all that deny us their eternal beauties, which are so much more attractive to look at than are the walls of our empty city. Moreover, the air is much fresher in the country, the necessities of life are more abundant, and the number of difficulties to contend with is smaller. Although the peasants are dying there in the same way that the city dwellers are here, our distress will be lessened if only because the houses and the people are fewer and farther between. Besides, if I am right, we will not be abandoning anyone here. Rather, we can truly say that we are the ones who have been abandoned, for our relatives, by dying or fleeing from death, have left us alone in the midst of this great affliction as if we were no kin of theirs. Nor will anyone reproach us if we adopt this plan, whereas if we do not, we will be facing sorrow and grief and possibly death itself.

"Consequently, if you please, I think it would be a good idea for us to do what I suggest, taking our maidservants with us and having everything we need sent after. We can live in one place today and another tomorrow, pursuing whatever pleasures and amusements the present times offer. And if death does not claim us before then, let us go on living this way until such time as we can perceive the end that Heaven has decreed for these events. Just remember that it is no less unseemly for us to go away and thus preserve our honor than for the great majority of the others to stay here and lose theirs."

Having listened to Pampinea, the other women not only applauded her advice, but were so eager to take it that they were already beginning to work out the details among themselves, as though they were going to get right up out of their seats and set off at once. But Filomena, who was very prudent, declared: "Ladies, although what Pampinea has argued is very well said, that is no reason for us to rush into it, as you seem to want to do. Remember, we are all women, and every one of us is sufficiently adult to recognize how women, when left to themselves in a group, can be quite irrational, and how, without a man to look after them, they can be terribly disorganized. Since we are fickle, quarrelsome, suspicious, weak, and fearful, I am really worried that if we take no guide along with us other than ourselves, this company will fall apart much more quickly, and with much less credit to ourselves, than would otherwise be the case. We would be well advised to deal with this problem before we start."

"It is certainly true," said Elissa, "that man is the head of woman, and without a man to guide us, only rarely does anything we do accord us praise.° But how are we to get hold of these men? As we all know, the majority of our male relatives are dead, and the others who remain alive not only have no idea where we are, but are fleeing in scattered little groups from exactly the same thing we seek to avoid ourselves. Nor would it be seemly for us to take up with those who are not our kin. Therefore, if self-preservation is the purpose of our flight, we must find a way to arrange things so that no matter where we go in quest of fun and relaxation, trouble and scandal do not follow us there."

The ladies were engaged in their discussion, when lo and behold, who should come into the church but three young men, though none so young as to be under twenty-five, in whom neither the horrors of the times, nor the loss of friends and relatives, nor fear for their own lives had been able to cool down, let alone extinguish, the love they felt. The first was named Panfilo, the second Filostrato, and the last Dioneo, all of them very pleasant and well bred. In the midst of all this turbulence, they were seeking the solace, sweet beyond measure, of catching a glimpse of the ladies they loved, all three of whom just so happened to be among the seven previously mentioned, while several of the others were close relatives of one or another of the men. No sooner did they catch sight of the ladies than the ladies caught sight of them, whereupon Pampinea smiled and began: "Look how Fortune favors us right from the start in placing before us three discreet and worthy young men who will gladly guide us and serve us if we are not too proud to ask them to do so."

Neifile's entire face had turned scarlet with embarrassment because she was the object of one of the youths' affections. "Pampinea, for the love of God," she said, "be careful about what you are saying. I know for certain that nothing but good can be said of any one of them, and I believe they are more than competent to carry out this task. I also think they would provide good, honest company not only for us but for many women more beautiful and finer than we are. But since it is perfectly obvious that they are in love with some of us here, I am afraid that if we were to take them with us, through no fault of theirs or of our own, we would be exposed to censure and disgrace."

"That really does not matter in the least," said Filomena. "If I live like an honest woman and my conscience is clear, let people say what they like to the contrary, for God and Truth will take up arms on my behalf. Now, if only they were disposed to accompany us, then we could truly claim, as Pampinea has said, that Fortune favors our plan."

Having heard what Pampinea had to say, the other ladies stopped talking and unanimously agreed that the men should be called over, told about their intentions, and asked if they would like to accompany them on their expedition. And so, without another word, Pampinea, who was related by blood to one of the men, got up and went over to where they stood gazing at the women. After giving them a cheerful greeting, Pampinea explained their plan and asked them on behalf of all the women if, in a spirit of pure, brotherly affection, they might be disposed to accompany them.

At first the young men thought they were being mocked, but when they saw that Pampinea was speaking in earnest, they replied happily that they were ready to go. In order to avoid delaying their project, they all made arrangements then and there for what they had to do before their departure. The next day, which was a Wednesday, after having carefully prepared everything they needed down to the last detail and sent it all on ahead to the place where they were going, they left the city at the crack of dawn and started on their way, the ladies traveling with a few of their maids, the three youths with three of their servants. Nor did they go more than two short miles from the city before they arrived at their first destination.

The place in question was some distance from any road, situated on a little mountain that was quite a pleasant sight to see with all its shrubs and trees decked out in their green foliage.° At the top there was a palace, built around a large, lovely courtyard, containing loggias, great halls, and bedchambers, all of which were beautifully proportioned and adorned with charming paintings of happy scenes. Surrounded by meadows and marvelous gardens, the palace had wells of the coolest water and vaulted cellars stocked with precious wines, wines more suitable for connoisseurs than for honest, sober ladies. When they got there, the company discovered to their great delight that the palace had been swept clean from top to bottom, the beds had been made up in their chambers, every room had been adorned with seasonal flowers, and the floors had been carpeted with rushes.

Soon after reaching the palace, they sat down, and Dioneo, who was the merriest of the young men and had the readiest wit, said: "Ladies, we have been led here more by your good sense than by our own foresight. Now, I do not know what you intend to do with all your troubles, but I left mine inside the city gates when I passed through them with you just a short while ago. Hence, you must either prepare to have fun and to laugh and sing along with me—as much as is consistent, of course, with your dignity—or you should give me leave to go back there to reclaim my troubles and stay in our afflicted city."

As though she, too, had gotten rid of such thoughts herself, Pampinea replied to him gaily: "Very well said, Dioneo. We should have fun while we are living here, for that is the very reason we fled our sorrows back there. But since things that lack order will not last long, and since I am the one who initiated the discussions that led to the formation of this fair company, I think that if we are to preserve our happiness, we have to choose a leader from among ourselves, someone whom we will honor and obey as our superior and whose every thought will be aimed at enabling us to pass our time together agreeably. Moreover, to allow us all to experience the heavy burden as well as the pleasure of being in command, and thereby to prevent those who are not in charge from envying the person who is, I think that the burden and the honor should be assigned to each of us in turn for just one day. The first ruler is someone we should all elect, but as for those who follow, the person who has been in charge on a particular day should, when the hour of vespers approaches, choose his or her successor.° Then this new ruler will be free to determine the place where we will go and to dictate the manner in which we are to live during the period of his or her reign."

They were all quite happy with Pampinea's proposal and unanimously elected her Queen for the first day, whereupon Filomena quickly ran over to a laurel tree, for she had often heard people say that its leaves were quite venerable and conferred great honor on those worthy individuals who were crowned with them. Having gathered a few branches, she made a magnificent garland of honor, which, during the time the company remained together, was placed on each person's head as a clear sign of royal sovereignty and authority.°

Once she had been crowned Queen, Pampinea summoned the servants of the three men as well as the women's maids, who were four in number. She then ordered everyone to be silent, and when they were, she said:

"So that I may begin by setting an example for you all that will allow our company to be able to live free from shame and will make our experience here an ever more orderly and pleasurable one for as long as we choose to stay together, let me first appoint Parmeno, Dioneo's servant, as my steward and entrust him with the care and management of our entire household as well as everything pertaining to the service of our dining hall.° I want Sirisco, Panfilo's servant, to be our buyer and treasurer and to carry out Parmeno's orders. Tindaro, who is in Filostrato's service, shall take care of his master's bedchamber as well as those of the other two men whenever their own servants are prevented by their duties from doing so. My maid Misia will be in the kitchen fulltime with Filomena's maid Licisca, where they will diligently prepare all the dishes ordered by Parmeno. We want Chimera, Lauretta's maid, and Stratilia, Fiammetta's, to act as the ladies' chambermaids and to clean all the places we frequent. Finally, if they wish to stay in our good graces, we desire and command all of the servants to take care that, no matter what they see or hear in their comings and goings, no news from the outside world should ever reach us unless that news is good."°

Having summarily given out her orders, which everyone commended, she rose gaily to her feet and declared: "Here there are gardens and meadows and lots of other truly delightful spots in which we are free to walk and enjoy ourselves. However, at the stroke of tierce, let us all return here so that we can eat while it is still cool."°

After the merry company was given leave to go by the Queen, the young men and their lovely companions set off on a leisurely walk through one of the gardens, talking of pleasant matters, making lovely garlands out of various types of foliage for one another, and singing songs of love. Then, when they had spent as much time there as the Queen had allotted them, they returned to their lodging where they found Parmeno had been quite diligent in carrying out his duties, for when they entered one of the great halls on the ground floor, they saw that tables had been set up, laid with the whitest tablecloths on which there were goblets gleaming like silver, and that the whole room had been adorned with broom blossoms. At the Queen's behest they rinsed their hands in water and went to sit in the places Parmeno had assigned them.

Exquisitely prepared dishes were brought in, the finest wines were at the ready, and without a sound the three servants began waiting on them. The entire company was delighted that everything was so beautiful and so well presented, and all through the meal there was a great deal of pleasant talk and much good cheer. Since everyone knew how to dance, as soon as the tables were cleared away, the Queen sent for musical instruments so that a few of their number who were well versed in music could play and sing, while all the rest, the ladies together with the young men, could dance a *carola*.° At her request, Dioneo took up a lute and Fiammetta a viol, and the pair began playing a melodious dance tune together, whereupon the Queen, having sent the servants away to eat, formed a circle with the other ladies and the two young men, and all began dancing at a stately pace.° After that, they sang a number of pleasant, happy little songs and continued to entertain themselves in this manner until the Queen, thinking it was time for a nap, dismissed them. The three young men consequently retired to their bedchambers, which were separated from those of the ladies. There they found not merely that their beds had been neatly made, but that their rooms were as full of flowers as the hall had been, and the ladies made a similar discovery, whereupon the entire company undressed and lay down to rest.

Not long after nones had struck, the Queen got up and had the young men and all the other women awakened, declaring that it was harmful to sleep too much during the day.° They then went off to a little meadow where the grass, shaded everywhere from the sun, grew lush and green, and where, feeling a gentle breeze wafting over them, the Queen asked them to sit down in a circle on the green grass. She then spoke to them as follows:

"As you can see, the sun is high, the heat is intense, and nothing can be heard but the cicadas up in the olive trees. To take a walk and go somewhere else right now would be the height of folly, since it is so lovely and cool here, and besides, as you can see, there are boards set up for backgammon and chess. However, although we are free to amuse ourselves in whatever way we like, if you would take my advice in this, we should not spend the hot part of the day playing games, for they necessarily leave one of the players feeling miffed, without giving that much pleasure either to his opponent or to those who are watching. Rather, we should tell stories, for even though just one person is doing the talking, all the others will still have the pleasure of listening. And by the time each one of you will have told his or her little tale, the sun will be setting, the heat will have abated, and we will be able to go and amuse ourselves wherever you choose. Now, if you like what I am proposing, let us put it into effect, but if you dislike it, since my only desire is to carry out your wishes, let us all go and spend our time doing whatever we please until the hour of vespers."

The entire company, the ladies and the young men alike, praised the idea of telling stories.

"Then, if that is your pleasure," said the Queen, "my wish is that, on this first day, we should all be free to speak on whatever topic each of us finds most agreeable."

Turning to Panfilo, who was seated to her right, the Queen graciously asked him to start things off with one of his stories. Upon hearing her command, Panfilo responded with alacrity, and as all the others listened, he began speaking as follows.

Story 1

SER CEPPARELLO DECEIVES A HOLY FRIAR WITH A
FALSE CONFESSION AND DIES, AND ALTHOUGH HE WAS ONE
OF THE WORST OF MEN DURING HIS LIFE, HE IS REPUTED
AFTER HIS DEATH TO BE A SAINT AND IS CALLED SAINT
CIAPPELLETTO.°

Dearest ladies, it is fitting that everything man does should take as its origin the wonderful and holy name of Him who was the maker of all things. Thus, since I am the first and must begin our storytelling, I intend to start off with one of His marvelous works so that, once you have heard it, our hope in Him, as in that which is immutable, will be strengthened, and we will forever praise His name. Now, it is clear that the things of this world are all transitory and fading, so that both in themselves and in what they give rise to, they are filled with suffering, anguish, and toil, as well as being subject to countless dangers. We, who live in the midst of these things and are a part of them, would certainly not be able to resist and defend ourselves against them, if the special grace of God did not lend us strength and discernment. It is wrong to believe that this grace descends to us and enters us because of any merit of our own. Rather, it is sent by His loving kindness and is obtained through the prayers of those who, though mortal like us, truly followed His will while they were alive and now enjoy eternal bliss with Him. To them, as to advocates informed by experience of our frailty, we offer up prayers about our concerns, perhaps because we do not dare to present them personally before the sight of so great a judge. And yet in Him, who is generous and filled with pity for us, we perceive something more. Although human sight is not sharp enough to penetrate the secrets of the divine mind in any way, it sometimes happens that we are deceived by popular opinion into making someone our advocate before Him in all His majesty whom He has cast into eternal exile. And yet He, from whom nothing is hidden, pays more attention to the purity of the supplicant than to his ignorance or to the damned state of his intercessor, listening to those who pray as if their advocate were actually blessed in His sight. All of this will appear clearly in the tale I intend to tell—clearly, I say, not in keeping with the judgment of God, but with that of men.

The story is told that Musciatto Franzesi, an extremely rich and celebrated merchant in France, who had been made a knight, was once supposed to move to Tuscany with Lord Charles Sans Terre, the King of France's brother, whom Pope Boniface had sent for and was encouraging to come.° Musciatto recognized that his affairs, as those of merchants often are, were tangled up here and there and could not be put right quickly and easily, but he thought of a number of different people to whom he could entrust them and thus found a way to take care of everything. There was, however, one exception. He was unsure whom he could leave behind to recover the loans he had made to quite a few people in Burgundy. The reason for his uncertainty was that he had heard the Burgundians were a quarrelsome lot, evil by nature and untrustworthy, and he could think of no one he could rely on who would be sufficiently wicked that his wickedness would match theirs. After he had given the matter a great deal of thought, there came to mind a certain Ser Cepparello da Prato, who was often a guest in his house in Paris.° Because the man was small of stature and dressed like a dandy, the French, not knowing what "Cepparello" signified and thinking it meant "hat," that is, "garland," in their language, called him, because he was small as we have said, not Ciappello, but Ciappelletto. And so, he was called Ciappelletto everywhere, while only a select few knew he was really Ser Cepparello.°

Let me tell you about the kind of life this Ciappelletto led. A notary, he would feel the greatest shame if even one of the very few legal documents he drew up was found to be other than false. He had composed as many of these phony ones as people requested, and he did so for free more willingly than someone else would have done for a sizable payment. Furthermore, he supplied false testimony with the greatest delight, whether it was asked for or not, and since people in France in those days placed the greatest trust in oaths, and since he did not care if his were false, he won a great many law cases through his wickedness whenever he was asked to swear upon his oath to tell the truth. Because it gave him real pleasure, he went to great lengths to stir up bad feelings, hatred, and scandals among friends and relations and everyone else, and the greater the evils he saw arise as a result, the greater his happiness. Invited to be an accomplice in a murder or some other criminal act, he would never refuse to go. Indeed, he would do so with a ready will and often found himself happily wounding or killing men with his own hands. He was the greatest blasphemer of God and the Saints, and since he would do so at the slightest provocation, he came off as the most irascible man alive. He never went to church and used abominable words to mock all its sacraments as being beneath contempt. On the other hand, he happily spent time in taverns and frequented other places of ill repute. Of women, he was as fond as dogs are of being beaten with a stick, and he took more delight in their opposite than any degenerate ever did. He would rob and steal with a conscience like that of a holy man giving alms. He was a total glutton and a great drinker, so much so that sometimes it would make him disgustingly ill. Plus, he was a devout cardsharp and gambled with loaded dice. But why do I lavish so many words on him? He was perhaps the worst man who had ever been born. For a long time his wickedness had preserved the wealth and rank of Messer Musciatto who often protected him from both private persons, who were frequently the victims of his abuse, and from the courts, which always were.

Thus, when this Ser Cepparello crossed the mind of Messer Musciatto, who was well acquainted with his life, he thought to himself that this would be just the man he needed to deal with the wickedness of the Burgundians. He therefore had Ciappelletto sent for and spoke to him as follows:

"Ser Ciappelletto, as you know, I am about to leave here for good, and since, among others, I have to deal with the Burgundians, who are full of tricks, I know of no one more qualified than you to recover my money from them. Since you're not doing anything at present, if you take care of this business for me, I intend to obtain the favor of the court for you here and to award you a fair portion of what you recover."

Ser Ciappelletto, who was indeed unemployed and in short supply of worldly goods, saw the man who had long been his refuge and defense about to depart, and so, without a moment's hesitation, constrained, as it were, by necessity, he made up his mind and said he would be more than willing to do what Musciatto wanted. The two of them then worked out the details of their agreement, and Ser Ciappelletto received Musciatto's power of attorney as well as letters of introduction from the King. Soon after Messer Musciatto's departure, Ciappelletto went off to Burgundy, where almost no one knew him. There, in a kind and gentle manner quite beyond his nature, as though he were holding back his wrath till the end, he began recovering Musciatto's money and taking care of what he had been sent to do.

Before long, while he was lodging in the house of two Florentine brothers who lent money at interest and who treated him with great respect out of love for Messer Musciatto, he happened to fall ill. The two brothers immediately sent for doctors and servants to take care of him and to provide him with everything he might need to recover his health. All their help was in vain, however, for, in the opinion of the doctors, the good man, who was already old and had lived a disorderly life, was going from bad to worse every day, as people did who had a fatal illness. The two brothers were very upset about this, and one day, right next to the bedroom in which Ser Ciappelletto lay sick, they began talking together.

"What are we going to do about this guy?" said the one of them to the other. "We've got a terrible mess on our hands on account of him, because if we kick him out of our house, as sick as he is, people would condemn us for doing it. Plus, they'd really think we're stupid since we didn't just take him in at first, but also went to great lengths to find servants and doctors for him, and now, although he couldn't have done anything to offend us, they see him suddenly kicked out of our house when he's deathly ill. On the other hand, he's been such a bad man that he won't want to make his confession or receive any of the sacraments of the Church, and if he dies without confession, no church will want to receive his body, and they'll wind up tossing him into some garbage pit like a dog.° But if he goes ahead and makes his confession, the same thing will happen. Since his sins are so many and so horrible, no friar or priest will be willing or able to absolve him, and so, without absolution, he'll be tossed into a garbage pit just the same. And when that happens, the people of this town—both because of our profession, which they think is truly wicked and which they bad-mouth all day long, and because of their desire to rob us— well, they'll rise up and riot when they see it. And as they come running to our house, they'll be screaming, 'These Lombard dogs that the Church refuses to accept, we won't put up with them any longer!' And maybe they won't just steal our stuff, but on top of that, they'll take our lives. So, no matter how things work out, it'll be bad for us if this guy dies."

Ser Ciappelletto, who, as we said, was lying close to where they were talking, and whose hearing was sharp, as it often is in those who are sick, caught every word they were saying about him and reacted by sending for them to come to him.

"I don't want you to fear anything on my account," he told them, "or to be afraid you'll be harmed because of me. I heard what you were saying about me, and I'm very sure that the outcome will be exactly what you've predicted if things happen the way you've been imagining them. However, it's all going to turn out differently. I've done the Lord God so many injuries during my lifetime that doing Him one more at the hour of my death won't make a difference to Him one way or the other. So go and arrange for the holiest and worthiest friar you can find to come to me—if such a one exists—and leave everything to me, for I'm sure I can set both your affairs and my own in order so that all will be well and you'll be satisfied with the result."   ·

Although the two brothers did not derive much hope from this, they nevertheless went off to a monastery and asked for a wise and holy man to hear the confession of a Lombard who was sick in their house. They were assigned an elderly friar, a grand master of the Scriptures, who had lived a good and holy life and was a very venerable figure toward whom all the townspeople felt an immense special devotion, and they took this man back home with them.

When the friar reached the bedroom where Ser Ciappelletto was lying, he seated himself beside the sick man, and after speaking some words of comfort, asked him how much time had passed since he had made his last confession. Ser Ciappelletto, who had never been to confession, replied to him: "Father, it used to be my custom to go to confession at least once a week, without counting the many weeks in which I went more often. Since I've been sick for about a week now, the truth is that the suffering I've endured from my illness has been so great that it has prevented me from going to confession."

"My son," said the friar, "you've done well, and you should continue that practice in the future. Considering how often you've made your confession, I don't think it will be a lot of trouble for me to hear it and to examine you."

"Messer Friar," said Ser Ciappelletto, "don't speak like that. Although I've gone to confession many, many times, I've always had a longing to make a general confession of all the sins I could remember, starting from the day of my birth and coming right down to the present. Therefore, my good father, I beg you to examine me point by point about everything just as if I'd never been to confession. And don't be concerned about me because I'm sick, for I would much rather mortify this flesh of mine than indulge it by doing something that might lead to the perdition of my soul, which my Savior redeemed with His precious blood."°

These words pleased the holy man immensely and seemed to him to argue a well-disposed mind. Consequently, after commending Ser Ciappelletto warmly for making frequent confessions, he began by asking him if he had ever committed the sin of lust with a woman.°

"Father," Ser Ciappelletto replied with a sigh, "I'm ashamed to tell you the truth on this subject for fear I might be committing the sin of pride."

"Don't be afraid to speak," said the holy friar. "Telling the truth was never a sin either in confession or anywhere else."

"Since you give me such reassurance," said Ser Ciappelletto, "I'll go ahead and tell you: I'm as much a virgin today as when I came forth from my mama's body."

"Oh, God's blessings on you!" said the friar. "What a good man you've been! In fact, by acting as you have, you are all the more meritorious, because, if you had wanted to, you had more freedom to do the opposite than we and others like us do, since we are bound by the vows of religion."

Next, he asked Ciappelletto if he had displeased God through the sin of gluttony. Breathing a heavy sigh, Ser Ciappelletto replied that he had done so many times. For although it was his habit to fast on bread and water at least three days a week, in addition to doing so during the periods of fasting that devout people observed on holy days throughout the year, he had nevertheless drunk that water with as much delight and gusto as any great wine drinker ever drank his wine, and especially if he was exhausted from performing acts of devotion or making a pilgrimage. Moreover, he was often filled with a longing to have those little salads of baby field greens that women fix when they go to the country, and sometimes, as he ate them, doing so seemed better to him than it should have seemed to someone, like himself, who fasted out of piety, which was the precise reason why he was fasting.

"My son," replied the friar, "these sins are natural and quite trivial, so I don't want you to burden your conscience with them any more than necessary. No matter how truly holy a man may be, eating after a long fast and drinking after hard work will always seem good to him."

"Oh, father," said Ser Ciappelletto, "don't say that just to console me. Surely you must realize that I know how every act we perform in the service of God has to be done wholeheartedly and with an unspotted soul, and how anybody who does otherwise is committing a sin."

Feeling quite content, the friar said: "I am overjoyed that you think like this. It pleases me greatly that on this topic your conscience is pure and good. But tell me: have you committed the sin of avarice by desiring more than what was proper or by keeping what you should not have kept?"

"Father," said Ser Ciappelletto, "I don't want you to suspect me of this because I'm living in the house of these usurers. I'm not here to do business. On the contrary, I've come with the intention of admonishing and chastising them and of leading them away from their abominable moneymaking. What is more, I think I would have succeeded if God had not visited this tribulation upon me. Now, you should know that although my father left me a rich man, I gave away the greater part of what he had to charity after his death. Then, however, in order to sustain my life and to be able to aid Christ's poor, I've done a little bit of trading, and in doing so, I did indeed desire to make money. But I've always divided what I earned down the middle with God's poor, devoting my half to my needs and giving the other half to them, and my Creator has aided me so well in this that my business has continually gotten better and better."

"Well done," said the friar. "But say, how often have you gotten angry?"

"Oh," said Ser Ciappelletto, "that's something, just let me tell you, that's happened to me a lot. For who could restrain himself, seeing the disgusting things men do all day long, neither observing God's commandments, nor fearing His chastisement? There've been many days when I would have preferred to die rather than live to listen to young people swearing and forswearing themselves, and to watch them pursuing vanities, frequenting taverns rather than going to church, and following the ways of the world rather than those of God."

"My son," said the friar, "this is righteous anger, and for my part, I cannot impose any penance on account of it. But was there ever a case in which your anger led you to commit murder or to hurl abuse at anyone or to do them any other sort of injury?"

Ser Ciappelletto answered him: "Alas, sir, how can you, who appear to be a man of God, speak such words? If I'd had even the teeniest little thought about doing any one of the things you've mentioned, do you think I'd believe that God would have shown me so much favor? Those are things that thugs and criminals would do, and whenever I've come upon a person of that sort, I've always said, 'Be gone! And may God convert you.'"

"God bless you, my son!" said the friar. "Now tell me: have you ever borne false witness against anyone or spoken ill of others or taken things from them without their permission?"

"Yes, sir," replied Ser Ciappelletto, "I really have spoken ill of others. Because once I had a neighbor who, without the least justification, was forever beating his wife, and so one time, I criticized him to his wife's family because of the great pity I felt for the wretched creature. Whenever he'd had too much to drink, God alone could tell you how he used to smack her around."

"Well, then," said the friar, "you tell me you've been a merchant. Have you ever deceived anyone, as merchants do?"

"Yes, sir, by gosh," replied Ser Ciappelletto, "but I don't know who he was, except that he was a man who brought me money he owed me for some cloth I'd sold him, and I put it in a box without counting it. Then, a good month later, I discovered that there were four more pennies in it than there should have been. Well, I kept them for an entire year with the intention of returning them to him, but when I never saw him again, I gave them away to charity."

"That was a trifle," said the friar, "and you did well to have acted as you did."

On top of this, the holy friar went on to ask him about many other things and got the same kind of reply in each case. But then, just as he was about to proceed to absolution, Ser Ciappelletto said: "I still have a sin or two more, sir, that I haven't told you about."

The friar asked him what they were, and Ciappelletto replied: "I remember how one Saturday I didn't show proper reverence for the Holy Sabbath because after nones I had my servant sweep the house."°

"Oh, my son," said the friar, "that's a trifle."

"No," said Ser Ciappelletto, "don't call it a trifle, for the Sabbath cannot be honored too much, seeing that it was on just such a day our Savior came back to life from the dead."

Then the friar asked: "Have you done anything else?"

"Yes, sir," replied Ser Ciappelletto. "Once, not thinking about what I was doing, I spat in the house of God."

The friar smiled and said: "My son, that's nothing to worry about. We, who are in holy orders, spit there all day long."

"And what you're doing is vile," said Ser Ciappelletto, "for nothing should be kept as clean as the Holy Temple in which we offer sacrifice to God."

In brief, he told the holy friar many things of this sort, until he finally began sighing and then burst into tears—for he was someone who knew only too well how to do this when he wanted to.

"My son," said the holy friar, "what's wrong?"

"Alas, sir," Ser Ciappelletto replied, "there's still one sin of mine remaining that I've never confessed because I feel so much shame in speaking about it. As you can see, every time I remember it, it makes me weep, and I think there can be no doubt that God will never have mercy on me because of it."

"Come on now, son," said the holy friar, "what are you talking about? If all the sins that have ever been committed by all of humanity, or that will be committed by them as long as the world lasts, were united in one single man, and yet he were as penitent and contrite as I see you are, then truly the benignity and mercy of God are so great that if that man were to confess them, he would be forgiven willingly. Therefore, don't be afraid to speak."

Ser Ciappelletto continued to weep violently as he replied: "Alas, father, my sin is so great that I can hardly believe God will ever pardon it unless you use your prayers on my behalf."

"Speak freely," said the friar, "for I promise I'll pray to God for you."

Ser Ciappelletto just kept on crying and refusing to talk about it, and the friar went on encouraging him to speak. Then, after Ser Ciappelletto had kept the friar in suspense with his weeping for a very long time, he heaved a great sigh and said: "Father, since you've promised to pray to God for me, I will tell you about it. You should know that when I was a little boy, I once cursed my mama." And having said this, he started weeping violently all over again.

"Oh, my son," said the friar, "does this seem such a great sin to you? Why, men curse God all day long, and yet He freely pardons anyone who repents of having cursed Him. And you don't think that He will pardon you for this? Don't weep and don't worry, for surely, even if you had been one of those who placed Him on the cross, He would pardon you because of the contrition I see in you."

"Alas, father," replied Ser Ciappelletto, "what are you saying? My sweet mama, who carried me in her body, day and night, for nine months, and who held me in her arms more than a hundred times—I was too wicked when I cursed her! My sin is too great! And if you don't pray to God for me, it will not be forgiven."

When the friar saw that there was nothing left to say to Ser Ciappelletto, he absolved him and gave him his blessing, taking him to be a very holy man, for he fully believed that what Ser Ciappelletto had said was true—and who would not have believed it, seeing a man at the point of death speak like that?

Then, after all this, the friar said to him: "Ser Ciappelletto, with the help of God you'll soon be well, but if it should happen that God calls that blessed, well-disposed soul of yours to Him, would you like to have your body buried at our monastery?"

"Yes, sir," replied Ser Ciappelletto. "In fact, I wouldn't want to be anywhere else, since you've promised to pray to God for me, not to mention the fact that I have always been especially devoted to your order. Therefore, when you return to your monastery, I beg you to have them send me that most true body of Christ that you consecrate upon the altar every morning, for, although I'm unworthy of it, I would like, with your permission, to partake of it, and afterward, to receive Holy Extreme Unction so that if I have lived a sinner, at least I may die a Christian."°

The holy man said he was greatly pleased that Ser Ciappelletto had spoken so well and told him that he would arrange for the Host to be brought to him right away. And so it was.

The two brothers, who were afraid that Ser Ciappelletto was going to deceive them, had placed themselves near a partition that divided the room where he was lying from the one they were in, and as they eavesdropped, they were able to understand everything he said to the friar. Upon hearing him confess the things he had done, they sometimes had such a desire to laugh that they almost burst, and from time to time they would say to one another: "What kind of man is this, whom neither old age, nor sickness, nor the fear of death, which is imminent, nor the fear of God, before whose judgment he must stand in just a short while, could induce him to give up his wickedness and want to die any differently than he lived?" But, seeing as how he had spoken in such a way that he would be received for burial in a church, everything else was of no consequence to them.

A little later Ser Ciappelletto took Communion, and as his condition was rapidly deteriorating, he received Extreme Unction and then died just a little after vespers of the day on which he had made his good confession. Using Ser Ciappelletto's own money, the two brothers took care of all the arrangements necessary for him to be given an honorable burial and sent word to the friars' house that they should come in the evening to perform the customary wake and take away the body in the morning.

The holy friar who had confessed Ser Ciappelletto, having heard that he had passed away, came to an understanding with the Prior of the monastery, and after the chapterhouse bell had been rung and the friars were gathered together, he explained to them how Ser Ciappelletto had been a holy man, according to what he had deduced from the confession he had heard. And in the hope that the Lord God was going to perform many miracles through Ser Ciappelletto, he persuaded the others to receive the body with the greatest reverence and devotion. The credulous Prior and the other friars agreed to this plan, and in the evening they all went to the room where Ser Ciappelletto's body was laid and held a great and solemn vigil over it. Then, in the morning, they got dressed in their surplices and copes, and with their books in their hands and the cross before them, they went for the body, chanting along the way, after which they carried it to their church with the greatest ceremony and solemnity, followed by almost all the people of the city, men and women alike. Once the body had been placed in the church, the holy friar who had confessed Ser Ciappelletto mounted the pulpit and began to preach marvelous things about him, about his life, his fasts, his virginity, his simplicity and innocence and sanctity, recounting, among other things, what he had confessed to him in tears as his greatest sin, and how he had scarcely been able to get it into his head that God would forgive him for it. After this, the holy friar took the opportunity to reprimand the people who were listening. "And you, wretched sinners," he said, "for every blade of straw your feet trip over, you blaspheme against God and His Mother and all the Saints in Paradise."

Besides this, the holy friar said many other things about Ser Ciappelletto's faith and purity, so that in short, by means of his words, which the people of the countryside believed absolutely, he managed to plant the image of Ser Ciappelletto so deeply inside the minds and hearts of everyone present that when the service was over, there was a huge stampede as the people rushed forward to kiss Ser Ciappelletto's hands and feet. They tore off all the clothing he had on, each one thinking himself blessed if he just got a little piece of it. Furthermore, the body had to be kept there all day long so that everyone could come to see him. Finally, when night fell, he was given an honorable burial in a marble tomb located in one of the chapels. The next day people immediately began going there to light candles and pray to him, and later they made vows to him and hung up ex-votos of wax in fulfillment of the promises they had made.° So great did the fame of Ciappelletto's holiness and the people's devotion to him grow that there was almost no one in some sort of difficulty who did not make a vow to him rather than to some other saint. In the end, they called him Saint Ciappelletto, as they still do, and claim that God has performed many miracles through him and will perform them every day for those who devoutly entrust themselves to him.

Thus lived and died Ser Cepparello da Prato who, as you have heard, became a saint.° Nor do I wish to deny the possibility that he sits among the Blessed in the presence of God. For although his life was wicked and depraved, it is possible that at the very point of death he became so contrite that God took pity on him and accepted him into His kingdom. However, since this is hidden from us, what I will say in this case, on the basis of appearances, is that he is more likely in the hands of the Devil down in Hell than up there in Paradise. And if that is so, then we may recognize how very great God's loving kindness is toward us, in that He does not consider our sinfulness, but the purity of our faith, and even though we make our intercessor one of His enemies, thinking him His friend, God still grants our prayers as if we were asking a true saint to obtain His grace for us. And therefore, so that all of us in this merry company may, by His grace, be kept safe and sound during our present troubles, let us praise His name, which is what we began with, and venerate Him, commending ourselves to Him in our need, in the certain knowledge that we will be heard.

And at this point he fell silent.°

Story 2

ABRAHAM THE JEW, URGED ON BY GIANNOTTO DI CIVIGNÌ,
GOES TO THE COURT OF ROME, AND AFTER HAVING SEEN
THE WICKEDNESS OF THE CLERGY, RETURNS TO PARIS AND
BECOMES A CHRISTIAN.°

The ladies laughed at parts of Panfilo's story while praising it in its entirety. They had given it their full attention, and once it came to an end, the Queen commanded Neifile, who was sitting next to Panfilo, to continue the order of the entertainment they had begun by telling a story of her own. Being no less endowed with courtly manners than beauty, Neifile replied gaily that she would do so with pleasure and began in this fashion:

In his storytelling Panfilo has shown us how the benevolence of God disregards our errors when they result from something we cannot understand, and in mine, I intend to show you how this same benevolence gives proof of its infallible truth by patiently enduring the faults of those who, although they ought to serve as true witnesses to it in both word and deed, do just the opposite. And I tell it in the hope that we will all put what we believe into practice with greater conviction.

I have heard it said, gracious ladies, that in Paris there once lived a great merchant, a good man named Giannotto di Civignì.° Extremely honest and upright, he ran a flourishing cloth business and had the greatest friendship with a very rich Jew named Abraham who was likewise a merchant and an extremely upright and honest man. Recognizing Abraham's honesty and upright character, Giannotto began to feel deep regret that the soul of such a worthy man, who was as good as he was wise, should go to perdition because of his lack of faith. And so, he started pleading with Abraham in an amiable manner to leave behind the errors of the Jewish faith and convert to the Christian truth, which, as something good and holy, was always prospering and increasing, as Abraham could see for himself, whereas clearly his own religion, by contrast, was on the decline and would come to nothing.

The Jew replied that he believed no faith to be either good or holy except the Jewish one, that having been born into it, he intended to live and die in it, and that nothing would ever make him abandon it. Nevertheless, Giannotto did not give up, and a few days later he addressed similar words to Abraham, speaking to him bluntly, as most merchants know how to do, and demonstrating to him how our faith is better than the Jewish one. Although the Jew was a grand master of the Jewish law, he actually began to find Giannotto's arguments compelling, either because he was moved by his great friendship with Giannotto, or perhaps because of the words that the Holy Spirit put into the mouth of that simple man. Still, however, the Jew clung stubbornly to his faith and would not allow himself to be converted.

The more obstinate he remained, the more Giannotto continued to entreat him, until the Jew was finally overcome by his continual insistence. "Look here, Giannotto," he said, "you'd like me to become a Christian. Well, I'm willing to do so, but on one condition: first, I want to go to Rome to see the man who you say is the Vicar of God on earth, and to observe his life and habits and likewise those of his brothers, the cardinals.° Then, if they seem to me to be such men that, between what you've said and what I'm able to observe about them for myself, I can see that your faith is better than mine—which is what you've been trying so hard to show me—I'll do what I've promised you. But if things should turn out differently, I'll remain the Jew that I am."

When Giannotto heard this, he was stricken with a deep sadness. "I've lost all the pains that I thought were so well taken," he said to himself. "I think I've converted him, and yet, if he goes to the court of Rome and sees the wicked and filthy lives of the clergy, not only won't he change from a Jew into a Christian, but if he had already become a Christian, he would, without fail, go back to being a Jew again."

Then, turning to Abraham, he said: "Come on, my friend, why do you want to go to all the trouble and expense you'll have in traveling from here to Rome? Not to mention the fact that both by sea and by land, the journey is filled with dangers for a rich man like you. Don't you think you'll find someone here to baptize you? And if, perhaps, you have doubts about the faith that I've explained to you, where are there more teachers and more learned men than right here who can answer your questions and tell you what you want to know?° Therefore, in my opinion, your trip is unnecessary. Remember that the prelates there are just like the ones you've seen here over the years, although those there are admittedly better insofar as they are closer to the Chief Shepherd. So, my counsel is that you should save your energy now, and at some other time you should go on a pilgrimage to seek an indulgence, when I, perhaps, will be able to keep you company."

"Giannotto," the Jew replied, "I do believe everything you've been saying is true, but to sum it all up in a word: if you want me to do what you've begged me to do so often, I absolutely must go there. Otherwise, I shall do nothing about it."

Seeing his determination, Giannotto said: "Go, then, and good luck to you!" Meanwhile, he thought to himself that Abraham would never want to become a Christian once he had seen the court of Rome, but since there was nothing to be lost if he went there, Giannotto stopped arguing.°

Mounting his horse, the Jew set off as quickly as he could for the court of Rome, where, upon his arrival, he was given an honorable reception by his Jewish friends. He settled in, and without telling anyone why he had come, he began carefully scrutinizing the behavior of the Pope, the cardinals, the other prelates, and all their courtiers. Between what he himself observed—for he was a keenly perceptive man—and the information he obtained from others, he discovered that from the highest to the lowest, all of the clergy, unrestrained by any sense of shame or remorse, committed the sin of lust in great wickedness, and not just the natural variety, but also the sodomitical, such that the influence of whores and boys was of no little importance in obtaining great favors from them. Besides this, he saw clearly that the clergy were all gluttons, drunks, and sots, who, like brute beasts, served their bellies more than anything else except for their lust. On closer inspection, he also discovered that they were all so avaricious and money grubbing that they would as readily buy and sell human blood, that is to say the blood of Christians, as they would sacred objects, whether the sacraments or benefices were involved. In these matters they did more business and employed more middlemen than could be found in any Paris market, including that of the cloth trade. They gave the name of "procurement" to their buying and selling of Church offices, and of "daily rations" to their gluttony, as if, no matter what their words actually referred to, God could not understand the intentions in their wicked hearts and would allow Himself to be deceived, just as men are, by the names that are given to things.° These failings, together with many others it is best to pass over in silence, were highly displeasing to the Jew, who was a sober and temperate man. When he finally felt that he had seen enough, he decided to return to Paris, which is just what he did.

Upon learning that Abraham had returned, Giannotto came to see him, thinking nothing less likely than that he had turned

Christian. The two men greeted one another with the greatest warmth, and then, after letting him have a few days to rest, Giannotto asked him what he thought about the Holy Father and the cardinals and the other courtiers.

"I think they're a curse—which is what I wish God would pronounce on all of them!" the Jew promptly replied. "I'm telling you this, because, if I'm any kind of judge, I saw no holiness there, no devotion, no good works or models of life—or of anything else—in any member of the clergy. Instead, it seemed to me that lust, avarice, gluttony, fraud, envy, pride, and the like, and worse, if anything worse is possible, had such power over everyone that I consider the place a forge of diabolical works rather than divine ones. The way it looks to me, your Shepherd, and all of the others, too, are only interested in reducing the Christian religion to nothing and use all their wits and all their skill to drive it from the world, just when they should be serving as its foundation and support. Still, since I see that what they are trying to do hasn't happened, and the fact is that your religion is constantly growing and becoming more resplendent and illustrious, I think I'm right to conclude that the Holy Spirit must indeed be its foundation and support, for it is truer and holier than any other.° Therefore, whereas I used to stand firm and unyielding against all your entreaties, refusing to become a Christian, now I tell you frankly that I wouldn't let anything get in the way of my becoming one. So, let's go to church, and there I'll have myself baptized according to the customary rites of your holy faith."

When Giannotto, who was expecting precisely the opposite conclusion, heard him say this, he was the happiest man there ever was, and off he went together with Abraham to Notre Dame de Paris where he asked the priests to baptize his friend. Once they learned that Abraham himself wanted it done, they performed the ceremony right away, and as Giannotto raised him from the sacred font, he named him Giovanni.° Giannotto then had the most learned men instruct him thoroughly about our faith, which he quickly mastered, and from that time on, Giovanni was not just a good and worthy man, but one who lived a holy life as well.

Story 3

MELCHISEDECH THE JEW USES A STORY ABOUT THREE RINGS
TO AVOID A VERY DANGEROUS TRAP SET FOR HIM BY
SALADIN.°

After Neifile had fallen silent and everyone had finished praising her story, Filomena, at the Queen's command, began to speak as follows:

The story told by Neifile calls to mind one about the dangerous straits that a Jew once found himself in. Since we have already spoken quite well about God and the truth of our faith, no one should object if at this point we descend to worldly events and the deeds of men. Once you have heard the story I am going to tell you, perhaps you will become more cautious in responding to questions that are put to you.

It is a fact, my dear companions, that just as stupidity will often take a person from a state of happiness and cast him into the greatest misery, so intelligence will extricate him from the gravest dangers and lead him to a state of peace and perfect security. Now, it is so clear that stupidity leads people from happiness into misery that I feel no need to demonstrate the truth of that notion by means of a tale, especially since you can easily find a thousand examples of it every day. Instead, as I promised, by means of a little story, I will show you in brief how intelligence can be our salvation.

Although Saladin's talents were so great that they enabled him to rise from humble beginnings and become the Sultan of Babylon,° while helping him gain many victories over both Saracen and Christian kings, on one occasion he discovered himself in need of a large sum of money, for his entire treasury had been used up in his wars and grand displays of munificence. Unable to see where he could get such a sum in short order, he happened to recall a rich Jew named Melchisedech who had a money-lending business in Alexandria.° Saladin thought this man might just be of service to him if he were willing to provide the money, but the Jew was so miserly he would never do so of his own free will, and Saladin was reluctant to use force. Since his needs were pressing, however, he racked his brains to find a way to get the Jew to be of service and finally decided to use force, but force disguised as reason.

Saladin sent for Melchisedech, and after having received him in an amicable manner, had the Jew sit down beside him. "You're a worthy man," said Saladin, "and many people have told me about your great wisdom and your deep knowledge of the ways of God. Consequently, I would gladly learn from you which of the three laws—the Jewish, the Saracen, or the Christian—you think to be the true one."

The Jew, who really was a wise man, knew only too well that Saladin was looking to catch him making some verbal slip in order to pick a quarrel with him, and he realized that if he praised one of the three more than the other two, he would enable Saladin to achieve his goal. Therefore, knowing that he needed a response that would enable him to avoid being caught, Melchisedech sharpened his wits, and in no time at all came up with just what he needed to say.

"My lord," he replied, "the question you've put to me is a beauty. However, if I'm to reveal to you what I think about it, I must first ask you to listen to the little story you're about to hear.

"Unless I'm mistaken, I remember having heard many times about how there was once a great and wealthy man who had a very beautiful, precious ring that was among the finest jewels in his treasury. Because of its value and its beauty, he wanted to do it the honor of leaving it in perpetuity to his descendants. Consequently, he announced that he would bequeath it to one of his sons, that whoever was discovered to have the ring in his possession should be considered his heir, and that all the others should honor and respect him as the head of the family.

"The son to whom he left the ring then made a similar arrangement for his descendants, doing exactly what his father had done, and thus the ring was passed down through many succeeding generations, ultimately arriving in the hands of a man who had three handsome, virtuous, very obedient sons, all of whom he loved equally. Since the three young men knew about the tradition of the ring, they were all eager to be singled out as the most honored heir and did their utmost to persuade their father, who was by now an old man, to leave them the ring when he died. The worthy man, who loved all his sons equally and could not make up his mind which one to bequeath it to, decided, after having promised it to each of them, that he would attempt to satisfy all three. Accordingly, he had a master craftsman secretly make two other rings that were so similar to the first that he himself, who had ordered them made, was scarcely able to identify the true one. Then, when he was dying, in private he gave each of his sons a ring of his own.

"After their father's death, they all claimed the inheritance and the title, while denying the claims of their brothers, and each one produced his ring as proof that he was right. But when they found the rings were so similar to one another that they could not tell which was the true one, the question of which son was their father's real heir was left pending. And so it still is to this day.

"Now, I say the same thing, my lord, about the three laws given by God the Father to the three peoples about whom you questioned me. Each one believes itself to be the rightful possessor of His inheritance, His true law, and His commandments, but as with the rings, the question of who is right is still pending."

Realizing that the Jew had cleverly figured out how to avoid the snare that was spread out before his feet, Saladin decided instead to say openly what it was he needed and to see if Melchisedech would be willing to be of service to him. And that is just what he did, while also admitting what he had planned to do if Melchisedech had not responded as discreetly as he had.

Melchisedech willingly gave Saladin every last bit of the money he asked for, which Saladin later paid back in full. What is more, Saladin bestowed the most lavish gifts on Melchisedech, became his lifelong friend, and kept him at his side in a lofty position of honor.

Story 4

A MONK, HAVING COMMITTED A SIN DESERVING THE
GRAVEST PUNISHMENT, ESCAPES PAYING ANY PENALTY FOR
IT BY JUSTLY REBUKING HIS ABBOT FOR THE SAME FAULT.°

When she finished her story, Filomena fell silent. Dioneo was sitting next to her, and since he knew from the order they had established that it was his turn, he did not wait for a command from the Queen, but immediately began speaking as follows:

Dear ladies, if I have truly understood your scheme, our purpose here is to amuse ourselves by telling stories. Therefore, as long as we do nothing contrary to this, I think each of us is permitted to do what our Queen has said we could do just a little while ago, namely, to tell whatever stories we think will be the most amusing. Having now heard how Abraham saved his soul through the good advice of Giannotto di Civignì, and how Melchisedech used his wits to defend his wealth from Saladin's snares, I intend, without fear of your censure, to tell a brief tale about how cleverly a monk saved his body from the gravest punishment.°

In Lunigiana, a place not very far from here, there was a monastery that once contained more monks, not to mention more holiness, than it does today.° In it there was a young monk whose vigor and freshness neither fasts nor vigils were able to diminish. By chance, one day around noon, when all the others were sleeping and the young monk was walking all by himself about the church, which was in a very isolated location, he caught sight of an extremely beautiful young woman. Perhaps the daughter of one of the local laborers, she was going through the fields collecting greens of various sorts, and as soon as he laid eyes on her, he was fiercely assaulted by carnal desire.

The monk approached the girl and struck up a conversation with her. One thing led to another until they reached an understanding, after which, making sure no one noticed them, he took her with him back to his cell. As he was sporting with her, however, he got carried away by his inordinate desire and threw caution to the winds, with the result that the Abbot, who had gotten up from his nap and happened to be walking quietly past the monk's cell, heard the racket they were making together. In order to distinguish their voices better, the Abbot stealthily approached the entrance to the cell where he could listen to them. When he realized there was a woman inside, at first he was tempted to order them to open the door. But then he decided on a different approach, and returning to his room, he waited there for the monk to come out.

Although the monk was busy entertaining himself with the girl, to his very great pleasure and delight, he nevertheless suspected that something was up because he thought he heard the shuffling of feet in the corridor. Putting his eye to a tiny hole in the wall, he looked through it and saw the Abbot as clear as day, standing there listening. He realized that the Abbot must have discovered that the girl was in his cell, and he was, consequently, extremely anxious, afraid that he would be severely punished for what he had done. Without revealing his concern to the girl, he ran over a number of different options in his mind, looking for one that might save him. Suddenly, a new kind of trick occurred to him that would hit the target he was aiming at right in the center.

Pretending that he had had enough fun with the girl, the monk said to her: "I want to go and try to find a way for you to get out of here without being seen. Just stay put and keep quiet till I return." After leaving his cell and locking it behind him, however, he went straight to the Abbot's room and gave him the key, as the monks usually did when they went outside. Then, with a straight face, he said: "Sir, this morning I was not able to bring back all the wood that I had them cut. With your permission, I'd like to go to the forest and have it brought here."

Thinking that the monk did not know that he had been observed, the Abbot rejoiced at this turn of events, because it would give him a chance to inform himself more fully about the sin that the monk had committed. He gladly took the key and at the same time gave the monk permission to go. After watching him leave, the Abbot was faced with the decision of what to do next: whether to open the cell in the presence of all the others and let them see the monk's guilt, so that they would have no reason to grumble when he was punished, or rather, before doing that, to get the girl to give him an account of the affair. On reflecting that she might be a respectable woman or the daughter of some important man, and not wishing to shame such a lady by putting her on display in front of all the monks, he decided first to see who she was and then to make up his mind. He therefore went quietly to the cell, opened the door, and went in, locking the door behind him.

When the girl saw the Abbot, she was scared out of her wits and began crying for shame. Messer Abbot looked her over, and noticing how fresh and beautiful she was, he immediately felt, despite his years, the prickings of the flesh that burned in him as much as in the young monk.° "Well, why shouldn't I enjoy myself when I can?" he thought to himself. "After all, sorrow and suffering are always available around here whenever I want them. This gal's a beauty, and nobody really knows she's here. If I can get her to have some fun with me, I don't know why I shouldn't do it. Who is there to know? No one is ever going to find out about it, and 'a sin that's hidden is half forgiven.'° Since I may never have such an opportunity again, I think it the part of a wise man to get some benefit from gifts that God has given to others."

After these reflections, he completely changed the purpose he had originally had in going to the cell. Approaching the girl, he asked her not to cry and gently began sweet-talking her. As one word led to another, he managed to convey to her just what it was he wanted, and the girl, who was hardly made of iron or diamond, gave in very easily to his desires. Embracing her and kissing her repeatedly, he climbed into the monk's little bed with her. Then, perhaps out of regard for the heavy burden of his dignity and the tender years of the girl, or perhaps fearing that he might harm her because of his excessive corpulence, he did not get on top of her but put her on top of him, and for a long time, amused himself with her.

The young monk had only pretended to go to the woods and had hidden himself instead in the corridor. When he saw the

Abbot enter the cell alone, he felt pretty sure that his plan was going to succeed. Indeed, when he saw the door being locked, he was absolutely certain it would. Coming out from his hiding place, he quietly went up to a hole in the wall through which he could see and hear what the Abbot was up to.

Meanwhile, the Abbot, having decided that he had been with the girl long enough, locked her in the cell and returned to his own room. A bit later he heard the monk, who he thought was coming back from the woods. In order to keep for himself alone the booty that both of them had won, the Abbot decided to give the monk a good scolding and then have him locked up. Accordingly, he had the monk summoned before him, put on a stern face, and after rebuking him severely, ordered them to put him in prison.°

The monk responded with the greatest alacrity: "Master, I've not yet been in the Order of Saint Benedict long enough to have learned every particular detail of its rules. Up to now you hadn't shown me how monks are supposed to support women just as they support fasts and vigils. But now that you've shown me how, I promise you that if you pardon me this time, I'll never sin that way again. On the contrary, I'll always do exactly what I saw you doing."

The Abbot, who was a clever man, knew at once that the monk had outsmarted him and had seen what he had done, and since he also felt some degree of remorse because of his own guilt, he was ashamed to inflict a punishment on the monk that he himself deserved just as much. Consequently, he pardoned the monk and imposed a vow of silence on him about what he had seen. Then they got the young girl out of there quite unobtrusively—but you had better believe that afterward they frequently had her back in again.

Story 5

BY MEANS OF A BANQUET CONSISTING ENTIRELY OF HENS, PLUS A FEW SPRIGHTLY LITTLE WORDS, THE MARCHIONESS OF MONFERRATO CURBS THE FOOLISH LOVE OF THE KING OF FRANCE.°

As the ladies listened to Dioneo's story, at first it made them feel a twinge of embarrassment, which manifested itself in their faces as a modest blush, but after a while, that was replaced by a malicious grin, and as they glanced back and forth at one another, they were scarcely able to keep from laughing. Nevertheless, once Dioneo had finished, they scolded him with a few gentle little words, making it clear that such stories were not the sort to be told in the presence of ladies. The Queen then turned to Fiammetta, who was seated next to Dioneo on the grass, and told her to take her turn. With a cheerful expression on her face, Fiammetta graciously began:

Whereas in men it is a sign of great wisdom to court women whose social position is higher than their own, women show how very discerning they are by means of their ability to protect themselves from the love of men stationed above them. For this reason, and also because I am quite pleased to see us using our stories to demonstrate the power of prompt and witty retorts, it occurred to me that I could use the story I have to tell in order to show you, lovely ladies, how a noble woman defended herself by both word and deed from that sort of love and dispelled it in her suitor as well.

The Marquis of Monferrato was a very worthy man who, as a Gonfalonier of the Church, had sailed across the seas leading a Christian army on a Crusade.° Some time after that, when people were talking one day about his merits at the court of Philippe le Borgne, who was himself preparing to leave France and join the Crusade, a knight remarked that there was no couple beneath the stars like the Marquis and his wife, for just as the Marquis was famed among knights for every virtue, so his wife was considered more beautiful and worthy of more respect than any other woman in the world. These words penetrated the heart of the French King so deeply that without his ever having seen her, he immediately began to love her with a passion and decided that he would not set sail for the Crusade he was about to go on from any port except Genoa, because in traveling overland to that city he would have an honest excuse for going to see the Marchioness, and with the Marquis out of the way, he thought he would have a good opportunity to satisfy his desires.°

The King put his plan into effect, sending his men on ahead and setting out afterward himself with a small retinue, including a few noblemen. As he approached the territory of the Marquis, he sent word to the Marchioness a day in advance that she should expect him for dinner the next morning. Being both wise and prudent, the lady sent back a cheerful reply, saying that this would be an honor beyond any other and that he would be truly welcome. Then, however, she started wondering what it meant that such a great king would come to visit her when her husband was not at home. Nor did she deceive herself when she reached the conclusion that he had been drawn there by her reputation for beauty. Nevertheless, like the worthy woman she was, she prepared to receive him, and after having summoned the gentlemen who still remained in her court, she solicited their advice, after which she gave orders for all the necessary arrangements to be made, at the same time declaring that she would take care of the banquet and the details of the menu by herself. Then, without a moment's hesitation she had all the hens in the countryside rounded up and ordered her cooks to make a series of different dishes out of them for the royal feast.

The King arrived on the appointed day and was honorably and ceremoniously received by the lady. Now that he actually saw her, it seemed to him that her beauty, worth, and refinement went far beyond anything he had imagined on the basis of the knight's words. Awestruck, he complimented her lavishly, for he was even more inflamed with passion on finding that the lady transcended his expectations of her. After a short rest in his chambers, which were richly furnished in a manner appropriate for the reception of so great a king, it was time for dinner, and the King sat down at one table with the Marchioness, while the remaining guests were given seats of honor at the other tables according to their rank.

As he was served an elaborate series of dishes one after the other, all accompanied by the finest, most precious wines, the King gazed contentedly from time to time at the radiantly beautiful Marchioness, which filled him with the most intense pleasure. However, as one course succeeded another, he found himself increasingly baffled by the fact that, however different the preparations were, hens supplied the main ingredient in all of them. The King was well enough acquainted with that region to know that it had to have an abundant supply of game of all sorts, and by announcing his arrival to the lady in advance, he had given her plenty of time to organize a hunt. Nevertheless, although he was truly puzzled, he had no desire to do anything except to get her to say something about her hens. So, with a smile on his face, he turned to her and said: "My lady, are hens alone born in this country, and never any cocks at all?"

The Marchioness, who understood perfectly well what he was asking, realized that God had given her just the opportunity she desired to explain what she intended. Turning boldly to the King, she replied to his question: "No, my lord, although they differ from others somewhat in their rank and style of clothing, for all that, the females here are made the same way they are everywhere else."°

On hearing this, the King understood clearly the reason for the banquet of hens as well as the virtue concealed beneath the Marchioness's words. He realized that persuasion would be wasted on such a woman and that force was out of the question. And so, just as he had been foolishly inflamed because of her, he now decided wisely that, for the sake of his honor, his ill-conceived fire had to be extinguished. Fearing her retorts, he refrained from teasing her any further, and with all his hopes dashed, concentrated on eating his dinner. As soon as the meal was finished, in order to cover the dishonorable way he had come by means of a hasty departure, he thanked her for her hospitality, she wished him Godspeed, and off he went to Genoa.

Story 7

WITH A STORY ABOUT PRIMASSO AND THE ABBOT OF
CLUNY, BERGAMINO JUSTLY REBUKES MESSER CAN DELLA
SCALA FOR AN UNEXPECTED FIT OF AVARICE.°

*   *   *

It is a fine thing, worthy ladies, to hit a target that never moves, but it is quasi-miraculous when some unexpected object appears all of a sudden and an archer hits it in a flash. The vicious and filthy life of the clergy is in many regards just such a fixed target of wickedness, so that it is not especially difficult for anyone so inclined to speak out, attack, and reproach them for it. Therefore, if the good man did well to rebuke the Inquisitor for the hypocritical charity of the friars, because they offered the poor what should have been given to the pigs or just thrown out, then I think the person of whom I shall speak, and of whom I was reminded by the last tale, is worthy of much more praise. For this man rebuked Messer Can della Scala, a great lord, for a sudden and atypical fit of avarice by telling a charming story in which he represented, through its characters, what he wanted to say about himself and his lord.° And the story goes as follows.

Practically everyone in the world knows of the great fame of Messer Can della Scala, a man whom Fortune favored in so many ways and who had the reputation of being one of the most distinguished and magnificent lords Italy has seen since the time of the Emperor Frederick II.° Messer Cane decided to stage a splendid festival in Verona, one that would be truly memorable, and he invited many people to it from all over, and especially court entertainers of every stripe. However, a sudden whim led him to change his mind, and after partially reimbursing his guests with token gifts, he sent them all away. Only one man remained behind, an entertainer named Bergamino, whose mastery of impromptu, yet polished speech was so impressive that you would only believe it if you heard him talk.° Since he had neither received a gift nor been given leave to depart, he hoped that this meant there was still some future benefit in store for him. However, the idea had somehow gotten itself into Messer Cane's head that anything he might give the man would be more surely wasted than if he had thrown it into the fire. Still, Messer Cane did not say anything to Bergamino about this, nor did he have anyone else do so.

After several days, Bergamino began to grow melancholy, for he was not sent for and asked to give a professional performance, and he realized he was using up all of his money just staying at the inn with his servants and horses. Nevertheless, he continued to wait, since it did not seem like a good idea for him to leave. In order to make an honorable appearance at the festival, he had brought with him three beautiful, expensive suits of clothes, which had been given to him by other lords, and since the innkeeper was asking to be paid, Bergamino started out by giving him one of them. Then, as the waiting continued a while longer, he was obliged, if he wanted to keep his room at the inn, to give him the second one. Finally, Bergamino started living off the third suit, having decided to stay until he saw how long it would last him and to go away after that.

Now, while he was consuming his third suit of clothes, he just happened to be standing one day by the table where Messer Cane was eating his dinner. Upon seeing Bergamino with a very melancholy look on his face, Messer Cane said, more to mock him than to be entertained by one of his witty remarks: "Bergamino, what's wrong? You look so melancholy. Tell us about it."

Without reflecting for more than a split second, yet speaking as though he had spent a great deal of time thinking about what he would say, Bergamino told this story, which fit his situation to a tee.

"My lord," he said, "let me begin by telling you about Primasso, a most worthy grammar master who had no equal at composing verse and was able to produce it with greater facility than anyone else.° His talents had made him so respected and so famous that even where he was not known by sight, there was almost no one who did not know him by name and reputation.

"Now it happened that one day when Primasso was in Paris, living in poverty—indeed, most of the time his livelihood depended on a talent that was little appreciated by those who had the means to help him—he heard mention of the Abbot of Cluny, a man who was thought to have so much income from his estates that he was the richest prelate, except for the Pope, in God's Church.° He heard people saying marvelous, magnificent things about the Abbot, such as how he was always holding court and how no one who went there was ever denied food and drink, provided he asked for them while the Abbot himself was dining.

"When Primasso heard these things, being a man who enjoyed associating with gentlemen and lords, he decided to go and see just how magnificent a lifestyle this Abbot had. He asked how far away the Abbot's residence was from Paris, and on being told that it was a distance of perhaps six miles, he calculated that he could get there by the dinner hour if he set out early in the morning. He was shown which road to take, but when he couldn't find anyone going in that direction, he was afraid that he might have the bad luck to get lost and wind up in a place where it would be difficult to find something to eat. Therefore, to be on the safe side, he decided to make sure he wouldn't lack for food by taking three loaves of bread with him, being convinced at the same time that he would always be able to find water to drink, even though it was not something he especially cared for.°

"Tucking the three loaves into his shirt, he started on his journey and made such progress that he arrived at the Abbot's residence before the dinner hour. Once inside, he went about inspecting everything, and when he discovered that a very large number of tables had been set, great preparations were under way in the kitchen, and many other things were being made ready for the meal, he said to himself: 'Truly, this man is as magnificent as people say he is.' For a while he just stood there, watching intently everything that was going on, until it was time to eat, at which point the Abbot's steward ordered water for all of them to wash their hands and then seated them at the tables.

"By chance, Primasso was given a seat right opposite the doorway through which the Abbot would pass when he entered the dining room. They had a custom in his court of never putting wine or bread or anything else to eat or drink on the tables before the Abbot himself had come in and sat down. Thus, when the tables were set, the steward sent word to the Abbot, informing him that the food was ready and he could come whenever he pleased. The Abbot had a servant open the door so that he could enter the room, and as he walked in, looking straight ahead of him, the very first man his eyes happened to light on was the shabbily dressed Primasso, whom he did not recognize by sight. As he stared at Primasso, a mean thought suddenly popped into his head, the kind of thought he had never had before, and he said to himself: 'Just look at the guy I'm giving my food to!' Then, turning on his heels, he ordered his servants to shut the door behind him, after which he asked them if anyone recognized the ragamuffin who was seated at the table directly opposite the entrance to the room. None of them, however, knew who the man was.

"Primasso had worked up quite an appetite because of his walk, and he wasn't in the habit of fasting, so after waiting a bit and seeing no sign of the Abbot coming back, he took one of the three loaves he'd carried with him out of his shirt and began to eat it. Meanwhile, the Abbot, who had paused a moment, ordered one of his servants to go and see if Primasso had left. The servant replied, 'No, sir. On the contrary, he's eating some bread that he must have brought with him.' 'Well,' said the Abbot, 'let him eat his own food, if he's got any, because he's not going to eat any of ours today.'

"The Abbot would have preferred to have Primasso leave of his own accord, for it seemed discourteous to send him away. By this time, Primasso had finished the first loaf, and there being no sign of the Abbot, began to eat the second. This fact was likewise reported to the Abbot who had sent a servant to see if the man had left. Finally, when the Abbot still did not come, Primasso, who had polished off the second loaf, started on the third. This fact was also reported to the Abbot, who, after pondering what it meant, said to himself, 'Now what's this strange thing that's gotten into me today? Why am I being such a miser? Why do I feel all this contempt? And for whom? I've given my food to anyone who wanted it for many years now without asking if he was a gentleman or a peasant, rich or poor, merchant or huckster. With my own eyes, I've seen any number of tramps devouring my food, and never once did I feel the way I do about this one. Since I would never have been afflicted with such stinginess by a man of no moment, this one, whom I've been regarding as a good-for-nothing, must really be somebody, for me to have set my heart against offering him my hospitality.'

"After these reflections, the Abbot really wanted to find out who the man might be, and when he discovered it was Primasso, who had come to see if what he had heard about the Abbot's magnificence were true, he felt a deep sense of shame, for he had long been aware of Primasso's reputation as a worthy man. Desirous of making amends, the Abbot contrived all sorts of ways to honor him, and after a dinner in keeping with Primasso's merits, he had him outfitted like a gentleman, provided him with money and a saddle horse, and told him he was free to come and go as he pleased.° More than satisfied, Primasso gave the Abbot the most heartfelt thanks, after which he returned to Paris on horseback, from which he had come on foot."

Messer Cane, a most perceptive lord, did not need an explanation to grasp what Bergamino meant, and with a broad smile said to him: "Bergamino, you've given an apt demonstration of the wrongs you've suffered, while at the same time showing us your virtues, my miserliness, and what it is you want from me. Honestly, never before have I been afflicted with the avarice I felt today on your account, but I will beat it away, using the stick you yourself have provided." Then, having paid off the innkeeper, Messer Cane had Bergamino dressed most nobly in one of his own suits of clothes, provided him with money and a saddle horse, and told him he was free to come and go as he pleased for the rest of his stay.

Conclusion

The sun was already sinking as vespers approached, and the heat had largely dissipated, when the young women and the three young men found that their storytelling had come to an end. Accordingly, the Queen addressed them in pleasant tones:

"Now, my dear companions, nothing remains for me to do during my reign today except to present you with a new Queen who will decide how her time and ours should be spent in honest pleasures tomorrow. And although my reign would seem to last until nightfall, I think this is the best hour for us to begin ruling from now on, so that we can make preparations for whatever topic the new Queen thinks appropriate for the next day. After all, those who do not set aside time for things beforehand will not be able to provide adequately for the future.° Therefore, in reverence for Him through Whom all things live, and for the sake of your pleasure, I say that the most prudent Filomena shall govern our realm on this, our second day."°

When she had finished speaking, she rose to her feet, and taking her garland of laurel, placed it reverently on Filomena, whom she and all the other ladies, and the men as well, hailed as their Queen, after which they happily pledged that they would obey her.

Blushing a bit because of her embarrassment at seeing herself crowned Queen, Filomena remembered the words spoken by Pampinea just a little earlier, and in order not to appear dull, she plucked up her courage and began by confirming the orders Pampinea had given. Then, seeing that they would continue to stay in their present lodging, she made arrangements for what they would eat the next morning as well as for their supper later that day, after which she spoke to them as follows:

"My dear, dear companions, although Pampinea, more out of kindness than because of my merits, has made me Queen over you, I am disinclined to rely on my judgment alone as to how we should spend our time, and instead, want us to make all our decisions together. In order to give you a chance to add things to my plan and to subtract things from it as you wish, let me briefly explain what I think we should do. Now, unless I am mistaken, the formalities observed by Pampinea today seem to me to have been both praiseworthy and delightful, and as long as they do not become tedious, either because we repeat them too often or for some other reason, in my judgment we should not make any changes.

"Given, then, the order that we have already begun to follow, we should get up now and go off in search of ways to amuse ourselves for a while. At about the time the sun is setting, we should eat our supper out of doors, after which we will have a few little songs and other entertainment until it is time for us to go to bed.

Tomorrow morning, we will get up while it is still cool, and once again we will all go off and amuse ourselves in whatever ways we think best. Then, just as we did today, we will return at the appointed hour to eat and dance, and after we have arisen from our nap, we will come back here to tell stories, which always, in my opinion, provide us with a great deal of pleasure as well as profit.

"Speaking frankly, I wish to initiate a practice that Pampinea could not introduce because she was elected Queen so late, and that is, I want to restrict within definite limits the subject matter of the stories we are going to tell. This way, because the theme will be announced in advance, each of you will have time to think up a fine story to tell about the topic that has been proposed. And this, if you please, is what it shall be: since from the beginning of time men have been subject to the whims of Fortune, as they will be to the very end, each one of us should speak about people who, after suffering through many misfortunes, arrive at a happy end beyond anything they could have hoped for."

All of them, both the women and the men, praised this arrangement and agreed to abide by it, except for Dioneo, who said, when the rest were silent: "My lady, like everyone else, I, too, say that the order you have established is quite pleasing and praiseworthy. But I beg you to grant me a special favor, which I would like to see confirmed for as long as this company stays together, namely, that if I do not want to be, I will not be forced by our arrangement to tell a story on the theme proposed, but can tell one on whatever topic I wish. Moreover, so that no one thinks I want this favor because I am the kind of person who does not have a lot of stories at hand, from now on I am willing always to be the last one to speak."

With the consent of all the others, the Queen happily granted him his wish, knowing that he was an entertaining and jovial person and clearly perceiving that he was only asking for such a favor so that, if the company ever got tired of talking on their chosen theme, he could cheer them up with a tale that would make them laugh. Then she stood up, and they all walked off at a leisurely pace toward a stream of crystal-clear water, whose banks were lined with smooth stones and verdant grasses, and that flowed down from a little mountain into the shade of a thickly wooded valley. There, with their feet and arms bare, they waded into the water and started playing all sorts of games with one another. Later, as the time for supper drew near, they returned to the palace where they ate together merrily.

When their meal was finished, they called for instruments, and the Queen had them begin a dance, which Lauretta was to lead, while Emilia would sing a song accompanied by Dioneo on the lute. Obedient to the Queen's command, Lauretta began dancing at once, while Emilia sang the following song in amorous tones:

> I'm so enamored of my loveliness
> That I will never care for other loves
> Or ever feel desire for them.
> When in my looking glass I view myself,
> I see the good that makes the mind content,
> Nor can some new event or some old thought
> Serve to deprive me of such dear delight.
> What other pleasing object, then,
> Could ever come in view
> To fill my heart with new desire?
> This good will never flee when I desire
> The consolation of its sight. Instead,
> To my delight, it moves toward me
> And is so sweet, I feel no words can say
> What it may be, or if they could, be grasped
> By any mortal living here
> Who did not burn with similar desire.
> And as I gaze more fixedly at it,
> My flame burns fiercer every hour.
> To it I give myself, to it surrender,
> Already tasting what it's promised me,
> And hoping that a greater joy than this,
> Whose equal no one ever felt,
> May come from such desire for loveliness.°

Even though the words of the little song made some of them ponder its meaning, they all cheerfully joined together in singing the refrains. When they were done, they did a few little dances for a while, and then, a portion of the short night having already passed, the Queen was pleased to proclaim that the end of the first day had been reached. Having called for torches to be lit, she ordered them all to go to bed, and after returning to their rooms, that is what they did.

Day 2

* * *

Story 1

PRETENDING TO BE A CRIPPLE, MARTELLINO MAKES IT SEEM
AS THOUGH HE IS CURED AFTER HAVING BEEN PLACED ON
THE BODY OF SAINT ARRIGO. WHEN HIS RUSE IS DISCOVERED,
HE IS BEATEN AND THEN ARRESTED, AND THOUGH IN
DANGER OF BEING HANGED, HE GETS OFF IN THE END.°

Dearest ladies, it often happens that those who try to make fools of
others, and especially in matters worthy of reverence, wind up not

only being made fools of themselves, but sometimes come to harm as well. Therefore, in obedience to the Queen's command, I will begin our storytelling on the chosen topic by telling you about what happened to a fellow citizen of ours who was at first quite unlucky, but wound up, beyond his wildest expectations, very happy indeed.

Not long ago there was a poor German named Arrigo living in Treviso, who worked as a porter, carrying heavy loads for anyone willing to pay, yet he was universally held to be a good man and was thought to have lived the most saintly of lives. Whether it was true or not, the Trevisans affirm that when he died, at the hour of his death all the bells of the Cathedral of Treviso began to ring even though no one was there pulling the ropes. Taking this to be a miracle, everyone said that Arrigo was a saint, and the entire populace of the city ran to the house in which his corpse was lying and carried it to the cathedral as if it were indeed the body of a saint. The lame, the crippled, and the blind were brought there, along with others suffering from all manner of illnesses and infirmities, in the belief that they would all be healed merely by touching his body.

In the midst of all this turmoil, with people coming and going, three of our fellow citizens happened to arrive in Treviso, the first named Stecchi, the second Martellino, and the third Marchese, all of whom used to frequent various noblemen's courts, entertaining the spectators there by putting on disguises and using strange gestures and expressions to impersonate anyone they pleased. They had never been to Treviso before and were surprised to see everyone running about, but as soon as they learned the reason why, they were eager to go and see for themselves.

After they had deposited their belongings at an inn, Marchese said: "We may want to go and have a look at this saint, but for my part, I don't see how we're going to get to him because from what I've heard, the square is full of Germans as well as lots of armed men whom the ruler of the city has stationed there to prevent disturbances.° And besides that, the church is said to be so packed with people that no one else can get inside."

"Don't give up just for that," said Martellino, who was eager to see what was going on. "I'm certain I can find a way to reach the saint's body."

"How?" asked Marchese.

"I'll tell you how," Martellino replied. "I'm going to disguise myself like a cripple, and then, with you on one side and Stecchi on the other, you'll go along holding me up as if I couldn't walk on my own, pretending that you want to take me where I can be healed by the saint. Anybody seeing us will get out of the way and let us through."

Marchese and Stecchi liked the plan, so the three of them promptly left the inn, and as soon as they reached a deserted spot, Martellino twisted up not only his hands, fingers, arms, and legs, but his mouth, eyes, and entire face as well, making himself look so horrific that anyone who saw him would have believed his body was crippled and hopelessly paralyzed. When he was ready, Marchese and Stecchi picked him up, and with the most pitiful expressions on their faces, made their way to the church, humbly asking all those in front of them, for the love of God, to let them through. They got people to move out the way without difficulty, and in short, accompanied by shouts of "Make way! Make way!" and with all eyes turned to look at them, they managed to reach the spot where the body of Saint Arrigo had been placed. There some gentlemen standing around the body immediately grabbed Martellino and put him on top of it so that he might benefit from contact with its holiness.

For some time Martellino just lay there while everyone stared at him, waiting to see what would happen. Then, like the expert performer he was, he began his show, pretending to straighten one of his fingers, then a hand, then an arm, and so on, until he had unwound himself completely. When the people saw this, they made so much noise in praise of Saint Arrigo that a thunderclap could not have been heard over it.

By chance, there was a Florentine nearby who was well acquainted with Martellino, but who had failed to recognize him when they brought him in because he had disguised himself so well. But when he saw Martellino standing up straight, he recognized who it was and burst out laughing. "Goddamn the guy!" he said. "Who would've believed that when he came here he wasn't a real cripple?"

"What?" exclaimed several Trevisans who had overheard what he had said. "Do you mean to say he wasn't a cripple?"

"Heaven forbid!" the Florentine replied. "He's always stood as straight as any one of us. But as you've just seen, he knows better than anybody how to play these tricks and can disguise himself any way he wants to."

That was all they needed to hear. Forcing their way to the front, they shouted: "Seize the traitor, this guy who mocks God and the Saints. He wasn't a cripple; he just came here disguised as one to make fun of us and our saint." And so saying, they grabbed him and dragged him down from where he was standing. Holding him by the hair, they tore all the clothes off his back and started punching and kicking him. To Martellino it seemed as though everybody there had rushed up to join in the fray. "Mercy," he cried, "for the love of God!" But although he did his best to defend himself, it was no use, and the crowd on top of him just kept getting bigger and bigger.

When Stecchi and Marchese saw what was happening, they realized that things were not looking good, but since they feared for their own safety, they did not dare to help Martellino, and in fact, along with everyone else, they were screaming that he deserved to be killed. At the very same time, however, they were trying to think of a way to get him out of the people's hands, who would surely have slain him if, all of a sudden, a plan had not occurred to Marchese. Since the entire watch of the city was posted outside the church, he went as quickly as he could to the lieutenant who had been put in charge by the *podestà,* and said to him, "Help me, for God's sake!° There's a crook here who's cut my purse, and it had at least a hundred gold florins in it. Arrest him, please. I want to get my money back."

On hearing this, a good dozen watchmen immediately ran over to where the wretched Martellino was being given a thorough shellacking.° They had the greatest difficulty in the world forcing their way through the crowd, but they managed to get him away from them and dragged him off to the palace, all bruised and battered. Many who felt he had been mocking them followed him there, and when they heard that he had been arrested as a cutpurse, they all began saying that he had cut their purses, too, since they had no other warrant to make trouble for him. When the *podestà*'s judge, a tough customer himself, heard these accusations, he immediately took Martellino aside and began interrogating him. But Martellino answered back with smart talk, as though he thought his arrest were no big deal. This infuriated the judge, who had him tied to the strappado and given a series of good, hard jerks.° The judge's intention was to get Martellino to confess to what his accusers were saying and then to have him hanged.

When Martellino was down on the ground again, the judge asked him if what his accusers were saying against him was true. Since denials would have been useless, Martellino replied: "My lord, I'm ready to confess the truth. But first, make everyone who's accusing me say when and where I cut his purse, and then I'll tell you whether I did it or not."

"Good idea," said the judge and had a number of them brought forward. One said that his purse had been cut a week before, another six days, another four, and several, that very day.

When Martellino heard them, he said: "My lord, they're lying through their teeth, and I can prove it! The truth is that I've never set foot inside this town—and I wish I'd never done so—until just a little while ago, and the moment I arrived, I went to see the body of this saint, where I had the bad luck to get a thorough shellacking, as you can see for yourself. Everything I'm telling you can be verified by the gatekeeper, who keeps tabs on all the foreigners coming into the city, and you can check his register, and ask my innkeeper, too. And then, if you conclude that I'm telling you the truth, please don't have me tortured and put to death because of the accusations of these wicked men."

While things were in this state, word had reached Marchese and Stecchi that the judge was giving Martellino a very rough time and had already had him tortured on the strappado. "What a mess we've made of it," they said, terrified, to one another. "We've taken him out of the frying pan and thrown him into the fire." Proceeding with the utmost caution, they then located the innkeeper and explained to him what had happened. Once he stopped laughing, he took them to a certain Sandro Agolanti, who lived in Treviso and had great credit with the ruler of the city.° The innkeeper told Sandro the whole story and with the other two begged him to intervene on Martellino's behalf.

After a hearty laugh, Sandro went to the ruler and asked him to send for Martellino, which he did. The men who went to fetch him found him standing before the judge in nothing but his shirt, thoroughly terrified and dismayed because the judge would not listen to anything that was said in his defense. On the contrary, since the judge just happened to have some sort of grudge against Florentines, he was absolutely determined to have Martellino hanged, and until forced to do so, he stubbornly refused to release him. When Martellino stood before the ruler, he told him the whole story and begged him, as a special favor, to be allowed to leave, because, he said, until he was in Florence again, he would always feel he had a noose around his neck. The ruler laughed long and hard over his misadventures, and then had each one of the Florentines given a new suit of clothes. Thus, beyond anything they could have expected, all three of them escaped from their terrible ordeal and returned home safe and sound.

Story 2

AFTER BEING ROBBED, RINALDO D'ASTI TURNS UP AT CASTEL
GUIGLIELMO, WHERE HE IS GIVEN LODGING BY A WIDOW,
AND THEN, AFTER HAVING RECOVERED HIS POSSESSIONS,
RETURNS HOME SAFE AND SOUND.°

The ladies laughed heartily at Neifile's account of Martellino's misadventures, as did the young men, and especially Filostrato, who was sitting next to her and was then ordered by the Queen to continue the storytelling. Without a moment's hesitation, he began:

My fair ladies, the story that attracts my interest involves a mixture of piety, misfortune, and love. Perhaps all there is to say for it is that it will be profitable for those who hear it and especially for those who have wandered through the hazardous lands of love, where anyone who has not said the Prayer of Saint Julian over and over again will find bad lodging no matter how good his bed may be.°

During the rule of the Marquis Azzo da Ferrara, a merchant named Rinaldo d'Asti was returning home from Bologna where he had gone to take care of some business.° He had already left Ferrara behind and was riding toward Verona when he happened to run into some men who looked to him like merchants but were actually bandits, a trio of wicked and particularly disreputable individuals. Rinaldo struck up a conversation with them and then foolishly decided to ride along in their company.

Seeing that Rinaldo was a merchant, the bandits guessed that he had money on him and decided they would rob him when the first opportunity presented itself. Meanwhile, to prevent him from getting suspicious, they assumed an air of modesty and propriety, and as they rode along, spoke with him only about matters involving honesty and trust, doing their best to make themselves seem humble and unthreatening. Since Rinaldo was traveling alone, accompanied by only a single servant on horseback, he concluded that his running into them was quite a stroke of good luck.

As they rode on, the conversation passed from one topic to another as it tends to do, until they got into a discussion of the prayers men say to God, at which point one of the three thieves addressed Rinaldo: "And you, my good sir, what prayer do you usually say when you're traveling?"

"To tell the truth," Rinaldo replied, "in such matters I'm pretty simple and down to earth, the old-fashioned kind of guy who'll tell you that two *soldi* are twenty-four *denari,* and so, I don't have many prayers on hand.° Still, when I'm traveling, it's always been my custom never to leave my lodging in the morning without

saying an Our Father and a Hail Mary for the souls of Saint Julian's
father and mother. After that, I pray to the saint himself and to God
to send me good lodging on the night to come. During my travels
I've spent a lot of days exposed to grave dangers, but I've escaped
all of them and invariably found myself at night in a safe place
where there was a comfortable inn. I therefore firmly believe that
Saint Julian, in whose honor I always say my prayer, interceded
with God to obtain this grace for me, and that if I fail to say that
prayer in the morning, I doubt the day would go well for me or I'd
arrive safely at night."

"And did you say it this morning?" asked the man who had
questioned him.

"Yes, indeed," replied Rinaldo.

Then the bandit, who already knew what was going to happen,
said to himself: "You're really going to need that prayer, because if
our plan succeeds, I think you're going to find pretty bad lodging
tonight."

"I've done a lot of traveling, too," he said to Rinaldo, "and
although I've never recited that prayer, which I've heard many
people praise, I myself have never wound up with a bad inn. Perhaps this evening you'll be able to discover which of us finds the
better one, you who have said the prayer, or I who have not. Truth
to tell, though, instead of that one of yours, I do say the *Dirupisti*
or the *'Ntemerata* or the *De profundis,* which are all very effective,
or so my old grandmother used to tell me."°

As they continued on their way, talking with Rinaldo of this
and that, the bandits were constantly on the lookout for a suitable
time and place to carry out their evil plan. It was already getting
late when they reached a river crossing beyond Castel Guiglielmo.
Seeing that it was almost night and that the spot they had reached
was deserted and out of the way, the three of them assaulted Rinaldo
and robbed him, leaving him on foot with nothing but his shirt.
Riding off, they said: "Now go and see if your Saint Julian will give
you good lodging tonight; our saint is certainly going to provide it
for us." And crossing the river, away they went.

When Rinaldo's coward of a servant saw him being attacked,

instead of coming to his master's aid, he turned his horse around, and galloping off in the direction they had come from, did not stop until he reached Castel Guiglielmo. Since it was already evening when he entered the fortress, he went and found himself an inn for the night and never gave what had happened another thought.

Rinaldo, barefooted and wearing only his shirt, was at his wits' end, for night had already fallen, the cold was intense, and the heavy snow kept falling and falling. Shivering all over, his teeth chattering, he decided to look around for some sort of shelter where he could spend the night and not die from the cold. But since there had recently been a war in the surrounding countryside, everything had been burned to the ground, and there was no shelter to be found. Setting off at a trot because of the frigid temperature, Rinaldo headed in the direction of Castel Guiglielmo. He did not know whether his servant had fled there or elsewhere, but he thought that if he could just get inside, then perhaps God would send him some sort of relief. However, by the middle of the night he was still a mile away, and when he finally did arrive, he could not get in because it was now so late that the gates had been locked and the drawbridges raised. Grief-stricken and weeping inconsolably, he was looking around for a place where he could at least get out of the snow, when by chance he caught sight of a house jutting out from the top of the castle walls. He decided he would go there and take shelter under it until the morning. When he reached the spot and discovered that there was a locked door beneath the overhang, he gathered some straw together that was on the ground nearby and sat down on it in front of the door, repeatedly complaining to Saint Julian in sad and mournful tones and saying that this was not what he deserved for all his faith and devotion. Saint Julian was, however, keeping an eye on him and did not wait long to supply him with good lodging.

In that fortress there was a widow whose beauty surpassed that of all other women, and Marquis Azzo, having fallen passionately in love with her, had set her up, for his pleasure, in the very house under whose overhang Rinaldo had taken refuge. By chance, the Marquis had come to the fortress during the day with the intention of spending the night with her and had made secret arrangements to have a bath and a magnificent supper prepared in her house. But just when everything was ready and she was anticipating his arrival, a servant showed up at the town gates with a message for the Marquis requiring him to leave immediately, and he quickly rode off on his horse, having first sent word to the lady that she should not wait up for him. Rather disconsolate and not knowing quite what to do with herself, the lady finally decided to get into the bath prepared for the Marquis, after which she would eat supper and go to bed.

The bath she got into was located near the door next to which the wretched Rinaldo sat huddled together on the other side of the town wall. As the lady lay there, she could hear someone who was weeping and whose teeth were chattering so badly that he sounded as if he had been turned into a stork clacking its beak. She called her maid and said: "Go upstairs, take a look over the wall, and see who's on the other side of this door. Then find out who he is and what he's doing there."

The maid went, and thanks to the clear night air, she could see Rinaldo sitting just as we said he was, barefooted, with nothing on but his shirt, and shivering violently. She asked him who he was, and Rinaldo, shaking so badly that he could scarcely pronounce the words, told her as quickly as he could who he was, how he had come there, and why. He then begged her in a pitiful voice to do whatever she could to prevent his being left there all night to die from the cold.

The maid, feeling quite sorry for him, returned and told her mistress everything, which moved her to feel sorry for Rinaldo as well. Recalling that she had the key to that door, which the Marquis sometimes used for his clandestine visits, she said: "Go and let him in, but do it quietly. We have this supper here with no one to eat it, and there's plenty of room to put him up."

The maid lavishly praised her lady for the humanity of her deed and then went directly to open the door for Rinaldo. Once they got him inside and saw that he was almost frozen to death, the lady said to him: "Quickly, my good man, get into this bath while it's still warm."

More than willing to get in, Rinaldo did not need a second invitation. There, as the heat of the bath succeeded in reviving him, he felt like a dead man who had come back to life. The lady then had him supplied with clothes that had once belonged to her recently deceased husband, and when Rinaldo put them on, he found that they fit as though they had been made to measure for him. While he waited for further instructions from the lady, he fell to thanking God and Saint Julian for having saved him from the horrible night he had been expecting and for leading him to what seemed like very good lodging, indeed.

Meanwhile, the lady had ordered her maid to light a great fire in one of her rooms and had gone off to take a short nap. When she returned, she asked at once how the gentleman was doing.

"He's dressed, my lady," her maid responded, "and he's oh so handsome and looks just like a proper gentleman."

"Well, go and call him," said the lady. "Tell him to come here and have some supper by the fire, since I know he hasn't had anything to eat."

When Rinaldo entered the room and saw the lady, who seemed from her appearance to be a person of quality, he greeted her respectfully and offered her his most sincere thanks for the kindness she had done him. Looking him over as he spoke, the lady concluded he was everything her maid had said he was, and after welcoming him cordially, she had him take a comfortable seat beside her by the fire and asked him to tell her all about the misfortune that had brought him there. In response, Rinaldo told her the whole story from beginning to end.

Since the lady had already learned something about what had happened because of the arrival of Rinaldo's servant at the fortress, she had no difficulty believing everything he said. In turn, she told him what she knew about his servant, adding that it would be easy to find him the next morning. But now that the table was set, they washed their hands, and at the lady's invitation, Rinaldo sat down and had supper with her.

Rinaldo was a fine, tall, handsome man in the prime of life, with impeccable manners, and as the lady repeatedly glanced over at him, she saw a lot there to like. Furthermore, since thoughts of the Marquis, who was to have come and slept with her that night, had already aroused her carnal appetite, after supper, she got up from the table and went to consult her maid, asking her if she thought it a good idea to make use of the gift that Fortune had sent her, seeing as how the Marquis had left her high and dry. The maid understood what her lady wanted and did everything she could to encourage her to go after it for all she was worth.

Consequently, the lady returned to the fire where she had left Rinaldo all alone, and as she looked at him, her eyes brimming with desire, she said: "Oh, Rinaldo, why are you so pensive? Don't you think you can find something to compensate for the loss of a horse and a few clothes? Relax and cheer up. I'd like you to feel you're right at home here. Actually, there's something more I want to say to you. Seeing you there in those clothes, I'm reminded so much of my late husband that I've wanted to give you a hug and a kiss at least a hundred times this evening. In fact, if I hadn't been afraid you'd dislike it, I would have done so for sure."

Upon hearing these words and seeing the gleam in the lady's eyes, Rinaldo, who was no fool, approached her with open arms. "My lady, I shall always have you to thank for my life," he said, "and when I consider the situation you've rescued me from, I think it would be very discourteous of me indeed not to try as hard as I can to do whatever gives you pleasure. So, come hug and kiss me to your heart's content, and I'll be more than happy to do the same in return."

After this, there was no need for them to go on talking. The lady, who was burning with amorous desire, immediately threw herself into his arms, and embracing him passionately, gave him a thousand kisses and received as many back from him. Then they got up from their seats and went off into the bedroom, where they lost no time getting into bed, and before the night was over, they had satisfied their desires to the fullest many times over.

As soon as dawn began to break, however, they arose in keeping with the lady's wishes, for she did not want anyone to get wind of what had happened. After giving Rinaldo some fairly shabby clothes, she filled his purse with money, telling him to keep it hidden, and then showed him which road he should take so that he could find his servant in the fortress. Finally, she let him out through the door by which he had entered, imploring him to keep their encounter a secret.

When it was broad daylight and the gates were open, Rinaldo entered the fortress, pretending he was coming from some distance away, and located his servant. Having put on some of his own clothes, which were in his saddlebags, he was about to mount his servant's horse when, by some divine miracle, the three bandits were brought to the fortress, having been arrested for some other crime they had committed shortly after they had robbed him the previous evening. They made a voluntary confession of what they had done, and as a result, Rinaldo got his horse, his clothes, and his money back, and wound up losing only a pair of garters, which the bandits could not account for.

Thus it was that Rinaldo, giving thanks to God and Saint Julian, mounted his horse and returned home safe and sound, whereas the next day the three bandits were left kicking their heels in the north wind.°

Story 4

LANDOLFO RUFOLO IS IMPOVERISHED, BECOMES A PIRATE, AND IS SHIPWRECKED AFTER BEING CAPTURED BY THE GENOESE. HE ESCAPES, HOWEVER, ON A CHEST FILLED WITH VERY PRECIOUS JEWELS, IS CARED FOR BY A WOMAN ON CORFU, AND FINALLY RETURNS HOME A RICH MAN.°

* * *

Most gracious ladies, in my opinion none of Fortune's deeds appears greater than the spectacle of someone being taken from the depths of poverty and raised up to a kingly throne, which is what Pampinea's story has shown us happened to Alessandro. And since no one telling stories on our announced topic will be able to go beyond the extremes of high and low that she has described, I shall not feel any shame if I tell you a story that, while containing even greater misfortunes than hers did, does not come to so splendid a conclusion. When I consider the previous story, I realize that mine will be followed less attentively, but I will be excused since I simply cannot do any better.

The seacoast between Reggio and Gaeta is thought to be just about the most delightful part of Italy. Quite close to Salerno there is a stretch of it overlooking the sea, which the inhabitants call the Amalfi coast and which contains many small towns, adorned with gardens and fountains, where countless merchants live, as wealthy and enterprising a group as you will find anywhere. Among those small towns there is one called Ravello, and although many men living there today are very well off, the town used to count among its citizens a man named Landolfo Rufolo who was really extraordinarily rich.° Not satisfied with the wealth he had, however, he sought to double it, and as a result, he came close to losing not just everything he possessed, but his very own life in the bargain.

Having made all the necessary preliminary calculations that merchants typically make, he bought a very large ship, loaded it full of merchandise of all sorts that he had purchased using his own money, and sailed with it to Cyprus. There he discovered that other ships had arrived with exactly the same kind of merchandise he had brought, so that not only did he have to sell what he had for cheap, but by the end he practically had to give it away in order to get rid of it, coming close to being ruined as a result.

Being extremely distressed over what had happened, not knowing what to do, and finding himself, one of the richest of men, virtually impoverished, he finally decided he would either restore his losses by means of piracy or die in the attempt. He was determined, having left his home a rich man, not to return to it a poor one. And so, he located a buyer for his boat, and with the money he got for it and from the sale of his merchandise, he bought a small, fast pirate ship that he armed as well as he could and equipped with everything else necessary for such an enterprise. Then he dedicated himself to making other people's property his own, and especially that belonging to the Turks.

In this undertaking, Fortune was much more favorable to him than she had been when he was a merchant. Within the space of about a year, he had captured and plundered so many Turkish ships that he not only regained what he had lost in trading, but discovered that he had more than doubled it. Chastened by the pain he had suffered before from his losses, he reckoned he now had enough to avoid a repetition of his former experience, and having persuaded himself to rest content with what he had and not to seek anything more, he decided to take his loot and return home.

Wary of commercial ventures, he did not bother to invest his money, but had the crew put the oars into the water and set off at once for home in the little boat with which he had gained his wealth. One evening, after having come as far as the Archipelago, he ran into a fierce south wind that was blowing head-on.° With his little boat hardly able to make any progress against the heavy sea swells, he took shelter in a cove on the leeward side of a little island, where he intended to wait for better winds. He had been there only a short while when two large Genoese merchant ships returning from Constantinople struggled into the cove to escape the same storm Landolfo had fled. The crews on board the two ships recognized his little boat and had heard rumors about his fabulous wealth. Being greedy and rapacious by nature, they blocked his way out of the cove and made preparations to capture him. They put a party of men ashore, well armed with crossbows, positioning them so that anyone trying to get off the little boat would be shot with their arrows. Then they launched dinghies, by means of which, aided by the current, they drew up alongside Landolfo's little boat, and in short order they seized it and its entire crew without much of a struggle and without losing a single man themselves. They brought Landolfo, dressed in a ragged old doublet, aboard one of their ships, and after removing all the cargo from the boat, sent it to the bottom.

When the wind changed the next day, the two merchant ships

set sail on a westerly course. They made good progress all day long, but in the evening a gale arose, producing high seas that separated the two ships from one another. By a stroke of bad luck, the ship on which the wretched, destitute Landolfo was sailing was taken by the winds and hurled with tremendous force onto the shoals off the island of Cephalonia, where it split apart and was smashed to bits, like a piece of glass shattered against a wall.° As usually happens in such cases, the sea was strewn with chests and planks and merchandise, and although the night was pitch black and there was an extremely heavy swell, the miserable wretches who had been on board, or at least those who knew how to swim, grabbed onto anything within reach that happened to float by.

Among those wretches was poor Landolfo, who had called on death repeatedly throughout the day, preferring to die rather than return home as poor as he was. Now that death was imminent, however, he was afraid, and like the others, he seized the first plank that floated his way, in the hope that if he put off drowning a while, God would somehow come to his rescue. Straddling the plank, he did his best to hold on till daybreak, despite being tossed hither and thither by sea and wind. When it was light, he took a look around, but all he could see was the clouds and the sea, and a chest that was bobbing on the waves. He was terrified because the chest would occasionally get close, and he was afraid he would be injured if it hit him. Although he did not have much strength left, he did his best to push it away with his hand whenever it came too near.

But as luck would have it, all of a sudden a violent gust of wind caused a sea swell that drove the chest right into the plank Landolfo was sitting on and turned it upside down. Losing his grip, he went under, and when he was able to swim back up, aided more by his terror than by his strength, he saw that the plank had floated some distance away. Fearing he would never be able to reach it, he made for the chest, which was quite close, got the upper part of his body onto the lid, and using his arms, did his best to hold it upright. And in this fashion, unable to eat because he had no food on him, forced to drink more than he would have wished, and unsure where he was because all he could see around him was water, he spent the whole of that day and the following night being tossed this way and that way by the sea.

By the next day Landolfo had almost turned into a sponge, when, either thanks to the benevolence of God or through the power of the wind, he reached the coast of the island of Corfu, still clinging to the chest, holding its edges tightly with both hands just as we see people do who are in danger of drowning. By chance, a poor little woman, who happened to be there cleaning and polishing her pots and pans in the sand and salt water, caught sight of him. At first she could not make out what sort of creature was approaching and ran back screaming in fear. Landolfo said nothing to her, for he was unable to speak and scarcely able to see. But as the sea brought him closer to the land, she began to make out the chest by its shape, and as she stared at it more intently, first she recognized a pair of arms stretched across it, then picked out a face, and finally realized just what it was.

Prompted by compassion, the woman waded out some distance into the sea, which had now become calm, seized Landolfo by the hair, and dragged him to the shore, chest and all. With some difficulty, she unhooked his hands from the chest, which she took and placed on the head of her young daughter, who was there with her, while she herself picked Landolfo up like a little child and carried him back to her village. Having put him into a hot bath, she rubbed and washed him in the warm water with such vigor that the bodily heat he had lost returned and he regained a portion of his former strength. When the time seemed right, she took him out and gave him some good wine and sweets to help him recuperate. For several days she did her best to take care of him until he fully recovered his strength and understood where he was. At that point, the good woman felt she ought to give him back his chest, which she had saved for him, and tell him it was time for him to fend for himself. And that is just what she did.

Landolfo remembered nothing about the chest, but accepted it anyway when the good woman presented it to him, thinking that it had to be worth enough to pay his expenses for a few days at least.

When he found it to be very light, however, his hopes were seriously dampened. All the same, once the good woman was out of the house, he pried it open to see what it contained and found a great many precious stones inside, some of them loose and others in settings. Being quite knowledgeable on the subject of jewels, Landolfo realized from the moment he saw them that they were extremely valuable. This discovery really raised his spirits, and he praised God for not having decided to abandon him yet. Still, as a man whom Fortune had cruelly made her target twice already, he feared a third encounter and decided he would have to proceed with great caution if he wanted to bring those things home with him. So, he wrapped them up as carefully as he could in some old rags and told the good woman that he no longer needed the chest, and that she was welcome to keep it if she gave him a sack in its place.

The good woman was happy to make the exchange, and Landolfo, after thanking her profusely for all the help she had given him, slung the sack over his shoulder and departed, first taking a boat to Brindisi and from there traveling along the coastline until he finally arrived in Trani, where he ran into some cloth merchants who turned out to be fellow townsmen.° Without mentioning the chest, he narrated all his adventures to them, moving them for the love of God to give him a new suit of clothes. They also lent him a horse and found him an escort to take him all the way back to Ravello, to which he wanted to return at all costs.

Finding himself safe at home, Landolfo thanked God for having brought him that far and then opened up his little sack. Examining everything with greater care than he had done before, he discovered that the stones were so numerous and of such quality, that if he sold them for their fair market value, or even for less, he would still be twice as rich as he had been when he first set out. After he found a way to dispose of the jewels, he sent a tidy sum of money as payment for services rendered to the good woman in Corfu who had pulled him out of the sea, and he did something similar for the merchants in Trani who had given him the new clothes. Then, abandoning any thought of being a merchant, he kept the rest of the money and was able to live on it in becoming prosperity for the rest of his life.

Story 5

ANDREUCCIO DA PERUGIA COMES TO BUY HORSES IN NAPLES
WHERE, DURING A SINGLE NIGHT, HE IS CAUGHT IN THREE
SERIOUS MISADVENTURES, MANAGES TO EXTRICATE
HIMSELF FROM ALL OF THEM, AND RETURNS HOME
WITH A RUBY.°

The stones found by Landolfo—began Fiammetta, for it was her
turn to tell a story—reminded me of a tale that contains almost as
many perils as the one narrated by Lauretta, but differs from hers
in that the misadventures she recounted happened over the course
of many years, whereas those in this tale, as you are about to
hear, occurred in the space of a single night.°

According to what I have been told, there once lived in Perugia
a young man named Andreuccio di Pietro, a horse trader by profession.° Having heard that horses were cheap in Naples, he put
five hundred gold florins in his purse, and despite never having
been away from home before, set off for that city with several
other merchants. He arrived there one Sunday evening around
vespers, and the next morning, following the directions given to
him by his innkeeper, went to the marketplace. Although he saw
quite a few horses there, many of which he liked, he was finally
unable to conclude a single deal despite having made offers on a
number of them. During the negotiations, in order to show that he
had the wherewithal to make a purchase, he kept pulling out his
purse full of florins in front of all the passersby, a sure sign of his
inexperience and lack of caution.

While he was thus engaged in bargaining, with his purse on
full display, a young Sicilian woman, who was not only very beautiful, but was willing to satisfy any man for a modest sum, happened
to walk by. Although he took no notice of her, she caught sight of
his purse and immediately said to herself: "Who'd be better off
than I would be if that money were mine?" She then walked right
on by him.

There was an old woman with her, however, also a Sicilian, and when she saw Andreuccio, she let her young companion go ahead while she herself ran up to him and gave him a warm embrace. On seeing this, the young woman did not say a thing, but simply stood off to the side, waiting for her companion. Andreuccio, having turned around and recognized the old woman, greeted her heartily and got her to promise him to come and see him at the inn. After a brief conversation with him, she went away, while Andreuccio returned to his trading, although he did not wind up buying anything that morning.

The young woman, who had initially seen Andreuccio's purse, had also noted the friendly greeting he had exchanged with her old companion, and since she was determined to figure out a way to get hold of his money, or at least some part of it, she cautiously began questioning her friend, asking her who he was, where he came from, what he was doing in Naples, and how she happened to know him. The old woman, who had lived with Andreuccio's father in Sicily for a long time, and later on in Perugia as well, gave her a full report about him, almost as good a one as he himself might have given, letting her know where he was staying and why he had come to Naples.

Now that she was fully informed about Andreuccio's family, down to the names of all his relatives, the cunning young woman devised a clever plan, based on what she had learned, to get the prize she desired. Upon returning home, she gave the old woman enough work to do for the rest of the day in order to keep her from going back to see Andreuccio. Then she took aside a young maid-servant of hers, whom she had trained thoroughly for such purposes, and around the hour of vespers, sent her to the inn where Andreuccio was staying.

When the girl arrived there, she ran into him by chance, all alone, at the door and asked him if Andreuccio was in. When he told her he was that very man, she drew him aside and said: "Sir, there's a gentlewoman in this city who would be happy to speak with you, if you please." When he heard this, Andreuccio immediately assumed, looking himself over from head to foot and thinking he was a pretty good-looking guy, that the lady had to be in love with him—as if he were the only handsome young man to be found in Naples at that time. So, without hesitation, he told the girl he was ready to go and asked her where and when the lady would speak with him.

"Whenever you wish to come, sir," said the girl, "she'll be there at home, waiting for you."

Without mentioning anything to the people at the inn, Andreuccio replied at once: "You go ahead and lead the way. I'll be coming right behind you."

The girl led him to the woman's house in a quarter of the city called Malpertugio whose name alone reveals how honest a place it is.° Knowing nothing about it, Andreuccio did not suspect a thing, but believed he was going to meet a proper lady in a very respectable area of the city. Thus, with the servant girl leading him, he entered her house without a second thought. The girl had already called out to the lady, saying, "Look, Andreuccio's here," and as he climbed the stairs, he saw her come out on the landing to wait for him.

The woman was still young and rather tall, with a gorgeous face, and her clothing and jewelry were all quite proper looking. As Andreuccio approached her, she descended three steps to meet him with her arms wide open. Clasping him about the neck, she stood there for some time without saying anything as though she were overwhelmed by tender feelings. Finally, as she wept, she kissed him on the forehead and said in a broken voice: "O my Andreuccio, how happy I am to see you."

Marveling at her tender caresses, the dumbfounded Andreuccio replied: "My lady, the pleasure is mine."

Taking him by the hand, she led him up to the main living room, and from there, without uttering a word, she entered her bedroom, which was redolent with the fragrance of roses and orange blossoms and other lovely scents. In the room he could see a handsome curtained bed, a large number of dresses hanging up on pegs, as was the custom there, plus many other beautiful, luxurious furnishings. Judging by what he saw, Andreuccio, like the greenhorn he was, firmly believed that she was nothing less than a great lady.

She had him sit beside her on a chest at the foot of her bed and began speaking as follows:

"Andreuccio, I'm quite sure you're amazed at my embracing you like this and shedding all these tears, for you don't know me, and it may be that no one's ever mentioned me to you. But you're about to hear something that will probably make you even more amazed: the simple fact is that I'm your sister. For a long time I've wanted to meet all my brothers, and since God has now granted me the favor of allowing me to see one of them before I die, I can tell you that I'll die content when the hour arrives. But in case you've never heard anything about this before, let me tell you my story.

"Pietro, who is my father as well as yours, lived for a long time in Palermo, as I believe you may know. Being a good and amiable man, he was greatly loved by everyone who knew him there, and to this day he still is. Among the people who were attracted to him, no one loved him more than my mother, a gentlewoman who was at that time a widow. In fact, she loved him so much that she cast off her honor as well as her fear of her father and her brothers, and became so intimate with him that it led to the birth of the person you see before you.

"When I was still a little girl, Pietro was called away from Palermo and returned to Perugia on some business or other, leaving me behind with my mother, nor, from what I've been able to discover, did he ever think of me or of her again. This is why, if he were not my father, I'd reproach him bitterly, considering his ingratitude toward my mother, for she was moved by the most devoted love for him to put herself and all her worldly goods into his hands without otherwise knowing anything about him. I'll say nothing about the affection he ought to feel for me, his daughter, since I'm not the child of a serving maid or some low-class woman.

"But what's the point of all this? It's a whole lot easier to condemn wrongs done a long time ago than to right them now. In any case, what happened was that when I was a little girl, he left me in Palermo where I grew up and have spent most of my time until fairly recently. My mother, being a wealthy woman, arranged my marriage to a well-heeled gentleman from Agrigento, who, out of love for my mother and me, came to live in Palermo. He was a staunch supporter of the Guelfs and entered into secret negotiations with our King Charles, but King Frederick got wind of the plot before it could be carried out, and we had to flee Sicily just when I thought I was going to be the grandest lady ever on the island.° We carried away what few things we could—I say 'few' in comparison to the huge number of things we owned there—and leaving behind our lands and palaces, we became refugees in this country. Here we've found King Charles to be so grateful to us as to give us houses and lands in partial compensation for the losses we suffered on his account, and as you will soon see for yourself, he continues to provide a substantial allowance for my husband, who is also, of course, your brother-in-law. So, that's how I came to be in Naples where, thanks more to God than to you, my sweet brother, I have met you at last."

Having said all this, she embraced him again, and weeping tenderly, once more kissed him on the forehead. She had recounted her fable in an orderly and artful manner, never stammering or stumbling over a word at any point, and for his part, Andreuccio not only remembered that his father really had been in Palermo, but knew from his own experience how easily, and lightly, young men fall in love during their youth. So, what with her tender tears and embraces and the honest kisses she gave him, as Andreuccio listened to her, he was convinced that what she was saying was truer than truth. When she fell silent, he replied:

"My lady, don't take it too hard that I'm amazed by all this, for to tell the truth, up to now I've had no more knowledge of you than if you'd never existed. For whatever reason, my father never talked about your mother and you, or if he did, I never heard a word about it. But I'm all the more delighted to have found my sister here because I'm completely on my own and was never expecting anything like this to happen. In fact, although I'm just a small-time merchant, I really can't imagine anyone, no matter how exalted his station, who wouldn't treasure you. There is one thing, however, that I'd ask you to clarify for me, please. How did you know I was here?"

"I was told about it this morning by a poor woman who often comes to see me," the lady replied, "because, according to what she tells me, she had spent a lot of time with our father in Palermo and Perugia. And if it had not seemed more honorable for you to make your way to me here, where you'd be at home, than for me to visit you in someone else's place, I would have come to see you long before now."

After saying this, she began inquiring about all his relatives individually by name, and as Andreuccio answered her questions one after the other, he came to believe even more firmly that which he should never have believed at all.

Since it was hot and they had been talking for a while, she sent for sweets and Greco wine, making sure that Andreuccio was given some of it to drink.° After that he wanted to leave because it was time for supper, but she would not hear of it, and making a show of being very upset, she threw her arms around his neck.

"Alas!" she said. "Now I see clearly how little you care for me. What else am I to think when you are with a sister of yours whom you've never seen before, and in her own house, where you should have been staying from the moment you arrived here, and yet you want to leave her in order to go get supper at some inn? Really! You are going to eat with me. And although my husband's away, which is something I regret very much, and although I'm just a woman, I'm still capable of showing you at least a little hospitality."

Not knowing what else to say to this, Andreuccio replied: "You are as precious to me as a sister should be, but if I don't go, they'll be waiting there the entire evening for me to come to supper, and I'll be behaving like a boor."

"God be praised!" she said. "As if I didn't have someone in the house who could be sent there to tell them not to expect you! But it would be a greater courtesy on your part, and no more than your duty, if you sent for your companions and told them to come here for supper. Afterward, if you still wanted to leave, you could all go back together as a group."

Andreuccio replied that he did not want his companions there that evening, saying he would place himself at her disposal if that was what she wished. She pretended to send word to the inn not to expect him for supper, and then, after they had talked for quite some time, they sat down to a splendid meal, consisting of multiple courses, which she cleverly prolonged until night had fallen. When they got up from the table, Andreuccio indicated that he would have to go, but she said that under no circumstances would she permit it, because Naples was no place to wander about in at night, especially for a stranger. Furthermore, she said that when she had sent word to the inn not to expect him for supper, she had told them the same thing about his returning to sleep there.

Andreuccio believed everything she said, and since, in his deluded state, he was enjoying her company, he stayed put. After supper was over, she deliberately kept him talking and talking into the wee hours of the night, at which point she left him to sleep in her bedroom, with a little boy to attend him and show him where to find whatever he needed, while she herself went off into another bedroom with her maidservants.

The heat was intense, and so, as soon as Andreuccio was alone, he quickly stripped down to his doublet, removing his breeches and stockings and placing his clothes at the head of the bed. Then, feeling a natural urge to dispose of the extra load in his belly, he asked where he should do it, and the boy, motioning toward a door in one of the corners of the room, said: "Go in there." The unsuspecting Andreuccio did so and chanced to set his foot down on a plank that came away at its other end from the beam that supported it, so that it flew up into the air, flipped upside down, and went tumbling to the ground, taking Andreuccio along with it. Despite having fallen from quite a height, by the grace of God he did not get hurt, but he did get covered from head to toe with the muck that filled up the place where he fell.

To give you a better picture both of what had happened and of what is about to follow, let me describe what that place was like. In a narrow alleyway, such as we often see between two houses, they had taken some planks and nailed them to two beams stretching from one house to the other, and had put a place to sit on top of them. It was one of those planks that had fallen with Andreuccio to the bottom.°

Finding himself down there in the alley, Andreuccio bemoaned his bad luck and started calling for the boy. But the boy, as soon as he had heard Andreuccio fall, had gone scurrying off to tell the lady. She immediately ran into her bedroom and checked to see if Andreuccio's clothes were there. She found them, and with them all his money, which he had been so stupid as to carry on him because he did not trust anyone else with it. Now that this woman from Palermo, who had transformed herself into the sister of a man from Perugia, had gotten what she had set her snares for, she did not give him another thought but quickly went and closed the door that he had passed through before his fall.

When the boy did not respond, Andreuccio started calling louder, but to no avail. Growing suspicious, he began to realize, now when it was too late, that he had been tricked, and having climbed over a little wall that closed the alley off from the street, he scrambled down to the ground and went up to the front door, which he recognized readily enough. There he remained for a long time, vainly calling out while he repeatedly shook and pounded on the door. Now he saw his misfortune clearly, and starting to weep, he said: "Alas, poor me! Look how little time it took me to lose five hundred florins, and a sister, too!"

After saying quite a bit more, he started to shout and to beat on the door all over again, keeping it up for so long that he awoke many of the people living nearby who got up out of bed because they could not stand the racket. One of the lady's maids, who looked very sleepy, came to the window and said, in a scolding voice: "Who's that knocking down there?"

"Oh," said Andreuccio, "don't you recognize me? I'm Andreuccio, Madama Fiordaliso's brother."°

"Listen, buddy," she replied, "if you've had too much to drink, go sleep it off, and come back tomorrow morning. I don't know any Andreuccio. You're talking nonsense. For goodness' sake, please go away and let us sleep."

"What," said Andreuccio, "you don't know what I'm talking

about? Sure you do. But look, even if people from Sicily can forget
the relatives they've just acquired in such a short space of time, at
least give me the clothes I left there, and then, in God's name, I'll
go away gladly."

"You must be dreaming, buddy," she said, scarcely able to keep
from laughing.

As she said this, she simultaneously shut the window and
went back inside, which made Andreuccio, who was now more
certain than ever that he had lost everything, so upset that what
had been intense anger before turned into a towering rage. Deciding that if he wanted to get his belongings back, force would be
more effective than words had been, he got a large rock and
began frantically beating on the door all over again, this time
hitting it harder than ever. Disturbed by his hammering, many
of the neighbors, who had been awakened and gotten up before,
decided he was a troublemaker who had invented some story to
make life difficult for the good lady there. Coming to their windows, they began to shout at him, like all the dogs in the neighborhood barking at a stray:

"You really ought to be ashamed of yourself, buddy, coming
around at this hour to the homes of good women and talking this
nonsense. For the love of God, please go away and let us sleep. If
you have any business with her, come back tomorrow, and stop
bothering us like this tonight."

Perhaps encouraged by these words, the good woman's pimp,
who was inside the house and whom Andreuccio had neither seen
nor heard, came to the window and said, in a horrible, rough, savage growl: "Who's that down there?"

Hearing that voice, Andreuccio raised his head and saw someone who, as far as he could tell, seemed like some sort of big shot.
His face was covered with a thick, black beard, and he was yawning
and rubbing his eyes as though he had been awakened from a deep
sleep and had just gotten out of bed. Somewhat fearfully, Andreuccio replied: "I'm the brother of the lady who lives here."

But the man did not wait for Andreuccio to finish. Instead,
more fiercely than before, he said: "I don't know what's keeping

me from coming down there and beating you with a stick until you can't move any longer, you stupid, drunken ass. Nobody can get any sleep here tonight because of you." Then he turned around and went inside, locking the window behind him.

Some of the neighbors, who knew more about the kind of man he was, said to Andreuccio, speaking in a whisper: "For God's sake, buddy, take off, unless you want to get yourself killed here tonight. For your own good, go away."

Terrified by the man's voice and appearance, and urged on by the advice of the neighbors, who seemed to speak to him out of charity, Andreuccio set off to return to the inn, feeling he was the most wretched man alive and filled with despair about the money he had lost. Not really sure where to go, he walked in the direction of the place from which he had come following the serving girl the previous day.

Disgusted by himself because of the stench he was giving off, he thought he would head for the sea where he could wash himself off, and so he made a turn to the left and went up a street called Ruga Catalana.° As he walked toward the upper part of the city, by chance he saw two men coming toward him with lanterns in their hands, and fearing that they were members of the watch or else men who might do him harm, he decided to avoid them and quietly took refuge in an abandoned hut he saw nearby. But the two men were headed for the same spot and also entered the hut. After they were inside, one of them put down the iron tools he had been carrying over his shoulders, and then the two of them began talking together as they inspected them.

Right in the middle of their discussion, the first one said: "What's going on here? That's the worst stench I think I've ever smelled." Having said this, he lifted up his lantern a bit, and they caught sight of the wretched Andreuccio. Astonished by what they saw, they asked: "Who's that there?"

Andreuccio remained silent, but when they came closer to him with the light and asked him what he was doing there, covered in filth as he was, he told them the whole story of what had happened to him. The two of them, who could easily imagine where all this must have taken place, said to one another: "It must have happened at Boss Buttafuoco's house."°

Then they turned to Andreuccio, and one of them said: "Listen, buddy, you may have lost your money, but you should really thank God for the accident that happened to you when you fell down and couldn't get back into the house. Because if you hadn't fallen, you may rest assured that as soon as you were asleep, you would have been killed, and in that case you would have lost your life as well as your money. But what's the use of crying over it now? You have about as much chance of getting a penny of your money back as you have of plucking the stars out of the sky. And there's a very good chance you'll be killed if that guy ever finds out you've said a word about it."

When he had finished speaking, they had a brief discussion among themselves and then said to Andreuccio: "Look, we're feeling sorry for you, and since we were on our way to do a job, if you're willing to go along with us, we can pretty much guarantee that your share will amount to a lot more than what you've lost." Feeling desperate, Andreuccio responded that he was ready to go.

Earlier that day an archbishop from Naples named Messer Filippo Minutolo had been buried.° He had been interred in very expensive vestments and had a ruby on his finger worth more than five hundred gold florins, which was the booty the two of them were after. They communicated their plan to Andreuccio, and he, more avaricious than wise, set off with them. As they were on their way to the cathedral and Andreuccio was still smelling pretty awful, one of them said: "Couldn't we find a way for this guy to wash up a bit somewhere or other so he wouldn't stink so horribly?"

"Sure," said the other, "not far from here there's a well that always used to have a pulley and a large bucket. Let's go there and give him a quick wash."

When they reached the well, they found that the rope was still there, but someone had removed the bucket. The idea occurred to them of tying Andreuccio to the rope and lowering him into the well so that he could wash himself off down below. When he had finished washing, he was to give the rope a tug, and they would haul him up.

But as they were proceeding to do this and had just lowered him into the well, several members of the watch happened to show up. They were thirsty because of the heat and because they had just been chasing somebody, and they were coming to the well for a drink. When the pair caught sight of them, they immediately ran away, making their escape without being seen by the watchmen as they approached the well. Down at the bottom, Andreuccio had finished washing himself and gave a tug on the rope. The watchmen, who had put down their shields and weapons and taken off their surcoats, started to pull it up, thinking there was a bucket full of water hanging from it. When Andreuccio saw himself nearing the top of the well, he let go of the rope and used his hands to heave himself onto the rim. On seeing him appear all of a sudden, the terrified watchmen immediately let go of the rope and without saying a word began running away as fast as they could. Andreuccio was so surprised by this that if he had not held on tightly, he would have fallen back down to the bottom and been seriously injured or even killed himself. However, when he managed to get out of the well, he was even more surprised to discover the weapons, for he knew his companions had not brought them. Lamenting his misfortune and fearing lest something worse should occur, Andreuccio decided to leave without touching a thing. And so off he went, although he did not have the slightest idea where he was going.

As he was walking along, he happened to run into his two companions who were coming back to haul him out of the well. When they saw him, they were amazed and asked him who had pulled him up. Andreuccio replied that he did not know and gave them a detailed account of everything that had occurred, describing what he had found lying next to the well. They figured out what had really happened and had a good laugh as they told him why they had fled and who was responsible for having pulled him out of the well. Then, without wasting any more time talking, since it was already midnight, they made their way to the cathedral and got in without difficulty. Going up to the tomb, which was made of marble and was very large, they took out their iron bars and lifted its enormously heavy lid, propping it open just enough to allow a man to get inside.

This done, one of them asked: "Who's going to go in?"

"Not me," replied the other.

"Not me, either," said the first. "Let's have Andreuccio do it."

"No, I won't do it," said Andreuccio, at which point both of them then rounded on him and said:

"What do you mean you won't do it? I swear to God, if you don't, we're going to bash in your head with one of these rods, and we'll just keep on hitting you until you fall down and die."

The terrified Andreuccio climbed in, thinking to himself as he did so: "These guys are making me do this in order to trick me, because once I've handed them all the stuff from inside, they'll go off about their business, leaving me struggling to get out of the tomb, and I'll wind up with nothing." Consequently, he decided to make sure he got his own share first, and recalling what he had heard them saying about an expensive ring, as soon as he climbed down into the tomb, he took it off the Archbishop's finger and put it on his own. Then he gave them the Archbishop's crosier, miter, and gloves, and having stripped him of everything else down to his shirt, he passed it all out to his companions. When he said there was nothing left, they insisted the ring had to be there and told him to look all over for it. But he replied that he was unable to find it and kept them waiting quite some time as he made a show of searching for it. They were just as wily as Andreuccio, however, and while they went on telling him to look really hard for it, they seized the opportunity to pull out the prop that was holding up the lid. At that point they fled, leaving Andreuccio shut up inside the tomb.

When Andreuccio realized what had happened, you can imagine how he felt. Again and again he tried, first using his head and then his shoulders, to raise the lid, but he labored in vain, until finally, overcome by deep despair, he fainted and fell down on top of the Archbishop's corpse. Anyone seeing the two of them there would have had trouble telling which of the two, Andreuccio or the Archbishop, was really the dead man. When Andreuccio came to, he burst into a flood of tears, for he had no doubt that one of two ends was in store for him: either no one would come to open the tomb, and he would die there from hunger and from the stench, covered by the worms from the dead body, or else some-one would come and find him inside, and then he would be hanged as a thief.

As these sad thoughts were going through Andreuccio's mind, making him feel terribly despondent, he heard a number of people talking to one another and moving about the church. He quickly concluded that they were coming to do just what he and his companions had already done, a realization that only increased his fears. But having opened the tomb and propped up the lid, they got into an argument about who was going to climb in. No one wanted to do it, until finally, after a long debate, a priest said: "What are you afraid of? Do you think he's going to eat you? The dead don't eat people. I'll go inside there myself." Having said this, he placed his chest on the rim of the tomb and swiveled around, turning his head to face out while thrusting his legs inside, ready to make his descent.

When Andreuccio saw this, he stood up, grabbed the priest by one of his legs, and pretended he was trying to pull him down into the tomb. The priest no sooner felt Andreuccio's hands than he let out an earsplitting scream and instantly hurled himself out of the tomb. This terrified all the others, and leaving the tomb wide open, they ran away as if they were being chased by a hundred thousand devils.

Happy beyond his wildest hopes when he saw what had happened, Andreuccio quickly threw himself out of the tomb and left the church by the way he had come in. Day was already starting to break as he went wandering aimlessly about with the ring on his finger. Eventually, he reached the waterfront where he stumbled upon his inn and discovered that his companions and the inn-keeper had spent the entire night up, worried about what had become of him. After he told them what had happened, the innkeeper counseled him to leave Naples right away. Andreuccio did so at once and returned home to Perugia, having invested his money in a ring rather than in the horses he had set out to buy.

Story 7

THE SULTAN OF BABYLON SENDS ONE OF HIS DAUGHTERS TO BE MARRIED TO THE KING OF ALGARVE, AND IN A SERIES OF MISADVENTURES SPANNING A PERIOD OF FOUR YEARS, SHE PASSES THROUGH THE HANDS OF NINE MEN IN VARIOUS PLACES, UNTIL SHE IS FINALLY RESTORED TO HER FATHER AS A VIRGIN AND GOES OFF, AS SHE WAS DOING AT THE START, TO MARRY THE KING OF ALGARVE.°

* * *

It is difficult, charming ladies, for us to know what is truly in our best interest. For, as we have frequently observed, there are many who have thought that if only they were rich, they would be able to lead secure, trouble-free lives, and they have not just prayed to God for wealth but have made every effort to acquire it, sparing themselves neither effort nor danger in the process. However, no sooner did they succeed than the prospect of a substantial legacy led to their being murdered by people who would never have considered harming them before then. Others have risen from low estate to the heights of power, passing through the dangers of a thousand battles and shedding the blood of their brothers and friends to get there, all because of their belief that to rule was felicity itself. And yet, as they could have seen and heard for themselves, it was a felicity fraught with endless cares and fears, and when it cost them their lives, they finally realized that at the tables of royalty chalices may contain poison, even though they are made of gold.° Again, there have been many who have ardently yearned for physical strength and beauty, while others have sought bodily ornaments with equal passion, only to discover that the things they unwisely desired were the cause of misery or even death.

But to avoid reviewing every conceivable human desire, let me simply affirm that no person alive can choose any one of them in complete confidence that it will remain immune from the vicissitudes of Fortune. Thus, if we wish to live upright lives, we should resign ourselves to acquiring and preserving whatever is bestowed on us by the One who alone knows what we need and has the ability to provide it for us. However, just as there are myriad ways in which men are driven to sin because of their desires, so you, gracious ladies, sin above all in one particular way, namely, in your desire to be beautiful, for finding that the attractions bestowed on you by Nature are insufficient, you make use of the most extraordinary art trying to improve on them. And therefore, I would like to tell you a tale about a Saracen girl's unfortunate beauty, which in the space of about four years turned her into a newlywed nine separate times.

A long time ago Babylon was ruled by a Sultan named Beminedab, in whose reign very little happened that went contrary to his wishes.° Among his many children of both sexes, he had a daughter named Alatiel who was at that time, according to what everyone said who saw her, the most beautiful woman in the world. The Sultan had been recently attacked by a huge army of Arabs, but thanks to the timely assistance of the King of Algarve, he had been able to defeat them decisively.° Consequently, when, as a special favor, the King asked to be given Alatiel as his wife, the Sultan agreed, and after having seen her aboard a well-armed, well-equipped ship and having provided her with an honorable escort of men and women as well as with many elegant and expensive trappings, he commended her to God's protection and sent her on her way.

When the sailors saw that the weather was favorable, they unfurled their sails into the wind, and for some while after leaving the port of Alexandria, their voyage prospered. One day, however, after they had already passed Sardinia and seemed close to their journey's end, crosswinds suddenly arose that were so violent and buffeted the ship so badly that time and again not only the lady, but the crew thought they were done for. Nevertheless, they held out valiantly, and by marshaling all their skill and all their strength, they resisted the onslaught of the heavy seas for two days. As night approached for the third time since the start of the storm, however, not only did it not abate, but rather, it kept growing stronger, until they felt the ship beginning to break apart. Although they were not far to the north of Majorca, the sailors had no idea of their location, and because it was a dark night and the sky was covered with thick clouds, they were unable to determine their position either by using nautical instruments or by making visual observations.

It now became a case of every man for himself, and the officers, seeing no other means of escape, lowered a dinghy into the water and jumped into it, choosing to put their faith in it rather than in the foundering ship. Right behind them, however, came all the other men on board, leaping down into the boat one after the other, despite the fact that those who had gotten there first were trying, knife in hand, to fend them off. Although they all thought this was the way to escape death, they actually ran right into it, for the dinghy, not built to hold so many people in such weather, went down, taking everyone with it.

Meanwhile, the ship, though torn open and almost completely filled with water, was being blown swiftly along by a fierce wind that finally drove it aground on a beach on the island of Majorca. At this point the only people remaining on board were the lady and her female attendants, all of whom lay prostrate, looking as if they were dead, overcome by both the tempest and their fear. The ship's impetus had been so great that it had thrust itself deep into the sand almost a stone's throw from the shore, where, now that the wind could no longer make it budge, it remained all night long, relentlessly pounded by the sea.

By daybreak the tempest had calmed down considerably, and the lady, who was feeling half dead, raised her head and, weak though she was, began calling to her servants one after the other. She did so in vain, however, because they were too far away to hear her. Puzzled when she got no reply and could see no one about, she began to feel quite panic-stricken, staggered to her feet, and finally discovered her ladies-in-waiting as well as all the other women lying about everywhere. As she went from one to the other, she called and shook them repeatedly. Few, however, showed any sign of life, most having died from a combination of terror and horrible stomach convulsions, a discovery that only served to intensify the lady's fears. Since she was all alone there and had no idea of her whereabouts, she felt a desperate need of assistance and prodded those who were still alive until she got them to their feet. But when she realized that no one knew where the men had gone and saw that the boat was stuck in the sand and full of water, she began weeping and wailing along with all the rest of them.

The hour of nones was already upon them before they saw anyone on the shore or elsewhere in the vicinity who might be moved to pity them and come to their assistance, for by chance, at that very hour, a nobleman named Pericone da Vislago, who was returning from one of his estates, happened to come riding by on horseback, accompanied by several of his servants.° The instant he saw the ship, he figured out what had happened and ordered one of his men to climb aboard without delay and to report what he discovered there. Although the servant had to struggle, he managed to get onto the ship, where he found the young noblewoman, frightened out of her wits, hiding with her few remaining companions under the end of the bowsprit. On seeing him, they started weeping and repeatedly begged him for mercy, although when they realized he could not understand them, nor they him, they tried to explain their misfortune by means of gestures.

Once he had assessed the situation to the best of his ability, the servant reported what he had discovered up there to Pericone, who promptly had his men bring the women down, along with the most valuable objects they could salvage from the ship. Then he escorted the women to one of his castles where he arranged for them to be fed and allowed to rest in order to restore their spirits. From their rich attire he deduced that he had stumbled across some great lady, and he quickly recognized which one she was by the deference that the other women paid to her alone. Although she was pallid and extremely disheveled because of her exhausting experiences at sea, her features still struck Pericone as extremely beautiful, and for this reason he resolved on the spot to take her to wife if she had no husband, and if marriage were out of the question, to make her his mistress.

Quite a robust man with a commanding presence, Pericone had her waited on hand and foot, and when, after a few days, she had recovered completely, he found her to be more beautiful than he could have imagined. Although it pained him that they could not understand one another and he could not determine who she was, nevertheless, her beauty had set him all ablaze, and he tried, by means of pleasant, loving gestures, to coax her to give in to his desires without a struggle. But it was all in vain: she kept refusing to let him get on familiar terms with her, and in the meantime, Pericone's passion just got hotter and hotter.

The lady had no idea where she was, but she guessed, after having observed the local customs for a few days, that she was among Christians and in a place where she saw that there was little to be gained by revealing her identity, even if she had known how to do so. She recognized what was going on with Pericone, and although she concluded that eventually either force or love was going to make her satisfy his desires, nevertheless, she proudly resolved to rise above her wretched predicament. To her three remaining women, she gave orders never to reveal their identities to anyone unless they found themselves in a place where doing so would clearly help them gain their freedom. Beyond that, she implored them to preserve their chastity, declaring that she herself was determined to let no one except her husband ever enjoy her favors. Her women commended her resolve and said they would do their utmost to follow her instructions.

Pericone's passion was burning more fiercely from day to day, growing hotter and hotter as he got closer to the object of his desire and it was ever more firmly denied him. When he saw that his flattering her was getting him nowhere, he sharpened his wits and decided to make use of deception, keeping force in reserve as a last resort. On several occasions he had noticed that the lady liked wine, which she was unaccustomed to drinking because the laws of her religion forbade it, and by using it as Venus's assistant, he thought he would be able to have his way with her.° Thus, one evening, pretending not to care about the very thing for which she had shown such distaste, he arranged for a splendid supper in the manner of a holiday celebration, which the lady attended. Since the meal was graced with a wide array of dishes, he ordered the man who was serving her to give her a variety of different kinds of wine to drink with them. The man did his job extremely well, and the lady, caught off guard and carried away by the pleasures of drinking, consumed more wine than was consistent with her honor. Forgetting all the adversities she had been through, she became positively merry, and when she saw other women doing Majorcan dances, she herself did one in the Alexandrian manner.°

On seeing this, Pericone thought he was getting close to what he wanted, and calling for more food and drink, he prolonged the banquet into the wee hours of the night. Finally, after the guests were gone, he accompanied her, alone, to her bedroom. There, unhindered by any feeling of shame, and more heated by the wine than restrained by her sense of honor, she undressed in front of him as if he were one of her women, and got into bed. Pericone was not slow to follow her, and after extinguishing the lights, he quickly got in from the other side. Lying down beside her, he took her in his arms, and with no resistance whatsoever on her part, began playing the game of love with her. Up until that moment, she had no conception of the kind of horn men do their butting with, but once she did, she almost regretted not having given in to Pericone's solicitations. And from then on, she would no longer wait for an invitation to enjoy such sweet nights, but often issued the invitation herself, not by means of words, since she did not know how to make herself understood, but by means of actions.

Fortune, however, was not content to have made the wife of a king into the mistress of a lord, but was preparing a crueler alliance for the lady in place of the very pleasurable one she had with Pericone. For Pericone had a twenty-five-year-old brother named Marato, fair and fresh as a rose, who had seen the lady and felt powerfully attracted to her. As far as he could judge from her reactions, it seemed very likely to him that he stood in her good graces, and since he thought the only thing between him and what he desired was the strict watch that Pericone kept over her, he devised a cruel plan that he quickly turned into a terrible reality.

There happened to be a ship down in the port just then that was loaded up with merchandise and bound for Chiarenza in Romania.° Although it had already hoisted sail, ready to depart with the first favorable wind, Marato made a deal with its two young Genoese masters for them to take himself and the lady on board the following night. With this out of the way, Marato made up his mind about how he would proceed, and as soon as night fell, he wandered unobserved over to Pericone's house, taking along with him several of his most trusted companions whom he had enlisted specifically to help him carry out his plan. Since Pericone had no reason to be on his guard, Marato was able to hide himself inside the house just as he had told his men he was going to do. Then, in the dead of night, he opened the door and led them to the room in which Pericone and the lady were sleeping. They slew Pericone in his bed and seized the lady, now wide awake and in tears, threatening to kill her if she made any noise. Then, after taking many of Pericone's most precious possessions, they left the house without being heard and hurried down to the harbor where Marato and the lady immediately boarded the ship while his companions returned to the city. The crew set sail, and with a good, fresh wind behind them, began their voyage.

The lady grieved bitterly over this second misfortune, just as she had over the first one, but Marato made good use of Saint Grows-in-the-Hand, God's gift to all of us, and began consoling her in such a way that she was soon on intimate terms with him and forgot all about Pericone. Things thus seemed to be going pretty well for her, but Fortune, not content it seems with the lady's previous tribulations, was already preparing her a new one. For what with her beauty, which was, as we have said many times before, quite stunning, and her extremely refined manners, the two young masters of the ship contracted such a violent love for her that they forgot about everything else and sought only to serve her and provide for her pleasures, at the same time, however, making sure that Marato never caught on to what they were doing.

When they discovered they were both in love with her, they talked things over in secret and agreed to make the acquisition of her love a joint venture—as if love could be shared like merchandise or money. The fact that Marato kept a close watch on her hindered their plan, but one day, when the ship was sailing ahead at full speed and he stood at the stern gazing out to sea, never suspecting that there was a plot against him, they both crept up on him, grabbed him quickly from behind, and threw him into the water. By the time anyone noticed that he had fallen overboard, they were already more than a mile away. When the lady heard what had happened and realized that there was no way of going to his rescue, she began filling the ship once more with the sound of her mourning.

Her two lovers came straightway to console her, and with the aid of sweet words and the most extravagant promises, of which she understood very little, they worked at getting her to calm down. She was really lamenting her own misfortune more than the loss of Marato, and when, after their lengthy speeches, which they repeated twice over, she seemed much less distressed to them, the pair had a private discussion to decide who would be the first one to take her to bed with him. Each man wanted that honor, and failing to reach an agreement, they started a violent argument about it. Their words kept fanning the flames of their anger until they reached for their knives and in a fury hurled themselves at one another, and before any of the ship's crew could separate them, they had both been stabbed repeatedly. One of them died instantly from his wounds, and although the other survived, he was left with serious injuries to many parts of his body.

The lady was very upset over what had happened, for she could see that she was all alone there now, with no one to turn to for aid or advice, and she was terrified that the relations and friends of the two masters would take their anger out on her. However, partly because of the injured man's pleas on her behalf and partly because the ship quickly reached Chiarenza, she escaped the danger of being killed. Upon arriving, she disembarked with the injured man and went to stay with him at an inn, from which rumors of her stunning beauty spread throughout the city, eventually reaching the ears of the Prince of Morea who was living in Chiarenza at the time. He insisted on seeing her, and once he had, not only did he find that her beauty surpassed anything he had heard about it, but he immediately fell in love with her so passionately that he could think of nothing else.

Having learned about the circumstances of her arrival in the city, he saw no reason why he should not be able to have her, and in fact, while he was still trying to figure out a way to do so, the family of the injured man discovered what he was up to and sent the lady to him without a moment's hesitation. The Prince was absolutely delighted by this turn of events, as was the lady, who felt she had escaped a very dangerous situation indeed. Observing that she was endowed with refined manners as well as beauty, the Prince concluded, not having any other way to determine her identity, that she had to be a noblewoman, which had the effect of redoubling his love for her and led not only to his keeping her in high style, but to his treating her more like a wife than a mistress.

When the lady compared her present situation with the awful experiences she had been through, she considered herself pretty well off, and now that she had recovered fully and felt happy again, her beauty flowered to such an extent that all of Romania seemed to be talking about nothing else. And that is why the Duke of Athens, a handsome, well-built youth, who was a friend and relative of the Prince, was moved by a desire to see her. And so, under the pretext that he was just paying a visit to the Prince, as he used to do on occasion, he arrived in Chiarenza at the head of a splendid, noble retinue, and was received there with honor amid great rejoicing.°

A few days later, the two men fell to talking about the lady's beauty, and the Duke asked if she was really so marvelous an object as people said. "Far more so!" replied the Prince. "But rather than take my word for it, I'd prefer it if you judged with your own eyes."

The Prince invited the Duke to follow him, and together they went to the place where she was staying. Having already been informed of their approach, she welcomed them with the greatest civility, her face glowing with happiness. They had her sit down between them, but took no pleasure in conversing with her since she understood little or nothing of their language. Instead, as if she were some marvelous creature, they wound up simply gazing at her, and especially the Duke, who could hardly bring himself to believe she was a mere mortal. He did not realize he was drinking down the poison of Love through his eyes as he stared at her, and although he may have believed he could satisfy his desire simply by looking, the wretch was actually being caught up in the snare of her beauty and was falling passionately in love with her.° After he and the Prince had taken their leave and he had had some time for reflection, he concluded that the Prince was the happiest of men in having such a beautiful creature at his beck and call. Many and varied were his thoughts on the subject until his burning passion finally overcame his sense of honor, and he decided that, whatever the consequences, he would do everything in his power to deprive the Prince of that happiness and make it his own.

Determined to move with dispatch, he set aside all considerations of reason and justice, concentrating entirely on his treachery, and one day, in furtherance of his wicked plan, made arrangements with one of the Prince's most trusted servants, a man named Ciuriaci, to have his horses and baggage secretly readied for a sudden departure. When night fell, Ciuriaci, whom we just mentioned, silently let him and an accomplice, both fully armed, into the Prince's chamber. It was a very hot night, and while the lady lay sleeping, the Duke saw the Prince standing completely naked next to a window that faced the sea, enjoying a light breeze coming from that direction. The Duke, who had told his accomplice what to do ahead of time, stole quietly across the room to the window and thrust a dagger into the Prince's back with such force that it went straight through him, after which he quickly picked him up and hurled him out of the window. The palace stood high above the sea, and the window by which the Prince had been standing overlooked a cluster of houses that had been reduced to ruins by the pounding of the waves. People went there seldom, if ever, and consequently, as the Duke had foreseen, no one noticed the Prince's body as it fell, for there was no one there to see it.

When the Duke's accomplice saw that the deed was done, he quickly took out a noose he had brought with him for the purpose, and while pretending to embrace Ciuriaci, threw it around his neck, and drew it so tight that the man could not make a sound. The Duke then came over, and together they strangled Ciuriaci before throwing him down where the Prince had just been thrown. Once this was done, and they were absolutely certain that neither the lady nor anyone else had heard them, the Duke took up a lantern, carried it over to the bed, and quietly took all the covers off of her as she lay there sound asleep. Looking her over from head to toe, he was enraptured, and if he had found her attractive when dressed, now that she was naked, his admiration knew no bounds. The flames of the Duke's desire were burning even more fiercely than before, and unperturbed by the crime he had just committed, he lay down beside her, his hands still bloody, and made love to her, while she, half asleep, thought he was the Prince.

After a while, having enjoyed himself to the limit with her, the Duke got up and summoned a few of his men whom he ordered to hold the lady in such a way that she could not make a sound and to carry her out through the secret door by which he had entered. Then, making as little noise as possible, they put her on a horse, and the Duke led them all in the direction of Athens. Since he already had a wife, however, he did not take this unhappiest of ladies to Athens itself, but to an extraordinarily beautiful villa he had, not far from the city, that overlooked the sea. There he kept her hidden away, but ordered that she be treated with respect and given everything she needed.

The next day the Prince's courtiers waited until nones for him to get up, but when they still heard no sound coming from his room, they pushed open the doors, which were unlocked, only to discover that no one was there. Working on the assumption that he had gone off somewhere in secret to spend a few days in the happy company of his beautiful mistress, they did not give the matter a second thought.

Things stood thus until the next day, when a madman, who had wandered into the ruins where the bodies of the Prince and Ciuri-aci were lying, dragged Ciuriaci out by the rope around his neck, and walked about, pulling the body behind him. When people recognized who it was, they were dumbfounded and managed to coax the madman into taking them to the place from which he had brought the body. There, to the immense sorrow of the entire city, they found the dead Prince. After burying him with full hon-ors, they opened an investigation to discover who was responsible for the heinous crime, and when they learned that the Duke of Athens, who had departed in secret, was nowhere to be found, they concluded correctly that he was the culprit and that he must have taken the lady away with him. After hastily choosing a brother of their dead Prince as their new ruler, they urged him with all the eloquence at their command to seek revenge. And when yet more evidence appeared, confirming that their suspicions were true, the new Prince summoned his friends, relations, and servants from various places to support his cause, quickly assembling a splendid, large, and powerful army, with which he set out to wage war against the Duke of Athens.

The moment the Duke heard what was happening, he, too, mobilized his entire army for his defense. Many noblemen came to his aid, including two who were sent by the Emperor of Con-stantinople, namely his son Constantine and his nephew Manuel, who arrived at the head of a fine large force.° They were warmly welcomed by the Duke, and even more so by the Duchess, who was Constantine's sister.

As war came closer day by day, the Duchess found a convenient moment to invite the two young men to her room, where she told them the entire story in great detail. Weeping copiously as she explained the causes of the war, she complained bitterly about the disrespect the Duke was showing her by having some woman as his mistress, whose existence he thought he was managing to keep hidden from her, and she begged them, for the sake of the Duke's honor and her own happiness, to take whatever measures were necessary to set things right. Since the young men already knew the whole story, they did not ask her very many questions, but did their best to comfort her and give her every reason to be hopeful. Then, after being informed as to where the lady was staying, they took their leave of her.

Since they had often heard the lady praised for her marvelous beauty, they were actually quite eager to see her and begged the Duke to present her to them. He promised he would, forgetting what had happened to the Prince for having done something similar. And the next morning, after arranging to have a magnificent banquet served in a lovely garden that was on the estate where the lady was staying, he took the two young men, along with a few other companions, to dine with her there. Sitting down next to her, Constantine stared at her in wonder, vowing to himself that he had never seen anything so lovely and that no one would blame the Duke, or anybody else, for resorting to treachery and other dishonest means in order to gain possession of so beautiful an object. And as he looked her over again and again, each time he admired her more than the time before, until finally the same thing happened to him that had happened to the Duke. As a result, by the time he left, he was so much in love with her that he abandoned any thought of going to war and concentrated on how he might take her away from the Duke, all the while doing a very good job of concealing his passion from everyone.

As Constantine was burning in this fire, the moment arrived to march against the Prince, who had by now almost reached the Duke's territories. In accordance with their strategic plan, the Duke, Constantine, and all the others left Athens and went to take up positions along certain stretches of the frontier where they intended to block the Prince's advance. While they waited there for several days, Constantine, whose thoughts and feelings were entirely focused on the lady, fancied that since the Duke was no longer anywhere near her, he now had an excellent opportunity to get what he wanted. Pretending to be seriously ill in order to have a pretext for returning to Athens, he got permission from the

Duke, handed his command over to Manuel, and went back to stay with his sister in the city. Several days later, after he got her talking about the disrespect she thought the Duke was showing her with his kept woman, he told her that if she wanted, he could certainly be of considerable assistance to her in this business, for he could have the woman removed from where she was staying and taken elsewhere. Thinking that Constantine was prompted by his love for her rather than for the lady, the Duchess said that it would please her very much, provided it was done in such a way that the Duke never found out she had given her consent to the scheme. Constantine reassured her completely on this point, and accordingly, the Duchess gave him permission to proceed in whatever way he thought best.

Constantine had a swift boat fitted out in secret, and one evening, after giving those of his men who were on board their instructions, he sent it to a spot near the garden on the estate where the lady was staying. Then, with another group of men, he went to her villa, where he was warmly received by her servants and by the lady herself, who at his request, went with him and his men to take a walk in the garden, accompanied by her servants.

Pretending he wanted to speak to her on behalf of the Duke, he led her down toward a gate overlooking the sea that had been unlocked earlier by one of his crew. There, at a given signal, the boat pulled up, and Constantine had his men seize her and quickly put her on board. Then he turned to her servants and said: "Don't anyone move or make a sound unless you want to be killed. My intention here is not to steal the Duke's mistress, but to take away the shame he's inflicted on my sister."

Seeing that no one dared to respond to him, he boarded the boat with his men, and sitting down beside the weeping lady, he ordered them to put their oars into the water and get under way. They did not row so much as fly along, arriving at Aegina just before dawn the next day.°

Disembarking there in order to rest, Constantine had his fun with the lady, who did nothing but lament her unlucky beauty. Then they boarded the boat once again and in just a few days reached Chios, where Constantine decided to put up, thinking he would be safe there both from his father's reprimands and from the possibility that someone might take away from him the lady he himself had stolen. For several days the beauty bewailed her misfortune, but eventually, thanks to Constantine's unremitting efforts to console her, she began to enjoy, as she had every other time, the lot that Fortune had assigned her.

This was the state of affairs when Osbech, at that time the King of the Turks, who was constantly at war with the Emperor, chanced to come to Smyrna, where he learned that Constantine was leading a dissolute life on Chios with some woman of his whom he had abducted and that he had consequently not bothered to set up any defenses there.° Arriving one night with a squadron of light warships, Osbech quietly entered the town with his men, capturing many people in their beds before they were even aware that the enemy was upon them, and killing those who awoke in time to run and get their weapons.° They then set fire to the town, loaded their booty and their prisoners onto the ships, and went back to Smyrna. Upon reviewing their spoils after their return, the young Osbech was delighted to discover the beautiful lady, whom he recognized as being the one he had captured in bed together with Constantine as they lay sleeping. He married her on the spot and after the wedding spent the next several months very happily sleeping with her.

In the period before these events occurred, the Emperor had been negotiating a pact with Basano, the King of Cappadocia, to have his forces attack Osbech from one direction while the Emperor assaulted him from the other.° He had not yet brought their negotiations to a conclusion, however, because he would not agree to some of Basano's demands that he found quite unreasonable. But on hearing what had happened to his son, the Emperor was so distraught that he accepted the King of Cappadocia's terms at once and urged him to attack Osbech as soon as he possibly could, while he himself made preparations to come down on Osbech from the other direction.

When Osbech heard about all this, rather than let himself get caught in the middle between two powerful rulers, he assembled

his army and marched against the King of Cappadocia, leaving
the lovely lady at Smyrna under the protection of a loyal retainer
and friend. Some time later, he confronted the King of Cappadocia and attacked him, but in the battle his army was defeated and
put to flight, and he himself was killed. Unopposed, the victorious
Basano then marched on Smyrna, and as he went, all the peoples
along the way submitted to him as their conqueror.

The retainer in whose care Osbech had left the lovely lady, a
man named Antioco, was so taken with her beauty that he
betrayed the trust of his friend and master, and despite his
advanced years, fell in love with her. It pleased her immensely that
he knew her language, because for a number of years she had been
forced to live as if she were a deaf-mute, incapable of understanding others or getting them to understand her. Spurred on by love,
in the first few days Antioco began taking so many liberties with
her that before long they had cast aside any concern for their
master, who was away fighting in the war, and became not merely
friends, but lovers who gave one another the greatest pleasure
imaginable over and over again as they lay together between the
sheets.

When they heard that Osbech had been defeated and killed,
however, and that Basano was on his way, carrying everything
before him, they were of one mind in deciding to leave rather than
wait for his arrival. Taking with them a substantial quantity of
Osbech's most valuable possessions, they fled together in secret to
Rhodes, where they had not been very long before Antioco contracted a fatal illness.° At the time he happened to have a Cypriot
merchant staying in his house, a very close friend whom he loved
dearly, and as Antioco felt the end approaching, he decided to
leave his friend both his possessions and his beloved lady. And so,
when he felt his death was imminent, he summoned the two of
them and said:

"I have no doubt that my strength is failing, which saddens me
because my life has never been as happy as it's been of late. Truth-
fully, though, there's one thing that reconciles me to my death,
and it's that since I'm going to die, I will do so in the arms of the

two people I love more than anyone else in the world, that is, in your arms, my dear, dear friend, and in those of this lady, whom I've loved more than I love myself for as long as I've known her. But still, what really continues to trouble me is that when I die, she'll be left all alone here in a strange land, with no one to turn to for help or counsel. And this worry would weigh on me even more than it does if I didn't have you here, because I believe that, out of love for me, you will take good care of her just as you would of me. Consequently, in the event of my death, I commit her, together with all my worldly goods, to your charge, and I entreat you as earnestly as I can to make use of them in whatever way you think will offer my soul some measure of consolation. And as for you, my dearest lady, I beg you not to forget me after my death, for then I can boast up there that I have been loved down here by the most beautiful woman ever fashioned by Nature. And now, if both of you will just reassure me on these two points, you may have no doubt but that I will die content."

Both Antioco's merchant friend and the lady wept as they listened to his words, and when he was finished, they comforted him and swore on their honor to do what he requested if he should happen to die. And not long after this, he did, in fact, pass away, and they saw to it that he was given an honorable burial.

A few days later, when the Cypriot merchant had taken care of all his business in Rhodes, he decided to take ship on a Catalan merchant vessel then in port that was about to sail to Cyprus.° He asked the lady what she wanted to do, in light of the fact that he was compelled to return to Cyprus, and she replied that if he had no objection, she would gladly go with him, because she hoped that, out of love for Antioco, he would think of her like a sister and would treat her accordingly. The merchant said he would be happy to do whatever she wished, and in order to protect her from any harm that might befall her before they reached Cyprus, he told everyone she was his wife. When they got on board, they were, consequently, assigned a small cabin in the stern, and to ensure that their actions were consistent with their words, he slept in the same narrow little bunk with her. What happened next was something that neither one of them had intended when they left Rhodes. Stimulated by the darkness as well as by the warmth and comfort of the bed, which are forces not to be underestimated, they were both seized by the same desires, and forgetting all about the loyalty and love they owed Antioco, before long they were fondling one another, with the inevitable result that even before they reached Paphos, the Cypriot's hometown, they were sleeping together like a regular married couple.° Indeed, for quite some time after they reached their destination, she went on living with the merchant in his house.

By chance, a gentleman named Antigono happened to come to Paphos on some business or other at a time when the Cypriot merchant was away on a trading mission in Armenia. An elderly man, Antigono had acquired even more wisdom than years, albeit very little wealth in the process, because every time he had undertaken a commission in the service of the King of Cyprus, Fortune had always been his enemy.° One day, as he was passing by the house where the lovely lady was staying, he happened to catch sight of her at one of the windows. He just could not stop staring at her, not only because she was so beautiful, but also because he had a vague recollection that he had seen her at some other time, although he could by no means remember where that had been.

For a long while, the lovely lady had been Fortune's plaything, but the moment was approaching when her sufferings would be over. Observing Antigono, she recalled having seen him in Alexandria where he had served her father in a position of some importance, and all of a sudden she was filled with hope that there might be some possibility of her returning once more to her royal station with the help of this man's advice. Since her merchant was out of the way, she sent for the old counselor at the first opportunity, and when he arrived, she asked him shyly if he was, as she thought, Antigono di Famagosto. Antigono replied that he was, adding: "My lady, I think I've seen you before, but I can't, for the life of me, remember where. Please be good enough, therefore, unless you have some objection, to remind me who you are."

When the lady heard that he was indeed Antigono, to his

complete astonishment she burst into tears and threw her arms about his neck. Then, after a moment, she asked him if he had ever seen her in Alexandria. The instant Antigono heard her question, he recognized that she was Alatiel, the Sultan's daughter, who everybody thought had died at sea. He tried to bow to her as court etiquette required, but she would not permit it, inviting him, instead, to sit down beside her for a while. When he was seated, he asked her with due reverence how and when and from where she had come to Cyprus, for all of Egypt was convinced that she had drowned at sea many years before.

"I really wish that had happened," replied the lady, "instead of my having led the sort of life I've led. Furthermore, I think my father would agree with me if he ever found out about it." Then, having said this, she began weeping prodigiously once again.

"My lady, don't distress yourself unnecessarily," said Antigono. "Tell me about your misfortunes, if you like, and about the life you've led. Perhaps things can be handled in such a way that, with God's help, we'll be able to find a solution for your problem."

"Antigono," said the lovely lady, "when I first saw you here, I felt I was looking at my own father, and although I could have concealed my identity from you, I was moved to reveal it by the same love and tender affection I am bound to feel for him. Actually, there are few people I would have been as happy to have seen here as I am to have seen you, and therefore, I'm going to reveal to you, as to a father, the story of my terrible misfortunes, which I've always kept hidden from everyone else. If, after you've heard it, you can see any means of restoring me to my pristine condition, I implore you to make use of it. If not, I beg you never to tell anyone that you've either seen me or heard anything about me."

This said, she gave him an account, without ever ceasing to weep, of everything that had happened to her from the day she was shipwrecked off Majorca up to the present moment. Her story made Antigono start weeping himself out of pity for her, and after pondering the matter awhile, he said: "My lady, since no one ever knew who you were during all your misadventures, have no doubt but that I can restore you, more precious than ever, first to your father and then, as his bride, to the King of Algarve."

Questioned by her as to how he would manage this, he explained in detail just what she had to do. Then, to prevent anything from happening that might cause a delay, Antigono returned at once to Famagosto where he presented himself before the King. "My lord," he said, "if it please you, you can do something at very little cost that will greatly redound to your honor, while simultaneously being of inestimable benefit to me, who have grown poor while I've been in your service."

When the King asked how this might be done, Antigono answered: "The beautiful young daughter of the Sultan, who was long thought to have drowned at sea, has turned up in Paphos. For many years she has suffered through extreme hardships in order to preserve her honor, and now she is living here in poverty and wants to return to her father. If it should be your pleasure to send her back to him under my escort, it would greatly enhance your honor and would mean a rich reward for me. It is, moreover, inconceivable that the Sultan would ever forget such a service."

Moved by regal feelings of magnanimity, the King said that it was indeed his pleasure to send the lady home, and he dispatched an honor guard to accompany her to Famagosto where he and the Queen received her with the most incredible pomp and circumstance. When they asked her about her adventures, she replied by recounting the whole story just as Antigono had taught her to tell it.

A few days later, at her request, the King sent her back to the Sultan under Antigono's protection and with a splendid retinue of distinguished gentlemen and ladies. No one need ask how warm a welcome she got there or how Antigono and her entire entourage were received. After letting her rest awhile, the Sultan wanted to know how it had come about that she was still alive, where she had been living for all that time, and why she had never sent him word about her situation.

The lady, who had memorized Antigono's instructions to the letter, answered the Sultan as follows: "Father, some twenty days after I left you, our ship foundered in a fierce storm and ran aground one night on some beach or other in the West near a place called Aigues-Mortes.° I never found out what happened to the men who were on board. All I do remember is that when dawn arrived, I felt as though I was rising from the dead and returning to life. Some peasants, who had spotted the wrecked ship, came running from all over to plunder it. When I was put ashore with two of my women, they were instantly snatched up by some young men who then fled, carrying them off in different directions, and I never discovered what became of them. As for me, although I tried to fight them off, two young men grabbed me and started to drag me away by my hair. I was weeping violently the whole time, but then, just as they started heading down a road in the direction of a very dense forest, four horsemen happened to come riding by, and the instant my abductors caught sight of them, they let go of me and immediately fled away.

"When they saw what was happening, the four horsemen, who seemed like persons of some authority, galloped over to me. They asked me a lot of questions, and I gave them a lot of answers, but it was impossible for us to understand one another. Then, after a long consultation among themselves, they put me on one of their horses and led me to a convent of women who practiced these men's religion. I have no idea what they said there, but the women gave me a very kind welcome and always treated me with respect. While I was in the convent, I joined them in reverently worshipping Saint Grows-in-the-Deep-Valley, to whom the women of that country are passionately devoted.° After I'd lived there awhile and had learned something of their language, they asked me who I was and what country I'd come from. Knowing where I was, I feared that if I told them the truth, they might expel me as an enemy to their religion, and so I replied that I was the daughter of an important nobleman of Cyprus, who had been sending me to be married in Crete when, unfortunately, we were driven onto their shores by a storm and shipwrecked.

"Fearful of a worse fate, I made a regular habit of observing their customs of every sort until, eventually, I was asked by the women's superior, whom they call their Abbess, whether I wanted to return to Cyprus, and I replied that there was nothing I desired more. Out of concern for my honor, however, she was unwilling to entrust me to just anyone coming to Cyprus, at least up until about two months ago, when certain French gentlemen, some of whom were related to the Abbess, arrived there with their wives. When she heard that they were going to Jerusalem to visit the Sepulcher, where the man they consider their God was buried after the Jews had killed Him, she placed me in their care and asked them to hand me over to my father in Cyprus.

"It would make too long a story if I were to describe how much I was honored and how warm a welcome I was given by these noblemen and their wives. Suffice it to say that we all took ship and in just a few days reached Paphos, where it suddenly hit me that I'd come to a place where I didn't know anyone and thus had no idea what to tell the noblemen who wanted to follow the venerable lady's instructions and hand me over to my father. Perhaps God took pity on me, however, for he arranged to have Antigono there on the shore at Paphos at the precise moment we were getting off the ship. I called out to him at once, using our own language so as not to be understood by the noblemen and their wives, and told him to welcome me as his daughter. He grasped my meaning instantly and made a tremendous fuss over me. After entertaining those noblemen and their wives as well as his limited means allowed, he took me to the King of Cyprus, and I couldn't begin to describe how much he honored me, not only with the welcome he gave me there, but by sending me back here to you. If anything else remains to be said, I leave it to Antigono, for he has heard me recount my adventures time and time again."

"My lord," said Antigono, turning to the Sultan, "she has now told you exactly the same story she's recounted to me many times and what the noblemen who were accompanying her told me as well. There's only one part that she's left out, which I think she omitted because it would not be appropriate for her to talk about it, and that is how much praise the gentlemen and ladies with whom she was traveling lavished on her not just because of the honest life she'd led with the pious women, but also because of her virtue and her laudable character. She also failed to mention how all of them, the men as well as the women, grieved and wept bitter tears when the time came to say farewell to her and place her in my charge. Were I to recount in detail everything they told me on this subject, I'd be talking not only all day, but all night, too. Let it suffice for me to say just this much, that from what their words have revealed to me, and from what I myself have been able to see, you may boast of having a daughter who is far lovelier, chaster, and more courageous than that of any monarch wearing a crown today."

The Sultan was absolutely overjoyed to hear these things, and he repeatedly asked God to grant him the grace to bestow proper rewards on all those who had treated his daughter so honorably, and in particular on the King of Cyprus who had sent her home with such pomp and ceremony. A few days later, having ordered the most lavish gifts for Antigono, he gave him leave to return to Cyprus, sending letters and special envoys along with him to convey his most sincere gratitude to the King for what he had done for his daughter. Then, since he wanted to bring what he had started long before to its conclusion, namely to make her the wife of the King of Algarve, he wrote to the King, explaining everything that had happened, and adding that if he still wished to have her, he should send his envoys to fetch her. The King of Algarve was quite delighted by this proposition, sent an honorable escort for her, and gave her a joyous welcome. Thus, although she had slept with eight men perhaps ten thousand times, she not only came to the King's bed as if she were a virgin, but made him believe she really was one, and for a good many years after that, lived a perfectly happy life with him as his Queen. And that is the reason why we say:

A mouth that's been kissed never loses its charm,
But just like the moon, it's forever renewed.°

Story 10

PAGANINO DA MONACO ABDUCTS THE WIFE OF MESSER
RICCIARDO DI CHINZICA, WHO, AFTER FINDING OUT WHERE
SHE IS, GOES AND BEFRIENDS HER ABDUCTOR. WHEN HE
ASKS PAGANINO TO GIVE HER BACK, THE LATTER AGREES TO
DO SO, PROVIDED THAT SHE WANTS TO GO. SHE REFUSES TO
RETURN TO MESSER RICCIARDO, HOWEVER, AND AFTER HIS
DEATH, BECOMES PAGANINO'S WIFE.°

*   *   *

Lovely ladies, there was one part of the Queen's story that has
led me to change my mind and substitute a different tale for the
one I had thought to tell. And that is the part about the stupidity
of Bernabò and of all those other men who believe the same thing
that he apparently did, namely, that when they go about the world,
enjoying themselves with one woman here and another there,
they imagine that the wives they left at home are just sitting on
their hands. Albeit things turned out well enough for Bernabò,
we, who are born and grow up and live our lives surrounded by
women, know what it is they really hanker for. By telling this
story, I will show you just how foolish such men are, and at the
same time, I will reveal the even greater folly of those who not
only think they are stronger than Nature and convince themselves
by means of specious arguments that they can do the impossible,
but actually work directly against Nature by striving to get others
to be just like them.

In Pisa there was once a judge named Messer Ricciardo di
Chinzica who was endowed with more intelligence than physical
strength and may well have believed that he could satisfy a wife
with the same sort of effort he used to put into his studies. Because
he was also very rich, he went to a great deal of trouble to find
himself a woman to marry who possessed both youth and beauty,
although if he had been capable of giving himself the good counsel

he normally gave others, those are two attributes he would have absolutely avoided in a bride. Well, success came his way, for Messer Lotto Gualandi let him marry one of his daughters, a girl named Bartolomea, who was one of the most beautiful and charming young women in Pisa, a city where most of the women are as ugly as little wormy lizards.° The judge brought her home with great festivity, and the wedding was grand and beautiful. However, on the first night, when he attempted to consummate their marriage, he barely managed to score one random hit, and even then, it came very close to being a complete stalemate. Moreover, the next morning, this skinny, feeble, dried-up old man had to drink a quantity of Vernaccia wine and eat lots of sweets as well as other restoratives before he could return to the land of the living.°

So now, this Messer Judge guy, having achieved a deeper understanding of his own strength than ever before, started teaching his wife about the kind of calendar that schoolboys like to consult and that may have once been used at Ravenna.° As he explained it to her, every single day in it was the feast day of at least one, if not more, saints, and out of reverence for them, he said, supplying her with a host of arguments, men and women ought to abstain from conjugal relations. Then, on top of those days, he added in all days of fasting, and the four Ember Days, and the vigils held for the Apostles and for a thousand other saints, and the Friday, Saturday, and Sunday of Our Lord, and the whole of Lent, plus certain phases of the moon as well as many other special occasions, possibly because he thought that men should take a holiday from bedding their wives just as he sometimes used to take a holiday from pleading civil cases in the law courts.° He adhered to this schedule for a long time, which made his wife profoundly depressed, since her turn came up perhaps just once a month, and all the while he kept a close watch on her in case someone else should try to teach her how to observe workdays the way he had taught her about holidays.

It just so happened that one day, during a hot spell, Messer Ricciardo was suddenly seized by a desire to go to a fine estate he had near Monte Nero and spend a few days there, relaxing and enjoying the fresh country air.° He took his lovely lady along with him, and after they had been there for a while, he decided to arrange a fishing excursion as a little diversion for her. They set out on two little boats in order to watch it, he on the one with the fishermen and she with several women on the other, and they got so absorbed in the delightful experience that, before they realized it, they had gone several miles out to sea.

At the precise moment when they were most intent on watching the fishermen, a small galley belonging to Paganino da Mare, a notorious pirate in those days, suddenly arrived on the scene.° Upon catching sight of the boats, he headed in their direction, and although they fled away, they were not fast enough to keep him from overtaking the one carrying the women. As soon as he spotted the lovely lady on it, he had no interest in anything else, and while Messer Ricciardo watched from the shore, which he had already managed to reach, Paganino took her on board his galley and sailed away. There is no need to ask if Messer Judge was distressed by what he saw, for he was such a jealous man that to him even the air around his wife was suspect. But although he went about Pisa and elsewhere, bemoaning the wickedness of pirates, it was all in vain, for he had no idea who had abducted his wife or where he had taken her.

When Paganino saw how truly beautiful the lady was, he felt he was a pretty lucky guy, and having no wife of his own, decided to keep her for himself permanently. Since she was weeping bitter tears, he immediately tried using sweet talk to comfort her, but by nightfall, he had reached the conclusion that the words he had been using all day long were getting him nowhere. Instead, he turned to consoling her with deeds, for this guy had lost his calendar and had long since forgotten about feast days and holidays.° In fact, he was so good at consoling her in this fashion that before they reached Monaco, she had completely forgotten about the judge and his laws, and was happier living with Paganino than anyone in the world could be. And once they were in Monaco, not only did he console her both day and night, but he also treated her as honorably as if she were his wife.

Some time later, when news reached the ears of Messer Ricciardo concerning the whereabouts of his wife, he was filled with the most passionate desire and decided, since he did not think anyone else was truly capable of doing everything that would be necessary, to go and fetch her himself. Ready to spend whatever amount of money it took to ransom her, he set sail for Monaco, where he caught sight of her soon after his arrival. She also caught sight of him and later that same evening informed Paganino both about what had happened and about what her intentions were. The next morning, Messer Ricciardo ran into Paganino and started a conversation with him, becoming his bosom buddy in short order, although Paganino, who pretended not to know him, was just waiting to see what he would do. At the earliest opportunity, Messer Ricciardo revealed the real reason why he had come, and in his best, most polite manner, told Paganino that he could have whatever ransom he wanted if he would just give back the lady.

"You're most welcome here, sir," replied Paganino, with a smile on his face. "And as for what you are asking, I will answer you briefly and tell you this much. While it's true that I have a young lady at my house, I can't really say whether she's your wife or not, for I don't know you, and all I know about her is that she's been living with me here for some time now. Since you seem like an amiable gentleman, I'll take you to her, and if you are her husband, as you say, I feel certain she'll recognize you without difficulty. What's more, if she says your story is true and wants to go with you, then, because you're such an amiable man, you can give me whatever you like as her ransom. However, if your story's not true, it would be wicked for you to try and take her from me, because I'm a young man who's just as capable of keeping a woman as anyone else, and especially this woman, for she's the nicest one I've ever seen."

"Of course she's my wife," said Messer Ricciardo, "and you'll soon see that she is, because if you take me to her, she'll throw her arms about my neck right away. And that's why I'm perfectly happy to agree to what you yourself are proposing."

"In that case," said Paganino, "let's go."

And so off they went to Paganino's house. After entering one of its great halls, he sent for the lady, who came in from another room, elegantly dressed and completely composed, and walked over to join the two men where they were waiting. She said no more to Messer Ricciardo, however, than she would have said to some complete stranger who had come home with Paganino. On seeing this, the judge was dumbfounded, for he had expected her to make an enormous fuss over him when she saw him. "Perhaps," he thought to himself, "my melancholy and the prolonged suffering I've been through since I lost her have changed my appearance so much that she doesn't recognize me." Consequently, he said to her:

"Wife, taking you fishing has cost me plenty. Nobody's ever experienced so much grief as I have since I lost you, and now it appears, from the cool reception you've just given me, that you have no idea who I am. Don't you see that I'm your own Messer Ricciardo, and that I've come here, to this gentleman's house, willing to pay him whatever he wants to let me take you away and bring you back home with me again? And for his part, he's been kind enough to hand you over for whatever I choose to give him."

Turning to him, the lady replied, with just the faintest suggestion of a smile: "Are you speaking to me, sir? Be careful not to confuse me with somebody else, because as far as I'm concerned, I can't remember ever having seen you before."

"Watch what you're saying," replied Messer Ricciardo. "Just take a good look at me, and if you try really hard to remember, you'll see for sure that I'm your very own Ricciardo di Chinzica."

"You must forgive me, sir," said the lady, "but for me to stare at you may not be so proper as you think it is. Nevertheless, I have looked you over sufficiently to know that I've never seen you before."

Messer Ricciardo thought she was doing all this because she was afraid of Paganino, in whose presence she did not want to admit that she recognized him, and so, after a while, he asked Paganino to be so kind as to allow him to speak all alone with her in another room. Paganino said that they could do so, provided Messer

Ricciardo did not try to kiss her against her will. Then he told her
to go into her room with Messer Ricciardo, listen to what he had
to say, and freely give him whatever answer she wished.

The lady and Messer Ricciardo went to the room by themselves
and sat down.

"Oh, sweetheart, my soul mate, my angel," he said, "do you still
not recognize your Ricciardo now, your Ricciardo who loves you
more than life itself? How is it possible? Can I have changed so
much? Oh, light of my life, just take another little look at me."

The lady started laughing and cut him off.

"Surely," she said, "you don't think I'm so scatterbrained that
I don't know you're my husband Messer Ricciardo di Chinzica,
even though you showed little sign of knowing me when I was
living with you. Because if either now or then you were as wise as
you want people to think you are, you should have been smart
enough to see that fresh, lively young women like me need more
than food and clothing, even if modesty prevents them from saying so. And you know what you did to take care of that.

"If studying the law appealed to you more than your wife did,
you should never have gotten married. To my mind, though, you
never really did seem like much of a judge, but more like a town
crier whose job it was to announce feast days and holidays—now
that's something you really knew all about—to say nothing of fasts
and vigils. And let me tell you, if you had given the laborers who
work on your estates as many holidays as you gave the guy who
had the job of tending my little field, you would never have har-
vested a single grain of wheat.

"But God looked down with pity on my youth, and by His will
I chanced upon the man I share this room with, in which holy
days are unheard of—I mean those holy days, of course, that you
used to celebrate so religiously, since you were always more
devoted to the service of God than the servicing of women. And
not only has that door over there remained shut to keep out Saturdays and Fridays and vigils and the four Ember Days, not to mention Lent, which just goes on and on and on, but inside we're
always at work together, giving the wool a good whacking day and

night.° In fact, from the time matins was rung early this morning, I can't begin to tell you how much wool we've whacked since we did it the first time.

"So that's why I intend to stay with him and to keep working away at it while I'm still young. I'll take holy days and fasting as well as making pilgrimages to obtain indulgences, and reserve them all for when I'm an old woman. As for you, be so good as clear out of here as soon as you can, and good luck to you. Go and celebrate as many holy days as you like, just so long as you're not doing it with me."

As he listened to these words, Messer Ricciardo was suffering an unbearable agony, and when he saw she had finished, he said: "Oh, sweetheart, do you realize what you're saying? Have you no concern for your parents' honor or your own? Do you want to live here in mortal sin as this guy's whore rather than come to Pisa where you'll be my wife? When this guy's tired of you, he'll humiliate you by tossing you out, whereas I will always cherish you, and you'll always be the mistress of my household, no matter what. Do you really mean to abandon not just your honor but me, too, someone who loves you more than life itself, for the sake of this unbridled, dishonorable appetite of yours? Oh, my angel, don't say things like that anymore. Just agree to come away with me, and since I know what you want, from now on I'll make a really big effort. Please, sweetheart, change your mind and come with me, for I've been miserable ever since you were taken from me."

"As for my honor," the lady replied, "no one's going to defend the little that's left of it more than I'm going to do. I just wish my family had taken greater care of it when they gave me to you! But since they weren't concerned about my honor in the past, I don't intend to worry about theirs in the present. Furthermore, if I'm living now in *mortar* sin, I guess I'll just have to live with the *pestle's-in*, too.° So don't you go getting any more concerned about it than I am. And let me tell you this: here I really do feel like Paganino's wife, whereas in Pisa I used to feel like your whore. There we were always using the phases of the moon and making geometrical measurements to determine whether we could bring our planets into conjunction with one another. By contrast, here Paganino holds me in his arms all night long, hugging me and giving me little love bites, and God alone can tell you how he services me.

"You say you'll make a really big effort. But how? By coming up empty after three feeble bouts and having to give it quite a whacking to make it stand up?° From what I can see here, you've become quite the sturdy rider since the last time I saw you! Go away, and put all that energy of yours into just staying alive, for it seems as if you're barely hanging on there, that's how rundown and droopy you look to me. And I'll tell you this as well: if this guy should ever leave me—and he doesn't seem inclined to do so, as long as I want to stay—I have no intention of ever returning to you. For if you were squeezed till you were dry, they couldn't get a spoonful of sauce out of you. My life with you amounted to nothing but one giant loss, including both principal and interest, so next time I'll go looking somewhere else for my profit. Once and for all, then, let me tell you that I intend to stay here where there aren't any holy days or vigils. Now, good-bye, and go away as quickly as you can, because if you don't, I'm going to scream that you're trying to rape me."

Seeing that the situation was hopeless and finally realizing what a fool he had been to have married a young woman when he was so feeble, Messer Ricciardo left her room feeling sad and forlorn, and although he talked for a long time with Paganino, it was just so much whistling in the wind.° Finally, having accomplished absolutely nothing, he left the lady there and returned to Pisa, where his grief caused him to fall into such a state of madness that whenever anyone greeted him or asked him about something as he was walking about the city, he would always reply with the same words: "The evil hole never takes a holiday."° Not long after that he died, and when the news reached Paganino, knowing how much the lady loved him, he took her as his lawful wedded wife. And without ever paying attention to holy days and vigils or observing Lent, the two of them had a jolly life together, working away at it as long as their legs could support them.

And that is why, dear ladies, in my opinion, when Ser Bernabò was arguing against Ambruogiuolo, he was making a complete fool of himself.°

Conclusion

This story gave the entire company so much to laugh about that there was no one whose jaws did not ache, and all the ladies unanimously agreed that Dioneo was right and that Bernabò had been an ass. When the story was finished, the Queen waited awhile for the laughter to subside. Then, seeing that the hour was late, and realizing that since everyone had told a story, her reign had come to its end, she took the garland from her head and, according to the rules they had agreed on, placed it on Neifile's, saying with a happy smile: "Now, my dear friend, you are the ruler of this tiny nation." After that, she sat back down again.

Neifile blushed a little on receiving this honor, so that her face looked like a fresh rose blooming just at daybreak in April or May, while her beautiful eyes, which she had lowered slightly, glittered like the morning star.° Once the respectful round of applause from her companions, who were happy to show their approval of her as Queen, had died down, and she had regained her composure, she took her seat in a slightly more elevated position than her usual one, and said:

"I have no desire to depart from the ways of my predecessors whose rule you approve of as you have shown by means of your obedience. But since I am now indeed your Queen, I shall take just a few words to acquaint you with what I propose to do, and if it meets with your approval, then we shall put it into effect.

"As you know, tomorrow is Friday and the next day, Saturday, both of which most people consider to be rather tedious because of the food we normally eat then.° Moreover, since Friday should be revered by us because it is the day when He who died that we might live suffered His Passion, I would consider it right and proper for us to honor God and set aside that day, devoting it to prayers rather than stories. As for Saturday, it is customary for women to wash their hair then and get rid of all the dust and grime that have accumulated from the work they did the preceding week. Besides, many of them also fast on Saturday in honor of the Virgin Mother of the Son of God, and for the remainder of the day they rest from their labors in honor of the approaching Sabbath. Since, therefore, it is impossible for us to lead our lives on Saturdays completely in accordance with the plan we adopted, I think it would be a good idea for us to take a break from storytelling on that day, too.

"Then, seeing as how we will have been here four days, if we want to avoid the possibility that other people might join us, I think it would be an opportune moment for us to leave and go elsewhere—and I have already thought about where that elsewhere would be and have made arrangements for us to go there.

"As we were telling our stories today, we had quite a wide field to wander in, but when we get together in our new location after our nap on Sunday, you will have had more time for reflection, and I have therefore decided that since it will be much nicer if we place some restrictions on the freedom we had in our storytelling today, we should focus on just one of the many facets of Fortune and should talk about people who have relied on their resourcefulness to acquire something they really desired or recover something they had lost.° On this topic each of us should think up a story that might be useful, or at least enjoyable, for the entire company to hear, an exception always being made for Dioneo and his privilege."

Everyone praised what the Queen had said and adopted her proposal. She then summoned the steward, and after deciding where to put the tables that evening, gave him detailed instructions about what to do during the course of her reign. That done, she rose to her feet, as did the rest of the company, and gave them leave to go and enjoy themselves however they wished.

Both the ladies and the men made their way down a path that led to a little garden where they amused themselves for a while until the hour for supper had arrived. They ate their meal amid laughter and merriment, and when they had risen from the table, at the Queen's request Emilia led them in a *carola*,° while Pampinea sang the following song, joined by all the others for the chorus.

What lady sings except for me alone,
Since each desire of mine is satisfied?
  Come, then, O Love, source of my joy,
Of all my hopes and every happiness,
Let's jointly sing awhile,
Though not of sighs or of love's suffering,
Which now for me make sweeter your delights,
But just of love's clear flame,
In which I burn and revel joyfully,
Adoring you as if you were my god.

  It's you, O Love, who placed before my eyes,
That day I started burning in your fire,
A youth who did possess
Such talent, ardor, and such valor, too,
That no man greater ever could be found,
Not one to equal him.
For him I've burned so bright that now
I gladly sing of him with you, my Lord.

  And what in all this pleases me the most
Is that I please him as he pleases me,
For which I thank you, Love.
Since in this world, I now have all I could
Desire, and in the next I hope for peace
Through that unbroken faith
I bear for him—which God, who sees all this,
Will grant us from His Kingdom up above.°

When Pampinea had finished, they sang many other songs, danced a number of dances, and played several tunes, until the Queen decided it was time for them to go to bed. Then, carrying torches to light their way, they went to their respective rooms, and for the next two days they attended to the matters the Queen had previously spoken of, although all of them were looking forward eagerly to Sunday.

Day 3

HERE ENDS THE SECOND DAY OF THE *DECAMERON*, AND THE
THIRD BEGINS, IN WHICH, UNDER THE RULE OF NEIFILE,
THEY SPEAK OF PEOPLE WHO HAVE RELIED ON THEIR
RESOURCEFULNESS TO ACQUIRE SOMETHING THEY REALLY
DESIRED OR RECOVER SOMETHING THEY HAD LOST.

On Sunday, just as dawn was beginning to turn from vermilion to
orange at the approach of the sun, the Queen arose and had the
entire company awakened. Quite some time before then, the steward had sent a great many of the things they would need on ahead
to their new residence, together with servants to make all the necessary preparations for them. When he saw that the Queen was
already on her way, he quickly had everything else loaded up, as
though he were striking camp, and set out behind the ladies and
gentlemen with the baggage and the rest of the servants.

Accompanied by the ladies and the three young men, all of

whom were following behind her, the Queen made her way west-
ward at a leisurely pace, guided by the song of perhaps a score of
nightingales and other birds. As she chatted and joked and laughed
with her companions, she walked down a little-used path over soft
green grass in which a host of flowers were all beginning to open
in response to the rising sun. When they had gone no more than
two thousand paces, and it was still well before even halfway to
the hour of tierce, she brought them to a most beautiful, ornate
palace, situated slightly above the plain on a little hill.°

Entering the palace, they went from one end of it to the other,
filled with admiration for its great halls as well as for its clean, elegant bedrooms, complete with all the necessary furnishings, which
led them to conclude that its owner knew how to live in the grand
style.° Then, when they went below and observed the extremely spa-
cious, cheery courtyard, the vaulted cellars stocked with the finest
wine, and the spring bubbling up with an abundant supply of ice-
cold water, they praised it even more. Finally, by way of repose, they
seated themselves on a loggia covered with seasonal flowers and
foliage that overlooked the entire courtyard below, and there the
thoughtful steward came to receive them and to offer them the most
delectable sweets and the choicest wines for their refreshment.

Afterward, a walled garden attached to the palace was opened
up for them, and when they went inside, it seemed at first glance a
thing of such wondrous beauty that they set out to explore it in
detail. There were wide walks both running around the garden
and intersecting one another in the middle, all straight as arrows
and covered over with trellised vines that gave every promise of
producing grapes in abundance that year. They were all then in
flower and filled the garden with a fragrance that, mingling with
the odors of the many other sweet-smelling plants that were growing there, made them feel as if they were standing in the midst of
all the spices that ever grew in the East. The sides of the walks
were almost completely enclosed by red and white rosebushes and
by jasmine, so that one could walk along any of them in pleasant,
sweet-smelling shade without ever being touched by the sun, not
just in the morning but even at high noon.

It would take a long time to describe how numerous and varied the plants were that grew in the garden, or how they were arranged, but all the most attractive ones that flourish in our climate were there in profusion. At its center was located not the least, but actually the most praiseworthy of its features, namely, a lawn of exceptionally fine grass, so intensely green that it seemed almost black. It was sprinkled all over with perhaps a thousand kinds of flowers and surrounded by luxuriantly growing, bright green orange and lemon trees that were covered with blossoms as well as both mature and ripening fruit, and that provided a pleasant shade for the eyes as well as delightful odors for them to smell.

In the middle of this lawn there stood a fountain of gleaming white marble, covered with marvelous bas-reliefs. Out of a figure placed on a column at its center, a jet of water shot high into the sky and then fell back down again into the limpid pool below with a delightful splashing sound. I do not know whether it came from some natural source or was conveyed there by artificial means, but it was powerful enough to have turned a water mill. The water that overflowed the brimming fountain was carried away from it through a hidden conduit and then rose to the surface in a series of beautiful, ingeniously contrived little channels that completely encircled the lawn. After that, it coursed along similar channels that ran through almost every section of the garden until it all eventually came together again in one single spot. From there it finally flowed out of that beautiful place in a crystal-clear stream, descending with such tremendous force toward the plain below that it turned two water mills situated along the way, to the considerable advantage of the owner.

The sight of this garden, so beautifully arranged, with its plants and its fountain and the little streams that flowed out of it, gave so much pleasure to the ladies and the three young men that with one voice they declared that they did not think the beauty of the place could be improved on, and that if Paradise could be created on earth, they could not imagine it having any other form. As they wandered contentedly through it, making the loveliest garlands for themselves from the foliage of various trees, and listening to perhaps twenty different kinds of songs sung by the birds who seemed to be having a singing contest among themselves, they became aware of yet another delightful feature of the garden, which, being wonder struck by all the others, they had not noticed before: they saw that it was filled with perhaps as many as a hundred varieties of beautiful animals, which they began pointing out to one another. There were rabbits coming into the open in one spot, hares running in another, deer lying here, and young fawns grazing there, and apart from these, they saw many harmless creatures of other sorts roaming about at leisure in pursuit of their own pleasures as if they were tame, all of which added immensely to their already abundant delight.

When, however, they had wandered about the garden for quite some time, examining one thing and then another, they arranged for tables to be set up around the lovely fountain, where, having first sung half a dozen little songs and done a number of dances, at the Queen's command they sat down to eat. A series of choice and dainty dishes, all carefully prepared and beautifully presented, were served them in order, after which they got up, merrier than before, and devoted themselves once again to making music, singing, and dancing. Eventually, however, with the heat of the day approaching, the Queen thought that the hour had come for those who felt like it to take a nap. Some of them, accordingly, retired, but the rest were so taken with the beauty of the place that they did not want to leave, and while the others were sleeping, they stayed where they were and passed the time reading romances or playing chess and backgammon.

A little after nones they all got up, and having refreshed themselves by washing their faces in the cool water, at the Queen's command they assembled on the lawn next to the fountain, where they seated themselves in their customary manner and waited to start telling stories on the theme she had proposed. The first one to whom the Queen assigned this task was Filostrato, who began in this way.

Story 1

MASETTO DA LAMPORECCHIO PRETENDS HE IS A
DEAF-MUTE AND BECOMES THE GARDENER IN A CONVENT
WHERE THE NUNS ALL RACE ONE ANOTHER TO GET TO
SLEEP WITH HIM.°

Loveliest of ladies, there are many men and women who are so
stupid as to really believe that when a young woman has the white
veil placed on her head and the black cowl on her back, she is no
longer a woman and no longer feels female cravings, as though,
when she became a nun, she was turned into a stone. And if they
should hear anything that runs counter to this belief of theirs,
they get as angry as they would if some enormous, horrific crime
had been committed against Nature. They never stop to think
about themselves and reflect on how they are never satisfied despite
having complete freedom to do whatever they want, nor do they
consider how potent the forces produced by idleness and confine-
ment can be. Likewise, there are a whole lot of people who believe
only too readily that the hoe and the spade, coarse food, and hard
living eliminate all carnal desires in those who work the land and
make them dim-witted and unperceptive. But now, since the Queen
has ordered me to speak, I would like to tell you a tiny little story
that is quite in keeping with the topic she has chosen and that will
make it clear to you just how deluded all those people are who
believe such things.

Here in this countryside of ours there was, and still is, a convent
quite renowned for holiness, which I will not name in order not to
diminish its reputation in any way. Not so long ago it housed only
eight nuns and their Abbess, all of them still young women, as
well as a good little guy who tended their resplendent garden. Not
content with his salary, he settled his accounts with the nuns'
steward and returned to his native village of Lamporecchio.° Among
the others who gave him a warm welcome home, there was a
young laborer named Masetto who was strong and hardy and, for
a peasant, quite handsome. He asked the good man, whose name

was Nuto, where he had been for such a long time, and after Nuto told him, Masetto wanted to know how he was employed in the convent.

"I used to work in a great big beautiful garden of theirs," replied Nuto, "and besides that, I sometimes used to go to the forest for firewood, or I'd draw water and do other little chores of that sort, but the women gave me such a small salary that I hardly had enough to pay for shoe leather. And another thing, they're all young and I think they all had the Devil inside them because no matter what I did, it never suited them. Sometimes when I was working in the vegetable garden, one of them would say, 'Put this here,' and another would say, 'Put that here,' and yet a third would snatch the hoe from my hand and tell me, 'You're doing it all wrong.' And they'd make themselves such a pain that I'd stop working and leave the garden. Well, what with one thing and another, I decided it was time to quit. As I was about to set off to come back here, their steward asked me to see whether I could find somebody who did that sort of work when I got home, and if so, he told me I should send the guy to him. Although I did promise him I'd do it, I'm not going to, because unless God gives the guy one heck of a constitution, you won't find me sending him there."°

As he listened to Nuto's story, Masetto was filled with such a desire to go and spend time with those nuns that it completely consumed him, for it was clear from what he had heard that he would have no difficulty in getting just what he wanted out of them. But realizing that his plan would go nowhere if he told Nuto anything about it, he said: "It sure was a good idea of yours to come back here. What kind of life can a man lead when he's surrounded by women? He'd be better off with a pack of devils. Six times out of seven they themselves don't know what they want."

Once they had finished talking, Masetto started thinking about what he needed to do in order to get to stay in the nunnery. Since he knew he was capable of doing the chores mentioned by Nuto, he had no worries about being rejected on that score, but he was afraid that he would not be hired because he was too young and attractive. After having pondered a number of options, an idea occurred to him: "The place is pretty far away, and no one there knows me. If I pretend I'm a deaf-mute, they'll take me on for sure."

Having settled on this plan, he dressed himself like a poor man, slung one of his axes over his shoulder, and without telling anyone where he was going, set off for the convent. When he arrived and entered the courtyard, he chanced to come upon the steward, and by using signs the way deaf-mutes do, made a show of asking him, for the love of God, to give him something to eat in return for which he would chop whatever wood they happened to need. The steward was perfectly willing to feed him, after which he presented him with a pile of logs that Nuto had not been able to split, but that Masetto, who was quite strong, managed to take care of in no time at all. The steward had to go to the forest, and taking Masetto along with him, he had him cut some firewood, while he himself went to bring up the donkey and by making certain signs, got Masetto to understand that he was to haul it all back to the convent. Masetto acquitted himself so well that the steward kept him around for several more days in order to take care of some chores he needed to have done, and it was on one of those days that the Abbess saw him and asked the steward who he was.

"My lady," said the steward, "he's a poor deaf-mute, one of those who came here a day or two ago begging for alms, and not only did I give him some, but I've had him take care of a bunch of chores that needed doing. If he knew how to tend the garden and wanted to stay on, I'm convinced we'd get good work out of him, because he's just what we need, a strong man who could be made to do our bidding. Besides, you wouldn't have to worry about him joking around with these young ladies of yours."

"I swear to God," said the Abbess, "you're telling the truth. Find out if he knows how to garden, and do your very best to make him stay here. Give him a pair of shoes plus some old hood or other, and be sure to flatter him and pamper him and give him plenty to eat."

The steward said he would take care of it. Masetto was not very far away, and although he was pretending to sweep the courtyard, he was really eavesdropping on their entire conversation. "Once you put me inside there," he said to himself gleefully, "I'm going to work your garden for you better than it's ever been worked before."

After the steward had confirmed that Masetto really knew how to do the work, he asked him by means of gestures if he wanted to stay on, and Masetto, using gestures to reply, said he would do whatever the steward wanted. The steward therefore hired him and ordered him to go and work in the garden, showing him what he needed to do there, after which he left Masetto alone and went to attend to other business for the convent.

As Masetto worked there day after day, the nuns started pestering him and making fun of him, something people frequently do with deaf-mutes, and since they were certain he could not understand them, they did not hesitate to use the worst language in the world in front of him. For her part, the Abbess paid little or no attention to what they were doing, perhaps because she was under the impression that Masetto had lost his tail just as he had lost his tongue.

One day, after he had been working hard and was taking a rest, two young nuns, who were walking through the garden, happened to approach the spot where he was lying. Since he appeared to be asleep, they gave him a good looking over, and the bolder of the two said to the other: "If I thought you could keep a secret, I'd share an idea with you that's often crossed my mind and that might work out to our mutual benefit."

"Don't worry about telling me," the other replied, "because I'm certainly not going to reveal it to anybody else."

Then the bold one began: "I don't know if you've ever spent much time thinking about how strictly we're confined here and how the only men who ever dare to set foot inside the convent are the steward, who's elderly, and this deaf-mute. Now, I've often heard many of the women who come to visit us say that all the other pleasures in the world are a joke compared to the one women experience when they're with a man. That's why I've frequently thought about putting it to the test with this deaf-mute here, seeing as how nobody else is available. He's actually the best one in the world for it, because he couldn't reveal it even if he wanted to. In fact, he wouldn't even know how, since you can see he's just a big dumb clod whose body's grown a lot faster than his brain. Anyway, I'd be glad to know what you think about all this."

"Oh, my goodness," said the other, "what are you saying? Don't you know that we've promised our virginity to God?"

"Oh," replied the first, "think about how many promises are made to Him every day, and not one of them is ever kept. So what if we've made promises to Him? He can always find lots of others who will keep theirs."

"But what if we get pregnant?" said her companion. "What'll we do then?"

"You're beginning to worry about difficulties before they've even happened," replied the other. "If and when they occur, that'll be the time to think about them. And there are a thousand ways to keep people from getting wind of what's going on, provided we don't talk about it ourselves."

With every word, her companion's desire became ever greater to find out what sort of beast a man might be. "So, how will we do it?" she asked.

"As you see, it's just about nones," the other replied, "and I'm sure that all the sisters are sleeping except for us. Let's have a look around the garden to see if anyone's here, and if there isn't, all we have to do is to take him by the hand and lead him into this hut where he stays when he wants to get out of the rain. Then one of us can go inside with him while the other stands guard, and he's such a simpleton that he'll do whatever we want."

Having heard their entire conversation, Masetto was quite eager to obey and was only waiting for one of them to come and get him. Meanwhile, the nuns had a good look around, and when they were sure they could not be seen from any direction, the one who had initiated their conversation approached Masetto and woke him up. He got to his feet right away, at which point she seized his hand and with all sorts of seductive gestures led him, giggling like an idiot, to the hut, where he did not need an invitation to do her bidding. When she had gotten what she wanted, like the loyal friend she was, she made way for her companion, and Masetto, still playing the simpleton, did what they asked him to do. And before the two of them finally left, each one made additional trials of just how good a rider the deaf-mute was. Later on, talking it over with one another, they both agreed that the experience really was as sweet as people said it was, if not more so. And from then on, whenever the opportunity presented itself, they went and amused themselves with him.

One day it just so happened that one of their sisters saw what they were up to from a window of her cell and showed the spectacle to two others. At first they thought to denounce the pair to the Abbess, but then they changed their minds and worked out an arrangement with the first two nuns whereby they would all have a share in Masetto's farm. And at different times by a variety of routes the last three nuns came to join them.

Finally, on one particularly hot day, the Abbess, who was still unaware of these goings-on, was walking by herself through the garden when she came upon Masetto. Because of all the riding he had been doing at night, even the little bit of work he engaged in during the day was proving too much for him, and so there he lay, fast asleep, stretched out under the shade of an almond tree. The front part of his tunic was blown back by the wind, leaving him entirely exposed, and the Abbess, who found herself quite alone, kept staring at it, until she succumbed to the same carnal appetite that the first two nuns had experienced. Consequently, she awoke Masetto and took him with her back to her room, where she kept him for several days, thereby provoking serious complaints on the part of the nuns because the gardener had stopped coming to work in the garden.

After repeatedly sampling the very sweetness she used to criticize in other women before then, the Abbess finally sent Masetto back to his own room. Still, she wanted to have him return again and again and was getting more than her fair share out of him, until Masetto, who was unable to satisfy so many women, realized that his playing the deaf-mute could wind up causing him irreparable damage if he continued to do so much longer. Consequently, one night, when he was with the Abbess, he untied his tongue and began to speak:

"My lady, it's my understanding that one cock is enough for ten hens, but that ten men will have a hard time satisfying one woman, and yet, it's my job to offer my services to no fewer than nine of them. Well, there's no way in the world I can keep it up any longer, and as a matter of fact, from doing what I've been doing up to now, I've reached the point where I can't do just about anything anymore. So, you should either say good-bye to me and let me go, or find some way to solve this problem."

Since the Abbess had always thought he was a deaf-mute, she was completely dumbfounded when she heard him speak. "What's all this?" she asked. "I thought you were a deaf-mute."

"I really was, my lady," replied Masetto, "but I wasn't born that way. I lost the ability to speak because of an illness, and I thank God from the bottom of my heart that on this very night, for the first time, I've managed to recover it."

The Abbess believed his story and then asked him what he meant when he said he had to offer his services to nine of them. Masetto explained how things stood, and as the Abbess listened, she realized that all of her nuns were much smarter than she was. Being a prudent woman, she then decided that rather than let Masetto go, in which case he might say something damaging to the reputation of the convent, she would work out some sort of arrangement with her nuns.

Their old steward had recently died, and so, with Masetto's consent, now that they all knew what they had all been doing in the past, the nuns decided unanimously to persuade the people living thereabouts that although Masetto had long been a deaf-mute, his speech had been restored through their prayers and through the intervention of the saint for whom the convent was named. Furthermore, they made Masetto their steward, but divided up his labors in such a way that he could take care of them all, and although he sired quite a few monklets and nunlets, the whole matter was handled with such discretion that no one heard anything about it until after the death of the Abbess, at a time when Masetto, now pretty well off, was approaching old age and was eager to return home. And once they knew what he wanted, he easily obtained their permission to go.

Thus, because he was clever and had figured out how he could put his youth to good use, Masetto, who had come from Lamporecchio with nothing more than an ax on his shoulder, returned home a rich, old man who had fathered numerous children, but spared himself the trouble of feeding them and the expense of raising them. And this was the way, he maintained, that Christ treated anyone who set a pair of cuckold's horns on His crown.

Story 2

A GROOM SLEEPS WITH THE WIFE OF KING AGILULF. WHEN THE KING FINDS OUT ABOUT IT, HE SAYS NOTHING, BUT TRACKS DOWN THE GUILTY PARTY AND SHEARS OFF SOME OF HIS HAIR. THE SHORN ONE THEN SHEARS ALL THE OTHERS AND THUS ESCAPES A TERRIBLE FATE.°

Some parts of Filostrato's tale caused the ladies to blush a bit, while others made them laugh. When he finished, it was the Queen's pleasure to have Pampinea continue the storytelling, and she, with a smile on her face, began as follows:

Some people are so lacking in discretion that when they have discovered or heard about things that they were better off not knowing, they feel compelled to reveal their knowledge at any cost, with the result that they sometimes censure faults in others no one else would have noticed, and although their goal in doing so is to lessen their own shame, they actually increase it out of all proportion. And now, pretty ladies, what I propose is to prove the truth of this to you by actually describing the contrary state of affairs in which the wisdom of a worthy king was matched by the cleverness of a man whose social position may have been even lower than Masetto's.

When he became the King of the Lombards, Agilulf followed the example of his ancestors and chose Pavia, a city in Lombardy, as the seat of his reign, having meanwhile married Theodolinda, who was the widow of Authari, the former Lombard ruler.° An exceptionally beautiful woman, Theodolinda was both wise and very honest, but she had a stroke of very bad luck with a man who had fallen in love with her.

At a time when Lombardy had been enjoying a long period of peace and prosperity, thanks to the valor and wisdom of King Agilulf, it just so happened that one of the Queen's grooms, a man who was as tall and handsome as the King himself, fell for her and loved her to distraction. Though of exceedingly low birth, the groom was in other respects vastly superior to his base occupation, and since his lowly condition did not prevent him from seeing that this love of his went well beyond the bounds of propriety, he wisely refrained from disclosing it to anyone and did not even dare to cast revealing glances in the lady's direction. Nevertheless, although he lived without any hope of ever winning her favor, deep inside he gloried that he had raised his thoughts to such a lofty height.° Burning all over in Love's fire, he showed himself more zealous than any of his companions in doing whatever he thought would give the Queen pleasure. And thus it came about that because the Queen preferred to ride the palfrey that was in his care rather than any of the others whenever she was obliged to go out on horseback, on those occasions, the groom felt that she was doing him the greatest of favors and would stand close by her stirrup, thinking himself blessed if he was merely able to touch her clothing.

However, what we see all too often is that as hope diminishes, love increases, and that is what happened with the poor groom, to the extent that, without a shred of hope to sustain him, he had the utmost difficulty controlling the powerful desire he kept hidden inside him, and on more than one occasion, being unable to free himself from this passion, he felt like killing himself. As he pondered the ways and means to do just that, he concluded that the circumstances leading up to his death should be such as to make everyone understand that it was the result of the love he had always borne for the Queen. At the same time, he was resolved to try his luck and see if those circumstances might also offer him an opportunity to wholly, or at least partially, gratify his desires. He had no intention of saying anything to the Queen or declaring his love for her by means of letters, for he realized that speaking or writing to her would be in vain, and so, instead, he concentrated on getting into her bed by means of some stratagem or other. Since he knew that the King did not spend every single night with his wife, he concluded that the one and only stratagem with a chance of success was for him to find some way to impersonate the King so that he would be free to approach her and gain access to her bedroom.

With the aim of discovering how the King was dressed and the routine he followed when he visited the Queen, the groom hid himself for several nights in a great hall of the palace that was situated between the two royal bedchambers. On one of those nights he saw the King come out of his room wrapped up in a large cloak, carrying a small lighted torch in one hand and a rod in the other. He walked over to the Queen's chamber, and without saying a word, knocked once or twice at the entrance with the rod, whereupon the door was opened at once and the torch taken from his hand.

Having observed what the King had done, and having likewise seen him return to his room some time later, the groom decided he would adopt the very same procedure. He managed to acquire a cloak that resembled the King's as well as a torch and a stick, and after first washing himself thoroughly in a hot bath so that the odor of dung would not repel the Queen or make her suspect a trick, he took his things to the great hall and hid himself in the usual place.

When the groom thought that everyone was asleep and that the time had come for him either to gratify his desires or to find a noble path to the death he had long sought, he used a piece of flint and steel he had brought with him to make a small fire by means of which he lit his torch. Then, wrapping himself up tightly in his cloak, he walked over to the entrance to the bedroom and knocked twice with his rod. The door was opened for him by a chamber-maid who, more asleep than awake, took his light and covered it up, after which, without saying a thing, he stepped inside the curtains, took off his cloak, and got into the bed where the Queen lay sleeping. Knowing that it was not the King's habit to engage in conversation whenever he was angry about something, the groom made a show of being irritated as he took the Queen lustfully in his arms, and then, without either one of them ever uttering a single word, he had carnal knowledge of her over and over again. Although he was very loath to leave her, he was afraid that if he stayed there too long, the joy he had experienced might be turned into sorrow. Consequently, he got up, and after he had retrieved his cloak and his torch, he went away, still without saying a word, and returned to his bed as quickly as he could.

The groom could scarcely have reached it when, to the Queen's utter amazement, the King showed up in her chamber and gave her a cheerful greeting as he got into bed with her. "O my lord," she said, encouraged by his good humor, "what's the meaning of this change tonight? You've only just left me after having enjoyed me more than you usually do, and here you are, coming back for more. You should be careful what you're doing."

On hearing these words, the King immediately inferred that the Queen had been deceived by someone who had looked and behaved like him. He was a wise man, however, and since neither she nor anyone else had noticed the substitution, he decided on the spot that he would not reveal it to her. Many a fool would have acted differently and said: "That wasn't me. Who was the man who was here? What happened? Who was it who came?" This would have given rise to a great many complications that would have upset the lady unnecessarily and might have given her a reason to want to repeat the experience she had just had. And besides, it allowed him to avoid disgracing himself by not talking about something that, as long as it remained unsaid, would never have been able to cause him shame.

Thus, giving no sign of his inner turmoil either by the way he spoke or by his facial expression, the King answered her: "Wife, don't you think I'm man enough to come back here a second time after having been with you once before?"

"Yes, my lord," the lady replied, "but nevertheless I beg you to be careful with your health."

"I'm happy to follow your advice," said the King, "and so, this time I'll go away and won't bother you any further."

As he picked up his cloak and left the room, the King was seething with rage, indignant over what he saw had been done to him and determined to go quietly and search for the culprit, operating on the assumption that the man had to be a member of his household and that, no matter who he was, he would not have been able to get out of the palace. Taking a little lantern that shed only a very faint light, he went to a long dormitory located over the palace stables where almost all of his servants were asleep, each in his own bed. And since he surmised that neither the pulse nor the heart rate of whoever had done the deed reported by the Queen could have returned to normal after all his exertions, the King started at one end of the room and began quietly walking along, feeling everyone's chest to see if it was still throbbing.

Although all the others were sound asleep, the one who had been with the Queen was still awake, and when he saw the King coming and realized what he was looking for, he became so frightened that the terror he felt made his heart, which was already pounding because of his recent exercise, beat even harder. He was absolutely convinced that if the King noticed it, he would be instantly put to death, and thoughts about various possible courses of action went racing through his mind. Upon observing, however, that the King was unarmed, he decided to pretend he was asleep and wait to see what the King would do.

Having already examined a large number of the sleepers and concluded that none of them was the man he was seeking, the King finally reached the groom. When he discovered how hard the man's heart was beating, he said to himself, "This is the one." However, he did not want to let anybody know what his intentions were, and so, the only thing he did was to take a small pair of scissors he had brought with him and cut off a lock of hair on one side of the groom's head. Since people wore their hair very long in those days, that would be a sign by which the King would be able to recognize the culprit the next morning. Then, once he was done, he made his exit and returned to his own room.

Having witnessed everything that had happened, the groom, who was very shrewd, had no doubt as to why he had been marked in this manner. Therefore, he did not hesitate for a moment, but got up, and having located one of several pairs of scissors they happened to keep in the stables for tending to the horses, he went through the room from one man to the next as they lay sleeping and quietly cut off their hair just above the ear in the same way his own had been. Having finished what he was doing without having been observed by anyone, he returned to his bed and went to sleep.

The moment the King arose in the morning, he gave orders that the palace gates should remain closed until the members of his household were assembled before him. When they had all arrived and were standing bareheaded in his presence, he began looking them over with the intention of identifying the man whose hair he had cut off. To his amazement, however, he discovered that the vast majority of them had had their hair sheared in exactly the same way. "The man I'm looking for may well be lowborn," he said to himself, "but he's demonstrated that he has quite a lofty intellect."

Then, since he realized that he could not achieve what he wanted without making a scene, he decided he would not expose himself to so great a disgrace in order to take his revenge on so petty a person. Instead, he contented himself with giving the man a stern word of warning to show him that his deed had not gone unobserved.

"Whoever did it," he said, addressing the entire assembly, "he'd better not do it ever again. Now go, and may God be with you."

Another man would have had them all put on the strappado, tortured, examined, and interrogated, but in doing so, he would have brought out into the open something that people should make every effort to conceal, for even if, by revealing the whole story, he had been able to revenge himself to the full, he would not have lessened his shame. On the contrary, he would have greatly increased it and would have sullied his lady's reputation to boot.

Those who heard the King's speech were amazed by it, and for a long time afterward they debated among themselves what he had meant. There was no one, however, who understood it except for the one person it really concerned, and he, wise man that he was, never revealed its meaning as long as the King was alive, nor did he ever put his life at risk by performing any such deed again.

Story 4

DOM FELICE TEACHES FRATE PUCCIO HOW TO
ACHIEVE BLESSEDNESS BY PERFORMING AN ACT OF
PENANCE HE DEVISES FOR HIM, AND WHILE FRATE PUCCIO
IS CARRYING IT OUT, DOM FELICE HAS A GOOD TIME WITH
THE FRIAR'S WIFE.°

* * *

My lady, there are a great many people who, while they are striving mightily to get into Paradise, unwittingly send others there instead—which is what happened to a lady in our city not so very long ago, as you are about to hear.

According to what I have been told, there used to be a good man, and a rich one, too, living close by San Pancrazio who was called Puccio di Rinieri. In his later years, he devoted himself wholly to matters of the spirit and became a Tertiary of the Franciscan Order, taking the name of Frate Puccio.° Since his family consisted only of his wife and a single maidservant, which relieved him of the necessity of practicing a trade, he spent a great deal of time at church so that he could pursue that spiritual life of his. Being a simple, rather slow-witted person, he used to recite his Our Fathers, attend sermons, and go to Mass, nor would he ever fail to show up when the lay brothers were chanting lauds.° What is more, he would fast and mortify his flesh, and it was whispered about that he was one of the Flagellants.°

His wife, Monna Isabetta by name, was still a young woman of about twenty-eight to thirty, and she was as fresh and pretty and plump as an apple from Casole.° Because of her husband's holy life, and possibly also on account of his age, she frequently had to go on much longer diets than she would have liked, and when she was in the mood to sleep or perhaps to play around with him, he would rehearse the life of Christ to her, followed by the sermons of Frate Nastagio, or the Lament of the Mary Magdalene, or things of that sort.°

About this time, a good-looking young monk called Dom Felice, a conventual brother at San Pancrazio, who was sharp-witted and deeply learned, returned from Paris. Frate Puccio formed a close friendship with him, and since Dom Felice, who was quite good at resolving all his friend's doubts, knew what his character was like, he made a great show of holiness himself as well. Frate Puccio consequently started taking him home with him, offering him a dinner or a supper, depending on the time of day, and out of love for her husband, Frate Puccio's wife likewise became his friend and was happy to entertain him.

In the course of his visits to Frate Puccio's house, the monk observed how fresh and plump his friend's wife was, and realizing what it was that she lacked the most, he decided that he would do his best to save Frate Puccio the trouble by making up for that deficiency himself. And so, proceeding with great caution, he began giving her the eye from time to time until he kindled the same desire in her mind that was burning in his. Then, when he perceived it was working, he seized the first opportunity that came his way and spoke to her about what he wanted. Although he found her quite willing to put his proposals into effect, it was impossible to do so, since she would not risk having an assignation with him anywhere except in her own home, and they could not do it there because Frate Puccio never left town. All of this made the monk quite melancholy, but although it took quite a while, a plan finally occurred to him as to how he could spend time with the lady in her own house and not have to worry even though her husband happened to be there, too. And so, one day, when Frate Puccio had come to visit him, he spoke to him as follows:

"It's been my understanding for some time, Frate Puccio, that your one overwhelming desire is to achieve saintliness, but you seem to me to be trying to reach this goal by taking the long route to get there, even though there's a very short one that the Pope and his chief prelates know about and make use of themselves. They don't want it revealed to others, however, for the clergy, who live for the most part on charitable donations, would be instantly undone, in that laymen would no longer support them by means of alms or anything else. But since you're my friend and have given me such honorable entertainment, I'd be willing to teach you the way, although only if I were sure that you really wanted to give it a try and would never reveal it to anyone else."

Eager to hear all about it, Frate Puccio began earnestly begging his friend to tell him how to do it, and then went on to swear he would never talk about it to anyone without Dom Felice's permission, affirming at the same time that he would really apply himself to it, provided it were the sort of thing he could manage.

"Since you've given me your promise," said the monk, "I'll let you in on the secret. Be aware that the Doctors of the Church maintain that anyone who wishes to achieve blessedness must perform the penance I'm about to describe. But don't misunderstand me: I'm not saying that after your penance you will no longer be a sinner just as you are right now. Rather, what will happen is that all the sins you've committed up to the time you perform your penance will be purged and remitted because of it. And as for those you commit afterward, they won't be written down against you and lead to your damnation. On the contrary, they'll be removed with holy water the way venial ones are now.

"What's really essential for the man who's about to start his penance is to be extremely diligent in confessing his sins, after which he must begin a fast and practice a very strict form of abstinence that is to continue for forty days, during which time you must abstain from touching not just other women, but even your own wife. Moreover, you've got to have some place in your house from which you can see the heavens at night and to which you will go at about the hour of compline.° There you will have a broad plank set up in such a way that you can stand with your back against it, and while keeping your feet on the ground, stretch out your arms in the manner of the Crucifixion. Should you wish to rest them on pegs of some sort, you may do so, but you must remain absolutely immobile in that position, looking up at the heavens, until matins. If you were a scholar, you would be obliged, in the course of the night, to recite certain prayers I'd give you, but since you're not, you're going to have to say three hundred Our Fathers and three hundred Hail Marys in honor of the Trinity. And while you're gazing at the heavens, you must always remember that God was the Creator of heaven and earth, and be mindful of the passion of Christ, since you will be in the same position he was in when he hung on the cross.

"As soon as matins is rung, you may, if you wish, go and throw yourself on your bed, dressed just as you are, and get some sleep. But later that morning, you must go to church, listen to three Masses, and say fifty Our Fathers and as many Hail Marys. Then, you may quietly go about your own business, should you happen to have any, after which you will have dinner and go to church again around vespers in order to say certain prayers I'll give to you in writing, without which the whole thing won't work. Finally, toward compline, you must go back and begin all over again. Now, I've done this myself, and if you carry it out with sufficient devotion, then I'm hopeful that even before your penance comes to an end, you will experience a marvelous sensation of eternal blessedness."

"This isn't a very difficult task," said Frate Puccio, "nor is it going to last all that long. And so, since it should be fairly easy to manage, I propose, in God's name, to start on Sunday."

After leaving Dom Felice, he returned home where, having first obtained the monk's permission, he recounted everything in great detail to his wife. The lady understood only too well what the monk meant, especially the part about his standing still and not moving at all until matins, and since it seemed like an excellent arrangement to her, she told him that she was pleased with it, as she was with whatever he did for the good of his soul. Furthermore, she said that in order to persuade God to make his penance profitable, she was willing to join in his fast, although that was as much as she would do.

Thus, it was all settled, and when Sunday came, Frate Puccio began his penance. As for Messer Monk, having made prior arrangements with the lady, on most nights he would show up at an hour when he could get inside unobserved, and would always bring plenty of good things to eat and drink along with him. Then, after the two of them had had their supper together, he would sleep with her until matins, at which point he would get up and go away before Frate Puccio returned to bed.

The place that Frate Puccio had chosen for his penance was next door to the bedroom in which the lady slept, separated from it by only the thinnest of walls. And one time, while Messer Monk was romping with her, having cast all restraints aside, just as she had with him, Frate Puccio thought he could feel the floor of the house shaking. When he finished reciting one hundred of his Our Fathers, he came to a stop, and without stirring from his spot, he called out to his wife and asked her what she was doing. The lady, who had a talent for making witty remarks, and who at the moment may have been riding Saint Benedict's ass or, even better, Saint Giovanni Gualberto's,° replied: "By gosh, husband, I'm tossing about here for all I'm worth."

"Tossing about?" asked Frate Puccio. "What's the meaning of all this tossing about?"

The lady started laughing, not only because she was a lively, jolly person, but also, most likely, because she had a pretty good reason to do so. "How is it possible you don't know what it means?" she replied. "Why, I've heard you say a thousand times, 'If you don't eat at night, you'll toss till daylight.'"

Frate Puccio was convinced that her fasting was the reason for her inability to sleep, which was, in turn, causing her to toss about in her bed, and so he said to her in good faith: "Wife, I told you, 'Don't fast.' But since you've chosen to do so anyway, stop thinking about it, and concentrate, instead, on getting some rest. You're tossing about in bed so much that you're making the whole house shake."

"No, no, don't you worry about it," said the lady. "I know exactly what I'm doing. You just keep up your good work, and as for me, I'll do the best I can with mine."

So Frate Puccio said no more and turned his attention to his Our Fathers once again. From that night on, however, for as long as his penance lasted, the lady and Messer Monk, who had had a bed set up in another part of the house, would go there and have themselves a ball until it was time for the monk to take off and for the lady to return to her bed, where she was joined by Frate Puccio shortly after his nightly vigil came to an end. Thus, while he carried on with his penance this way, his wife carried on her pleasant affair with the monk, during which she would quip to him from time to time: "You made Frate Puccio do the penance, but we're the ones who've gained Paradise."

The lady thought that things had never been better for her, and since she had been kept on a very lengthy diet by her husband, she wound up getting so accustomed to the monk's fare that even when Frate Puccio's penance was done, she found a way to keep on feasting with the monk in another location, and she was sufficiently discreet in managing the affair that she was able to go on enjoying herself with him for a long time afterward.

And so, to make the last words of my story accord with the first, this is how it came about that Frate Puccio, who thought he was getting into Paradise by doing his penance, actually showed the way there both to the monk, who had revealed the shortcut to him, and to his own wife, who lived with her husband in a state of scarcity, wanting that which Messer Monk, who was the soul of charity, supplied her with in great abundance.

Story 8

HAVING CONSUMED A CERTAIN POWDER, FERONDO IS BURIED
FOR DEAD, BUT THE ABBOT, WHO HAS BEEN ENJOYING HIS
WIFE, REMOVES HIM FROM HIS TOMB, IMPRISONS HIM, AND
MAKES HIM BELIEVE HE IS IN PURGATORY, UNTIL HE IS
FINALLY RESUSCITATED AND THEN RAISES AS HIS OWN A
CHILD HIS WIFE HAD WITH THE ABBOT.°

*   *   *

My dearest ladies, I find myself faced with the task of having to recount a true story that looks more like a lie than was actually the case and of which I was reminded when I heard about the man who had been mourned and buried in place of another. My story, then, is concerned with a living person who was buried because he was presumed dead, and who later, after he had emerged from the tomb, believed that he had been brought back to life, although he had actually been alive all along, a belief that was shared by many others who adored him as a saint when they should have blamed him for his folly.

In Tuscany, then, there was once—and there still is today—an abbey, situated, as we see so many of them are, in a place little frequented by people. Its newly created Abbot was a monk who was extremely saintly in every way except when it came to women, but he was so cautious with every move he made that hardly anyone suspected, let alone knew, what was going on, so that he was considered to be not merely just, but the holiest of men in every respect.

Now, the Abbot happened to develop a close relationship with a very wealthy peasant named Ferondo, an exceedingly coarse and dim-witted individual, whose friendship he enjoyed only because he was occasionally amused by the man's simplicity. During the course of his association with Ferondo, the Abbot discovered that he was married to a very beautiful woman, and he fell so passionately in love with her that day and night he thought of nothing else. When he found out, however, that although Ferondo was simpleminded and stupid in every other regard, he was as shrewd as can be when it came to loving his wife and always keeping a strict watch over her, the Abbot was close to despair, but since he was very shrewd himself, he managed to persuade Ferondo to bring his wife on occasion to enjoy the pleasures of the abbey's garden. There, adopting an unassuming manner, the Abbot would talk to them about the blessedness of the life eternal and the most holy deeds of men and women from times past, until eventually the lady was seized by a desire to make her confession to him, and she asked and received Ferondo's permission to do so.

Thus, to the Abbot's boundless delight, the lady came to him in order to make her confession. Seating herself at his feet, before she went on to say anything else, she began as follows: "Sir, if God had given me a proper husband, or none at all, perhaps it might be easy for me, with the help of your teaching, to start down the road you've told us about that leads to the life eternal.° But considering the kind of person Ferondo is and his utter stupidity, I might as well call myself a widow, for even though I'm married, I can't have any other husband except that half-wit as long as he's alive, and he, for no good reason, is so extraordinarily jealous of me that my life with him amounts to endless suffering and misery. Therefore, before I get to the rest of my confession, I beg you in all humility to be so kind as to give me some advice on this subject, because if I can't find some means here for me to start improving my life, then confessions and other good deeds won't do me much good."

This declaration filled the Abbot's heart with glee and made him feel that Fortune had opened the way for him to fulfill his greatest desire. "My daughter," he said, "I do think it's a terrible affliction for a beautiful and delicate lady like you to have an idiot for a husband, but it's even worse, in my opinion, to have one who's jealous, and since you have both kinds in the same man, it's not hard for me to believe what you're saying about how much you suffer. But there's only one piece of advice, only one remedy, I can suggest, and that is, in a word, to cure Ferondo of his jealousy. Now, I know perfectly well how to make the medicine needed to do it, provided you have it in you to keep what I'm about to tell you a secret."

"Don't worry about that, father," said the lady, "because I'd sooner die than tell anyone something you've asked me not to repeat. So, how is this going to be done?"

"If we want to cure him," replied the Abbot, "he'll have to go to Purgatory."

"And just how can he do that, while he's still alive?" asked the lady.

"He's got to die," said the Abbot. "That's how he'll get there. And when he's suffered enough pain to purge him of his jealousy, we'll recite certain prayers and ask God to restore him to life, and God will do it."

"Then I'll be left a widow?" the lady declared.

"Yes, for a certain length of time," replied the Abbot, "but during that period you must really take care not to let them marry you off again, because God would take it badly. Furthermore, when Ferondo returned, you'd have to go back to him, and he'd be more jealous than ever."

"As long as he gets cured of this malady of his," said the lady, "and I don't have to spend the rest of my life living like a prisoner, it's fine with me. Do as you please."

"And I will," said the Abbot. "But what reward am I to have from you for such a service?"

"Whatever you want, father," she replied, "provided it lies within my power. But what gift can a woman like me give that would be suitable for a man in your position?"

"My lady," he said, "you can do as much for me as I am going to do for you. Just as I'm preparing to provide for your welfare and your happiness, you, too, can do something that will rescue me and save my life."

"If that's the case," said the lady, "I'm ready to do it."

"Then, give me your love," said the Abbot, "and let me enjoy you, for I'm all on fire, consumed with desire for you."

Completely dumbfounded by what she had heard, the lady exclaimed: "Oh no, father, whatever are you asking me to do? I always thought you were a saint—and is it really proper for saints to make such a request of ladies who come to them for advice?"

"Don't be so surprised, sweetheart," replied the Abbot. "This isn't something that diminishes saintliness, for that resides in the soul, and what I'm asking you for is a sin of the flesh. But in any case, your beauty is so ravishing, so powerful, that love forces me to act like this, and let me tell you, when you consider how pleasing your loveliness is to saints, who are used to seeing the beauties of heaven, you have more reason to be proud of it than any other woman. Furthermore, although I'm an Abbot, I'm still a man just like the others, and as you can see, not all that old. So, you shouldn't find this a burden; on the contrary, you should be looking forward to it, because while Ferondo's in Purgatory, I'll be keeping you company at night and providing you with the kind of consolation he should be giving you. No one will ever notice what's going on, either, because they all believe in my saintliness just as much as—in fact, more than—you did a short while ago. Don't reject the grace that God is bestowing upon you, for you've been offered something that plenty of women long for, and if you're sensible enough to follow my advice, it'll be yours. Besides, I have some beautiful jewels, expensive ones, and I don't intend to give them to anyone but you. Therefore, my sweet hope, don't refuse to do for me what I'll gladly do for you."

The lady kept her eyes fixed on the ground, for although she did not know how to refuse him, she still felt it was wrong for her to grant his request. As the Abbot observed her listening to his proposition and hesitating about how to respond to it, he felt she was already half converted. He therefore added a great deal to his former arguments, and by the time he stopped talking, he had gotten it into her head that it was all right for her to comply with his wishes. And so she said, rather bashfully, that she was ready to obey his every command, although she could not do so before Ferondo had gone to Purgatory.

"Well," said the Abbot gleefully, "we'll see to it that he goes there right away. Just arrange for him to come here and stay with me either tomorrow or the next day."

That said, he slipped a very beautiful ring into her hand on the sly and sent her away. Delighted by the gift, and looking forward to receiving others, the lady returned to her companions, and as they made their way home together, she told them all sorts of marvelous things about the Abbot's saintliness.

A few days later, Ferondo came to the abbey, and the moment the Abbot caught sight of him, he decided to send him off to Purgatory. Consequently, he went to get a wondrous powder he had, which had been given to him in the East by a great prince who maintained that the Old Man of the Mountain would use it whenever he wanted to send people to his Paradise in their sleep or to bring them back from it again.° The prince had also said that by varying the dose, one could make them sleep for longer or shorter periods without suffering any sort of harm, and that as long as the powder's effect lasted, nobody would ever think they were alive. The Abbot took a quantity of it sufficient to make a man sleep for three days, added it to a glass of somewhat cloudy wine, and gave it to the unsuspecting Ferondo to drink while they were in his cell. He then led him into the cloister where he and some of his monks began amusing themselves at Ferondo's expense and making fun of his foolishness. This had not gone on for long, however, before the powder began to work, and all of a sudden, Ferondo's faculties were overwhelmed by such a powerful sensation of drowsiness that he dozed off while he was still standing, then fell to the ground, fast asleep.

Pretending to be upset over what had happened, the Abbot had them loosen Ferondo's clothes, sent for cold water, and had them throw it in his face. He then had them try a variety of other remedies he knew, acting as if he wanted to restore the life and feeling that had been taken away from Ferondo by some expulsion of gas out of his stomach or by whatever else it was that might have afflicted him. But when the Abbot and the monks saw that despite all their efforts he did not come to and that when they felt his pulse, it did not seem to be beating, they all concluded that he was dead. Accordingly, they sent word to his wife and family, all of whom came rushing to the scene. A little later, after the lady and her female relations had finished weeping, the Abbot had Ferondo placed in a tomb, dressed in the same clothes he had been wearing.

The lady returned home and announced that she would never part from the little boy she had had with Ferondo. And so, she remained there in the house, planning to take care of her child and to manage the fortune her husband had left her.

That night the Abbot got up quietly, and with the assistance of a monk from Bologna who enjoyed his full confidence and who had just come from there that very same day, he dragged Ferondo from his tomb and carried him to a lightless underground vault that had been built as a prison to punish monks for their transgressions. They removed his clothes, dressed him in one of their habits, and left him lying on a bundle of straw until he recovered his senses. In the meantime, unobserved by anyone else there, the monk from Bologna waited for Ferondo to come to, having been told everything he needed to do by the Abbot.

The next day the Abbot pretended he was making a pastoral visitation, and attended by a group of his monks, went to the lady's house, where he found her dressed in black and overcome with grief. He comforted her for a while, and when he was done, quietly reminded her of her promise. Realizing that she was now free, unhindered by Ferondo or anyone else, and spotting another fine ring on the Abbot's finger, the lady told him that she was ready to do it and arranged for him to pay her a visit that evening.

After dark, therefore, the Abbot disguised himself in Ferondo's clothes and went to her house, accompanied by his monk. There he lay with her in the utmost pleasure and delight all night long, returning to the abbey just before matins. And from then on, he frequently traveled down the same road to perform the same service. Although people occasionally encountered him on his way back and forth, they always believed it was Ferondo who was wandering about the area, doing penance of some sort, and before long, many strange stories sprang up among the simple people from the village, some of which were reported to his wife, who knew very well what was really going on.

When Ferondo regained consciousness, he did not have the faintest idea where he was, and at just that moment, the monk from Bologna entered the room with a horrible roar, and clutching a bundle of sticks in his hand, gave him a terrible beating.

As he wept and wailed, Ferondo kept on asking: "Where am I?"

"You're in Purgatory," said the monk.

"What? Am I dead, then?" asked Ferondo.

"You sure are," said the monk, at which point Ferondo started weeping for himself and for his wife and son, and saying some of the strangest things in the world as he did.

The monk then brought him something to eat and drink, and when Ferondo saw it, he asked: "Oh, do dead people get to eat?"

"Yes," replied the monk. "In fact, the food I'm giving you here was sent to the church this morning by the lady who was once your wife in order to have Masses said for your soul. And the Lord God wants you to have it."

"May God give her a year's worth of blessings!" said Ferondo. "I really loved her a whole bunch before I died. Why, I used to hold her in my arms all night long and never stop kissing her, and when I felt the urge, I'd occasionally do something else as well."

Then, being very hungry, he began eating and drinking, but when he discovered that the wine was not very good, he exclaimed: "Goddamn her! She didn't give the priest the wine from the cask that's next to the wall."

When he finished his meal, the monk brandished his sticks again, seized him a second time, and gave him another terrible beating.

"Hey," said Ferondo, after screaming for quite a while, "why are you doing this to me?"

"Because the Lord God has decreed that you should get it twice a day," said the monk.

"And for what reason?" asked Ferondo.

"Because you were jealous of your wife, even though you had the finest woman in the area," answered the monk.

"Alas, you're telling the truth there," said Ferondo. "She was the sweetest, too—in fact, sweeter than a sugarplum. But I would never have been jealous if I had known that God Almighty was offended by it."

"You should have thought of that yourself and mended your ways while you were still down there," said the monk. "If you should ever happen to return, make sure you remember what I'm doing to you now, and don't you ever be jealous again."

"Oh! Do the dead ever return to life?" asked Ferondo.

"Yes, the ones God chooses," replied the monk.

"Oh! Well, if I ever go back," said Ferondo, "I'll be the best husband in the world. I'll never beat her, never scold her, except about the wine she sent here this morning, and also for not sending me any candles so that I was forced to eat in the dark."

"Yes, she did send some," said the monk, "but they were used up during the Masses."

"Oh, yes," said Ferondo, "you must be right. Well, if I ever do get back there, I'll be sure to let her do whatever she wants. But tell me, who are you, and why are you treating me like this?"

"I'm dead, too," said the monk. "I used to live in Sardinia, and because I praised one of my masters to the skies for his jealousy, I've been condemned by God to be punished by giving you food and drink and these beatings until He decides otherwise about you and me."

"Isn't there anyone here besides the two of us?" asked Ferondo.

"Yes, thousands," replied the monk, "but you can't see or hear them any more than they can see or hear you."

"Oh, how far are we from our homes?" asked Ferondo.

"Oh my, oh my!" said the monk. "We're more miles away than we can crap."

"By gosh!" said Ferondo. "That's a lot! If we're that far away, I think we really must be out of the world."

Thus, what with discussions of this sort and others like them, they kept Ferondo there for ten months, alternately feeding and beating him, while the Abbot, being quite the enterprising type, paid countless visits to the lady and had himself the jolliest time in the world with her. But accidents will happen, and the lady got pregnant. She told the Abbot about it as soon as she was aware of her condition, and both of them concluded that Ferondo should be brought back to life from Purgatory without delay and reunited with her, and furthermore, that she should tell him that it was he who had gotten her with child.

Consequently, the following night, the Abbot went to Ferondo in his prison, and disguising his voice, spoke to him.

"Be of good cheer, Ferondo," he said, "for it is God's pleasure that you should go back to earth, where, after your return, your wife will present you with a son. And you shall name him Benedetto, for God is bestowing this grace on you in answer to the prayers of your reverend Abbot and your wife, and out of His love for San Benedetto."°

When he heard this, Ferondo was overjoyed.

"This really makes me happy!" he declared. "May God give a

year's worth of blessings to Messer God Almighty and the Abbot and San Benedetto and my cheesy-weesy, sweet honeybun of a wife."

Having put enough of the powder in the wine he had sent Ferondo to make him sleep for four hours or so, the Abbot dressed him in his own clothes again, and aided by the monk, quietly carried him back to the tomb in which he had been buried. At daybreak the next morning, Ferondo came to his senses and saw that light was coming in through a chink in the tomb. Not having seen such a thing for a good ten months, he concluded that he had to be alive and began shouting, "Open up! Open up!" At the same time he pressed his head up against the lid of the sarcophagus, which was not very secure, and shoved it so hard that it began to move. He had just about pushed it off when the monks, who had finished reciting matins, rushed to the scene, recognized Ferondo's voice, and saw him emerging from the tomb. They were all so frightened by this unexpected event that they took to their heels and ran off to find the Abbot.

The Abbot pretended he was just rising up from prayer. "Be not afraid, my sons," he said. "Take up the cross and the holy water and follow me. Let's go and see what God Almighty wants to show us." And away he went.

In the meantime, Ferondo, who was deathly pale from having spent so much time without seeing the sky, had gotten out of the tomb. When he saw the Abbot, he threw himself at his feet and declared: "Father, I've been rescued from the pains of Purgatory and brought back to life, and it's been revealed to me that your prayers, along with those of San Benedetto and my wife, were responsible for it. And so, I pray to God that He send you a good year, and good months, both now and forever."

"Praised be the power of God!" exclaimed the Abbot. "Now that He has sent you back here, my son, you should go and comfort your wife, who has done nothing but weep since you departed this life. And from now on may you live to serve God and preserve His friendship from this day forth."

"That's exactly what I've been told to do, sir," said Ferondo.

"Just let me handle it. As soon as I find her, I'm going to give her a great big kiss. I love her so much."

The Abbot acted as if what had happened was a miracle, and as soon as he was alone with his monks, he had them devoutly sing the *Miserere*.°

When Ferondo returned to his village, everyone who caught sight of him fled away, as from some horrible vision, and his wife, too, seemed terrified, but he called them all back and assured them that he had, indeed, been restored to life. Then, once they all felt more comfortable being around him and saw that he really was alive, they plied him with questions, all of which he answered as if he were some sage returned from the grave, giving them news about the souls of their relatives, and inventing the most beautiful fables in the world about the goings-on in Purgatory. And he gave the assembled populace a full account of the revelation that he had received straight from the mouth of the Ark-Ranger Bagriel just before he came back to life.°

Having returned home with his wife and taken possession once again of his property, he proceeded to get her pregnant—or so he imagined. And by chance he happened to arrive not a moment too soon, for his wife, confirming the opinion of fools who believe that women carry their babies for precisely nine months, gave birth to a son, who was named Benedetto Ferondi.

Since almost everyone believed that Ferondo had really come back from the dead, his return and the stories he told enhanced immeasurably the Abbot's fame for holiness. Moreover, Ferondo was cured of his jealousy by the countless beatings he had received, and never behaved like that toward his wife again, just as the Abbot had promised her he would not. The lady was pleased with this turn of events, and from then on she lived with Ferondo no less chastely than she had in the past, except that, whenever she could do so conveniently, she was always happy to spend time with the Abbot who had attended to her greatest needs with such skill and diligence.

Story 10

ALIBECH BECOMES A RECLUSE, AND RUSTICO, A MONK,
TEACHES HER HOW TO PUT THE DEVIL BACK IN HELL. SHE IS
THEN LED AWAY FROM THERE AND BECOMES THE WIFE OF
NEERBALE.°

* * *

Gracious ladies, perhaps you've never heard anyone explain
how the Devil is put back in Hell, and therefore, without departing from the topic you've all been talking about today, I want to
tell you how to do it. Perhaps you'll even be able to save your souls
once you've learned it. You'll also learn that although Love prefers
to dwell in gay palaces and voluptuous bedchambers more than in
poor huts, for all that, he sometimes makes his powers felt in
dense forests, on rugged mountains, and in desert caves—from
which you'll be able to see that everything is subject to his power.

Now, to get to the point: let me tell you that there once lived in
the city of Capsa in Barbary a very rich man who, among his many
children, had a beautiful and graceful little daughter named Alibech.° She was not a Christian, but having heard how greatly the
Christian faith and the service of God were praised by the numerous Christians living in the city, one day she asked one of them
how God could be served best and with the least difficulty. He
replied that those served God best who fled farthest from the
things of this world, as did the people who had gone to live in the
desert around Thebes. The young girl of about fourteen was
extremely naive, and the following morning, moved not by a reasonable desire, but rather by a childish whim, she set out secretly
for the Theban desert all by herself without letting anyone know
what she was doing.

With great difficulty, but sustained by her desire, she reached
that solitary place several days later. Catching sight of a hut in the
distance, she went up to it and found a holy man on the threshold
who was amazed to see her there and asked her what she was

looking for. She answered that, inspired by God, she wanted to enter His service and was seeking someone who would teach her how to do that. Seeing how young and very beautiful she was, and fearing that the Devil would tempt him if he kept her there, the worthy man praised her good intentions, and after giving her some roots of herbs and wild apples and dates to eat along with some water to drink, he said to her: "My daughter, not very far from here there is a holy man who is much more capable than I am of teaching you what you want to know. You should go to him." And he sent her on her way.

When she reached the second man, she heard the same thing from him, and so she went farther on until she reached the cell of a young hermit, a truly good and devout person named Rustico, whom she asked the same question she had asked the others. Eager to put the firmness of his religious vow to a very demanding test, Rustico, unlike the first two, did not send her away or direct her to go farther on, but kept her with him in his cell. And when night came, he made her a little bed out of palm fronds on one side of it and told her to sleep there.

Once these things were done, temptations did not wait long before launching an attack on his powers, whose strength he found he had greatly overestimated, so that after a very few assaults, he turned tail and surrendered. Casting aside holy thoughts and prayers and penitential discipline, he began contemplating her youth and beauty, and beyond that, what ways and means he might employ in dealing with her so that she would not see just how dissolute he was as he went about getting what he wanted from her. After first testing her by asking certain questions that showed she had never had carnal knowledge of a man and was just as naive as she appeared to be, he came up with a plan by means of which, under the pretext of serving God, she would have to satisfy his desires. He started out with long speeches, demonstrating to her how great an enemy the Devil was to the Lord God, and finally giving her to understand that the most pleasing service she could offer Him would be to put the Devil back in the Hell to which the Lord God had damned him.

The young girl asked him how this might be done, and he replied: "You'll soon find out. Just do whatever you see me do." And he began to take off the few clothes he had on until he was completely naked, while the girl did the same thing. Then he knelt down as if he wanted to worship, and he made her position herself right in front of him. And as they knelt in this way, and Rustico felt his desire growing hotter than ever at the sight of her beauty, the resurrection of the flesh took place.° Staring at it in amazement, she said, "Rustico, what's that thing I see sticking out in front of you, the thing I don't have?"

"O my daughter," said Rustico, "this is the Devil I told you about, and now you can see for yourself how he's tormenting me so much that I can scarcely endure it."

Then the girl said, "Oh, praised be God, for I see I'm better off than you are, since I don't have any such Devil."

"That's the truth," said Rustico, "but you do have something else I don't have, and you have it in place of this."

"Oh," said Alibech, "what's that?"

"You've got Hell there," Rustico said to her. "And let me tell you, I believe God has sent you here for the salvation of my soul. For this Devil is giving me such pain that if you'll take pity on me and allow me to put him back in Hell, you'll give me the greatest relief. Plus, you'll please God by performing an immense service, if you really came here to do that, as you say."

"Oh, Father," replied the young girl in good faith, "since I've got that Hell, just do it whenever you please."

"Bless you, my daughter," said Rustico. "Let's go ahead and put him back in there so that he'll finally leave me in peace."

And with those words, he led her up onto one of their little beds and taught her what she should do to incarcerate that evil spirit cursed by God. The young girl, who had never, ever put any Devil in Hell, felt a little pain the first time, and because of it she said to Rustico: "Surely, Father, this Devil must be a wicked thing and truly the enemy of God, for he not only hurts others, but he even hurts Hell when he's put inside it."

"My daughter," said Rustico, "it won't always be like that." And to ensure that it would not be, they put the Devil back in there a good six times before they got out of the bed, so that, when they were done, they had forced him to lower his proud head, and he was content to be quiet a while.

The Devil's pride often came right back up during the next few days, however, and the young girl, who was obedient and always willing to take it down for him, began to enjoy the game and would say to Rustico: "Now I certainly see that those worthy men in Capsa were telling the truth about how sweet a thing it is to serve God, for I'm sure I can't recall any other thing I've done that has been so delightful or given me so much pleasure as putting the Devil back in Hell. And for that reason, in my judgment, anyone interested in doing something other than serving God is an ass."

Repeatedly approaching Rustico with this purpose in mind, she would say to him, "Father, I've come here to serve God and not to remain idle. Let's go and put the Devil back in Hell." While they were engaged in doing it, she would sometimes remark, "Rustico, I don't know why the Devil wants to escape from Hell, for if he liked being inside it as much as Hell likes taking him in and holding him there, he'd never want to leave."

Thus, by inviting Rustico to play the game over and over again, always encouraging him to serve God in this way, she took so much padding out of his doublet that he started feeling cold whereas anyone else would have been sweating. Consequently, he tried telling her that the Devil was only to be punished and put back in Hell when he raised his head in pride: "And we have so humiliated him, by the grace of God, that he is begging the Lord to be left in peace."

In this way he was able to keep the girl quiet for a while. But one day, when she realized that Rustico was no longer asking her to put the Devil back in Hell, she said to him, "Rustico, though your Devil has been punished and is no longer making you suffer, this Hell of mine is giving me no peace. So, you would do a good deed if you, with your Devil, helped to quench the fury of my Hell, just as I, with my Hell, helped you lower the pride of your Devil."

Now Rustico was living on the roots of herbs and spring water, so that her invitations could hardly get a rise out of him. He told her that it would take an awful lot of Devils to quench the fires of her Hell, but said that he would do what he could for her. Thus, he was sometimes able to satisfy her, but it was so seldom that it amounted to little more than tossing a bean into the mouth of a lion. Consequently, the young girl, feeling she was not getting to serve God as much as she wanted to, went around grumbling more often than not.

While this dispute went on between Rustico's Devil and Alibech's Hell, the result of too much desire on the one side and too little potency on the other, a fire happened to break out in Capsa that burned Alibech's father to death in his own house, together with all his children and the rest of his household, leaving Alibech the heir to his entire estate. Because of this, a youth named Neerbale, who had spent his entire substance in sumptuous living and who had heard that she was alive, set out in search of her and found her before the courts could confiscate her father's property because he had died without an heir. To the great relief of Rustico, though much against her will, Neerbale brought Alibech back to Capsa and took her as his wife, and together with her he became the heir to her enormous patrimony.

Before Neerbale slept with her, however, she was asked by some women how she used to serve God out in the desert. She replied that she served Him by putting the Devil back in Hell and that Neerbale had committed a great sin in taking her away from such a fine service. The women asked her how the Devil is put back in Hell, and when, between her words and her gestures, the girl showed them how, they laughed so much that they are still laughing to this day. Then they said, "Don't feel sad, child, no, for they do it pretty well here, too. Neerbale will serve the Lord God with you just fine."

Then one woman told this story to another throughout the city until they turned it into a common saying, namely that the most delightful service one could perform for God was to put the Devil back in Hell. This saying, which has crossed the sea from there, is still current. And so, young ladies, you who need God's grace, learn to put the Devil back in Hell, because this is greatly pleasing to God and a pleasure for those who are doing it, and much good may arise and come out of it.

Conclusion

So apt and well chosen were Dioneo's words that his story moved the virtuous ladies to laughter a thousand times or more. When he reached the conclusion, the Queen, recognizing that the term of her reign had come to an end, took the laurel crown from her head and very graciously placed it on Filostrato's, saying: "We will soon see if the wolf knows how to guide the sheep better than the sheep did the wolves."

On hearing her remark, Filostrato laughed and said: "Had they listened to me, the wolves would have taught the sheep how to put the Devil in Hell no worse than Rustico did with Alibech. But you should not call us wolves, since you have not been acting like sheep. Still, now that you have entrusted the kingdom to my care, I will govern it to the best of my ability."

"Listen, Filostrato," replied Neifile, "if you men had tried to teach us to put the Devil in Hell, you might have learned a lesson from us the way Masetto da Lamporecchio did from the nuns, for you would have recovered your ability to speak at just about the time when the wind would have been whistling through your hollow bones."°

On perceiving that the ladies' scythes were as sharp as his arrows, Filostrato stopped making witty quips and addressed himself to the business of ruling the kingdom entrusted to him. Summoning the steward, he asked how matters stood, after which he discreetly gave him his orders, basing them on what he thought would be worthwhile and would give satisfaction to the company during the term of his reign. Then he turned to the ladies and said:

"Loving ladies, ever since I could distinguish good from evil, it has been my misfortune, because of the beauty possessed by one of your number, to be perpetually enslaved to Love. I have been humble and obedient and followed his rules, to the extent that I understood them, but all to no avail, for first I would be abandoned for another lover, and then things would always go from bad to worse for me—and I think they will continue to do so from now on until the day I die. Consequently, it is my pleasure that the subject for us to talk about tomorrow should be none other than the one that fits my situation best, namely, those whose love came to an unhappy end. For I myself expect a most unhappy one in the long run, and that is the reason why the name you use to address me was conferred on me by someone who certainly knew what it meant."° Then, having finished speaking, Filostrato got to his feet and dismissed everyone until suppertime.

The garden was so beautiful and delightful that no one chose to leave it in search of greater pleasures elsewhere. On the contrary, since the sun's heat had already abated, making it much less trouble to go hunting, some of the ladies set off in pursuit of the deer and the rabbits and the other animals that were in the garden and that had startled them perhaps a hundred times by jumping into their midst while they were sitting. Dioneo and Fiammetta began singing a song about Messer Guiglielmo and the Lady of Vergiù, while Filomena and Panfilo devoted themselves to a game of chess.° So intent were they on their various activities that the time flew by, and when the hour arrived for supper, it caught them unawares. Tables were then set up around the lovely fountain, and there, in the evening, they ate their meal with the greatest delight.

Once the tables were cleared away, Filostrato, not wishing to stray from the path taken by the ladies who had ruled as queens before him, ordered Lauretta to lead a dance and sing them a song.

"My lord," she said, "I only know songs I have composed myself, and I cannot recall any of mine that are really suitable for such a merry company. Still, if you are willing to accept those I know, I will be happy to sing one of them for you."

"Nothing of yours could be anything other than beautiful and pleasing," replied the King, "so sing whatever you have for us, just as it is."

Then, in very sweet, but rather doleful tones, Lauretta began as follows, while the other ladies joined her in the refrains.

No lady all forlorn
Could grieve more than I do,
Who sigh here all in vain, cast down by Love.°
He who moves heaven and all of its stars
Made me, for His delight,
Refined and charming, graceful, too, and fair,
To give to lofty spirits here below
A certain sign of that
Beauty abiding ever in His sight.
But mortals imperfect,
Who can't see what I am,
Find me unpleasing, nay, treat me with scorn.

There once was one who cherished me, was glad,
When I was young, to hold
Me in his arms and fix me in his thoughts,
And from my eyes he caught such searing heat
That he spent all his time,
Which lightly flies away, in wooing me.
And I, in courtesy,
Deemed him a worthy mate,
But now, alas! I've been bereft of him.

A youth did then present himself to me,
Presumptuous and proud,
Boasting himself a brave and noble man.
He took me captive and through false surmise
Succumbed to jealousy,
Which brings me almost to despair, alas!
For I see clearly how,
Although I'd come to earth
For all men's good, of one I'm now the slave.

And so I curse my luckless nuptial hour
When I said yes and changed
My widow's weeds, for dressed in garments black,
I was so fair and gay, but wearing these,
I lead a harsh life here
And others think me much less honest now.

O mournful bridal day,
I wish that I had died
Before I'd seen you in such dire straits.
        O dearest love, with whom I was content
Beyond all women once,
Since now you are in Heaven with the One
Who fashioned us, alas! take pity please
On me, for I cannot
Forget you for another. Make me see
How flames I kindled once
In you still burn unquenched:
Obtain for me my swift return above.°

Everyone had been listening attentively to Lauretta's song, and when she finished, they all interpreted it in different ways. Some wanted to take it in the Milanese fashion as meaning that it was better to have a good pig than a pretty gal, while others gave it a finer, more sublime, and truer sense, which need not be rehearsed at present.° Next, the King called for a large number of lighted torches to be set on the lawn and in among the flowers, after which, at his command, the other ladies continued the singing until every star that had risen had begun its descent.° Then, thinking it was time to go to sleep, he bid them goodnight and told them all to return to their rooms.

Day 4

Introduction

HERE ENDS THE THIRD DAY OF THE *DECAMERON*
AND THE FOURTH BEGINS, IN WHICH, UNDER THE RULE
OF FILOSTRATO, THEY SPEAK OF THOSE WHOSE LOVE
CAME TO AN UNHAPPY END.

Dearest ladies, both from what I have heard wise men say as well as from everything I have often read and seen for myself, I have always thought that the fierce, scorching wind of envy assaulted only lofty towers and the highest treetops.° I have found myself deceived in this judgment, however. For whenever I fled—and I have always done my best to flee—the wild buffetings of this furious storm, I have tried to go about my affairs quietly and unobtrusively, not just staying on the plains, but seeking out the deepest valleys. This should be patently clear to anyone who casts an eye on these little stories of mine, which lack a title and were written in the Florentine vernacular, in prose, and in the homeliest and lowest style possible.° Yet in spite of all this, I have not been able to avoid being violently shaken and almost uprooted by that wind and practically torn to pieces by the fangs of envy. Consequently, I now see clearly the truth of what wise men have frequently said, namely that misery alone is free of envy in this our present life.°

Discerning ladies, there are those who, upon reading these little stories, have claimed that I like you too much and that it is improper for me to take so much delight in entertaining and consoling you, and even worse, in praising you as I do. Others, wishing to make it seem as though their judgment were more mature, have said that it is inappropriate for someone of my years to occupy my time with such things, that is, with talking about women and finding ways to please them. There are many who present themselves as being very concerned about my renown and who say that it would be wiser for me to stay with the Muses in Parnassus than to be with you and to busy myself with this nonsense. And yet others, who speak more out of scorn than wisdom, have said that it would be more prudent for me to think about where I am going to obtain my daily bread than to pursue these trifles and feed myself on mere wind. Finally, there are certain people who, in order to disparage my efforts, endeavor to show that the things I have told you about did not happen in the way I said they did.

Thus, worthy ladies, while I have been fighting in your service, I have been blown about and battered by all these gusts, cut to the quick by these cruel, sharp teeth. God knows my mind has remained serene while I have listened to and made a record of their criticisms. Now, although I depend entirely upon you for my defense, nevertheless I have no desire to spare myself any pains, and so, while I will not respond to my critics as fully as they deserve, I intend to offer a few slight rejoinders to them in order to secure my ears from all their noise—and to do so right away. For if there are so many of them and they are already so presumptuous before I have even completed a third of my labors, I can only suppose that unless they encounter some resistance now, they will have multiplied to such an extent before I reach the end that they will be able to lay me low with only the slightest of efforts, and your power, great though it may be, will not suffice to withstand them.

Before responding to any of my critics, however, as a matter of self-defense I would like to recount not an entire story, lest it seem as though I would equate my own stories with those of the very distinguished company I have been telling you about, but merely part of one, whose very incompleteness will reveal that it is not one of theirs. Thus, for the benefit of my assailants, let me say that a man called Filippo Balducci once lived in our city quite some time ago.° His social position was rather modest, but he was rich and prosperous and knowledgeable about everything pertaining to his station in life. Furthermore, he had a wife whom he loved devotedly, as she loved him, and the two of them had a peaceful life together, their only desire being to make one another as happy as possible.

Now it so happened, as it will happen to all of us, that the good woman departed this life, leaving nothing of herself to Filippo except the single son whom she had had with him and who was about two years of age. No one has ever been more distressed by the loss of the thing he loved than Filippo was by the death of his wife. Seeing himself bereft of the companion who was so dear to him, he resolved to withdraw from the world in order to devote himself to the service of God, and to do the same thing with his little boy.

Having given away everything he owned for the love of God, Filippo went straightway up to the top of Monte Asinaio and installed himself in a tiny little cell with his son.° There he lived on alms, fasting and praying, and taking the greatest pains, whenever his son was present, never to discuss worldly matters or to let him see such things, so that they would not distract him from his devotions. Instead, he always spoke to him about the glory of the life eternal and about God and the Saints, nor did he ever teach him anything other than holy prayers. And for many years he kept this up, never letting his son out of their cell or allowing him to see anything except his father.

From time to time the worthy man would come to Florence,

and after various friends of God had supplied him with the things he needed, he would return to his cell. One day, when the boy was eighteen, he happened to ask his father where he was going, and Filippo, who had become an old man by this time, told him.

"Father," said his son, "since you're an elderly man now and have trouble dealing with such hardships, why don't you take me with you on one of your trips to Florence? Once you've introduced me to those friends of yours who are devout followers of God, then, seeing as how I'm young and better able to put up with such toil than you are, I can go to Florence and get what we need whenever you like, while you stay here."

Thinking that his son, who was now grown up, was so accustomed to serving God that the things of this world would have difficulty attracting him, the worthy man said to himself, "He's got a point." And since he had to go to Florence anyway, he took his son along with him.

When the young man saw the palaces, the houses, the churches, and all the other things that abound in the city, he could not remember ever having seen such things before and was truly amazed by them. He questioned his father about many of them and wanted to know what every one of them was and what it was called. His father told him, and once the boy heard each explanation, he was content, but then went on immediately to ask about something else.

As the pair walked along thus, the son asking questions and the father answering them, by chance they came upon a company of beautiful, well-dressed young women who were returning from a wedding somewhere. As soon as the boy saw them, he asked his father what they were.

"My son," replied his father, "keep your eyes on the ground and don't look at them, for they are evil."

"Oh," asked his son, "what are they called?"

In order to avoid awakening some less than useful desire from among his son's carnal appetites, the father was unwilling to give them their proper name, that is, women, and answered instead: "They're called goslings."°

How wonderful! He who had never before set eyes on a woman was no longer interested in the palaces, the oxen, the horses, the asses, the money, or any of the other things he had seen, but said straight out: "Father, please arrange it so that I can have one of those goslings."

"Oh no, my son!" said his father. "Be quiet. They're evil."

"Is that what evil things are like?" asked his curious son.

"Yes," replied his father.

"I don't understand what you're saying," his son replied, "or why they're evil. As far as I know, I've never seen anything so beautiful or attractive. They're lovelier than the painted angels you've frequently pointed out to me. Oh, if you care for me at all, arrange it so that we can bring one of these goslings back up there with us, and I'll take care of feeding it."

"No, I won't do it," said his father. "You don't know how they do their pecking." And right then and there he realized that his wits were no match for Nature, and he regretted that he had ever brought his son to Florence.

But let what I have told of the present story suffice, so that I may return to those for whose sake I recounted it.

Now, many of my detractors say that I am wrong for doing my best to entertain you, O my young ladies, and for being too fond of you. I confess this most freely, for I am indeed fond of you, and I do take pains to please you. But what, I ask, do they really find so astonishing about this, when you consider that a young man, who was nurtured and reared on top of a savage, solitary mountain, grew up within the limits of a tiny cell, and had no company other than his father, no sooner caught sight of you than you became the only thing he wanted, the only thing he asked for, the only thing he pursued with passion? As for us, my sweetest ladies, even if we set aside the amorous kisses, the pleasant embraces, and the blissful couplings we have frequently enjoyed with you, one need only think about how we are continually exposed to the vision of your refined manners, your charming beauty, and your elegant grace, not to mention your womanly decorum, to understand our affection for you.

   Will they reproach and bite and tear me if I am fond of you and strive to please you, when Heaven has given me a body fit for loving you, and when I have devoted my soul to you from my childhood, having felt the power that comes from the light shining in your eyes, from the sweetness of your mellifluent speech, and from the fire kindled by your compassionate sighs—especially considering how you first pleased a young hermit, a witless youth, in fact a savage animal, more than anything else ever did? Those who scold me are surely people who, being entirely ignorant about the pleasures and power of natural affection, neither love you nor desire your love in return, and about such people I care very little.

   As for those who keep harping on my age, they simply reveal what they do not know, namely that although the head of the leek is white, its tail is still green.° But joking aside, I will respond to them by saying that to the very end of my life I will never be ashamed of seeking to give pleasure to those whom Guido Cavalcanti and Dante Alighieri, when they were already old men, and Messer Cino da Pistoia, when he was very aged indeed, found it an honor to serve and whose beauty was so dear to them.° And if it did not require that I depart from the customary mode of debate, I would turn to history and show how it is filled with countless examples of worthy men from antiquity who even in their most mature years still strove with all their might to give pleasure to the ladies. And if my critics are ignorant of such things, let them go and learn about them.

   That I should dwell with the Muses on Parnassus is good counsel, I agree, but we cannot always live with the Muses, any more than they can live with us. And so, if a man sometimes happens to leave them, he is not to be blamed if he delights in seeing that which resembles them, for the Muses are women, and although women are not as worthy as the Muses, yet at first sight they do look like them, so that if they pleased me for no other reason, they should do so on this score. Besides, women have been the occasion of my composing a thousand lines of poetry, whereas the Muses never caused me to write anything. To be sure, they have assisted me and shown me how to compose those thousand lines, and perhaps in writing these stories here, no matter how very humble they may be, the Muses have stayed with me on several occasions possibly because they acknowledge and honor the likeness that women bear to them. Consequently, as I go weaving these tales together, I do not stray so far away from Mount Parnassus or from the Muses as many may chance to think.

But what shall we say to those who feel so much pity for me because of my supposed hunger that they advise me to make provision for my daily bread? I certainly do not know how to answer them except to say that when I try to imagine how they would respond if I, were I in need, should ask them for food, I conclude that their answer would be: "Go look for it among the fables." And yet, poets have always found more to nourish them among their fables than many rich men have among their treasures, and quite a few have lived to a ripe old age by pursuing their fables, whereas, on the contrary, many who sought more bread than they needed have died young. But what more is there to say? Let them chase me away if ever I ask them for food, although in any case, I thank God that I still have no need of it. And even if I did, I know, in the words of the Apostle, both how to abound and to suffer need, and therefore, let no one worry more about me than I do about myself.°

As for those who say these stories never happened the way I have narrated them, I would appreciate it if they would produce the original versions, and if the latter proved to be different from what I have written, then I would grant that this criticism is just and would do everything in my power to mend my ways. But since thus far I have seen nothing but words, I will leave them to their opinion and will stick to my own, and I will say precisely the same thing about them that they have been saying about me.

For the time being, since I think I have supplied a sufficient response to my critics, let me say that with God's assistance, and with yours, my most noble ladies, in which I place all my hope, I will go forward with my work, fortified with good patience, turning my back to this storm and letting it blow as much as it likes. For I do not see that anything can happen to me that is different from what happens to fine dust in a whirlwind. Either it remains where it is on the ground, or if it is moved, it is carried aloft and often deposited on the heads of men, on the crowns of kings and emperors, sometimes even on high palaces and lofty towers, from which, if it falls, it cannot go lower than the place from which it was lifted up.

And if I have ever been disposed to use all my strength in order to serve your pleasure in any way, I am now more inclined to do so than ever, because I know that no one can justly say anything about me or any of the others who love you except that we are acting naturally. In order to oppose the laws of Nature, one has to have exceptional powers, and they are often employed not only in vain, but to the greatest harm of the person who makes use of them. Such strength I confess I lack, nor do I have any desire to acquire it for such a purpose. In fact, even if I did possess it, I would lend it to others rather than use it myself. Therefore, let my detractors be silent, and if they cannot find any warmth in themselves,° let them live in their cold rancor, and while they pursue their own delights, or rather, their corrupt appetites, may they allow me to pursue mine during the brief life that is granted to us.

But we have wandered quite far afield, O my lovely ladies, and now it is time for us to return to our point of departure and continue along our pre-established course.

The sun had already chased all the stars from the sky and had driven the humid shadow of night from the earth, when Filostrato arose and had the entire company awakened. They then went off to the fair garden, where they proceeded to entertain themselves until the hour for dinner arrived, which they ate in the same spot where they had taken their supper the previous evening. While the sun was at its highest, they took their nap, after which, having gotten up, they went and seated themselves in their usual order beside the lovely fountain. There Filostrato ordered Fiammetta to begin the storytelling, and without waiting for him to say another word, she displayed all her feminine grace and began to speak as follows.

Story 1

Our King has certainly given us a harsh topic to speak about today, especially when we consider that, having come together in order to cheer ourselves up, we are obliged to recount stories about others' tears, stories that cannot be told without awakening feelings of pity in speaker and listener alike. Perhaps he chose this topic to temper somewhat the gaiety of the past few days. However, no matter what moved him to do so, since it is not appropriate for me to alter the topic that it is his pleasure to have chosen, I will recount an incident that was not only pitiful, but disastrous, and entirely worthy of our tears.

Tancredi, Prince of Salerno, was a man of benevolent character and a ruler known for his humanity, except that in his old age he sullied his hands with the blood of lovers. In the entire course of his life, he had only a single daughter, and he would have been happier if he had never had her at all. He loved the girl more tenderly than any daughter was ever loved by her father, and not knowing how to part with her because of this tender love, he refused to arrange a marriage for her, even when she was well beyond the age when she should have wed. At long last, he gave her away in marriage to one of the sons of the Duke of Capua, but she lived with him for only a short while before she was left a widow and returned to her father.

Her face and her body were as beautiful as those of any other woman who has ever lived. Youthful and vivacious, and wiser than might have been appropriate in a woman, she lived like a great lady with her doting father in the midst of real luxury. When she saw, however, that because of his devotion to her, he was not giving much thought to arranging a new marriage for her, and since she thought it unseemly for her to ask him to do so, she decided that she would try to find a clandestine lover for herself who was worthy of her affection.

After looking over all the men, both noble and non-noble, who frequented her father's court, men of the sort we see in courts everywhere, and after considering the manners and conduct of quite a number of them, she found herself attracted to one of her father's young valets above all the rest. He was named Guiscardo, and although his origins were humble, his virtues and his manners sufficed to ennoble him. By dint of seeing him often, she soon became secretly inflamed with the most passionate love for him, and her admiration for the way he comported himself grew greater every day. As for the young man himself, he was by no means unperceptive, and from the moment he noticed her interest in him, he took her so deeply into his heart that he thought of virtually nothing else except his love for her.

In this way, then, the two of them went on secretly loving one another. The young girl wished for nothing more than to be together with her beloved, but since she was unwilling to make anyone her confidant in the matter, she thought up a new trick by means of which she could communicate her plan to him. She composed a letter in which she explained what he had to do in order to be with her on the following day, and then she inserted it into the hollow center of a reed, which she gave to Guiscardo, telling him in a joking manner: "Make a bellows of this for your servant girl, and she'll rekindle your fire with it this evening."

Guiscardo took it, and thinking that she would not have given it to him and spoken to him as she did without good reason, he left the room and returned to his lodging with it. When he examined the reed and discovered that there was a crack in it, he opened it up and found her letter inside. As he read it and noted what she wanted him to do, he was the happiest man who ever lived, and he immediately set about making preparations to meet with her, following all the details of the plan she had laid out for him.

Next to the Prince's palace there was a mountain containing a grotto that had been formed in the distant past and that was faintly illuminated by an air shaft, which had been dug out of the solid rock. The grotto, however, had been abandoned, and the mouth of the shaft was almost completely blocked by the brambles and weeds growing over it. From one of the ground-floor rooms of the palace that were occupied by the lady, a hidden stairway led into the grotto, although its entrance was barred by a very strong door. So much time had passed since the stairway had been used that there was virtually no one who still remembered it. Love, however, from whose eyes nothing can be concealed, had reminded the enamored lady of its existence.

To keep anyone else from noticing what was going on, she spent several days working hard on the door with various implements until she finally got it open. Once she had done so, and had climbed down alone into the grotto and seen the shaft, she sent word about it to Guiscardo, letting him know approximately how high its mouth was from the ground and telling him he should make every effort to get in by that route. With this end in mind, Guiscardo lost no time in obtaining a rope and tying knots and loops in it so that he could use it to descend and climb back out again. Then, without arousing anyone's suspicion about what was going on, the next night he went to the shaft, wearing a leather suit to protect himself from the brambles. After securely tying one end of the rope to a sturdy bush growing out of its mouth, he used the rope to lower himself into the grotto and waited there for the lady to appear.

The next day the lady sent her ladies-in-waiting away on the pretext that she wanted to take a nap, and having locked herself alone in her bedroom, she opened the door to the stairway and descended into the grotto where she found Guiscardo waiting for her. The two of them greeted one another with wonderfully warm affection and then went to her bedroom together where they spent the greater part of the day enjoying themselves in utter delight. After they had agreed on the most prudent plan for keeping their love affair a secret, Guiscardo went back to the grotto, while the lady locked the door and came out to rejoin her attendants. Then, after nightfall, Guiscardo used the rope to climb out of the shaft, exited from the place where he had come in, and returned to his lodging.

Having mastered this route, Guiscardo made the return journey many times after that. Fortune, however, was envious of such great and long-lived happiness, and made use of a calamity to transform the two lovers' joy into tears of sorrow.

From time to time, Tancredi was in the habit of going alone to his daughter's bedroom, where he would stay and chat with her for a while before he left. One day he went down there after dinner, and having entered her room without being seen or heard by anyone, he discovered that the lady, whose name was Ghismunda, was out in one of her gardens with all of her ladies-in-waiting. Not wishing to deprive her of her recreation, he sat down to wait on a stool located at the foot of the bed near one of its corners. The windows of the room were closed and the bed curtains drawn aside, and after a while Tancredi pulled one of them over him almost as if he were deliberately trying to hide, lay his head against the bed, and fell asleep.

Unfortunately, Ghismunda had arranged to have Guiscardo meet her that day, and as Tancredi was sleeping, she left her ladies-in-waiting in the garden and quietly returned to her room. Without noticing that anyone was there, she locked herself in and opened the door for Guiscardo, who was waiting for her. The two of them got into bed as they usually did, and while they were playing and enjoying themselves together, Tancredi happened to wake up. When he saw and heard what Guiscardo and his daughter were doing, his grief overwhelmed him. His first impulse was to scream at them, but then he decided to hold his peace and, if possible, remain hidden, because a plan had already taken shape in his mind and he wanted to proceed with more caution, and with less shame to himself, as he put it into effect.

The two lovers remained together a long time, as they usually did, without ever once noticing Tancredi. When they felt it was time to part, they got out of bed, after which Guiscardo returned to the grotto, and the lady left her room. Despite his advanced age, Tancredi then lowered himself down from a window into the garden, and without being seen, returned to his room, sick to death with grief.

At Tancredi's orders, that night around bedtime two of his men seized Guiscardo, who, encumbered by his leather suit, was just coming out of the shaft. They then brought him in secret to Tancredi, who said to him, practically in tears:

"Guiscardo, the kindness I've shown you did not deserve the outrage and dishonor that you've done to what belongs to me, and that I witnessed today with my very own eyes."

All that Guiscardo offered by way of reply was to say: "Love is much more powerful than either you or I."°

Tancredi ordered his men to take Guiscardo to an inner room, where he would be guarded in secret, and they took him away.

Ghismunda knew nothing of all this, and after dinner the next day, Tancredi, who had spent time thinking up all sorts of strange and terrible possibilities, went to his daughter's room just as he usually did. Having sent for her, he locked her in with him and began weeping.

"I never doubted your virtue and honesty, Ghismunda," he sobbed, "and so, no matter what anyone might have said, it would never have occurred to me that you could have thought of yielding to any man other than your husband, let alone actually doing it. But now that I've seen it with my own eyes, I will be grief stricken whenever I recall it during the little bit of life that is left to me in my old age.

"I would to God that if you had to commit such a dishonorable act, you had chosen a man whose rank was suited to your nobility. Instead, from among all the people who frequent my court, you selected Guiscardo, a young man of the basest condition who has been raised in our court as an act of charity from the time he was a small child right up to the present. Your behavior has created the most distressing dilemma for me, in that I simply don't know what I'm going to do about you. As for Guiscardo, I had him apprehended last night as he was coming out of the grotto and put in prison, and I've already made up my mind what I will do about him. But God knows, I have no idea how I'm going to deal with you. I am moved, on the one hand, by the love I've always felt for you, a love greater than that which any father ever felt for his daughter. On the other, I'm filled with righteous indignation because of your folly. My love prompts me to pardon you, while my anger wants me to go against my nature and show you no pity. Still, before I reach any decision about you, I'd like to hear what you have to say in reply."

When he finished speaking, Tancredi, like a child who has just been given a sound beating, lowered his head and wept bitter tears.

As she listened to her father, Ghismunda realized not merely that her secret love had been discovered, but that Guiscardo had been captured. This filled her with such incalculable grief that she was frequently on the point of expressing it by screaming and weeping, as most women usually do. Her lofty soul enabled her to triumph over such base behavior, however, and instead, making a marvelous effort to keep her countenance unchanged, she decided that she would sooner die than make any sort of plea on her own behalf, convinced as she was that her Guiscardo was already dead. Thus, presenting herself not like a grief-stricken woman who had been rebuked for a fault but like an undaunted figure of courage, she turned to her father with dry eyes and a fearless look on her face that did not betray the least hint of any distress.

"Tancredi," she said, "I am disposed neither to argue with you nor to beg, because the first won't help me and I don't want the second to do so. I intend no appeal to either your mercy or your love. Rather, I will tell you the truth, and after defending my reputation with sound arguments, I will then, by means of my actions, resolutely follow the lofty promptings of my heart. It's true that I have loved—and still love—Guiscardo. In fact, as long as I shall live, which will not be long, I shall continue to love him. And if there is love after death, my affection for him will never cease. I have been brought to act as I did not so much by my womanly frailty as by your lack of concern to see me married as well as by Guiscardo's own worth.

"It should have been clear enough to you, Tancredi, as a creature of flesh and blood, that you have produced a daughter of flesh and blood, not one of stone or iron. And even though you are now an old man, you should have been mindful all along of the nature and the strength of the laws of youth. As a man, you may have spent a portion of your best years in martial activity, but you should still be aware of the powerful effects that idleness and luxury can have on old and young alike.

"Being your daughter, I am a creature of flesh and blood, and what is more, I am still quite a young woman. Now, for both of those reasons I am filled with carnal desires whose force has been enormously increased by the fact that I was once married and have known the pleasure that comes from satisfying them. Not being able to resist their force, I decided, being a woman in the prime of life, to follow where they led me, and as a result, I fell in love. But insofar as I was able, I certainly did everything in my power to prevent that to which I was being drawn by my natural sinfulness from conferring shame on either you or me. To that end I was assisted by compassionate Love and benevolent Fortune who found out and showed me how to satisfy my desires in perfect secrecy. No matter who revealed this to you or however you came to know about it, I do not deny that this is what happened.

"I did not take a lover at random, as many women do, but made a deliberate choice of Guiscardo, selecting him ahead of everyone else. With thoughtful planning I drew him to me, and by dint of prudence and persistence on both of our parts, I have been satisfying my desires with him for a long time now. What you are blaming me for with such bitterness, far more than for my carnal sin itself, is that I am consorting with a man of base condition, as if it wouldn't have bothered you for me to have chosen a nobleman as my lover. In doing this, you are following common opinion rather than the truth, for you fail to see that you are not really blaming my sin, but Fortune, who has very frequently raised the unworthy to great heights, while keeping the most deserving down low.

"But leaving all this aside, just consider the basic principles involved, and you will see that we are all made of one flesh and that the same Creator has created all our souls, giving them equal faculties, powers, and virtues. Since we are all born equal, and always have been, it is virtue that made the first distinctions among us, and those who not only had, but actually made use of a greater portion of it were the ones considered noble, while the rest were not. Since then, practices to the contrary have obscured this law, but it has never been erased from Nature or good manners, so that a person who behaves virtuously shows unmistakably that he is noble, and if anyone calls him something else, then that person, not the other, is in the wrong.

"Just take a look at your noblemen, and compare their lives, manners, and general behavior with those of Guiscardo. If you judge them all without prejudice, you will say that he is the true nobleman and the rest of them are mere commoners. In estimating the virtues and valor of Guiscardo, I did not trust the judgment of other people, but that which was contained in your own words and which my own eyes have confirmed. What person ever commended him as much as you did for performing all those praiseworthy deeds for which men of valor merit commendation? And you were certainly not wrong to do that, because if my eyes have not deceived me, you have never praised him for something I didn't actually see him do, and usually in a manner more wonderful than your words could ever express. Thus, if I was ever deceived at all in this, you were the one who deceived me.

"Will you say, then, that I have allied myself with a man of base condition? Well, you're simply not telling the truth. Perhaps if you'd said I'd done so with a poor man, that might be conceded— but it would be conceded to your shame, because it reveals you have failed to reward such a worthy servant with the advancement he deserves. In any case, poverty does not take away a man's nobility of character; only wealth can do that. There have been many kings, many great princes, who were once poor, and many a farmer and many a shepherd were once immensely wealthy and are so again.

"As for the last doubt you entertain, namely, about what you should do with me, banish it altogether. If you are ready in your extreme old age to do what you were never accustomed to do when you were young, that is, to treat me with savage cruelty, then go ahead and use all of it on me, since I myself am the real cause of this supposed sin. I am determined not to offer you any sort of plea for mercy, and I swear to you that whatever you have done to Guiscardo, or are planning to do to him, if you don't do the same thing to me, I will do it to myself with my very own hands. Now get out of here. Go shed your tears with the women. And then, when you are inclined to cruelty again, kill us both with the same blow if you think we've merited it."

The Prince recognized the lofty nature of his daughter's spirit, but for all that, he doubted she was so resolute as to do what her words suggested. As a result, once he left her, he lost any desire he had to take out his anger on her and decided, instead, that he would cool off her fervent love by punishing her lover. Consequently, he ordered the two men who were guarding Guiscardo to strangle him noiselessly that night, and then to take out Guiscardo's heart and bring it to him. The two of them did as they were ordered, and the next day the Prince sent for a beautiful large chalice made of gold, into which he put the heart. Then he had one of his most trusted servants take it to her, bidding him to say the following words as he handed it over: "Your father sends you this to comfort you for the loss of the thing you love best, just as you have comforted him for the loss of what he loved best."

After her father had left her, Ghismunda, who was unflinching in her fierce resolve, had them bring her poisonous herbs and roots, which she distilled into a liquid so as to have it at the ready in case what she feared actually came to pass. When the servant then appeared and presented her with the cup and the Prince's message, she took it, and with her countenance unchanged, removed the cover. As soon as she saw what it contained, she understood the meaning of the Prince's words and had no doubt whatsoever that this was Guiscardo's heart. Raising her head, she looked straight at the servant.

"A heart like this," she said, "deserves nothing less splendid than a sepulcher of gold. At least in this case, my father has acted wisely." And having spoken, she raised the heart to her lips and kissed it.

"In every respect," she said, "right down to the very end of my life, I have always found my father's love for me to be most tender, and now it is more so than ever. Consequently, on my behalf, I ask you to give him the last thanks I shall ever give him for so great a gift." Having said this, she turned to the chalice, which she held firmly in her grip, and stared at the heart.

"Ah," she said, "sweetest vessel of all my pleasures, I curse the cruelty of the man who now compels me to look at you with the eyes of my body! It was enough for me to have beheld you at all hours with those of my mind. You have finished the course of the life that Fortune has allotted you, you have reached the end to which everyone hastens, and having left behind all the misery and weariness of the world, you have received from your enemy himself the sepulcher that your worth deserves. Your funeral rites lacked nothing but the tears of the woman you loved so dearly while you were alive, and God prompted my pitiless father to send you to me so that you might have them now. I shall weep for you, even though I intended to die with my eyes dry and my countenance completely unmarked by fear. But once I have paid you the tears I owe you, I will make no delay in sending my soul, with your help, to join the one that you have guarded so tenderly.° Is there another companion with whom I would be happier or more secure as I travel to that unknown place? I am certain that your soul is nearby right now, looking down on the scene of all the delights we shared, and since I am sure it loved me, I know that it awaits my soul, which loves it beyond all measure."

When Ghismunda finished speaking, she bent her head over the chalice, and suppressing all sounds of womanly grief, she began weeping in a way that was wondrous to behold. As her tears poured forth like water from some fountain in her head, all the while she gave the dead heart an infinite number of kisses. Her ladies, who were standing around her, did not understand whose heart it was or what her words meant, but overcome with pity, they, too, began to weep. Filled with compassion, they asked her to reveal the cause of her lamentation, but it was all in vain, nor could they comfort her, despite all their best efforts to do so.

When Ghismunda had wept her fill, she raised her head and dried her eyes.

"O my dearly beloved heart," she said, "now that I have discharged the duty I owe you, the only thing I have left to do is to send my soul to you and unite it with yours as your eternal companion."

Having made this pronouncement, she sent for the little vial containing the liquid she had made the day before, and poured it into the chalice where lay the heart she had bathed with so many of her tears. Then, without a trace of fear, she brought it to her lips and drained it dry, after which, with the chalice still in her hand, she climbed up onto her bed. There she arranged her body as decorously as she could, placed the heart of her dead lover next to her own, and without saying another word, waited for death.

When her ladies had seen and heard all these things, even though they did not know the nature of the liquid that she had drunk, they sent word of it to Tancredi. He was afraid of what was in fact transpiring and immediately descended to his daughter's room, arriving just as she was positioning herself on her bed. When he saw the condition she was in, he tried—too late—to comfort her with sweet words, and then dissolved in a flood of bitter tears.

"Tancredi," said the lady, "save your tears for some misfortune less desired than mine is. Just don't shed them for me, for I don't want them. Who ever heard of anyone, aside from you, weeping when he gets what he wanted? But if you still retain even a bit of the love you used to feel for me, grant me one last gift: since it displeased you that I lived quietly with Guiscardo in secret, let my body be publicly laid to rest beside his wherever it may be that you had them throw it after his death."

His anguished sobbing did not permit the Prince to respond, whereupon the young lady, who felt her end approaching, pressed the dead heart to her bosom, and said: "God be with you, for now I take my leave of you." Then, her vision grew blurry, her senses failed, and she left this life of sorrow behind her.

Thus, as you have heard, the love between Guiscardo and Ghismunda came to its sad conclusion. Tancredi grieved deeply over what had happened, and although his repentance for his cruelty came too late, he did have the couple honorably buried in the same tomb, to the universal mourning of all the people of Salerno.

Story 2

FRATE ALBERTO, HAVING GIVEN A LADY TO
UNDERSTAND THAT THE ANGEL GABRIEL IS IN LOVE WITH
HER, ASSUMES THE ANGEL'S FORM HIMSELF AND SLEEPS
WITH HER ON NUMEROUS OCCASIONS, UNTIL, SCARED BY
HER RELATIVES, HE THROWS HIMSELF OUT OF HER HOUSE
AND TAKES REFUGE IN THAT OF A POOR MAN. THE NEXT
DAY THE LATTER LEADS HIM TO THE PIAZZA DRESSED UP
LIKE A WILD MAN, WHERE HE IS RECOGNIZED AND
APPREHENDED BY HIS FELLOW FRIARS WHO PROCEED TO
INCARCERATE HIM.°

More than once, Fiammetta's story had brought tears to the eyes of her companions, but when it was done, the King looked at them sternly and declared:

"I think it would be a small price to pay if I were to give up my life in exchange for even half the pleasure that Ghismunda had with Guiscardo. Nor should any of you find this surprising, seeing as how every hour of my life I die a thousand deaths without ever having received even a tiny morsel of pleasure. However, setting my affairs aside for the present, I want Pampinea to continue the storytelling with some savage tale that partly resembles my own predicament, and if she will just follow Fiammetta down the way she has set out on, I shall doubtless begin to feel some drops of dew falling upon the fire that burns within me."

Because of the way she felt herself, Pampinea was far more responsive to her companions' mood than to the King's after what he had just said, and so, when she heard herself ordered to speak, although she was perfectly willing to obey his command, she was more inclined to amuse them a bit than to satisfy him. Consequently, she decided that, without straying from the prescribed theme, she would tell them a tale that would make them laugh, and thus, she began:

The people have a proverb that goes like this:

A man who's wicked, yet thought to be good,
Can always do wrong: no one thinks that he would.

This proverb provides me not just with ample material to discuss in connection with the theme that has been proposed, but also with an opportunity to reveal both the nature and the extent of the clergy's hypocrisy. When they go about begging, they don long, flowing robes, make their faces look pale by artificial means, and keep their voices mild and low, but they become loud and haughty when they attack others for their own vices, or show how the people will achieve salvation by giving alms to them, while they do so by taking alms from the people. Furthermore, unlike the rest of us, they do not act as if they have to work to get into Paradise, but as if they already owned it and had been made its rulers, assigning everyone who dies a better or a worse place depending on the amount of money he has bequeathed to them. In this they make every effort to deceive, first, themselves, if they really believe what they say, and then, all those who put faith in their words. If I were permitted to reveal their tricks, I would soon open the eyes of many simple people and show them just what it is that they keep hidden underneath those ample habits of theirs.

But now, may it please God that what happened to a Franciscan should happen to them on account of all of their lies.° No longer a young man, that friar was considered to be among the most authoritative churchmen in Venice, and it will give me the greatest pleasure to tell you a story about him so that your spirits, which have been filled with pity for the death of Ghismunda, may perhaps be lifted up to some degree if I can get you to laugh and enjoy yourselves.°

In Imola, worthy ladies, there once lived a wicked, corrupt man by the name of Berto della Massa whose ignominious deeds were so well known to the people of the town that no one there was willing to believe anything he said, no matter whether he was lying or telling the truth.° When he perceived that his scams would no longer work in Imola, as a last resort he moved to Venice, that receptacle of every sort of filth, thinking he would find a different way to practice fraud there than he had anywhere else before then.° And so, pretending he was conscience stricken because of his past misdeeds, he gave everyone the impression that he was overcome by the utmost feeling of humility, and then, as if he were the most pious man alive, he went and became a Franciscan, adopting the name of Frate Alberto da Imola. Wearing the habit of that order, he put on a show of living an austere life, greatly commending both penance and abstinence, and never eating meat or drinking wine, at least when he did not find any to his taste.

Almost no one perceived that the man who had suddenly turned into a great preacher had been a thief, a pimp, a forger, and a murderer, let alone that he had never really abandoned any of his vices, which he would practice on the sly whenever he could. To top it off, after being ordained a priest, every time he went up to the altar to celebrate the Mass, provided that there were a lot of people present, he would weep over the Passion of Our Savior, for he was the kind of guy it cost very little to shed tears whenever he wanted. In short, between his sermons and his tears, he knew how to lure in the Venetians so successfully that not only was he made the trustee and executor of practically every will written in the city, but many people asked him to safeguard their money, and the vast majority of both men and women named him their confessor and adviser. Having thus changed from a wolf into a shepherd, he acted in such a way that he gained a reputation for holiness in those parts much greater than that which Saint Francis had ever enjoyed in Assisi.

Now it just so happened that a group of women went to this holy friar one day in order to be confessed, and among them there was a frivolous, empty-headed young lady named Madonna Lisetta da Ca' Quirino, the wife of an important merchant who had sailed away to Flanders with his galleys.° She was kneeling at his feet, and being a Venetian, all of whom are chatterboxes, she had only gotten through a few of the things she had done, when Frate Alberto asked her whether she had a lover.

"Hey, Messer Friar," replied Madonna Lisetta, giving him a black look, "don't you have eyes in your head? Do you think my

charms are just like everybody else's? I could have lovers to spare
if I wanted, but my kind of beauty is not something for just anybody who happens to be attracted to it. How many women have
you seen whose good looks are anything like mine? Why, I'd be
counted a beauty even in Paradise." And she added so much more
about this beauty of hers that it was a pain to listen to her.

Frate Alberto saw immediately that this one was something of
an idiot, and since she seemed like good soil for him to plow, he
fell passionately in love with her then and there. He decided, however, to postpone any courtship until a more suitable moment.
Instead, in order to keep up his saintly appearance for the time
being, he began scolding her, telling her this was all vainglory and
making her listen to a lot more of his nonsense. In reply, the lady
told him that he was an ass and that he could not tell one woman's
beauty from another's. Since he wanted to avoid irritating her
unduly, Frate Alberto heard the rest of her confession and allowed
her to go on her way with the other women.

A few days later, Frate Alberto went to Madonna Lisetta's house
with a trusted companion, and withdrawing into a separate room
with her where he could not be seen by anybody, he threw himself on his knees before her.

"My lady," he said, "I beg you for God's sake to forgive me for
what I said to you on Sunday when you were talking to me about
your beauty. I was punished so severely for it the following night
that I have not been able to get out of my bed until today."

"And who was it who punished you like that?" asked Lady
Blockhead.

"I'll tell you," replied Frate Alberto. "When I was praying that
night, as I usually do, all of a sudden I was aware of a great light
shining in my cell, and before I could turn around to see what it
was, there was an incredibly beautiful young man standing over
me with a large club in his hand. He grabbed me by my habit, pulled
me down to the floor at his feet, and really let me have it until he'd
bruised practically every bone in my body. When I asked him why
he had treated me like that, he replied, 'Because today you presumed to disparage the celestial beauty of Madonna Lisetta, and

except for God Himself, there is no one in the world I love more than her.'

"'Who are you?' I asked, and he replied that he was the Angel Gabriel.

"'O my lord,' I said, 'I beg you to forgive me.'

"'I forgive you on this condition,' he replied, 'that you go to her as soon as you can and persuade her to forgive you. And if she doesn't, I'm going to come back here and give it to you so soundly that you'll be sorry for the rest of your life.' What he said to me after that I don't dare to tell you unless you forgive me first."

Lady Pumpkinhead, who was somewhat lacking in wit, was enormously gratified upon hearing his words and took them all to be the utter truth.

"Well, Frate Alberto," she said, after a brief pause, "I told you that my beauty was celestial, didn't I? But so help me God, I do feel sorry for you, and in order to spare you any further injury, I will forgive you, but only on the condition that you tell me what else the angel said to you."

"Now that you've pardoned me, my lady," replied Frate Alberto, "I'll do so gladly. But let me ask you to bear one thing in mind, and that is never to tell anyone in the world what I'm about to say to you, if you don't want to ruin everything for yourself. Truly, you're the luckiest lady alive, for the Angel Gabriel told me to tell you how he'd taken such a liking to you that he would have come to spend the night with you on many occasions if he hadn't been worried about frightening you. Now he's sent me to inform you that he wants to come one night and spend time in your company, and because he's an angel and you would not be able to touch him in that form, he says that for your own pleasure he would like to come in the form of a man. Therefore, you should let him know when you want him to be here and in whose shape, and he'll do it. And so, now you know why you should consider yourself more blessed than any other woman alive."

Madonna Simple declared she was very pleased that the Angel Gabriel loved her, seeing how she certainly loved him and never let the opportunity go by to light a four-penny candle for him wherever she saw his image in a painting. And he would be very welcome to visit her whenever he pleased, and he would always find her all alone in her room. Nevertheless, there was this proviso, that he would not leave her for the Virgin Mary, whom, it was said, he loved very much, and it did appear that way because wherever she saw him, he was always on his knees in front of her.° For the rest, she said, it was up to him to come in whatever form he wanted as long as she would not be frightened.

"Spoken like a wise woman, my lady," said Frate Alberto. "I'll be sure to arrange everything with him just as you've suggested. But you can do me a great favor that will cost you nothing, namely, you should have him use this body of mine when he comes to you. Let me explain how you'll be doing me a favor: the moment he enters my body, he's going to remove my soul and place it in Paradise, where it will remain for as long as he's down here with you."

"What a good idea," said Madonna Noodlepate. "I'd really like you to have this consolation to compensate for all the blows he gave you on my account."

"You should make sure he'll find the door to your house open tonight so that he can get in," said Frate Alberto, "because he'll be coming in human form, and when he arrives, he'll have to enter that way."

The lady replied that she would take care of it, and after Frate Alberto left, she strutted around so high and mighty that her shift did not reach down to cover her butt. And still, to her it seemed like a thousand years before the Angel Gabriel arrived.

Thinking he was going to play the horseman, not the angel, that night, Frate Alberto fortified himself with sweets and other delicacies so that he would not be easily thrown from his mount. Then, at nightfall, after having obtained permission to leave the monastery, he went with a trusted companion to the house of a lady friend of his, a place he often used as a starting post for racing after his fillies, and when the time seemed right, from there he went on in disguise to the lady's house. Once inside, he transformed himself into an angel by putting on the gewgaws he had brought with him, after which he climbed up the stairs and entered the lady's room.

When she saw the brilliantly white object in front of her, she fell on her knees before it. The angel gave her his blessing, raised her to her feet, and gestured to her to get into bed. Eager to obey, she did so immediately, and the angel lay down beside his devotee. Frate Alberto was a physically attractive man, quite robust, and with a more than sufficiently sturdy pair of legs on him, so that when he was with Madonna Lisetta, who was herself soft and fresh, he showed himself to be quite a different partner in bed than her husband. Many times that night he took flight without wings, causing the lady to cry out loud with satisfaction at what he did, which he supplemented by telling her all about the glories of Heaven. Then, as day approached, having made arrangements for his return, he took all his gear and went to rejoin his companion to whom the good lady of the house had offered her friendly company in bed so that he would not feel frightened if he had to sleep all by himself.

As soon as she had eaten, the lady went with her maidservant to see Frate Alberto and told him her news about the Angel Gabriel. She rehearsed what he had said about the glories of the life eternal and described his appearance, while adding to her account all sorts of marvelous inventions of her own.

"My lady," said Frate Alberto, "I don't know how you fared with him. What I do know is that when he came to me last night and I gave him your message, in an instant he transported my soul among so many more flowers and so many more roses than have ever been seen down here, and there, in one of the most delightful spots that ever existed, he permitted my soul to remain until matins this morning. As for what happened to my body, I just don't know."

"Isn't that what I've been telling you?" said the lady. "Your body, with the Angel Gabriel inside, spent the entire night in my arms. And if you don't believe me, take a look under your left breast where I gave the angel such a passionate kiss that its mark is going to be there for days to come."

"Well, then," said Frate Alberto, "today I'm going to do what I haven't done in a long time, and that is, I'm going to undress myself to see if you're telling the truth."

Finally, after a lot more chitchat, the lady returned home, which, from that day on, is where Frate Alberto also went to pay her many a visit, unimpeded, in the form of the angel.

One day, however, when Madonna Lisetta was talking with a close friend of hers, engaged in a dispute about physical beauty, she was determined to place her own charms up above everyone else's, and having precious little wit in her pumpkinhead, she declared: "If you only knew who was taken with my beauty, you'd certainly stop talking about how attractive other women are."°

Because her friend certainly understood the kind of woman she was dealing with, she was very curious about what Madonna Lisetta had to say.

"My lady," she said, "you may well be telling the truth, but still, since his identity remains unknown, it's difficult for one to change one's opinion."

"I shouldn't be telling you this, neighbor," replied Madonna Lisetta, who got all worked up very easily, "but my sweetheart is the Angel Gabriel, who loves me more than he loves himself, and according to what he tells me, it's all because I'm the most beautiful woman to be found anywhere in the world or in the Maremma."°

Her friend wanted to laugh, but held herself in check so that Madonna Lisetta would continue talking.

"I swear to God, my lady," she said, "if the Angel Gabriel is your sweetheart and tells you that, then it must be true. But I didn't think that the angels did such things."

"That's where you've got it wrong, neighbor," replied Madonna Lisetta. "By God's wounds, he does it better than my husband, and in fact, he tells me they all do it up there, too. And because he thinks I'm more beautiful than anyone in Heaven, he's fallen in love with me and frequently comes to stay with me. Now do you get it?"

After her friend left Madonna Lisetta's, it seemed like a

thousand years before she found someone to whom she could repeat what she had heard. Finally, while attending a party where there was a large group of women, she told them the entire story from start to finish. These women told it to their husbands and to other women, and they told it to yet others, and thus in less than two days the news was all over Venice. But among those whose ears it reached were Madonna Lisetta's brothers-in-law. Without saying a word about it to her, they decided they would find that angel and discover if he really could fly, and for the next few nights in a row they lay in wait for him.

Some vague news about all this happened to reach the ears of Frate Alberto, and so he went one night to give her a scolding. No sooner had he undressed, however, than her in-laws, who had spotted him coming, were at the door to the room and in the process of opening it. When Frate Alberto heard them and realized what was up, he got out of bed, and seeing no other way to escape, opened a window overlooking the Grand Canal and threw himself into the water. Since the canal was deep there, and he was a good swimmer, he got away without suffering any harm. Having swum over to the other side of the canal, he hurried through the open door of a house and begged the good man he found inside, for the love of God, to save his life, making up some tall tale about how he had come there at that hour and why he was completely naked. The good man took pity on him, and since he was obliged to go off and tend to some affairs of his, he had Frate Alberto get into his bed and told him to stay there until he returned. Then, after locking him in the house, he went about his business.

When the lady's in-laws entered her room, they found that the Angel Gabriel had flown away, leaving his wings behind. Disconcerted, they directed a stream of verbal abuse at the lady, after which they took the angel's trappings and returned home, leaving her all alone in a state of utter dejection. By now it was broad daylight, and while the good man was on the Rialto, he heard the story about how the Angel Gabriel had gone to bed that night with Madonna Lisetta and been discovered there by her brothers-in-law, how he had been terrified and thrown himself into the canal, and how no one knew what had become of him.° He immediately realized that this was the guy he had in his house. Upon his return he confirmed his suspicions, and after listening to a lot more stories from Frate Alberto, he got him to send for fifty ducats if he wanted to avoid being handed over to the lady's in-laws. Once the money was taken care of, Frate Alberto was anxious to get away.

"There's only one way for you to do that," said the good man, "provided you're willing to go along with my plan. Today we're holding a festival in which people will be led about in various disguises, one dressed up like a bear, someone else like a wild man, and so on, and so on. Then they'll stage a hunt in the Piazza San Marco, and when that's over, the festival will come to an end, and everyone will be free to take the person he brought there with him and go wherever he wants.° So, if you're willing to have me lead you around wearing one of those disguises, I can take you away wherever you want to go before someone spots you. Otherwise, I can't see any way for you to get out of here without being recognized, because the lady's in-laws have concluded that you're somewhere in this quarter, and they've placed guards all over the place in order to capture you."

Although it seemed hard to Frate Alberto to go about in such a disguise, nevertheless his fear of the lady's relations persuaded him to do so, and he told the good man where he wanted to go, leaving the choice of a disguise up to him. The good man then smeared Frate Alberto from top to toe with honey, scattered downy feathers all over him, and after attaching a chain to his neck and putting a mask over his face, gave him a large club to hold in one hand and two huge dogs in the other that he had gotten from the slaughter-house.° Then he sent a man ahead to the Rialto to announce that whoever wanted to see the Angel Gabriel should go to the Piazza San Marco—that was Venetian trustworthiness for you!

Once everything was ready, the good man waited a bit longer and then took Frate Alberto outside, making him lead the way while holding him from behind by the chain. As they went along, they stirred up a lot of commotion among the throngs of people there, all of whom were asking, "What's that? What's that?" The good man led Frate Alberto on toward the piazza, where, between those who were following them from behind and those who had heard the announcement and had come from the Rialto, the crowd had grown so large that it was impossible to count all the people in it. When they finally arrived at the piazza, the good man tied his wild man to a column in an elevated spot where everyone could see him. Then, he pretended to wait for the hunt to begin, while Frate Alberto, because he was smeared all over with honey, was suffering intense pain from all the gnats and gadflies.

When the good man saw that the piazza was almost completely full, he made as if he was going to unchain his wild man, but pulled off Frate Alberto's mask instead and declared:

"Gentlemen, since the boar is not going to make an appearance, there won't be any hunt today. However, I didn't want you to have come here in vain, and so I've decided to let you have a look at the Angel Gabriel who descends at night from Heaven to earth in order to console the women of Venice."

No sooner was his mask off than Frate Alberto was instantly recognized by everybody, who all started yelling at him, using the foulest words and the worst insults ever hurled at any scoundrel, at the same time throwing filth of every sort in his face. They kept this up for a very long time until, by chance, the news reached his fellow friars. As many as six or so of them came to the piazza, threw a cloak over his shoulders, and unchained him, after which, followed by a general hue and cry, they led him to their monastery where they locked him up. And there it is believed he finally died, having spent the remainder of his life in utter misery.

Thus this guy, whose evil deeds were never believed because he was thought to be a good man, had dared to turn himself into the Angel Gabriel. After being transformed into a wild man, however, he was put to shame as he deserved to be, and for a very long time he wept in vain for the sins he had committed. May it please God that the same thing should befall all the others like him.°

Story 5

AFTER LISABETTA'S BROTHERS KILL HER LOVER,
HE APPEARS TO HER IN A DREAM AND SHOWS HER WHERE
HE IS BURIED. SHE SECRETLY DIGS UP HIS HEAD AND PUTS
IT IN A POT OF BASIL, WEEPING OVER IT FOR HOURS EVERY
DAY, BUT WHEN HER BROTHERS TAKE IT AWAY FROM HER,
SHORTLY AFTERWARD SHE HERSELF DIES OF GRIEF.°

* * *

There once lived in Messina three young men who were brothers. All of them were merchants and had been left very rich after the death of their father, who had come there from San Gimignano.° They also had a sister named Lisabetta, but although she was a young woman who was quite beautiful and well mannered, for some reason or other, they had still not arranged for her to be married.

In addition to the three brothers, there was a young Pisan named Lorenzo in their trading establishment who oversaw and managed all of their operations, and who, being quite handsome and charming, had often caught Lisabetta's eye. Having noticed from time to time that she was unusually attracted to him, he abandoned all his other love relationships and in like fashion set his heart on her. And thus the business went on in such a way that with the two of them equally drawn to one another, it was not long before they took all the necessary precautions and did what each of them desired to do more than anything else.

As they continued their affair, to their mutual joy and pleasure, they did everything they could to keep it a secret, but one night, as Lisabetta was making her way to Lorenzo's sleeping quarters, she was observed, without knowing it, by her eldest brother. This young man was quite discreet, and however great the distress he felt over his discovery, he made the prudent decision, out of concern for their family honor, not to make a sound, let alone to say anything about it, and he bided his time all night long, turning over in his mind many possible responses to what had happened.

The next morning he told his brothers what he had seen of Lisabetta and Lorenzo the night before, and the three of them discussed the matter at great length. Determined to spare both themselves and their sister any loss of reputation, he decided they would pass it over in silence and act as if they had neither seen nor heard anything at all until such time as it would be safe and convenient for them to rid themselves of this shame before it went any further.

Keeping to their plan, the three of them chatted and joked around with Lorenzo just as they always used to do until one day came when they pretended they were going on an outing to the country and took Lorenzo along with them. Once they had reached a very remote and isolated spot, they saw their opportunity, and catching Lorenzo off guard, they killed him and buried his body, doing it all in such a way that no one had any idea what had happened. On their return to Messina, they put it about that they had sent Lorenzo away on business, something people readily believed, since the brothers frequently used to have him make such trips for them.

Lorenzo's failure to return weighed heavily on Lisabetta, and in her anxiety, she kept asking her brothers about him. One day, when she happened to be particularly persistent in questioning them, one of her brothers said to her:

"What's the meaning of all this? What do you have to do with Lorenzo that you keep asking about him all the time? If you question us any more on the subject, we'll give you the kind of answer you deserve."

This made the young woman sad and miserable, and from then on, filled with fear and foreboding, she refrained from asking them about him. At night, however, she would repeatedly call out to him in a pitiful voice and beg him to come to her, occasionally dissolving in a flood of tears because of her grief over his absence. Nor was anything capable of cheering her up, as she went on and on, waiting for him to return.

One night, after crying so much over Lorenzo's absence that she finally cried herself to sleep, he appeared to her in a dream, pallid and terribly disheveled, his clothes torn to shreds and rotting, and it seemed to her that he said: "Oh, Lisabetta, you do nothing but call out to me, bemoaning my long absence and cruelly accusing me with your tears. You should know that I can't ever come back here, because on the day when you saw me for the last time, I was killed by your brothers." He then described to her the place where they had buried him, told her not to call him or wait for him any longer, and disappeared. Lisabetta awoke, and believing that the vision she had seen was true, wept bitter tears.

When she got up the next morning, she decided to go to the place Lorenzo had shown her and seek confirmation of what she had seen in her dream. She did not dare to say anything about it to her brothers, but got their permission to go on a little outing in the country, accompanied by a maid who had served the two lovers at one time and was privy to all her affairs. She went to the spot as quickly as she could, and after clearing away the dry leaves, began digging where the soil seemed looser. Nor did she have to dig very deep before she uncovered her unfortunate lover's body, which as yet showed no sign of decay or decomposition and offered her clear proof that her vision had been true.

Lisabetta was the saddest woman alive, but knew that this was no time for tears. Although she would have willingly taken the entire body away and given it a proper burial if she had been able to do so, she realized how impossible that would be. And so, instead, she took out a knife, and after severing the head from the trunk as best she could, she wrapped it up in a towel and gave it to her maid to hold. She then covered the rest of the body with dirt, after which, unobserved, she left the scene and made her way home.

Taking the head to her room, she shut herself in and cried bitterly, weeping so profusely that she bathed it thoroughly with her tears, and at the same time planting a thousand kisses all over it. Then she wrapped it in a lovely piece of cloth and put it inside a beautiful large pot of the sort people use for growing marjoram and basil. Covering it with soil, she planted in it a number of sprigs of the finest basil from Salerno, and refused to sprinkle anything on it other than the water of roses or orange blossoms, or her own tears.° It became her custom to sit with this pot always by her side and to stare at it, concentrating all her desire on it, since her Lorenzo lay concealed within. After she had gazed at it raptly for a long period, she would bend over it and begin to weep, and would go on weeping until the basil was thoroughly watered by her tears.

Because of the constant, unremitting care she gave it, and because the soil was enriched by the decomposing head inside the pot, the basil grew luxuriantly and was exceptionally fragrant. And as the young woman maintained this routine consistently, on several occasions it came to the attention of her neighbors, who reported it to her brothers. "We've noticed," they said, "that she keeps doing the same thing every day."

The brothers had been puzzled by the fact that Lisabetta was losing her looks and that her eyes had become sunken in her head. When they heard their neighbors' account and then observed her behavior for themselves, they chided her for it several times, but to no avail, which prompted them to have the pot secretly removed from her room. Upon discovering that it was missing, she kept asking to have it back with the greatest insistence, but they refused to return it to her. And so, she went on crying and lamenting until she fell ill, and from her sickbed all she ever asked for was her pot of basil.

The brothers were very puzzled by her persistent entreaties and decided to find out what was inside the pot. When they dumped out the soil, they saw the cloth and the head wrapped inside it, which was not yet sufficiently decomposed that they could not help but identify it, from the curly hair, as being Lorenzo's. Utterly confounded by what they had discovered, and fearful that news of it would get around, they buried the head, after which, without saying another word, they made all the arrangements for an orderly departure from Messina, secretly left the city, and moved to Naples.

The young woman never stopped weeping and asking over and over again for that pot of hers. And so weeping, she died, thus bringing her ill-fated love to its end. In the course of time, however, people did learn the truth about the affair, and one of them composed the song that we still sing today, which goes:

Who was that wicked Christian man
Who stole my pot of herbs from me, etc.°

Story 9

MESSER GUIGLIELMO ROSSIGLIONE SLAYS HIS WIFE'S LOVER,
MESSER GUIGLIELMO GUARDASTAGNO, AND GIVES HER HIS
HEART TO EAT, BUT WHEN SHE FINDS OUT ABOUT IT LATER,
SHE THROWS HERSELF DOWN TO THE GROUND FROM A HIGH
WINDOW, AND AFTER HER DEATH, IS BURIED WITH
HER BELOVED.°

* * *

Considering how much you are saddened, my most compassionate ladies, by lovers' misfortunes, the tale that presents itself to me will make you feel at least as much pity as the last one did, since the people involved in the events I am about to relate were of loftier rank and met with a crueler fate than those of whom we have already spoken.

You must know, then, that according to the people of Provence, there were once two noble knights living in that region, each of whom had a castle and a large number of vassals under him. One was named Messer Guiglielmo Rossiglione and the other Messer Guiglielmo Guardastagno, and since both excelled in feats of arms, they used to arm themselves from head to toe, and not only would they go together to tournaments and jousts and other contests involving martial prowess, but they would do so wearing exactly the same device.°

Although the castles in which the two of them resided were a good ten miles apart, Messer Guiglielmo Guardastagno chanced to fall madly in love with Messer Guiglielmo Rossiglione's very beautiful and charming wife, and despite all the affection and camaraderie the men shared, he made use of one means and then another to make her aware of his feelings. The lady, knowing him to be a most gallant knight, was pleased by this and soon became so infatuated with him that there was nothing she burned and yearned for more, until the only thing she was still waiting for was to have him proposition her. Nor was it very long before he did, after which they met with some frequency and made passionate love together.

Since they were not very discreet in their encounters, one day her husband chanced to discover them and became so deeply incensed that the great love he felt for Guardastagno was transformed into mortal hatred. Better at keeping it hidden, however, than the two lovers had been with their affair, he decided, no matter what, that he would kill the man.

With Rossiglione in this frame of mind, a grand tournament happened to be announced in France. He immediately sent word of it to Guardastagno, asking him if he would like to come to his castle where the two of them could decide together whether they wanted to go and how they would get there. Quite delighted, Guardastagno replied that he would come without fail the next day and have supper with him.

When he received Guardastagno's message, Rossiglione thought the time had come to kill him. The next day, after arming himself, he got on his horse, and with a few of his men he went about a mile away from his castle, where he set up an ambush in a wood through which Guardastagno was bound to pass. After a long wait, he caught sight of him approaching, unarmed, followed by two servants, who were likewise unarmed, because he never thought for a moment that he might need to protect himself against his friend. When Rossiglione saw that Guardastagno had reached the spot he had chosen, he rushed out at him, with murder and vengeance in his heart, holding his lance above his head and shouting, "Traitor, you're a dead man!" And before the words were even out of his mouth, he thrust his lance straight through Guardastagno's chest.

Unable to defend himself, let alone even utter a word, Guardastagno fell, impaled on the lance, and died almost instantly, at which point his servants, without waiting to see who had killed him, turned their horses' heads around and fled back to their master's castle as fast as they could.

After dismounting from his horse, Rossiglione cut open Guardastagno's chest with a knife, tore out the heart with his own hands, and wrapping it up in a banderole, told one of his men to take it with him. Having given them all strict instructions not to dare to say so much as a word about what had happened, he got back on his horse and returned to his castle, by which time it was nightfall.

The lady, who had heard that Guardastagno was supposed to come to supper, was waiting for him with the greatest impatience. When he did not show up with her husband, she was quite surprised and asked him: "How is it, sir, that Guardastagno hasn't arrived?"

"Wife," replied her husband, "I've received word from him that he can't be here until tomorrow"—a statement that left her feeling somewhat perturbed.

After he had dismounted, Rossiglione had his cook summoned and said to him: "Take this boar's heart and make sure that you prepare the finest, most delectable dish you can with it. Then, when I'm seated at table, send it to me on a silver serving plate." The cook took the heart, and calling upon all his knowledge and all his skill, he minced it, seasoned it with a number of savory spices, and made a very tasty dish out of it indeed.

When it was time to eat, Messer Guiglielmo sat down at the table with his wife. The meal was served, but he was preoccupied with the crime he had committed and ate very little. The cook then sent him the special dish, and he had it placed before the lady, saying he had no appetite that evening. He heartily commended the dish, however, and the lady, who did have an appetite, started to eat it, and finding it quite tasty, consumed every last morsel.

When the knight saw that his wife had finished the whole thing, he asked her: "Wife, what did you think of the dish?"

"In good faith, my lord," she replied, "I liked it very much."

"So help me God," said the knight, "I do believe you did. But

I'm really not surprised that you liked it dead, because you liked it when it was alive more than anything else in the world."

Upon hearing these words, the lady hesitated a moment. Then she asked: "How's that? What's this thing you've had me eat?"

"What you ate," said the knight, "was actually the heart of Messer Guiglielmo Guardastagno, whom you, like the faithless woman you are, were so infatuated with. And you may rest assured that it really was his, because I ripped it out of his chest myself, with these hands, just a little while before I came back here."

When she heard what had happened to the man she loved more than anything else in the world, there's no need to ask if she was grief stricken. After a brief pause, she said: "In doing what you did, you've behaved like a wicked, faithless knight, for if I was not forced into it by him, but freely chose to abuse you by making him the master of my love, then you should have punished me for it, not him. But now that I've eaten such a noble dish, made from the heart of so gallant and courteous a knight as Messer Guiglielmo Guardastagno, God forbid that any food should ever pass my lips again."

Then she stood up, and going to a window right behind her, without the slightest hesitation she let herself fall backward out of it. Because it was so high above the ground, the lady did not merely die, but was completely dashed to pieces.

Messer Guiglielmo was profoundly shaken by what he had witnessed and conscience stricken over having done wrong. Moreover, he feared what his fellow countrymen and the Count of Provence might do. Consequently, he had his horses saddled and rode away.°

By the next morning, news of what had happened had spread throughout the entire region, and people came from both Messer Guiglielmo Guardastagno's castle and that of the lady's family to gather up the two bodies, which were taken, amid a great outpouring of grief and lamentation, to the chapel inside the lady's castle and buried there in a single tomb together. Upon it there was an inscription in verse, indicating who was buried inside and the manner as well as the cause of their deaths.

Conclusion

*   *   *

Perceiving that the sun was fading to yellow and the end of his reign had come, the King offered the lovely ladies the most courteous apology for what he had done, that is, for having made them speak on so harsh a subject as the misfortunes of lovers. Having thus excused himself, he got to his feet and removed the laurel wreath from his head. Then, as the ladies waited to see whom he would bestow it on next, he set it graciously on Fiammetta's brilliantly blond hair, and said to her: "I now place this crown upon you because you will know better than anyone how to console our companions tomorrow for the disagreeable experience we have had today."

Fiammetta, who had long, golden curls that tumbled down over her delicate, white shoulders, a softly rounded face resplendent with the authentic hues of white lilies and crimson roses, a pair of eyes in her head that were like those of a peregrine falcon, and a dainty little mouth with lips like two tiny rubies, answered him with a smile:

"I am happy to accept it, Filostrato. And to make you even more aware of just what it is that you have done, I desire and decree forthwith that each of us should be ready tomorrow to recount the stories of lovers who, after terrible accidents or misfortunes, finally found happiness."

Everyone liked Fiammetta's proposal, and after summoning the steward and making all the necessary arrangements with him, she got up from her seat and gaily dismissed the entire company until suppertime.

All of them went off to amuse themselves in whatever ways they wished, some of them strolling through the garden, whose beauties never seemed stale to them, while others walked in the direction of the mills, which were grinding away outside. When the hour for supper arrived, they reassembled as usual next to the beautiful fountain and had their meal, which was very well served and which they ate with the greatest pleasure.

After getting up from the table, they devoted themselves, as was their custom, to singing and dancing. As Filomena took the lead, the Queen said:

"Filostrato, I have no intention of departing from the ways of my predecessors. Just like them, I intend to have a song performed at my command, and since I am certain that your songs are just like your stories, it is our pleasure that you should choose the one you like best and sing it for us now. Thus we will not have any more days, other than this one, that will be disturbed by your woes."

Filostrato replied that he was quite willing to do so, and immediately began a song that went this way:

> By weeping I can show
> How very much my heart is right to grieve,
> Betrayed, O Love, despite your promises.
>
> When first you found within my heart, O Love,
> A special place for her for whom I sigh
> In vain, deprived of hope,
> You made her seem so full of virtue then
> That I considered all those torments light
> With which you filled my breast
> Whose suffering still goes on
> Unchecked today. But I have gravely erred
> And realize it now in all my pain.
>
> You made me recognize her treachery
> And understand that she, my only hope,
> Had then abandoned me
> Just when I thought that I for sure enjoyed
> Her favor and was held her servant true.
> I could not see what pain
> And suffering I would have,
> When finding she'd embraced another's worth
> Within her heart, and cast me out of it.
>
> And when I knew that I'd been spurned by her,
> A sad lament welled up within my heart,
> And there it lingers on.

That day and hour I curse and curse again
When first I saw that lovely face of hers,
With lofty beauty graced,
Radiant beyond compare.
And so, my faith, my ardor, and my hope,
My dying soul will go on cursing you.
   Just how bereft of comfort in my woe
I am, my Lord, you know, for calling you,
My voice is filled with grief.
  I tell you that I burn with so much pain
The death I seek's the lesser martyrdom.
Come, Death, and take from me
My cruel, my wretched life,
And end as well my madness with your stroke;
Wherever I may go, I'll feel it less.
      No other course than death remains for me,
No other comfort's left for all my grief.
Then grant it to me now,
And with it put an end, Love, to my woes—
From such a wretched life release my heart.
Since wrongly I'm deprived
Of joy and solace, too,
Ah, do it, Lord; let my death give her joy
As did the new love whom you sent to her.
      O song of mine, I do not care if no
One ever learns to sing you, for they could
Not sing you as I do.
There's one sole task I wish to give to you:
May you find Love and unto him alone
Explain how little worth
My sad and bitter life
Still has for me, and for his honor's sake,
Beg him to steer me to a better port.

The words of this song quite clearly revealed Filostrato's state of
mind as well as what was causing it, and perhaps the face of a

certain lady among the dancers would have revealed even more if the darkness of the night, which had come upon them, had not concealed the blush that was spread across it. When his song was done, they sang many another until it was time to go to bed, at which point, in response to the Queen's command, they all retired to their own individual rooms.

Day 5

Story 1

CIMONE ACQUIRES WISDOM THROUGH HIS LOVE FOR HIS
LADY EFIGENIA, WHOM HE THEN ABDUCTS AT SEA.
IMPRISONED IN RHODES, HE IS FREED BY LISIMACO, WITH
WHOM HE ONCE AGAIN ABDUCTS BOTH EFIGENIA AND
CASSANDREA DURING THEIR WEDDING. THEY THEN FLEE
WITH THEIR LADIES TO CRETE, WHERE THEY GET MARRIED,
AFTER WHICH THEY ARE SUMMONED TO COME BACK TO
THEIR HOMES WITH THEIR WIVES.°

There are many tales I can think of telling you, delightful ladies,
which would make an appropriate beginning for so happy a day as

this is going to be. There is one, however, that is, to my mind, especially appealing, for not only will it enable you to perceive the happy goal at which all the storytelling we are now about to begin is aimed, but it will allow you to see just how divine, how powerful, and how beneficial the forces of Love can be, even though many people, who speak out of ignorance, mistakenly condemn and revile them. All of this, if I am not mistaken, you ladies should find quite agreeable, for I believe that you are yourselves in love.

As we have read in the ancient chronicles of Cyprus, there was once a very noble gentleman by the name of Aristippo living on that island who was far richer in worldly possessions than any of his countrymen, and who might have considered himself the happiest man alive if Fortune had not given him one particular source of grief. And this was that among his children, he had a son, taller and much better looking than all the other young men, who was, for all intents and purposes, an imbecile. His case appeared hopeless, and neither his tutor's efforts, nor his father's cajoling and whippings, nor the ingenious stratagems others devised had been able to beat one jot of learning or good manners into his head. On the contrary, they left him with a coarse, uncouth mode of speech and manners more suitable to a wild beast than a man, so that although his real name was Galeso, he was contemptuously referred to as Cimone by everyone, because in their language that meant the same thing as "stupid ass" in ours.° His waste of a life was a matter of the gravest concern to his father, but since he had by now given up all hope for his son and did not wish to have the source of his grief constantly in front of him, he ordered him to go and live among the peasants on his country estate. Cimone was overjoyed to do so, for he found the customs and practices of rustics more to his liking than those of city dwellers.

And so, off to the country went Cimone, where he busied himself with whatever work needed doing on the estate. One day in the early afternoon, while he was walking from one farm to another with his staff slung over his shoulder, he chanced to enter a little wood, the most beautiful in the area, where, since it happened to be the month of May, everything was in full leaf. As he went along, seemingly guided there by Fortune, he came upon a clearing surrounded by extremely tall trees, in a corner of which there was a very lovely, cool fountain. Beside it, sleeping on the green grass, he saw an exquisitely beautiful young lady who was wearing a dress made of such sheer fabric that it concealed almost nothing of the white flesh beneath it. From the waist down, she was covered by a pure white quilt of equally transparent material, and at her feet, likewise fast asleep, lay two women and a man, who were her attendants.

On catching sight of her, Cimone stopped, leaned on his staff, and without saying a word, began staring at her with the greatest intensity, utterly rapt in admiration, as though he had never before seen a woman's form. And within his rustic breast, on which, despite a thousand lessons, no touch of civilized pleasure had been able to make the slightest impression, he felt the awakening of a sentiment that spoke to his gross, uncouth mind and informed it that she was the most beautiful thing any mortal had ever seen. Cimone then proceeded to examine her features, admiring her hair, which he thought was made of gold, her brow, her nose and mouth, her neck and arms, and especially her breasts, still not fully developed. Having been instantaneously transformed from a peasant into a connoisseur of beauty, he desired more than anything to see her eyes, which she kept closed under the weight of a profound slumber. More than once he was moved to wake her up in order to observe them, but as she seemed far more beautiful to him than any other woman he had ever seen before, he feared that she might be some goddess, and he had enough sense to know that divine things merit greater respect than those of this world. He therefore refrained, waiting for her to wake up of her own accord, and even though the wait seemed to go on forever, he was so taken by the unfamiliar pleasure he felt that he was incapable of tearing himself away.

It took a long while before the young lady, whose name was Efigenia, woke up. Her servants were still sleeping as she raised her head and opened her eyes, and when she caught sight of Cimone standing there before her, leaning on his staff, she was utterly astonished.

"Cimone," she said, "what are you going about looking for in these woods here at this hour?"

Cimone, who was known to practically everyone in the area by reason of his good looks and his coarse manners as well as his father's nobility and wealth, said nothing in reply to Efigenia's question. But seeing that her eyes were now open, he proceeded to gaze into them with great intensity, for it seemed to him that there was a sweetness emanating from them that filled him with a pleasure he had never experienced before.

When the young lady noticed how fixedly he was staring at her, she began to worry that his rusticity might move him to do something that could bring dishonor upon her. Consequently, after calling her women, she got to her feet and said: "God keep you, Cimone, farewell."°

"I'm going to come along with you," he replied.

Still afraid of him, the young lady refused his company, but she was unable to get rid of him until he had escorted her all the way back home. From there, he went to his father's house, where he announced that he would on no account ever go back to the country again. Although his father and his family were upset by this, they nevertheless allowed him to stay and waited to see what might have caused him to change his mind.

Now that Cimone's heart, which no amount of schooling had been able to penetrate, had been pierced by Love's arrow through the medium of Efigenia's beauty, he underwent a swift mental development, coming up with one new idea after another that simply astonished his father, his whole family, and everyone else who knew him. First, he asked his father if he could wear the same type of clothing and all the other kinds of ornaments as his brothers, and his father was only too happy to oblige. He then started spending time with worthy young men, observing the manners appropriate to gentlemen, especially gentlemen in love, and to everyone's absolute amazement, in a very short space of time not only did he acquire the rudiments of learning, but he was more than able to hold his own with students of philosophy. The next thing he did—and this, too, was the result of the love he bore for Efigenia—was to transform his coarse, rustic mode of speech into one that was more seemly and civilized, while also becoming an accomplished singer and musician, and he soon distinguished himself in horsemanship and the martial arts, whether on sea or land, by means of his great skill and daring. In brief, without going into all the particulars of his many virtues, it took less than four years from the day he had first fallen in love for him to turn into the most refined, well-mannered, multitalented young man on the island of Cyprus.

What then, charming ladies, shall we say about Cimone? Surely, nothing except that the lofty virtues instilled by Heaven in his valiant spirit had been tied tightly together and locked away by envious Fortune in a tiny little corner of his heart, and that Love, who is by far the mightier of the two, had burst those bonds and torn them asunder. As the awakener of sleeping talents, Love had taken Cimone's virtues out of the cruel darkness in which they lay concealed, and with his power he had forced them into the light, clearly showing from what sort of place he will extract those spirits who are subject to his rule and where he will lead them with his radiant beams.

Although with his passion for Efigenia Cimone went to extremes in some respects, as young men in love often do, nevertheless Aristippo thought of how Love had transformed him from a muttonhead into a man and did not merely bear his extravagances with patience, but encouraged him to pursue Love and all of its pleasures. Cimone, however, who refused to be called Galeso because he remembered how Efigenia had used that name when she spoke to him, was determined to bring his desires to an honorable conclusion and tried on many occasions to persuade Cipseo, Efigenia's father, to allow him to marry her. Every time, however, Cipseo replied that he had promised her to Pasimunda, a young nobleman from Rhodes, and he had no intention of going back on his word.

When the time arrived for Efigenia's arranged marriage to take place, and her husband had sent to fetch her, Cimone said to himself: "O Efigenia, now is the time for me to show you just how much I love you. Because of you I've become a man, and if I can make you mine, then I have no doubt I will achieve a glory greater than that of any god. What's certain is that I'll have you, or else I'll die."

Thus resolved, he quietly went about recruiting a number of young noblemen who were friends of his and had a ship fitted out in secret with everything necessary for a naval battle. He then put out to sea where he lay in wait for the vessel that was supposed to convey Efigenia to her husband in Rhodes.

After Pasimunda's friends had been lavishly entertained by her father and had taken her on board, they aimed their prow in the direction of Rhodes and departed. Ever on the alert, Cimone overtook them the next day, and from up on the bow of his ship, he shouted in a loud voice to the sailors over on Efigenia's: "Strike your sails and heave to, or prepare to be captured and sunk."

Since Cimone's opponents had brought weapons up on deck and were preparing to defend themselves, he followed up his words by seizing a grappling iron, which he threw onto the poop deck of their vessel as it was rapidly pulling away, and thus secured it tightly to the prow of his own. Spurred on by Love, he did not wait for anyone to follow him, but leaped aboard the Rhodians' ship as if he took no account of any opposition they might offer. Then, like a ferocious lion, he fell upon his enemies in an amazing display of force, and sword in hand, struck them down one after the other, slaughtering them like so many sheep. Seeing this, all the Rhodians threw down their weapons, and, practically with one voice, declared themselves his prisoners.

Cimone then addressed them. "Young men," he said, "it was not any desire for plunder, or any hatred I feel toward you, that made me leave Cyprus and subject you to an armed assault here on the high seas. My only motive was to acquire something that I value very highly, and that you can easily, and peacefully, surrender to me. And that something is Efigenia, whom I love more than anything in the world. Since I could not obtain her from her father by friendly and pacific means, Love has compelled me to take her from you as your enemy and by force of arms. And now I intend to be for her what your Pasimunda was to have been. So, give her to me, and may God's grace go with you."

Yielding to force more than acting out of generosity, the young men handed the weeping Efigenia over to Cimone. "Noble lady," he said, seeing her in tears, "don't be upset. I am your own Cimone, and my long love for you has given me a much greater right to have you than anything Pasimunda has because of the pledge that was made to him."

Having watched her taken aboard his ship, Cimone returned to his comrades himself, and without touching anything else that belonged to the Rhodians, he allowed them to depart. The acquisition of so dear a prize made him the happiest man alive, and after spending quite a while consoling his tearful lady, he and his comrades decided not to return to Cyprus for the time being. Instead, they all agreed together that they would turn the prow of their ship in the direction of Crete, where they believed they would be safe with Efigenia, for almost all of them, and especially Cimone, had both long-established and more recent family ties there as well as a large number of friends.

But Fortune is fickle, and although she was quite happy to let Cimone acquire the lady, all of a sudden she transformed the young lover's incalculable joy into sadness and bitter weeping. Scarcely four hours had passed since he had parted company with the Rhodians when, as night approached, from which Cimone was expecting more pleasure than he had ever experienced before, an extremely violent storm arose, filling the sky with clouds and sweeping the sea with furious winds. It was impossible for those on board to see what they were doing or where they were going or even how they could manage to stay on their feet long enough to carry out any of their duties on the ship.

There is no need to ask how much this turn of events upset Cimone. It seemed as if the gods had granted his desire, but only to make him feel all the more distressed at the prospect of his death, which before, without Efigenia, would have mattered very little to him. Although his comrades were equally downcast, the most disconsolate of all was Efigenia, who was weeping violently and shuddering with fear every time they were battered by the waves. Between her tears she bitterly cursed Cimone's love and condemned his rash behavior, proclaiming that the furious storm had arisen because his wish to marry her was contrary to the will of the gods, and that they were determined not merely to prevent him from deriving any joy from his presumptuous desire, but to make him witness her death before coming to a miserable end himself.

The laments went on and on, including some that were even more vehement, until, with the wind growing ever stronger, the sailors not knowing what to do, and no one having the slightest idea of their location and how they should direct their course, they finally arrived off the coast of Rhodes. Failing to recognize the island, they did everything they could possibly do to reach land and thus save their lives.

Fortune favored their efforts and led them into a little bay that the Rhodians who had been released by Cimone had entered with their own vessel just a little while before. Dawn was breaking, and as the sky grew lighter, not only did they realize that they were at the island of Rhodes, but they saw they were no more than a bow shot away from the ship they had parted from the previous day. Distressed beyond measure by this discovery, and fearing the very fate that did in fact befall him, Cimone ordered his crew to make every effort to get out of there and let Fortune carry them wherever she wished, since they could not be in a worse place than the one they were in. Although they strove with might and main to escape, it was all to no avail, for a violent gale was blowing against them with such force that not only did it prevent them from getting out of the little bay, but it drove them relentlessly, against their will, toward the shore.

The moment they reached it, they were recognized by the Rhodian sailors who had by now disembarked from their ship. One of them immediately ran off to find the young noblemen from Rhodes, who had gone earlier to a nearby village, and told them that, as luck would have it, the ship carrying Cimone and Efigenia had, like their own, arrived in the little bay. Overjoyed to hear this news, the young Rhodians assembled a large number of the villagers and were back down at the shore in no time. In the meantime, although Cimone and his men had left their ship and were intent upon fleeing into some neighboring woods, they were all seized, together with Efigenia, and brought back to the village. From there, Cimone and his entire crew were taken by Lisimaco, the chief magistrate of the island for that year, who had come up from the city, and they were led away to prison under the escort of a very large company of men-at-arms, all of which had been arranged by Pasimunda who had gone and lodged a complaint with the Senate of Rhodes as soon as he had heard the news.

And so it came about that the wretched Cimone lost his beloved Efigenia only a little while after winning her, without ever getting anything more than a kiss or two out of her. As for Efigenia, she was welcomed by numerous Rhodian noblewomen who helped her recover from the painful experience of being abducted as well as from the fatigue she had endured during the storm. And with them she remained until the day appointed for her wedding.

Pasimunda did everything in his power to have Cimone and his comrades executed, and although their lives were spared because they had set the young gentlemen from Rhodes free the day before, they were still condemned to life in prison. And there, it is easy to believe, they led a wretched existence, with little hope of ever knowing happiness again.

While Pasimunda was doing all he could to hasten the preparations for his upcoming marriage, Fortune, as if repenting of the sudden blow she had dealt Cimone, came up with a novel way to save him. Pasimunda had a brother named Ormisda, a younger but no less worthy man, who had long sought the hand of a beautiful young noblewoman from the city called Cassandrea, with whom Lisimaco was also very deeply in love. The wedding had been postponed many times, however, thanks to a variety of unexpected events.

Seeing that he was now about to have an extremely lavish banquet in order to celebrate his own wedding, Pasimunda thought it would be an excellent idea to arrange for Ormisda to get married as well on the same occasion, thus allowing him to avoid a repetition of the festivities and all the expenses involved. Consequently, he reopened negotiations with Cassandrea's family and came to an understanding with them, after which all the parties agreed that Ormisda should marry Cassandrea on the same day that Pasimunda married Efigenia.

When Lisimaco heard about this plan, he was desperately unhappy, because he saw himself deprived of the hope he had preserved, namely, that if Ormisda did not marry Cassandrea, he would surely be able to have her himself. He was wise enough, however, to keep his suffering hidden, and began thinking of ways to prevent the wedding, ultimately concluding that the only possible solution was to abduct her. This course of action seemed quite feasible to him because of the office he held, although he would have considered it a far less dishonorable thing to do if he were not the chief magistrate. But finally, after a great deal of deliberation, honor gave way to love, and he resolved that, come what may, he would carry off Cassandrea. Moreover, as he was thinking about the companions he needed to do this and about the strategy he would adopt, he remembered that he had imprisoned Cimone, together with his men, and it occurred to him that for an undertaking like this one, he could not find a better or more loyal confederate.

And so, that night, he had Cimone secretly brought to his chamber and proceeded to speak with him in this fashion:

"Cimone, not only are the gods extraordinarily free and generous in bestowing their gifts on men, but they are also extremely wise when they put men's virtues to the test. And those whom they find to be firm and constant in all circumstances, since they are the most valiant, are considered worthy of receiving the greatest rewards. The gods wanted a surer proof of your mettle than what you could display while confined to the house owned by your father, whom I know to be immensely rich. And so, having first transformed you, as I've been told, from a senseless beast into a man through the bittersweet stimulus of Love, now they wish to see whether, after the harsh misfortune you've suffered and the pain of your present imprisonment, your spirit has been changed from what it was when you were made happy for a brief time with the spoils you'd won. So, if it is indeed what it once was, they are preparing to bestow a boon on you that will make you even happier than anything they gave you before. And I intend to explain what it is in order to help you recover your former strength and regain your courage.

"Pasimunda, who rejoices over your misfortune and has been zealously urging that you be put to death, is doing everything he can to advance the date for the celebration of his marriage to your Efigenia, so that he may enjoy the prize that Fortune was originally happy to grant you and then suddenly snatched away again in anger. If you are as much in love as I think you are, then I know from my own experience just how much pain this would cause you, for his brother Ormisda is preparing to do a similar wrong to me on the very same day by marrying Cassandrea, whom I love more than anything else in the world. Nor do I see how we can prevent Fortune from dealing us such a painful blow except to take the only way she has left open for us, and that is to rely on our stout hearts and our strong right hands, with which we must seize our swords and force open a path to our ladies, so that you may abduct yours for the second time, and I may carry off mine for the first. Consequently, if you value the recovery of—I won't say your freedom, because I believe that would mean little to you without your lady—but the recovery of your lady herself, then the gods have placed her within your grasp, provided you are willing to second me in my enterprise."

These words completely restored any spirits Cimone had lost, and with scarcely a moment's hesitation, he replied: "Lisimaco, if the reward you speak of really does come my way, you cannot have a hardier or more trustworthy comrade than I will be in such an undertaking. Therefore, impose on me whatever task you think I should perform, and you'll marvel at the vigor I'll display in carrying it out."

"Two days from now," Lisimaco replied, "the new brides will go to their husbands' homes for the very first time. As evening is approaching, we'll enter the house ourselves, fully armed, you with your comrades, and I with those of mine whom I trust the most. Then we'll seize the ladies right in the midst of all the guests and carry them off to a ship I've had fitted out in secret, killing anyone who should dare to stand in our way." Cimone liked the plan and remained quietly in prison, waiting for the appointed time.

When the wedding day arrived, it was celebrated with so much pomp and splendor that every corner of the house belonging to the two brothers resounded with their joyous revelry. Having completed all his preparations, Lisimaco delivered a lengthy harangue to Cimone and his comrades, as well as his own friends, in order to fire them up with enthusiasm for his plan. Then, when the time seemed right, he divided the men, all of whom came carrying arms concealed beneath their clothing, into three groups. One of the three he prudently sent to the port so that no one could prevent them from getting on the ship when it was time to leave. Arriving at Pasimunda's house with the other two, he left one group posted at the main entrance to prevent anyone inside from closing it behind them or barring their retreat, and with the rest, including Cimone, he climbed the stairs. In the hall the new brides were already seated at their allotted places with a large number of other ladies and were preparing to dine, when Pasimunda's company arrived and forced their way in. Hurling the tables to the floor, each man seized his lady, handed her over to his comrades, and ordered them to carry the two women off at once to the waiting ship.

The new brides began crying and screaming, as did the other women and the servants, and in an instant the entire place was in an uproar, filled with the sound of their wailing. But Cimone, Lisimaco, and their comrades drew out their swords, and as everyone stood aside to let them pass, they made their way over to the stairs unopposed. They were just in the process of descending, when they were met by Pasimunda, who had been attracted by all the noise and came carrying a large staff in his hand, but Cimone gave him such a vigorous blow on the head that a good half of it was sliced off and he fell dead at Cimone's feet. Rushing up to his brother's assistance, the wretched Ormisda was likewise killed by Cimone with a single blow, while a handful of others who ventured to approach were driven back, wounded, by his followers and by those of Lisimaco.

Leaving the house full of blood and noise, tears and sorrow, they made their way unimpeded to the ship, maintaining a tight formation as they carried their booty along with them. After getting the ladies on board, Cimone, Lisimaco, and their comrades followed, and then, just as the shore was filling up with armed men who were coming to rescue the ladies, they put their oars into the water and cheerfully made their escape.

When they arrived in Crete, they were given an ecstatic welcome by their many friends and relations, and after they had married their ladies and held a grand wedding feast, they happily enjoyed the spoils they had taken.

In Cyprus and Rhodes their deeds gave rise to a great deal of clamor and commotion that continued unabated for quite some time. Finally, however, their friends and relations, interceding for them on the two islands, found a way for Cimone, after a period of exile, to make a joyful return to Cyprus with Efigenia and for Lisimaco, similarly, to go back to Rhodes with Cassandrea. And each of them lived a good long life, happy and contented with his lady in the country of his birth.

Story 2

GOSTANZA IS IN LOVE WITH MARTUCCIO GOMITO, BUT WHEN SHE HEARS THAT HE HAS DIED, IN HER DESPAIR SHE SETS OFF ALONE IN A BOAT, WHICH IS CARRIED BY THE WIND TO SUSA. UPON FINDING HIM ALIVE IN TUNIS, SHE REVEALS HERSELF TO HIM, AND HE, WHO WAS A GREAT FAVORITE OF THE KING'S BECAUSE OF THE ADVICE HE HAD GIVEN HIM, MARRIES HER AND THEN, HAVING BECOME A RICH MAN, RETURNS WITH HER TO LIPARI.°

Seeing that Panfilo's story had come to an end, the Queen gave it high praise, after which she ordered Emilia to follow his lead and tell another one. Emilia thus began:

It is only right for people to rejoice when they see an undertaking obtain rewards appropriate to the emotions that inspired it, and since love deserves to be crowned with happiness in the long run, rather than with misery, it gives me much greater pleasure to obey the Queen and speak on the present topic than it did yesterday when I obeyed the King and spoke on the one he chose.

You must know then, gentle ladies, that there is a little island near Sicily called Lipari, where, not so very long ago, there lived a very beautiful girl named Gostanza who was born into one of its noblest families. There was also a young man living on that island, a certain Martuccio Gomito, who was a skilled craftsman as well as being both well mannered and exceptionally handsome.° Now, Martuccio fell in love with Gostanza, and she likewise burned for him, so much so that she felt miserable whenever he was out of her sight. Wishing to make her his wife, Martuccio asked her father for her hand, but was told he was too poor to have her.

Indignant at seeing his offer rejected on the grounds of his poverty, Martuccio fitted out a little ship with certain friends and relations of his, and swore never to return to Lipari until he was rich. After leaving the island, he proceeded to become a pirate and sailed up and down the Barbary coast, robbing anyone whose forces were weaker than his own. In this endeavor Fortune was quite favorably disposed to him, had he only known how to place some sort of limit on his successes. Not satisfied, however, with having grown extremely wealthy in just a short time, Martuccio and his companions went on seeking to become even wealthier, when they chanced to run into a Saracen fleet, by which, after a lengthy defense, they were captured and plundered. The vast majority of the crew were then thrown into the sea, their ship sunk, and Martuccio himself taken to Tunis where he was held in prison for a long time under miserable conditions.

The news was brought back to Lipari, not just by one or two, but by many different people, that every last man on board the little ship with Martuccio had drowned. Upon hearing that her beloved and his companions were dead, Gostanza, whose grief over his departure had known no bounds, wept and wept, until she finally resolved to take her own life. Since she did not have the courage to lay violent hands on herself, she came up with a novel but seemingly infallible way to procure the death she desired. Slipping secretly out of her father's house one night, she went down to the port, where by chance she found a little fishing boat lying some distance away from the other ships. The owners had just gone ashore, and Gostanza discovered that the boat was still equipped with its mast as well as its sails and oars. Since she had some knowledge of the rudiments of seamanship, as all the women living on the island generally do, she quickly climbed on board, rowed a little way out to sea, and raised the sail, after which she threw the oars and the rudder overboard, abandoning herself to the mercy of the wind. She was convinced that one of two things was bound to happen: either the boat, having neither ballast nor steersman, would capsize because of the wind, or it would be driven onto the rocks somewhere and smashed to pieces. And in both cases she would necessarily wind up drowning, for she would not be able to save herself even if she wanted to. Then, having wrapped a cloak around her head, she lay down, weeping, in the bottom of the boat.

Everything turned out differently, however, than she had imagined. For the wind blew so gently from the north that there was hardly a wave, the boat maintained an even keel, and the next day around vespers it brought her ashore near a city called Susa, a good hundred miles beyond Tunis.° The girl was not aware that she was now more on land than at sea, for nothing had occurred to make her raise her head from the position in which it was lying, nor did she have any intention of doing so, no matter what happened.

By chance, when the boat ran aground on the shore, there was a poor woman down by the seaside gathering up the nets that had been left in the sun by the fishermen she worked for. Seeing the boat, she wondered how anyone could have allowed it to run up onto the beach under full sail, and thinking that some fishermen were sleeping on board, she went over to it and discovered that the only person there was this young lady, fast asleep. By calling to her repeatedly, she finally got her to wake up, and since she could see from her clothing that the girl was a Christian, she asked her in Italian how she had managed to get there, and in that boat, all by herself. When the girl heard the woman speaking her language, she wondered whether a shift in the wind had taken her back to Lipari. She got to her feet at once and looked all around her, and seeing that she was on land, but in unfamiliar territory, she asked the good woman where she was.

"My daughter," the woman replied, "you're in Barbary, not far from Susa."

When she heard these words, the girl, dismayed that God had refused to allow her to die, began to fear for her honor, but since she had no idea what to do, she simply sat down by the keel of her boat and began to cry. Upon seeing this, the good woman took pity on her and got her, after a great deal of begging and pleading, to accompany her to her little hut where she coaxed her into explaining how she had come to be there. Realizing that the girl had to be hungry, the woman set some dry bread, water, and a few fish before her, and eventually persuaded her to eat a little.

Gostanza then asked her who she was and how she spoke Italian like that, to which the woman replied that she came from Trapani, her name was Carapresa, and she worked for certain fishermen who were Christians.° Although the girl was generally feeling very sad, when she heard the woman say "Carapresa," she took it, without knowing why, as a good omen. Indeed, for reasons she could not comprehend she began to feel hopeful and was no longer quite so intent on dying. Without revealing who she was or where she had come from, she earnestly begged the good woman to have pity on her youth for the love of God and to advise her as to what she could do in order to protect her honor.

Responding to the girl's request like the good woman she was, Carapresa left her in the hut while she quickly gathered up her nets, but the moment she returned, she wrapped the girl up in her own cloak from top to bottom, and then took her with her to Susa. When they arrived in the city, she said: "Gostanza, I'm going to take you to the home of a very nice, elderly Saracen lady, who frequently employs me to do various chores for her. She's an extremely compassionate person, and since I'm going to recommend you to her as warmly as I can, I feel quite certain that she'll be glad to take you in and treat you like a daughter. For your part, while you stay with her, you must serve her to the best of your ability so as to win and retain her favor until such time as God sends you better luck."

Carapresa was as good as her word, and when the lady, who was indeed well on in years, had heard Gostanza's story, she looked the girl in the face and started weeping. Then, taking her by the hand, she kissed her on the forehead and led her into her house, where she lived with several other women, no men being allowed to reside on the premises. The women did various types of work with their hands, producing articles of all kinds from silk and palm leaves and leather, and within a few days, having learned how to make some of those things herself, the girl began working right there alongside them. It was marvelous to see with what kindness and affection the lady and the other women treated her, and thanks to their instruction, in a relatively short space of time, Gostanza also managed to learn their language.

Now, while the girl was living in Susa, having long since been mourned by her family, who considered her dead and gone forever, it just so happened that the King of Tunis, whose name was Meriabdela, was threatened by a young man of considerable power, the scion of an important family in Granada.° Having decided that the Kingdom of Tunis belonged to him, he had assembled a vast army and was marching on the King, intent upon driving him from his realm.

News of this development reached the ears of Martuccio Gomito where he lay in prison, and since he knew the language of Barbary quite well, when he heard that the King of Tunis was making enormous efforts to prepare his defenses, he spoke to one of the men who were guarding him and his companions. "If I might speak with the King," he said, "I feel confident I can give him the advice he needs to win this war of his."

The guard repeated these words to his superior, who immediately relayed them to the King. In response, the King ordered them to bring Martuccio to him and asked him what his advice might be.

"My lord," he replied, "I used to visit this country of yours in the past, and if I've correctly observed the tactics you employ in your battles, it seems to me that you rely on your archers more than anything else to do the fighting. Consequently, if you can find a way to deprive your adversaries of arrows, while your own troops have more than enough, I know you'd win the battle."

"If this could be done," said the King, "I have no doubt but that I'd be victorious."

"My lord," replied Martuccio, "if you so desire, it certainly can be done. Listen, and I'll tell you how. You must equip your archers' bows with much finer strings than those that are normally used, and then have arrows made with notches that will only fit these finer strings. All of this must be done in secrecy so that your enemy doesn't get wind of your plan, because otherwise, he'll find a way to get around it. Now, here's the reason why I'm making this recommendation. As you know, when your enemy's archers have used up all their arrows, and ours have shot theirs, for the battle to continue, they'll have to collect all the arrows your troops have shot, just as ours will have to collect theirs. But the enemy won't be able to use what your men shot at them because their bowstrings will be too thick to fit into the narrow notches of your arrows, whereas just the opposite will happen for us, since our fine strings will easily fit into the wide notches of theirs. Thus, your troops will have a plentiful supply of arrows, and the others won't have any."

A wise ruler, the King approved of Martuccio's plan, and by following it to the letter, he managed to win his war. As a result, Martuccio became one of the King's greatest favorites, and consequently acquired wealth and a position of considerable importance.

News of these events spread throughout the country, and when it reached Gostanza's ears that Martuccio Gomito, whom she had long believed dead, was actually alive, the love she felt for him, which had cooled off in her heart, instantly flared up again, burning with a hotter flame than ever and bringing all her dead hopes back to life. She therefore gave the good woman with whom she was staying a full account of all the events she had been through, and then told her that she wanted to go to Tunis so that she might feast her eyes with looking on that which she longed to see because of the report she had heard with her own ears. The lady approved her request with enthusiasm, and acting as if she were Gostanza's mother, embarked with her for Tunis, where the two of them were honorably received in the home of one of the lady's relatives. She then sent Carapresa, who had accompanied them there, to find out what she could about Martuccio. When she reported back that he was alive and occupied a high place in the kingdom, the gentlewoman decided that she would be the one to have the pleasure of telling Martuccio about the arrival of his Gostanza. And so, one day she went around to where he was living and said to him: "Martuccio, a servant of yours from Lipari has turned up in my house and would like to speak with you there in private. And since he didn't want me to entrust this to anyone else, I've come here to tell you about it myself." Martuccio thanked her and followed her back to her house.

When the girl saw him, she almost died of happiness. Overcome by her emotions, she ran right up to him, flung her arms about his neck, and embraced him. Then, incapable of uttering a word, she gently began to weep, both because of her sorrowful memories of the misfortunes she had been through and because of all the joy she felt in the present moment.

When Martuccio recognized who it was, for a while he was struck dumb with amazement and did not make a move. But at last he heaved a sigh and said, "O Gostanza, are you really alive? I was told a good long time ago that you had vanished, and since then, no one at home has heard anything about you." Then, having managed to say this much, he, too, shed gentle tears as he held her in his arms and kissed her.

Gostanza told him about everything that had happened to her and about the honorable treatment she had received from the gentlewoman with whom she had been staying. Martuccio spent a long time talking with her, after which he went to the King, his master, and gave him a full account both of his own ups and downs and of those the girl had endured, adding that he intended, with the King's permission, to marry her in accordance with the laws of our religion.

Truly amazed by what he heard, the King summoned the girl, and when he discovered that everything was exactly the way Martuccio had described it, he said to her, "Well, then, you've certainly earned the right to have him as your husband." The King proceeded to send for the most opulent and noble of gifts, some of which he bestowed on her, and some on Martuccio. He then gave the couple permission to arrange their affairs between them in whatever way they pleased.

After lavishly entertaining the gentlewoman with whom Gostanza had been staying, not only did Martuccio thank her for what she had done to assist the girl, but he gave her presents suitable for a person of her station. Then, while Gostanza shed many a tear, he said good-bye to the lady and departed. Finally, with the King's leave, the couple embarked on a small boat, taking Carapresa with them, and thanks to a favorable breeze, they quickly returned to Lipari, where the rejoicing was so great that no words could ever describe it.

There, Martuccio and Gostanza were married and celebrated their nuptials with great pomp and splendor, after which, for many a day, the two of them enjoyed the love they bore one another in peace and tranquility.

Story 3

FLEEING WITH AGNOLELLA, PIETRO BOCCAMAZZA RUNS INTO A GANG OF THIEVES, AND WHILE THE GIRL ESCAPES THROUGH A FOREST AND IS LED TO A CASTLE, PIETRO IS CAPTURED BY THEM. HE MANAGES TO GET OUT OF THEIR CLUTCHES, HOWEVER, AND AFTER ONE OR TWO MORE ADVENTURES, HE HAPPENS UPON THE CASTLE WHERE AGNOLELLA IS STAYING, GETS MARRIED TO HER, AND RETURNS WITH HER TO ROME.°

There was no one in the company who did not praise Emilia's story, and when the Queen saw that it was finished, she turned to Elissa and told her to continue. Eager to obey, Elissa began:

The tale that presents itself to me, charming ladies, concerns a terrible night spent by two somewhat indiscreet young people, but since it was succeeded by many days of happiness, it fits our topic, and I should like to tell you about it.

Not long ago, in Rome—once the head of the world, but now its tail—there lived a young man named Pietro Boccamazza, a member of an illustrious Roman family, who fell in love with a very beautiful, charming girl named Agnolella, the daughter of a certain Gigliuozzo Saullo, who, though a plebeian, was held in high repute by his fellow citizens.° Having fallen for the girl, Pietro was so skillful in courting her that she soon came to love him as much as he did her. Spurred on by his burning passion, and no longer willing to endure the harsh pain of his desire for her, he asked for her hand in marriage. But when his relations found out about it, they all came to him and gave him a good scolding for what he wanted to do, at the same time letting Gigliuozzo Saullo know that he should on no account take what Pietro said seriously, because if he did, they would never acknowledge him as a friend or a kinsman.

When Pietro saw that the only way he could think of to obtain what he desired was blocked, he was ready to die of grief. If he could have just obtained Gigliuozzo's consent, he would have married the girl, even if it displeased every last one of his relations. But in any case, he made up his mind that he would do whatever was necessary to achieve his goal, provided the girl was willing, and when he learned through a third party that she was, he got her to agree to elope from Rome with him.

Having made all the preparations, Pietro arose very early one morning, saddled up a pair of horses, and the two of them took off down the road toward Anagni, where Pietro had certain friends of his whom he trusted implicitly.° Since they were afraid of being pursued, they had no time to stop and get married, so they simply talked together about their love for one another, exchanging the occasional kiss as they went riding along.

Now, Pietro did not know the route very well, and when they were about eight miles away from Rome, they happened to take a road that went off to the left when they should have gone to the right. They had only ridden a little more than two miles when they saw a small castle from which, the moment they were sighted, about a dozen soldiers sallied forth. Just as they were about to intercept the couple, the girl spotted them and yelled, "Pietro, let's get out of here, we're being attacked!" To the best of her ability, she turned her nag's head in the direction of a vast forest nearby, grabbed onto the saddle horn, and dug her spurs into his flanks. When the animal felt her jabbing him, he took off at a gallop and carried her into the woods.

Pietro, who had been riding along looking at Agnolella's face more than the road, was not as quick as she had been to notice the approaching soldiers, and so, he was still looking around to see where they were coming from and was unable to locate them, when he was overtaken, captured, and forced to get down off his horse. They asked him who he was, and as soon as he told them, they began conferring among themselves.

"This guy's one of the friends of the Orsini," they said. "What better way to spite our enemies than to take his clothes and this nag of his, and to string him up on one of these oaks?"°

They all agreed on this plan and ordered Pietro to take his clothes off. Well aware of what was in store for him, he began undressing, when all of a sudden, a good twenty-five soldiers, who had been waiting in ambush, fell upon them with shouts of "Kill them! Kill them!" Taken by surprise, Pietro's captors abandoned him and turned to defend themselves, but seeing that they were greatly outnumbered, they took to their heels, with their attackers in hot pursuit. When Pietro saw this, he quickly picked up his things, jumped on his horse, and fled as fast as he could down the road he had seen the girl taking.

Upon reaching the woods, however, and finding no sign there of a road or a path, or even a horse's hoofprints, let alone the girl, Pietro was the saddest man alive, and as soon as he thought he was safely beyond the reach of his captors and their assailants, he began weeping. He continued to wander through the woods, calling her name here, there, and everywhere, but no one answered him, and since he did not dare to turn back, he rode on without having the slightest idea of where he was going. What is more, he was afraid, both for his own sake and for that of his beloved, of the wild animals that generally lurk in the forest, and at every moment he imagined some bear or wolf seizing her and ripping open her throat.

Thus the unfortunate Pietro spent the entire day meandering through the forest, shouting and calling her name, sometimes going backward just when he thought he was going forward, until at last, what with his yelling and his weeping and his fear and his lack of food, he was so exhausted that he could go no farther. Seeing that night had fallen, and not knowing what else to do, he found a large oak, got off his nag, and tied him to the tree. Then he climbed up into the branches to avoid being devoured by wild animals during the night. Afraid of falling, Pietro did not dare to let himself go to sleep, although that would have been impossible in any case because of all his grief and anxiety about Agnolella. And so, after the moon rose a little later in the cloudless sky, he remained awake, sighing and weeping and cursing his misfortune.

Meanwhile, the girl, who, as we said before, had fled with no idea where she was going, simply allowed her horse to carry her wherever he wanted until she had gone so far into the forest that she could no longer see the spot where she had entered it. Thus, she spent the entire day just as Pietro had done, wandering round and round that wilderness, now pausing and now moving on, weeping and calling his name and bemoaning her misfortune. Finally, as evening was falling and Pietro had still not come, she stumbled upon a little path that her horse turned into and began to follow, until after riding more than two miles, she caught sight of a cottage up ahead of her in the distance. She made her way to it as quickly as she could, and there she found a good man, well along in years, with a wife no younger than he was.

When they saw she was by herself, they said: "Oh, child, where are you going in these parts, all alone, at this hour?" Weeping, the girl replied that she had lost her escort in the woods, and asked them how far it was to Anagni.

"My child," said the good man, "this isn't the road to Anagni. It's more than twelve miles away from here."

"Then how far is it to the nearest house where I could find lodging?" asked the girl.

"There's nothing around here that's close enough for you to reach before nightfall," he answered.

"Since I have nowhere else to go," said the girl, "would you, for the love of God, be so kind as to let me stay here tonight?"

"Young lady," replied the good man, "we would be delighted to have you stay the night with us, but all the same, we must warn you that these parts are overrun by gangs of bandits, some of whom are allied to one another, while others are mortal foes, and all of them go about day and night doing us injuries and causing a great deal of damage. If we were unlucky enough to have one of those gangs come here while you're staying with us, and they were to see how young and beautiful you are, they might harm you and dishonor you, and there'd be no way for us to help you. We wanted to tell you this so that if something like that should happen, you wouldn't blame us for it."

The old man's words terrified her, but seeing how late the hour was, Agnolella said: "God willing, He will protect all of us from such harm, but even if such a thing should happen to me, it's much better to be mistreated by men than torn to pieces by wild beasts in the forest."

Having said this, she got off her horse and went into the poor man's house. There she supped with them on what little food they had, after which, fully clothed, she threw herself down on their little bed where she lay with them, sighing and weeping all night long over both her own misfortunes and Pietro's, to whom she could only suppose that the very worst must have happened.

Just a little before matins, she heard a loud sound of people walking around, which led her to get up and make her way into a large yard at the rear of the cottage. On one of its sides, she spied a big pile of hay and went over to hide in it, thinking that if those people were to come in, this would make it more difficult for them to find her. Scarcely had she finished concealing herself than the men, a large gang of bandits, were at the door of the cottage. After forcing the old people to open it, they came inside, where they discovered the girl's horse still fully saddled and demanded to know who was there.

Seeing no sign of the girl, the good man answered: "There's nobody here except us. But this nag, which must have run away from somebody, showed up here yesterday evening, and we brought him into the house to keep the wolves from devouring him."

"In that case, since he doesn't belong to anyone else," said the leader of the gang, "he'll do quite well for us."

Then the men spread out all over the cottage, some of them finding their way into the yard, where they put down their lances and wooden shields. One of them, having nothing better to do, happened to toss his lance into the hay where it came within an inch of killing the girl who was hiding there and who almost gave herself away when the head of the lance went right by her left breast, so close to her body that it tore her clothing. Fearing that she had been wounded, she was at the point of screaming out loud, when she remembered where she was, and getting a grip on herself, she kept quiet.

The gang cooked kid as well as some other meat they had with them, and after having eaten and had something to drink, they took the girl's horse with them and went about their business, some going one way, some another. Once they were fairly far away, the first thing the good man did was to ask his wife: "Whatever happened to that young lady of ours who showed up here yesterday evening? I haven't seen her since we got out of bed." The good woman replied that she did not know and went off to look for her.

When the girl realized that the gang had gone, she climbed out from under the hay. The old man was greatly relieved to see that she had not fallen into their hands, and since it was then getting light, he said to her: "Now that day is breaking, we'll accompany you, if you like, to a castle just five miles from here where you'll be safe. But you're going to have to go there on foot, because that gang of bandits who just left here took your horse with them." Resigning herself to the loss, the girl asked them in God's name to lead her to the castle, for which they set out at once, reaching it halfway between prime and tierce.

The castle belonged to a member of the Orsini family named Liello di Campo di Fiore, whose wife, a very good and pious woman, just happened to be staying there at the time.° On seeing Agnolella, she recognized the girl right away and gave her a hearty welcome, after which she insisted on knowing precisely how she came to be there. In response, the girl told her the entire story. The lady, who also knew Pietro because he was a friend of her husband's, was distressed to learn what had happened, and when she was told where Pietro had been captured, she was convinced he must have been killed. So she said to the girl: "Since you don't know what's happened to Pietro, you must stay here with me until such time as it's possible for me to send you safely back to Rome."

Meanwhile, Pietro had been sitting in the oak tree, as sad as sad could be, and at just about the time he would normally have fallen asleep, he saw a good twenty wolves approaching. When they caught sight of the horse, they came up on him from all sides, but he heard them coming, and yanking his neck, he snapped his reins and made an attempt to flee. Since they had him surrounded, he could not get away, and although he defended himself for quite some time with his teeth and hooves, they finally brought him down, ripped out his throat, and quickly gutted him. Then, they all gorged themselves on him until they had picked him clean, after which they took off, leaving nothing but his bones behind. Pietro was utterly dismayed by what he saw, for to him the horse had been a companion and a prop in his troubles, and now he began to think that he would never succeed in getting out of the woods.

He continued to keep a lookout in every direction, however, and a little before dawn, when he was dying from the cold up there in the oak, he caught sight of a huge fire perhaps a mile from where he was sitting. Consequently, as soon as it was completely light out, he climbed down from the tree, even though he felt pretty apprehensive as he did so, and set off in that direction. When he reached the spot, he saw a band of shepherds who were sitting around the fire, eating and making merry. The shepherds took pity on him and invited him to join them.

Once Pietro had eaten and warmed himself, he gave them an account of his misadventures and how he had come there all by himself, after which he asked them if there was a village or a castle in those parts to which he might go. The shepherds said that about three miles away there was a castle belonging to Liello di Campo di Fiore whose wife was staying there at present. Overjoyed, Pietro asked if any of the shepherds would accompany him to the castle, and two of them did so with a ready will.

When Pietro reached the castle, he ran into a few people he knew, and as he was trying to make arrangements with them to go out and search for the girl in the forest, he was told that Liello's wife wanted to see him. He went to her at once, and on finding that she had Agnolella with her, there has never been a man whose happiness was equal to his. He longed to take her in his arms, but he refrained because he felt too embarrassed to do so in the presence of the lady. And if he was ecstatic, the girl was no less delighted to see him.

The noble lady gave him a warm welcome and took him in, although after listening to what had happened to him, she rebuked him sternly for seeking to defy the wishes of his family. But when she saw that he was determined to do so anyway, and that it was what the girl wanted, too, she said to herself: "Why should I give myself all this trouble? The two of them are in love, they understand one another, they're both friends of my husband, and their intentions are honorable. Besides, I believe that what they want must be pleasing to God, seeing as how the one of them was saved from a hanging, the other from being killed by a lance, and both of them from being devoured by wild beasts. So, let them do as they wish." Then, turning to the couple, she said: "If it's still your desire to be joined together as husband and wife, well, so be it. I'm in favor of it, too, and in fact, we can celebrate your wedding right here at Liello's expense. After that, you can safely leave everything to me, and I'll make peace between you and your families."

The jubilant Pietro and his Agnolella, who was even happier, got married then and there, and the noble lady gave them the most honorable wedding one could have in the mountains. And that is where they tasted the incomparable sweetness of the first fruits of their love.

Several days later, accompanied by a substantial escort, they and the lady set off on horseback and returned to Rome. Although she found that Pietro's relatives were very angry with him for what he had done, she managed to restore him to their good graces. And after that he lived with his Agnolella to a ripe old age in perfect peace and pleasure.

Story 4

RICCIARDO MANARDI IS DISCOVERED BY MESSER LIZIO DA VALBONA WITH HIS DAUGHTER, WHOM RICCIARDO MARRIES, THUS REMAINING ON GOOD TERMS WITH HER FATHER.°

Having fallen silent, Elissa listened as her companions praised her tale, after which the Queen ordered Filostrato to tell a story, who laughed and began as follows:

I have been scolded so often, and by so many of you, because I imposed the topic of sad stories on you and made you weep, that I feel myself obliged to make amends to some extent for the sorrow you experienced by telling you a tale that will make you laugh a little. Consequently, I am going to recount a very short love story in which the only unpleasant things are the lovers' sighs and their brief experience of fear and shame before the tale proceeds directly to its happy ending.

Not so very long ago, worthy ladies, there was a quite reputable, well-bred knight living in Romagna who was called Messer Lizio da Valbona.° When he was at the threshold of old age, it was his good fortune that his wife, named Madonna Giacomina, gave birth to a daughter who, as she grew up, turned out to be more beautiful and charming than any other girl in those parts. And since she was the only daughter left to her father and mother, not only did they love and cherish her very dearly, but they took extraordinary care in guarding her, for they hoped to be able to arrange a great match for her.

Now, there was a handsome, lively young man named Ricciardo, from the Manardi da Brettinoro family, who used to frequent Messer Lizio's house and spend a great deal of time in his company, and neither Messer Lizio nor his wife kept watch on Ricciardo any more than they would have if he had been one of their own sons. On more than one occasion, Ricciardo noticed the girl, who he knew was of marriageable age, and as he observed how beautiful and graceful she was, and how admirable her manners and comportment, he fell passionately in love with her. Although he took the greatest care to keep his love hidden, the girl perceived it, and making no effort to ward off the emotion, she fell for him as well, to Ricciardo's great delight.

Ricciardo had often wanted to say something about his feelings to her, but he remained silent out of fear, until one day, summoning up the courage, he seized the opportunity to speak. "Caterina," he said, "I implore you, don't let me die of love."

"May God grant that you don't let me die of it first!" she promptly replied.

This response only served to increase Ricciardo's love and desire, and he said to her: "There's nothing I wouldn't undertake to do if it would give you pleasure, but it's up to you to find a way to save both your life and mine."

"Ricciardo," the girl replied, "you see how closely I'm being watched, so closely that I can't really imagine any way for you to come to me. But if you can think up something I can do without exposing myself to shame, tell me, and I'll do it."

After considering a number of options, all of a sudden Ricciardo declared: "My sweet Caterina, I don't know of anything better except for you to go and sleep on the balcony that overlooks your father's garden, or at least to find some means to get out onto it. For although it's very high up, if I knew you were going to be spending the night there, I would certainly find a way to reach you."

"If you have the courage for such a climb," replied Caterina, "I'm sure I can arrange things so that I can get to sleep there."

Ricciardo swore he would do it, after which they gave one another a quick kiss on the sly and parted.

It was already close to the end of May, and the next day, the girl began complaining to her mother about how she had not been able to sleep the night before because of the stifling heat.

"Daughter of mine," said her mother, "what's this heat you're talking about? It wasn't hot at all."

"Mother of mine," replied Caterina, "you should say 'in my opinion,' and then you might be speaking the truth. But you should remember how much hotter girls are than older women."°

"My child," the lady answered, "that's certainly true. But I can't make it hot or cold at my whim, as you might want me to do. You just have to take whatever weather comes with the seasons. Maybe it'll be cooler tonight, and you'll sleep better."

"Now, God grant that may be the case," said Caterina, "but it's not normal for the nights to get cooler as summer approaches."

"Well," said the lady, "what do you want us to do about it?"

"If you and my father wouldn't object," replied Caterina, "I'd like to have a little cot made up out on the balcony that is next to his room and overlooks his garden, and I'll go to sleep there. I'll certainly be better off in that nice cool place, listening to the song of the nightingale, than I would be in your bedroom."

"Cheer up, my child," said her mother. "I'll speak to your father, and we'll do whatever he decides."

Perhaps because Messer Lizio, as an old man, was inclined to be somewhat surly, he listened to what his wife had to say and then remarked: "What's this nightingale she wants to listen to when she goes to sleep? I'll make her go to sleep listening to the song of the cicadas."

When Caterina found out what he had said, not only did she not go to sleep the following night, but acting more out of spite than because of the heat, she kept complaining about how hot it was, thus preventing her mother from sleeping as well. In response to her daughter's complaints, the next morning her mother went to Messer Lizio and said:

"Sir, you can't be very fond of this young daughter of yours. What difference does it make to you if she sleeps out on the balcony? All night long she didn't get any rest because of the heat. And besides, why are you surprised that she should take pleasure in hearing the nightingale sing? She's just a little girl, and young people like things that are just like them."

"All right, then," replied Messer Lizio, after he had heard her out. "Have whatever kind of bed you want set up for her out there, and have them hang a light curtain around it. She can sleep there and listen to the song of the nightingale to her heart's content."

Once the girl heard what her father's decision was, she promptly had a bed made up for herself on the balcony, and since she was planning to sleep there that night, she waited until she saw Ricciardo, at which point she gave him the signal they had arranged between themselves to let him know what he had to do.

As soon as Messer Lizio heard his daughter getting into bed, he locked the door that led from his bedroom to the balcony, and then he, too, retired for the night.

When Ricciardo saw that all was quiet, he got up onto a wall with the aid of a ladder, from which, with great difficulty and always in danger of falling, he climbed up another wall by holding on to certain stones that jutted out from it. Finally, he reached the balcony where he was received by the girl in silence, but with the greatest joy imaginable. After a multitude of kisses, the two of them lay down together, and for virtually the entire night, they took their pleasure of one another, delightedly making the nightingale sing over and over again.

The nights were so short at that time of year, and their enjoyment of one another lasted such a long time, that it was almost daybreak before they fell asleep, completely unaware of what time it was. They did not have a stitch of clothing on, for they had gotten heated up both by the weather and by all the fun they had been having together, and as she slept, Caterina cradled Ricciardo's neck in her right arm, while with her left hand she held him by that thing which you ladies are too embarrassed to name when you are in the presence of men.

They went on sleeping in that position and did not wake even after dawn arrived. Messer Lizio, however, did get up, and when he recalled that his daughter was sleeping out on the balcony, he quietly opened the door, saying to himself as he did so: "Let's just see how the nightingale helped Caterina sleep last night." He walked over to the bed, and when he lifted up the curtain that surrounded it, he saw his daughter and Ricciardo, naked and uncovered, fast asleep there, embracing one another in the way that has just been described. Having clearly recognized Ricciardo, he left them there and went to his wife's bedroom, where he called her and said: "Quick, woman, get up. Come see how fond your daughter is of the nightingale, for she's captured it, and she's holding it in her hand."

"How is that possible?" the lady replied.

"You'll see," said Messer Lizio, "if you come quickly."

The lady got dressed in a hurry and quietly followed Messer Lizio until they reached the bed. When the curtain was raised, she saw plainly enough how her daughter had captured and was still holding on to the nightingale whose song she had so wanted to hear.

Feeling herself terribly deceived by Ricciardo, Madonna Giacomina wanted to shout insults at him, but Messer Lizio said to her: "Woman, if you value my love, don't make a sound, because now that she's caught him, he's going to be hers for keeps. Ricciardo is young and rich and noble, so a match with him can only be to our advantage. If he wants to part with me on good terms, he's going to have to marry her first, and this way he'll discover that he's put the nightingale into his own cage, not into somebody else's."

The lady was reassured to see that her husband was not upset about what had happened, and when she considered that her daughter had had a good night, was now well rested, and had caught the nightingale, Madonna Giacomina held her peace.

They did not have to wait long after this exchange before Ricciardo woke up. As soon as he saw that it was broad daylight, he thought he was as good as dead, and calling to Caterina, he said, "Oh, my darling, day has come and caught me here. What are we going to do?"

At these words, Messer Lizio approached the bed, raised the curtain, and replied: "We are going to do just fine."

When Ricciardo saw him, he felt as though his heart had been ripped out of his body, and sitting up straight in bed, he said: "My lord, I beg you, in God's name, have mercy on me. I know that I deserve to die because of my wickedness and disloyalty, so you should do whatever you want with me. And yet, I implore you to spare my life, if it's possible. Please don't let me die."

"Ricciardo," said Messer Lizio, "this deed was not worthy of the love I bore you and the trust I placed in you. But what's done is done, and since it's your youth that moved you to commit such a fault, there's a way for you to save yourself from death, and me from dishonor: you must take Caterina as your lawful wedded wife. That way, for the rest of her life she'll be yours just as she has been yours tonight, and as a result, you'll be able to secure both my pardon and your own safety. But if you don't agree to do this, then you'd better commend your soul to God."

While the two men were speaking, Caterina let go of the nightingale, and after covering herself up, she burst into tears and begged her father to forgive Ricciardo, at the same time beseeching her lover to do as Messer Lizio wished so that the two of them could spend many more nights like this one together in perfect safety.

All this pleading was not really necessary, however, for Ricciardo readily agreed, without so much as a moment's hesitation, to accept Messer Lizio's proposal, being moved to do so not just by his shame over his misdeed and his desire to make amends for it, but also by his fear of death and his desire to escape with his life, to say nothing of the ardent love he felt and his yearning to possess the object of his affections.

Consequently, Messer Lizio borrowed one of Madonna Giacomina's rings, and Ricciardo did not budge from the bed, but took Caterina as his wife right there and then in the presence of her parents. With the marriage thus sealed, Messer Lizio and his wife left the young couple, saying as they went: "You should get some rest now, for you probably need that more than you need to get up."

As soon as they were gone, the two young people embraced one another again, and since they had traveled only six miles that night, they went two more before they finally got out of bed—which is how they brought their first day together to a close.

Once they were up, Ricciardo discussed things in greater detail with Messer Lizio, and a few days later, as was proper, he went through the full ceremony of marrying the girl again in the presence of all their friends and relations. Then, with great pomp, he brought her to his house where their nuptials were celebrated in splendor and dignity. And for many years after that he lived with her in peace and happiness, catching nightingales both day and night to his heart's content.°

Story 8

IN LOVE WITH A LADY FROM THE TRAVERSARI FAMILY,
NASTAGIO DEGLI ONESTI SPENDS ALL HIS WEALTH WITHOUT
OBTAINING HER LOVE IN RETURN. AT THE URGING OF HIS
FRIENDS AND FAMILY, HE GOES AWAY TO CHIASSI WHERE
HE SEES A YOUNG WOMAN BEING HUNTED DOWN AND
KILLED BY A KNIGHT AND DEVOURED BY TWO DOGS.
NASTAGIO THEN INVITES HIS RELATIONS AS WELL AS HIS
BELOVED TO A BANQUET WHERE SHE SEES THAT SAME
YOUNG WOMAN BEING TORN APART AND, FEARING A
SIMILAR FATE, ACCEPTS NASTAGIO AS HER HUSBAND.°

* * *

Amiable ladies, just as we are commended for our pity, so our cruelty is also punished rigorously by divine justice. In order to prove this to you and to give you a reason for ridding yourselves of every last trace of cruelty, I would like to tell you a story that is no less moving than delightful.

In Ravenna, a very ancient city in Romagna, there once lived a great many noblemen and gentlemen, among whom was a youth named Nastagio degli Onesti who had been left rich beyond all measure by the deaths of his father and one of his uncles.° He was as yet unmarried, and as often happens to young men, he fell in love with one of the daughters of Messer Paolo Traversari, a young lady much more noble than he was, whom he hoped to persuade to love him by virtue of his accomplishments. But no matter how magnificent, splendid, and commendable his deeds, not only did they not help him, but they actually seemed harmful, so cruel and hard and unyielding did the girl he loved show herself to him. In fact, perhaps because of either her singular beauty or her noble rank, she became so haughty and disdainful that she took a dislike both to him and to everything he cared for. This was so hard for Nastagio to bear that at times, after having wallowed in grief, he would be filled with despair and be seized by a desire to kill himself. Nevertheless, he repressed this urge and instead frequently resolved to give her up altogether or, if he could manage it, to hate her the way she hated him. But he made such resolutions in vain, for it seemed that the more his hope dwindled, the more his love increased.

The young man persisted in both loving and spending lavishly, until it seemed to certain of his friends and relations that he was in danger of exhausting both himself and his fortune. Consequently, they offered him their counsel over and over again, imploring him to leave Ravenna and to go and stay somewhere else for a while, in the expectation that if he did so, both his love and his expenditures would decrease. Nastagio repeatedly rejected their advice with scorn, but he was solicited so earnestly that, finally, he could no longer say no to them and agreed to do as they suggested. After having had enormous preparations made, as if he were intending to go to France or Spain or some other far-away land, he mounted his horse and left the city, accompanied by many of his friends. Having arrived at a place some three miles outside of Ravenna called Chiassi, he sent for his tents and pavilions, and informed those who had accompanied him that he intended to stay there and that they were free to return to the city.

Once he had set up his camp, he began living in as elegant and magnificent a style as any man ever did, inviting different groups of friends to come and have dinner or supper with him, as he had been accustomed to doing.

Now it happened that one Friday near the beginning of May, when the weather was very fine, Nastagio fell to brooding about the cruelty of his lady, and having ordered all his attendants to leave him alone so that he could meditate without being disturbed, he wandered, lost in thought, and was transported, step by step, into the pine forest.° The fifth hour of the day had almost passed, and he had gone a good half mile into the woods, oblivious of food or anything else, when all of a sudden he seemed to hear the loud wailing and earsplitting shrieks of a woman.° His sweet reverie thus interrupted, he raised his head to see what was happening and was surprised to discover himself in the woods. But then, when he looked straight ahead of him, he caught sight of a very beautiful young woman, stark naked, who was running through a dense thicket of bushes and brambles toward the very spot on which he was standing. Her hair was disheveled, her flesh was all torn by the branches and the briars, and she was weeping and screaming for mercy. Nor was this all, for he saw two huge, fierce mastiffs chasing after her in a fury, one on either flank, who would catch up to her every so often and bite her savagely. Behind her he saw a swarthy knight, his face contorted with anger, come riding on a black courser. He held a sword in his hand and was threatening her with death in the most terrifying and abusive language.

This sight filled Nastagio's mind with both wonder and terror at once and then moved him to feel compassion for the unfortunate lady, which engendered, in turn, a desire to save her, if he could, from such horrible suffering and the threat of death. On finding himself unarmed, he ran and took up a branch from a tree to use in place of a cudgel, preparing to ward off the dogs and set himself in opposition to the knight. When the latter saw this, he shouted to him from the distance: "Don't get in the way here, Nastagio. Leave it to me and the dogs to give this wicked woman what she deserves."

And even as he was speaking, the dogs seized the woman so hard by the flanks that they halted her in her flight. When the knight had come up and dismounted from his horse, Nastagio approached him and said: "I don't know who you are or how you know me by name, but I'll say this much, that it's base cowardice for an armed knight to seek to slay a naked woman and set his dogs on her as if she were a wild beast. I'm certainly going to do all I can to defend her."

"Nastagio," the knight replied, "I lived in the same city as you do, and my name was Messer Guido degli Anastagi. You were still a little boy when I fell far more passionately in love with this woman than you did with that Traversari girl. Her pride and cruelty reduced me to such a miserable state that one day I took this sword, which you see in my hand, and in despair I killed myself with it, for which I have thus been condemned to eternal punishment. Nor was it long before she, who derived immeasurable happiness from my death, died as well, and for her cruelty and the joy she got from my torments, sins for which she never repented since she thought her behavior meritorious rather than sinful, she, too, has been condemned to the pains of Hell.°

"No sooner had she been cast down there than it was ordained for our punishments that she was to flee from me, and I, who once loved her so dearly, was to pursue her as my mortal enemy rather than the woman I once loved. And every time I catch up to her, I kill her with this same sword with which I slew myself. Then I rip open her back, and as you are about to see for yourself, I tear from her body that cold, hard heart of hers, which neither love nor pity could ever penetrate, and together with the rest of her inner organs, I give it to these dogs to eat. In a short space of time, as the justice and power of God ordain, she rises up as if she had never died and begins her woeful flight all over again, with the dogs and me in pursuit.

"Now it just so happens that every Friday around this hour I overtake her in this spot where I slaughter her in the way you are about to observe. Do not imagine, however, that we are resting on the other days, for then I hunt her down in different places where she either practiced her cruelty against me or thought up ways to do so. As you can see, I have now been turned from her friend into her enemy, and I must go on like this for a number of years equal to the number of months she treated me with such cruelty. Now allow me to carry out the decree of divine justice, and do not think to oppose what you could never prevent."

On hearing these words, Nastagio was so frightened that there was scarcely a hair on his head that was not standing on end, and stepping back, he stared at the wretched young woman in terror as he waited to see what the knight would do. Having finished speaking, the latter, with sword in hand, pounced like a mad dog upon the girl who was kneeling before him, held tightly by the two mastiffs, and crying for mercy. With all his strength he stabbed her right in the middle of her chest, causing his blade to pass right through her body and come out the other side. After receiving this blow, she fell down face forward, still weeping and screaming, at which point the knight, having laid hold of a knife, slit open her back, ripped out her heart and everything else around it, and threw it all to the two famished dogs who devoured it at once. Before very long, however, the young woman suddenly rose to her feet as though none of this had happened, and began fleeing toward the sea, with the dogs right after her, tearing at her flesh. Having picked up his sword and gotten back on his horse, the knight set off in pursuit, and a short while later they were so far away that Nastagio could no longer see them.

Nastagio stood there meditating for a long time on what he had seen, divided between pity and fear, but after a bit it occurred to him that since this scene was enacted every Friday, it might well be very useful for him. Consequently, once he had marked the spot, he returned to his attendants, after which, when the time seemed ripe, he sent for a number of his friends and relations.

"For a long time now," he said to them, "you've been urging me to stop loving this enemy of mine and to put an end to all my expenditures on her. Well, I'm ready to do it, provided that you obtain a favor for me, which is this: that you arrange for Messer Paolo Traversari, his wife and daughter, and all their female relations, as well as any other women you like, to come here and dine with me next Friday. You'll see for yourselves later on why I want you to do this."

To all of them this seemed like a small enough commission to carry out, and they promised him they would do it. After returning to Ravenna, in due course they invited all those whom Nastagio wanted as his guests. Although it was no easy matter to persuade the girl he loved to go there, in the end she went along with the others.

Nastagio had them prepare a magnificent feast and had the tables set under the pine trees around the spot where he had witnessed the slaughter of the cruel lady. Moreover, when the men and women were being seated at the tables, he arranged to have his beloved seated directly in front of the spot where the spectacle was going to take place.

They had just been served the last course when they all began to hear the despairing cries of the young woman as she was being chased. Everyone was greatly astonished and asked what it could be, but since no one seemed to know the answer, they all got to their feet in order to see what was happening and caught sight of the weeping girl, the knight, and the dogs who in no time at all arrived in their midst. The spectators made a loud outcry against the dogs and the knight, and many of them rushed forward to help the girl, but the knight, speaking to them just as he had spoken to Nastagio, not only got them to fall back but terrified every last one of them and filled them with amazement. When he then did to the girl what he had done to her before, all the women present, many of whom were related to either the suffering young woman or the knight, recalled both his love for her and his death, and began to weep as piteously as though what they were witnessing were happening to them.

When the spectacle had come to an end, and the lady and the knight had departed, they all started talking and offering different opinions about what they had seen. Among those who had been the most terrified, however, was the cruel young woman loved by Nastagio, for she had seen and heard everything distinctly, and as she recalled the cruelty with which she had always treated him, she realized that what had happened applied to her more than to anyone else there. And it made her feel as though she was already fleeing from her furious lover, with the two mastiffs at her flanks.

So great was the fear engendered in her by this spectacle that in order to prevent a similar fate from happening to her, she transformed her hatred into love, and seizing the earliest opportunity, which was granted to her that very evening, she secretly sent a trusted chambermaid of hers to Nastagio, asking him on her behalf to be so kind as to come to her, for she was ready to do everything he desired. Nastagio replied to her that this was very gratifying, but that, if she agreed, he preferred to take his pleasure of her in a way that would be consistent with her honor, in other words, by marrying her. Knowing that it was no one's fault but her own that she had not already become Nastagio's wife, the young lady replied to him that she consented. And so, acting as her own intermediary, she told her father and mother that she was happy to become Nastagio's bride, which made the two of them quite happy as well.

The following Sunday Nastagio married her, and after celebrating their nuptials, he lived happily with her for a very long time. Nor was this the only good that came from that fearful spectacle, for indeed, all the women of Ravenna were so frightened because of it that from then on they were far more willing to yield themselves to men's pleasures than they had ever been before.

Story 9

IN LOVE WITH A LADY WHO DOES NOT RETURN HIS
AFFECTION, FEDERIGO DEGLI ALBERIGHI CONSUMES HIS
FORTUNE, SPENDING IT ALL ON COURTING HER, UNTIL THE
ONLY THING HE HAS LEFT IS A SINGLE FALCON. WHEN SHE
COMES TO CALL ON HIM AT HIS HOUSE, HE SERVES IT TO
HER TO EAT BECAUSE HE HAS NOTHING ELSE TO OFFER
HER. UPON DISCOVERING WHAT HE HAS DONE, SHE HAS A
CHANGE OF HEART, TAKES HIM AS HER HUSBAND, AND
MAKES HIM A RICH MAN.°

Once Filomena had stopped speaking, the Queen saw that no one else was left except for Dioneo, who had his privilege, and so she said, with a cheerful expression on her face:

Since it is now my turn to speak, dearest ladies, I shall do so gladly and shall tell you a story that partly resembles the preceding one. I do not do so just to make you realize what an effect your charms have on noble hearts, but to teach you how you should, when it is fitting, decide for yourselves how to bestow your favors rather than always allowing Fortune to direct you, for she, as it happens, almost always distributes her gifts with more abundance than discretion.

You should know, then, that Coppo di Borghese Domenichi, who used to live in our city, and perhaps lives there still, was one of the most distinguished and highly respected men of our times, an illustrious person who deserved eternal fame more because of his character and abilities than his noble lineage.° When he was well advanced in years, he often derived great pleasure from talking with his neighbors, and with others as well, about incidents from the past. In this he excelled other men, for he had a good sense of how to order things, possessed a capacious memory, and was quite eloquent. Among his many fine stories, there was one he used to tell about a young man who once lived in Florence named Federigo, the son of Messer Filippo Alberighi, who for feats of arms and courtly manners was more highly spoken of than any other squire in Tuscany.°

As often happens with gentlemen, Federigo fell in love with a noble lady named Monna Giovanna, who was in her time considered to be one of the most beautiful and refined women in Florence. In an attempt to earn her love, he participated in jousts and tournaments, held banquets, lavished gifts on people, and spent his wealth without restraint. She, however, who was no less honest than beautiful, took no notice of either the things that were done for her or the person who did them.

As Federigo continued to spend money well beyond his means, while acquiring nothing from his lady in return, he went through his entire fortune, as can easily happen, and wound up a poor man, left with nothing except a tiny little farm, the income from which was just enough for him to live very frugally, and a single falcon, which was among the finest in the world. More in love with the lady than ever, but knowing that he could no longer live in the city in the style he preferred, he moved out to Campi where his little farm was located.° There he would go hunting with his falcon whenever he could, and without asking assistance from anyone, he bore his poverty with patience.

One day, while Federigo was living in these extremely strait-ened circumstances, Monna Giovanna's husband, who was very rich, happened to fall ill, and seeing death approach, drew up his will. In it he left his entire estate to his son, who was still a growing boy, and since he also loved his wife very dearly, he made her his heir in the case that his son should die without lawful issue. Then, shortly after that, he passed away.

Monna Giovanna was left a widow, and as our women nor-mally do every year, she went to the country during the summer, taking her son with her to an estate of theirs not far from Federi-go's farm. Consequently, the little boy happened to strike up a friendship with Federigo and developed a passionate interest in birds and dogs. He had often seen Federigo's falcon in flight and was so taken with it that he longed to have it for his own, but since he realized how dear it was to Federigo, he never dared to ask him for it.

So things stood, when, to his mother's deep distress, the boy happened to fall ill. Since he was her only child and she loved him as much as one possibly could, she hovered about him all day long, never ceasing to comfort him. Every so often she asked him if there was anything he wanted, imploring him to tell her, because if it was possible to acquire it, she would see about getting it for him.

Finally, after hearing her make this offer over and over again, the boy said: "Mother, if you could arrange for me to have Federi-go's falcon, I think I'd soon get better."

When she heard his request, the lady pondered it a great while as she tried to figure out what she should do in response. Knowing that Federigo had been in love with her for a long time and had not received even a single passing glance from her, she said to herself: "How can I send someone to him, let alone go there myself and ask him for his falcon, which is, from everything I've heard, the finest that ever flew, and more than that, the only thing keeping him alive? How can I be so insensitive as to want to deprive such a noble man of his one remaining pleasure?"

Stuck in this quandary, she remained silent, not knowing what to say in answer to her son's request, even though she was certain the falcon was hers for the asking. Finally, however, her love for her son got the better of her, and she decided to satisfy him, come what may, not by sending someone for the falcon, but by going there herself to get it and bring it back to him. "Cheer up, my son," she said, "and just think about getting better. I promise you I'll go to fetch it first thing in the morning, and I'll bring it back here to you for sure." The boy was overjoyed, and that very same day, began showing signs of improvement.

The next morning, taking another woman along with her as company, the lady went over to Federigo's little cottage and asked for him just as though it were nothing more than a casual visit. Since the weather had not been right for hawking for several days, Federigo was in his kitchen garden taking care of one or two little chores, but the moment he heard, to his utter astonishment, that Monna Giovanna was at the door and wanted to see him, he was so happy that he ran there at once to meet her.

When she saw him coming, she got up to meet him with womanly grace. After receiving his respectful greeting, she said, "I hope you are well, Federigo." Then she continued: "I have come to make amends for the harm you have suffered on my account in loving me more than you should have. What I offer you by way of compensation is that I and my companion should like to have a simple dinner here at home with you this morning."

"My lady," replied Federigo in all humility, "I cannot recall ever having suffered any harm on account of you. On the contrary, I have received so much good that if I have ever proved myself worthy in any way, it was entirely due to your merit and to the love I bore you. Moreover, let me assure you that this visit, which is such a generous gesture on your part, is even more precious to me than it would be if I were once again able to spend as much as I have in the past, although on this occasion you have come to a very poor host indeed."

When he finished speaking, he humbly welcomed her into his house and from there led her into his garden, where, not having anyone to keep her company, he said: "My lady, since there is no one else available, this good woman, who is the wife of this farmhand here, will keep you company, while I go to see about having the table set."

Although his poverty was dire, until then Federigo had not realized how desperately needy he had made himself by squandering all his wealth. That morning, however, when he discovered that he had nothing with which he could honor the lady, for whose love he had entertained countless people in the past, he was forced to realize just what it was that he had done. Distressed beyond measure, he silently cursed his fortune, as he ran here and there like a man out of his senses, but he had no success in finding either money or something to pawn. It was already late in the morning, and he was still determined to honor the noble lady with a meal of some sort without asking for assistance from his own farmhand, let alone anyone else, when his eye happened to fall upon his precious falcon sitting on its perch in the little room where he kept it. Since he had no other recourse, he seized the bird, and finding it nice and plump, decided it would make a worthy dish for such a lady. So, without giving the matter a second thought, he wrung its neck and promptly gave it to a maidservant to be plucked, dressed, and carefully roasted on a spit. Then, when the table was laid with the whitest linen—for he still had some of that in his possession—he returned to the lady in the garden and with a smile on his face told her that their dinner, such as he could prepare for her, was ready.

The lady and her companion arose and came to the table. Then, together with Federigo, who served them with the greatest devotion, they ate the fine falcon without knowing what it was they were eating.

After they had finished dining and the two women had chatted pleasantly with Federigo for a while, the lady felt it was the right time to tell him her reason for coming. Thus, in an affable manner, she began speaking to him:

"Federigo, I haven't the slightest doubt but that you are going to marvel at my presumption when you hear the principal reason for my coming here, especially when you recall your past life and my honesty, which you may have interpreted as harshness and cruelty. But if you had children, or if you had ever had any, you would recognize just how powerful the love one bears for them can be, and on that account, I feel certain you would, to some extent, forgive me.

"Although you have no children, I, who do have a son, am not exempt from the laws common to all other mothers, and since I have no choice but to obey them, I am forced, against my will and contrary to all the rules of decency and decorum, to ask you to make me a gift of something to which I know you are deeply attached—and with good reason, for it is the only delight, the only recreation, the only consolation left you after the loss of your entire fortune. And that gift is your falcon, for which my son has such a longing that if I do not bring it back to him, I fear his sickness is going to get so much worse that I might well lose him. And therefore, not because of the love you bear me, which places you under no obligation to me, but because of your nobility, by which you have shown yourself superior to everyone else in performing acts of courtesy, I implore you to be so kind as to give it to me so that I may be able to say I have preserved my son's life by means of this gift and have thereby placed him forever in your debt."

When he heard what the lady wanted from him and realized that there was no way for him to be of service to her because he had given her the falcon to eat, Federigo began weeping in her presence before he could so much as utter a word in reply. The lady at first believed his tears arose more from his grief over having to part with his prized falcon than from any other motive, and she was on the point of telling him she no longer wanted it. She held herself back, however, and waited to see how Federigo would respond once he stopped crying.

"My lady," he said, "ever since it pleased God that I should make you the object of my love, I have repeatedly complained that Fortune has been my enemy, but everything she did is trivial in comparison with what she has done to me just now. Nor shall I ever be able to forgive her, for I cannot help thinking of how you have come here to my poor house, which you never deigned to visit when it was rich, and how you want only a trifling gift from me, but she has arranged things so that I cannot give it to you. Why I cannot do so, I will explain to you in just a few words.

"When you did me the kindness of saying you wished to dine with me, I deemed it right and proper, in consideration of your distinction and your merit, to honor you by doing all I could to provide you with choicer fare than that which I generally serve other people. Calling to mind the excellence of the falcon you asked me for, I decided it would make a worthy dish for you, and so, this morning I had it roasted and served to you on a trencher, which was, I thought, the best way to present it. But now, I realize that you wanted to have it in a different sense, and I am so distressed by my inability to be of service to you that I do not believe I shall ever forgive myself."

After he finished speaking, he had the feathers, the talons, and the beak placed before her as evidence. On seeing and hearing all this, although the lady initially reproached him for having killed such a falcon simply in order to feed a woman, she then began commending him to herself and was soon filled with admiration for his magnanimity, which his poverty had not been able to diminish, nor ever would. Now, however, that she could not hope to obtain the falcon, she feared that her son's health was therefore in jeopardy, and so, after thanking Federigo for both his hospitality and his good intentions, she took her leave of him, utterly despondent, and returned to her child. To the immeasurable grief of his mother, in the space of a few days, whether it was the result of his depression because he could not have the falcon, or simply the case that his illness would have inevitably led him to such a pass, the boy departed from this life.

After a period of bitter mourning and endless tears, the lady was urged by her brothers on more than one occasion to remarry, since she had been left very rich and was still a young woman. Although she would have preferred to remain a widow, they importuned her so insistently that finally, recalling Federigo's great worth and his last act of generosity, that is, his having killed such a splendid falcon in her honor, she said to them: "I would gladly abstain from marriage, if only that would please you, but since you really want me to choose a husband, you may be certain that I shall never take any man other than Federigo degli Alberighi."

"What are you saying, you silly woman?" said her brothers, making fun of her. "How can you want someone who doesn't have a thing in the world?"

"My brothers," she replied, "I am well aware of the truth of what you're saying, but I'd rather have a man without riches than riches without a man."

Seeing that her mind was made up and knowing Federigo to be a very worthy gentleman, despite his poverty, the brothers acceded to her wishes and gave her to him, together with all her wealth. And so, Federigo, finding himself not just married to the great lady he had loved so dearly, but a very rich man to boot, managed his fortune more prudently than he had before and lived with her happily to the end of his days.

Story 10

AFTER PIETRO DI VINCIOLO GOES OUT TO HAVE SUPPER, HIS WIFE INVITES A YOUNG MAN TO COME TO HER HOUSE, BUT HIDES HIM UNDERNEATH A CHICKEN COOP WHEN HER HUSBAND RETURNS. PIETRO TELLS HER THAT WHILE HE WAS EATING AT ERCOLANO'S PLACE, THEY DISCOVERED A YOUNG MAN WHO HAD BEEN BROUGHT THERE BY HIS WIFE. PIETRO'S WIFE CRITICIZES HER SEVERELY, BUT THEN AN ASS UNFORTUNATELY STEPS ON THE FINGERS OF THE YOUNG MAN UNDERNEATH THE COOP, AND WHEN HE SCREAMS, PIETRO RUNS OUT AND SEES HIM, THUS DISCOVERING HIS

WIFE'S DECEPTION. IN THE END, HOWEVER, BECAUSE
OF HIS OWN PERVERSION, HE REACHES AN
UNDERSTANDING WITH HER.°

When the Queen's story had come to its conclusion, and everyone had praised God for having given Federigo the reward he deserved, Dioneo, who never waited around to be asked, began speaking:

I do not know whether to term it an accidental failing stemming from our bad habits, or a defect in our nature as human beings, but the fact is that we are more inclined to laugh about bad behavior than about good deeds, and especially when we ourselves are not involved. And since the sole purpose of the task I am about to undertake, as I have undertaken it on previous occasions, is to dispel your melancholy, loving ladies, and to provide you with laughter and merriment, I am going to tell you the following story, for even though the subject matter is a little unseemly, it may well give you pleasure. As you listen to it, you should do what you would normally do when you go out into your gardens, where you stretch out your delicate hands to pluck the roses, but leave the thorns alone. This you will do if you leave the wicked husband to his ill-fated, degenerate behavior, while laughing merrily at the amorous tricks of his wife, and feeling compassion, as need be, for the misfortunes of others.

There once lived in Perugia, not so very long ago, a rich man named Pietro di Vinciolo who got married, perhaps to deceive his fellow citizens and to improve the low opinion they all had of him, more than because of any desire he had to take a wife.° And Fortune showed herself to be in such conformity with his proclivities that the wife he chose for himself was a buxom young woman with red hair and a fiery complexion who would have preferred to have two husbands rather than one, and who now found herself with a man whose inclinations led him elsewhere rather than in her direction.

In the course of time the wife came to understand the way things stood, and since she was well aware of just how fresh and lovely she was, and how lusty and lively she felt, she got so upset about it that every once in a while, she would quarrel with her husband and call him filthy names. She was miserable practically every moment until it finally dawned on her that if she went on like this, it might well lead to her prostration rather than any reformation of her husband's vice, and so, she said to herself:

"Since this sorry pervert abandons me to go up the dry path in his clogs, I'll do my best to get others to board my boat and carry them through the rain.° I took him as my husband and brought him a fine large dowry, acting on the assumption that he was a man and believing he was interested in the kind of thing men generally like, as they certainly should. After all, if I hadn't thought he was a man, I would never have married him. Furthermore, he knew I was a woman, and if women weren't to his taste, why did he ever take me as his wife? I'm not going to put up with this. Had I wanted to turn my back on the world, I would have become a nun, but in choosing to live in it as I do, if I expect any fun and games out of this guy, I'll probably still be waiting in vain for that when I'm an old woman. And what good will it do me, in my old age, to look back and grieve over having wasted my youth, especially since this husband of mine here has actually been a really good teacher and shown me precisely how I ought to console myself? I should get my pleasure from the same thing he delights in, but whereas that pleasure will be strongly condemned in his case, in mine it will be commendable, for I will merely be breaking the laws of marriage, while he breaks those of Nature as well."

These, then, were the good lady's thoughts, to which she probably returned on more than one occasion, and in order to put them into effect on the sly, she made the acquaintance of an old woman who gave every indication of being a Saint Verdiana feeding the serpents, for she would go around to every pardoning service at church, always carrying her rosary in her hand, and never talking about anything except the lives of the Holy Fathers and the wounds of Saint Francis, with the result that virtually everyone considered her a saint.° When the time seemed right, the wife revealed her intentions in full to the old woman, who said in reply:

"My child, God knows—and He knows everything—that

what you'll be doing is right, because even if you had no other
reason, you're bound to do it, you and every other young woman,
rather than fritter away your youth. To anyone who's had any
experience of such matters, there's no grief equal to that of having let your time go to waste. After all, what the devil are we
women good for in our old age except to sit around the fire and
stare at the ashes? If there are any women who know this and
can prove it to you, I'm certainly one of them. Now that I'm old,
I experience the sharpest, most bitter pangs of regret in my heart
whenever I realize, all to no avail, how many opportunities I let
slip by. Actually, I didn't waste all of them—I wouldn't want you
to think me a complete idiot—but I still didn't do as much as I
could have. And so, when I recall the past and then contemplate
the state you see me in today, God only knows how sorry I feel
that I can't find anyone nowadays to light my fire for me.°

"It's not like that for men. They're born with a thousand different talents besides this, and for the most part, the older ones are
worth much more than the young. But women are born just to do
this single thing, and to make babies, and that's the only reason
why they're cherished. Now, if nothing else will convince you of
this, then you ought to consider the fact that we women are always
ready for it, which is not the case with men. What's more, one
woman could exhaust a host of men, whereas a host of men can't
tire out a single woman. And since this is the purpose for which
we are born, I repeat that you'll be doing the right thing if you give
your husband tit for tat, for that way, when you grow old, your
heart won't have any reason to lodge a complaint against your
flesh.

"In this world, you only get what you grab for, especially in the
case of women, so it's far more important for them than for men
to make the best use of their opportunities while they've still got
some, because as you can see for yourself, when we get old, neither
our husbands nor any other man can bear the sight of us. On the
contrary, they chase us away into the kitchen to tell tales to the cat
and to count the pots and pans. What's worse, they make up
rhymes about us and sing:

> For young gals, all the best mouthfuls in town;
> For old ones, stuff that gets stuck halfway down.

And they have lots of other sayings just like that.

"But to avoid detaining you any longer with my chatter, let me tell you that you couldn't have revealed your thoughts to anybody else in the world who was better able to help you. For there's no man so refined that I would hesitate to tell him what's required of him, nor is there anyone so hard and churlish that I couldn't really soften him up and get him to do what I want. All you have to do is to show me which one you like, and then leave the rest to me. But let me ask one thing of you, my child, and that is to always keep me in mind, for I'm a poor old woman, and from now on I want you to take a share in all of my indulgences and all the Our Fathers I recite, so that God may turn them into so many lights and candles for your own dear departed ones."

When the old woman had had her say, the young lady came to an understanding with her, telling her that if she ever happened to see a certain young fellow who often walked through that part of the city and whose features the young lady described to her in great detail, she would know what she had to do. She then gave the old woman a piece of salted meat and sent her on her way with God's blessings.

It only took a few days for the old woman, acting on the sly, to get the guy the young lady had been talking about into her bedroom, and then, a little after that, another one and yet another one, as they happened to catch the young lady's fancy. And although she lived in constant fear of her husband, she never failed to take advantage of any opportunity that presented itself to her.

One evening, when her husband was supposed to go out to have supper with a friend of his named Ercolano, the wife gave the old woman the order to bring her one of the prettiest, most agreeable youths in Perugia, an order that she carried out with alacrity.° But the wife had just sat down at the supper table with the young man when, lo and behold, there was Pietro at the entrance shouting for her to open the door.

When she heard her husband's voice, the lady thought she was as good as dead, but all the same, she wanted to conceal the young man if she could, and since she did not see how she could send him away or think of any other place for him to hide, she got him to take refuge underneath a chicken coop in the shed adjoining the room in which they were having supper. Then she took the cover of a straw mattress, whose contents had been emptied out earlier that day, and threw it over him. This done, she rushed to the door and opened it for her husband, saying to him as he entered the house: "You sure gulped down that supper of yours in a big hurry."

"We didn't even get to taste it," he replied.

"How come?" the lady asked.

"I'll tell you how come," he said. "We'd just sat down at the table, Ercolano, his wife, and I, when we heard someone sneezing nearby. We took no notice of it the first time, or the second, but when the guy who had sneezed did it again a third and then a fourth and a fifth time, and a good many more times after that, it got us all to wondering. Already a little irritated by his wife because she'd left us standing in the entryway for ages before opening the door, Ercolano just about flew into a rage and blurted out, 'What's the meaning of this? Who's doing all that sneezing?' Then he got up from the table and walked over to some stairs nearby, which had an enclosure made of wooden boards at the bottom, the sort of thing we often see people use for storage when they're tidying up their houses.

"Since it seemed to Ercolano that the sneezing was coming from inside there, he opened the little door, and the moment he did, out flew the worst smell of sulfur in the world. We had actually gotten a whiff of the stench before then, but when we had complained about it, Ercolano's wife had said, 'That's because I was using sulfur earlier to bleach my veils, and even though I sprinkled it over them in a large pan so they would absorb the fumes and then placed it under the stairs, it's still giving off an odor.'

"Since Ercolano had opened the closet door and the fumes had now dispersed to some extent, he looked inside and caught sight of the guy who'd been sneezing. In fact, he was still doing it because of the overpowering stench of the sulfur, and despite all his sneezing, the sulfur was choking him to the point that if he'd stayed in there much longer, he wouldn't have sneezed, or done anything else for that matter, ever again.

"The moment he saw the guy, Ercolano yelled: 'Now I see, woman, why you made us wait so long outside the door just now before you got around to opening it. But I'm going to pay you back for this, if it's the last thing I do!' When his wife heard this threat and realized that her sin had been discovered, she got up from the table without saying a word to excuse herself and fled away, nor do I have the slightest idea where she went. Not noticing that she'd taken off, Ercolano repeatedly told the guy who was sneezing to come out, but he was on his last legs and didn't budge no matter what Ercolano said. So, Ercolano grabbed him by one of his feet, dragged him out, and then ran off for a knife with the intention of killing him. But I was afraid we'd be arrested by the watch, myself included, and so I got up and wouldn't let him murder the guy or even do him any harm. In fact, as I was defending him from Ercolano, it was my shouting that brought some of the neighbors to the scene, and they picked up the young man, who was now more dead than alive, and carried him to some place out of the house, although I have no idea where. Because of all these goings-on, our supper was disrupted, and as I said before, not only did I not gulp it down, I didn't even get to taste it."

When the wife heard her husband's story, she realized that there were other women who were just as clever as she was, even though some of their plans occasionally met with misfortune. She would have been glad to speak out in defense of Ercolano's wife, but thinking that if she condemned someone else's misdeeds, she would have a freer scope for her own, she said:

"What fine goings-on! What a good, saintly person that woman must be! What a faithful, honest spouse! Why, I was practically ready to make my confession to her, she seemed so devout! And the worst part of it is that someone her age should be setting such a fine example for young women! I curse the hour she came into the world, and curse the wicked, deceitful woman for allowing herself to become a universal figure of shame and scorn for all the women in the city! Not only has she thrown away any concern for her honor, the vow of fidelity she made when she got married, and her reputation in society, but she felt no remorse at involving her husband in her disgrace, despite the fact that he's treated her very well and is such a proper man and a well-respected citizen—and all for the sake of some other guy! So help me God, women of that sort should be shown no mercy. They should be killed. In fact, they should be burned alive until they're reduced to ashes!"

Then, recollecting that she had concealed her lover underneath the chicken coop next to the room they were in, she began coaxing Pietro to go to bed, telling him that it was time to do so. But he was much more interested in food than in sleep and kept asking her whether there was anything for supper.

"Sure, we've got something for supper!" she replied. "We always go ahead and make supper when you're not here! What do you take me for, Ercolano's wife? So, why don't you just go off to bed for tonight? It would be a lot better for you!"

Now, that evening, it just so happened that some of the farmhands who worked for Pietro had brought him a load of provisions from his farm and had tethered their asses in a little stable located next to the shed. They had not bothered to give the animals anything to drink, and one of them, desperately thirsty, had slipped its head out of its halter, strayed away from the stable, and gone sniffing around everywhere to see if it could find water. As it went roaming about, it wound up, by chance, bumping into the chicken coop under which the young man was hiding. Since he was forced to crouch there on all fours, the fingers of one of his hands, which he had stretched out on the ground, were protruding slightly from underneath the coop, and it was just his luck—or rather, his bad luck, we should say—that the ass stepped right on them with his hoof, causing the young man such excruciating pain that he started shrieking at the top of his lungs.

When he heard the noise, Pietro was astonished, and realizing that it was coming from the interior of the house, he went outside the room, where the guy was still howling, for the ass had not yet lifted up its hoof from off his fingers and was continuing to press down on them just as hard as ever. "Who's that there?" yelled

Pietro, and he ran right over to the coop, lifted it up, and discovered the young man who was not only suffering from the pain of having his fingers crushed by the ass's hoof, but was shaking all over with fear that Pietro might do him some injury. Recognizing the young man as someone he had long pursued for his own wicked purposes, Pietro asked him, "What are you doing here?" The young man said nothing in reply to this question, but instead, begged Pietro, for the love of God, not to harm him.

"Get up," said Pietro. "There's no reason to worry. I'm not going to hurt you. Just tell me how you wound up in here, and why."

The young man told him everything, and Pietro, who was as happy to have discovered him there as his wife was upset about it, took him by the hand and led him back into the room where she was waiting for him, just as frightened as she could be. Pietro sat down right in front of her and said: "When you were cursing out Ercolano's wife just now, saying that she should be burned and that she was a disgrace to all you women, why didn't you say the same things about yourself? Or if you wanted to avoid speaking about yourself, how did you have the gall to talk about her since you knew you'd done exactly what she did? The only reason you said it, of course, is that you women are all alike: you're always looking to use other people's faults to cover up your own transgressions. I wish that Heaven would send down a fire and burn up the whole disgusting lot of you!"

Seeing that in the first flush of his anger Pietro had done nothing worse than abuse her verbally, and sensing that he was thoroughly delighted to be holding such a good-looking youth by the hand, his wife took heart and said: "I'm not surprised that you'd like to have a fire come down from Heaven and burn us all up, because you're the kind of guy who's as fond of women as a dog is of a cudgel, but by God's Cross, you're not going to see that wish of yours fulfilled. Still, I'd like to discuss this with you a bit more, because I want to know what it is you're complaining about. As far as I'm concerned, it would certainly be fine with me if you wanted to put me on an equal footing with Ercolano's wife, because at least that breast-beating old hypocrite gets what she wants out of her husband, and he's as fond of her as any man is of his spouse—which is more than can be said in my case. Sure, I grant you do a good job of providing me with clothes and shoes, but you know only too well how I'm doing in another respect and how long it's been since the last time you slept with me. I'd rather go around barefoot and in rags, and have you treat me well in bed, than to have all that stuff and to be treated by you the way I am. Now, you need to understand me clearly here, Pietro: I'm a woman just like the rest, and I want the same thing they do. And if I can't get it from you, you have no cause to bad-mouth me just because I go and find it for myself somewhere else. At least I do you the honor of not getting involved with stable boys and other riffraff."

Pietro realized that she could go on talking like this all night long, and since he was not particularly interested in her anyway, he said: "All right, woman, that's enough. I'll make sure that you get what'll really satisfy you. But now, will you be so kind as to arrange for us to have something to eat, because it seems to me that this young man here hasn't had any more supper than I have."

"Of course he hasn't had any supper yet," said the lady, "because we were just sitting down at the table to eat when you showed up, damn you."

"Well go then," said Pietro, "and see to it that we get some food. After that, I'll take care of things so that you won't have any more reason to complain."

Seeing that her husband was content, the lady got up and soon had the table set again. Once it was spread with the food that she had prepared, she ate supper merrily with her pervert of a husband and the young man.

What exactly Pietro had worked out to satisfy all three of them after supper has slipped my mind, but this much I do know. When the young man was escorted back to the piazza the next morning, he was not entirely sure whether he had been more of a wife or a husband that night. And that's why my advice to you, dear ladies, is to do unto others as they do unto you. And if you can't do it right then and there, bear it in mind until you can. That way, just like that ass bumping into the wall, you'll give as good as you get.°

Day 6

Introduction

HERE ENDS THE FIFTH DAY OF THE *DECAMERON* AND THE
SIXTH BEGINS, IN WHICH, UNDER THE RULE OF ELISSA, THEY
SPEAK OF THOSE WHO, HAVING BEEN PROVOKED BY SOME
ELEGANT WITTICISM, HAVE REPLIED IN KIND, OR WHO,
WITH A PROMPT RETORT OR A STRATEGIC MANEUVER,
HAVE MANAGED TO AVOID DANGER, LOSS, OR RIDICULE.

The moon, which was still in the middle of the sky, had lost its radiance, and the new light of dawn was already shining brightly everywhere in our hemisphere, when the Queen got up and had her companions summoned. After leaving the beautiful palace, they strolled for a while at a leisurely pace through the dewy grass, conversing together on a variety of topics, debating which of the stories they had heard were the most beautiful and which the least, and laughing anew over the many different incidents recounted in them, until, as the sun climbed higher and it was starting to get warm, they all decided they needed to go back. Consequently, they retraced their steps and returned to the palace, where the tables had already been set and fragrant herbs and beautiful flowers had been strewn all about. At the Queen's command they all addressed themselves to their dinner before the heat of the day set in, and then, having finished their merry meal, they first of all sang a number of beautiful, sprightly little songs, after which some of them went to take a nap and others played chess and dice games, while Dioneo, together with Lauretta, began singing about Troilus and Cressida.°

When the hour arrived for them to reassemble, the Queen had them summoned, and in their usual way they all sat down around the fountain. As she was about to call for the first story, however, something happened that had never happened before: namely, she and all the others heard a huge racket coming from among their maids and serving men in the kitchen.° She sent for the steward and asked him who was doing the screaming and what the uproar was all about. He replied that Licisca and Tindaro were having an argument, but that he did not know what had caused it, for just as he had arrived on the scene to make them quiet down, he had been summoned to appear before the Queen. Consequently, she ordered him to have Licisca and Tindaro brought before her at once, and when they arrived, she asked them to explain what they had been arguing about.

Tindaro was about to reply, when Licisca, who was no spring chicken and was rather full of herself, and who had, besides, gotten heated from all the yelling, turned on him and gave him a withering look. "Look, you ass of a man," she said, "how dare you, in my presence, speak before I do! Just let me talk." Then, turning back to the Queen, she went on:

"My lady, this guy wants to teach me all about Sicofante's wife, and just as if I wasn't acquainted with her at all, he would have me believe that the first night Sicofante went to bed with her, Messer Mace entered Black Mountain by force and with much bloodshed.° But let me tell you, that's not true: he entered it peacefully and to the general contentment of those inside. What's more, this guy is such an ass that he really believes young women are all so foolish that they're willing to waste their time waiting around for their fathers and brothers to marry them off, which six times out of seven takes them three or four years longer than it should. Brother, they'd be in a fine state if they postponed it that long! I swear to Christ—and I should really know what I'm talking about when I swear like that—I don't have a single neighbor who was a virgin when she got married, and as for the married ones, I sure know about all the different kinds of tricks they play on their husbands and how often they play them. Yet this muttonhead wants to teach me about women as if I were born yesterday!"

While Licisca was talking, the women were laughing so hard that you could have reached in their mouths and yanked out all their teeth. The Queen imposed silence on her a good half-dozen times, but all to no avail, for she would not stop until she had had her say.

When she was finally done, the Queen turned to Dioneo with a laugh and said: "Dioneo, this is a dispute for you to settle, and so, when our storytelling is over, I want you to pronounce the final judgment on it."

"My lady, there's no need for another word," replied Dioneo without hesitation. "Judgment has already been given. I declare that Licisca is in the right, and not only do I believe that things are the way she says, but I also agree that Tindaro is an ass."

When Licisca heard this, she burst out laughing, and turning to Tindaro, she said: "Didn't I tell you so? Now get along, and God be with you. Do you really think you know more than I do, when you're still wet behind the ears? Thank goodness, I haven't lived for nothing, no, not me."

With a stern look that by itself imposed silence on her, the Queen commanded Licisca not to utter another sound, let alone a word, unless she wanted to be whipped, and then sent her and Tindaro away. Indeed, had she not done so, the company would not have had anything else to do for the rest of the day but listen to Licisca talk. Then, when the two servants were gone, the Queen ordered Filomena to start the storytelling, which she cheerfully began as follows.

Story 1

A KNIGHT OFFERS MADONNA ORETTA A HORSEBACK RIDE IN THE FORM OF A STORY, BUT HE TELLS IT IN SO DISORDERLY A FASHION THAT SHE BEGS HIM TO SET HER DOWN ON FOOT.°

Young ladies, just as heaven is decorated with stars on cloudless nights and in the spring the green meadows are brightened with flowers and the hills with saplings dressed in their new foliage, so good manners and pleasant conversation are adorned with clever quips. These, because they are brief, are much better suited to women than to men, whereas it is much less becoming for the former than the latter to give elaborate speeches. Truth to tell, for whatever reason, whether because of the defectiveness of our wits or the singular hatred that the heavens bear toward our age, to our universal shame, there are few, if any, women left who know how to deliver a quip at the right time or are able to grasp one correctly after it has been delivered. Since Pampinea has already spoken at length on this subject, however, I do not intend to say any more about it. But in order to show you how beautiful a witticism can be when delivered at the right moment, I would like to tell you about the courteous way a gentlewoman once imposed silence on a knight.

As many of you know, having either met her or heard about her, not long ago there lived in our city a lady who was not only wellborn and well bred, but well-spoken, too, and who, for all her fine qualities, deserves to be identified by name. She was called Madonna Oretta and was the wife of Messer Geri Spina. Like us, she happened to be in the country at one point, where, as a form of recreation, she was going from one spot to another with a party of ladies and knights whom she had had to dinner at her house earlier that day. Since the trip between the place from which they had just come and the one to which they all wanted to go was rather long on foot, one of the knights in the company said to her:

"Madonna Oretta, if you like, I'll carry you through most of what remains of our journey by giving you a horseback ride there astride one of the finest stories in the world."

"Sir," the lady replied, "I beg you most earnestly to do so, for I would look upon it as a great favor."

Consequently, this Messer Knight, who was perhaps no better at using the sword by his side than he was at using his tongue to tell stories, began reciting one of his tales to her. It was, admittedly, very beautiful in itself, but by repeating the same word three, four, or even six times, and going back to start sections over again, and sometimes declaring "I haven't got it right," and often getting lost in all the names, and confusing one person with another, he was well on his way to ruining it completely. Besides, his mode of delivery was terribly unsuited to the different characters and incidents he was describing.°

As Madonna Oretta listened to the knight's narration, she repeatedly broke out in a sweat and experienced heart palpitations, as if she had become ill and was almost at the point of death. When she finally could not endure it anymore, seeing that the knight had gotten bogged down in the mire° and was not about to extract himself from it, she said to him in a pleasant manner: "Sir, this horse of yours has too hard a trot. Please be so good as to set me down."

The knight, who just happened to be much better at interpretation than at storytelling, understood her quip, and treating it as a joke, took it in good humor. He then began rehearsing other stories and left unfinished the one he had begun and was narrating so badly.

Story 2

BY MEANS OF A SINGLE PHRASE, CISTI THE BAKER
MAKES MESSER GERI SPINA SEE HOW HE HAS MADE
AN INAPPROPRIATE REQUEST.°

Madonna Oretta's remark received high praise from all the women as well as the men. When the Queen then ordered Pampinea to follow suit, she began as follows:

Lovely ladies, for my part I am unable to decide which sin is greater, that of Nature in assigning a noble spirit to an inferior body, or that of Fortune in assigning a body endowed with a noble spirit to an inferior profession. The latter happened in the case of our fellow citizen Cisti, as well as in many others we have had occasion to observe, for although Cisti was endowed with a most exalted spirit, Fortune made him a baker.

I would certainly curse Nature and Fortune alike if I did not know that the former is very discerning and the latter has a thousand eyes, albeit fools picture her as being blind. I am convinced that since both are very shrewd, they do what mortals do when they are unsure about the future. For they often bury their most precious belongings in the most unprepossessing places in their homes, places where one would least expect to find them, so that then, when the need is greatest, they can be brought out again, the humble nature of their hiding place having kept them safer than if they had been in some elegant chamber. In the same way, the two arbiters of all worldly things often hide their most precious treasures beneath the shadow of the basest professions, so that when the need arises for them to be brought forth, their splendor will be all the more apparent. I will prove this to you by means of a very short tale, which I was reminded of by the last story we heard. It involves an episode, in itself of no great importance, in which Cisti the baker got Geri Spina, who was Madonna Oretta's husband, to open the eyes of his mind and see the truth.

Let me say, then, that when Pope Boniface, who held Messer Geri Spina in the highest esteem, sent certain noblemen as his ambassadors to Florence on urgent papal business, they stayed at Messer Geri's house.° He joined them in their negotiations, and almost every morning, for one reason or another, it just so happened that they would all walk past Santa Maria Ughi where Cisti the baker had his shop and plied his trade in person.

Although Fortune had assigned Cisti to a very humble profession, she had been sufficiently kind to him as he practiced it that he had become extremely wealthy, and while he felt no desire to change his profession for any other, he nevertheless lived in the most splendid style and had, among all the other fine things he called his own, the best white and red wines to be found in Florence or the surrounding region. As he watched Messer Geri and the Pope's ambassadors walking past his door every morning, it occurred to him that it would be very courteous on his part, seeing how hot the weather was, to offer them a drink of his good white wine. But being conscious of the difference in social rank between himself and Messer Geri, he felt it would be an unseemly act of presumption for him to make such an invitation, and so he thought up a plan, instead, by means of which he could induce Messer Geri to make the proposal himself.

Accordingly, every morning, Cisti would always put on the whitest of doublets and a freshly washed apron, which made him look more like a miller than a baker, and around the time he thought Messer Geri was going to walk past with the ambassadors, he would station himself near the entrance to his shop where a shiny tin pail of fresh water had been set up alongside a new little Bolognese pitcher filled with his good white wine and two goblets so luminous they seemed made of silver. There he would sit, and as they passed by, after clearing his throat once or twice, he would start drinking this wine of his with such gusto that he would have made the dead feel thirsty.

After Messer Geri had observed this two mornings in a row, on the third he asked: "How is it, Cisti? Is it good?"

"Yes, sir," replied Cisti, springing to his feet, "but I can't really make you understand just how good it is unless you taste some of it."

Whether it was the weather, or his having exerted himself more than usual, or maybe the sight of Cisti drinking with so much relish, Messer Geri had developed such a thirst that he turned to the ambassadors with a smile and said: "Gentlemen, we would do well to sample this worthy man's wine. Perhaps it's such that we won't regret having done so."

Messer Geri and the ambassadors all walked over to Cisti, who immediately had an attractive bench brought out from inside the shop and invited them to have a seat. He then turned to their servants, who were already coming up to wash the glasses, and told them:

"Stand aside, friends, and leave this duty for me to take care of, because I know as much about serving wine as I do about baking. As for you, just don't you think that you're going to taste a drop of this yourselves!"

After he had spoken, Cisti washed four beautiful new goblets with his own hands, had a little pitcher of his good wine brought out for them, and with meticulous care, poured some of it for Messer Geri and his companions, none of whom had drunk anything that fine in years. Messer Geri was enthusiastic in his praise of the wine, and for the rest of the time that the ambassadors were in Florence, he went there with them almost every morning to drink it.

When the ambassadors had finished their business and were about to depart, Messer Geri held a magnificent banquet for them to which he invited a number of the most prominent citizens. He also sent an invitation to Cisti, who could not be persuaded to come under any circumstances. Whereupon Messer Geri ordered one of his servants to go for a flask of Cisti's wine and to give half a glass of it to each person during the first course.

The servant, who was perhaps annoyed that he had never been allowed to taste the wine, took a large flagon with him, and as soon as Cisti saw it, he said: "Son, Messer Geri's not sending you to me."

The servant kept insisting that Messer Geri had indeed done so, but when he could not extract any other answer from Cisti, he returned to his master. After the servant explained what Cisti had said, Messer Geri told him: "Go back to him and tell him that I really did send you to him, and if he still responds like that, ask him to whom I'm sending you."

The servant returned and said: "Cisti, I assure you that Messer Geri really is sending me to you."

"And I assure you, son," replied Cisti, "he's really not."

"Then," said the servant, "to whom is he sending me?"

"To the Arno," replied Cisti.°

When the servant reported this exchange to Messer Geri, the

eyes of his mind were immediately opened, and he said to the man: "Let me see the flask you're taking to him." The instant he saw it, Messer Geri declared, "Cisti's right," and then, after giving the servant a scolding, he had him take a flask of a suitable size.

When he saw the flask, Cisti said, "Now I'm certain he's sending you to me," and happily filled it up for him.

Later the same day, Cisti had a little cask filled with a wine of the same vintage and had it carefully transported to Messer Geri's house. He followed right behind, and upon encountering Messer Geri in person, he said to him: "I wouldn't want you to think, sir, that I was taken aback by that large flagon this morning. It's just that I thought you'd forgotten what I've shown you over the last few days with the help of my little pitchers, namely that this is no wine for servants. All I wanted to do this morning was to refresh your memory. Now, since I don't intend to be the guardian of this wine for you any longer, I've had it all brought here, and from this point forward, you may dispose of it as you please."°

Deeply appreciative of Cisti's gift, Messer Geri thanked him in an appropriate manner, and from that time forth he held Cisti in high esteem and considered him his friend forever.

Story 4

CHICHIBIO, CURRADO GIANFIGLIAZZI'S COOK, SAVES HIMSELF BY MEANS OF A PROMPT RETORT THAT CONVERTS HIS MASTER'S ANGER INTO LAUGHTER, ALLOWING HIM TO ESCAPE THE UNPLEASANT FATE WITH WHICH CURRADO HAD THREATENED HIM.°

* * *

Affectionate ladies, although a ready wit will often supply a speaker with things to say that are useful, beautiful, and appropriate for the circumstances, it sometimes happens that Fortune will come to the aid of people who are scared and will suddenly put words in their mouths that they would never have been able to come up with if they were not under pressure—which is what I want to show you with this story of mine.

As all of you ladies will have heard and seen for yourselves, Currado Gianfigliazzi has long been a noteworthy citizen of Florence, a generous and magnanimous individual who always led the life of a gentleman and delighted in hawks and hounds, to say nothing for the moment of his more significant activities. One day a falcon he owned brought down a crane in the vicinity of Peretola, and finding it to be young and plump, he sent it to an accomplished cook of his, a Venetian named Chichibio, ordering him to dress it well and then roast it for supper.°

Chichibio, who was as much of a birdbrain as he looked, prepared the crane, set it over the fire, and began to cook it with great care. When it was almost done and was giving off a most appetizing smell, a little gal from the country named Brunetta, with whom Chichibio was utterly infatuated, happened to come into the kitchen. On catching sight of the crane and sniffing its aroma, she pleaded lovingly with him to give her one of its thighs.

Chichibio replied to her in his singsong way and said: "You're not a-goin' a get it from me, Donna Brunetta, you're not a-goin' a get it from me."°

Donna Brunetta was rather peeved and said, "I swear to God, if you don't give it to me, you'll never get what you want out of me ever again." In short, they went on exchanging words like this until finally Chichibio, not wishing to anger his ladylove, cut off one of the crane's legs and gave it to her.

A little later, when the crane was set before Currado and his guests, he was surprised to find that one of its legs was missing. He had Chichibio summoned and asked him what had happened to it, and the lying Venetian promptly replied: "My lord, cranes only have one thigh and one leg."

"What the devil do you mean they have only one thigh and one leg?" said Currado in a rage. "Do you think I've never seen any cranes except this one?"

"It's just the way I'm telling you it is, sir," continued Chichibio. "If you like, we can go and see some live ones, and I'll show you."

Out of consideration for his guests, Currado decided not to pursue the argument any further, but said: "I've never seen or even heard of any one-legged cranes, but since you've said you'll show me some live ones, I want to see them tomorrow morning for myself, and then I'll be satisfied. But I swear by the body of Christ that if you don't prove it, I'll have them take care of you in such a way that you'll feel sorry every time you call my name to mind for the rest of your life."

Thus, the discussion was closed for that evening, but the next morning, as soon as it was light, Currado, whose anger had not abated while he slept, got out of bed, and still seething with rage, ordered them to bring the horses. After making Chichibio mount an old nag, he led him toward a riverbank where cranes could always be spotted at daybreak, and said to him: "We'll soon see which one of us was lying last night."

Perceiving that Currado was still angry and that he was going to have to make good on his lie, Chichibio, who had no idea how to manage it, was in a state of absolute terror as he rode along behind his master. If he could have run away, he would have done so gladly, but since that was impossible, he kept looking ahead of him and behind him and on either side, and everywhere he turned, the cranes he saw all seemed to be standing on two legs.

But just as they were approaching the river, Chichibio spotted a dozen cranes or more on its bank well before anyone else did, and all of them were standing on one leg as they normally do when they are sleeping. Chichibio immediately pointed them out to Currado and announced: "Now, if you'll take a look at those cranes over there, sir, you can see quite clearly that I was telling you the truth last night when I said that they have only one thigh and one foot."

Currado looked at them and said, "Wait a bit, and I'll show you they have two." Then, moving a little closer to them, he shouted, "Ho, ho!" At this outburst, the cranes put down their other feet, and after taking a couple of steps, they all began flying away. After that, Currado turned to Chichibio and said: "What do you say to that, you gluttonous rogue?° Do they have two legs, or not?"

Chichibio was utterly confounded, but managed to come up

with a reply even though he did not have the slightest idea where the words were coming from.

"They do indeed, sir," he said, "but you didn't cry 'Ho, ho!' to the one last night. Had you yelled like that, it would have stuck out its other thigh and its other foot just the way these here did."

Currado enjoyed this answer so much that all his anger was transformed into merry laughter.

"You're right, Chichibio," he said. "That's exactly what I should have done."

Thus, by means of his prompt and amusing reply, Chichibio made peace with his master and avoided an unpleasant fate.

Story 5

MESSER FORESE DA RABATTA AND MASTER GIOTTO THE
PAINTER, RETURNING FROM MUGELLO, CLEVERLY MOCK
ONE ANOTHER'S DISREPUTABLE APPEARANCE.°

The ladies were greatly amused by Chichibio's retort, and as soon as Neifile fell silent, Panfilo, in deference to the Queen's wishes, began speaking:

My dearest ladies, just as Fortune sometimes hides the most precious virtues in those who practice humble trades, which is what Pampinea showed us just a little while ago, so, too, one often discovers that Nature has located the most marvelous intelligence in the ugliest of men.°

This was plainly to be observed in two of our fellow citizens, about whom I intend to tell you a short tale. One of them, Messer Forese da Rabatta by name, had such a small, deformed body and such a flat, snub-nosed face that he would have been considered repulsive next to the ugliest of the Baronci, although he was so knowledgeable a jurist that people considered him a veritable encyclopedia of civil law.° The other, named Giotto, possessed a genius so lofty that there was nothing he could not represent with his lead stylus, his pen, or his paintbrush. Indeed, whatever Nature might produce—and she is the mother and mover of all things, determining their operations through the continual revolutions of the heavens—he was able to imitate it, or rather, to make his work resemble the thing itself so closely that he often deceived men's eyes, making them think that what he painted was real.

Hence, by virtue of the fact that he brought back into the light of day an art that had been buried for many centuries beneath the errors of those who painted more to delight the eyes of the ignorant than to please the understanding of the wise, Giotto may justly be considered one of the shining glories of Florence—and all the more so because, despite his having achieved that glory and having been the master of other artists while he lived, he always displayed the utmost humility by refusing to be called "Master." In fact, this title, which he rejected, shone all the more resplendently in him when one compares his modesty to the overweening ambition and greed that led not just those who knew less than he did, but his very own pupils, to usurp it. However great his art may have been, nevertheless, he did not, for all that, have a body or a face that were any more attractive than those of Messer Forese.

Turning now to our story, I should tell you that both Messer Forese and Giotto had property in the region of Mugello. One summer, during the period when the law courts are suspended for the holidays, Messer Forese went there to visit his estates. As he was returning to Florence on a wretched nag he had rented, he ran into the Giotto I have been speaking of, who was also on his way back from a similar visit and whose horse and clothes were in no way any better than Messer Forese's. The two of them fell in together, and like the old men they were, they jogged along toward home at a very slow pace.

As chance would have it, they were caught by surprise in a sudden rainstorm of the sort we often see during the summer, and they took shelter as soon as they could in the house of a peasant, who was an acquaintance, indeed a friend, of both men. After a while, however, as the rain showed no sign of letting up, and they wanted to get back to Florence before nightfall, they borrowed two shabby old woolen cloaks and two hats, threadbare with age, from their host, who had nothing better to offer them, and set off again on their journey.

After they had traveled some distance, they found themselves thoroughly soaked and covered with vast quantities of mud that their nags' hooves had kicked up—things that normally do not make people appear more reputable to others. When the sky brightened a little, the two of them, having gone on in silence for quite some time, began to chat. As Messer Forese rode along, listening to Giotto, who was quite a wonderful talker, he began looking him over, going from one side to the other and from head to foot, taking him in from every direction. When he saw how disreputable and unkempt his companion seemed, he started laughing and said, without thinking once about his own appearance:

"Giotto, what if we were to meet some stranger who had never seen you before, do you think he'd ever believe that you were the greatest painter in the world, as you really are?"

"Sir," Giotto promptly replied, "I think he'd believe it if, after looking you over, he gave you credit for even knowing your ABCs."

On hearing this, Messer Forese recognized his mistake and perceived that he had gotten as good as he gave.°

Story 7

WHEN MADONNA FILIPPA'S HUSBAND DISCOVERS HER WITH
A LOVER, SHE IS CALLED BEFORE A JUDGE, BUT SECURES
HER FREEDOM BY MEANS OF A PROMPT AND AMUSING
REPLY, WHILE ALSO GETTING THE STATUTE CHANGED
AT THE SAME TIME.°

*   *   *

Worthy ladies, it is a fine thing to be able to speak well in all circumstances, but it is even better, I think, to know how to do so when necessity requires. A noblewoman I am going to tell you about knew this art so well that she did not merely entertain her auditors and make them laugh, but as you are about to hear, she extricated herself from the snare of a shameful death.

In the city of Prato there was once a statute, no less reprehensible than harsh, that condemned women taken in adultery to be burned alive, making no distinction between one whose husband caught her with her lover and one who was doing it with somebody for money. And while this statute was in force, a case occurred in which a gentlewoman named Madonna Filippa, who was not just beautiful, but exceptionally amorous by nature, was discovered one night in her own bedroom by her husband, Rinaldo de' Pugliesi, in the arms of Lazzarino de' Guazzagliotri, a handsome, young nobleman from that city, whom she loved as much as life itself.° When Rinaldo saw the two of them together, he was so deeply disturbed that he could scarcely keep himself from rushing upon them and killing them, and if he had not been afraid of what could happen to him, he might have given in to his angry impulse and done it. Although he kept this urge under control, however, he could not be restrained from seeking the death of his wife, and as it was unlawful for him to kill her, he was determined to use the city's statute in order to get what he wanted.

Since Rinaldo had more than sufficient evidence to prove that Madonna Filippa was guilty, he sought no further counsel, but denounced her the next morning and had a summons issued for her. Like most women who are truly in love, the lady was possessed of a lofty spirit, and even though many of her friends and relations discouraged her from doing so, she was firmly resolved to appear in court, confess the truth, and die bravely rather than flee like a coward and live in exile because she had defied the law, thus showing herself unworthy of such a lover as the man in whose arms she had been the night before.

Escorted by a large group of men and women, all of whom were encouraging her to deny the charge, she went before the *podestà* and with a steady gaze and a firm voice asked him what he wanted to question her about. As he gazed at her and noted that she was not only very beautiful and extremely well mannered, but possessed a lofty spirit, to which her words bore witness, he began to feel pity for her and was afraid that she would confess to something for which, if he wanted to do his duty as a judge, he would have to condemn her to death.

Since he could not, however, refuse to interrogate her about what she was charged with, he said: "My lady, as you can see, your husband Rinaldo is here, and he's lodged a complaint against you, alleging that he caught you committing adultery with another man. Consequently, he's demanding that I punish you according to the requirements of a statute that's in force here and have you put to death. I can't do that, however, unless you confess. So, be very careful now about how you reply, and tell me if what your husband accuses you of is true."

In no way intimidated, the lady replied in a pleasant voice:

"Sir, it's true that Rinaldo is my husband and that he found me last night in Lazzarino's arms, where I have been many times because of the deep and perfect love I bear him. Nor is this something I would ever deny. But as I'm sure you know, laws should be impartial and should only be enacted with the consent of those affected by them. In the present case, these conditions have not been met because this law applies only to us poor women who are much better than men at giving satisfaction to a whole host of lovers. Moreover, when it was passed, not only were there no women present to give their consent to it, but since then, not once have they ever been consulted about it. And that's why, for all these reasons, it could with justice be called a bad law.

"If, however, to the detriment of my body and your soul, you choose to implement it, that's your business. But before you arrive at any sort of verdict, I beg you to grant me a small favor, and that is to ask my husband whether or not I ever told him no and refused to give myself fully and completely to him whenever, and however many times, he liked."

Without waiting for the *podestà* to ask the question, Rinaldo promptly replied that without doubt, she had always satisfied his every desire and given herself to him whenever he requested it.

"Then I ask you, Messer *Podestà*," she continued without a pause, "if he's always obtained what he needed from me and was pleased with it, what was I supposed to do—in fact, what am I to do now—with the leftovers? Should I throw them to the dogs?° Isn't it much better to serve some of them up to a gentleman who loves me more than his very own life than to let them go to waste or have them spoil?"

The nature of the case and the lady's fame were such that practically all the citizens of Prato had flocked to the trial, and when they heard her amusing questions, they had a good laugh over them, after which they immediately shouted with one voice that she was right and that it was all well said. Then, at the suggestion of the *podestà,* before they left, they modified their cruel statute, restricting it so that it only applied to those women who betrayed their husbands for money.

Thus, having made a fool of himself with what he had tried to do, Rinaldo left the courtroom feeling utterly abashed, whereas his wife was now happy and free, and having been, as it were, resurrected from the flames, she returned to her house in triumph.°

Story 9

WITH A CLEVER QUIP, GUIDO CAVALCANTI JUSTLY
PUTS DOWN A GROUP OF FLORENTINE GENTLEMEN
WHO HAD TAKEN HIM BY SURPRISE.°

*   *   *

Graceful ladies, although you deprived me of at least two of the stories I intended to tell today, I still have one I can recount, which ends with a clever quip that is more profound, perhaps, than any we have heard so far.

Let me remind you that in the past we used to have a number of truly splendid and commendable customs in our city, all of which have now disappeared thanks to the avarice that has grown right along with our wealth and has driven them all away.° One of these customs was that in various places throughout Florence the gentlemen living in different quarters of the city used to get together in fairly exclusive companies, taking care to include in their number only those who could, without difficulty, support the expense of offering a banquet to the entire group, one of them doing so today, another tomorrow, and then all the rest of the company in turn. At these banquets they often honored foreign gentlemen who visited the city as well as their fellow citizens. Moreover, at least once a year they would all wear the same kind of clothing, and on holidays they would ride in procession through the city, sometimes holding tournaments, especially on the greater feast days or when the city had received the happy news of a victory or something of that sort.

Among these companies there was one led by Messer Betto Brunelleschi, who, together with his companions, had made every effort to get Guido, the son of Messer Cavalcante de' Cavalcanti, to join them.° Nor did they do so without reason, for leaving aside the fact that he was one of the best logicians in the world and an excellent natural philosopher—things that did not much interest the company—he was the most refined man, both well-mannered and well-spoken, and he exceeded all the rest in any gentlemanly activity he set his mind to undertake. Finally, to top it all off, he was extremely rich and capable of entertaining anyone he thought deserved it in as lavish a fashion as you can imagine.

Messer Betto, however, had never succeeded in getting him to join his group, a resistance that he and his companions thought was due to Guido's sometime engagement in philosophical speculation, which would cut him off from his fellow human beings. Moreover, because Guido was somewhat inclined to the opinions of the Epicureans, it was said among the common people that all his speculating had no other goal than to see whether he could show that God did not exist.

One day it just so happened that Guido had left Orsanmichele, and taking his usual route, was walking along the Corso degli

Adimari heading for San Giovanni, around which there were many large marble sarcophaguses, including those that are located today in Santa Reparata.° Guido had reached a spot among the tombs, in between the porphyry columns that have been placed there and the door of San Giovanni, which was locked, when Messer Betto and his company came up on horseback through the Piazza of Santa Reparata. As soon as they caught sight of him, they said, "Let's go give him a hard time," and spurring on their horses in a mock assault, they were upon him almost before he noticed them.

"Guido," they said, "you can refuse to be part of our company, but look, when you've discovered that God doesn't exist, what will you have accomplished?"

Seeing himself hemmed in by them, Guido promptly replied, "Gentlemen, you may say whatever you please to me in your own house." Then, he placed his hand on one of the tombs, which were quite high, and being very nimble, he leaped up and vaulted over it onto the other side. Thus, having freed himself from them, he went on his way.

The others were left staring at one another. Then they started saying that he was out of his mind and that his remark was meaningless since the spot they were on had no more to do with them than with any of their fellow citizens, and least of all with Guido. But Messer Betto turned on them and said:

"You're the ones who are out of your minds, if you didn't understand him, for in just a few words, he has justly given us the greatest put-down in the world. If you think about it, these tombs are the houses of the dead, for this is where they are laid to rest and where they reside. When he said that this is our house, what he wanted to show us was that in comparison to him and the rest of the learned, all men who are as ignorant and uneducated as ourselves are worse than the dead. Thus, when we're here, we really are in our own house."

Now that they all understood what Guido had meant, they were quite abashed and never gave him a hard time again. And what is more, from that time forward, they considered Messer Betto to be a gentleman of subtle, discerning intelligence.

Story 10

FRATE CIPOLLA PROMISES A GROUP OF PEASANTS THAT HE
WILL SHOW THEM A FEATHER BELONGING TO THE ANGEL
GABRIEL, BUT WHEN HE FINDS LUMPS OF COAL IN ITS
PLACE, HE DECLARES THAT THEY WERE THE ONES USED TO
ROAST SAINT LAWRENCE.°

Now that each member of the company had told a story, Dioneo
knew that it was his turn to speak, and so, without waiting for a
formal command, he imposed silence on those who were praising
Guido's pithy retort and began as follows:

Charming ladies, although it is my privilege to speak about
whatever I please, today I do not propose to depart from the topic
that all of you have spoken about so very fittingly. On the contrary, following in your footsteps, I intend to show you how one of
the friars of Saint Anthony, with a quick bit of thinking, found a
clever way to avoid a humiliating trap laid for him by two young
men. And if I speak at greater length in order to tell you the whole
story as it should be told, you should not feel this is a burden, for if
you take a look at the sun, you will see that it is still in mid-heaven.

Certaldo, as you may perhaps have heard, is a fortified town in
the Val d'Elsa, located in our territory, and although it is small, the
people living there were once noble and pretty well-to-do.° Because
it offered him such rich pickings, one of the friars of Saint Anthony
used to go to Certaldo once a year to collect the alms that all the
people were simpleminded enough to donate to his order. His
name was Frate Cipolla, and the people used to give him a warm
welcome there perhaps as much for his name as for any pious sentiment they felt, since the soil in those parts produced onions that
are famous all over Tuscany.° Small of stature, this Frate Cipolla
had red hair and a merry face, and was really the most sociable
scoundrel in the world. What is more, although he was not learned,
he was such a fine speaker and had such a ready wit that someone
unacquainted with him would have concluded not just that he was
a grand master of rhetoric, but that he was Cicero himself or maybe

Quintilian.° And there was almost no one in those parts who did not consider him a good buddy, a friend, or at least a nodding acquaintance.

As was his custom, he went there for one of his visits in the month of August, and on a Sunday morning, when all the good men and women from the surrounding villages had gathered in the parish church to hear Mass, he waited for a suitable moment and then came forward.

"Ladies and gentlemen," he said, "it is, as you know, your yearly custom to send some of your wheat and oats to the poor of our Lord and Master Saint Anthony,° some of you giving more and some of you less, according to your ability and your devotion, in exchange for which the Blessed Saint Anthony will keep your oxen, asses, pigs, and sheep from harm. It's also customary, especially for those of you who are enrolled as members in our confraternity, to pay the small sum that constitutes your annual dues. Now, I've been sent to collect this money on behalf of my superior, that is, Messer Abbot. And so, with God's blessing, I want you to come outside after nones, when you hear the bells ring, and assemble in front of the church where I will, as usual, preach my sermon and you will kiss the cross. What's more, because I know how deeply devoted you all are to our Lord and Master Saint Anthony, I will, as an act of special grace, show you a beautiful and extremely sacred relic that I myself brought from the Holy Land across the sea, and that is nothing less than one of the Angel Gabriel's feathers that was left behind in the Virgin Mary's bedchamber when he came to Nazareth to perform the Annunciation." And having said all this, he fell silent and then returned to celebrating the Mass.

Among the large number of people present in the church while Frate Cipolla was speaking were two very clever young men, one of them named Giovanni del Bragoniera and the other, Biagio Pizzini.° After having had a good laugh between themselves about Frate Cipolla's relic, they decided, even though they were very close friends and cronies of his, to make use of the feather in order to play a practical joke on him.

They knew that Frate Cipolla was going to dine that morning up in the citadel with one of his friends, and as soon as they knew he was at the table, they went down into the street and made their way to the inn where he was staying. Their plan was for Biagio to keep Frate Cipolla's servant occupied in conversation while Giovanni looked through the friar's belongings for the feather, or whatever it was, and stole it so that they could see later on how he was going to explain what had happened to the people.

Frate Cipolla had a servant whom some called Guccio the Whale, others Guccio the Slob, and yet others Guccio the Pig.° He was such a bad character that Lippo the Mouse never came close to being his match. When chatting with his cronies, Frate Cipolla would often make jokes about him.

"My servant," he would say, "has nine failings, and if any one of them had been found in Solomon or Aristotle or Seneca, it would have been sufficient to ruin all the ingenuity, all the wisdom, and all the sanctity they possessed. So, just think what sort of man he must be, who not only lacks these three qualities, but has nine failings altogether!"

On occasion, someone asked him what the nine were, and he would respond with a rhyme he had made up.

"I'll tell you," he would say. "He's slothful, untruthful, and crude; neglectful, disrespectful, and lewd; careless and witless and rude.° Apart from this, he has some other little black marks it would be better not to talk about. But the funniest thing about him is that wherever he goes, he's always looking to find a wife and rent a house, and since he has a big, black, greasy beard, he thinks he's very handsome and attractive, and that every woman who sees him is in love with him. In fact, if you let him have his way, he'd be chasing after all of them so hard that he wouldn't even notice it when his pants fell down. Truth to tell, though, he's very helpful to me because whenever anyone wants to impart something in secret to me, he always wants to hear his share of it, and if I'm ever asked a question, he's so afraid I won't be able to answer it that he immediately replies yes or no, just as he sees fit."

When Frate Cipolla had left his servant at the inn, he had been told that on no account was anyone to be allowed to touch any of his master's belongings, and especially his saddlebags, which contained the sacred objects. But Guccio the Slob was fonder of the kitchen than any nightingale is of the green branches, especially if he smelled out some serving girl there, and he had indeed caught sight of one about the inn. She was fat and coarse, short and deformed, with a pair of boobs that looked like two big dung baskets and a face like one of the Baronci's, all sweaty and greasy and covered with soot.° And so, Guccio did not bother to lock the door behind him, but left Frate Cipolla's room and all of his things to take care of themselves, and like a vulture pouncing on carrion, swooped down on the kitchen. Even though it was August, he took a seat next to the fire and struck up a conversation with the girl, whose name was Nuta, telling her he was a gentleman by proxy, that he had more than a gazillion and nine florins, not counting those he owed others, which were greater in number, and that he knew how to say and do more stuff than his master could.°

Despite the fact that his cowl was covered with so much grease it would have served as seasoning for the soup caldron of Altopascio, and that his doublet was torn and patched, glazed with filth around the neck and under the armpits, and stained in more colors than cloth from Tartary or India, and that his shoes were falling apart and his stockings all in tatters—despite all this, he told her, as though he were the Lord of Châtillon, that he wanted to buy her some new clothes, set her up properly, release her from this servitude of always waiting on others, and while she would not have much of her own, put her in hope of a better fortune.° Nevertheless, although he said all this, and much more besides, with great emotion, everything turned out to be as insubstantial as the wind, and like most of his undertakings, it came to nothing.

Upon discovering Guccio the Pig thus occupied with Nuta, the two young men were quite pleased because it meant that half their work was done for them. With no one to get in their way, they entered Frate Cipolla's room, which had been left open, and the first thing they came upon in their search was the saddlebag containing the feather. When they opened it, they found a tiny casket inside wrapped up in many folds of taffeta, and when they opened that in turn, they found one of the tail feathers of a parrot inside, which they concluded had to be the one he had promised to show the people of Certaldo.

And without a doubt, in those days he could have easily made them believe what he said about it, because the luxuries of Egypt had only just begun to make their way into Tuscany, as they have since done in great quantities everywhere, to the ruin of the whole of Italy. And if such things were little known elsewhere, in that town the people were not acquainted with them at all. In fact, since the rough, honest ways of their forefathers were still followed there, the vast majority had never seen a parrot, let alone heard people mention one.

Delighted to have found the feather, the young men took it out, and to avoid leaving the casket empty, filled it with some lumps of coal they saw in a corner of the room. Then they shut the lid, and after arranging everything the way it had been, went off gleefully with the feather, unnoticed by anyone, after which they waited to see what Frate Cipolla was going to say when he found the coals in its place.

The simple men and women who were in the church, hearing that they were going to see one of the Angel Gabriel's feathers after nones, returned home when Mass was over and spread the news from friend to friend and neighbor to neighbor.° Then, once they had all finished eating, they thronged the citadel in such numbers that it could scarcely hold them, men and women both, every last one of them desperate to see that feather.

Having had a good dinner and taken a short nap, Frate Cipolla arose a little after nones. When he learned that a huge crowd of peasants had come to see the feather, he ordered Guccio the Slob to come up to him and to bring the bells and the saddlebags with him. Tearing himself away from the kitchen and from Nuta with difficulty, Guccio struggled up with the things he was asked to bring. His body was so bloated from all the water he had drunk that when he arrived, he was completely out of breath. Still, at Frate Cipolla's command, he went to the church door and began vigorously ringing the bells.

Once all of the people were assembled, Frate Cipolla began his sermon and said a great deal to serve his own purposes, never noticing that any of his things had been tampered with. As he was approaching the moment to show them the Angel Gabriel's feather, first he recited the *Confiteor* with great solemnity and had two large candles lit.° Then, having thrown back his cowl, he slowly unfolded the taffeta wrapping, brought out the casket, and after reciting a short, laudatory speech in praise of the Angel Gabriel and his relic, proceeded to open it. When he saw it was filled with lumps of coal, he did not suspect that Guccio the Whale had done this to him, because he did not think the man capable of rising to such heights, nor did he blame him for having done a bad job of preventing others from playing such a trick. Instead, he silently cursed himself for having trusted Guccio to safeguard his belongings since he knew the man was neglectful, disrespectful, careless, and witless. Without changing color, however, he raised his hands and his eyes to heaven and said in a voice that all could hear, "O God, blessed be Thy power forever and ever." Then he closed the casket and turned to the people.

"Ladies and gentlemen," he said, "I want you to know that when I was still quite young, I was sent by my superior into those parts of the world where the sun rises, and at his express command I was charged to seek out the Privileges of the Porcellana, which, although they cost nothing to seal, are much more useful to others than to us.° I set out on my journey to find them, departing from Venice and going through Greekburg, after which, riding from there through the Kingdom of Algarve and Baghdad, I arrived in Parione, from which I made it to Sardinia after a while, though not without suffering great thirst.

"But why should I go through every particular country I visited? After having passed the Straits of Saint George, I came to Conland and Clownland, which are populous countries inhabited by a great many people, and from there I went to Liarland, where I found a large number of friars, including many who belonged to our own order, all of whom were bent on forsaking a life of discomfort for the love of God, and cared little about others' troubles wherever they saw they could pursue their own advantage.° And in all of those countries I only spent money that had not been minted. Next I came to the Land of Abruzzi, where men and women climb up the mountains in clogs and clothe pigs in their own guts, and a little farther on I found a people who carry bread on sticks and wine in a sack, after which I arrived at the Basqueworm Mountains where all the water flows downhill.° In short, I went so far in those parts that I even reached India Parsinippia where I swear to you by the habit I'm wearing that I saw pruningbills fly, which is quite unbelievable if you haven't seen it—and Maso del Saggio will second me on this, for I met him there and he's a great merchant who cracks nuts and sells their shells retail.°

"But because I couldn't find what I was sent for, and because from that point on you have to go by water, I turned back and came to the Holy Land where in summertime cold bread costs you four pennies, but when it's hot, it doesn't cost you a thing. There I met with the Reverend Father Messer Dontblameme Ifyouplease, the most worshipful Patriarch of Jerusalem, who, out of respect for the habit of our Lord and Master Saint Anthony, which I've always worn, wanted me to see all the relics he had about him.° They were so numerous that if I tried to count them all, it would take me miles till I got to the end. Still, since I don't want to disappoint the ladies, I'll tell you about a few of them.

"First of all, he showed me the finger of the Holy Spirit, as whole and sound as it ever was; then the forelock of the seraphim who appeared to Saint Francis; and one of the fingernails of the cherubims; and one of the ribs of the Word-made-flesh-go-right-out-the-window; and the vestments of the Holy Catholic Faith; and some of the rays from the star that appeared to the three Magi in the East; and a vial of Saint Michael's sweat from when he fought with the Devil; and the jawbone of the Death of Saint Lazarus; and lots of others as well.°

And because I freely gave him *The Dingle of Mount Morello* in the vernacular and several chapters from the *Oldgoatius,* which he had long been seeking, he made me a part-sharer in his holy relics. He gave me one of the teeth of the Holy Cross, and in a little vial a bit of the sound of the bells from the temple of Solomon, and the feather of the Angel Gabriel, which I've already told you about, and one of the clogs of Saint Gherardo da Villamagna, which a little while ago I gave to Gherardo di Bonsi in Florence, who is particularly devoted to the saint.° Finally, he let me have some of the coals on which the most blessed martyr Saint Lawrence was roasted. With the greatest devotion, I brought these things back from over there, and I still have them all in my possession.

"True, my superior has never allowed me to display them until such time as they were verified as authentic, or not, but now that this has been established to his satisfaction by means of certain miracles they have wrought, and by letters sent to us from the Patriarch, he's given me permission to show them. But I'm afraid to entrust them to anyone else and always keep them with me.

"Now, as a matter of fact, I carry the Angel Gabriel's feather in one casket to prevent it from being damaged, and I have the coals on which Saint Lawrence was roasted in another. The two caskets are so much alike that I often mistake one for the other, and that's what happened to me today, for although I thought I was bringing you the casket with the feather, I actually brought the one with the coals.

"I don't think this was a mistake, however. On the contrary, it's clear to me that it was the will of God and that He Himself placed the casket containing the coals in my hands, for I've only now remembered that the Feast of Saint Lawrence is just two days away.° And since God wanted me to show you the coals on which the saint was roasted and thus rekindle the devotion you should feel for him in your hearts, He had me bring here, not the feather I intended to take, but those blessed coals, which were extinguished by the humors that came from the saint's most sacred body.° Therefore, my blessed children, you should take off your caps, and then you may, with reverence, come forward to behold them. But first, I want you to know that whoever is marked with the sign of the cross by these coals may rest assured that for an entire year he won't be burned by fire he doesn't feel."

When Frate Cipolla was finished speaking, he chanted a hymn

in praise of Saint Lawrence, opened the casket, and displayed the coals. For a little while, the foolish multitude gazed at them in reverent wonder, after which they all pressed forward in a huge crowd around Frate Cipolla, and giving him much better offerings than usual, begged him to touch each one of them with the coals. Accordingly, Frate Cipolla picked up the coals with his hand and began making the largest crosses he could manage on their white smocks and doublets and on the women's veils, declaring that, as he had seen it happen many times, no matter how much the coals were worn away from making those crosses, they would grow to their former size again in the casket.

Thus, thanks to his quick-wittedness, Frate Cipolla not only profited enormously by scrawling crosses on the people of Certaldo, but made fools of those who thought they had made a fool of him. The two young men had attended his sermon, and as they had listened to the ingenious and truly far-fetched verbal display he used to turn the situation to his advantage, they had laughed so hard they thought their jaws would break. Then, after the crowd had dispersed, they went up to him, as merry as could be, and revealed what they had done, after which they gave him back his feather, which proved no less lucrative to him the following year than the coals had been that day.

Conclusion

The entire company was greatly pleased and entertained by Dioneo's story, and they all laughed heartily about Frate Cipolla, especially about his pilgrimage and his relics, both the ones he had seen and those he had brought back with him. When the Queen realized that the tale was finished and that her reign had likewise come to an end, she got to her feet, removed her crown, and placed it on Dioneo's head.

"The time has come, Dioneo," she declared, laughing all the while, "for you to find out what a burden it is to have ladies to govern and guide. Therefore, you will be our King, and may your rule be such that when it has come to an end, we will all have reason to praise it."

After taking the crown, Dioneo responded with a laugh: "I am pretty sure you have had many opportunities to see kings who are worth a lot more than I am—kings on a chessboard, I mean. But I have no doubt that if you were to obey me as a real king should be obeyed, I would make sure that you had a chance to enjoy that without which no entertainment can ever be truly happy and complete. But enough of such talk. I shall rule over you to the best of my ability."

Then, in accordance with their usual practice, he sent for the steward and gave him orders about what his duties would be during the course of his reign, after which he said:

"Worthy ladies, we have already talked so much and spoken in so many different ways about both the resourcefulness of our fellow human beings and the vicissitudes of Fortune that if Madonna Licisca had not come here just a little while ago and said something that provided me with material for our discussions tomorrow, I suspect it would have been very difficult for me to have found a topic to speak on. As you heard, she claims that none of the girls in her neighborhood was a virgin when she got married, and she added that she knew all about the many different tricks wives play on their husbands. Now, if we set aside the first thing she said, which is a subject that concerns children, I reckon the second one should be a pleasant topic to discuss, and therefore, taking our cue from Madonna Licisca, tomorrow I want us to talk about the tricks that women, either for the sake of love or for their self-preservation, have played on their husbands, whether those tricks were ever discovered by them or not."°

Speaking about such a subject seemed quite unsuitable to some of the ladies, and they asked him to change the topic he had proposed.

"Ladies," said the King in reply, "I am just as aware as you are of what it is that I have chosen as our theme, but the objection you have raised would not have prevented me from selecting it, for I think that as long as men and women take pains to ensure that their behavior is honest, the times we are going through permit all subjects to be freely discussed. Are you not aware that since everything has been turned upside down nowadays, judges have forsaken their tribunals, the laws, divine as well as human, have fallen silent, and everyone has been granted ample license to preserve his life however he can? Consequently, if you go somewhat beyond the bounds of decorum in speaking, not with the intention of behaving indecently, but only of providing pleasure for yourselves and others, I do not see what plausible argument anyone in the future could make to criticize you.

"Furthermore, from the first day up to now our company has been the epitome of honesty, for no matter what we have said, our honor has never been sullied by anything we did—nor, with God's help, will it ever be. Besides, is there anyone who is unaware of your virtue? I doubt that even the fear of death, let alone these pleasant discussions of ours, could ever shake it.

"The truth of the matter is that if anyone were to discover that you had refrained at some point from talking about these trifles, he might suspect that you did not want to discuss them because you were actually guilty of having misbehaved. Not to mention the fact that you would be paying me quite a pretty compliment if now, after I have been so obedient to you all, and after you have chosen me as your King and made me your lawgiver, you refuse to talk about the subject I proposed. So, set aside these scruples, which are more appropriate for the wicked than for us, and may you all have the good fortune to think up some beautiful tale to tell."

After listening to Dioneo's arguments, the ladies agreed to do what he wished, at which point he gave them all permission to pursue their own pleasures until suppertime.

The sun was still high in the sky, because their storytelling had been brief, and so, once Dioneo and the other young men had started playing a game of backgammon, Elissa called the other ladies aside.

"From the day we arrived here," she said, "I have been wanting to take you to a place called the Valley of the Ladies where I think none of you has ever been. Although it is not very far away, I did not see an opportunity until today, the sun being still very high, to take you there. So, if you would like to come, I am completely

confident that once you are there you will be very happy to have
made the journey."

The ladies replied that they were ready to go, and without telling the men a thing about it, they summoned one of their maids
and set out, reaching the Valley of the Ladies before they had traveled much more than a mile. They entered it by way of a narrow
path on one side of which there flowed a crystal-clear stream, and
they found what they saw there to be as lovely and delightful, especially then when it was so very hot, as could possibly be imagined.
According to what one of them told me afterward, the floor of the
valley was as round as if it had been drawn with a compass,
although it looked more like Nature's artwork than something
from the hand of man. A little more than half a mile in circumfer-
ence, the valley was surrounded by six little hills, none of them
very high, and on each of the summits there was a palace built
more or less in the form of a lovely little castle.°

The sides of those hills sloped gradually down toward the floor
of the valley in a regular sequence of terraces, arranged like the
tiers in an amphitheater, their circumferences steadily decreasing
in size as one went from top to bottom. The slopes that faced the
southern sky were so full of grapevines and of olive, almond,
cherry, fig, and many other species of fruit trees, that there was
scarcely a handsbreadth of land left uncultivated between them.
The slopes that looked toward the North Star were covered over
with groves of oak saplings, ashes, and other trees, all as green and
straight as could be. The plain below, which had no entrances
other than the one through which the ladies had come, was filled
with firs, cypresses, and laurels, plus a small number of pines,
which were all so neatly arranged and symmetrically disposed
that it seemed as if they had been planted there by the most skillful forester. And when the sun was high overhead, very little, if
any, of its light shone through their foliage and reached the ground
below, which was one continuous meadow of the finest grass
abounding in flowers of every description, many of them purple
in color.

Besides all this, what gave them just as much pleasure was a stream that cascaded down over the living rock of a gorge separating two of the little hills, for it made a most delectable sound to hear, and from a distance it looked as if its waters were being sprayed under pressure into a mist of fine quicksilver. When the stream finally reached the floor of the valley, it was collected into a lovely little channel along which it flowed quite swiftly toward the center of the small plain where it formed a diminutive lake like one of those fishponds that townspeople sometimes construct in their gardens when they can afford to do so.

The lake was not very deep, for its waters came up only chest high, and since it had no impurities in it, its bed of exceptionally fine gravel was so crystal clear that a man with nothing else to occupy him could have counted every last grain of it, had he wanted to do so. But in addition to the bed of the lake, on looking down into the water, one could see a large number of fish darting here and there, a sight not just delightful, but marvelous to behold. Nor was the lake enclosed by any bank other than the soil of the meadow that was all the more luxuriant around it because there was so much more moisture there. And the water that flowed out of the lake was collected in another little channel through which it issued from the valley and ran down into the lowlands.

This, then, was the place to which the ladies had come. After gazing all around at everything and heaping praise on it, they found themselves looking at the little lake that was right there in front of them, and since it was very hot, and they were in no danger of being observed, they decided to go for a swim. First, they ordered their maid to station herself above the path by which they had entered the valley, so that she could keep watch over it and warn them if someone was coming. Then, all seven of them got undressed and went into the lake, which concealed their pure white bodies no better than a thin sheet of glass would conceal a bright red rose.

Once in the water, which nevertheless remained as crystal clear as before, they started swimming as best they could, going in every direction after the fish, which had trouble finding a place to hide, and attempting to grab them with their bare hands. After they had spent some time amusing themselves this way and had caught some of the fish, they got out and put their clothes on again. Unable to praise the spot any more highly than they had already done, they decided it was time for them to go back. Consequently, they set off down the path at a leisurely pace, talking all the while about how beautiful the place was.

It was as yet quite early when they reached the palace and found the young men still playing there just as they had left them. With a laugh, Pampinea said to them: "We really managed to trick you today."°

"What?" said Dioneo. "Have you started off by doing precisely what you are going to be talking about later on?"

"Yes, Your Majesty," replied Pampinea. And she gave him a lengthy description of the place they had come from, telling him how far away it was and what they had been doing there.

When the King heard her describe the beauty of the spot, he was so eager to see it that he had supper served at once. They all ate it with great pleasure, and the instant they were done, the three young men and their servants left the ladies and went off to the valley. None of them had ever been there before, and after examining every aspect of it, they praised it as being one of the most beautiful sights in the world. Then, after they had gone for a swim and had gotten dressed again, since it was getting late, they returned to the palace, where they found the ladies dancing a *carola* to an air sung by Fiammetta. Once it was finished, they entered into a discussion of the Valley of the Ladies, saying many good things in praise of it. Consequently, the King sent for the steward and ordered him to have everything set up in the valley the following morning and to have beds carried there in case anyone wanted to lie down for a while or take a nap in the middle of the day. Then he had them bring lights, wine, and sweets, and when everyone had taken a little refreshment, he ordered them all to join in the dancing. At his request, Panfilo began the first dance, after which the King turned to Elissa and said to her pleasantly:

"My fair young lady, today you honored me with the crown, and now, this evening, I want to honor you by asking you to sing.

So, give us a song, and make it one about the person you like the best."

Smiling, Elissa replied that she would do so gladly, and in a sweet voice thus she began:

> If ever I escape your claws, O Love,
> I never will be caught,
> I do believe, on any other hook.
>   When still a girl, I went to join your wars.
> Thinking to find there sweet and perfect peace,
> Upon the ground I laid down all my arms,
> Naively trusting your assurances,
> But you, rapacious tyrant, harsh and false,
> With cruel claws outstretched,
> And bearing arms, pounced on me instantly.
>   Then after I'd been fettered in your chains,
> You gave me, bound and weeping bitter tears,
> To him who for my very death was born.
> Now full of pain, I'm living in his power,
> And over me his rule has been so cruel
> That he could not be moved
> By sighs and tears that wear me quite away.
>   My prayers to him the winds all carry off;
> To none of them he listens, never will,
> Which makes my torment grow relentlessly.
> My life's reduced to pain, yet I can't die.
> Ah, Lord, take pity on my suffering
> And do what I cannot:
> Give him to me bound tightly in your chains.
>   If this you will not do, at least release
> Me from the bonds of hope that tie me down.
> Ah, Lord, I beg you, grant me this one gift,
> For if you do, then I shall still have hope
> To be again the beauty I once was,
> And when my grief is gone,
> To deck myself with flowers red and white.°

Elissa brought her song to an end with a very plaintive sigh, and although everyone wondered about her words, no one could guess what caused her to sing as she did. The King, however, who was in a merry mood, sent for Tindaro and ordered him to produce his bagpipe. To its strains he then had them all do a fair number of dances, after which, since a good part of the night had already passed, he told them, each and every one, that they should go to sleep.

Day 7

Introduction

HERE ENDS THE SIXTH DAY OF THE *DECAMERON* AND THE
SEVENTH BEGINS, IN WHICH, UNDER THE RULE OF DIONEO,
THEY SPEAK ABOUT THE TRICKS THAT WOMEN, EITHER FOR
THE SAKE OF LOVE OR FOR THEIR SELF-PRESERVATION,
HAVE PLAYED ON THEIR HUSBANDS, WHETHER THOSE
TRICKS WERE EVER DISCOVERED BY THEM OR NOT.

All the stars had vanished from the eastern skies except for the one
we call Lucifer,° which was still gleaming in the increasingly white
light of dawn, when the steward arose and went with a large baggage train to the Valley of the Ladies, intent upon arranging everything there in accordance with the orders and instructions he had
received from his master. After his departure, it was not long before
the King, who had been awakened by the noise of the animals and
of the servants who were loading them, got out of bed himself.
Once up, he had them rouse all the ladies as well as the young men.

The rays of the sun had not yet quite begun to shine when they all took to the road, and it seemed to them that the nightingales and the other birds had never sung so gaily as they did that morning. Those songs accompanied them all along the way to the Valley of the Ladies, where they were greeted by many more, who sang to them and seemed to rejoice at their coming.

After they had roamed around the place, examining it in detail once again, they thought it even lovelier than the day before, inasmuch as the hour was better for showing off its beauties. Then, when they had broken their fast with some good wine and assorted sweets, so as not to be outdone by the birds, they, too, began a song, which the valley took up with them, repeating the very strains they were singing, and to which all the birds added their sweet, new notes, as though they were determined not to be bested.

When the dinner hour arrived, they went and sat down at the tables that had been set at the King's command under the verdant laurels and the other fair trees beside the pretty little lake. As they ate, they watched the fish swimming through it in great shoals, which not only attracted their attention, but prompted discussion from time to time. With their meal at an end, and the food and tables removed, they began to sing even more merrily than before, after which they played music on their instruments and danced.

The prudent steward had arranged for beds to be set up in various locations throughout the little valley, all of them surrounded by curtains and covered by canopies of French serge, in which those who were so inclined were given permission by the King to go and take a nap, while those who had no interest in sleeping were free to entertain themselves to their hearts' content with any one of their usual pastimes.

Finally, when the hour had come for them to assemble and turn their attention again to storytelling, they all got up and took their seats on the carpets that, at the King's command, had been spread on the grass beside the lake, not very far from the place where they had eaten. The King then asked Emilia to start them off, and with a smile, she gaily began as follows.

Story 1

GIANNI LOTTERINGHI HEARS A KNOCKING AT HIS DOOR
DURING THE NIGHT AND AWAKENS HIS WIFE. SHE
MAKES HIM BELIEVE IT IS THE BOGEYMAN, AND
AFTER THEY GO AND EXORCISE IT WITH A PRAYER,
THE KNOCKING STOPS.°

My lord, had it been your pleasure, I would have greatly preferred
for you to have asked someone else to introduce so splendid a topic
as the one we are supposed to speak on, but since it is your desire
that I should provide an encouraging example for all the other
women, I shall gladly do so. Moreover, I shall try my best, dearest
ladies, to say something that might be useful to you in the future,
for if other women are like me, they are all easily frightened, and
especially of the bogeyman. Now, even though God knows I have
no idea what sort of creature that is, nor have I ever met any woman
who does, all of us are afraid of him just the same. But if you want
to chase him away when he comes to visit you, you should pay attention to my story, for it will teach you a good, holy, and extremely
effective prayer for the purpose.

There once lived in Florence, in the quarter of San Pancrazio,
a wool dealer named Gianni Lotteringhi, who was more successful in his trade than sensible in other matters, for despite being
something of a simpleton, he was frequently made the leader of
the Laud Singers of Santa Maria Novella, was charged with over-
seeing their performances, and had many other trivial duties of
the same sort.° The result was that he had a very high opinion of
himself, although all these offices came his way simply because,
being a man of substance, he frequently treated the friars to a
good meal. Since they often used to get a pair of stockings, or a
cowl, or a scapular out of him, in return they taught him a few
good prayers and gave him a copy of the Lord's Prayer in the vernacular as well as the Song of Saint Alexis, the Lament of Saint
Bernard, the Laud of the Lady Matilda, and lots of other nonsense like that.° He, however, considered all these things very

precious and exercised great care in keeping them safe for the sake of his soul's salvation.

Now, this man had a very beautiful, charming wife, an intelligent, perceptive woman called Monna Tessa who was the daughter of Mannuccio dalla Cuculia.° Knowing how simple her husband was, and having fallen for Federigo di Neri Pegolotti, a handsome, lusty young man, who was likewise in love with her, she made arrangements through one of her maids for Federigo to come and see her at a very lovely villa Gianni had in Camerata.° She used to stay there the entire summer, and Gianni would occasionally join her to have supper and spend the night before going back to his shop in the morning or sometimes to his laud singers.

Federigo, who desired nothing better than to spend time with Gianni's wife, seized the opportunity to do so one day, when she had sent for him, and went up to Camerata a little before vespers. Since Gianni was not coming that evening, Federigo felt entirely at his ease, and after having eaten a very enjoyable supper there, he spent an equally enjoyable night with the lady, who lay in his arms and taught him how to sing a good half-dozen of her husband's hymns.

Neither she nor Federigo intended this to be their first and last time together, and since they did not want to have her constantly sending the maidservant for him, they worked out the following arrangement. Every day, on his way to or from a place he had that was a little farther up the road, he would keep his eye on a vineyard next to her house, where he could see the skull of an ass set on one of the stakes that held up the vines.° When he saw its muzzle turned in the direction of Florence, that meant it was safe, and so, he would not fail to come and see her that evening after dark. If he discovered that the door was locked, he would knock softly three times, and she would open it for him. When he saw the muzzle of the ass turned toward Fiesole, however, he would stay away because this meant that Gianni would be there. Thus, by using this system, they managed to get together with some frequency.

But one time, when Federigo was supposed to have supper with Monna Tessa and she had arranged to have two fat capons cooked for him, it just so happened, much to the lady's distress, that Gianni showed up unexpectedly when it was already quite late. She had a little salted meat boiled separately and supped on it with her husband. Meanwhile, she ordered her maidservant to wrap the two cooked capons in a white tablecloth and carry them, together with a quantity of fresh eggs and a good flask of wine, into her garden that could be reached without going through the house and where she occasionally used to have supper with Federigo. She told the maidservant to leave everything at the foot of a peach tree that grew next to a little meadow, but she was so upset because of what had happened that she forgot to tell the maidservant to wait until Federigo showed up so that she could let him know that Gianni was inside and that he was to take the things in the garden away with him.

Not long after she, Gianni, and the maidservant had gone to bed, Federigo arrived and knocked once softly at the door. It was so close to the bedroom that Gianni heard it immediately, as did the lady, although she pretended to be asleep so that her husband would have no reason to suspect her of anything. After waiting a short while, Federigo knocked a second time. This really puzzled Gianni, who gave his wife a little poke and asked her: "Tessa, do you hear what I'm hearing? It sounds like somebody's knocking at our door."

The lady, who had heard it much better than he had, pretended to be waking up, and muttered: "What's that you say? Huh?"

"I'm saying," replied Gianni, "that it sounds like somebody's knocking at our door."

"Knocking?" said the lady. "Oh no, Gianni dear, don't you know what it is? It's the bogeyman. He's been giving me the fright of my life these last few nights. And every time I heard him, I stuck my head under the covers and didn't dare take it out again until it was broad daylight."

"Come on, woman," replied Gianni, "if that's what it is, there's no need to be afraid, because I said the *Te lucis* and the *'Ntemerata* and lots of other good prayers before we got into bed—plus, I made the sign of the cross from one corner of it to the other in the name of the Father and the Son and the Holy Ghost—so there's no reason to fear he can harm us, no matter how powerful he may be."°

To make sure there was no chance that Federigo would become suspicious and get angry with her, the lady decided that she absolutely had to get out of bed and let him know that Gianni was in the house. Consequently, she said to her husband: "That's all very well. You just go ahead and say those words of yours. But as far as I'm concerned, I'll never feel safe and secure until we exorcise him, and now that you're here, that's just what we're going to do."

"How are we going to perform an exorcism?" asked Gianni.

"I know exactly what to do," replied the lady, "because the other day, when I went to the pardoning service at Fiesole, one of those hermit women, who's the saintliest creature, Gianni dear, as God is my witness, saw how frightened I was and taught me a good, holy prayer. She said she'd used it many times before becoming a hermit and that it had always worked for her. Still, God knows, I would never have had the courage to go and try it out all by myself, but now that you're here, I want us to go and exorcise him."

Gianni said he really liked her idea, after which the two of them got out of bed and crept quietly to the door. On the other side of it Federigo was waiting and beginning to get suspicious. When they had reached a spot right next to the door, Gianni's wife said to him: "Now you go ahead and spit when I tell you to."°

"All right," replied Gianni.

Then the lady began the exorcism, saying:

Bogeyman, bogeyman, who goes walking by night,
Tail erect you came here, tail erect take your flight.
Go into the garden to the foot of the tree,
Where the peaches are growing, and here's what
  you'll see:
Greasy grease plus the droppings, five score, from
  my hen.
Put the flask to your lips, and just go away then.
And don't do any harm to my Gianni or me.

When she finished speaking, she told her husband, "Now spit, Gianni," and Gianni spat.

Federigo, who was listening to her words on the other side of the door, had stopped feeling jealous, and despite all his disappointment, he had such an urge to laugh that he thought he was going to burst. Then, just as Gianni spat, Federigo muttered under his breath, "Your teeth!"° Finally, after the lady had exorcised the bogeyman three times this way, she went back to bed with her husband.

Federigo had not yet eaten because he had expected to have supper with her, but since he understood exactly what the words of the exorcism meant, he went right into the garden where he found the two capons at the foot of the great peach tree together with the wine and the eggs. He took it all home with him and had his supper there in complete comfort. On many later occasions when he was with the lady, they used to have a good laugh together about this exorcism of hers.

Truth to tell, some people say that the lady had turned the skull of the ass toward Fiesole, but a farmhand, passing through the vineyard, had poked a stick up inside it and made it spin around and around until it wound up facing in the direction of Florence, which is why Federigo, believing he had been summoned, had come to her house. They also claim that the lady's prayer went this way:

> Bogeyman, bogeyman, in God's name leave us be,
> For the head of the ass was not turned 'round by me.
> It was somebody else, and may God make him pine,
> While I stay here in bed with this Gianni of mine.

In response, Federigo went away, losing his supper as well as his lodging there for the night.

However, a neighbor of mine, a very old woman, tells me that from everything she had learned as a girl, both stories are true, although the second one did not involve Gianni Lotteringhi, but a certain Gianni di Nello, who lived at Porta San Piero and who was no less a pea brain than Gianni Lotteringhi.°

It is therefore up to you, my dear ladies, to choose which exorcism of the two you like best, or to use both of them if you prefer, for as you have heard, experience shows they are extremely effective in such cases. You should learn them by heart, then, for they may be able to help you in times to come.

Story 2

WHEN HER HUSBAND RETURNS HOME UNEXPECTEDLY,
PERONELLA STASHES HER LOVER IN A BARREL. HER
HUSBAND HAS SOLD IT, BUT SHE SAYS THAT SHE
HERSELF HAD ALREADY DONE SO TO A MAN WHO
HAD CLIMBED INSIDE TO SEE IF IT WAS IN GOOD CONDITION.
LEAPING OUT OF THE BARREL, THE LOVER GETS THE
HUSBAND TO SCRAPE IT OUT AND THEN TO CARRY
IT BACK HOME FOR HIM.°

Emilia's story was received with gales of laughter. When it was finished, and everyone had praised the prayer as being indeed a good and holy one, the King asked Filostrato to continue, who began as follows:

My dearest ladies, so numerous are the tricks that men, and husbands in particular, play on you that when a woman sometimes happens to play one on her husband, you should not only be glad to have heard about what had occurred, but you should go around telling the story everywhere yourselves, so that men will come to realize that if they know how to do such things, for their part, women know how to do them, too. All of this cannot help but be advantageous to you, for when a man recognizes that others are equally in the know, he will not lightly undertake to deceive them. Who, then, can doubt that if men could hear what we are going to say today on this topic, they would have every reason to refrain from deceiving you, knowing that you also are capable of tricking them if you want to? It is therefore my intention to tell you about what a young woman, though of low birth, did to her husband on the spur of the moment in order to save herself.

Not so very long ago in Naples, a poor man took to wife a beautiful, charming young girl named Peronella.° Although they did not earn very much, the two of them, he by plying his trade as a mason, and she by spinning, supported themselves as best they could. One day this Peronella caught the eye of a young man-about-town who, finding her very attractive, fell in love with her, and by soliciting her one way and another, soon managed to get on familiar terms with her. In order to be able to spend time together, the two of them came up with this plan: since her husband got up early every morning either to go to work or to look for a job, the young man would station himself in a place from which he could see him leaving the house, and as the neighborhood where she lived, which is called Avorio, was pretty deserted, the young man would go to her house as soon as the husband left. And that is just what they did on many occasions.

One particular morning, however, when the good man was out of the house and Giannello Scrignario—for that was the young man's name—had gone inside to spend some time with Peronella, the husband, who was usually away all day, happened to return after just a short absence.° Upon finding the door locked from within, he knocked on it, and after doing so, he said to himself: "O God, praised be Your name forever, for although You've ordained that I should be poor, at least You've given me the consolation of having a good, honest young woman as a wife! You see how quickly she locked the door from the inside as soon as I left so that nobody could get in and cause her trouble."

Peronella knew it was her husband from the way he was knocking, and said: "O no, Giannello my love, I'm a dead woman! Look, it's my husband there, goddamn him. He's come back home, and I really don't know what that means, because he's never returned at this hour. Maybe he caught sight of you when you came in! But no matter what the reason may be, for the love of God, get into this barrel you see here, while I go and open the door. Then we'll find out what's brought him back home so early this morning."

Giannello promptly climbed into the barrel, after which Peronella went to the door and opened it for her husband. Giving him a withering look, she said: "What's the story here? Why have you come back home so early like this? It seems to me, seeing you here with your tools in your hands, that you want to take the day off. If you carry on like this, how are we going to live? Where are we supposed to get our bread from? Do you think I'm going to let you pawn my gown and the other rags I have for clothing, when I do nothing all day and night but spin until I've worked my fingers to the bone, just so there's enough oil to keep our lamp burning? Husband, husband, there's no woman in the neighborhood who doesn't marvel at it and make fun of me for all the work I put up with, and you, you come home with your hands dangling uselessly by your sides when you should be out working."

After she finished, she started to cry, but then she started up all over again: "Oh, alas, poor me! In what an evil hour was I born! Under what evil star did I come into the world! I could have had a proper young man, but turned him down and came instead to this guy who never gives a second thought to the woman he's taken into his home! Other women have a good time with their lovers—and there's no one around here who doesn't have two or three of them—and they enjoy themselves while they make their husbands think the moon is the sun. But me, poor little me, because I'm a good girl and don't get involved in such hanky-panky, I'm the one who gets to suffer, I'm the one with all the bad luck. I don't know why I don't get me one of these lovers the way other women do! Listen up, husband of mine, if I wanted to be bad, I'd soon find someone to do it with, for there are plenty of good-looking guys here who are in love with me and are my admirers. They've sent me offers of lots of money, or dresses and jewels if I prefer, but my heart's never allowed me to do it, because I'm not the daughter of that kind of lady. And here you come home to me when you should be out working!"

"Oh, for God's sake, woman," replied her husband, "don't get down in the dumps about it. Believe me, I know you and the kind of woman you are, and as a matter of fact, I saw proof of it this very morning. Now, it's true that I went out to work, but what you don't seem to realize, any more than I did, is that today is the festival of Saint Galeone, and since everyone's taking a holiday, that's why I came back home at this hour.° But even so, I've been a good provider and found a way to keep us in bread for more than a month, for I've sold the barrel, which you know has been cluttering up our house for some time now, to the man you see here with me, and he'll give me five silver ducats for it."°

"Well, that really makes me mad," said Peronella. "You'd think that since you're a man and you get around, you'd know how the world works, and yet here you've gone and sold the barrel for five ducats. Now, I'm merely a woman, and I've hardly ever gone beyond our threshold, but I, too, could see that the barrel was cluttering up our house, and so I sold it to a good man here for a full seven ducats. In fact, when you came home, he had just climbed inside to see if it was in good condition."

Upon hearing this, her husband was overjoyed and turned to the man who had come with him for the barrel.

"God be with you, my good man," he said. "You heard my wife. She's sold it for seven, and the most you offered me for it was five."

"All right, then," replied the good man, and away he went.

"Now that you're home," said Peronella to her husband, "come on up here and take care of this business with him yourself."

While he was waiting, Giannello had been keeping his ears open in case there was anything he had to fear or needed to prepare himself to deal with. On hearing Peronella's words, he immediately leaped out of the barrel, and then, as if he had not heard anything about her husband's return, he said: "Where are you, my good woman?"

"Here I am," said the husband, who was just coming up. "What can I do for you?"

"Who are you?" asked Giannello. "I'd like to see the lady who was selling me this barrel."

"Don't worry," the good man answered, "you can deal with me, because I'm her husband."

"The barrel seems in pretty good condition to me," said Giannello, "but I think you let the lees from the wine remain in it, because it's entirely crusted over with something or other that's dried onto it, and it's so hard I can't get it off even if I use my nails. Now, unless it's cleaned out first, I'm not going to take it."

"Our bargain's not going to fall through just because of that," said Peronella. "My husband will clean the whole thing for you."

"That I will," declared her husband, who laid his tools down and stripped to his shirt. Then, after asking for a lighted lamp and a scraper, he got into the barrel and started working away at it. Pretending she wanted to watch what he was doing, Peronella leaned her head over the edge of the barrel, which was not very wide, along with one of her arms and shoulders.

"Scrape here, and here, and over there," she said to him, and "Look, there's still a little bit left here."

While she was standing there, giving her husband directions and telling him where to scrape, Giannello, who had not fully satisfied his desires that morning before the husband had arrived, and realizing that he could not do it the way he wanted to now, decided to take care of things as best he could. So, he came up behind Peronella, who was blocking off the entire mouth of the barrel, and just as the unbridled stallions of Parthia, burning with love, assail the mares in the open fields, so he satisfied his youthful appetite, which reached its climax almost at the very same moment that the scraping of the barrel was finished, at which point he backed off, Peronella removed her head from the barrel, and her husband climbed out.°

"Take this light, my good man," said Peronella to Giannello, "and see if it's all been cleaned out to your satisfaction."

After taking a look inside, Giannello said that everything was fine and that he was indeed satisfied. He then gave the husband seven ducats and got him to carry the barrel home for him.°

Story 4

TOFANO LOCKS HIS WIFE OUT OF THE HOUSE ONE
NIGHT, AND WHEN SHE CANNOT GET BACK IN DESPITE
ALL HER PLEADING WITH HIM, SHE PRETENDS TO
THROW HERSELF DOWN A WELL, BUT DROPS A LARGE

ROCK INTO IT INSTEAD. TOFANO COMES OUT OF THE
HOUSE AND RUSHES OVER TO THE SPOT, AT WHICH
POINT SHE SLIPS BACK INSIDE, LOCKS HIM OUT,
AND SCREAMS INSULTS AT HIM.°

* * *

O Love, how great and varied are your powers, how wonderful
your counsels and insights! What philosopher, what artist could
have ever imagined the stratagems, the subterfuges, and the arguments that you supply in an instant to those who follow in your
footsteps? There can be no doubt but that everyone else's teaching
is slow in comparison with yours, as may clearly be deduced from
the cases that have already been brought to our attention. And to
those cases, dear ladies, I will now add yet another, this one involving a woman of quite ordinary intelligence who came up with a
stratagem that only Love could have revealed to her.

In Arezzo, then, there once lived a rich man by the name of
Tofano, who took an exceptionally beautiful woman called
Monna Ghita to wife and then promptly became jealous of her for
no particular reason.° When she found out about it, she got angry,
and repeatedly asked him to explain why he felt as he did. Since
the only explanations he came up with were vague and uncon-
vincing, however, she resolved to make him die from the very illness that up to then he had had no real cause to fear.

Having noticed that a young man, a very agreeable person to
her way of thinking, was quite attracted to her, the lady discreetly
arranged to make his acquaintance, and when things between
them had advanced to the point that nothing remained for them
to do but to translate words into deeds, she turned her attention to
devising a way to bring this about as well. Since she knew that one
of her husband's bad habits was his fondness for drink, not only
did she start commending it to him, but she would cleverly
encourage him to indulge as often as she could. In fact, she became
so expert at doing this that practically any time she wanted to, she
got him to drink himself into a stupor, after which, once she saw

that he was good and drunk, she would put him to bed and go off to meet her lover. After their first time together, she felt secure enough to go on seeing him again and again. Indeed, she became so confident, because of her husband's weakness for drink, that she made bold not merely to bring her lover into the house, but on occasion to spend a large part of the night with him at his place, which was not very far away.

The amorous lady had been carrying on like this for some time, when her wretched husband happened to notice that although she encouraged him to drink, for all that, she never touched a drop herself. This made him suspect what was indeed the case, namely that his wife was getting him drunk so that afterward she could do what she wanted while he was asleep. Wishing to put this supposition to the test, he returned home one evening, having refrained from drinking all day long, and pretended by the way he spoke and acted that he was as drunk as could be. She was taken in by his show, and concluding that he did not need another drop to make him sleep soundly, she quickly put him to bed, after which, just as she had done on many other occasions, she left her house and went to her lover's place, where she remained until the middle of the night.

Once he no longer heard his wife about the place, Tofano got up, went over to the door, and after locking it from the inside, stationed himself at the window so he could see her when she came back and let her know that he was well aware of what she was up to. And there he stayed until she returned.

His wife eventually came home, and when she found herself locked out, she got very upset and started trying to force the door open. After putting up with this for a while, Tofano said: "You're wasting your energy, woman, because there's no way you can possibly get in. Go back to wherever it is you've been staying until now, and rest assured that you're never going to return to this house until I've honored you just as you deserve for this affair right in front of your family and neighbors."

The lady began pleading with him, for the love of God, to please open the door for her, saying that she was not coming from the place where he thought she had been. Instead, she had been sitting up with a neighbor of hers, who could not sleep the whole night through because it lasted so long and who did not want to sit up in her house all alone. The lady's prayers were completely unavailing, however, because the stupid brute was perfectly willing to have all of Arezzo learn about their shame, even though, so far, no one knew anything about it.

When she saw that her pleading was getting her nowhere, the lady resorted to threats. "If you don't open up for me," she said, "I'm going to make you the sorriest man alive."

"And just what can you possibly do to me?" asked Tofano.

Love had sharpened the lady's wits with his counsel, and she replied: "Before I'll allow myself to suffer the shame that you wrongly wish to inflict on me, I'll throw myself down this well here, and when they find me dead inside, they'll all think that you got drunk and threw me into it. Then, either you're going to have to run away, and you'll forfeit all your possessions and live in exile, or they'll wind up chopping off your head for having murdered me, which is, in effect, what you really will have done."

When all of her words failed to make Tofano budge one bit from his stupid decision, she said: "Look here, I'm not going to let you torment me like this any longer. May God pardon you! I'm leaving my distaff behind here, and you can put it back where it belongs."

The night was so dark that people could hardly see one another passing in the street, and having uttered these words, the lady made her way over to the well, picked up a huge rock that was lying next to it, and shouting "God forgive me!" let it fall in.

When Tofano heard the enormous splash the rock made as it struck the water, he was firmly convinced that she had thrown herself in, and snatching up his bucket and rope, he flung himself out of the house and rushed over to the well to help her. His wife had hidden herself near the front door, and the moment she saw him running to the well, she slipped inside the house, locked herself in, and went over to the window.

"You should add water to your wine when you're drinking it," she said, "and not later on in the middle of the night."

When Tofano heard what she said, he realized that she had made a fool of him and went back to the front door. On finding that he could not open it, he told her to let him in. Although she had been talking quietly up to that point, now, however, she began shrieking.

"By God's Cross, you repulsive drunk," she said, "you're not getting in here tonight. I won't put up with your antics anymore. I'm going to show everybody the kind of a man you are and let them see just what time of night it is when you come back home."

Now Tofano got angry, too, and began screaming insults at her, with the result that the neighbors, men and women alike, hearing all the noise, got up, went over to their windows, and demanded to know what the matter was.

The lady began crying and said: "The matter is this wretch of a husband of mine who comes home drunk every evening, or else he falls asleep in some tavern and only gets back at this hour. I've put up with this for years without being able to make him change, and I just can't take it anymore. So I decided to shame him by locking him out of the house to see whether he'll mend his ways."

The asinine Tofano, for his part, told them what had actually happened, while continuing to threaten her in the worst way. His wife then turned to the neighbors and said: "Now you see the kind of man he is! What would you think if I were out in the street like him, and he were in the house like me? I swear to God, I have no doubt you'd believe he was telling the truth. So, you can see just how clever he is! For here he is, saying that I did the very thing I'm pretty sure he did himself. He thought he could frighten me by throwing something or other into the well, but I would to God he'd really thrown himself down there and drowned, so that all that wine he's drunk far too much of would be well and truly diluted with water."

Without exception, all the neighbors who were present, both the men and the women, began scolding Tofano, blaming him for what had happened and reviling him because of what he was saying about his wife, and in short, they created such an uproar that it spread from one person to another until it eventually reached the lady's family. They hurried to the scene, and after they had put together the story from the accounts several of the neighbors gave them, they grabbed Tofano and beat him until he was completely covered with bruises. Then they went into the house, gathered up all the lady's belongings, and took her back home with them, threatening Tofano with even worse to come.

Seeing that he had gotten the worst of it and that his jealousy had brought him to a sorry pass, Tofano, who was really very fond of his wife, got some friends to act as intermediaries, and thanks to them he managed to make peace and arrange for her to come back home. And not only did he promise her that he would never be jealous again, but what is more, he gave her permission to do whatever she liked, as long as she was so discreet that he never found out anything about it. Thus, just like the peasant who was a dunce, having been beaten, he made peace at once. So, long live Love, and death to Avarice and all his company!°

Story 5

DISGUISED AS A PRIEST, A JEALOUS MAN HEARS HIS WIFE'S
CONFESSION AND IS GIVEN TO UNDERSTAND THAT SHE IS
IN LOVE WITH A PRIEST WHO COMES TO SEE HER EVERY
NIGHT. THEN, WHILE HER HUSBAND IS SECRETLY KEEPING
WATCH BY THE FRONT DOOR, THE WIFE HAS HER
LOVER COME TO HER ACROSS THE ROOF AND
PASSES THE TIME WITH HIM.°

Lauretta had ended her tale, and after everyone had praised the lady for treating that bad husband of hers just as he deserved, the King, who did not want to waste time, turned to Fiammetta and graciously assigned her the task of telling the next story, which she began as follows:

Noblest of ladies, the preceding tale prompts me to tell a similar one about a jealous husband, for in my opinion, whatever their wives do to them is well done indeed, especially when they become jealous for no reason at all. And if lawgivers had taken everything into consideration, then I think that the punishment they established for wives in such cases would not have differed from the one they prescribed for a person who attacks another in self-defense. For jealous men plot against the very lives of their young wives and will stop at nothing in seeking their deaths.

Like everyone else, after spending the entire week cooped up in their houses attending to the needs of their families and taking care of domestic chores, those wives long for peace and relaxation on holidays and want to have a little fun, just like the workers in the fields, the artisans in the cities, and the magistrates in the courts, indeed, just as God Himself did when He rested on the seventh day from all His labors. Both canon and civil law, which seek to promote the honor of God and the general welfare of the people, want there to be a distinction between workdays and days of rest.

Jealous men will have none of this, however, but on precisely those days when other women are enjoying themselves, they keep their wives under lock and key not just in their houses, but in their rooms, making those days even more wretched and miserable for them, and only those poor creatures who have had to endure such treatment know how wearing it is. To sum it all up: whatever a wife does to a husband who is jealous without cause is surely to be praised rather than censored.

There was once a very wealthy merchant and landowner living in Rimini, who, having married an extremely beautiful woman, became inordinately jealous of her. And the only reason for it was that, since he loved her passionately, thought she was simply gorgeous, and knew that she did everything in her power to please him, he imagined that all the men were in love with her, that she seemed beautiful to every last one of them, and that she would do as much as she could to please them just as she did for him. This was the thinking of a wicked, insensitive man, who, in his jealousy, watched her so carefully and placed such restraints on her that I doubt whether prisoners sentenced to death are guarded so closely by their jailors. It was not merely that she was unable to attend weddings or parties, or go to church, or even set foot beyond her door at all, but she did not dare to show herself at a window or look outside her house for any reason. As a result, her life was pure misery, and she endured her suffering with less and less patience insofar as she knew she was innocent.

To console herself, seeing how unjustly her husband was persecuting her, she decided to find some way, if any could be found, to provide him with a real reason for treating her as he did. Since she could not appear at a window, she had no means of giving any sign of encouragement to a potential lover who might be passing through the neighborhood. Knowing, however, that a handsome, agreeable young man lived next door, she thought that if she could find a hole in the wall that divided her house from his, she could go on peeping through it until she caught sight of him. She would then have an opportunity to speak with him and offer him her love, if he were prepared to accept it, after which, should a way be found to do so, they could get together from time to time. And in this fashion she would be able to get through her unhappy life until the demon who possessed her husband left him.

And so, when her husband was not around, she went from one spot to another in her house examining the wall, until she discovered, in a fairly remote location, a place where there was a crack. Peering through it, she had a hard time making out what was on the other side, but she finally determined that it was a bedroom, and said to herself, "If this were Filippo's room"—that being the name of the young man who was her neighbor—"I'd be halfway there."

The wife got one of her maidservants, a woman who felt sorry for her, secretly to keep watch by the crack, and discovered that it was indeed the young man's bedroom and that he slept there all by himself. By paying frequent visits to the crack, and dropping pebbles and little pieces of straw through it whenever she heard the young man on the other side, she finally managed to get him to come over and see what was going on. Then she quietly called out to him, and when the young man, recognizing her voice, replied, she seized her opportunity and in short order told him everything that was on her mind. Overjoyed, the young man began to enlarge the hole from his side of the wall, but always in such a way that no one would notice what he was doing. And there, on numerous occasions, the two of them would talk and touch one another's hands, although they could go no further because of the strict surveillance maintained by her jealous husband.

Now, seeing as how Christmas was approaching, the lady told her husband that, if he approved, she would like to attend church on that morning so that she could go to confession and take Communion just like every other Christian.

"And what sins have you committed," asked the jealous husband, "that you want to go to confession?"

"What!" she replied. "Do you think I'm a saint just because you keep me locked up? You know very well that I commit sins like everyone else down here, but I have no intention of telling them to you since you're no priest."

His suspicions being aroused by her words, the jealous husband decided he would try to discover just what those sins were that she had committed. Having thought up a way to do it, he responded to her request by saying that he approved of it, but that he wanted her to go to their own chapel rather than some other church. Moreover, she was to get there early in the morning and make her confession to their chaplain, or to whatever priest the chaplain assigned her, and to no one else, after which she was to return home straightway. The lady had an inkling that he was up to something, but without saying anything further on the subject, she replied that she would do as he wished.

When Christmas morning arrived, the lady arose at daybreak, put on some nice clothes, and went to the church her jealous husband had insisted on. As for him, he, too, had gotten up and gone to the same church, arriving there ahead of her. He had already arranged things with the chaplain and quickly put on one of his robes. It had a large hood that covered his cheeks, like the ones we see priests wearing nowadays, and after pulling it forward a bit over his head, he took a seat in the choir stalls.

Upon entering the church, the lady asked for the chaplain, and when he arrived and heard that she wanted to make her confession, he told her he could not hear it himself, but would send her one of his fellow priests. Then away he went and sent the jealous husband, unfortunately for him, to speak with her instead. But even though he walked up to her with great solemnity, and the day was not particularly bright, and he had pulled the hood down well over his eyes, he was still unable to disguise himself so completely as to prevent the lady from recognizing him at once. The moment she realized who it was, she said to herself: "Praise be to God, this guy's turned from a jealous husband into a priest! But never mind, I'm going to see that he gets what he's looking for."

Pretending not to recognize him, she sat down at his feet.° Messer Jealous had put some pebbles in his mouth so that they would interfere with his speech a bit in order to keep his wife from identifying him by his voice, and he thought his disguise was otherwise so perfect that she would not be able to make him out.

But to come now to the confession: having first explained that she was married, the lady told him, among other things, that she was in love with a priest who came to sleep with her every night. When her jealous husband heard this, he felt as though someone had taken a knife and stabbed him through the heart, and if it were not for the fact that he was driven by his desire to know more about it, he would have abandoned the confession and gone away. Instead, he stayed put and asked her: "How's that? Doesn't your husband sleep with you?"

"Yes, Father," replied the lady.

"Well, then," said the jealous man, "how can the priest sleep with you, too?"

"Father," said the lady, "I don't know what art the priest makes use of, but there's not a door in the house so securely locked that it won't open the instant he touches it. What's more, he tells me that when he arrives at the one to my bedroom, he recites certain words before unlocking it that immediately make my husband doze off, and as soon as he hears him sleeping, he opens the door, comes inside, and lies down with me. And this procedure of his never fails."

"My lady," said the jealous husband, "this is very wrong, and you must give it up completely."

"Father," said the lady, "I don't think I could ever do that because I love him too much."

"Then I won't be able to give you absolution," replied the jealous husband.

"I'm sorry about that," she said, "but I didn't come here to tell you lies. If I thought I could do what you ask, I'd tell you so."

"I am truly sorry for you, my lady," he said, "for I see you losing your soul by taking this course of action. But I will do you a favor and go to the trouble of saying some special prayers of mine to God on your behalf, which may possibly do you some good. Also, I'll be sending you one of my young clerks from time to time.° You're to report to him whether or not the prayers are helping you, and if they are, then we'll take it from there."

"Don't do it, father," she replied. "Don't send anyone to me at the house, because if my husband found out about it, he's so insanely jealous that nothing in the world would ever dislodge the idea from his head that the boy had some evil design in going there, and he'd give me no peace for the rest of the year."

"Don't worry about that, my lady," he said. "I'll make sure to arrange things in such a way that you'll never hear a word about it from him."

"If you're confident you can do that," said the lady, "then it's all right with me." And having recited the *Confiteor* and received her penance, she got to her feet and went to hear Mass.°

Fuming with jealousy, the hapless husband headed off as well, and after removing his priest's robes, he returned home, determined to find a way to catch the priest and his wife together and to do the pair of them a bad turn. When the lady came back from church, she saw quite clearly from the look on her husband's face that she had spoiled his holiday for him, although he did his best to conceal what he had done and what he thought he knew.°

Having made up his mind to spend the following night waiting near the front door to see whether the priest would show up, he said to his wife: "Tonight I have to go out for supper, and I'll be sleeping elsewhere as well, so be sure you do a good job of locking up not just the front door, but the one on the landing and the one to the bedroom. Then, whenever you feel like it, you can go to bed."

"Very well," replied the lady.

As soon as she had the chance, she went to the hole in the wall and gave the usual signal. When he heard it, Filippo came at once, and the lady told him what she had done that morning as well as what her husband had told her after they had eaten.

"I'm certain he won't leave the house," she said. "Instead, he's going to keep watch by the front door. So, find some way to get in here tonight by climbing up over the roof, and then we can be together."

"Leave it to me, my lady," said the young man, who was thoroughly delighted by this development.

At nightfall, the jealous husband quietly concealed himself with his weapons in one of the rooms on the ground floor, while his wife locked up all the doors, and especially the one on the landing, so that he could not come back up, and in due time, the young man appeared, having made his way to her very cautiously by climbing over the roof from his side of it. Then the two of them went to bed, where they took their pleasure of one another, enjoying themselves until daybreak, at which point the young man returned to his house.

The jealous husband, freezing to death, aching, and supperless, spent practically the entire night with his weapons next to the front door, waiting for the priest to show up, but as dawn approached, incapable of staying awake any longer, he fell asleep in the ground-floor room. It was close to tierce when he awoke, and finding that the front door was now open, he acted as if he were just coming back home, went upstairs, and had something to eat. A little later he sent a servant boy of his, pretending to be the young clerk of the priest who had heard his wife's confession, to ask her if a certain person she knew about had come around again. The lady, who recognized the messenger quite easily, replied that he had not been there that night and that if he continued to behave like this, she might just wind up forgetting all about him, even though she did not particularly want to.

Now, what more is there to tell you? While the lady was having a good time with her lover, her jealous husband spent night after night at the front door trying to catch the priest, until he finally could not take it any longer, and with a look of fury on his face, demanded to know what his wife had said to the priest on the morning when she had gone to confession. The lady answered that she did not want to tell him because doing so was neither right nor proper.

"You wicked woman," said the jealous husband, "whether you like it or not, I know what you said to him, and I absolutely insist that you tell me, because unless you give me the name of the priest whom you're so much in love with and who uses incantations every night so he can sleep with you, I'll slit your throat."

The lady said it was simply not true that she was in love with a priest. "What?" asked her husband. "Didn't you say thus and such to the priest who was hearing your confession?"

"Yes, I sure did," she said, "not that he would have ever told you about it. All that would have really been required was for you to have been present and to have heard it for yourself."

"Then, tell me who this priest is," said the jealous man, "and be quick about it."

The lady began to smile, and said: "It's really very gratifying for me to see a simple woman lead a wise man around in the same way that a ram is led by the horns to the slaughter—not that you're a wise man, nor have you ever been one since the hour you allowed the evil spirit of jealousy to enter your breast, without there being any reason for it. And the more foolish and asinine you are, the less my accomplishment amounts to.

"Husband, do you really believe that the eyes in my head are as blind as the ones in your brain? They sure aren't. Because at first glance I recognized the priest who was hearing my confession and knew it was you, but I made up my mind to give you exactly what you were looking for—and that's just what I did. However, if you'd been as smart as you think you are, you would never have tried to find out your good wife's secrets by that means, and instead of succumbing to baseless suspicion, you would have realized that she was confessing the truth to you and hadn't committed a sin at all.

"I told you I was in love with a priest, and you, whom I'm greatly at fault for loving as I do, hadn't you turned yourself into a priest? I told you that no door in my house would remain locked when he wanted to sleep with me, and which door in your house was ever closed to you when you wanted to come to me, wherever I might happen to be? I told you that the priest slept with me every night, and was there ever a night when you didn't sleep with me? And every time you sent your clerk to me, you know it was always when you were not sleeping with me, and so, I sent him to tell you that the priest had not been here.

"How could anyone except you, a man who's let himself be blinded by jealousy, have been so foolish as to have failed to understand these things? And you, you've been in the house every night keeping watch by the front door, and you actually think you made me believe that you'd gone elsewhere to have supper and spend the night!

"It's time you took a good look at yourself and went back to behaving like a man the way you used to do. Stop allowing yourself to be made a fool of by someone who knows you as well as I do. And give up all this strict surveillance of yours, because I swear to God that if I had any desire to make you a cuckold, I'd find a way to enjoy myself without your ever noticing it, even though you had a hundred eyes instead of just a single pair."°

After listening to what she had to say, the jealous wretch, who thought he had been so very clever in discovering his wife's secret, realized that he had been made a laughingstock, and without saying another word by way of reply, he concluded that she was not only sagacious, but virtuous as well. And so, now that he really needed it, he divested himself completely of his jealousy, just as he had put it on before, when it was unnecessary. Consequently, his clever wife, having acquired, as it were, a license to pursue her pleasures, no longer had her lover come over the roof like a cat in order to visit her, but ushered him right straight in through the front door. And from then on, always acting with discretion, she had lots of good times with him and spent many a merry hour in his company.

Story 8

A MAN BECOMES JEALOUS OF HIS WIFE WHEN HE DISCOVERS
THAT SHE HAS BEEN TYING A PIECE OF STRING TO HER TOE
AT NIGHT SO THAT SHE WILL KNOW WHEN HER LOVER HAS
ARRIVED. WHILE HER HUSBAND IS OFF PURSUING HIM, THE
LADY GETS ANOTHER WOMAN TO TAKE HER PLACE IN BED.
THE HUSBAND BEATS THE WOMAN, AND HAVING CUT OFF
SOME OF HER HAIR, GOES TO FETCH HIS WIFE'S BROTHERS,
BUT WHEN THEY DISCOVER THAT HIS STORY IS UNTRUE,
THEY DIRECT A STREAM OF INSULTS AT HIM.°

*   *   *

Lovely ladies, if I am to entertain you with a story as fine as the ones that my predecessors have already produced, I am facing quite a heavy responsibility, but with God's help, I hope to carry it off successfully.

You must know, then, that in our city there once lived an extremely wealthy merchant named Arriguccio Berlinghieri who foolishly thought to ennoble himself by marrying into the aristocracy, as his counterparts have been doing continuously down to this very day, and who took to wife a young noblewoman, quite unsuited to him, by the name of Monna Sismonda.° Since her husband was often on the road, as merchants commonly are, and spent little time at home with her, she fell in love with a young man called Ruberto, who had been courting her for a long time.

Soon on intimate terms with him, Monna Sismonda took such delight in his company that she possibly became somewhat careless, and Arriguccio, whether he had by chance gotten wind of the affair or for some other reason, became the most jealous man in the world. He stopped traveling about, abandoned every single one of his other concerns, and devoted all his care to keeping his wife under close surveillance, nor would he ever go to sleep until after he had felt her climb into bed. She was, as a result, in the deepest distress, for there was no possible way for her to get together with her Ruberto.

But having devoted a great deal of thought to finding some means to be with him, and being eagerly urged on by him to do so as well, she finally hit upon the following plan: since her bedroom overlooked the street, and she had frequently noticed that Arriguccio slept very soundly once he overcame the difficulty he had in getting to sleep, she decided that she would ask Ruberto to come to the front door of the house around midnight, and she would go and open it for him. In this way, she could spend time with him while her husband was sound asleep. And so that she would know when he had arrived, she came up with the idea of dangling a thin string out of the bedroom window in such a way that no one would notice it. Allowing one of its ends to almost touch the ground, she would run it low across the floor of the room until it reached the bed, where she would bring its other end up under the covers, and as soon as she was in bed, she would tie it to her big toe. She sent word of this plan to Ruberto, telling him that when he came, he was to pull the string, and if her husband was sleeping, she would release it and go to open the door for him, but if her husband was awake, she would hold it taut and pull it in to let him know that he was not to wait for her. Ruberto liked the plan and stopped by her house quite frequently, sometimes being able to spend time with her, and sometimes not.

They continued to make use of this elaborate stratagem until finally, one night, while the lady was sleeping, Arriguccio just happened to stretch his foot down in the bed and discovered the string. Reaching down for it with his hand, he found it was attached to his wife's toe and said to himself, "This must be some sort of trick." When he then noticed how the string went out through the window, he was sure of it, and so he quietly cut it off from his wife's toe, tied it to his own, and waited vigilantly to see what would happen next. It did not take long for Ruberto to arrive, and when he tugged on the string as usual, it gave Arriguccio quite a start.

He had not tied it properly to his toe, however, and since Ruberto had given it a hard jerk and the string had come down into his hands, he assumed he was to wait. And so he did.

Leaping out of bed and grabbing his weapons, Arriguccio ran to the front door to see who it was, intent upon doing him some injury. Now, for all that he was a merchant, Arriguccio was a strong, savage man, and when he reached the front door, he did not open it quietly the way his wife always did. Ruberto was waiting outside, and the moment he heard the noise, he divined what it meant, namely that Arriguccio was the one who had opened the door, and he instantly took off, with Arriguccio in hot pursuit. At last, after running quite some distance without managing to shake off his pursuer, Ruberto, who was armed as well, drew out his sword and turned around, and the two of them began to fight, with Arriguccio on the attack and Ruberto defending himself.

Meanwhile, when Arriguccio opened the bedroom door, the lady woke up to find that the string attached to her toe had been cut, and she immediately realized that her ruse had been discovered. Hearing Arriguccio running after Ruberto, she got out of bed in haste, and anticipating what was likely to happen, she called to her maid, who knew the entire story, and prevailed upon her to take her own place in the bed, begging her not to reveal her identity, but to patiently endure all the blows that Arriguccio might inflict on her, in exchange for which she would receive such a reward that she would have no cause for complaint. Then, having extinguished the light that was burning in the bedroom, she went and hid herself in another part of the house, waiting to see what was going to happen.

While Arriguccio and Ruberto were scuffling, the people in the neighborhood heard the noise, got out of bed, and started cursing them out. Afraid that he might be recognized, Arriguccio stopped the fight and returned home, full of rage and indignation, without having been able to discover who the young man was or to inflict the slightest injury on him. When he reached the bedroom, he started shouting angrily: "Where are you, you evil woman? You put out the light to prevent me from finding you, but you've got that one wrong!"

Going over to the bed, he grabbed the maid, thinking he had hold of his wife, and hit her and kicked her, giving her as many blows with his hands and feet as he could manage, until he had completely smashed in her face. Finally, he cut off her hair, all the while calling her the foulest names that were ever directed at an unchaste woman.

The maid was weeping bitterly, as she had every reason to, and although now and again she said, "Alas! For God's sake, have mercy!" or "No more!" her speech was so broken up by her sobbing, and Arriguccio was so blinded by his fury, that he did not realize that the voice belonged to some other woman, not his wife. Having thus beaten the living daylights out of her and cut off her hair, as we said before, he exclaimed: "You wicked woman, I have no intention of laying another hand on you, but I'll go fetch your brothers and tell them about the fine way you behave. Furthermore, I'll tell them to come for you and to do with you whatever they think their honor requires. Then I want them to take you away from here, for let me assure you, you're not going to stay in this house any longer." When he was finished speaking, he left the bedroom, locked it from the outside, and set off down the road all by himself.

Monna Sismonda had heard everything, and as soon as she knew that her husband had left the house, she opened the bedroom door, and having lit the lamp again, she found her maid there, bruised all over and weeping bitterly. She consoled her as best she could and led her back to her own bedroom, where, afterward, she secretly arranged for her to be waited on and given medical treatment, compensating her with Arriguccio's own money so handsomely that the maid declared she was quite satisfied.

Once the maid had been reinstalled in her own room, the lady quickly tidied up her bedchamber, remade the bed, and arranged everything as if no one had slept there that night. Having relit the lamp, she got dressed and fixed herself up to make it appear that she had not yet gone to bed, after which she lit another lamp, picked up her sewing, and sitting down at the head of the stairs, she began working on it as she waited to see how things would turn out.

Meanwhile, after leaving his house, Arriguccio had gone as quickly as possible to that of his wife's brothers, and once there, knocked away on the door until someone heard him and let him in. When the lady's brothers, all three of them, and her mother learned that Arriguccio was in the house, they got out of bed, called for lamps to be lit, and came down to see him and ask him what had brought him there, all alone, and at such an hour.

Beginning with the string he had found tied to Monna Sismonda's toe, Arriguccio went on to tell them the entire story about what he had discovered and what he had done. To supply them with conclusive proof of what had happened, he took the hair that he thought he had cut off his wife's head and handed it over to them, adding that they should come to get her and should deal with her in a way they thought consistent with their honor, for he had no intention of keeping her in his house any longer.

Believing every word of Arriguccio's story, the lady's brothers got very upset about what they had been told, and filled with rage at their sister, they called for torches to be lit and set out to accompany Arriguccio to his house with the intention of really giving her a bad time. Upon seeing their reaction, their mother started out after them, weeping and begging them, each in turn, not to be in such a rush to believe these things without seeing more evidence or learning more about what had happened. She noted that the husband might have had some other reason to be angry with their sister, and having treated her badly, he could now be blaming her in order to excuse his own behavior. She also said that she was truly amazed how such a thing could have happened, knowing her daughter as well as she did, and having raised her from the time she was a little girl. And she went on making many more remarks in a similar vein.

Upon reaching Arriguccio's house, they went inside and began climbing the stairs. When Monna Sismonda heard them coming, she asked, "Who's there?"

"You're going to find out soon enough who it is, you evil woman," replied one of her brothers.

"God help us! What's this all about?" she said, and getting to her feet, she went on: "Brothers, how nice to see you. But what can have brought the three of you here at this hour?"

When they saw her sitting there and sewing, without any sign of a beating on her face, although Arriguccio had said he had really pummeled her, they were initially somewhat taken aback, and restraining the vehemence of their anger, they asked her for an explanation in response to the complaint that Arriguccio had made about her, threatening her with dire consequences if she did not tell them the whole story.

"I don't know what I'm supposed to say to you," the lady replied, "or why Arriguccio should have complained to you about me."

Arriguccio was looking at her, staring like someone who had lost his mind, for he recalled having punched her maybe a thousand times in the face and having scratched her and given her the world's worst beating, but now she looked as though nothing had happened to her.

In brief, the brothers told her what Arriguccio had said to them about the string, the beating, and all the rest. Turning to her husband, the lady exclaimed: "Alas, husband, what's this I'm hearing? Why are you bringing so much shame on yourself by presenting me as some evil woman even though I'm nothing of the sort, while making yourself out to be a cruel, wicked man, even though you're not like that, either? And when were you ever in this house tonight until just now, let alone with me? And when was it that you gave me a beating? For my part, I have no recollection of it."

"What, you evil woman," Arriguccio started to say, "didn't we go to bed together? Didn't I come back here after giving chase to your lover? Didn't I punch you repeatedly and cut off your hair?"

"You didn't go to bed in this house last night," replied the lady. "But let's leave that be, since I have nothing but my own words to prove it's true, and let's come to what you said about beating me and cutting off my hair. You never hit me, and I ask everyone here, including you, to observe whether I have any sign of a beating anywhere on my body. Nor would I advise you to be so bold as to lay a hand on me, for by God's Cross, I'd scratch your face to pieces. And you didn't cut off my hair, either, as far as I felt or saw anything, although perhaps you did it without my noticing it. Let me see whether it's cut or not." Then, lifting her veils from off her head, she showed that her hair was all there and that not a single strand of it had been cut.

When her brothers and her mother saw and heard all this, they turned on Arriguccio and started in with: "What are you saying, Arriguccio? This doesn't jibe with what you came and told us you'd done, and we have no idea how you can possibly prove the rest of it." Arriguccio stood there like someone lost in a dream, and although he wanted very much to say something, on seeing that what he had thought he could prove true was not the case, he did not dare to utter a single word.

Turning back to her brothers, his wife said: "Now I see, brothers, what he's been looking for. He wants me to do something that I, myself, have never had any desire to do, which is to tell you all about his wicked, dishonorable behavior. And I'll do it, for I firmly believe that the story he told you about what happened to him is actually true and that he did do all the things he said he did. Just listen, and I'll explain how.

"This worthy man, to whom it was my misfortune to have been given by you in marriage, and who calls himself a merchant and wishes to be thought creditworthy—which means he should be more temperate than a monk and chaster than a maid—well, there are few evenings when he doesn't go from tavern to tavern getting drunk and consorting with one harlot after another. And he keeps me waiting up for him, just the way you saw me now, for half the night and sometimes all the way to matins.

"I'm sure that when he was good and drunk, he went to sleep with one of his trollops and that when he woke up and found the string on her foot, he did all those brave feats he told you about, after which he returned to her, beat her up, and cut off her hair. And since he was still in his cups, he believed—and I'm sure he still does—that he'd done those things to me. In fact, if you take a good look at his face, you'll see he's still half drunk. But all the same, whatever he may have said about me, I want you to think of it as nothing more than the words of a lush, and since I forgive him myself, you must do so, too."

In response to her speech, her mother started raising a stink and said: "By God's Cross, my daughter, that's not what should be done. Instead, this obnoxious cur, this nobody, who was completely unworthy of having a girl like you, he ought to be killed. Brother, this is just great! You'd think he'd picked you up out of the mud! May he rot in Hell before you have to put up with the foul slander of some petty dealer in donkey droppings. These yokels come up here from some country lord's gang of thugs and go around dressed in cheap clothes and baggy breeches with their quill pens stuck in their butts.° As soon as they've got three *soldi,* they want the daughters of noblemen and fine ladies for their wives, and they make up coats of arms for themselves, and they go around saying, 'I'm one of the so-and-sos,' and 'The people from my house did thus and such.'

"I really wish my sons had followed my advice, for they could have set you up just as honorably in the house of one of the Guidi counts even though you had no more than a piece of bread for your dowry.° Instead, they wanted to give you to this lovely jewel, this guy who's got the best, most virtuous girl in Florence, but who's not ashamed, and in the middle of the night, to say that you're a whore, as if we didn't know you. By God, if they took my word for it, he'd get such a beating that he'd be stinking from it for days."

Then she turned to the lady's brothers and said: "Boys, I told you all along that this couldn't be true. Have you been listening to how your sister is treated by this fine brother-in-law of yours? By this two-bit peddler here, which is what he is. Because, if I were you, after hearing what he says about her and what he's doing to her, I'd never rest content or consider myself satisfied until I'd wiped him off the face of the earth. And if I were as much of a man as I am a woman, I'd take care of this mess myself and wouldn't let anyone get in my way. God, damn him to Hell, the miserable, shameless drunk!"

Having taken everything in, the young men turned to Arriguccio and gave him the worst tongue-lashing any bad man has ever received. They then concluded, however, by saying: "We forgive you this time because you were drunk, but as you value your life, from now on you better watch out that we never hear any more stories like this, for if another one ever reaches our ears, you may rest assured we'll pay you back for that one, and for this one as well."

Having said their piece, away they went, leaving Arriguccio standing there like someone who had lost his mind, unsure if what he had done was real or if he had been dreaming, and without uttering another word on the subject, from then on he left his wife in peace. Thus, thanks to her quick-wittedness, not only did Monna Sismonda manage to escape her imminent peril, but she opened the way to enjoy herself as much as she liked and never had to fear her husband again.

Story 9

NICOSTRATO'S WIFE, LIDIA, IS IN LOVE WITH PIRRO, WHO
ASKS HER TO DO THREE THINGS TO PERSUADE HIM THAT
SHE IS SINCERE, AND NOT ONLY DOES SHE DO ALL OF THEM,
BUT IN ADDITION, SHE MAKES LOVE TO HIM WHILE
NICOSTRATO IS WATCHING AND GETS HER HUSBAND
TO BELIEVE THAT WHAT HE SAW WAS UNREAL.°

The ladies enjoyed Neifile's story so much that they simply could not stop laughing and talking about it, even though the King, who had ordered Panfilo to tell his own tale, repeatedly called for them to be silent. Once they finally quieted down, however, Panfilo began as follows:

I do not believe, esteemed ladies, that there is any enterprise, no matter how difficult or dangerous, that someone passionately in love would not dare to undertake. Although this has been shown in many of our stories, nevertheless, I believe I can offer even better proof with the one I intend to tell you. In it you will hear about a lady whose deeds were far more favored by Fortune than guided by reason, which is why I do not advise any of you to risk following in her footsteps, because Fortune is not always so well disposed, nor are all the men in the world equally gullible.

In Argos, that most ancient Greek city, whose former kings brought it great renown despite its small size, there once lived a nobleman by the name of Nicostrato, on whom, as he was approaching old age, Fortune bestowed a wife of distinction, a woman who was no less bold than beautiful, and who was called Lidia.° As befits a man both rich and noble, he maintained a large household, owned numerous hawks and hounds, and took the greatest delight in hunting. One of his retainers was a lively, elegant young man named Pirro, who was handsome and adept at whatever activity he chose to pursue, and Nicostrato loved and trusted him above all the others.

Lidia fell so passionately in love with this Pirro that she could think of nothing else day and night. Pirro, however, showed no interest in her passion, either because he did not notice it, or because he did not want to, and this filled the lady's heart with unbearable pain. Fully determined to make him aware of her feelings, she summoned one of her chambermaids, a woman named Lusca, who was her close confidante, and said to her:

"Lusca, all the favors you've had from me in the past should have earned me your loyalty and obedience, and therefore, you must take care that no one ever hears what I am about to tell you, except for the man to whom I will ask you to repeat it. As you can see, Lusca, I'm young and vigorous, as well as being abundantly supplied with everything a woman could desire. In short, I have nothing to complain about, with one exception, which is that my husband is much too old for me, so that I have been getting far too little of that which gives young women the greatest pleasure. And because I desire it no less than others do, I made up my mind long ago that since Fortune didn't show herself my friend when she bestowed such an elderly husband on me, I should at least avoid being my own worst enemy and try to find another way to obtain my happiness and my salvation. Now, to make sure that my enjoyment in this should be as complete as it is in everything else, I've decided that our Pirro is the one to take care of my needs with his embraces, for he is worthier in this regard than any other man, and such is the love I bear him that I feel sick whenever I'm not gazing at him or thinking about him. In fact, unless I can be with him very soon, I truly believe I'm going to die. Therefore, if you value my life, you must acquaint him with my love for him in whatever way you think best, and beg him on my behalf to be so good as to come to me whenever you go to fetch him."

The maid said she would be happy to do it, and as soon as she found a convenient time and place, she took Pirro aside and, to the best of her ability, delivered her mistress's message. Pirro was completely taken by surprise when he heard it, for such a thing had never occurred to him, and he was worried that the lady might have sent him the message in order to test him. Consequently, speaking harshly, he gave quite an abrupt reply: "Lusca, I can't believe these words come from my lady, so you'd better be careful about what you're saying. Even if they really did come from her, I don't believe she was sincere when she spoke with you. And even if she was, my lord has done me so much more honor than I deserve that I would never, on my life, commit such an outrage against him. So, you watch out and never talk to me about such things again."

"Pirro," said Lusca, undeterred by the severity of his speech, "if my lady orders me to speak to you about this, or about anything else, I'll do so as often as she tells me to, whether you like it or not. But you now, you really are an ass!"

Somewhat chagrined by what Pirro had said, Lusca returned to her mistress, who simply wanted to die when she heard his answer. A few days later, however, she spoke to her chambermaid about the matter once more.

"You know, Lusca," she said, "it's not the first stroke that fells the oak. So it seems to me you should go back again to this man who has such a strange way of wanting to prove his loyalty at my expense. Find a convenient time to give him a full account of my passion, and do your best to make sure you succeed. For if things remain as they are, I'm going to die, and he'll just think we were making a fool of him, so that instead of the love we're seeking, we'll wind up earning his hatred."

After comforting her mistress, the maid went in search of Pirro, and when she found him in a cheerful and agreeable mood, she said to him: "Pirro, a few days ago I explained to you how your lady and mine was being consumed by the flames of the love she feels for you, and I'm here to assure you yet again that if you remain as unyielding as you were the other day, she won't be alive much longer. I therefore implore you to be so kind as to provide her with the solace she desires. I used to consider you very wise, but if you persist in being stubborn like this, I will take you for an utter fool.

"What greater glory can you have than to be loved above everything else by such a lady, who's so beautiful and noble and rich? Furthermore, don't you realize how grateful you should be to Fortune for having given you quite a valuable prize, a woman who is perfectly suited to your youthful desires and who will also provide you with a secure refuge from all your material needs? How many of your peers will have a life more blissful than yours, if you'll just act and use your intelligence here? Which of them will be your equal when it comes to arms and horses, clothing and money, if you will just grant her your love? So, open your heart to my words, and return to your senses. Remember that Fortune greets a man only once with a smiling face and open arms, and if he does not know how to accept what she gives him and later on winds up an impoverished beggar, he has only himself, not her, to blame.

"Besides, there doesn't have to be the same sort of loyalty between servants and masters as that which exists between friends and family. On the contrary, to the extent that they can, servants ought to treat their masters the same way their masters treat them. If you had a beautiful wife, or a mother or daughter or sister, and Nicostrato took a liking to her, do you really believe he'd spend as much time thinking about loyalty as you are doing with regard to his wife? You're a fool if you give it a moment's thought, for you can be sure that if his flattery and entreaties weren't sufficient, he'd make use of force on her, no matter what you might think about it. So let's treat them and their belongings the same way they treat us and ours. Make the most of what Fortune's offering you, and don't chase my mistress away. Go out and meet her half-way as she approaches, because you may be sure that if you don't do that, not only will her death be inevitable, but you'll wind up reproaching yourself so often for what you did that you, too, will want to die."

Pirro had spent a great deal of time mulling over what Lusca had said to him during their previous exchange, and he had already made up his mind that if she ever approached him again, he would give her a different answer and would do everything he could to satisfy the lady, provided that it could be proved she was not simply testing him. And so, he replied by saying: "Look here, Lusca, I recognize the truth in everything you've said to me, but on the other hand, I also know that my master is not merely very wise, but very shrewd as well, and since he has placed the managing of all of his affairs in my hands, I'm really afraid that Lidia is doing all this with his advice and consent so as to put me to the test. However, if she's willing to do three things I'll ask of her in order to reassure me, then you may depend on me to do whatever she wishes without a moment's hesitation. And these are the three things I want her to do: first, she must kill Nicostrato's fine sparrow hawk right in front of his eyes; then she should send me a tuft of hairs from his beard; and finally, she should get me one of the soundest teeth he has left."

These terms seemed hard to Lusca and much, much harder to her mistress, but Love, that great provider of comfort and excellent teacher of cunning, made her resolve to attempt it. Consequently, she sent Pirro word through her maid that she would do everything he asked, and soon. Furthermore, since he thought Nicostrato was so smart, she told him that she would arrange for them to make love right in front of him and get him to believe that it was not really happening.

Pirro therefore waited to see what the lady would do, and a few days later, when Nicostrato was entertaining certain gentlemen at one of the great banquets he used to give with some frequency, the tables had no sooner been cleared away than the lady came out of her room, wearing a green velvet dress richly adorned with jewels, and entered the hall where the gentlemen had been dining. Then, as Pirro and all the others watched, she went over to the perch where the sparrow hawk that Nicostrato treasured so much was sitting, untied it as if she intended to set it on her hand, and having seized it by the jesses, dashed it against the wall and killed it.°

Nicostrato shouted at her, "Oh no, woman, what have you done?" She, however, said nothing in response, but turned instead to the gentlemen with whom he had been dining and said: "My lords, I'd hardly be able to revenge myself on a king who insulted me if I lacked the courage to take it out on a sparrow hawk. What you need to know is that this bird has long deprived me of the attention that men should devote to their ladies' pleasure, for Nicostrato always gets up at the crack of dawn, mounts his horse, and with his sparrow hawk on his hand, rides off to the open plains in order to watch it fly, leaving me behind in my bed, just as you see me here, all alone and discontent. That's why I have often wanted to do what I did just now, and all I was waiting for was a chance to do it in the presence of men who would judge my cause justly, as I trust you will do."

Supposing that her feelings for her husband were exactly what her words implied, the gentlemen all started to laugh, and turning to the angry Nicostrato, they said, "Come on now, your wife did the right thing to avenge her wrongs by killing the sparrow hawk!" And with a host of witty remarks on the subject—the lady having returned to her room in the meantime—they managed to transform Nicostrato's irritation into laughter.

Pirro, who had observed all this, said to himself: "My lady has given my happy love a noble start. May God let her stay the course!"

Not many days after killing the sparrow hawk, Lidia found herself in her bedroom with Nicostrato, and when she began caressing and joking around with him, he gave her hair a playful little tug, which provided her with an opportunity to fulfill the second of Pirro's demands. She then promptly took hold of a little tuft of hairs in his beard, and laughing all the while, pulled it so hard that she tore it right out of his chin. In response to Nicostrato's complaints, she said: "Now what's the matter with you that you're making such a face? Just because I tore maybe half a dozen hairs out of your beard? That's nothing compared to what I felt when you were yanking at my hair just a moment ago." And so, they continued jesting and playing around with one another. Meanwhile, the lady carefully preserved the tuft of hairs she had pulled from his beard and sent it to her precious beloved the very same day.

The third task gave the lady a lot more to think about, but since she was a person of superior intelligence and Love had made her wits even sharper, she figured out a way to take care of it.

In his house Nicostrato had two young boys of gentle birth who had been entrusted to him by their fathers so that they might learn proper manners, and when he was dining, one of them used to carve for him, while the other poured him his drink. Having sent for them, the lady gave them to understand that their breath stank, and taught them that whenever they served Nicostrato, they were to hold their heads as far back as possible, and also, that they were never to mention the subject to anyone.

The boys believed her and began acting as she had told them to, until eventually, one day, she asked Nicostrato: "Have you noticed what these boys do when they're waiting on you?"

"I certainly have," said Nicostrato, "and in fact, I've been meaning to ask them why they do it."

"Don't bother," said the lady, "because I myself can tell you why. I've kept quiet about it for quite some time because I didn't want to upset you, but now that I see others are starting to notice, there's no reason to hide it from you any longer. This is all happening to you simply because your breath smells atrocious. Now, I don't know why it does, because it never used to, but it really is terrible, and since you spend your time in the company of gentlemen, we've got to figure out some way to cure it."

"What could be causing it?" said Nicostrato. "I wonder if one of the teeth in my mouth is rotten."

"Perhaps it is," replied Lidia, and leading him to a window, she made him open his mouth. After having inspected both sides of it, she said: "Oh, Nicostrato, how can you have put up with it for so long? You've got one on this side, and as far as I can see, it's not just decayed, but rotten through and through. If it stays in your mouth much longer, it'll be sure to ruin the teeth on either side. So, my advice to you is to have it out before it gets any worse."

"If that's what you think," said Nicostrato, "well, then, I agree. Send for a surgeon right away and have him extract it for me."°

"God forbid that we should have a surgeon come here and do that," replied the lady. "The way your tooth looks to me, I think I can do a very good job of pulling it out myself and won't need help from anyone else. Besides, those surgeons are so cruel when they perform such operations that I'd be utterly heartsick and couldn't bear to see and hear you suffering at their hands. No, I absolutely insist on doing it myself, because then, if you're in too much pain, I'll stop at once, which is something a surgeon would never do."

She then had them bring her the necessary instruments and sent everyone out of room except for Lusca, whom she kept right by her side. After locking the door, they made Nicostrato stretch out on a table, put the pincers in his mouth, and grabbed one of his teeth with them. And although he roared out loud because of the pain, one of the women held him firmly down, while the other, using all her might, yanked out a tooth, which she hid away and replaced with another one, horribly decayed, that she had been holding in her hand. She showed it to Nicostrato, who was whimpering, practically half dead, and said to him: "Look at what you've had in your mouth for all this time."

Nicostrato did not doubt her story, and although the pain he was suffering was excruciating and he was still complaining bitterly about it, now that the tooth was out, he felt as if he were cured. And so, after he had been consoled in one way and another, and his pain had diminished, he left the room. The lady then took the tooth and promptly sent it to her lover who was now completely convinced of her affection for him and declared that he was prepared to minister to her every pleasure.

The lady wanted to reassure him even more, however, and although every hour she was not with him seemed like a thousand to her, she was determined to keep the promise she had made to him. Consequently, she pretended to be sick, and one day, when Nicostrato came to visit her after dinner, and she saw that there was no one with him except Pirro, she asked him if they would help her down to the garden in order to give her some relief in her illness. And so, with Nicostrato supporting her on one side and Pirro on the other, they carried her into the garden and placed her on the lawn at the foot of a lovely pear tree. After sitting there for a while, the lady addressed herself to Pirro, to whom she had already sent word about what he was to do. "Pirro," she said, "I have a great longing for a couple of those pears, so would you climb up there and throw down some of them."

Pirro immediately scampered up and began tossing down the pears, and as he was doing so, he said: "Hey, what are you doing there, sir? And you, my lady, aren't you ashamed to permit it in my presence? Do you two think I'm blind? Up until a moment ago you were terribly sick: how did you get well so quickly that you can do such things? Really, if you want to carry on like that, you've got plenty of fine bedrooms. Why don't you go and do it in one of those? That would be much more decent than doing it in front of me!"

The lady turned to her husband and said: "What's Pirro talking about? Has he gone crazy?"

"No, my lady, I'm not crazy," replied Pirro. "Do you think I can't see you?"

"Pirro," said Nicostrato, who was completely baffled, "I really do think you're dreaming."

"No, my lord," Pirro replied, "I'm not dreaming, not one little bit, and neither are you. In fact, you're doing it with so much vigor that if this tree were shaking like that, there wouldn't be a single pear left on it."

"What can this mean?" said the lady. "Can he really be seeing what he says he's seeing? God help me, if my health were what it was before, I'd climb up there and see these marvels that he claims to be observing."

Meanwhile, from up in the pear tree, Pirro kept talking and telling them the same strange story, until Nicostrato said, "Come down." When Pirro was on the ground, Nicostrato asked him, "Now what is it you say you saw?"

"I do believe that you two take me for a madman or a dreamer," replied Pirro, "but since you force me to tell you, I saw you there on top of your wife, and then, when I was descending, you got off and sat down here where you are now."

"You really were out of your mind," said Nicostrato, "because from the time you climbed into the pear tree, we haven't budged from this spot."

"What's the point of having this debate?" said Pirro. "I really did see you, and if I did, then what I saw was you there on top of yours."°

Nicostrato grew more and more astonished. Finally, he declared: "I want to find out for myself if this pear tree is enchanted and what kind of marvels you can see from it!"

So up he went, and no sooner was he in the tree than his wife and Pirro started to make love together.° Nicostrato saw it and began yelling at them: "Oh, you vile woman, what are you doing? And you, Pirro, whom I trusted more than anyone else?" And as he was speaking, he started to climb down again.

"We're just sitting here," said Pirro and the lady at first, but upon seeing him descend, they went and seated themselves the way they had been before. The moment that Nicostrato reached the ground and saw them sitting where he had left them, he fell to berating them.

"Nicostrato," said Pirro in response, "now I must confess that what you were saying before was right, that my eyes were, in fact, deceiving me when I was up in the pear tree. And my only reason for saying this is that I now know for a fact that you, too, have had the same experience I did. Moreover, to convince you that I'm telling the truth, just stop and think about your wife for a moment. If a woman of such unequaled honesty and wisdom as she is wished to commit an outrage in this way against your honor, do you really think she would ever bring herself to do it right before your eyes?

Of myself I say nothing, except that I would sooner allow myself to be drawn and quartered than even contemplate such a thing, let alone come and do it in your presence.

"Hence, whatever is causing our faulty perception must surely be emanating from the pear tree. For nothing in the world would have kept me from believing that you were having carnal relations with your wife here, until I heard you say that I myself appeared to be doing something that I know for sure I never did, let alone even thought of doing."

At this point the lady pretended to be terribly upset and got to her feet. "Damn you," she said, "for thinking me so stupid that, if I had wanted to engage in that disgusting behavior you claim to have seen, I'd come and do it right before your eyes. But there is one thing you can be certain of: should I ever feel such a desire, I wouldn't come out here to satisfy it. On the contrary, I think I'd be capable of finding one of our bedrooms and arranging to do it there in such a way that I'd be very surprised if you ever found out about it."

Nicostrato believed that the two of them were telling the truth and that they would never have brought themselves to commit such a deed in front of him. Consequently, he stopped shouting and berating them the way he had been doing, and instead began talking about the strangeness of what had happened and about the miraculous way people's eyesight was transformed when they climbed into the tree.

But his wife, who was still pretending to be upset over the opinion Nicostrato supposedly had of her, said: "If I can help it, there's absolutely no way this pear tree will ever put me or any other woman to shame again. Go, run and fetch an ax, Pirro, and at one stroke you can avenge both of us by chopping it down, although it would be much better if you took the ax and hit Nicostrato on the head with it for not giving the matter a second thought and allowing the eyes of his intellect to be blinded so easily. For although things may have appeared the way you said they did to those eyes in that head of yours, you should never have allowed the judgment of your mind to imagine, let alone admit, that they were true."

Pirro went for the ax as fast as he could and cut down the pear tree. And as soon as she saw it on the ground, the lady turned to Nicostrato and said: "Now that I've seen the fall of my honor's enemy, I'm not angry anymore." Then, she graciously pardoned Nicostrato, who had been begging her to do so, charging him never again to presume to think such thoughts about the woman who loved him more than her own life.

And so, the poor, deluded husband returned with his wife and her lover to the palace, where from that time on, it became much easier for Pirro to get together with Lidia at frequent intervals for their mutual pleasure and delight. And may God grant as much to all of us.

Conclusion

*   *   *

The sun was descending in the west and a gentle breeze had risen, when the King, who had finished his story and realized that there was no one else left to speak, removed the crown from his head and set it on Lauretta's. "My lady," he said, "with this, your namesake, I crown you Queen of our company.° And now, as our sovereign mistress, you may give orders for whatever you think will provide us all with pleasure and entertainment."

He then returned to his seat, and Lauretta, having become Queen, summoned the steward and ordered him to arrange to have the tables set up in the pleasant valley at a somewhat earlier hour than usual, so that they could return to the palace at their leisure. Next, she told him what he needed to do during the rest of her reign, after which she turned to the company and said:

"Yesterday, Dioneo proposed that we talk today about the tricks that women play on their husbands, and if it were not for the fact that I do not want to be thought of as belonging to that breed of snapping little curs who immediately want to retaliate for everything, I would insist that tomorrow we talk about the tricks men play on their wives. But letting that go, I want each of you, instead, to think up a story about the tricks that women are always playing on men, or men on women, or men on other men. This, without doubt, will be a topic just as pleasant to talk about as the one we had today." Having finished speaking, Lauretta got to her feet and dismissed the company until suppertime.

And so they all arose, the ladies and the men alike, and while some of them began wading barefoot through the clear water, others entertained themselves by roaming through the green meadow in among the lovely tall, straight trees, and Dioneo sang a lengthy song about Arcite and Palamon together with Fiammetta.° Thus, they all amused themselves in their several different ways, passing the time very agreeably until the hour for supper. When it arrived, they took their places at the tables next to the little lake, where they happily ate their meal at their ease, with never a fly to bother them, while they listened to the songs of a thousand birds and were cooled by a gentle breeze that flowed down continuously from the surrounding hills.

The tables were then cleared away, and since it was only half-way between nones and vespers and the sun was still up, they took a walk around the pleasant valley for a while, until the Queen gave the word and at a leisurely pace they went back down the road toward their usual lodging. Joking and chatting not only about what they had discussed that day, but about a thousand other things as well, they finally reached their lovely palace a little before nightfall. There they dispelled the fatigue of their brief journey with the coolest of wines and a variety of sweets, after which they immediately fell to dancing *carole* around the fair fountain, sometimes to the sound of Tindaro's bagpipes and sometimes to that of other instruments.°

At the end, however, the Queen ordered Filomena to sing a song, which she began this way:

> Alas, my life's forlorn!
> Oh, shall it ever be that I'll regain
> The place from which I had to part in grief?
> I'm far from sure I can return, alas,

Where I once was, despite the great desire
That burns within my breast.
O you, my precious Good, my sole Repose,
Who hold my heart bound tight,
Please answer me, for I don't dare to ask
Elsewhere, or know whom I
Might question. Oh, my Lord, please give me hope
So that my wandering soul may find relief.

     I can't describe how great the pleasure was
That has inflamed me so
That neither night nor day can I find rest.
For hearing, sight, and touch, my senses all,
With unfamiliar force,
Did kindle then new fires on their own,
So I burn everywhere.
There is no one but you to comfort me
Or to restore my shaken faculties.

     Please tell me if and when the time will come
I'll ever find you there
Where once I kissed those eyes that murdered me.
Tell me, my precious Good, O Soul of mine,
When you will come back there.
Please comfort me a little and say, "Soon."
May all the time be brief
Until you come, but then stay on, how long
I do not care—Love's wound's so deep in me!

     If I should happen once again to hold you,
I'll not be such a fool
As once I used to be and let you go.
I'll hold you fast, and then, let come what may,
For I must satisfy
All my desire on that sweet mouth of yours.
For now I'll say no more:
Come quickly therefore, come embrace me soon,
For just the thought of that moves me to sing.

This song made the entire company suspect that some pleasurable new love might have held Filomena in its grip. Indeed, the words seemed to imply to them that she had tasted more of love than just exchanging glances, and if they considered her all the happier for it, some of those present could not help but feel envious. When her song was finished, however, the Queen, remembering that the next day was Friday, graciously addressed the whole group:

"You know, noble ladies, and you young men as well, that tomorrow is the day consecrated to the Passion of Our Lord, and you will surely remember that we observed it devoutly when Neifile was Queen by refraining from these delightful discussions of ours, just as we did the following Saturday. Therefore, since I want to imitate the excellent example Neifile has given us, I think that for tomorrow and the day after, it would be proper for us to abstain from our pleasant storytelling, just as we did in the past, and to meditate instead on what was done on those two days for the salvation of our souls."

Everyone approved the devout words of their Queen, and since a good portion of the night had already passed, she dismissed them, and off they all went to take their rest.

Day 8

HERE ENDS THE SEVENTH DAY OF THE *DECAMERON* AND
THE EIGHTH BEGINS, IN WHICH, UNDER THE RULE OF
LAURETTA, THEY SPEAK OF THE TRICKS THAT WOMEN ARE
ALWAYS PLAYING ON MEN, OR MEN ON WOMEN, OR MEN ON
OTHER MEN.

* * *

Story 3

CALANDRINO, BRUNO, AND BUFFALMACCO GO DOWN
ALONG THE BANKS OF THE MUGNONE IN SEARCH OF THE
HELIOTROPE. BELIEVING HE HAS FOUND IT, CALANDRINO
RETURNS HOME WITH A LOAD OF STONES, AND WHEN HIS
WIFE SCOLDS HIM, HE GETS ANGRY AND BEATS HER.
FINALLY, HE TELLS HIS FRIENDS THE STORY, WHICH THEY
KNOW BETTER THAN HE DOES.°

* * *

My most pleasant ladies, I do not know whether, with a little story of mine, which is both true and entertaining, I will be able to make you laugh as much as Panfilo has done, but I will certainly try my best.

Not so very long ago, there lived in our city, where there has never been a lack of unusual customs and bizarre characters, a painter named Calandrino, a simpleminded man with some strange habits.° He used to hang out with two other painters named Bruno and Buffalmacco, a pair who were very merry, but who, being quite perceptive and shrewd, spent time with Calandrino because they often found his antics and his simplicity really funny.° At the same time there also lived in Florence a marvelously entertaining, astute, and capable young man named Maso del Saggio, who, having heard tales of Calandrino's simplicity, decided to go and amuse himself at Calandrino's expense by playing a practical joke on him or by getting him to believe some far-fetched notion.°

One day he came upon Calandrino by chance in the Church of San Giovanni where he was staring intently at the paintings and the bas-reliefs on the canopy that had recently been placed above the altar.° Maso felt that it was the right time and place for him to carry out his plan, and having informed a companion about what he intended to do, the two of them approached the place where Calandrino was sitting all by himself. Pretending not to see him, they started talking with one another about the powers of various stones, of which Maso spoke as authoritatively as if he were some important, well-known expert on the subject.

Hearing them talk, Calandrino pricked up his ears, and after a while, concluding that their conversation was not really private, he got to his feet and went over to join them, much to the delight of Maso, who was still holding forth when Calandrino asked him where these magical stones were to be found. Maso replied that most of them were in Gluttonia, the country of the Basques, which can be found in Gourmandistan, where the vines were tied up with sausages and a goose could be had for a penny, with a gosling thrown in for good measure.° In those parts they had a mountain made entirely of grated parmesan cheese where people did nothing except make gnocchi and ravioli that they cooked in capon broth. Then they would toss them down below, and the more you picked up, the more you had. And nearby there was a stream flowing with Vernaccia wine, the best you ever drank, without a single drop of water in it.°

"Oh!" said Calandrino. "What a wonderful country! But tell me: what happens to the capons they cook?"

"They're all eaten by the Basques," replied Maso.

"Were you ever there?" asked Calandrino.

"Was I ever there, you say?" Maso responded. "Why, if I've been there once, I've been there a thousand times."

"And how many miles away is it?" asked Calandrino.

"Of miles you count a thousandfold, which all the livelong night are told," replied Maso.°

"Then," said Calandrino, "it must be even farther away than Abruzzi."

"Sure is farther," Maso responded, "but it's really nothing."°

As he watched Maso say all this with a straight face, never laughing once, the simpleminded Calandrino believed absolutely everything Maso said, giving his words the kind of credence usually reserved for the most manifest of truths.

"As far as I'm concerned," Calandrino said, "that's just too far away. But if it were closer, you can bet I'd go there with you one of these days just to see those gnocchi come tumbling down and to get myself a bellyful of them. But tell me, God bless you, aren't any of those magical stones to be found in these parts?"

"Yes," replied Maso, "you can find two sorts of stones here that have extraordinary powers. They are the sandstones of Settignano and Montisci, by virtue of which, when they are turned into millstones, flour gets made, which is why they say in those parts over there that blessings come from God and millstones from Montisci.° But we've got so many of those sandstones around here that they're worth as little to us as emeralds are to them over there, where they have mountains of them higher than Monte Morello, and how they shine in the middle of the night, well, good night to you.° And you should know that if someone had the ability to make beautiful millstones and tie them together in a ring before the holes were bored in them, and then take them to the Sultan, he could get whatever he wanted for them.

"The other type is what we lapidaries call a heliotrope, a stone of such enormous power that no one can see you when you're not there, provided you keep it in your possession at all times."

"What amazing powers!" said Calandrino. "But this second one, where can you find it?"

Maso replied that they were commonly found in the valley of the Mugnone.

"How big is the stone?" asked Calandrino. "And what color is it?"

"They come in various sizes," replied Maso, "some bigger and some smaller, but all of them are nearly black in color."

Having made a mental note of all these details, Calandrino pretended he had other business to attend to and left Maso, determined to go and look for one of these stones. He did not want to do that, however, until he had informed Bruno and Buffalmacco about it, since they were his very closest friends. He therefore set out to find them so that they could all go and search for the stones at once before anyone else was able to do so, and he spent the rest of the morning hunting them down. Finally, some time after the hour of nones, he remembered that they were working in the convent at Faenza, so he dropped everything else he was doing, and although it was extremely hot, ran practically all the way there to find them.°

"Friends," he said, calling out to them, "if you'll trust me, we can become the richest men in Florence. Because I've heard it from a trustworthy guy that there's a stone in the valley of the Mugnone and that whoever has it on him will be completely invisible, so I reckon we should go and look for it right away before anybody else does. And since I know what it looks like, we're sure to find it, and once we do, what's to stop us from putting it in our purses, going to the money changers' tables, which are, you know, always loaded with groats and florins, and helping ourselves to as many as we want? No one's going to see us, and we'll be able to get rich quick and not have to spend every day sliming the walls like a bunch of snails."

As they listened to him, Bruno and Buffalmacco began laughing to themselves, but looking at one another, they pretended to be completely astonished and praised Calandrino's plan. Then Buffalmacco asked him what the stone was called, but like the dough-head he was, he had already forgotten its name.

"What does the name matter to us," he replied, "as long as we know about its powers? I think we should get a move on and go look for it rather than hang around here."

"All right, then," said Bruno, "so what does it look like?"

"They come in all shapes and sizes," Calandrino answered, "but since they're all more or less black, what we have to do, in my opinion, is to pick up all the black ones we see until we come across it. So let's get going and not waste any more time."

"Just wait a minute," replied Bruno and turned to Buffalmacco. "I think Calandrino's got a good idea," he said, "but it strikes me that this isn't the right time for it. The sun is high at this hour, and since it's shining straight down on the Mugnone, it will have dried out all the stones there, so that the ones that looked black this morning before the sun got to them will now appear to be white. Besides, since it's a workday, there are going to be a lot of people with business of one sort or another along the Mugnone, and if they see us, they might be able to guess what we've gone there to do. Then maybe they'll do it as well, and if they should get their hands on the stone, we would have wasted all our efforts.° So if you agree, it seems to me that this is a job we should do during the morning, when it will be easier to distinguish the black stones from the white ones, and on a holiday, when there won't be anyone around to see us."

After Buffalmacco praised Bruno's advice, Calandrino accepted it as well, and the three of them arranged to go together the following Sunday morning to look for the stone. Calandrino, however, begged them on no account to mention this to a living soul, as it had been imparted to him in the strictest confidence. After this, he went on to tell them what he had learned about

Gourmandistan, swearing an oath that it was all true. Once he had gone, the pair took time to work out the details of their plan together.

Calandrino waited impatiently for Sunday morning to arrive, and when it did, he got up near the crack of dawn and went to call on his friends. They left by the Porta San Gallo and went down to the Mugnone, where they followed its course as they began their search for the stone. The most eager of the three, Calandrino rushed on ahead, hopping nimbly from one place to the next. Whenever he spotted a black stone, he would throw himself to the ground, pick it up, and stuff it down the front of his shirt, while his companions followed behind, collecting the odd stone here and there. Calandrino had not gone very far before his shirt was filled to the brim with stones. He therefore pulled up the hem of its skirt—for it was not cut in the style of Hainault—and tucking it securely into his leather belt all around, he made a large pouch out of it, which he filled up with stones in no time.° After that, in the same way, he made another pouch out of his cloak and soon had it filled up as well.

Bruno and Buffalmacco could see that Calandrino was now loaded down with stones, and since the hour for dinner was approaching, Bruno set the plan they had agreed on in motion by asking Buffalmacco: "Where's Calandrino?" Although Buffalmacco could see Calandrino right there beside him, he turned around in one direction and then another, looking for him.

"I don't know," he replied. "He was right here in front of us just a little while ago."

"A little while ago, yeah!" said Bruno. "I'll bet he's at home now eating dinner and has left us here like a couple of idiots to go hunting for black stones down along the Mugnone."

"Well," said Buffalmacco, "it serves us right for him to play this practical joke on us and leave us here, since we were stupid enough to have believed him. Look, who besides us would've been so dumb as to have imagined you could find such a magical stone by the Mugnone?"

Hearing their words, Calandrino imagined that he had gotten

his hands on the stone and that because of its power they were unable to see him although he was right there just a short distance away. Overjoyed at such a stroke of luck, he decided to go home without saying a word to them, and turning on his heel, he started to walk back.

Buffalmacco observed this and said to Bruno: "What'll we do now? Why don't we leave, too?"

"Let's go," replied Bruno, "but I swear to God that Calandrino's never going to play another trick on me again. If I were as close to him now as I was this morning, I'd hit him so hard on the heels with this stone that he'd remember this practical joke for the next month or so."

And even as he spoke, he drew back his arm and threw a stone that hit Calandrino right on the heel. When he felt the pain, Calandrino jerked his foot high in the air and started panting and blowing, but he said nothing and kept on walking.

Buffalmacco took one of the stones they had gathered between his fingers and said to Bruno, "Just look at this nice sharp one. How I'd like to catch Calandrino in the back with it now just like this," and he let it fly, smacking Calandrino hard, right in between the kidneys. To make a long story short, they kept hurling stones at him in this fashion, now saying one thing and now another, all the way back up from the Mugnone to the Porta San Gallo. There, after they had dumped all the stones they had collected on the ground, they stopped to chat with the customs guards whom they had let in on the joke earlier and who allowed Calandrino to pass, pretending not to see him, though all the while they were roaring with laughter.

Without stopping, Calandrino went straight to his house, which was near the Canto alla Macina.° And Fortune favored the joke to such an extent that while he was walking along the river and then across the city, no one said anything to him, although he actually encountered very few people since almost everyone was home eating dinner.

When Calandrino entered his house with the load he was carrying, by chance his wife, a beautiful, virtuous woman named

Monna Tessa,° was at the head of the stairs, and as she was rather irritated because he had stayed out so long, no sooner did she see him come in than she began to scold him.

"Hey, brother, where the devil have you been?" she said. "Everybody else has finished dinner, and you're just getting home."

When Calandrino heard this and realized she could see him, he was filled with anger and dismay. Then he started shouting: "Oh no, you damned woman, why did you have to be there? You've ruined me. But I swear to God I'm going to pay you back for it."

He went upstairs, where he dumped the huge load of stones he had brought home in a little room, after which he ran at his wife in a rage. Grabbing her by the hair, he threw her to the ground at his feet, and then, for as long as he could move his arms and legs, he let her have it from head to foot. She cried to him for mercy and prayed to him with clasped hands, but it was all in vain, and he went on hitting her and kicking her until she did not have a hair left on her head that had not been torn or a bone that remained unbruised.

After having had a good laugh with the customs men at the gate, Bruno and Buffalmacco set off to follow Calandrino, walking at a leisurely pace and always staying some distance behind him. When they reached the steps leading up to his front door and heard the savage beating he was giving his wife, they called out to him, pretending they had just arrived. Soaked in sweat, red faced, and out of breath, Calandrino appeared at the window and invited them to come on up. Acting as though they were somewhat annoyed, they climbed the stairs and found the room full of stones, with the woman sobbing pitifully in a corner, her hair disheveled, her clothes torn, and her face all livid and bruised. On the opposite side sat Calandrino, whose belt was unfastened and who was panting with exhaustion.

After surveying the scene awhile, they said, "What's going on, Calandrino? Are you planning to build a wall with all these stones we see here?" And to this, then, they added: "And what's the matter with Monna Tessa? It looks as though you've given her a beating. What's the story here?"

Worn out by the weight of the stones he had carried, and the fury with which he had assaulted his wife, and the despair he felt over losing the fortune he thought he had acquired, Calandrino was unable to catch his breath and utter a single word in reply. So, after pausing a moment, Buffalmacco started in again.

"Calandrino," he said, "you shouldn't have played such a mean trick on us the way you did just because you were angry about something or other. First, you seduced us into looking for that precious stone with you, and then, without saying 'God be with you,' let alone 'the Devil take you,' you came back here, leaving us behind down by the Mugnone like a couple of jerks. We're pretty unhappy about the way you treated us, but you can be sure, this is the last time you're ever going to do such a thing to us."

Calandrino had to make quite an effort to respond, but finally he managed to say: "Don't be angry, friends. It's not the way you think. Poor unlucky me, I'd actually found the stone. Now, you just give a listen, and I'll prove to you that I'm telling the truth. When you two started asking one another where I'd gone, I was less than ten yards away from you. Then I noticed how you started walking home and didn't see me, so I got out in front of you and always stayed a little ahead of you all the way back here."

After that, he gave them a detailed account of everything they had said and done, beginning at the beginning and taking it right down to the end. He also showed them the welts the stones had made on his back and heel.

"And I'm telling you," he continued, "when I came through the gate, my shirt was filled with all these stones you see here, but nobody said a thing to me, and you yourselves know how unpleasant and annoying those customs men are, with their habit of demanding to inspect every last thing. And besides, I ran into lots of my friends and neighbors along the way, and they can always be depended on to say hello to me and invite me to go for a drink, yet none of them uttered a word to me, not so much as a syllable, just as though they didn't see me. Finally, when I arrived home, this devil of a woman, damn her, appeared in front of me and looked at me—and you know how everything loses its special power in the presence of women. So, where before I'd been thinking myself the luckiest man in Florence, I wound up becoming the unluckiest, and that's why I beat her until I couldn't move my hands anymore. In fact, I don't know what's keeping me from slitting her throat right now. I curse the hour I first laid eyes on her and the day she came into this house." And blazing with fresh anger, he was about to get up and start beating her all over again.

Bruno and Buffalmacco made a great pretense of being astonished as they listened to Calandrino's story, and repeatedly confirmed what he was telling them, though all the while they had such a desire to laugh that they almost burst. But when they saw him getting up in a fury to beat his wife a second time, they also stood up in order to block his way and hold him back, telling him it was not the lady's fault, but his, because he knew that things lose their power in the presence of women, and yet he had not told her to keep out of sight that day. It was God, they said, who had kept him from taking that precaution either because he did not deserve to have such good luck or because it had been his intention to deceive his friends, to whom he should have revealed his discovery as soon as he realized that he had found the stone. After much discussion, they finally managed, though not without a great deal of difficulty, to reconcile him and his grieving spouse. They then departed, leaving him in a melancholy state, with his house full of stones.

Story 5

THREE YOUNG MEN PULL DOWN THE BREECHES OF A JUDGE
FROM THE MARCHES WHILE HE IS SITTING ON THE BENCH
AND ADMINISTERING JUSTICE IN FLORENCE.°

*   *   *

Delightful ladies, the young man Elissa mentioned just a short while ago, that is, Maso del Saggio, has prompted me to pass over a story I intended to tell you in order to recount another one about him and some of his companions. Although the tale itself is not indecent, certain words do appear in it that you would be ashamed to use. Nevertheless, since it is so funny, I am going to tell it anyway.

As all of you may well have heard, the chief magistrates of our city very frequently come from The Marches, and they are generally mean-spirited men who lead such wretched, beggarly lives that everything they do looks like chicanery. And because of their innate miserliness and avarice, they bring judges and notaries along with them who seem to have been brought up behind the plow or taken from the cobbler's shop rather than from the law schools.

Now, one of them had come here as *podestà,* and among the numerous judges he brought with him, there was a man called Messer Niccola da San Lepidio who looked more like a smith than anything else, and he was assigned to go with the other judges and hear criminal cases.

It often happens that people go to the law courts although they have no business there at all, which is just what Maso del Saggio was doing one morning, for he had gone there to look for one of his friends. When he arrived, he happened to glance over to where this Messer Niccola was sitting, and thinking him a weird birdbrain, surveyed him from top to bottom. He noticed that the vair in the cap the man was wearing had been completely blackened by smoke,° that he had a pen case hanging down from his belt, that his gown was longer than his robe, and many other strange things that would be unbecoming in a proper, well-bred gentleman. The most noteworthy thing of all, in his opinion, was the pair of breeches the judge was wearing, for their crotch was halfway down his legs, something that Maso could easily see because the man's outer garments were so tight that when he sat down, they opened up all the way in the front.

Having seen all he needed to, Maso abandoned his first search for his friend, and setting out on a new one, ran into two of his buddies, named Ribi and Matteuzzo, both of whom loved to have fun as much as Maso did.°

"If you value my friendship," he said to them, "come with me to the courthouse, and I'll show you the weirdest jerk you've ever seen."

So off they went to the courthouse where Maso showed his friends the judge and his breeches. What they could see from a distance already got them laughing, and when they were closer to the platform on which Messer Judge was sitting, not only did they realize that it would be a very easy matter to crawl underneath it, but they also noticed that the plank on which Messer Judge was resting his feet was broken and had an opening in it through which someone could easily stick his hand and arm.

Accordingly, Maso said to his friends: "Let's go and pull his breeches all the way down. It'll be a snap to do it."

The other two had already figured out how it could be managed, and having arranged with one another what they were going to say and do, they returned there the next morning. The courtroom was crowded, allowing Matteuzzo to crawl under the platform without being seen by anyone and position himself right beneath the spot where the judge was resting his feet.

Then Maso approached Messer Judge from one side and seized the hem of his robe, while Ribi came up to him from the other and did the same thing.

"Your Honor, your Honor," Maso started to say, "I beg you in God's name, don't let that petty thief, the one over there on the other side of you, get away from here before you make him give me back the pair of boots he stole from me. He says he didn't do it, but I saw him getting them resoled less than a month ago."

On the other side, Ribi was yelling at the top of his lungs: "Your Honor, don't you believe him, the lousy crook. Just because he knows I've come to file a complaint against him for stealing a saddlebag of mine, he shows up here with this story about the boots, which I've had in my house for I don't know how long. And if you don't believe me, I can call up plenty of witnesses, like the lady from next door who's a fruit seller, and Fatty the tripe woman, and a street sweeper from around Santa Maria a Verzaia who saw him coming back from the country."°

Maso for his part was not prepared to let Ribi do all the talking, and started shouting, prompting Ribi to shout right back at him. Then, while the judge was standing up, leaning closer to them in order to hear them better, Matteuzzo seized the opportunity to stick his hand through the opening in the plank, grabbed the seat of the judge's breeches, and gave them a tremendous yank. Down they came in a flash, for the judge was a skinny guy, and he had really scrawny shanks. He felt his breeches slip, but had no idea how this had happened, and he tried to cover himself up by sitting back down and pulling his robe around in front of him. Maso and Ribi, however, were holding it tight on either side and yelling with all their might: "Your Honor, it's outrageous for you to refuse to listen to me and try to get away before giving me justice. Surely, you don't need to get written evidence in this town for a little case like this one."

While they were saying all this, they held him by his robe long enough for everyone in the tribunal to see that he did not have his breeches on. Matteuzzo, however, who had clung to them for some time, let them go and slipped outside without being seen, while Ribi, who thought he had done quite enough, exclaimed: "I swear to God I'm going to appeal this to the superior court!"° On the other side, Maso let go of the robe and declared: "Not me. I'm just going to keep coming back here until I find you less distracted than you seem to be this morning." And then, the two of them went off in opposite directions, leaving the tribunal as quickly as they could.

Only at this point, after Messer Judge had pulled up his breeches in front of everyone, as if he were just getting out of bed, did he realize what had happened and demanded to know the whereabouts of the two men who had been arguing about the boots and the saddlebag. Since they were nowhere to be found, he started swearing by God's guts that he would have liked it if somebody had told him it was the custom in Florence for people to pull down a judge's breeches when he was sitting on the seat of justice.

When the *podestà*, for his part, heard what had happened, he made a real stink about it, but his friends explained to him that it had only been done to show him that the Florentines knew how he had tried to save money by bringing stupid fools to town with him, instead of real judges. Consequently, he thought it best to say nothing more on the subject, and so, for the time being, that was as far as it went.

Story 6

BRUNO AND BUFFALMACCO STEAL A PIG FROM CALANDRINO, AND THEN, PRETENDING TO HELP HIM RECOVER IT, THEY GET HIM TO UNDERGO A TEST INVOLVING GINGER PILLS AND VERNACCIA WINE. THEY GIVE HIM TWO OF THE PILLS, ONE AFTER THE OTHER, CONSISTING OF DOG GINGER SEASONED WITH ALOES, WHICH MAKE IT APPEAR AS THOUGH HE HIMSELF HAD STOLEN IT. FINALLY, THEY FORCE HIM TO PAY THEM BLACKMAIL IF HE DOES NOT WANT THEM TO TELL HIS WIFE ABOUT IT.°

Filostrato's tale, which caused a great deal of laughter, had no sooner reached its conclusion than the Queen ordered Filomena to follow it with another one, and she began in this manner:

Gracious ladies, just as Filostrato was led by the mention of Maso's name to rehearse the story about him you just heard, I, too, have been led in exactly the same way by the one concerning Calandrino and his buddies to tell you another, which I believe you are really going to enjoy.

I do not have to explain to you who Calandrino, Bruno, and Buffalmacco were, since you have already heard quite a lot about them in the earlier tale. So, I shall get right on with my story and tell you that Calandrino had a little farm not very far from Florence that he had received from his wife as part of her dowry. Among many other things, it provided him with a pig every year, and it was his regular custom to take his wife and go to the country sometime around December in order to slaughter the animal and have it salted.

It happened that one of those years, when Calandrino's wife was not feeling very well, he went there by himself to slaughter the pig. Bruno and Buffalmacco heard he was going to the country, and when they found out that his wife would not be with him, they set off to spend a few days with a priest, a very close friend of theirs, who was one of Calandrino's neighbors.

Calandrino had killed the pig the very morning of the day they arrived, and on seeing them with the priest, he called out to them, saying: "A hearty welcome to you all. I want to show you what a terrific farmer I am." And he took them into the house, where he showed them the pig.

It was a very fine animal, as they could see for themselves, and when they understood from Calandrino that he wanted to have it salted for his family, Bruno said to him: "Hey, you must be nuts! Sell it, and let's have a good time on what you get for it. You can always tell your missus somebody stole it from you."

"No," replied Calandrino, "not only wouldn't she believe it, but she'd chase me out of the house. So, stop interfering, because I'm never going to do it."

They talked with him at great length, but it was all to no avail. Calandrino then invited them to have supper with him, but he did so with such reluctance that they decided not to accept and took their leave of him instead.

Bruno asked Buffalmacco: "What would you say to stealing that pig of his tonight?"

"But how could we do that?" said Buffalmacco.

"I've already got the how of it all worked out," said Bruno, "provided he doesn't move it from where it was just now."

"Let's do it, then," said Buffalmacco. "After all, why shouldn't we? And later on, we could enjoy the proceeds together with the *padre* here."

The priest declared he was all for it, after which Bruno said: "This will call for some cunning on our part. Now, you know, Buffalmacco, how stingy Calandrino is and how happy he is to have a drink when somebody else is paying. So, let's go and take him to the tavern, where the priest can pretend to be the host and offer free drinks to all of us. When Calandrino sees that he doesn't have to pay for a thing, he'll get drunk out of his mind, and then we can manage it easily enough because there's no one else with him in the house."

They all did just what Bruno suggested. When Calandrino saw that the priest would not let him pay for anything, he started doing some serious drinking, and although it normally did not take much to get him drunk, in this case he really got a load on. By the time they left the tavern, it was already the wee hours of the night, and Calandrino, who had no interest in having any other kind of supper, returned home and went to bed. As he came in, he left the door wide open, although he thought he had locked it up tight.

Buffalmacco and Bruno went off to have supper with the priest, and when they were finished, they quietly made their way to Calandrino's house, having collected the tools they needed so that they could break into it at the spot Bruno had decided on earlier. Upon discovering the door was open, however, they just walked in, took the pig down from its hook, and carried it over to the priest's house. Then, having stowed it away there, off they went to bed.

The next morning, after his head had cleared from the effects of the wine, Calandrino got up and went downstairs, where he looked around only to discover that the pig was gone and the door was standing wide open. He asked one person after another if they knew of anybody who might have taken it, and when he failed to find it, he started creating a ruckus, complaining about how miserable he was, alas! and lamenting that his pig had been stolen.

Meanwhile, Bruno and Buffalmacco got up and went over to Calandrino's to hear what he would say about the pig. As soon as he saw them, he called out to them, almost in tears, and said: "Alas, my friends, somebody's stolen my pig from me!"

Bruno sidled up to him and whispered, "It's a miracle! Here you are actually using your brains for a change!"

"Oh, woe is me," said Calandrino. "I'm telling you the absolute truth."

"That's the way to talk," replied Bruno. "Go ahead and shout, so people will think it really did happen."

"God's body, I'm telling you the truth," said Calandrino, howling even louder. "Somebody stole it from me."

"That's good, well said," replied Bruno. "You really need to talk like that. Yell it so loud that everyone can hear you, and that way they'll all believe it's true."

"You're going to drive me to perdition!" exclaimed Calandrino. "I say it, and you don't believe me. May I be hanged by the neck if my pig hasn't been stolen!"

"Come on! How is it possible?" said Bruno. "I saw the pig here myself only yesterday, and you think you can convince me that it's just flown away?"°

"It's exactly the way I've been telling you," said Calandrino.

"Really, is it possible?" asked Bruno.

"Yes, it sure is," replied Calandrino, "and I'm ruined because of it. I don't know how I can go back home, because my missus won't believe me, and even if she does, there'll be no peace between us for all of next year."

"God save me," said Bruno, "this is serious stuff if you're telling the truth. But you know, Calandrino, just yesterday I was advising you to say something like this, and I wouldn't want to think you were making fools of both your missus and us at the same time."

"Oh, you're driving me to despair," Calandrino started shouting. "You'll have me cursing God and the Saints and everything else. I'm telling you somebody stole the pig from me last night."

"If that's the case," said Buffalmacco, "then we'll have to see if we can't find some way to get it back again."

"Find a way?" asked Calandrino. "How can we do that?"

"Well, if anything's certain," replied Buffalmacco, "it's that the guy who took your pig didn't come here all the way from India. It must have been one of your neighbors. So, if you could manage to round them up, I know how to do the bread and cheese test, and then we'll see right away who took it."°

"Oh yes," said Bruno, "what a great idea, to use bread and cheese on the fine folks who live around here! It's certain that one of them took it, but he'd just see through what we're doing and refuse to come."

"So, what's to be done, then?" asked Buffalmacco.

"What we ought to do," said Bruno, "is to make use of some nice ginger pills along with some good Vernaccia wine and then invite them to come here for a drink.° That way they wouldn't suspect a thing, and they'd all come. And we could have the ginger pills blessed the same way the bread and cheese are."

"That's the way to do it, all right," said Buffalmacco. "And you, Calandrino, what do you say? Shall we give it a try?"

"Yes, for the love of God," said Calandrino, "I beg you to do it. If only I knew who took the pig, I wouldn't feel half so bad about it."

"Well, then," said Bruno, "just to oblige you, I'm ready to go all the way to Florence to get the things you need if you'll give me the money for them."

Calandrino had perhaps forty *soldi* on him, and he gave them to Bruno, who went to a friend of his in Florence, an apothecary, from whom he bought a pound of good ginger pills, but also had him make up two others out of dog ginger, seasoning them with fresh hepatic aloes.° Then he had the apothecary coat those two with sugar just like the other ones, and to keep them from being misplaced or getting confused with the good ones, he had him put a certain little mark on them so that he would have no trouble telling them apart. Finally, after purchasing a flask of good-quality Vernaccia wine, Bruno returned to Calandrino's place in the country and said to him: "See to it that you invite everybody who's a suspect to have a drink with you tomorrow morning. Since it's a holiday, they'll all be happy to come. Tonight, along with Buffalmacco, I will recite a spell over the pills, and bring them to your house in the morning. Because we're such good friends, I'll hand the pills out myself, and I'll do and say everything necessary."

Calandrino issued the invitations, and the next morning, a sizable group of people, including farmhands and young men from Florence who happened to be staying in the country, had already assembled around the elm in front of the church, when Bruno and Buffalmacco appeared, carrying the box of pills and the flask of wine. Then they made everyone stand around in a circle.

"Gentlemen," said Bruno, "it's my job to explain to you why you're here so that if something happens that's not to your liking, you'll have no cause to blame me for it. The night before last, Calandrino, who's right here, had a fine pig of his stolen from him and has been unable to discover who took it. Considering that it could only have been taken by someone here, he wants to find out who it was by having each of you in turn eat one of these pills and then have a drink. Now, let me explain right away that the one who took the pig will not be able to get it down. In fact, he'll find it's more bitter than poison, and he'll spit it out. So, before subjecting himself to such shame in the presence of so many people, it might be better for the person who took the pig to confess what he did to the *padre,* in which case I won't proceed any further with this business."

Everyone there declared that he was ready to eat the pills, after which Bruno made them stand in a line, placing Calandrino in among them, and then, starting at one end, he gave each person his pill. When he came up in front of Calandrino, he took out one of those containing dog ginger and put it in his hand. Without a moment's hesitation, Calandrino popped it into his mouth and started chewing on it, but as soon as he felt the aloes on his tongue, he could not stand the bitter taste and spat it out.

All the people were staring one another in the face to see if anyone would spit it out, when Bruno, who had not finished giving out the pills and was pretending not to notice what was going on, heard someone behind him say, "Ah, Calandrino, what's this all about?" Bruno quickly whirled around, and when he saw that Calandrino had spit his pill out, he said: "Hold on. Maybe he spat it out for some other reason. Here, have another one." And picking up the second pill, he put it in Calandrino's mouth, after which he continued distributing those that were left.

If the first pill had seemed bitter to Calandrino, this one appeared far, far worse. But since he was ashamed to spit it out, he kept it in his mouth for a while. As he chewed on it, he began shedding tears as big as hazelnuts, until finally, he could not stand it any longer and sent it flying out just like the first one.

Meanwhile, Buffalmacco was in the process of pouring drinks for everyone in the group, as was Bruno, and when they and all the others saw what happened, they all agreed that it had to be Calandrino who had stolen the pig himself. In fact, there were even some of them who criticized him harshly for having done so.

When the crowd had gone, however, leaving Bruno and Buffalmacco alone with Calandrino, Buffalmacco said to him: "I knew all along that you were the one who'd taken it and that you wanted to make us believe it had been stolen so you wouldn't have to stand us to a round of drinks with the money you were paid for it."

Calandrino, who had still not gotten all the bitter taste of the aloes out of his mouth, started swearing that he had not taken it. "On your honor, now, buddy," said Buffalmacco, "how much did you get for it? Did it amount to six florins?"° When he heard this, Calandrino felt close to despair.

"Now you just listen and get this straight, Calandrino," said Bruno. "There was a guy in the group of people who were eating and drinking with us, and he told me that you had some girl around here you were keeping at your disposal and that since you gave her whatever you could scrape together, he was certain that you'd sent her this pig of yours. You've become quite the trickster, haven't you? There was that time you led us down along the Mugnone to collect black stones, but after sending us on a wild-goose chase, you took off back home and tried to make us believe you'd found the thing. And now that you've given away the pig, or, what's more likely, sold it, once again you think that with all those oaths of yours you'll persuade us that it was actually stolen. We've caught on to your tricks, and now we know them when we see them, so you're never going to be able to pull one on us again. And to tell you the truth, that's why we took so much trouble with the magic spell, because unless you give us two pairs of capons for it, we're going to tell Monna Tessa everything."

Seeing that they would not believe him, and thinking that he had had enough grief already without getting a scolding from his wife on top of it, Calandrino gave them the two pairs of capons. Then, after they had salted the pig, they carried everything back with them to Florence, leaving Calandrino behind with nothing but his losses and his humiliation.°

Story 7

A SCHOLAR FALLS FOR A WIDOW WHO IS IN LOVE WITH
SOMEONE ELSE AND GETS THE SCHOLAR TO SPEND A
WINTER'S NIGHT WAITING FOR HER IN THE SNOW. LATER ON
HE PERSUADES HER TO FOLLOW HIS COUNSEL AND SPEND
AN ENTIRE DAY IN THE MIDDLE OF JULY, NAKED ATOP A
TOWER, EXPOSED TO FLIES AND GADFLIES AND THE SUN.°

The ladies had a good laugh about the hapless Calandrino and would have laughed even harder if they had not felt sorry for him because the people who had stolen his pig relieved him of his capons as well. But when the story came to an end, the Queen ordered Pampinea to tell hers, and she promptly began as follows:

Dearest ladies, since it often happens that one person's cunning makes someone else's seem ridiculous, it is unwise to take delight in causing others to look like fools. Although many of our little stories have made us laugh a great deal over the pranks that people have played, we have never talked about how any of the victims avenged themselves. I, however, intend to make you feel sympathy for an act of just retribution that was meted out to a woman from our city who almost died when the trick she played got turned around and used against her. Nor will this tale be unprofitable, for when you have heard it, you will be more hesitant about deceiving others and will thereby show your splendid good sense.

Not so many years ago there was a young woman living in Florence named Elena who was physically attractive, proud of spirit, well bred, and rather generously supplied with the goods of Fortune.° Having been left a widow by her husband's death, she decided never to marry again, having fallen in love with a handsome, charming young man of her own choosing. Now that she was free of all other cares, she managed, with the help of her maid, whom she trusted implicitly, to spend many wonderfully pleasurable hours with him to their mutual delight.

At that time it just so happened that a young nobleman of our city named Rinieri came back to Florence from Paris. He had been studying there for many years, not in order to sell his knowledge for profit, as many do, but to understand the nature of things and their causes, a most fitting pursuit for the well born. Greatly honored in Florence for both his nobility and his learning, he settled down to lead the life of a gentleman there.

It is often the case, however, that those who have the keenest understanding of life's profundities are the soonest caught in the halter of Love, and that is just what happened to Rinieri. For one day, seeking to amuse himself, he had gone to a banquet where who should appear before his eyes but this Elena, dressed all in black as our widows usually are. She seemed more beautiful and charming than any woman he had ever seen, and he said to himself that the man to whom God granted the grace of holding her naked in his arms might consider himself truly blessed. As he glanced at her cautiously over and over again, he thought to himself that things great and precious cannot be acquired without an effort, and he therefore made up his mind to devote all his care and attention to pleasing her, hoping that he would acquire her love in that way and thus be able to enjoy her to the full.

The young woman, who admired herself for all she was worth, if not more, was not in the habit of keeping her eyes directed down toward the nether regions.° Instead, she would dart coy glances in all directions, being quick to spot anyone who took pleasure in looking at her. Thus, when she noticed Rinieri, she laughed to herself and thought, "My coming here today wasn't a waste of time, because unless I'm mistaken, I'll soon be leading this gull around by the nose." She then started glancing at him every so often out of the corner of her eye and did her best to make it appear that she was interested in him, since it was her view that the more men she allured and captured with her charms, the more highly her beauty would be prized, and especially by the man on whom, together with her love, she had actually bestowed it.

The learned scholar, setting his philosophical speculations aside, devoted all his thoughts to the lady, and after discovering where her house was located, he invented a variety of pretexts to begin taking frequent walks by it, thinking he would please her. For the reason already mentioned, the lady was vain, and glorying in this, she pretended she was very happy to see him. Accordingly, the scholar found a way to strike up a friendship with her maid, revealed his love to her, and begged her to use her influence with her mistress in order to help him obtain her favor.

The maid was lavish with her promises and then went and reported everything to her mistress who had the heartiest laugh in the world about it.

"Have you noticed how he's managed to lose all the wisdom he brought back here from Paris with him?" said the lady. "Well, anyhow, let's give him what he's looking for. The next time he speaks to you, tell him I'm even more in love with him than he is with me, but that I have to safeguard my honor if I want to be able to hold my head up when I'm in the company of other women. And if he's as wise as people say he is, then that ought to make him value me even more."

Ah, the wretched, wretched woman! She really had no idea, dear ladies, what it means to tangle with scholars.

When the maid next encountered him, she carried out her mistress's orders, and the scholar, overjoyed, proceeded to make even warmer entreaties, writing letters and sending gifts to the lady, all of which she accepted. The only responses he got back from her were vague generalities, however, and thus she kept him feeding on hope for quite some time.

When the lady revealed everything that was going on to her lover, he got rather angry at her and was sufficiently jealous that she finally decided she had to do something to prove to him that his suspicions of her were wrong. Since the scholar was becoming ever more insistent with his entreaties, she sent her maid to tell him, on her mistress's behalf, that although from the time he had declared his love for her, she had not had a single opportunity to give him satisfaction, she hoped to spend time with him during

the Christmas holidays, which were fast approaching. If, therefore, he were willing to come to her courtyard after nightfall on
the day after Christmas, she would go to meet him there as soon
as she could. The scholar was the happiest man in the world, and
having gone to her house at the time specified, he was taken by the
maid to a courtyard, where he was locked in and began waiting
for the lady to appear.

The lady had sent for her lover that evening, and after the two of
them had happily eaten their supper, she told him what she was
planning to do that night, adding: "And so, now you'll be able to see
the true nature and intensity of the love I've felt—and still feel—
for the guy you were foolish enough to be jealous of." These words
filled the lover's heart to the brim with happiness and made him
eager to see how the lady would make good on what she had said.

By chance they had had a heavy snowfall during the day
that had covered everything, and as a result, the scholar was not
in the courtyard for very long before he started to feel colder
than he would have wished. Because he was expecting relief, however, he suffered it all with patience.

After a while, the lady said to her lover: "Let's go over to the
little window in the bedroom and watch the guy you're so jealous
of. From there we'll be able to see what kind of answer he'll give
the maid I just sent to have a chat with him." So off they went to the
little window, through which they could look out without being
seen, and heard the maid talking to the scholar from another
window.

"Rinieri," she was saying, "my lady is the unhappiest woman
there ever was, because one of her brothers came by this evening,
and after talking and talking to her, he decided to stay for supper, and although I think he'll be going pretty soon, he still
hasn't left, which is why she hasn't been able to make it here to see
you. She'll be coming down soon enough, though, and begs you
not to get upset for having to wait."

Believing the maid's story to be true, the scholar replied: "Tell
my lady not to give another thought to me until it's convenient for
her to come, but do ask her to come as soon as she can."

The maid drew her head back inside and went to bed. Then the lady said to her lover: "So, what do you say to that? Do you think I'd keep him down there, freezing in the cold, if I really cared for him, as you suspect I do?"

Her lover was now pretty well satisfied, and after she got into bed with him, the two of them amused themselves there for quite a long stretch, taking their pleasure of one another, while laughing and making fun of the hapless scholar.

Since there was no place for the scholar to sit down or find shelter from the open air, he kept moving in order to stay warm, and as he walked around the courtyard, he repeatedly cursed the lady's brother for staying with her for so long. Every time he heard a sound, he imagined it was his lady opening the door for him, but all his hopes were in vain.

After amusing herself with her lover until almost midnight, the lady said to him: "What do you think about this scholar of ours, my darling? Which do you think's greater, his wisdom or my love for him? Will the cold I'm making him suffer expel the cold that entered your heart because of the remarks I made about him in jest to you the other day?"

"Yes, indeed, sweetheart," replied her lover, "now I see clearly that you really are my treasure, my repose, my bliss, my every hope, just as I am yours."

"Then give me a thousand kisses at least," said the lady, "so I may see whether you're telling the truth." And in response, her lover held her tight in his embrace and kissed her not a thousand, but more than a hundred thousand times.

After they had carried on like that for quite a while, the lady said: "Come on, let's get up and take a moment to see if the fire, which this strange, new lover of mine says in his letters is always burning inside him, has been partly extinguished by now." And so, they got up and went over to the little window they had used before. Looking out into the courtyard, they saw the scholar down in the snow doing a brisk dance to the accompaniment of his chattering teeth. Because of the extreme cold, his movements were so lively and quick that they had never seen anything like it.

"What do you say to that, my sweet hope?" said the lady. "Wouldn't you agree that I can make men do a dance without hearing the sound of trumpets or bagpipes?"

"I do indeed, my darling," replied her lover with a laugh.

"Let's go down to the courtyard door," said the lady. "You keep quiet while I do the talking, and let's hear what he has to say. Perhaps we'll get as much fun out of it as we've had in watching him from up here."

Then they quietly left the bedroom and made their way down to the door, which the lady kept shut up tight. There was a tiny hole in it, however, and speaking through it, she called out to the scholar in a low voice. When he heard her summons, he believed all too readily that she was about to let him in, and thanking God, he walked over to the door. "Here I am, my lady," he said. "Open up, for the love of God, because I'm dying from the cold."

"Oh yeah," said the lady, "I'm sure you're awfully chilly! It must be really cold out there, all because of that little bit of snow! Well, I happen to know the snow's much worse in Paris. In any case, I can't open the door for you yet because this damned brother of mine, who came to have supper with me yesterday evening, still hasn't left. But he'll be going soon, and then I'll be down in a jiffy and let you in. I had a hard enough time slipping away from him just now so that I could come here to comfort you and tell you not to be upset over all the waiting you've had to do."

"Oh, my lady," replied the scholar, "I beg you, for God's sake, open the door and let me take shelter inside, for there's never been such a heavy snowfall as the one that started just a little while ago, and it's still coming down. I'll wait for you in there just as long as you please."

"Alas, my sweet, I can't do it," said the lady. "This door makes so much noise when it's opened that my brother would be sure to hear it. Anyway, what I want to do now is to go and tell him he has to leave. After that, I'll come back and let you in."

"Go quickly, then," said the scholar, "and I beg you, have them make up a good fire so that I can warm myself up when I come inside, for I've gotten so cold I scarcely have any feeling left in my body."

"I don't see how that's possible," replied the lady. "You've said over and over again in your letters that you're all on fire because of your love for me. But I feel certain you're just kidding me. In any case, I'm going now. Wait for me, and don't give up."

The lady's lover, who had heard everything, was as pleased as he could be and went right back to bed with her, although the two of them did not do much sleeping there that night. Instead, they spent almost the entire time, when they were not satisfying their desires, making fun of the scholar.

Finally realizing that he had been duped, the wretched scholar, whose teeth were chattering so badly that it sounded as if he had been turned into a stork, tried repeatedly to open the door while he looked around everywhere for another way to get out. When he could not find one, he began pacing up and down like a caged lion, cursing the state of the weather, the treachery of the lady, and the length of the night as well as his own simplemindedness. So intense was the anger he felt at her that his long-standing, fervent love was instantly transformed into bitter, unrelenting hatred, and he began mulling over a wide variety of schemes for revenge, which he now desired far more than he had ever longed to be with the lady in the past.

Although the night went on forever and ever, day eventually drew near, and when dawn began to appear, the maid, following her mistress's instructions, came down to the courtyard and opened the door.

"Curse that guy for coming here yesterday evening!" she said, pretending to feel sorry for the scholar. "He kept us on tenterhooks all night long while you were left to freeze out here. But you know what? Don't be discouraged, because if it didn't work out for you last night, it'll work out some other time. I know for a fact that nothing could have occurred that would have upset my lady as much as that."

The scholar was furious, but like the wise man he was, he knew that threats only serve to arm those who are threatened. Consequently, he kept his feelings locked up tight within his breast, feelings that would surely have burst out if he had not used all his willpower and done everything he could to restrain them.

"Truth to tell," he said in a low voice, without revealing the least hint of the anger he felt, "it was the worst night I've ever had, but I could certainly see that my lady was in no way to blame for what happened, inasmuch as she herself felt so sorry for me that she came down here to apologize and try to cheer me up. And since, as you say, what didn't work out for me last night will surely work out some other time, commend me to her, and may God be with you."

Almost completely numb from the cold, the scholar did what he could to make his way back to his own house, where, exhausted and dying from lack of sleep, he flung himself down on his bed to rest. When he awoke and discovered that he could hardly move his arms and legs, he sent for physicians, and after telling them about the cold he had been exposed to, he placed himself in their care. Although they gave him the most quick-acting and potent medicines, it was a long time before they managed to get his muscles to heal sufficiently so that he could straighten out his limbs once again, and if it had not been for his youth and the arrival of warm weather, the experience would have been too much for him to have borne. He did regain his health and vigor, however, and keeping his hatred down deep inside him, he pretended to be much more in love with his widow than ever before.

After a certain amount of time had passed, it just so happened that Fortune provided the scholar with an opportunity to get what he really desired. For the young man who was the object of the widow's affection, paying no heed whatsoever to her feelings for him, fell in love with another woman. Because he no longer had much interest in talking with the widow or doing anything else to please her, she pined away in tears and bitter sorrow. Her maid pitied her, but could find no way to assuage the grief her mistress felt over the loss of her lover. Then, however, she came up with the foolish idea that they could use some sort of necromantic spell to make the lover return to his former passion. Since she thought that the scholar, whom she would see walking through their neighborhood the way he used to, had to be a grand master of the art of magic, she explained all this to her mistress.

The lady, who was not very bright, did not once stop to think that if the scholar had known anything about necromancy, he would have used it on his own behalf. Therefore, taking her maid's advice, she told her to go at once and find out if he would be willing to do it, and to assure him that, in return for his help, her mistress would do whatever he wanted.

The maid was quite diligent in delivering the message. When he had heard it, the scholar was overjoyed and said to himself: "Praise be to God, for with Your assistance, the time has now come for me to punish that wicked woman for the harm she did to me as my reward for all the love I bore her." Then he said to the maid: "Tell my lady not to worry about it, for even if her lover were in India, I would make him come back at once and ask her to pardon him for what he's done to displease her. As for the course she has to take in this affair, however, I will wait to explain that to her at a time and place of her choosing. Say all this to her, and tell her, from me, not to worry."

The maid brought back his answer, and arrangements were made for them to meet in the Church of Santa Lucia near the Prato Gate. When they arrived there, the lady and the scholar went and spoke together in private. Forgetting that this was the man she had almost led to his death, she freely told him everything about her situation, explained what she wanted, and begged him to come to her rescue.

"My lady," the scholar said in reply, "it's true that necromancy was one of the subjects I studied in Paris, and you may rest assured that I know everything there is to know about it. But because that art is most displeasing to God, I've sworn never to practice it either for my own benefit or for anyone else's. Nevertheless, the love I bear for you is so strong that I find myself incapable of refusing to do anything you ask of me, and so, even though this deed alone would be enough to send me down to the Devil's domain,

I'm ready to perform it since that is your pleasure. Let me warn you, however, that this thing is harder to do than you may perhaps realize, especially when a woman wants to regain a man's love, or a man wants to regain a woman's, because it can't be done except by the person involved. Moreover, this person has to be very brave, for the ceremony must be performed at night in a solitary spot when no one else is around, and I don't know whether you are ready to do such things."

The lady, who was more in love than wise, replied: "I am spurred on by Love so hard that there's nothing I wouldn't do to get back the man who has wrongfully forsaken me. But tell me, please, how will I have to show that I'm brave?"

"My lady," said the scholar with diabolical cunning,° "it'll be my job to make a tin image of the man you wish to get back. Once it's been delivered to you, take it, and when the moon is on the wane, go all by yourself to a flowing stream, in which, about the time you would first go to sleep, you must immerse yourself seven times, completely naked. After that, still naked, you must climb up to the top of a tree or of some deserted house, where, facing north and still holding the image in your hand, you are to repeat seven times certain words that I'm going to give you in writing. Once you've said them, you'll be approached by two of the fairest damsels you've ever seen who'll greet you and ask you graciously what you want them to do. See that you explain your wishes to them as fully and as clearly as possible, taking care not to confuse the names. When you've told them everything, they'll depart, and you may descend to the spot where you left your clothes, get dressed again, and return home. And then, without a doubt, before the following night is half over, your lover will come to you in tears, asking for your forgiveness and begging you for mercy. From that moment on, I can assure you, he will never again leave you for another woman."

Believing wholeheartedly in everything she had heard, the lady felt as if she were already holding her lover in her arms again and that half her troubles were over.

"Never fear," she said. "I'll do everything you tell me down to the last detail. What's more I have the best place in the world to do it, for I own a farm in the upper valley of the Arno that is very close to the riverbank, and since it's only the beginning of July, it'll actually be a pleasure to go bathing in it. In fact, now I remember, there's a little tower not very far from the river that's been abandoned, except that every so often the shepherds will climb up a ladder made out of chestnut wood and get on a platform to look around for their lost sheep. It's all quite solitary and out of the way, and by going up there, I'll be able to carry out your instructions to perfection."

The scholar, who knew exactly where the lady's property and the little tower were located, was delighted that things were going according to plan.

"My lady," he said to her, "I've never been in those parts, so I'm not familiar with the farm or the little tower, but if everything's the way you describe it, then there couldn't be a better place in the whole world. Consequently, when the time is ripe, I'm going to send you the image and the spell. But I beseech you, when you've got what you desire and realize how well I've served you, do think of me and remember to keep the promise you've made me."

The lady said she would do so without fail, and, after taking her leave of him, returned home.

Delighted that his plan seemed about to produce results, the scholar created an image, marking it with various characters, and wrote some nonsense he made up by way of a spell. In due course he sent these things to the lady and told her not to wait but to carry out the instructions he had given her the very next night. Then, taking one of his servants with him, he went in secret to a friend's house, which was not very far from the little tower, in order to put his plan into action.

For her part, the lady set out with her maid and went to the farm. As soon as night had fallen, pretending that she was about to go to sleep herself, she sent the maid off to bed, and in the dead of night, she quietly left the house and made her way to a spot on the bank of the Arno that was quite close to the tower. Having first looked about with great care and having neither seen nor heard anyone, she got undressed and hid her clothes under a bush. Then, she took the image and immersed herself in the river with it seven times, after which, still naked and holding the image in her hand, she walked up to the little tower.

Meanwhile, the scholar was watching everything from the clump of willows and other trees near the tower where he had been hiding with his servant since nightfall. When the lady passed by right next to him, naked as she was, he was struck by the way the whiteness of her form overcame the gloom of the night, and as he stared at her bosom and the other parts of her body, impressed by just how beautiful they were, he thought to himself about what was going to happen to them in just a short while and began to feel a twinge of pity for her. At the same time, he suddenly found himself assailed by the prickings of the flesh, which made a certain something that had been lying down stand right up, so that he was tempted to leave his hiding place, seize her, and take his pleasure of her. Between them, these two promptings almost got the better of him, but when he remembered who he was, the injury he had received, and why, and at whose hands, his wrath was rekindled, dispelling both his pity and his carnal appetite. The result was that he clung firmly to his original resolve and allowed her to go on her way.

Having climbed to the top of the tower, the lady turned to the north and began reciting the spell given to her by the scholar, who had come in right behind her and was quietly dismantling the ladder, piece by piece, that led up to the platform where she stood. Then he waited to see what she would say and do.

The lady finished reciting the spell seven times and expected the two damsels to appear at any moment, but her wait went on so long that she started feeling far chillier than she would have liked, and she was still standing there when dawn arrived. Upset that things had not turned out as the scholar had told her they would, she said to herself: "I suspect he was trying to give me a night like the one I gave him. But if that was his intention, he had a pretty bad idea about how to go about avenging himself, because the night he spent was three times as long as this one, and the cold he had to deal with was really something else altogether."

Since she had no desire to be caught up there in broad daylight, she decided to climb down from the tower, only to discover that the ladder was gone. Feeling as though the earth beneath her feet had disappeared, she fell down in a faint onto the platform of the tower. As soon as she came back to her senses, she started weeping and wailing in the most pitiful fashion, and since she knew only too well that this had to be the work of the scholar, she began to regret the harm she had done as well as her willingness to trust someone she had had every good reason to consider her enemy. And thus she remained, meditating on all this, for a very long time.

After looking around for another way to get down and finding none, she began weeping again and thought bitterly to herself: "Oh, you unlucky woman, what are your brothers and relatives and neighbors, indeed what are people generally in Florence, going to say when they learn that you were found naked up here? They'll all know that your supposedly unimpeachable honesty was phony, and even if you tried to come up with some lying excuses for this—assuming you could find any—you'll be prevented from using them by that damned scholar who knows everything about you. Oh, you poor wretch, at one and the same time you've lost not only the young guy you stupidly chose as a lover, but your honor into the bargain." Having reached this conclusion, she felt so overcome with grief that she very nearly threw herself down from the tower onto the ground below.

Since the sun had already risen, the lady moved closer to the wall on one side of the tower, looking out in the hope that she might see some boy approaching with his flock of animals whom she could send to fetch her maid. Just then, the scholar, who had gone to sleep for a while underneath a bush, happened to wake up and catch sight of her at the very moment she caught sight of him.

"Good-day, my lady," he said to her. "Have the damsels arrived yet?"

When she saw him and heard what he said, she burst into tears once more and begged him to come inside the tower so that she could speak to him. With the utmost courtesy, the scholar granted her request, while the lady went and lay down prone on the platform in such a position that only her head showed through the opening.

"Rinieri," she said, sobbing, "if I gave you a bad night, surely you've gotten even with me. Even though it's July, I was convinced, standing naked up here last night, that I was going to freeze to death, not to mention the fact that I've wept so much over the trick I played on you and over my being such a fool as to believe you, that it's a miracle I still have any eyes left in my head. So, not for love of me, whom you have no reason to love, but for your self-esteem as a gentleman, I beseech you to let what you've done up to this point suffice as revenge for the injury I did you, and to have my clothes brought to me and allow me to climb down from here. Please don't deprive me of the one thing you could never restore to me later even if you wanted to, namely, my honor, because although I did prevent you from spending a night with me, I can offer you many others in exchange for it whenever you please. So, let this suffice for you, and like a gentleman, be satisfied that you were able to avenge yourself and make me fully aware of it. Don't employ all your strength against a woman: the eagle gets no glory from having defeated a dove. Therefore, for the love of God and for the sake of your own honor, have mercy on me."

His heart filled with hatred, the scholar had been brooding on the injury he had received, but when he perceived her tears and listened to her entreaties, he felt both pleasure and sorrow simultaneously, pleasure in his revenge, which he had longed for above all else, and sorrow because his sense of humanity moved him to feel compassion for her. His humanity, however, could not overcome his fierce desire for vengeance.

"Madonna Elena," he said to her in reply, "if my prayers, which, it is true, I did not know how to bathe with tears and coat with honey the way you do yours, had been able to persuade you to give me the slightest bit of shelter on that night when I was freezing to death out in your snow-filled courtyard, then it would be an easy matter for me now to answer your prayers. But if you are more concerned about your honor at present than you were in the past, and if it bothers you to be up there completely naked, why don't you direct your prayers to the man in whose arms, as you well remember, you did not mind being naked that night while you listened to me tramping back and forth, my teeth chattering, through the snow in your courtyard? Go get him to help you, get him to bring you your clothes, get him to put the ladder in place so that you can climb down. In fact, do everything you can to make him feel some concern for your good name even though you yourself never hesitated to place it in danger for his sake, not just now, but on a thousand other occasions.

"Why don't you call him to come to your rescue? What could be more fitting, since you are his, and if there's anything he's going to protect, it would have to be you? When you were enjoying yourself with him, you asked him what he thought was greater, my folly or your love for him, so go ahead and call him now, you silly woman, and find out whether the love you bear him, and your intelligence, combined with his, can save you from this folly of mine.° And don't think you can make me a generous offer now of something I no longer desire, although if I did want it, there's no way that you could refuse to give it to me. Save your nights for your lover, if you should happen to get out of here alive. The two of you are welcome to them. One night was more than enough for me, and I have no intention of being made a fool of a second time.

"What's more, with those cunning words of yours, you do your best to flatter me, calling me a gentleman and a man of honor, all in order to get my goodwill and quietly dissuade me from punishing you for your wickedness by appealing to my sense of magnanimity. But your flattering words will not cloud the eyes of my mind the way your treacherous promises once did. I really know myself now, for you taught me more about that subject in a single night than I ever learned during the whole of my stay in Paris.

"But even supposing I were a magnanimous man, you are not the kind of person who deserves to be treated with magnanimity. For a savage beast like you, the only fit punishment, the only just revenge, must be death, whereas if I were dealing with a human being, what I've already done, as you mentioned before, would suffice. Furthermore, I'm no eagle, and you're certainly no dove.

No, you're a poisonous serpent, and I intend to hunt you down with all my hatred and all my strength as if you were our oldest enemy.° Nevertheless, what I've done to you cannot properly be called revenge, but rather, retribution, for revenge should exceed the offense, and this will fall short of it. In fact, when I consider the peril you exposed me to, it would not suffice for me to take your life by way of revenge, nor a hundred lives just like yours, since I'd only be killing a vile, wicked, worthless little woman.

"Except for that tolerably pretty face of yours, which will be ruined and covered with wrinkles in just a few years, how the devil do you differ from any other poor, worthless serving girl? It was not for lack of trying that you almost caused the death of a gentleman, as you called me just a moment ago, who could be of more use to the world in a single day than a hundred thousand of your kind could be for as long as the earth shall last. Therefore, through the pain you're suffering now, I'm going to teach you what it means to make fun of men who have feelings, and especially scholars, and should you manage to escape from here with your life, I'll give you good cause never to stoop to such folly again.

"But if you are so anxious to come down, why don't you just throw yourself onto the ground here? That way, with God's help, you'll break your neck, and at one and the same time, you'll escape the pain you seem to be suffering while making me the happiest man in the world. That's all I have to say to you for the time being. I was smart enough to get you to climb up there; now let's see if you're as smart about getting down as you once were about making a fool of me."

As the scholar spoke, the wretched woman wept incessantly. Meanwhile, time was passing, and the sun was climbing higher and higher in the sky. When he finally stopped talking, she said: "Ah, what a cruel man you are! If you suffered so much on that damned night and if my fault seemed so serious to you that neither my youthful beauty, nor my bitter tears, nor my humble prayers can make you feel a touch of pity, at least you should be a little moved to treat me with less remorseless severity by the fact that I eventually trusted in you and revealed all of my secrets to you, thus giving you the means to satisfy your desire and show me how I've sinned. For if I hadn't trusted you, you wouldn't have had any way to avenge yourself on me, as you seemed so passionately intent upon doing.

"Ah, put aside your anger now and forgive me. Should you deign to pardon me and let me get down from here, I'm ready to abandon that faithless young man forever and to take you alone as my lover and my lord even though you disparage my beauty and say it's fleeting and of little value. Whatever it may be worth when you compare it to the beauty of other women, yet this much I do know: it should be prized, if for no other reason than that it is a joy and a plaything and a delight for men in their youth—and you're by no means an old man.

"However cruelly I've been treated by you, I still can't believe that you would want to see me die so shameful a death as to throw myself down there in despair right before your eyes, eyes which, if you were not a liar in the past as you have since become, once found me so very attractive. Ah, for the love of God, have mercy on me, for pity's sake! The sun is becoming unbearably hot, and it's beginning to make me feel as miserable now as the intense cold did last night."

"My lady," replied the scholar, who was only too delighted to chat with her, "you didn't place your trust in me just now because of the love you felt for me, but to get back the lover you'd lost, and that's why you deserve to be treated even more harshly. Furthermore, you're crazy if you think this was the one and only way I had to obtain the revenge I desired. I had a thousand others. Indeed, while I was pretending to love you, I had spread a thousand snares around your feet, so that if it hadn't happened now, you would have inevitably been caught in one of them.° Although you could have been snagged by many others that would have meant more suffering and shame than this one does, I did not choose it to make things easier for you, but because I wouldn't have to wait so long to be happy like this.

"Moreover, should all of my tricks have failed, I would still have had my pen, and with it I would have written such things about you in such profusion and in such a style that when they came to your notice, as they most certainly would have, you would have wished, a thousand times a day, that you had never been born. The power of the pen is very much greater than those people suppose who have not proved it by experience. I swear to God— and may He make my revenge as sweet right down to the end as He has made it here at the beginning—I would have written things about you that would have shamed you so much not only in others' sight, but in your own, that you would have gouged out your eyes so you would never have had to look at yourself again. Therefore, don't go blaming the sea because a tiny little stream has added to its waters.

"As for your love and your claim that you are mine, I couldn't care less, as I've already said. Go ahead and stay with the guy you belonged to before, if you can. Because of what he's done to you, I now love him as much as I once used to hate him. You women are always falling for young men and longing for them to love you in return, because you see their fresher complexions and blacker beards, their strutting about and dancing and jousting. Men who are more mature have been through all that, and now they know things that those others have yet to learn.

"What's more, you believe that the young are better riders and can do more miles in a day than men of riper years. But whereas I certainly confess that they can give your fur-trimmed gown a more vigorous shaking, older men, being more experienced, are superior when it comes to finding out where the fleas are hiding. Besides, it's far better to have a small portion that's tasty than a large one that's bland, and although a fast trot will tire and weaken a man, even if he's young, an easy gait may bring another somewhat later to the inn, but at least he'll be in good shape when he gets there.

"Witless creatures that you are, you women don't realize how much evil is hidden under that handsome appearance of theirs. Young men are never content with just a single woman, but want every one they see, thinking they deserve to have them all. Consequently, their love can never be stable, something to which you yourself can now testify as an expert witness, thanks to the experience you've had. Moreover, they think they have a right to be worshipped and pampered by their women, and believe there's no greater glory than bragging about all the ones they've had, a fault that has caused many women to go and spread themselves underneath some friar simply because he'll keep mum about it. Although you claim nobody knew anything about your love affairs except your maid and me, you are badly misinformed. You deceive yourself if that's what you believe, for in his neighborhood, they talk about almost nothing else, just as they do in yours, although the people most involved are usually the very last to have news about such things reach their ears. Moreover, young men will steal from you, whereas the older ones will give you presents. Consequently, since you've made a bad choice, you may stay with the guy you gave yourself to and leave me, whom you've spurned, for another, because I've found a woman who's worth a lot more than you are and who has understood me better than you ever did.

"Now, because it seems you don't believe what I've been telling you in the here and now, if you want to get a better idea of my feelings about you, you can do so in the next world. Just throw yourself down onto the ground here, and then your soul, which I truly believe is already in the Devil's arms, will be able to see whether or not your headlong fall will trouble these eyes of mine in any way. Still, since I don't believe you'll consent to make me such a happy man, let me say this to you, that if you find yourself beginning to burn up, just think back to the cold you made me endure, and then, if you mix it with this heat, you will, without doubt, make the sun feel more temperate."

On seeing that the scholar's words were always directed at the same cruel end, the disconsolate lady began weeping again. "Look," she said, "since there's nothing about me that is capable of making you feel pity, at least be moved by the love you bear that woman you've found who's wiser than I am and who, you say, returns your affection. Forgive me out of love for her, bring me my clothes so that I can get dressed again, and let me climb down from here."

This made the scholar burst out laughing, and observing that it was already well past the hour of tierce, he replied: "Well, there's no way I can refuse your request now that you've appealed to me in the name of my lady. So, if you'll tell me where your clothes are, I'll go fetch them and arrange for you to get down from there."

The lady believed him, and feeling somewhat reassured, she gave him precise directions to the place where she had put her clothes. Upon emerging from the tower, the scholar ordered his servant not to leave the area but to stay close by and do all he could to keep anyone else from getting in until he himself had returned. After he finished speaking, he walked over to his friend's house where he dined, completely at his ease, and then, in due course, went to take a nap.

Left atop the tower, the lady may have felt reassured to some degree because of her foolish hope, but since she was still terribly uncomfortable, she went over and sat next to that part of the wall that offered a little shade. There she settled down to wait, with nothing but her own exceedingly bitter thoughts as company, by turns brooding and weeping, now buoyed by hope and now in despair that the scholar would ever return with her clothes. As her mind flitted from one thought to another, she was finally overcome by her grief, and since she had been awake all night, fell fast asleep.

The sun was blazing hot, and when it reached its zenith, it beat straight down on the lady's tender, delicate body and her unprotected head, striking them with such intensity that it produced blisters on every last bit of her exposed flesh, causing countless tiny cracks to open up all over it. In fact, she was burned so badly that the pain forced her awake even though she was in a deep sleep.

Feeling her flesh on fire, she tried to move just a little, but when she did, it seemed that her scorched skin was cracking and bursting open all over, as if someone had taken a burned piece of parchment and was stretching it. Besides—and this was hardly surprising—her head hurt her so badly that she felt it was going to split in two. Since the floor of the platform atop the tower was so hot that she could not find a place to put her feet or any other part of her body, she was unable to stand still and kept shifting her position constantly, weeping with every step she took. Even worse, there was not a breath of wind, which allowed swarms of flies and gadflies, which had arrived in large numbers, to settle down inside the fissures in her flesh where they stung her so fiercely that every sting felt as if she were being stabbed with a spear. In response, she went flailing about with her hands, while she continually cursed herself, her life, her lover, and the scholar.

Being thus tormented and goaded and pierced to the quick by the incalculable heat, by the sun, by the flies and gadflies, and by her hunger, too, though much more by her thirst, and on top of all that, by a thousand distressing thoughts, the lady got to her feet, and standing up straight, she began looking everywhere she could, hoping to see or hear someone nearby, for she was ready to call out and ask for help, no matter what might happen to her as a result.

Even this, however, her enemy Fortune denied her. For the farmhands had all left the fields because of the heat, and in any case no one had actually gone to work anywhere near there that day, for they were all staying close to their houses in order to thresh their wheat. Consequently, the lady heard nothing but the cicadas and saw only the Arno, which filled her with a desire for its waters that only served to increase her thirst rather than diminish it. Here and there she saw woods and patches of shade and houses, all of which similarly caused her anguish because of the longing she felt for them.

Is there anything more for us to say about the hapless widow? What with the sun overhead and the hot platform beneath her, the stings of the flies and gadflies on every side, she was in such a sorry state that her skin, whose whiteness had overcome the gloom on the previous night, had now turned as red as madder and was so spotted everywhere with blood that she would have seemed to anyone who saw her the ugliest thing in the world.°

There she remained, bereft of counsel and hope, fully expecting to die, until halfway to the hour of nones. At that point, the scholar woke up, and calling his lady to mind, he returned to the tower to see how she was doing. When he spoke to his servant, who had not yet had his dinner, and told him to go and eat, the lady heard him, and even though she was weak and suffering terribly from the pain, she went over and sat down next to the opening.

"Rinieri," she said to him in tears, "surely you've taken your revenge beyond any conceivable limit. If I made you freeze in my courtyard all night, you didn't just stop at giving me a roasting, but you've had me burning up on this tower all day long, not to mention the fact that I'm dying from hunger and thirst. That's why I implore you, if only for the love of God, to climb up here, and since I don't have the heart to take my own life, to kill me yourself, for the torment I'm suffering is so horrible that what I want more than anything else is to die. Or if you won't bestow this grace on me, at least have someone bring me a cup of water so that I can moisten my mouth, for it's so parched and scorched that my tears aren't sufficient to do that."

The scholar could tell from her voice just how weak she was, and since he could also see part of her body that had been completely burned by the sun, he was moved by those things as well as by her humble prayers to feel a little pity for her. But nevertheless, he replied: "You wicked woman, you won't die at my hands, but at your own if that's what you really want. You're going to get just as much water from me to relieve you from the heat, as I got fire from you to relieve me from the cold. What I most regret is that the illness I suffered on account of the cold had to be treated with the warmth of stinking dung, whereas they'll heal the injuries you got from the heat by means of cool, sweet-smelling rose water. And while I practically lost my life as well as the use of my limbs, you will merely be flayed by this heat, and will wind up no less beautiful than a serpent who has shed her old skin."

"Oh, woe is me!" cried the lady. "May God take such beauty, acquired in such a way, and give it to all my worst enemies. But you, who are crueler than any wild beast, how could you bear to torture me this way? Is there a worse punishment you or anyone else could have inflicted on me if I had killed everyone in your family after subjecting them to the direst of torments? I certainly don't know what greater cruelty could have been used against a traitor who had put an entire city to the slaughter than the one you subjected me to. I've been roasted by the sun and devoured by the flies, and on top of that, you refuse to offer me a cup of water, although even condemned murderers on their way to be executed are often given wine to drink if they merely ask for it. But look, now that I see you are unwavering in your savage cruelty and my suffering is in no way capable of moving you, I will prepare myself to meet my death with resignation. May God have mercy on my soul, and may He look down, I pray, on what you are doing with the eyes of justice."

When she finished speaking, she dragged herself in agonizing pain, filled with despair that she would ever be able to survive the fiery heat, toward the middle of the platform, where, quite apart from her other torments, she felt she was going to faint from thirst, not once, but a thousand times. And all the while she wept bitter tears as she bemoaned her misfortune.

Finally, when vespers arrived, it seemed to the scholar that he had done enough. He therefore had his servant take her clothes and wrap them up in his cloak, and they set off for the hapless lady's house, where he found her maid, sad and forlorn, sitting on the doorstep, unable to determine what she should do.

"My good woman," he said to her, "what's become of your mistress?"

"Sir," replied the maid, "I don't know. This morning I expected to find her in her bed, where I thought I saw her going last night, but I didn't find her there or anywhere else, and since I don't know what's happened to her, I'm really very worried. But you, sir, is there anything you can tell me about her?"

"I just wish," replied the scholar, "that I'd had you up there where I put her so that I could have punished you for your sins the way I've punished her for hers! But you can bet you're not going to escape my clutches until I've made you pay such a price for what you did that you'll never make a fool of any man again without remembering me." And having said this, he told his servant: "Give her those clothes and tell her she can go for her mistress if she wants to."

The servant did as he was told and gave the clothes to the maid. When she recognized whose they were, she was so terrified that she could scarcely keep herself from screaming, for she was convinced, in light of what had been said, that they had killed her mistress. Then, as soon as the scholar had left, she burst into tears and immediately set off at a run for the tower, carrying the clothes along with her.

That same day, one of the lady's swineherds had had the misfortune to lose two of his pigs and had gone in search of them, arriving at the little tower just a short time after the scholar's departure. As he went looking for them all over the place, he heard the hapless lady's woeful moans, and climbing up as high as he could go, he shouted: "Who's that crying up there?"

Recognizing the farmhand's voice, the lady called to him by name. "For pity's sake," she said, "go find my maid and have her come to me up here."

The farmhand realized who it was and replied: "Oh no, my lady, who carried you up there? Your maid's been running around searching for you all day long. But who'd ever have guessed you were here?"

Taking the two uprights of the ladder, the peasant set them up in the proper position and began tying the rungs in place with bands of willow. As he was doing this, the maid arrived, and when she entered the tower, unable to restrain herself any longer, she cried out, while beating her head with the palms of her hands: "Alas, my sweet lady, where are you?"

On hearing her, the lady called out as loudly as she could: "Oh, my sister, I'm up here. Don't cry. Just bring me my clothes, and do it quickly."

Greatly relieved to hear her mistress's voice, the maid started climbing up the ladder, which the peasant had just about finished repairing, and with his help she managed to reach the platform. When she saw her mistress lying naked on the floor, utterly exhausted and defeated, looking less like a human being than a half-burned log, she dug her nails into her face and wept over her as if she were dead.

The lady begged her to be quiet, for God's sake, and to help her get dressed. Then, when she learned from the maid that no one else knew where she had been except the peasant and those who had brought her clothes, she felt somewhat relieved and begged them for God's sake never to say a word about this to anyone. Since the lady could not walk on her own, after much discussion the farmhand lifted her onto his shoulders and carried her safely down and out of the tower. The wretched maid, who had stayed behind, was less careful as she climbed down the ladder, with the result that her foot slipped and she fell to the ground, breaking her thigh.

Because of the pain she was experiencing, the maid began roaring like a lion, so that the farmhand, after having set the lady down on a plot of grass, went back to see what was wrong with her. Upon discovering that she had broken her thigh, he also brought her to the same spot and placed her on the grass beside her mistress. When the lady saw that, on top of all her other misfortunes, the person on whose assistance she most depended had broken her thigh, she felt unspeakably sad and began weeping once again so bitterly that not only was the swineherd incapable of consoling her, but he actually started crying himself.

Since the sun was already beginning to set, however, and the disconsolate lady did not want to be caught out there when night fell, she prevailed upon the farmhand to go back to his house. There he found his wife and two of his brothers who returned to the tower with him, carrying a plank on which they placed the maid and brought her home. The farmhand himself, having comforted the lady with words of sympathy and given her fresh water to drink, lifted her onto his shoulders and carried her to his wife's room, who gave her some sops of bread to eat, undressed her, and put her to bed. After that, they made arrangements for the lady and her maid to be taken to Florence that very night. And so they were.

Once she was back in the city, the lady, who had a plentiful supply of tricks, made up a yarn about herself and her maid that had nothing to do with what had actually happened, and managed to persuade her brothers and sisters and everyone else that it was all the result of diabolical spells.° The doctors lost no time in curing her of her raging fever and other ills, but since she shed her skin more than once in the process, leaving it stuck to the sheets, she suffered the greatest anguish and torment imaginable. They also took care of the maid with her broken thigh. As a result of her experience, the lady forgot all about her lover, and from then on she wisely refrained both from playing any more tricks and from falling in love with anyone. As for the scholar, once he found out that the maid had broken her thigh, he decided that his revenge was complete, and happy to leave it at that, he never said another word about it.

This, then, is what happened to the foolish young woman with all of her tricks, for she thought she could trifle with a scholar the way she could with anyone else, not realizing that scholars—not all of them, I say, but the vast majority—know where the Devil keeps his tail. Consequently, ladies, take care not to play such tricks yourselves, especially when you are dealing with scholars.°

Story 9

EAGER TO BE MADE A MEMBER OF A COMPANY OF
PRIVATEERS, MASTER SIMONE, A PHYSICIAN, IS PERSUADED
BY BRUNO AND BUFFALMACCO TO GO ONE NIGHT TO A
CERTAIN SPOT, WHERE HE IS THROWN INTO A DITCH BY
BUFFALMACCO AND LEFT TO WALLOW IN FILTH.°

* * *

Dear ladies, Spinelloccio richly deserved the prank that Zeppa played on him, and that is why, as Pampinea was trying to show just a little while ago, I believe we should not judge people too harshly who play tricks on others if the victim is asking for it or is getting his just deserts. Spinelloccio got what he deserved, and so, now I intend to tell you about someone who went around looking for it and whose deceivers, in my opinion, are consequently to be praised rather than blamed. The man in question was a physician who came to Florence from Bologna, covered in vair, like the stupid sheep he was, from head to toe.°

Every day we see our fellow citizens returning from Bologna, this one a judge, that one a physician, and yet another a notary, all sporting long, flowing robes of scarlet and vair as well as a host of other things designed to make a grand impression—and we likewise see every day just how much all this really amounts to in practice. A certain Master Simone da Villa was one of this sort, for his patrimony was far greater than his learning. He came here, not all that many years ago, dressed in a scarlet robe with a large hood, proclaimed himself a doctor of medicine, and rented a house in the street we now call Via del Cocomero.° Having just recently arrived, as I said, this Master Simone made it a practice, among his many other remarkable habits, of asking whomever he was with to identify all the people he saw passing in the street, and he would observe and remember everything they did as though he were going to make up the medications he had to give his patients on that basis.

Among those he eyed most intently were his two neighbors Bruno and Buffalmacco, the two painters about whom we have already told two stories today. The pair of them were constantly in one another's company, and since they seemed to him to be the most carefree people in the world and to lead happier lives than anyone else, as indeed they did, he made lots of inquiries about their situation and was told by everyone that they were just a couple of poor painters. Unable to comprehend how they could possibly lead such merry lives if they did not have much money, he concluded, having heard how clever they were, that they had to be extracting enormous profits from some source people knew nothing about. He was therefore very eager to strike up a friendship with one of them at least, if not with both, and finally managed to do so with Bruno.

It only took a few meetings with Master Simone for Bruno to conclude that he was an ass and to begin having a grand old time with him thanks to his very eccentric behavior. The doctor likewise found Bruno's company wonderfully entertaining, and after having invited him to dinner on several occasions, from which he assumed they could talk on familiar terms, Master Simone expressed his amazement at how the two painters could lead such merry lives despite being so very poor, and he asked Bruno to teach him how they did it.

Thinking that this was another one of the doctor's usual stupid, senseless questions, Bruno started to laugh. But then he decided he would reply to him as his asininity deserved.

"Master," he said, "I wouldn't tell many people how we manage it, but as you're my friend and I know you won't reveal it to anyone else, I won't keep it all to myself. Now it's true that the life I lead with my buddy is just as happy and contented as you suppose. Actually, it's even better than that. Still, we don't get enough money from our work or from the property we own even to pay for the water we consume. Not that I want you to think we're a couple of robbers; no, we simply go about privateering, and from that, without harming anyone, we don't just obtain the necessities of life, but many of the extras that give us pleasure as well. And that's how, as you've noticed, we've been able to lead such merry lives."

The doctor took in everything Bruno said, and since he believed him without knowing what he was really talking about, he was filled with amazement and promptly conceived an intense, burning desire to discover what it meant to go privateering, swearing to Bruno that he would never, ever tell anyone else about it.

"Oh no, Master," said Bruno, "what are you asking me to do? The secret you want me to reveal is so serious that if anyone were to find out about it, I'd be ruined, driven right off the face of the earth. I could even wind up in the jaws of the Lucifer at San Gallo.° Still, the love I bear your qualitative melonosity of Legnaia and the faith I have in you are so great that I feel myself obliged to grant your every wish.° So, I'll reveal the secret to you, but on this condition, that you swear to me by the cross at Montesone to keep your promise and never tell anyone."

The doctor swore he would not.

"Know then, my dull-cified Master," said Bruno, "that not long ago there was a grand master of necromancy in this city named Michael Scot, so-called because he came from Scotland.° He was received with the greatest hospitality here by many gentlemen, of whom only a few remain alive today. When the time came for him to depart, he was moved by their urgent entreaties to leave behind two quite capable disciples, charging them to grant, without a moment's hesitation, every wish those very noble men might have who had given him such an honorable reception.

"The disciples freely assisted the gentlemen I've referred to in certain love affairs of theirs as well as in other trifling matters, and after a while, having taken a liking to the city and its people's ways, they decided to settle down here permanently. They managed to form good, close friendships with a number of people, showing no concern for whether they were gentlemen or commoners, rich or poor, provided only that they all shared the same interests. And in order to please the friends they had made, they formed a company of some twenty-five men who were to meet at least twice a month in whatever place the pair selected. When they are all assembled, each man tells them what he wants, and the two of them immediately see about granting his wish that very night.

"Since Buffalmacco and I are on the most friendly and intimate terms with the pair, they made us members of their company, and we've belonged to it ever since. And let me tell you that whenever we get together, it's a wonderful thing to see the hangings all around the hall where we eat, the tables set for a king, and the noble array of handsome servants, both men and women, who are at the beck and call of everyone in the company, not to mention the bowls and pitchers, the flasks and cups, and the rest of the vessels we use for eating and drinking, all of them made of gold and silver. Finally, no less marvelous, there is the abundance and variety of the dishes that they set before us in their proper order, each one prepared according our own individual preferences. I couldn't begin to describe the range and variety of the sweet sounds coming from countless instruments and the melodious songs that we hear there, nor could I tell you how many wax candles are burned at those suppers, or the number of sweets consumed, or how costly the wines are that we drink. And I wouldn't want you to imagine, my dear sweet pumpkin, that we show up there in the same clothes you see us wearing right now. The poorest person at the dinner would look like an emperor to you, for we are decked out, each and every one of us, in expensive robes and other finery.

"But over and above all these delights, there are the beautiful women who are brought in from all over the world the moment anyone asks for them. Not only would you see the Lady of the Barbanichi, the Queen of the Basques, and the Consort of the Sultan, but also the Empress of Osbech, the Chitterchatterer of Norwega, the Semistanding of Gluttonia, and the Scapulathedral of Narsia. But why do I go on enumerating them to you? All the queens of the earth are there, I'm telling you, down to the Skinkimurra of Prester John.° Now, there's a sight for you! And once they've had something to drink and eaten some of the sweets, they do a dance or two, and then each of them goes off to her bedroom with the guy who wanted her brought to him there.

"And let me tell you, those rooms are so beautiful you'd think you were in Paradise, and they're as fragrant as the spice jars in your shop when you're grinding the cumin.° When we all lie down to rest, we do it in beds that would seem to you more beautiful than the one the Doge has in Venice. And I'll leave it to your imagination just how those lady weavers push your treadles and tug on your shuttle, pulling it toward them in order to make your fabric nice and tight!°

"But in my opinion, among the people who have the best time there you've got to count Buffalmacco and me, because he usually has them bring him the Queen of France, and I send for the Queen of England. They're two of the most beautiful women in the world, and we know how to handle them so they don't have eyes for anyone else but us. So, now you can decide for yourself whether we have good reason to be happier than other men as we go about our lives, considering that we have the love of two queens like that—not to mention the fact that whenever we want a thousand florins or two from them, it's because we haven't got them.

"And that's what, in our way of speaking, we call going about privateering. Just as pirates take everybody's goods, so do we, except that there's this much of a difference between us: they never give anything back, whereas we return what we've taken once we're finished with it. Now that you know what we mean, my good and simple Master, when we say we go about privateering, you can surely see for yourself how closely you've got to guard this secret, so there's no need for me to say anything more on that subject or ask you not to talk about it, either."

The doctor, whose knowledge of medicine most likely did not extend beyond treating babies for thrush infections, trusted Bruno's words as if they were truth itself, and was enflamed with an intense longing to be made a member of their company as though that were the most desirable thing in the world. Accordingly, while he told Bruno that he was no longer surprised that the two of them went about as happy as could be, it was only with the greatest difficulty that he could restrain himself from asking to be made a member of the company right then and there, rather than waiting until such time as he had shown Bruno more of his hospitality, after which he could plead his case with greater confidence that he would succeed. Having thus held himself in check, he began assiduously cultivating Bruno's friendship, inviting him over to eat both mornings and evenings, and displaying boundless affection toward him. In fact, they spent so much time with one another and got together so often that the doctor seemed incapable of living without him, indeed, that he could not even imagine doing so.

Bruno felt he was doing pretty well, and so, in order not to seem ungrateful for the hospitality the doctor had shown him, he painted the figure of Lent for him in his dining room, an *Agnus Dei* at the entrance to his bedroom, and a urine flask over the door to the street so that those people who needed a consultation could distinguish his house from the others. Moreover, in a small loggia of his, Bruno painted the battle of the cats and the mice, which seemed to the doctor beautiful beyond description.°

Bruno would sometimes say to him, when the two had not had supper together the previous evening: "Last night I was with the company, and since I'd gotten a little tired of the Queen of England, I had them send me the Gumedra of the Great Khan of Altarisi."°

"Gumedra," said the doctor, "what does that mean? I don't understand these names."

"I'm not surprised, my dear Master," said Bruno, "because I've been told that Hoggiphates and Avadinner don't say anything about it."°

"You mean Hippocrates and Avicenna," replied the doctor.

"By gosh," said Bruno, "I just don't know, for I'm as bad at your names as you are at mine. However, 'gumedra' in the language of the Great Khan means the same thing as 'empress' in ours. Oh, you'd really find her one good-looking gal! She'd make you forget all about your medicines and your enemas and your poultices, let me tell you."

Bruno went on talking to him like this from time to time in order to get him all fired up, until one evening, when he was paint-ing the battle of the cats and the mice, with Simone holding up a light for him to see by, Messer Doctor decided that, thanks to all his hospitality, he had Bruno sufficiently in his debt, and could open up and freely reveal his feelings. Since the two of them were all alone, he said: "Bruno, God knows there's no one alive today for whom I'd do all the things I'd be willing to do for you. If you asked me to go from here to Peretola, I don't think it would take much to get me to do it.° So, don't be surprised if I speak to you as a friend and ask you a favor in strict confidence. As you know, not so long ago you spoke to me about the activities of that merry company of yours, and it's filled me with a desire to become a member that's stronger than anything I've ever felt in my life. I have good reason for wanting to join, as you'll see for yourself if I should ever happen to get in, for I assure you here and now that if I don't have them bring me the prettiest serving girl you've seen in a long, long time, you can make me the butt of all your jokes from then on. I only caught sight of her just last year at Cacavincigli, but I fell passionately in love with her, and I swear by Christ's body

that I offered her ten Bolognese groats if she'd consent to give herself to me, but she didn't want to.°

"And so, I beg you from the bottom of my heart to tell me what
I have to do in order to join the company, and also, to use whatever influence you have to help me get in, for I can assure you that
you'll never have a better, more loyal member, nor one who'll
bring you more credit. First of all, you can see how handsome a
guy I am, what a fine pair of legs I've got under me, and that this
face of mine is just like a rose. Besides, I'm a doctor of medicine,
and I doubt you have any of them in your company. On top of
that, I know lots of good stories as well as some lovely little songs.
In fact, let me give you one of them right now"—and all of a sudden he started singing.

Bruno had such a tremendous urge to laugh that he could
hardly contain himself, although he nevertheless managed to do
so. Then, when the song was done, the Master asked him: "What
do you think of it?"

"Your barbartistic caterwarbling would sure put all the reed
whistles to shame," replied Bruno.°

"You would never have believed it," said the doctor, "if you
hadn't heard me yourself, would you?"

"You're certainly right about that," said Bruno.

"I know a whole lot of other ones," said the doctor, "but let's let
that be that for now. What you see here in me is what you get. My
father was a nobleman, although he lived in the country, and on
my mother's side I was born into a family from Vallecchio.° Furthermore, as you may have observed yourself, I've got the finest
books and the most beautiful wardrobe of any doctor in Florence.
I swear to God, I have a robe that cost me, all told, about a hundred *lire* in small change more than ten years ago! And that's why
I'm begging you from the bottom of my heart to have them make
me a member, and I swear to God that if you do get me in, I'll
never take a penny from you for my services, no matter how sick
you are."

Having listened to him run on, Bruno was as convinced as ever that the man was a pea brain, and said to him: "Master, give me a little more light over here, and if you'll just be patient until I've finished the tails of these mice, I'll give you your answer then."

When the tails were done, Bruno pretended he was very worried about the doctor's request. "I know all about the great things you'd do for me, Master," he said, "but nevertheless, what you're asking of me, although it may seem insignificant to a great mind like yours, is still a very big deal as far as I'm concerned. Now, even if I were in a position to grant it, I don't know of another person in the world for whom I'd do it except for you, not only because I love you as a good friend should, but also because your words are seasoned with so much wisdom that they would draw pious old ladies right out of their boots, let alone make me change my mind.° In fact, the more time I spend with you, the wiser you seem to me. And let me tell you this as well: even if I had no other reason to love you, I am bound to do so because you've fallen for such a beautiful creature as the one you described.

"I must point out, however, that I don't have as much influence in these matters as you think, which is why I can't do what's necessary for you. But if you'll promise me, on your solemn and tainted word, to keep it a secret, I'll explain how you can take care of it yourself, and since you have all those fine books and the other things you were telling me about earlier, I feel certain you'll succeed."°

"You can speak freely," said the doctor. "If you knew me better, then you'd know that I'm really good at keeping secrets. When Messer Guasparuolo da Saliceto was serving as a judge for the *podestà* of Forlimpopoli, there were very few things he did not tell me, because he found me such a good secretary.° And if you want proof, well, I was the first man he told that he was about to marry Bergamina. Now, what do you think of that?"

"Well, that settles it," said Bruno. "If a man like that confided in you, I can certainly do the same. Here's how you should go about it. In our company we always have a captain as well as two counselors who are replaced every six months, and we know for certain that on the first of next month, Buffalmacco is to be captain, and I'll be one of the counselors. Now, whoever becomes captain has a lot of influence over who gets to be admitted as a member, so, in my opinion, you should do everything you can to strike up a friendship with Buffalmacco and start entertaining him on a lavish scale. He's the kind of man who'll take a real liking to you from the moment he sees how intelligent you are, and once you've managed to advance your friendship with him by means of your wit as well as all those fine things you own, you can ask him to do it, and he won't know how to tell you no. I've already spoken to him about you, and he feels as well disposed toward you as can be, so, as soon as you've accomplished what I've told you to do, you can leave all the rest to the two of us."

"I'm really, really pleased with your plan," said the doctor, "for if he's a man who takes pleasure in the company of the wise, he has only to talk with me for a while, and I promise you he'll never want to let me out of his sight. I've got enough intelligence to supply an entire city, and I'd still remain as wise as they come."

Having arranged everything with the doctor, Bruno recounted the whole story in all its particulars to Buffalmacco, who was so eager to provide this Master Sappyhead with what he was looking for that every moment passing seemed like a thousand years to him.°

The doctor, who wanted more than anything to go privateering, did not rest until he had struck up a friendship with Buffalmacco, which, of course, he had no difficulty doing. He then began treating him, both morning and night, to the finest meals in the world and always invited Bruno to join them as well. For their part, knowing that Simone had an excellent wine cellar and many fat capons, not to mention a host of other good things, Bruno and Buffalmacco were happy to indulge themselves and live like lords, never needing much of an invitation to spend time in his company, although they constantly assured him that they would not have done such a thing for anyone else.

But eventually, when the time seemed right to the doctor, he made the same request to Buffalmacco that he had made before to Bruno. Upon hearing it, Buffalmacco pretended to be absolutely furious and blew up at Bruno.

"I swear by the High God of Passignano," he said, "I can barely keep myself from giving you such a wallop on your head that it'd knock your nose down to your heels, you traitor, because you're the only one who could've revealed these things to the Master."°

Simone, however, did his utmost to excuse Bruno, saying on his oath that he had learned everything from another source, and after many of those wise words of his, he finally managed to mollify Buffalmacco, who then turned to him and said: "My dear Master, it's pretty clear that you've been in Bologna and that you've been keeping your mouth shut since you came back to this town. And let me tell you something else: you didn't learn your ABCs by writing them on an apple, the way many fools try to do it, but instead, you used that great big, long melon of yours, and in fact, unless I'm badly deceived, you were baptized on a Sunday.° Bruno told me you studied medicine up there, but in my opinion you were really studying how to attract men to you, for what with your wisdom and your fine talk you do that better than any other man I've ever seen."

Cutting him off in midsentence, the doctor turned to Bruno and said: "What a thing it is to talk with wise men and to pass the time in their company! Who would've been able to read my mind down to the last little thought as promptly as this worthy man just did? You were not nearly so quick to perceive my true value as he was. But you might at least tell him what I said to you when you informed me that he takes pleasure in the company of the wise. Do you think I've been as good as my word?"

"Better," replied Bruno.

The Master then said to Buffalmacco: "You would have had even more to say, if you had seen me in Bologna, for there was no one, high or low, professor or student, who didn't think the world of me, because I could keep them entertained with my wit and wisdom. And I'll tell you something else: I never uttered a word there without making them all laugh, that's how much they enjoyed my company. As a result, when it was time for me to leave, they complained bitterly, and every last one of them begged me to stay, until it reached the point that to keep me there, they offered to let me alone do all the lecturing in the faculty of medicine. But I didn't want to, because I'd already decided to come here where I've got some very substantial estates that have been in my family forever. And that's just what I did."

"Now what do you think?" said Bruno to Buffalmacco. "I told you what he was like, but you wouldn't believe me. I swear on the Holy Gospel, there's not a doctor in these parts who knows his way around ass's urine in comparison to him. In fact, you wouldn't find his equal between here and the gates of Paris. Now just see if you can prevent yourself from doing whatever he wants!"

"Bruno's telling the truth," said the doctor, "but people don't give me the recognition I deserve around here. You all are a bunch of dummies. I just wish you could see me in my natural element, among my fellow doctors."

"Truly, Master," replied Buffalmacco, "you know far more than I would have ever imagined. Therefore, speaking frankastically— to use here the kind of language one should employ with wise men like yourself—let me tell you that without fail, I'll arrange for you to become a member of our company."°

After receiving this promise, the doctor lavished even more hospitality on the pair, who enjoyed themselves at his expense, persuading him to believe the most nonsensical things in the world, and promising that he would have as his mistress the Contessa di Crappa, who was the most beautiful thing to be found in the whole ass-sembly of the human race.°

When the doctor asked who this Countess was, Buffalmacco replied: "O my seed-filled cucumber, why she's so great a lady that there are few houses in the world that do not, at least to some extent, come within her jurisdiction. Indeed, even the Franciscans, to say nothing of all the others, pay her tribute to the sound of the kettledrum. And let me assure you that whenever she goes about, you'll certainly have some scents of her presence, albeit most of the time she keeps herself shut up tight inside. Although her usual residence is in Laterina, nevertheless, not so very long ago she passed right by the entrance to your house when she was making her way one night to the Arno to wash her feet and get a whiff of fresh air.°

You can frequently see her servants making their rounds, carrying her staff and pail as the sign of her authority, and everywhere you look, you'll find her noble retainers, such as Sir Dingleberry, Lord Turd, Viscount Broomhandle, Baron Squirts, and others with whom you are intimately acquainted, even if you may not recall them at the present moment.° So, you can forget all about that woman from Cacavincigli, for unless we're deceiving ourselves, we'll soon have you in the sweet embraces of that very great lady."

The doctor, who had been born and bred in Bologna, did not understand the meaning of their words, and told them that the lady would suit him to a tee. Nor did he have to wait very long after hearing their tall tales before the two painters brought him the news that he had been accepted into the company. On the day before the group's next evening get-together, Simone invited the pair to dinner, and when they were finished, asked them how he was supposed to get to the meeting.

"Look, Master," said Buffalmacco, "for reasons you are now about to hear, you've got to be very brave, because if you aren't, you might run into trouble, and you could make things very difficult for us as well. Tonight, around bedtime, you must find a way to get up onto one of those raised tombs they've recently erected outside of Santa Maria Novella, and be sure to wear one of your finest robes so that your first appearance before the company will be an honorable one, and also because the Countess is proposing, in light of the fact that you're a gentleman, to make you a Knight of the Bath at her own expense—or so we've been told, for we weren't actually there at the time.° And you're to wait at the tombs until we send someone to get you.

"Now, so you'll know exactly what to expect, let me tell you that a black beast with horns on its head is going to come for you, and though it isn't particularly large, it'll try to scare you by going up and down before you in the piazza, leaping high into the air and making loud hissing noises. When it sees you aren't afraid, however, it'll quiet down and come over to you. As soon as it's close enough, don't be frightened or call on God and the Saints, but get down from the tomb and climb right up onto its back.

After you've firmly seated yourself there, fold your arms across your chest the way courtiers do, and don't touch the beast again with your hands. Soon, it will set off at a slow pace and bring you right to us. But let me tell you, if you invoke God or the Saints, or show any sign of fear before you've arrived, it might throw you off or knock you into something, and then you'd be in a big stinking mess. So, unless you're sure you'll be brave, don't come, because you'd just make trouble for us and not do yourself the least bit of good."

"You still don't know me," replied the doctor. "Perhaps you're worried about me because of the gloves and the long robes I wear, but if you knew what I used to do in Bologna when I went around at night with my buddies on the lookout for women, you'd be amazed. I swear to God, I remember a night when there was one of them, a skinny gal, and what's worse, no taller than my fist, who didn't want to come with us. So, after giving her a few good punches to start with, I picked her up and carried her, I think, about as far as a crossbow shot, and finally made her agree to join us. Then, there was another time when I was all alone, except for one of my servants, and shortly after the "Ave Maria," I was passing by the Franciscans' cemetery, where they had just buried a woman that very day, and I wasn't the least bit afraid. So, you don't have to worry on that score: I've got courage and vigor to spare. As for my making an honorable appearance before you all, let me tell you, I'll put on the scarlet robe I wore when I graduated, and you'll soon see how happy the whole company will be the moment they catch sight of me and how they'll be making me their captain before too long. Just wait till I get there, and you'll see how things will go. After all, without ever having laid eyes on me, the Countess is already so in love with me that she wants to make me a Knight of the Bath. But perhaps you think knighthood won't suit me and that I won't know what to do with it once I've got it. Well, just leave it to me!"

"That's all very well said," replied Buffalmacco. "Only make sure you don't play a trick on us, either by not showing up or by not being around there when we send for you. I'm saying this because it's cold outside, and that's something you medical men are very sensitive to."

"God forbid!" said the doctor. "I'm not one of those chilly guys, so I don't really mind it. In fact, whenever I get up at night to relieve myself, as we men do sometimes, I almost never put anything on over my doublet except a fur gown. So rest assured, I'll be there."

The two men left, and as night began to fall, Master Simone found some excuse or other to make to his wife at home, and having secretly taken his splendid robe with him, he put it on when the time seemed right and made his way to one of the tombs. After climbing up on top, he sat down, all huddled together on the marble surface because of the bitter cold, and began waiting for the beast to show up.

Buffalmacco, who was tall and sturdily built, managed to get one of those masks that they used to wear in certain festivals we no longer celebrate nowadays, and having put on a black fur gown turned inside out, he got himself up to look exactly like a bear, except that his mask had the face of a devil and horns on top.° Thus disguised, off he went to the new piazza at Santa Maria Novella, with Bruno following right behind to see what was going to happen. As soon as Buffalmacco perceived that Messer Doctor was there, he began leaping madly up and down all around the piazza, hissing and howling and screeching like a man possessed.

When the Master, who was more fearful than a woman, saw and heard all this, every hair on his body stood on end, and he began shaking all over. For a moment he wished he had stayed at home, but now that he had come so far, he forced himself to buck up his courage, so great was his desire to see all the marvels that the two painters had told him about.

After raging around for a while in the manner just described, Buffalmacco pretended to calm down and moved toward the tomb on which the doctor was sitting, where he finally came to a stop. Master Simone was shaking all over from fear and could not make up his mind whether to climb up onto the beast or to stay put. Finally, since he was afraid that it would hurt him if he did not get on its back, this second fear drove out the first, and having slid down from the tomb, he mounted the creature, saying "God help me!" under his breath as he did so. Once he was securely seated there, still trembling all over, he folded his arms across his chest in a courtly fashion, just as he had been told to do.

Heading off in the direction of Santa Maria della Scala, Buffalmacco slowly crawled along on all fours until he had carried Master Simone almost as far as the nunnery at Ripoli.° In those days there were ditches in that quarter into which the farmhands would pour their offerings to the Contessa di Crappa in order to enrich their fields. When Buffalmacco reached the spot, he walked right up to the edge of one of them, and choosing his moment, he put his hand under one of the doctor's feet, used it to push him up off his back, and hurled him headfirst into the ditch. Then he began to snort ferociously, leaping about like a man possessed, as he made his way back past Santa Maria della Scala toward the meadow of Ognissanti. There he met up with Bruno, who had fled the scene because he could not contain his laughter, and after slapping one another on the back in glee, the two of them went and watched from a distance to see what the filth-bespattered doctor was going to do.

Finding himself in such a loathsome place, Messer Doctor struggled to his feet and tried to climb out, but he kept falling back down in one place after another until, finally, he managed to extricate himself from it. Grieving and miserable, he stood there covered in filth from head to foot, having swallowed several drams of the stuff and left his hood behind in the ditch. He proceeded to clean himself off with his hands as best he could, and then, not knowing what else to do, he made his way back home where he knocked on the door again and again until he was let in.

No sooner had he entered the house, stinking all over, and had the door shut behind him, than Bruno and Buffalmacco showed up to hear what kind of welcome the Master would get from his wife. As they stood there listening, they heard her giving him the worst tongue-lashing any wretch ever received. "Well, it serves you right!" she said. "Went to see some other woman and wanted to make a big impression with your scarlet robe, did you? So, I'm not enough for you? Brother, I could satisfy an entire parish, let alone you. Well, I wish they'd drowned you instead of just dumping you where you deserved to be put! Just look at the honorable physician here who has a wife of his own, but goes around at night chasing after other people's women." To these words she added many others, while the doctor was washing himself from head to foot, and she did not stop tormenting him until well into the middle of the night.

The next morning, Bruno and Buffalmacco painted bruises all over the parts of their bodies that were covered by their clothes to make it look as if they had been given a beating, after which they made their way to the doctor's house where they found him already up and about. From the moment they set foot inside, they were greeted by a foul stench coming from everything, because there had not been enough time to clean it all up and get rid of the smell.

When the doctor was told that they had come to see him, he went to greet them, bidding them a very good morning. By way of response, the two of them glared at him in anger, as they had planned to do. "We can't say the same to you," they replied. "On the contrary, we pray to God to give you years and years of misery and that you end up with your throat cut, because you're the most disloyal, vilest traitor alive. Although we did everything we could to make sure you were honored and entertained, it's no thanks to you that we barely escaped being killed like a couple of dogs. As a result of your treachery, we were punched so many times last night that you could have driven an ass from here to Rome with fewer blows, not to mention the fact that we were in danger of being kicked out of the company that we'd arranged for you to join. And if you don't believe us, take a look at our bodies and see what shape they're in." At this point they bared their chests in the dim light long enough for him to see all the bruises they had painted there, after which they hastily covered them up again.

The doctor attempted to apologize and tell them about his misfortunes and about how he had been dumped into a ditch, but Buffalmacco broke in with: "I wish he'd thrown you off the bridge into the Arno. Why did you call on God and the Saints? Didn't we warn you beforehand about that?"

"I swear to God," replied the doctor, "I did no such thing."

"What?" said Buffalmacco. "You weren't thinking about them? Well, here's something you should really remember: the man we sent for you told us you were shaking like a reed and had no idea where you were. Anyway, you've really put one over on us, but we're never going to let anyone ever do that to us again. And as for you, from now on we're going to give you precisely the kind of honorable treatment you deserve."

The doctor pleaded with them to pardon him and did his best to mollify them, using all the eloquence at his command. He begged them for God's sake not to shame him, and out of fear that they would make him into a public laughingstock, from then on he treated them to dinners and pampered them in even more lavish ways than he had ever done in the past.

So now you have heard how wisdom is learned by those who did not acquire very much of it in Bologna.

Day 9

HERE ENDS THE EIGHTH DAY OF THE *DECAMERON* AND
THE NINTH BEGINS, IN WHICH, UNDER THE RULE OF
EMILIA, THEY ALL SPEAK AS THEY WISH ON WHATEVER
TOPIC THEY LIKE THE MOST.

The light, whose splendor puts the night to flight, had already
changed the color of the entire eighth heaven from azure to pale
blue, and the little flowers scattered throughout the meadows had
started lifting up their heads, when Emilia arose and had both her
companions and the young men summoned to her.° Once everyone had arrived, they set off, following the Queen's leisurely steps,
and made their way to a little wood no great distance from the
palace. On entering it, they spotted roebucks and stags and other
wild animals, who, as though sensing they were safe from hunters
because of the widespread plague, stood waiting for them there as
if they had been tamed and rendered fearless. By approaching the

animals one after the other and pretending they were about to touch them, the members of the company made them run and leap, and in this way they amused themselves for a while until the sun had risen well into the sky, at which point they all agreed that it was a good time to return.

The members of the company were wearing garlands made of oak leaves, their hands full of either fragrant herbs or flowers, so that if anyone had encountered them, the only thing he could possibly have said was: "Either these people will not be vanquished by death, or they will die happy." And so back they came, step by leisurely step, singing and chatting and engaging in witty banter with one another, until they reached the palace, where they found everything set out in order and their servants in a gay and festive mood. The young men and the ladies rested there for a while, and would not go to the table before they had sung half a dozen songs, each one merrier than the last. But then, having washed their hands, on the Queen's instructions, they were seated by the steward, and when the food came, they happily ate their meal. Getting up from the table, they next devoted themselves for some time to dancing *carole* and making music until the Queen told those who wanted to rest that they had her permission to go and do so.°

When the customary hour arrived, however, they all went to the place where they usually gathered to tell stories. The Queen, looking over at Filomena, asked her to tell the first one of the day, and with a smile, she began in the following manner.

Story 1

MADONNA FRANCESCA IS COURTED BY A CERTAIN RINUCCIO
AND A CERTAIN ALESSANDRO, BUT IS NOT IN LOVE WITH
EITHER MAN, AND SINCE NEITHER ONE CAN COMPLETE THE
TASK SHE ASSIGNS HIM, THE FIRST BEING REQUIRED TO
ENTER A TOMB AND POSE THERE AS A CORPSE, WHILE THE
SECOND MUST CLIMB INSIDE AND CARRY OUT THE
SUPPOSEDLY DEAD MAN, SHE DISCREETLY RIDS HERSELF
OF BOTH OF THEM.°

Since it is your pleasure, my lady, I am delighted to be the first to joust in this free and open field for storytelling to which you, with your generosity, have brought us, and if I acquit myself with distinction, I have no doubt that those who come after me will do as well as I, and even better.

In the course of our discussions, charming ladies, although we have often seen how great and how varied Love's powers can be, I still do not believe that we have exhausted the topic or that we would be able to do so even if we were to speak of nothing else for an entire year. And since it not only leads lovers to risk their lives in perilous situations of every sort, but has even induced them to enter the houses of the dead by playing dead themselves, I should like to recount a story on the subject, in addition to all the others that have already been told, which will enable you not merely to comprehend Love's power, but to appreciate the ingenuity a worthy lady made use of in ridding herself of two unwanted suitors.

Let me say, then, that in the city of Pistoia there once lived a very beautiful widow, with whom, as chance would have it, two of our fellow citizens, who had settled there after having been exiled from Florence, had fallen very deeply in love. Their names were Rinuccio Palermini and Alessandro Chiarmontesi, and while they remained ignorant of one another's existence, each of them cautiously went on doing everything in his power to win her affection.°

The lady, who was named Francesca de' Lazzari, was constantly being pestered with their messages and entreaties, and having been fool enough, on occasion, to lend them a willing ear, she found she could not extricate herself from her relationship with them, which she now wisely wished to do, until a thought finally occurred to her as to how she might stop them from importuning her.° Her idea was to request that they perform a service for her, one that would not be impossible, but that they would be unable to do, so that when they failed, she would have an honorable, or at least a plausible, excuse for refusing to accept their advances. And this was her plan.

On the day the idea came to her, a man had died in the city who, despite having had noble ancestors, was reputed to be the worst person who had ever lived, not just in Pistoia, but in the whole wide world. Moreover, when he was alive, he was so deformed and had so hideous a face that anyone who did not already know him would have been filled with terror upon seeing him for the first time. He had been interred in a tomb outside the church of the Franciscans, which the lady felt would be quite useful in carrying out her scheme, and so she said to one of her maids: "As you know, I'm annoyed and tormented all day long by the messages that those two Florentines, Rinuccio and Alessandro, keep sending me. Since I have no intention of gratifying either one of them with my love, in order to get rid of them, I've decided to respond to the great protestations of affection they're always making by setting them a task that I'm certain they can't accomplish, and that way I'll stop them from pestering me. Now just listen to how I'll do it.

"You know that this morning Scannadio—for that was the name of the evil man we just mentioned—was buried at the monastery belonging to the Franciscans and that the mere sight of him, while he was alive, let alone now that he's dead, was enough to frighten the bravest men in this town.° So first, I want you to go in secret to Alessandro and say to him: 'Madonna Francesca sends me to tell you that the time has come for you to enjoy the love that you have so ardently desired, and that you can get to be with her, if you wish, in the following way. For reasons you'll be informed about later on, a relative of hers is supposed to fetch the body of Scannadio, who was buried this morning, and bring it to her house tonight. But since she's still terrified of him, even though he's dead, and she doesn't want him in the place, she implores you to do her a great favor. Namely, at bedtime this evening she wants you to be so good as to enter the tomb in which Scannadio has been interred, to put on his clothes, and to lie there impersonating him until someone comes to get you. Then, without saying a word or making a sound, you are to allow yourself to be taken out of it and carried to her house. She'll be there to welcome you, and you can stay with her for as long as you like, leaving the rest of the details for her to take care of.' Now, if he says he'll do it, well and good, but if he refuses, then tell him from me that he should stay

out of my sight, and if he values his life, he shouldn't send me any
more of his messages or entreaties.

"After that, you'll go to Rinuccio Palermini and tell him:
'Madonna Francesca says she's ready to comply with your every
desire, provided that you do her a great favor. Namely, around
midnight tonight you are to go to the tomb where Scannadio was
interred this morning, and without saying a word in response to
anything you see or hear, you are to remove the body ever so
gently and bring it to her at her house. There you'll discover why
she wants you to do this, and you'll be able to satisfy your desires
with her. But if you're not willing to do this, then from now on she
orders you never to send her any messages or entreaties again.'"

When the maid went to the two young men and delivered the
messages exactly as she had been instructed to do, in both cases
they replied that they would go as far as Hell itself, let alone climb
down into a tomb, if that would please her. The maid conveyed
their response to the lady who waited to see if the two of them
would be truly crazy enough to do it.

After nightfall, around the time when people have just gone to
sleep, Alessandro Chiarmontesi stripped down to his doublet and
left his house in order to go and take Scannadio's place inside
the tomb. As he went on his way, a terrifying thought entered his
head, and he began talking to himself: "Oh, why am I such an ass!
Where do I think I'm going? How do I know her relations haven't
discovered that I'm in love with her? Perhaps they believe things
that aren't true about what we've done, and they've forced her to
have me do this so they can murder me inside the tomb. If that
were to happen, I'd be the one to get the blame, since no one in the
world would know a thing about what happened, and they'd
escape scot-free. Or for all I know, perhaps one of my enemies has
set this up for me, and because she may be in love with him, she
wants to do this for him as a favor."

"But let's suppose," he continued, "that neither of these things is
the case, and that her relations really do intend to carry me to her
house. I can't believe they want to take Scannadio's body there so
they can clasp it in their arms, let alone put it in hers. The only

conclusion I can draw is that they want to do violence to it because of some wrong he did to them. She says I shouldn't make a sound no matter what happens to me, but where would I be if they were to pluck out my eyes or yank out my teeth or cut off my hands or play some other trick like that on me? How could I keep quiet? And if I speak, they'll recognize me, and perhaps they'll hurt me. But even if they don't, I won't have accomplished anything, for they're not going to leave me there with the lady in any case. And then she'll say I've disobeyed her orders, and she'll never do anything to please me."

Talking to himself this way, he was at the point of turning around and heading home, but the immense love he felt drove him on, providing counterarguments so strong that they brought him eventually right up to the tomb. Having opened it, he climbed inside, stripped off Scannadio's clothes, and dressed himself in them. Then, closing the tomb over his head, he lay down in Scannadio's place. As he began thinking about the kind of person the dead man had been and dwelling on the stories he had heard people tell concerning what happened at night not just among the tombs of the dead, but even outside them, pretty soon every hair on his body was standing on end, and he felt sure that at any moment Scannadio was going to rise up and slit his throat. But fortified by his fervent love, he overcame these as well as other terrifying thoughts, and lying there as if he were the corpse, he waited to see what was going to happen to him.

As midnight approached, Rinuccio left his house in order to carry out the orders that the lady had given him, and as he was walking along, he began mulling over the various things that could possibly happen to him, such as falling into the hands of the watch while he was carrying Scannadio's body on his shoulders, for which he would be condemned to be burned as a sorcerer, or incurring the wrath of the dead man's relations if they found out what he was doing. Several other thoughts of the same sort occurred to him, and he was almost deterred from going on, but then he changed his mind and said to himself: "What, shall I say no to the first request I've gotten from this gentlewoman, whom I love as deeply as ever, and especially when I'm going to win her favor if I do it? No, even if I should die for it, I'm determined to honor the promise I made her." And so, he continued walking on until he arrived at the tomb, which he then opened with ease.

As Alessandro heard the lid being moved, he was absolutely terrified, but managed nevertheless to remain perfectly still. Rinuccio climbed inside, and thinking he was picking up Scannadio's body, he grabbed Alessandro by the feet, dragged him out of the tomb, hoisted him up onto his shoulders, and began walking in the direction of the gentlewoman's house. Since the night was pitch black, he could not see where he was going, and as he went along, not taking much care with the body he was carrying, he frequently banged it against the edges of one or another of the benches that lined the street.

Waiting to see if he was actually going to bring Alessandro to her house, the gentlewoman was standing there at the window with her maid, already armed with an excuse to send the pair of them away, but just as Rinuccio was about to reach the first step leading up to her front door, the officers of the watch happened to hear the noise he was making with his feet as he went shuffling along. They had been placed on guard in the neighborhood, where they were quietly lying in wait in order to catch an outlaw, and they immediately produced a lantern to see what was going on and which direction they had to take. Picking up their shields and lances, they shouted, "Who goes there?" Rinuccio recognized who they were, and having no time to compose his thoughts, he dropped Alessandro and ran away as fast as his legs would carry him. Alessandro quickly leaped to his feet, and despite being hampered by the dead man's shroud, which was very long, he, too, took off.

By the light the watch was holding out, the lady had clearly observed Rinuccio carrying Alessandro on his shoulders, noting as well that the latter was dressed in Scannadio's clothing, and she was amazed at the courage displayed by the two men. For all her amazement, however, she had a good laugh when she saw Alessandro being dropped and then watched the two men take to their heels. Overjoyed at this turn of events, and praising God for having freed her from the awkward situation the pair had put her in, she turned from the window and went back to her room, agreeing with her maid that both of the men certainly loved her very much, for, as it appeared, they had done precisely what she had ordered them to do.

Heartbroken and cursing his bad luck, Rinuccio did not return home despite everything that had happened, but as soon as the watch had left the neighborhood, he returned to the spot where he had dumped Alessandro and groped around on all fours to see if he could find him and thus complete the task the lady had assigned him. But when he failed to locate the body, he supposed that it had been carried off by the watch, and sadly made his way back home.

Alessandro had no idea what else he could do, and so, without ever having discovered who had been carrying him, he likewise returned to his house, grief stricken over his terrible misfortune.

When Scannadio's tomb was found open the next morning and there was no sign of his body—for Alessandro had rolled it down to the bottom of the vault—the whole of Pistoia came up with various explanations for what had happened, the fools among them concluding that he had been carried off by devils. Each of the lady's lovers informed her of what he had done, and using the events that had occurred as an excuse for why he had not carried out her instructions to the full, he demanded her forgiveness and her love. But she pretended she did not believe either one, and by curtly responding that she had no desire to do anything for them since they had not completed the tasks she had assigned them, she managed to get the pair of them off her back.

Story 2

ARISING HURRIEDLY IN THE DARK, AN ABBESS RUSHES OUT TO CATCH ONE OF HER NUNS WHO WAS REPORTED TO BE IN BED WITH HER LOVER, BUT THE ABBESS HERSELF WAS WITH A PRIEST AT THE TIME AND PLACES HIS BREECHES ON HER HEAD, THINKING SHE IS PUTTING HER VEILS THERE, WITH THE RESULT THAT WHEN THE ACCUSED NUN SEES THEM

AND POINTS THEM OUT TO THE ABBESS, SHE IS ACQUITTED
AND FROM THEN ON IS ABLE TO SPEND TIME WITH HER
LOVER AT HER LEISURE.°

When Filomena was silent, the entire company praised the lady's intelligence in getting rid of the men she did not love, while, on the contrary, they all judged the men's daring presumption to be madness rather than love. Then, turning to Elissa, the Queen graciously said, "Continue, Elissa," and she promptly began speaking as follows:

My dearest ladies, as we have heard, Madonna Francesca certainly knew how to get rid of a nuisance by using her wits. Now, however, I am going to tell you about a young nun who, with Fortune's help, freed herself from imminent danger by means of a clever remark. You all know that there are plenty of very foolish people who take it upon themselves to instruct and correct others, but as you will learn from my story, from time to time Fortune justly puts them to shame—which is precisely what happened to the Abbess who was the superior of the nun I am going to tell you about.

You should know, then, that in Lombardy there used to be a convent, widely renowned for the holiness and religious zeal of its nuns, one of whom was a young woman of noble birth, endowed with wondrous beauty, who was named Isabetta. One day, having come to the grating to speak with a relative of hers, she fell in love with a handsome young man who was with him, and who, when he saw how very beautiful she was and understood what she was feeling from the look in her eyes, began burning with just as fierce a passion for her.

The two of them suffered intense anguish for quite some time because of this unfulfilled love of theirs, but it kept spurring them on until, finally, the young man thought of a way he could get together with his nun in secret. From that time on, with her full consent, he visited her not once, but many, many times, always to their mutual delight.

Things went on in this manner until one night, unbeknownst

to him or Isabetta, he happened to be spotted by one of the nuns after he had taken his leave and was going on his way. The nun communicated her discovery to several others, and their first thought was to denounce Isabetta to the Abbess, a certain Madonna Usimbalda, who was a good and pious woman in the opinion of the nuns and of everyone else who knew her.° On second thought, however, they decided to arrange for the Abbess to catch the girl with the young man so that there would be no room for her to deny it. Consequently, they held their peace and secretly took turns keeping her under close surveillance in the hope of taking her by surprise.

Now, Isabetta, who had no idea what was going on and was not on the lookout, happened to arrange one night for her lover to join her. The nuns who were keeping watch spotted him at once, but waited to act until the wee hours of the night. Then, when they thought the time was right, they divided themselves into two groups, the first standing guard by the entrance to Isabetta's cell while the second ran off to the Abbess's room. There they knocked on the door, and as soon as they heard her voice, they said: "Get up, Reverend Mother, and hurry. We've discovered Isabetta has a young man in her cell."

That night the Abbess was keeping company with a priest whom she often had brought to her inside a chest. When she heard all the racket, she was afraid that the nuns, in their haste and excessive zeal, would force the door open. Consequently, she got up in a rush and dressed herself as best she could in the dark. Thinking that she had picked up the pleated veils that nuns wear on their heads and are called psalters, she happened to grab the priest's breeches, and she was in such a hurry that without realizing what she was doing, she clapped them onto her head in place of her veils.° She exited the room, quickly locking the door behind her and exclaiming: "Where is that goddamned girl?"

Accompanied by the nuns, who were so fired up, so eager to see Isabetta caught in the act, that they took no notice of what the Abbess had on her head, she arrived at the entrance to the cell, and all of them together managed to push down the door. Upon entering the room, they found the two lovers in bed together, lying in one another's arms, so confused by this sudden and surprising turn of events that they had no idea what to do and just stayed where they were, unable to move.

The nuns immediately seized the girl and at the Abbess's orders led her to the chapterhouse. Meanwhile, the young man, who had stayed where he was, got dressed and waited to see what the outcome would be, fully resolved, if his young lady were harmed in any way, to make all the nuns he could get his hands on pay dearly for it, after which he would take her away with him.

Having assumed her seat in the chapterhouse surrounded by the nuns, all of whom had their eyes fixed on the accused, the Abbess launched into the severest scolding any woman has ever received, telling the girl that by her reprehensible, disgusting conduct—if people outside ever found out about it—she had sullied the sanctity, the honor, and the good reputation of the convent. And to these insults, the Abbess added the worst threats imaginable.

Knowing she was at fault, the girl had no idea how to respond, and as she stood there, fearful and ashamed, her silence was actually beginning to make the others feel sorry for her. After a while, however, as the Abbess went on and on multiplying her insults, the girl happened to raise her head and caught sight of what the Abbess had on her head, with its straps dangling down on either side. Realizing what was up, she completely recovered her composure and said: "God help you, Reverend Mother, would you tie up your cap, and then you may tell me whatever you want."

The Abbess had no idea what she meant and replied: "What cap, you vile woman? Do you have the cheek to make jokes now? Does it really seem to you that what you've done is some laughing matter?"

"Reverend Mother, I beg you," said the girl a second time, "tie up your cap. Then you can say anything you please to me."

At this point, several of the nuns raised their eyes and looked in the direction of the Abbess's head, while she simultaneously raised her hands up to it. And then all of them realized just what it was Isabetta had been referring to.

Recognizing that she was equally guilty and that there was no way for her to cover things up since everyone was staring at her, the Abbess changed her tune and began telling a very different story than she had before. When she reached the conclusion that it was impossible to defend oneself from the goadings of the flesh, she told them all that they should enjoy themselves whenever they could, provided it was done discreetly, as it had been up until then.

After setting Isabetta free, the Abbess returned to sleep with her priest, while the girl went off to rejoin her lover. And from then on, regardless of the envy felt by the nuns, Isabetta had him come back to see her at frequent intervals, and the others, who lacked lovers, did their best to find some sort of consolation for themselves in secret.

Story 3

EGGED ON BY BRUNO, BUFFALMACCO, AND NELLO, MASTER
SIMONE MAKES CALANDRINO BELIEVE HE IS PREGNANT.
CALANDRINO THEN GIVES THEM ALL CAPONS AND MONEY
IN RETURN FOR MEDICINE, AND HE IS CURED WITHOUT
HAVING TO GIVE BIRTH.°

When Elissa had finished, everyone thanked God for the young nun's happy escape from the fangs of her envious companions. At that point the Queen ordered Filostrato to continue, and he, without waiting to be asked again, began:

Loveliest of ladies, that boorish judge from The Marches about whom I spoke to you yesterday took a story about Calandrino that I was all prepared to tell you and snatched it right out of my mouth. We have, to be sure, heard quite a bit about him and his comrades, but since everything we say about him can only serve to increase the fun we are having, I am going to recount the story now that I intended to tell you then.

From what was previously said, you should have a very clear picture of Calandrino and of the others who are going to be the subject of this story. Consequently, I will get right to the point and tell you that one of Calandrino's aunts happened to die and leave him two hundred *lire* in small change, which prompted him to start talking about how he was going to buy himself a farm.° Acting as if he had ten thousand gold florins to spend, he entered into negotiations with all the brokers in Florence, although the deals always fell through as soon as they mentioned the asking price for the property. Bruno and Buffalmacco, who knew what had happened, had told him many times that it would be better for him to use the money in order to have a good time with them than to go and buy just enough land to make mud pies out of it.° But far from getting him to do what they proposed, they had never managed to persuade him to stand them to a single meal.

As they were griping about this one day, they were joined by a buddy of theirs, a painter named Nello, and the three of them decided they just had to find a way to stuff their snouts at Calandrino's expense.° It did not take them very long to work out a plan of action among themselves, and the next morning they were lying in wait for Calandrino as he left his house. Before he had gone even a short distance, Nello came up to him and said, "Goodday, Calandrino."

Calandrino replied by saying that God should give him a good day, and a good year, too, after which Nello paused for a moment and began looking Calandrino hard in the face.

"What are you staring at?" asked Calandrino.

"Did anything happen to you last night?" replied Nello. "You don't seem like your usual self."

Calandrino immediately started worrying and said, "Oh no! How's that? What do you think I've got?"

"Well, I'm not saying that you've got something," said Nello. "It's just that you look very different to me. Maybe it's nothing at all."

Nello let him go, and as Calandrino continued on his way, he was terribly upset, although he did not sense that there was anything at all wrong with him. Buffalmacco, however, was not far off, and when he saw Calandrino leave Nello, he walked up to him, greeted him, and asked him if he was feeling all right.

"I don't know," said Calandrino, "but just now Nello was tell-ing me that I looked all different to him. Is it possible I could have come down with something?"

"Yes, you could well have a little something or other," replied Buffalmacco. "You look half dead."

Calandrino had already started to feel feverish when lo and behold, Bruno appeared on the scene, and the first words out of his mouth were, "Calandrino, what a face! You look like death itself! How are you feeling?"

Having heard all of them say the same thing, Calandrino was now absolutely convinced that he was sick, and completely dis-mayed by the prospect, he asked them, "What shall I do?"

"In my opinion," said Bruno, "you should go right home, get into your bed, and cover yourself up good and tight. Then you should send a specimen of your urine to Master Simone who, as you know, is a very good buddy of ours and will soon tell you what you have to do.° Plus, we'll come with you, and if anything has to be done, we'll take care of it."

Nello soon joined them, and the three of them accompanied Calandrino back to his house where he made his way, utterly exhausted, to his bedroom. "Come and pile the covers over me," he said to his wife. "I'm feeling terribly ill."

After he got settled in his bed, he sent a serving girl with a specimen of his urine to Master Simone, who in those days had set up his practice in the Mercato Vecchio at the sign of the Melon.° Bruno turned to his buddies and said: "You stay here with him, while I go and see what the doctor has to say. If it's necessary, I'll escort him back here with me."

"Ah, yes, my friend," said Calandrino, "do go there and bring me back word about how things stand, because I'm feeling I've got something, I don't know what, inside me."

Bruno set off for Master Simone's, getting there ahead of the serving girl who was carrying the specimen, and explained to the doctor what they were up to. Thus, when the girl arrived, Master Simone examined the urine and said to her: "Go back and tell Calandrino that he should keep himself good and warm. I'm coming to see him right away to let him know what's wrong with him and what he has to do about it."

After the girl delivered the message, it was not long before the doctor, accompanied by Bruno, showed up. Sitting down beside Calandrino, he began taking his pulse, and then, after a pause, in the presence of Calandrino's wife, he said to him: "Look here, Calandrino, speaking to you as a friend, I'd say there's nothing wrong with you except for the fact that you're pregnant."

When Calandrino heard this, he began wailing in despair. "Oh no, Tessa," he exclaimed, "you did this to me. You always want to be on top, and I've told you clearly all along what would come of it." When she heard him say this, Calandrino's wife, who was a very modest woman, turned scarlet with shame, and lowering her gaze, left the room without saying a word.

Meanwhile, Calandrino went on with his lament. "Oh, poor me," he said, "what shall I do? How am I going to give birth to this child? Where will he come out? Now I see only too clearly that this wife of mine, what with that insatiable lust of hers, has been the death of me. May God make her as miserable as I wish to be happy. If I were well—which I'm not—I'd get up and give her such a beating I'd break every bone in her body. It does serve me right, though, because I should never have let her get up on top. Anyway, one thing's for certain: if I manage to get out of this alive, she can die of frustration before she ever gets to do it that way again."

As they listened to Calandrino, Bruno, Buffalmacco, and Nello had such a desire to laugh that they were ready to explode. They managed to contain themselves, however, but Master Simonkey guffawed, opening his mouth so wide that you could have pulled out every one of his teeth.° After a long while, Calandrino finally threw himself on the doctor's mercy and begged him for his advice and assistance.

"Calandrino," Master Simone told him, "there's no reason for you to get upset. God be praised, we diagnosed the problem early enough for me to set you right quite easily in just a few days. However, you're going to have to spend a little money on it."

"Oh yes, doctor," said Calandrino, "do it, for the love of God. I've got two hundred *lire* here that I thought of using to buy a farm. If you need them, you can have them all, just so long as I don't have to give birth. I don't know how I'd manage it, because I hear women making so much noise when they're having a baby, despite the fact that they have such a great big thing to use for it to come through, that I'm afraid if I suffered so much pain, I'd die before I got it out."

"Don't give it another thought," said the doctor. "I'll have a certain potion made up for you, a distillation that's good for such cases and very pleasant to drink. It'll take care of everything by the third morning and make you as healthy as a horse.° But see to it that you're wiser in the future and don't get into such foolish situations. Now, to prepare this medicine, we'll need three pairs of good, fat capons, and you must give one of your buddies here five of those *lire* to buy all the other ingredients that are needed. Then make sure that everything is taken around to my shop, and tomorrow morning, in God's name, I'll send you that distilled potion, which you should start drinking, a nice, big glassful at a time."

When Calandrino heard what Master Simone had to say, he declared, "Doctor, it's in your hands," and he gave Bruno the five *lire* as well as enough money for three pairs of capons, asking him to purchase everything and thanking him profusely for going to so much trouble on his behalf.

The doctor went away and had a little bit of spiced wine prepared, which he sent around to Calandrino.° As for Bruno, he went out and bought the capons as well as everything else necessary for a good meal, which he then proceeded to eat in the company of his two buddies and the doctor.

Calandrino drank the wine for three mornings in a row, after which the doctor came to see him, accompanied by his three comrades. Having taken Calandrino's pulse, he announced: "You're cured, Calandrino, no doubt about it. You may safely attend to your affairs today and don't have to stay home any longer."

The happy Calandrino got up and went about his business, and whenever he ran into anyone to talk to, he was full of praise for the wonderful way that Master Simone had cured him, because in just three days he had terminated his pregnancy with absolutely no pain at all. Bruno, Buffalmacco, and Nello were pleased to have found a clever plan to get around Calandrino's stinginess, but Monna Tessa had figured it out and did nothing but grumble to her husband about it.

Story 5

WHEN CALANDRINO FALLS IN LOVE WITH A YOUNG WOMAN, BRUNO MAKES A MAGIC SCROLL FOR HIM, WITH WHICH HE NO SOONER TOUCHES HER THAN SHE GOES OFF WITH HIM. THEN, HOWEVER, HE GETS CAUGHT BY HIS WIFE AND FINDS HIMSELF IN A VERY SERIOUS AND UNPLEASANT PREDICAMENT.°

* * *

Noblest of ladies, as I believe you already know, there is no subject, no matter how much has already been said about it, that will fail to provide even more pleasure if the person who wants to discuss it knows how to choose the right time and place to speak. Now, since the reason we are here is to enjoy ourselves and have some fun, then I reckon this is the proper time and place for any subject that would entertain us and give us pleasure, for even though the subject had been discussed a thousand times already, we could return to it a thousand times more and still find it delightful.

Now, despite the fact that we have talked quite a lot about Calandrino's antics, when you consider that everything he does is amusing, as Filostrato observed just a little while ago, then I shall be so bold as to add yet one more tale to the others we have heard about him. Had I wanted to depart from the truth, I could have easily disguised things with fictitious names, and I could still do so now. However, since a storyteller greatly diminishes the delight he gives his audience by departing from the truth of what really happened, I shall, for the reason I have just mentioned, tell you my story as it actually occurred.

A wealthy fellow citizen of ours named Niccolò Cornacchini had, among his many possessions, a fine piece of property at Camerata, on which he had a beautiful, stately mansion built for himself.° He arranged with Bruno and Buffalmacco to paint the entire building with frescoes, but since it was a very substantial job, they enlisted Nello and Calandrino to help them, and then the four of them got down to work. Although a few rooms in the house contained beds and other furnishings, none of the members of the household lived on the premises except for an old serving woman who stayed there to keep watch over the place. Consequently, from time to time, one of Niccolò's sons, a young bachelor named Filippo, was in the habit of bringing some woman or other there who would tend to his pleasures for a day or two before she was sent away.

On one of those occasions he happened to bring with him a certain Niccolosa who was kept by an unsavory character named Mangione at a house in Camaldoli from which he used to let her out for hire.° She had a beautiful figure and was nicely dressed, and for a woman of her sort she was polite and well-spoken. One day around noon she left the bedroom, wearing a white shift with her hair tied up around her head, and went to a well located in the courtyard of the house, where she was washing her hands and face, when Calandrino happened to come by to get some water. He gave her a friendly greeting, and after replying, she started to stare at him, not because she found him attractive, but because he seemed to her a very strange man indeed. Calandrino returned her gaze, and on seeing how beautiful she was, he came up with any number of excuses not to take the water back to his buddies. Since he did not know who she was, however, he could not pluck up the courage to address her. Noticing how he was staring at her, she decided to play a trick on him and started glancing over at him from time to time, heaving little sighs as she did so, with the result that Calandrino instantly fell head over heels for her and did not leave the courtyard until Filippo called her back to the bedroom.

Upon returning to work, Calandrino did nothing but breathe

out one huge sigh after another. Bruno took great delight in whatever Calandrino did and always kept his eye on him, and when he noticed this, he said: "What the devil's the matter with you, Calandrino, my friend? You do nothing but sigh all the time."

"If I could only find someone to help me, buddy," replied Calandrino, "I'd be all right."

"What do you mean?" asked Bruno.

"Don't tell anyone," said Calandrino, "but there's a young woman down there who's more beautiful than a fairy, and she's so much in love with me that it would astonish you.° I spotted her just now when I went for the water."

"Uh-oh," said Bruno, "you'd better be careful it isn't Filippo's wife."

"I think she is," said Calandrino, "because when he called her from his room, she went right in to him. But what difference does that make? In affairs like this, I'd put one over on Christ Himself, to say nothing of Filippo. Truth is, buddy, I couldn't begin to tell you how much I'm attracted to her."

"I'll find out who she is for you, buddy," said Bruno, "and if she's Filippo's wife, it'll only take me two words to fix things up for you, because she's a good friend of mine. But how will we manage it so that Buffalmacco doesn't find out? I never get a chance to speak with her except when he's around."

"I'm not worried about Buffalmacco," replied Calandrino, "but we've got to watch out for Nello, because he's one of Tessa's relatives and he'd ruin everything."°

"That's true," said Bruno.

Now, Bruno knew exactly who the girl was because he had seen her arrive, and besides, Filippo had told him all about her. Consequently, when Calandrino interrupted his work for a while in order to go and see if he could catch a glimpse of her, Bruno told everything to Nello and Buffalmacco, and together they secretly agreed on what they were going to do about this infatuation of his.

Upon his return, Bruno asked Calandrino in a whisper: "Did you get to see her?"

"Oh yes, alas," replied Calandrino, "and she's knocked me dead!"

"I'll just go and see if she really is the one I think she is," said Bruno. "And if that's the case, you can just leave everything to me."

Bruno went downstairs, and when he found Filippo and the girl, he explained precisely what kind of man Calandrino was and told them what he had said. Then Bruno arranged with each of them what they should say and do to have fun and enjoy the spectacle of Calandrino's infatuation. Afterward, returning to Calandrino, he said to him: "It's her, all right, and that's why we're going to have to proceed with great caution in this business, because if Filippo gets wind of it, all the water in the Arno won't wash us clean of it. But what do you want me to tell her from you if I should have a chance to speak with her?"

"By gosh," said Calandrino, "the very, very first thing to tell her is that I wish her a thousand bushels of that good stuff you get pregnant with, and then say that I'm her obedient server, and if there's anything she wants—you get my meaning?"°

"Yes," replied Bruno. "Leave it all to me."

When the hour for supper arrived, they stopped working for the day and went down into the courtyard where they found Filippo and Niccolosa and stayed awhile for Calandrino's benefit. Staring continually at Niccolosa, Calandrino began performing the oddest antics in the world. In fact, there were so many of them, and they were so weird, that even a blind man would have noticed them. As for Niccolosa, in light of what Bruno had told her, she did everything she thought would set Calandrino on fire, having the best time in her life because of his strange behavior. Meanwhile, Filippo pretended to be talking with Buffalmacco and the others, unaware of what was going on.

After a while, however, to Calandrino's very great disappointment, they left, and as the painters made their way back to Florence, Bruno said to him: "I have to tell you, you're making her melt like ice in the sun. By God's body, if you bring your rebeck here and sing some of those love songs of yours, you'll make her throw herself out the window and right down to the ground in order to get to you."°

"Do you think so, buddy?" said Calandrino. "Do you think I should bring it?"

"Yes, I do," replied Bruno.

"You didn't believe me today when I told you about it," said Calandrino. "But there's no doubt about it, buddy: I know better than any man alive how to get what I want. Who besides me would have discovered the way to make such a woman fall in love with him so quickly? Not these young guys. They're just a bunch of blowhards who go parading up and down all day long and wouldn't be able to pick up three handfuls of nuts in a thousand years. Just you watch me with my rebeck for a little while. I'll show you a trick or two! And I'll have you know I'm not as old as you think. She's certainly noticed it, she has, but in any case, I'll really prove it to her once I get my paws on her. I swear by the true body of Christ, I'm going to play such a game with her that she'll follow me around everywhere like the mad mother doting on her son."°

"Oh," said Bruno, "you'll stick your snout right into her. In fact, I can see you now, with those lute-peg teeth of yours, biting her little red mouth and those cheeks that look like two roses, and then devouring every last bit of her."

As he listened to Bruno's words, Calandrino thought he was already doing the deed, and he went around singing and skipping with such glee that he practically jumped right out of his hide. Moreover, the next day, he brought his rebeck along, and accompanying himself with it, he sang a number of songs, to the great delight of the entire group.

To cut the story short, Calandrino took so many breaks to go and see the girl as often as he could that he stopped working altogether. Instead, a thousand times a day, he would dash to the window, and then to the door, and then into the court, all in order to catch a glimpse of her, while she astutely followed Bruno's instructions and provided him with every opportunity to do so. For his part, Bruno would answer Calandrino's messages in her name and would sometimes carry notes to him as if they came from her.

When she was not around, which was mostly the case, he would have letters sent to Calandrino from her in which she filled him with the hope that he was going to be able to satisfy his desires, but explained that she was then staying at the house of some relatives and that he could not come to see her there.

In this way, Bruno and Buffalmacco managed the affair, deriving the greatest pleasure in the world from Calandrino's antics. Sometimes, they got him to give them gifts, pretending that she was asking for them. At one time it was an ivory comb, at another a purse, and at yet another a little knife, plus other trifles of that sort, in exchange for which they gave him some worthless little counterfeit rings, which made him deliriously happy. In addition, they got some nice meals out of him, and he showed them other little favors to encourage them to work diligently on his behalf.

They kept him on tenterhooks like this for a good two months without his making any more progress. When Calandrino saw that their work was at the point of completion, and realized that if he did not satisfy his desires before it was finished, he was never going to be able to do so, he started pressing Bruno as hard as possible for his help. Consequently, the next time the girl was there, Bruno made arrangements with her and Filippo about what they were to do.

"Look, buddy," he said to Calandrino, "this lady has promised me at least a thousand times that she's ready to give you what you want, and every time she does absolutely nothing about it. I think she's leading you around by the nose. So, if you're willing, seeing as how she isn't keeping her promises, we'll make her do it whether she wants to or not."

"Ah yes, for the love of God," replied Calandrino, "let's do it right away."

"Are you brave enough to touch her with a scroll I'll give you?" asked Bruno.

"Yes," answered Calandrino, "I sure am."

"Then," said Bruno, "go and fetch me a little piece of parchment from a stillborn lamb, a live bat, three grains of incense, and a candle that's been blessed. You can leave the rest to me."

Calandrino spent the whole of that evening trying to catch a bat by means of various contrivances. Finally, he managed to snag one and brought it to Bruno along with the other things. Withdrawing into another room, Bruno wrote some nonsense in made-up characters on the parchment and took it back to Calandrino.

"Now be aware, Calandrino," he said, "if you touch her with this scroll, she'll come with you immediately and do whatever you want. So, if Filippo should go off anywhere today, find some way to get close to her and touch her with it. Then go to the barn that's off to the side of the house. It's the best place for your purposes because no one ever goes there. You'll see that she'll come, too, and when she does, you know exactly what it is you have to do."

Calandrino was the happiest man in the world as he took the scroll. "Buddy," he said, "just leave it to me."

Nello, against whom Calandrino was constantly on guard, was enjoying the affair as much as the others, and like them, he had his hand in the trick they were playing. Thus, following Bruno's instructions, he went down to see Calandrino's wife in Florence.

"Tessa," he said to her, "you remember the terrible beating that Calandrino gave you, for no reason at all, the day he came back home from the Mugnone with all those stones? Well, I want to give you a chance now to get even with him, and if you don't take it, don't you ever call me your kinsman or your friend again. He's really fallen for some woman up there, and she's such a slut that she's been regularly shutting herself up in some room or other with him. As a matter of fact, just a little while ago, they arranged to get together very soon, and that's why I want you to come and see him, and then punish him the way he deserves."

When Monna Tessa heard this, it did not seem like a joke to her, and leaping to her feet, she blurted out: "Oh no, you common thief, you. So, this is how you treat me, is it? By God's Cross, you won't get away without paying for it."

Then she grabbed her cloak, and accompanied by a little maidservant, set off with Nello, rushing to the mansion at a furious pace. Bruno saw her coming in the distance and said to Filippo, "Look, here comes our friend." So Filippo went up to where

Calandrino and the others were working and said to them, "Masters, I have to go to Florence immediately. Keep up the hard work." As soon as he left them, he went and hid himself in a place from which, without being seen, he could observe what Calandrino would do.

When Calandrino thought that Filippo had gotten far enough away, he went down into the courtyard where he found Niccolosa alone and started chatting her up. She knew exactly what she was supposed to do, and sidling over to him, she treated him with greater familiarity than usual, at which point Calandrino touched her with the scroll. As soon as he had done so, without saying a word he turned and directed his steps toward the barn, with Niccolosa following right behind him. Once she had gotten inside and had closed the door behind them, she took him in her arms and threw him down on the straw that was lying on the floor. Then she climbed on top and straddled him. Placing her hands on his shoulders to hold him down and keep his face away from hers, she gazed at him as if he were her utmost desire.

"O my sweet Calandrino," she said, "heart of my body, my soul, my treasure, my comfort, how long have I wanted to have you all for myself and to clasp you to me like this! Your charms have got me wound around your little finger! You've chained up my heart with that rebeck of yours! Is it really possible that I'm here, holding you in my arms?"

"Ah, my sweet soul," said Calandrino, who was scarcely able to move, "let me kiss you."

"Oh, you're in such a rush!" said Niccolosa. "Let me first have my fill of gazing upon you! Let me sate my eyes with looking at that sweet face of yours!"

Bruno and Buffalmacco had gone to join Filippo, and the three of them were watching and listening to everything that was going on, when lo and behold, just as Calandrino was about to give Niccolosa a kiss, who should arrive but Nello and Monna Tessa.

"I swear to God the two of them are in there together," said Nello, as they approached the door to the barn. Fuming with rage, Monna Tessa gave it a shove with her hands that flung it wide open. When she entered the barn, she saw Calandrino lying there, straddled by Niccolosa, who no sooner caught sight of her than she sprang to her feet and ran off to join Filippo.

Before Calandrino could get up, Monna Tessa ran at him with her nails and clawed him all over his face. Then she seized him by the hair and started dragging him up and down. "You damned filthy dog, you!" she said to him. "So this is how you treat me? You old fool, I curse all the love I ever felt for you! Don't you think you've got enough to take care of at home, instead of going around lusting after other women? Just look at this fine lover! Don't you know who you are, you wretch? Don't you know yourself, you sad sack? Why, if you were completely squeezed dry, there wouldn't be enough juice to make a sauce. I swear to God, the woman who was getting you pregnant just now, that wasn't Tessa.° Whoever she is, may God make her suffer, because she must really be pretty pathetic to be attracted to a precious jewel like you!"

When he first saw his wife coming, Calandrino did not know whether he was alive or dead, and he did not have the courage to do anything to defend himself against her. But later, all scratched and scraped and disheveled, he gathered up his cloak, got to his feet, and began humbly begging her not to shout, unless she wanted to see him all cut up into little pieces, because the woman who had been with him was the wife of the master of the house.

"I don't care who she is," said Monna Tessa. "May God punish her!"

Bruno and Buffalmacco, who, along with Filippo and Niccolosa, had had their fill of laughing at this scene, came in, pretending they had been attracted there by all the noise. After a lot of talk back and forth, they managed to pacify the lady, and advised Calandrino to return to Florence and never come up there again, because if Filippo ever found out about the affair, he would certainly do him some harm.

Thus, the miserable, forlorn Calandrino, all scratched and scraped, made his way back to Florence and never dared to go up to Camerata again. Vexed and tormented night and day by his wife's reproaches, he put an end to his fervent love, having made himself a complete laughingstock not only for his companions, but for Niccolosa and Filippo as well.

Story 6

TWO YOUNG MEN FIND LODGING OVERNIGHT, AND WHILE ONE OF THEM GOES TO BED WITH THEIR HOST'S DAUGHTER, THE HOST'S WIFE INADVERTENTLY SLEEPS WITH THE OTHER. THEN THE YOUTH WHO WAS WITH THE DAUGHTER GETS INTO BED WITH HER FATHER, AND THINKING HE IS TALKING TO HIS COMPANION, TELLS HIM EVERYTHING. A GREAT COMMOTION ENSUES, AT WHICH POINT THE WIFE, REALIZING HER MISTAKE, GETS INTO BED WITH HER DAUGHTER AND BY MEANS OF A FEW CHOICE WORDS RESTORES THE PEACE.°

Just as he had done before, Calandrino made the entire company laugh once again. Then, when the ladies finally stopped talking about his antics, the Queen ordered Panfilo to speak, and he said:

Praiseworthy ladies, the name of Calandrino's beloved has brought to mind a story about another Niccolosa that I would like to recount for you, because in it you will see how a good woman's presence of mind enabled her to avert a great scandal.

Not so long ago, in the valley of the Mugnone there lived a worthy man who earned money by supplying travelers with food and drink, and although he was poor and his house tiny, he would sometimes put them up, but only in cases of urgent need and only if he knew who they were. The man was married to a most attractive woman, who had borne him two children, a lovely, charming young girl fifteen or sixteen years old who was still unmarried, and a tiny baby boy not yet one whom his mother was breast-feeding herself.

The girl had caught the eye of a young gentleman from our city, a lively, attractive youth who spent a lot of time in the countryside, and he fell passionately, fervently, in love with her. For her part, she took great pride in having won the affection of such a young man, and making every effort to keep his love for her alive by behaving with the greatest affability toward him, in the process she likewise fell in love with him. Now, on more than one occasion they would have consummated their love for one another, to the great delight of both parties, if Pinuccio—for that was the youth's name—had not been worried about exposing both the girl and himself to censure. His ardor, however, grew from day to day until he was simply overwhelmed by his desire to be with her. It therefore occurred to him that he just had to discover a way to find lodging at her father's house, for he knew its layout and thought that if he could just get inside, he and the girl could be together, and no one would be any the wiser. And in fact, no sooner did this idea enter his head than he promptly proceeded to put it into effect.

Late one evening, Pinuccio and a trusted companion of his named Adriano, who knew about his love for the girl, hired a couple of packhorses, placed a pair of saddlebags on them, which may have been filled with straw, and set out from Florence. After riding around in a large circle, they arrived at the valley of the Mugnone, reaching it sometime after nightfall. There, after turning their horses around as if they were returning from Romagna, they rode up to the worthy man's house and knocked on the door, which he opened right away since he was well acquainted with the pair.

"Look, you have to put us up for the night," Pinuccio told him. "We thought we would've reached Florence by this time, but as you can see, we couldn't ride fast enough to get any farther than here."

"Pinuccio," replied the host, "you must know how poorly provided I am to offer lodging to gentlemen like yourselves, but still, since you've been caught here at this hour, and there's no time for you to go anywhere else, I'm happy to do what I can to put you up for the night."

The two young men dismounted, and after having first seen to their horses, they entered the cottage where they got out the generous supper they had brought with them and ate it with their host. Now, the latter had only one tiny little bedroom, in which he had set up three small beds to the best of his ability, leaving so little space that it was a tight squeeze indeed to maneuver around them.

Two of the beds were next to one of the walls, while the third one stood on the opposite side of the room. The host then had the least uncomfortable bed made up for the two companions and invited them to sleep there. A little later, while the two of them were still wide awake, although they were pretending to be asleep, the host had his daughter settle down in one of the other beds, and he got into the third one with his wife, who placed the cradle holding their little baby son next to where she was sleeping.

After everything had been arranged in the room, Pinuccio made a mental note of it all and waited a little while until he thought everyone was asleep. At that point, he quietly got up, went over to the little bed where the girl he loved was sleeping, and lay down beside her. Although she was frightened, she gave him a joyous welcome, and there he stayed, taking his fill of that pleasure for which they had both been yearning for such a long time.

While Pinuccio was in bed with the girl, a cat happened to knock some things over. The noise woke up the wife, who was afraid that it was something else. She got out of bed in the dark, naked as she was, and headed for the place from which the sound had come.

By chance, Adriano also happened to get up, not for the same reason, but in response to a call of nature, and as he was going to take care of his business, he bumped into the cradle where the wife had placed it on the floor. Since he could not get past without moving it out of the way, he grabbed it, lifted it up from where the wife had set it, and put it down next to the bed in which he himself had been sleeping. Then, having finished what he had gotten up to do, he came back, and without giving any further thought to the cradle, climbed into bed.

After having searched the house for a while, the wife concluded that nothing of importance had fallen down, and having no desire to light a lamp in order to inspect things more closely, she yelled at the cat and then returned to the little bedroom, groping her way right up to the bed where her husband was sleeping. But when she failed to find the cradle there, she said to herself: "Oh no, stupid me! See what I was about to do! For God's sake, I was heading right for the bed where my guests are sleeping!" Moving forward a bit, she found the cradle, and then lay down with Adriano in the bed beside it, thinking she was lying down with her husband. Adriano had not yet gone back to sleep, and when he realized what had happened, he gave her a warm reception, after which, without uttering a single sound in the process, he yanked his rope until it was taut and his sail was all swollen out, much to the wife's great satisfaction.°

This was how matters stood when Pinuccio, who had enjoyed himself with the girl as much as he had wanted, started worrying that sleep might surprise him there with her. Consequently, he rose from her side in order to go back and rest in his own bed. When he got there, however, only to run into the cradle, he moved on, thinking it was the host's bed, and wound up getting in beside the host himself, who was awakened by his arrival. Being under the impression that the man who lay beside him was Adriano, Pinuccio said: "About that Niccolosa, I have to say, there's nothing could be sweeter, in any way.° By God's body, I've had more fun with her than any man's ever had with a woman. And let me assure you, since I left here, I've managed to get into her country house six times."

When the host heard this bit of news, he was not exactly pleased. First, he asked himself: "What the devil is this guy doing here?" Then, allowing his anger to get the better of his prudence, he said: "Pinuccio, what you've done is shameful. I don't know why you had to do it to me, but by God's body, I'm going to pay you back for it."

Pinuccio was not the smartest young man in the world, and when he realized his mistake, instead of trying to find the best remedy he could for it, he replied: "How're you going to pay me back? What could you do to me?"

The host's wife, who thought she was sleeping with her husband, said to Adriano: "Uh-oh! Just listen to the way our guests are quarreling with one another."

"Let 'em go ahead," said Adriano, with a laugh, "and to Hell with 'em. They had too much to drink last night."

The wife was thinking it was her husband's voice when she

heard him cursing them, but as soon as she heard Adriano's words, she immediately realized where she was and with whom. Wise woman that she was, however, she got up at once without saying another word and grabbed her baby son's cradle. Since there was absolutely no light in the room, she felt her way along, carrying the cradle to the side of the bed in which her daughter was sleeping. There she put it down and got into the bed with her. Then, pretending to have been awakened by the noise her husband was making, she called to him and asked him what he was having words with Pinuccio about.

"Didn't you hear what he says he did to Niccolosa tonight?" her husband replied.

"He's lying through his teeth," she said. "He didn't sleep with Niccolosa, because I've been lying here all this time and haven't slept a wink since I got in. You're a fool to believe him. You men drink so much in the evening that at night you do nothing but dream and walk about all over the place in your sleep without knowing where you are and imagine you've performed all sorts of miracles. It's a pity you don't break your necks! But what's Pinuccio doing over there? Why isn't he in his own bed?"

For his part, seeing how adroitly the woman was covering up both her own shame and her daughter's, Adriano added: "Pinuccio, I've told you a hundred times that you shouldn't be wandering about, because this vice of yours of sleepwalking and then recounting the fantasies that you've dreamed as though they were true is going to get you into trouble one of these days. Come back here, goddamn you."

When the host heard what his wife and Adriano were both saying, he started to think that Pinuccio really was dreaming. Consequently, taking him by the shoulders, he began to shake him and yell at him. "Wake up, Pinuccio," he said. "Get back in your own bed."

Having taken in everything they had said, Pinuccio began raving like someone who was dreaming, provoking the host to the heartiest laugh in the world. Finally, as if in response to the shaking he was being given, Pinuccio pretended to wake up, and shouting over to Adriano, he said: "Why are you calling me? Is it day already?"

"Yes, it is," said Adriano. "Come over here."

Feigning ignorance of what had happened and acting as if he were very drowsy, Pinuccio finally left the host's side and went back to bed with Adriano. When day came and everyone was up, the host started laughing and making fun of Pinuccio and his dreaming. And so, between one jest and another, the two young men got their horses ready and strapped on their saddlebags. Then, after having had a drink with the host, they mounted up and rode off to Florence, no less content with the way things happened than with the outcome of their night's adventures.

From then on, Pinuccio found other ways to spend time with Niccolosa, and since she swore to her mother that he had unquestionably been dreaming, her mother, who certainly recalled Adriano's embraces, was left with the conviction that she had been the only one awake that night.

Story 10

DONNO GIANNI IS PREVAILED UPON BY *COMPAR* PIETRO TO
USE AN INCANTATION IN ORDER TO TURN HIS WIFE INTO A
MARE, BUT WHEN THE PRIEST COMES TO STICK ON THE
TAIL, *COMPAR* PIETRO SAYS HE DID NOT WANT ONE AND
COMPLETELY RUINS THE SPELL.°

*   *   *

Graceful ladies, the beauty of a flock of white doves is enhanced more by a black crow than by a pure white swan, and in the same way, among many wise people, on occasion the presence of someone less wise will not only add splendor and beauty to their mature wisdom, but will be a source of delight and entertainment as well.

Now, you are all ladies of exceptional discretion and modesty, whereas I feel myself to be more the fool than not, and since I therefore make your virtue shine all the brighter in comparison with my deficiency, I ought to be dearer to you for that reason than if my superior worth made yours seem dimmer. Consequently, in telling the tale I am about to relate to you, I should have greater license to reveal myself such as I am, and you should display greater patience in tolerating me than if I were wiser. In any case, I am going to tell you a story that is not especially long, but that will teach you how carefully one must follow the instructions of those who do things by means of incantations and how making even one tiny mistake will ruin everything the magician has done.

A year or two ago in Barletta there was a priest called Donno Gianni di Barolo, who, because his church was poor, was forced to eke out a living for himself by carrying goods on his mare to fairs all over Apulia, and by buying and selling things.° In the course of his travels, he struck up a close friendship with a certain Pietro da Tresanti who plied the same trade, albeit in his case, he made use of an ass he owned. As a sign of their love and friendship, the priest adopted the Apulian custom of calling him *compar* Pietro, and every time the man came to Barletta, the priest always took him to his church, where he gave him lodging and entertained him to the best of his ability.°

Since *compar* Pietro, for his part, was exceedingly poor and had only a little cottage in Tresanti that scarcely sufficed for him, his beautiful young wife, and his ass, every time Donno Gianni showed up in town, he would take him to his house and entertain him there as well as he could, in recognition of the hospitality he had received from the priest in Barletta. With regard to lodging, however, *compar* Pietro could not take care of him in the way he would have liked, because he only had a tiny bed in which he slept with his pretty wife. Instead, Donno Gianni was obliged to go into the little stable where his mare was quartered next to the ass and to lie down beside her on a pile of straw. Knowing all about the hospitality the priest showed her husband, *compar* Pietro's wife had volunteered on more than one occasion, when he had come to stay with them, to go and sleep with a neighbor of hers named Zita Carapresa, the daughter of Giudice Leo, so that he would have been able to pass the night in the bed with her husband.° However, although she frequently said as much to him, Donno Gianni would never hear of it.

On one occasion like that, among many others, he said to her: "*Comar* Gemmata, don't trouble yourself about me. I'm doing just fine, because whenever I like, I change this mare into a beautiful gal and pass the time with her. Then, whenever I want to, I turn her into a mare again. And that's why I would never part from her."

The young woman was amazed, and believing every word of it, she told her husband what the priest had said, adding: "If he's such a good friend as you say, why don't you get him to teach you that magic spell so you can turn me into a mare, and then you can run your business with a mare as well as an ass? That way we'll earn twice as much, and when we got home, you could turn me back into a woman again just as I am now."

Compar Pietro, who was something of a dunce, believed the story, and taking his wife's advice, started begging Donno Gianni for all he was worth to teach him how to do it. Although the priest tried his best to talk him out of this foolishness, he was ultimately unable to do so. "Look," he said, "since that's what you want, we'll get up tomorrow before daybreak as usual, and then I'll teach you how it's done. However, to tell the truth, as you'll see for yourself, the most difficult thing to manage in this business is to stick on the tail."

Compar Pietro and *comar* Gemmata were looking forward so eagerly to what was going to happen that they hardly slept a wink that night, and when day was finally just about to dawn, they got out of bed and called Donno Gianni who, having just risen and still in his nightshirt, came to *compar* Pietro's little room. "I wouldn't do this for anybody else in the world," he said, "except for the two of you, and since you're so insistent, I'll go ahead with it for you. But if you really want it to work, you've got to obey my every order."

After the pair of them assured him that they would, Donno Gianni took a light, and said, as he was handing it to *compar* Pietro: "You should watch what I'm about to do very closely, and memorize carefully what I say. Furthermore, unless you want to ruin everything, make sure you don't utter a single word yourself, no matter what you see or hear. And pray to God that the tail really sticks on tight." Taking the light, *compar* Pietro promised to do as he was told.

Then, Donno Gianni made *comar* Gemmata strip off her clothes until she was completely naked and stand with her hands and feet on the ground just like a mare, similarly instructing her not to utter a sound no matter what happened. After that, he began passing his hands over her face and head, while saying:

"Let this be a fine mare's head."

Then, stroking her hair, he said:

"Let this be a fine mare's mane."

Next, he touched her arms, saying:

"Let these be a fine mare's legs and hooves."

When he came to her breasts, he found they were so firm and round that a certain uninvited something or other awoke and stood up, and he said:

"And let this be a fine mare's chest."

He then did the same thing to her back, her stomach, her hind-quarters, her thighs, and her legs. Finally, having nothing left to take care of but the tail, he whipped up his shirt, grabbed hold of the stick he used for planting men, and quickly stuck it into the furrow that was designed for it, saying:

"And let this be a fine mare's tail."

Up to this point, *compar* Pietro had been watching everything with the greatest attention, but when he saw this last bit, he took it amiss and exclaimed:

"Oh, Donno Gianni, no tail! I don't want a tail there!"

The vital fluid that all plants need to take root had already come by the time Donno Gianni pulled it out.

"Oh no, *compar* Pietro," he said, "what have you done? Didn't I tell you not to say a word no matter what you saw? The mare was just about finished, but now you've gone and ruined everything by talking, and there's no way for us to do it over ever again."

"That's all right," said *compar* Pietro, "I didn't want that tail there, no, not me. Why didn't you tell me, 'Do it yourself'? And besides, you were sticking it on too low."

"I didn't tell you because it was your first time," replied Donno Gianni, "and you wouldn't have known how to stick it on as well as I do."

After listening to their exchange, the young woman stood up and said to her husband in all seriousness:

"What a dope you are! Why did you have to go and ruin everything for the two of us? When did you ever see a mare without a tail? So help me God, you may be poor now, but you deserve to be even poorer."

Now that there was no longer any way for the young woman to be turned into a mare, thanks to the words that her husband had spoken, she got dressed, feeling downcast and melancholy, while *compar* Pietro prepared to ply his old trade again, taking with him his single ass, as usual. Then off he went to the fair at Bitonto together with Donno Gianni, and he never asked him for such a favor again.°

Conclusion

How the company laughed at this story, which the ladies understood better than Dioneo had intended, can be left to the imagination of that lady who has read it and is laughing at it still. But since their storytelling was now over and the sun's heat had started to abate, the Queen rose to her feet, and aware that her rule had come to an end, she took her crown and placed it on the head of Panfilo, who was the last one left to be granted this honor.

"My lord," she said, with a smile, "you are left with a great burden, for as the last ruler, you must make amends not just for my shortcomings, but for those of all the others who have held this office before you. May God grant you His grace in this undertaking, just as He has granted it to me in proclaiming you King."

Panfilo happily accepted the honor and replied: "Your own excellence and that of my other subjects will ensure that my reign will be as praiseworthy as all the others have been." And following the custom of his predecessors, he made all the necessary arrangements with the steward, after which he turned to the ladies who were waiting for him to address them.

"Loving ladies," he said, "the prudent Emilia, who has been our Queen today, gave you the freedom to talk about whatever you pleased so that you might rest your faculties awhile. But now that you have done so, I think it would be good to return to our customary rule, and I therefore want each of you to think up something to say tomorrow on the subject of those who have acted with liberality or magnificence, whether in matters of love or otherwise.

"Both the description of those actions and the actions in and of themselves will assuredly enflame you, well disposed as your spirits already are, to perform worthy deeds. And thus our lives, which cannot help but be brief in these mortal bodies of ours, will be preserved through the fame of our praiseworthy achievements—a goal that those who do not serve their bellies, like brute beasts, should not only desire, but zealously pursue and make every effort to attain."

The merry company approved of the theme, and with the new King's permission, they all got up from their seats and devoted themselves to their usual pleasures, all of them going wherever their desires led them, until it was time for supper, to which they returned in a festive mood. At the end of the meal, which had been served with care and in the proper order, they rose and danced as they normally did, and after they had sung perhaps a thousand little songs, more entertaining for their words than distinguished by their music, the King asked Neifile to sing one on her own account. And without a moment's hesitation, in a clear and joyful voice, she began singing pleasantly, as follows:

> A youthful maiden, I'm so happy now
> To sing and take delight in early spring,
> All thanks to Love and the sweet thoughts he brings.
> I walk through verdant meadows, looking at
> The white and yellow flowers and the red,
> The roses with their thorns, the lilies white,
> And I compare them, each and every one,
> Unto his face whose love has conquered me

And keeps me his forever, so that I
Now have no wish but to serve his delight.
      Whenever I find one among these blooms,
That to my mind is similar to him,
I pluck it, kiss it, and then speak to it,
And as I can, I open up my soul
Entirely and all my heart's desires.
I make a garland of it with the rest,
And bind them with my dainty golden hair.
      The pleasure that a flower naturally
Provides the eyes, that one bestows on me:
It's just as if I see him here himself,
The man who's fired me with his sweet love.
What more he does to me with his perfume
I never could express by means of words:
My sighs, though, bear true witness to its power.
      Those sighs will never issue from my breast
As other women's do, so sad and harsh,
But rather, warm and soft they come from me
And make their way into the presence of
My love, who, hearing them, moves instantly
To bring me pleasure, and arrives as I'm
About to say, "Ah, come, lest I despair!"

   The King and all the ladies bestowed lavish praise on Neifile's
song, after which, since much of the night was already spent, the
King ordered everyone to go and rest until morning.

Day 10

* * *

Story 3

ENVIOUS OF NATHAN'S REPUTATION FOR COURTESY,
MITHRIDANES SETS OUT TO MURDER HIM. AFTER
ACCIDENTALLY COMING ACROSS HIM WITHOUT
RECOGNIZING HIM, AND BEING INFORMED BY HIM AS TO
HOW HE MIGHT DO THE DEED, HE FINDS HIM, JUST AS
NATHAN HAD ARRANGED IT, IN A LITTLE WOOD. WHEN
MITHRIDANES REALIZES WHO IT IS, HE IS FILLED WITH
SHAME AND BECOMES NATHAN'S FRIEND.°

* * *

Noble ladies, although the munificence of the King of Spain was great and that of the Abbot of Cluny possibly unheard of, you will perhaps be no less amazed to hear about a man who, intent upon bestowing his generosity on a person who did not merely thirst for his blood, but for his very life, cleverly arranged to give it to him. Furthermore, as I intend to show you in a little story of mine, he would have done so if his adversary had desired to take it.

It is beyond doubt, if the reports of various men from Genoa and elsewhere who have been to those parts may be trusted, that in the region of Cathay there once lived a man of noble lineage named Nathan who was rich beyond compare.° He owned an estate close to a road along which everyone who wanted to go from west to east or east to west was more or less forced by necessity to pass, and since he had a lofty and magnanimous spirit, and wanted to be known for his deeds, he assembled a host of master builders there who in a short space of time erected one of the largest, most beautiful, and most luxurious palaces for him that had ever been seen, which he then had excellently furnished with everything suitable for the reception and honorable entertainment of gentlemen. Having engaged a large group of splendid servants, he saw to it that everyone passing by in either direction was received and made welcome there in a most agreeable and festive manner, a laudable practice he kept up until his reputation had soon spread not only throughout the East, but throughout most of the West as well.

When Nathan had already reached a ripe old age, without ever tiring of displaying such courtesy, his fame happened to reach the ears of a young man named Mithridanes who lived in a country not far from his. Knowing that he was just as rich as Nathan, he grew envious of Nathan's renown and his virtue, and he resolved that through an even greater display of liberality he would either obliterate the old man's renown or overshadow it. And so, after having had a palace built similar to Nathan's, he began to bestow the most extravagant courtesies ever seen on everyone who passed by, going in either direction, and there is no doubt that in a short time he became very famous.

Now one day, while the young man was all alone in the court-yard of his palace, a poor woman happened to come in through one of its gates and ask him for alms. Not only did she get them, but then, returning to him through a second gate, she received them yet again. This occurred twelve times in succession, and when she came back for the thirteenth, Mithridanes remarked, "My good woman, you're very persistent with this begging of yours," although he gave her alms just the same.

In response to his comment, the little old woman said: "Ah, Nathan's generosity, how wonderful you are! For his palace has thirty-two gates, just like this one, and even though I came in through every single one of them and asked for alms, I always got them without his ever giving any sign that he knew who I was. Here, by contrast, I've only come in through thirteen, and not only have I been recognized, but I've been given a scolding." Then, having said her piece, she left, never to return.

Mithridanes felt that the words he heard the old woman speak about Nathan's reputation only served to diminish his own, and they ignited a raging fury in him. "Oh, poor me!" he exclaimed. "How can I ever match Nathan's greatest acts of generosity, let alone surpass him as I've sought to do, when I can't come close to him in the smallest things? All my efforts will truly be in vain unless I wipe him off the face of the earth, and since old age isn't carrying him away all by itself, I'll have to do the job with my own hands, and that without delay."

Driven by this emotion, he leaped to his feet, and without communicating his plan to anyone, he set out on horseback, accompanied by only a small entourage. In three days they reached the place where Nathan lived, arriving there toward evening. Mithridanes instructed his followers to pretend that they were not with him and had no idea who he was, telling them to find some-where to stay until they received further orders from him. Left alone, he came upon Nathan not far from his magnificent palace, taking a leisurely stroll, unattended and dressed in simple clothing. Not realizing who it was, Mithridanes asked him if he could tell him where Nathan lived.

"My son," Nathan replied cheerfully, "nobody in these parts can show you the way better than I can, and so, whenever you wish, I'll take you there myself."

The young man said that he would like that very much, but that, if possible, he did not want Nathan to see him or to know that he was there.

"And this, too, I will do," replied Nathan, "since that's the way you want it."

Mithridanes then dismounted, and as they walked along, Nathan soon engaged him in the most pleasant conversation, until he reached his lovely palace. There Nathan got one of his servants to take Mithridanes's horse, and drawing close to the servant, he whispered in his ear, telling him to pass the word immediately that no one in his household should tell the young man that he himself was Nathan. His order was carried out, and once the two men had entered the palace, he had Mithridanes lodged in a very handsome room where no one saw him except those who were delegated to be his servants. And to make sure that the young man was entertained in the most honorable fashion, Nathan himself kept him company.

After they had spent some time together, although Mithridanes treated Nathan with all the reverence due to a father, he finally could not refrain from asking him who he was.

"I'm one of Nathan's menial servants," he replied, "but despite having been with him since my childhood and grown old in his service, he has never raised me above my present station, so, however much everyone else may praise him, I myself have little cause to do so."

These words raised Mithridanes's hopes that he could carry out his wicked plan with greater safety and assurance. When Nathan then asked him very politely who he was and what business brought him to that part of the world, offering to advise and assist him in whatever way he could, Mithridanes hesitated for a while before responding. Eventually, he decided to take Nathan into his confidence, and after much beating about the bush, he began by swearing the old man to secrecy, then asked him for his help and his counsel, and finally revealed everything about who he was, his purpose in coming there, and what had motivated him to do so.

Upon hearing Mithridanes speak and learning of his savage plan, Nathan was deeply disturbed, but he had a resolute spirit, and without changing the expression on his face, he scarcely paused a moment before replying.

"Mithridanes," he said, "your father was a noble man, and your desire to live up to his example is revealed by the lofty enterprise you have undertaken of bestowing your generosity on all comers. Moreover, I greatly commend the envy you have of Nathan's virtue, because if there were a great deal of that sort of feeling around, the world, which is quite a miserly place, would soon change for the better.°

"I shall certainly keep the plan you've revealed to me a secret, and although I can't offer you any substantial assistance with it, I can give you some useful advice, which is this. About half a mile from here you can see a little wood where practically every morning Nathan takes a long, leisurely walk all by himself. It'll be easy for you to find him there and deal with him as you please. If you kill him, however, and want to be able to return home without encountering any obstacles, you must leave the wood not by the road you took when you went there, but by the one you see over there to your left, because although it may be a bit rougher, it'll bring you out closer to your house and be safer for you."

Once he had given this information to Mithridanes, Nathan took his leave, and the young man secretly informed his companions, who were likewise staying in the palace, where they were to wait for him the following day. Nathan had no second thoughts about the advice he had given Mithridanes, and when the new day dawned, with his mind still unchanged, he set off alone for the little wood, there to meet his death.

Mithridanes had no other weapons other than his bow and his sword, and after he awoke, he collected them, mounted his horse, and rode off toward the little wood, where, from a distance, he caught sight of Nathan taking a stroll all by himself. Mithridanes raced toward him, but having decided that he would take a good look at him and hear him speak before attacking him, he seized him by the turban he had on his head and exclaimed: "Old man, you're as good as dead!"

To this, Nathan's only response was, "Then I must deserve it."

Upon hearing his voice and looking him in the face, Mithridanes instantly recognized him as the man who had received him with such kindness, had kept him company like a friend, and had advised him so faithfully. Consequently, his fury immediately subsided, and his anger was transformed into shame. Hurling away the sword, which he had already drawn out in order to strike his adversary, he dismounted and flung himself down in tears at Nathan's feet.

"Your generosity is only too clear to me now, dearest father," he said, "considering how prudently you arranged to come here in order to offer me your life, which I, despite having no reason to do so, wanted to take from you, as I told you myself. But at the point when my need was greatest, God showed He was more concerned about where my duty lay than I was myself and opened the eyes of my mind that wretched envy had sealed. Indeed, considering how ready you've been to comply with my desires, I am all the more cognizant of the debt of penance I owe you because of my fault. Therefore, take your revenge on me in whatever way you think appropriate for the sin I've committed."

After raising Mithridanes to his feet, Nathan embraced him and kissed him tenderly. "As far as your design here is concerned, my son," he said, "call it evil or not as you will, there's no need to ask for my forgiveness or for me to grant it, because you didn't pursue it out of hatred, but in order to be held in greater esteem. Live, then, and have no fear of me, for you may rest assured that there's no other man alive who loves you as much as I do, considering the lofty nature of your spirit, in that you have dedicated yourself not to the amassing of wealth, which is what misers do, but to spending what you have accumulated. Nor should you feel ashamed of having wanted to enhance your reputation by slaying me or imagine that I am surprised by it. In order to increase their realms, and thus their fame, the most illustrious of emperors and the greatest of kings have practiced almost no art other than killing, not just one man as you wanted to do, but an infinite number of them, as well as putting entire countries to the torch and razing cities to the ground. And so, if, to achieve renown, I was the only person you wanted to kill, you were not doing anything extraordinary or unusual, but something actually quite commonplace."

Without attempting to exculpate himself for his perverse desire, Mithridanes praised the honorable way Nathan had found of excusing it, and in the course of conversing with him finally reached the point of expressing his utter astonishment that Nathan had accepted it and was prepared not only to supply him with the means but also with advice for carrying out his plan.

"Mithridanes," replied Nathan, "neither my compliance nor my advice should astonish you, for ever since I've been my own master and had a mind to pursue the same goal that you, too, have been aiming at, I have always sought to satisfy anyone who showed up at my house, to the extent that I could, by giving him whatever he asked of me. You came here seeking my life, and as soon as I heard what it was that you wanted, I immediately resolved to give it to you, so that you wouldn't be the only person ever to leave my home unsatisfied. With that end in mind, I gave you advice I thought would be good for taking my life without losing your own. Therefore, I say to you yet again that if that's what you want, I implore you to give yourself the satisfaction of taking my life, for I can't think of how it might be better spent.

"I've had the use of my life now for some eighty years, spending it all on my own pleasures and comforts, and I know that as I follow the course of Nature just like other men, indeed like everything else in the world, it will only be mine to have for a little while longer. And that's why I think it's much better to give it away, just as I have always given away and spent my treasures, than to try to hold on to it until Nature takes it from me against my will.

"To give away even a hundred years is a trifle, and if so, how much less is it to give away six or eight of the ones remaining to me down here? Take my life, then, if you want it, I beg you, for during all the years I've been alive, I've never yet found anyone who wanted it, and if you don't take it, you who are actually asking for it, I have no idea when I'd ever be able to find someone who would. But even if I should happen to find such a person, I realize that the longer I keep it, the less value it will have. So take it, I implore you, before it depreciates even more."

"God forbid," said Mithridanes, feeling profoundly ashamed of himself, "that I should deprive you of so precious a thing as your life, let alone contemplate such a deed, which is what I was doing just a little while ago. In fact, far from wanting to shorten the years you have left, I'd gladly add some of my own to them if I could."

"And if you could," Nathan promptly replied, "would you really seek to add some of your years to mine? Why, then, you'd have me serve you in a way I've never served another human being, for you'd make me take something you possessed away from you, when I've never taken anything from anyone?"

"Yes," said Mithridanes, without a moment's hesitation.

"In that case, you must do what I tell you," said Nathan. "Remain here in my house, young as you are, and assume the name of Nathan, while I go to yours and from now on have myself called Mithridanes."

"If I knew how to comport myself as well as you do now, and as you've always done," replied Mithridanes, "I'd take your offer without giving it a second thought, but because I feel quite certain that my actions would only serve to diminish Nathan's fame, and because I have no intention of marring in another what I cannot make perfect in myself, I won't accept it."

After they had conversed agreeably on these and many other topics, the two of them returned together, as Nathan wished, to his palace, where for many days he entertained Mithridanes in the most honorable fashion, using all the wit and wisdom at his disposal to encourage the young man to pursue his grand and lofty enterprise. And when Mithridanes finally wanted to go back home with his companions, Nathan, having made it abundantly clear that his own liberality could never be surpassed, gave his guest leave to depart.

Story 4

MESSER GENTILE DE' CARISENDI COMES FROM MODENA AND
TAKES THE LADY HE LOVES OUT OF THE TOMB IN WHICH
SHE HAD BEEN BURIED FOR DEAD. AFTER SHE IS REVIVED
AND GIVES BIRTH TO A MALE CHILD, MESSER GENTILE
RESTORES BOTH HER AND HER LITTLE BOY TO NICCOLUCCIO
CACCIANEMICO, HER HUSBAND.°

It seemed miraculous to all of them that any person could be so liberal with his own blood as Nathan had been, and everyone agreed that his generosity had truly surpassed that of the King of Spain and the Abbot of Cluny. But then, after they had discussed the matter awhile, the King looked over in Lauretta's direction, indicating that he wished her to speak. In response, Lauretta began immediately:

Young ladies, we have been told about such beautiful and magnificent things, and heard stories that are filled with such lofty examples of magnanimity, that for those of us who have yet to speak, there is, I think, little terrain left for us to explore, unless we turn to the deeds of lovers, which will always provide a most copious supply of material on any topic. Consequently, for this reason, and also because our youth especially inclines us in that direction, I would like to tell you about a generous deed performed by a man who was in love. And if it is true that in order to obtain the object of their affections, men will give away fortunes, set aside enmities, and expose their very lives, their honor, and what is even more important, their reputation to a thousand dangers, then you may possibly conclude, all things considered, that this man's actions were in no way inferior to some of those already described.

In Bologna, then, that most noble city in Lombardy, there once lived a gentleman called Messer Gentile de' Carisendi who was quite noteworthy for his virtue and the nobility of his blood.° In his youth, he became enamored of a gentlewoman named Madonna Catalina, the wife of a certain Niccoluccio Caccianemico, and because his love for her was ill requited, he almost despaired of it, and went off to Modena, where he had been appointed the *podestà*.

At that time, Niccoluccio was away from Bologna, and his wife, being pregnant, had gone to stay on one of his estates about three miles outside the city. There she had the misfortune to be stricken all of a sudden by a terrible malady so virulent that it extinguished every sign of life in her, and she was pronounced dead by several different doctors. Since her closest female relations said that from what she had told them, she had not been pregnant long enough for her child to have been completely formed, they did not reflect further on that subject, but after a great deal of weeping, buried her in a tomb, just as she was, in a nearby church.

The news of her death was immediately reported to Messer Gentile by one of his friends, and despite the fact that he had never been the recipient of her favors, he was overcome with grief. At length, however, he said to himself: "So there you are, Madonna Catalina, you're dead. Well, I never managed to get as much as a single glance from you while you were alive, but now that you're dead and can't defend yourself, it's only right that I should take a kiss or two from you."

Night had already fallen as he said these things to himself, and so, after making arrangements to keep his departure a secret, he mounted his horse, accompanied by just one of his servants, and did not stop until he had reached the place where the lady was buried.° Having opened up the tomb, he cautiously went inside, and lying down beside her, he drew his face close to hers and kissed her again and again, all the while weeping profusely. But as we know, men's appetites—and especially those of lovers—are never content to stay within bounds, but always want to go further, and so, just as he was deciding that it was time to leave, he said to himself: "Ah, why don't I fondle her breast a little, seeing as how I'm here? I never touched her in the past, and I will never have the opportunity to do so again."

Thus, overcome by this desire, he placed his hand on her breast, and after keeping it there for some time, he thought he could sense her heart faintly beating. Having subdued his fears, he began examining her with greater care and discovered that she was in fact still alive, although the signs of life in her were minimal and very weak. Consequently, as gently as he could, he removed her from the tomb with the aid of his servant, and having set her across his horse in front of him, he carried her in secret to his house in Bologna.

His mother, a wise and worthy woman, was living there, and after she had heard her son's lengthy account of what had happened, she was moved to compassion and skillfully brought the lady back to life again with the aid of a series of warm baths and a good hot fire. When she came to, she heaved a great sigh and said: "Alas! Where am I now?"

"Don't worry," replied the worthy woman. "You're in a good place."

Having recovered her senses, the lady looked all around her and discovered, to her amazement, that she had no idea where she was, but seeing Messer Gentile standing before her, she asked his mother to tell her how she came to be there, which prompted Messer Gentile to give her a detailed account of everything that had happened. She was distressed over what she heard, but after a while, she thanked him as best she could and begged him, out of the love that he had borne for her and his own sense of honor, to do nothing to her in his house that would impair her honor or that of her husband, and to let her return home at daybreak.

"My lady," replied Messer Gentile, "whatever my desire may have been like in the past, seeing as how God has bestowed this grace on me of bringing you back to life because of the love I once bore you, I do not intend, either now or in the future, to treat you as anything other than a dear sister, whether here or elsewhere. But since the service I did for you tonight deserves some sort of reward, I hope you will not deny me the favor I'm about to ask of you."

The lady responded graciously that she was ready to grant his wish, provided that it lay in her power to do so and that there was nothing improper about it.

"My lady," said Messer Gentile, "since all of your relations, indeed, all the people in Bologna believe with utter certainty that you're dead, there's no one expecting you at your house any longer. Consequently, the favor I would ask of you is to be so good as to stay here quietly with my mother until I return from Modena, which will be fairly soon. And the reason I'm making this request of you is that I propose to stage a solemn ceremony in which I will make a precious gift of you to your husband in the presence of all the leading citizens in the town."

The lady truly longed to cheer up her family by showing them she was still alive, but realizing that she was in Messer Gentile's debt and that his request was honorable, she decided to do what he wanted and gave him her word of honor to that effect.

She had scarcely finished giving him her answer when she felt that she was about to have her baby, and not long afterward, with the tender assistance of Messer Gentile's mother, she gave birth to a handsome boy, which doubled and redoubled the joy both she and Messer Gentile felt. After ordering that she should have everything she needed and that she was to be treated as though she were his own wife, Messer Gentile then returned in secret to Modena.

When the term of his office there was finished and he was about to go back to Bologna, he arranged that on the morning of his return a grand, sumptuous banquet should be given at his house, to which he invited a host of gentlemen from the city, and among them, Niccoluccio Caccianemico. Upon his arrival, he dismounted and went to join his guests, although he first called on the lady and found that she was more beautiful and in better health than ever and that her little boy was thriving. Then, with a joy beyond compare, he showed his guests to their tables and offered them a magnificent feast served in multiple courses.

When they were close to the end of the meal, he began speaking to the group, after having first told the lady what he intended to do and having arranged with her how she should comport herself.

"Gentlemen," he said, "I remember having once been told that in Persia they have a custom, most agreeable in my opinion, which is that whenever someone wants to confer a special honor on one of his friends, he invites him to his house and shows him the thing he holds most dear, whether it's his wife or his mistress or his daughter or whatever it may be, declaring that just as he has shown him this thing, he would show him his heart even more readily if he could. Now this is a custom I would like us to observe here in Bologna. You have been so good as to honor my banquet with your presence, and I would like to honor you in the Persian fashion by showing you the most precious thing I have in the world or am ever likely to have.

"However, before I do so, I would ask you to tell me what you think about a problem I am going to place before you. A certain person has in his house a good and extremely faithful servant who becomes gravely ill; this person, without waiting for the servant to die, has him carried out into the middle of the street and takes no further interest in him; then a stranger comes along, and moved by compassion for the sick man, takes him to his house where, with much care and at great expense, he restores him to his former healthy condition. Now, what I should like to know is this: if the second master retains him and makes use of his services, does the first one have any right to complain or to blame the other one, should he refuse to give the servant back when he's asked to do so?"

After they had discussed the question from a variety of viewpoints among themselves, the gentlemen all reached the same conclusion, and since Niccoluccio Caccianemico was an eloquent and polished speaker, they entrusted him with their response.

Niccoluccio began by praising the Persian custom and then declared that he and the others were all of the same opinion that the first master no longer had any claim on his servant since in such a desperate situation he had not merely abandoned him, but cast him away. Moreover, because of the benefits conferred on him by the second master, they thought it just if he claimed the servant as his own, for in refusing to give him up, he was neither doing any harm, nor offering any insult or injury to the first master. All the others who were sitting around the tables—and there were many worthy gentlemen among them—all of them seconded the opinion that Niccoluccio had given.

Delighted with this answer and with the fact that it had come from Niccoluccio, Messer Gentile affirmed that he, too, shared their opinion, after which he declared: "Now it's time for me to honor you as I promised I would." And calling two of his servants, he sent them to the lady, who, at his command, had been decked out in magnificent clothing and jewelry, charging them to ask her if she would be so good as to come and gladden the gentlemen with her presence.

Taking her extraordinarily beautiful little boy in her arms, the lady entered the hall, accompanied by the two servants, and at Messer Gentile's bidding, sat down next to one of his distinguished guests.

"Gentlemen," he said, "this is the thing I value above all others and intend to treasure forever. Look for yourselves and see whether you think I'm right to do so."

The gentlemen welcomed her, praised her enthusiastically, and assured Messer Gentile that he was indeed right to cherish her. As they were gazing at her, there were quite a few of them who would have said that she was the very woman she was, except for the fact that they thought she was dead. No one scrutinized her so closely, however, as Niccoluccio, who was seized by a burning desire to find out who she was. As soon as Messer Gentile stepped aside for a moment, he was no longer able to contain himself and asked her whether she was from Bologna or a foreigner. On hearing this question being put to her by her husband, it was quite difficult for her to keep from responding, but she followed the instructions she had been given and remained silent. One of the other gentlemen asked her if the child were hers, and yet another, if she were Messer Gentile's wife or related to him in any way, but to both of them she made no reply.

When they were rejoined by Messer Gentile, however, one of his guests said to him: "Sir, this treasure of yours is a beauty, but she seems to be mute. Is that so?"

"Gentlemen," said Messer Gentile, "the fact that she has not spoken up to now is no small proof of her virtue."

"Then you must tell us who she is," replied the other.

"I'll do so gladly," said Messer Gentile, "but only if you promise me not to budge from your places, no matter what I say, until I've finished my story."

When they had all promised they would and the tables had been cleared away, Messer Gentile sat down beside the lady and said:

"Gentlemen, this lady is that loyal and faithful servant to whom I was referring in the question I put to you just now. Little prized by her own people, she was thrown out, like something vile and worthless, into the middle of the street from which I retrieved her, and through my care, I saved her from death with my own hands. Recognizing my pure affection, God has transformed her from a fearsome corpse into the beauty you see before you. But to give you a clearer understanding of what happened to me, I shall briefly explain it all to you."

Then, to the great amazement of his listeners, he narrated every detail of what had occurred, from his first falling in love with the lady up to the present moment, after which he added: "Consequently, unless you, and especially Niccoluccio, have changed the judgment you reached just a little while ago, I'm the one who deserves to have this lady, and no one can legitimately ask me to give her back."

To this no one offered a reply. Instead, all of them waited to see what he would say next. While Niccoluccio was weeping for pity, being joined in that by a few of the others as well as by the lady herself, Messer Gentile got to his feet, took the little boy in his arms, and led the lady by the hand over to where Niccoluccio was sitting.

"Stand up, *compare*," he said.° "I'm not giving you back your wife whom your family as well as hers threw away. Instead, I want to make you a gift of both this lady, my *comare,* and this little boy of hers, of whom you are assuredly the father and whom I held at his baptism and named Gentile.° And I beg you to prize her as much as ever, even though she has been in my house for almost three months, for I swear to you—by that God who perhaps made me fall in love with her so that my love might be, as indeed it has been, the cause of her salvation—she has never led a more virtuous life either with her father and mother or with you than she has with my mother here in my house."

Having said this, he then turned to Catalina and declared: "My lady, I now release you from every promise you made me and leave you free to return to Niccoluccio." And having left her and the baby in Niccoluccio's arms, he returned to his seat.

Niccoluccio eagerly embraced his wife and son, his present happiness being far greater than his hopelessness had been before, and he did the very best he could possibly do to thank the knight, while all the others, who were weeping for pity, were full of praise for what he had done, as was everyone else who came to hear about it. The lady was given a wonderfully festive reception upon her return home, and for a long time afterward the people of Bologna regarded her with awe as someone who had returned from the dead. As for Messer Gentile, for the rest of his life he remained a good friend of Niccoluccio, his family, and the lady's family as well.

So, what do you say now, gentle ladies? Do you think that a King's giving away his crown and scepter, or an Abbot's reconciling a malefactor with the Pope at no cost to himself, or an old man's exposing his throat to the knife of his enemy—can any of these match the deed performed by Messer Gentile? For he was a lusty young man who felt he had a legitimate claim to that which the negligence of others had thrown away and that he had had the good fortune to retrieve. Nevertheless, not only did he behave honorably in tempering his glowing ardor, but upon obtaining the object that he had always desired with all his heart and had long sought to steal for himself, he generously returned it. Surely, none of the acts of magnanimity about which we have spoken seems to me the equal of this one.

Story 5

MADONNA DIANORA ASKS MESSER ANSALDO FOR A GARDEN
IN JANUARY AS BEAUTIFUL AS IT WOULD BE IN MAY, AND HE
PROVIDES IT FOR HER BY HIRING A MAGICIAN. HER
HUSBAND THEN GIVES HER PERMISSION TO SATISFY MESSER
ANSALDO'S DESIRES, BUT UPON HEARING OF HER HUSBAND'S
GENEROSITY, MESSER ANSALDO RELEASES HER FROM HER
PROMISE, AND THE MAGICIAN RELEASES MESSER ANSALDO
FROM HIS, REFUSING TO ACCEPT ANY SORT OF PAYMENT
FROM HIM.°

Every member of the merry company praised Messer Gentile to
the skies, after which the King ordered Emilia to continue, and as
if she just could not wait to speak, she boldly began as follows:

Delicate ladies, no one can reasonably deny that Messer Gentile
acted with generosity, but if anyone should argue that doing more
than he did is impossible, it will perhaps not be all that difficult to
prove that his accomplishments can indeed be surpassed, as I propose to show you in a little story of mine.

In Friuli, which is a cold province, but one happily endowed with
beautiful mountains, numerous rivers, and clear springs, there is a
town called Udine where there once lived a beautiful, noble lady
called Madonna Dianora, the wife of a very wealthy man named Gilberto who was exceptionally pleasant and amiable.° Such was this
lady's worth that she attracted the most fervent love of a noble lord
named Messer Ansaldo Gradense, an important man of exalted station who was known everywhere for his feats of arms and his courtesy. Although he loved her passionately and did everything he could
to get her to return his affection, sending her frequent messages to
this end, all his efforts were in vain. Eventually, the lady found the
gentleman's solicitations wearisome, and realizing that despite refusing everything he asked of her, he nevertheless persisted in loving
her and would not stop importuning her, she came up with a novel
and, to her mind, impossible request as a way to get rid of him. So
one day she spoke to a woman who often came to her on his behalf.

"My good woman," she said, "you've assured me many times that Messer Ansaldo loves me more than anything else, and you've frequently offered me marvelous gifts on his behalf, which I'd prefer he kept for himself, because they could never induce me to love him or satisfy his desires. Were I certain, however, that he really did love me as much as you say he does, then I should undoubtedly bring myself to return his affection and do whatever he wished. Consequently, if he were willing to provide me with proof by doing what I intend to ask of him, I shall be only too ready to obey his commands."

"And just what is it, my lady, that you want him to do?" said the good woman.

"What I desire is this," she replied. "In the month of January that is now approaching, I want a garden, close to town here, that will be full of green grass and flowers and leafy trees just the way it would be in May. And if he can't produce it, then he's not to send you or anyone else to me ever again, because if he bothers me any more, I won't keep it a secret, as I have up to now, but instead, I'll seek to rid myself of him by complaining to my husband and my relatives."

When the gentleman heard what his lady was demanding as well as what she was offering in return, he felt that she was really asking him to do something quite difficult, indeed virtually impossible, and realized that the only reason she had for making such a request was to dash his hopes. Nevertheless, he resolved to try everything he could to fulfill it and had inquiries made throughout many parts of the world to see whether anyone could be found who might provide him with assistance or advice. Finally, he got hold of a man who offered to do what he wanted by means of necromancy, provided he was well paid for his services.

Having agreed to pay the magician a very large sum of money, Messer Ansaldo waited contentedly for the appointed time to arrive. On the night before the calends of January, when it was extremely cold and everything was covered with snow and ice, the worthy man went to work with his arts, and the very next morning, in a quite lovely meadow not far from the town, there appeared, according to the testimony of those who saw it, one of the most exquisite gardens anyone has ever seen, with grass and trees and fruit of every kind.°

After the ecstatic Messer Ansaldo had looked over it, he arranged for some of the finest fruit and the most beautiful flowers growing there to be picked and presented in secret to the lady, along with an invitation for her to come and see the garden that she had asked for. Thus she would not only realize how much he loved her, but she would remember the promise she had given him, which she had sealed with an oath, and would thus, as a woman of honor, find a way to keep her word.

The lady had already heard many reports about the wonderful garden, and when she saw the flowers and fruit, she began to repent of the promise she had made. Nevertheless, for all her repentance, being curious to see such novelties, she set off with a large group of ladies from the town to have a look at the garden, and after according it great praise and expressing no small astonishment over it, she returned home, the saddest woman alive as she thought of what it obliged her to do. So intense was her grief that she was unable to conceal it, and her husband, noticing how she looked, insisted on knowing the reason why. Deeply ashamed, she maintained her silence for a long time, but finally felt compelled to tell him everything down to the last detail.

As he listened to her story, Gilberto was initially enraged, but then, upon mature reflection, considering the purity of his wife's intentions, he cast off his anger and said: "Dianora, it's not the part of a discreet and honorable lady to listen to messages of that sort, or to make a bargain about her chastity with any man, under any condition. The power of words that the heart receives by way of the ears is greater than many people believe, and for those who are in love there's almost nothing they can't accomplish.° Thus, you did wrong, first of all by listening to him, and then by making that bargain. But because I know how pure your heart is, I'll allow you to do something to fulfill the promise you made, something that perhaps no other man would permit, albeit I'm also moved by my fear of the magician, for Messer Ansaldo might ask him to harm us if you played him for a fool. I therefore want you to go to him, and using any means at your disposal, I want you to do what you can to preserve your chastity and get him to release you from your promise. However, if that's not possible, then just this once you may yield your body, but not your heart, to him."

As she listened to her husband, the lady wept and insisted that she did not want such a favor from him. But no matter how vehemently she refused it, Gilberto remained adamant, and so, the next morning around dawn the lady set out, not having bothered to get especially dressed up, and made her way to Messer Ansaldo's house, preceded by just two of her servants and followed by a single chambermaid.

Messer Ansaldo was utterly astonished when he heard that his lady had come to him, and as soon as he got out of bed, he sent for the magician. "I want you to see for yourself what a wonderful prize your art has procured for me," he said. The two of them then went to meet her, and far from displaying anything like unbridled passion, Messer Ansaldo welcomed her with courtesy and reverence. After that, they went into a lovely room where a great fire was burning, and having offered her a place to sit, he said: "My lady, if the long love I have borne for you merits any sort of reward, I beseech you to do me the kindness of revealing the truth about what has brought you here at such an hour and with such a small escort as this."

Ashamed, her eyes welling up with tears, the lady replied: "Sir, I have not been led here because of any love I feel for you or because of the promise I gave you, but rather, because I was ordered to do so by my husband, who has more regard for the labors you've undertaken to satisfy your unbridled passion than he does for his own honor or for mine. And it is at his command that I am furthermore disposed, just this once, to satisfy your every desire."

If Messer Ansaldo had been astonished by the lady's coming to his house, his astonishment was much greater when he heard what she had to say, and he was so moved by Gilberto's liberality that his ardor gradually changed into compassion.

"My lady," he said, "things being the way you say they are, God forbid that I should mar the honor of a man who takes pity on my love. And so, for as long as you choose to stay here, you will be treated as if you were my sister, and whenever you please, you shall be free to depart, provided that you convey to your husband such thanks as you deem appropriate for the immense courtesy he has displayed and that from now on you always look upon me as your brother and servant."

Upon hearing his words, the lady was happier than she had ever been. "From what I've noted of your conduct," she replied, "nothing could ever make me believe that my coming here would have produced any result other than the response I see you've made to it, and for that, I will be eternally in your debt." The lady then took her leave and returned, now with an honorable escort, to Gilberto. She told him what had occurred, with the result that he and Messer Ansaldo became faithful friends, attached to one another by the closest of bonds.

The magician had observed Gilberto's liberality toward Messer Ansaldo as well as Messer Ansaldo's toward the lady, and so, just as Messer Ansaldo was preparing to give him the reward he had been promised, he declared: "Now that I've seen how generous Gilberto has been with regard to his honor and you with regard to your love, God forbid that I shouldn't also be equally generous as far as my remuneration is concerned. And considering how you deserve it, I intend to let you keep it for yourself."

This embarrassed the gentleman, who did everything he could to make him take either the entire sum, or at least part of it, but all his efforts were in vain. Consequently, when the magician, having removed his garden on the third day, expressed a wish to depart, Messer Ansaldo bid him Godspeed. And from then on, any carnal desire he felt for the lady having been extinguished in his heart, Messer Ansaldo burned only with honorable affection for her.

What, then, shall we conclude, loving ladies? Shall we take the case of a lady who was almost dead and a man's love for her that had already grown lukewarm because his hopes had waned, and shall we place it above the generosity of Messer Ansaldo, whose love was more fervent than ever, who burned, as it were, with even more hope than before, and who held the prey he had pursued for so long right there in his hands? It strikes me as foolish to believe that first example of generosity could be compared to this one.°

Story 6

THE VICTORIOUS KING CHARLES THE OLD, HAVING FALLEN
IN LOVE WITH A YOUNG GIRL, FEELS SHAME OVER HIS
FOOLISH FANCY AND ARRANGES HONORABLE MARRIAGES
FOR HER AND HER SISTER.°

It would take too long to give a full account of all the varied discussions among the ladies as to whether Gilberto, Messer Ansaldo, or the necromancer had displayed the greater liberality in the case of Madonna Dianora. After the King had allowed them to debate the question for a while, however, he looked over at Fiammetta and ordered her to put an end to their dispute by telling her story. Without a moment's hesitation, she began as follows:

Illustrious ladies, I have always been of the opinion that in companies like ours, we should talk in such general terms that what one person says never gives rise to arguments among the others because of its excessive subtlety, something that is much more appropriate for scholars in the schools than for us, since we have quite enough to do just to manage our distaffs and spindles. Consequently, although I have been thinking about a certain story, it is perhaps a trifle ambiguous, and seeing as how you are at odds over the ones we have already heard, I shall set it aside and tell you another that concerns the chivalrous deed, not of some man of little account, but of a valiant king whose reputation was in no way diminished by what he did.

Each of you must have heard tell many times of King Charles the Old, or King Charles the First, through whose magnificent campaign and the glorious victory he later achieved over King Manfred, the Ghibellines were driven out of Florence and the Guelfs allowed to return.° As a result, a knight named Messer Neri degli Uberti left the city, taking his entire household and a great deal of money with him, intent upon finding a refuge somewhere under the protection of King Charles.° Wishing to retire to a secluded spot where he could live out his life in peace, he went to Castellammare di Stabia, and there, perhaps a crossbow shot away from the other houses in the area, amid the olives and hazelnuts and chestnuts that abound in those parts, he purchased an estate on which he built a fine, comfortable mansion. Next to it he laid out a delightful garden, in the middle of which, there being a plentiful supply of fresh water, he constructed a beautiful, clear fishpond in our Florentine style, which he stocked in his own good time with an abundant supply of fish.°

While he went on dedicating himself every day to the task of making his garden more attractive, it just so happened that King Charles, in the heat of the summer, came to Castellammare for a bit of relaxation. Upon hearing how beautiful Messer Neri's garden was, he was quite eager to see it. Once he discovered who its owner was, however, he decided that since the knight belonged to the party opposed to his own, he would make his visit more informal. Consequently, he sent word to Messer Neri that on the following evening he and four of his companions desired to have a private supper with him in his garden.

Messer Neri was deeply appreciative of this gesture, and having made preparations for a magnificent feast and given instructions to his household about what was to be done, he received the King in his lovely garden as cordially as he possibly could. The King inspected the entire garden as well as Messer Neri's house, lavishing praise on everything he saw, after which he washed up and seated himself at one of the tables, which had been placed next to the fishpond. He ordered Count Guy de Monfort, one of his companions, to sit on one side of him, and Messer Neri on the other, and then he directed the other three who had come with him to wait upon them according to Messer Neri's instructions.° Exquisite dishes were then set before them, as were wines both costly and rare, all of which elicited great praise from the King, as did the service, which was fine and quite commendable, free from any noise or unpleasantness.

The King was happily eating his meal and enjoying the solitude of the place, when lo and behold, two young girls, both around fifteen years old, entered the garden. Their hair was a mass of ringlets that were as blond as spun gold and crowned with a dainty garland of periwinkle blossoms, and their features were so delicate and lovely that it made them seem more like angels than anything else. They were wearing gowns of sheer linen, that had close-fitting bodices and bell-shaped skirts stretching down to their feet, and that looked white as snow up against their skin. The girl in front had thrown a pair of fishnets over her shoulders, which she was holding on to with her left hand, while in her right she carried a long pole. The girl behind had a frying pan on her left shoulder, a bundle of sticks under her left arm, and a trivet in her left hand, while in the other, she held a flask of oil and a small lighted torch. The King was surprised by their appearance and waited in some suspense to see what it meant.

The girls came forward, chaste and modest in their bearing, and bowed before the King. Then they went over to the edge of the fishpond, where the one carrying the frying pan put it down along with the other things she had brought and took the pole from her companion, after which the two of them waded out into the water until it just came up to their breasts. One of Messer Neri's servants quickly lit a fire beside the pool, and pouring oil into the frying pan, he placed it on the trivet and waited for the girls to throw him some fish.

While the first girl poked around in places where she knew the fish were hiding, the other prepared her nets, and in no time at all, to the great delight of the King, who was watching them attentively, they had caught a large number of them. They threw some of their catch to the servant, who took them, still alive, and put them directly into the frying pan, after which the pair began picking out some of the finest specimens, as they had been instructed to do, and tossing them onto the table in front of the King, the Count, and their father.

The sight of the fish flopping about pleased the King no end, and he picked them up in his turn and politely tossed them back again to the girls. And in this fashion they went on playing for some time until the servant had finished cooking the ones that had been thrown to him. At Messer Neri's command the grilled fish were then placed before the King as an entremets or side dish rather than as a really fancy, delectable main course.

When the girls saw that the fish had been cooked and that there was no need for them to catch any more, they got out of the pond, their thin white garments clinging to their skin all over and revealing practically every last detail of their delicate bodies. After picking up the things they had brought with them, they walked shyly past the King and went back into the house.

The King, the Count, and the other gentlemen who were serving the meal had observed the young girls closely, and each one had secretly admired them for their beauty and shapeliness as well as for their charm and good manners. But they had made the deepest impression on the King, for when they had come out of the water, he had stared at their bodies up and down with such intensity that if someone had pricked him then, he would not have felt a thing.

The more the King's thoughts dwelt on the girls, without knowing who they were or how they had come to be there, the more he felt awakening in his heart the most fervent desire to please them, and because of this he knew full well that unless he was careful, he was going to fall in love with them. Nor could he decide which of the two he preferred, so closely did they resemble one another in every way. After brooding on this question for a while, however, he finally turned to Messer Neri and asked him who the two maidens were.

"My lord," replied Messer Neri, "these are my twin daughters, one of whom is called Ginevra the Fair and the other, Isotta the Blond."°

The King heaped praise on them and encouraged him to arrange marriages for them, to which Messer Neri replied apologetically that he no longer had the wherewithal to do so.

At that moment, when the supper was almost over and there was nothing left but the fruit course to bring to the table, the two girls returned. Wearing stunning gowns of fine silk, they carried two enormous silver trays piled high with every kind of fruit then in season. After the trays had been placed on the table before the King, the girls withdrew a short distance and started in on a song, which began with these words:

> O Love, the state that I have reached
> Could not be told in many, many words. . . .

They sang it so sweetly and pleasantly that to the King, who was watching and listening with delight, it seemed as if all the hierarchies of the angels had come down there to sing.° When they were finished, they knelt down and respectfully asked the King for permission to leave, and although he was sorry to see them go, he granted it, making a show of cheerfulness as he did so. Since supper was now over, the King and his companions mounted their horses, took their leave of Messer Neri, and returned to the royal residence, talking of various subjects as they rode along.

Still harboring his secret passion, the King was unable, even when important affairs of state supervened, to forget the beauty and charm of Ginevra the Fair, for whose sake he also loved the sister who resembled her. So entangled did he become in the snares of Love that he could scarcely think of anything else, and he invented various pretexts to cultivate a close relationship with Messer Neri and to visit him frequently in his lovely garden, all in order to catch a glimpse of Ginevra. Finally, unable to endure it any longer, he came to the conclusion that, for lack of any other alternative, he had to take not one, but both girls away from their father. He then revealed his love and his intention to Count Guy who, being the honorable man he was, said to him:

"My lord, I am utterly astonished by what you've told me, indeed, more astonished than someone else would be because I think I have a greater familiarity with your ways than any man alive, having known you intimately from your childhood up to the present day. I do not recall your ever having experienced such a passion in your youth, when it would have been easier for Love to have gotten its talons into you. To hear that you've actually fallen in love, now when you're on the verge of old age, seems so new and strange that it's nothing less than miraculous. And if the task of reprimanding you for it fell to me, I know exactly what I'd say to you, considering that you're still bearing arms in a realm you've just recently acquired, that you live among an alien people who are extremely wily and treacherous, and that you have been so completely preoccupied with the gravest concerns and the loftiest affairs of state that you have not yet been able simply to sit securely in the seat you occupy—and nevertheless, in the midst of all this, you've succumbed to the flattering allure of Love. This is not the behavior of a magnanimous king but of a weak-willed youth.

"What's far worse is that you say you've decided to abduct the two girls from the poor knight, who went beyond his means to honor you by entertaining you in his own home, indeed, who honored you even more by showing his daughters off to you practically naked, thereby demonstrating the great faith he has in you and how firmly he believes you to be a king and not a rapacious wolf. Have you forgotten so soon how the gates of this kingdom were opened to you because Manfred violated the women here? Has anyone ever committed an act of betrayal worthier of eternal punishment than this deed of yours would be: to deprive the man who honored you not only of his own honor, but of his hope and his consolation? What would people say of you if you did this?

"Perhaps you think it would be a sufficient excuse for you to say: 'I did it because he's a Ghibelline.' Now, is it consistent with a king's justice that those who turn to him for protection, whoever they may be, should receive this kind of treatment? Let me remind you, my King, that although you achieved the greatest glory in conquering Manfred and defeating Conradin, it is far more glorious to conquer oneself.° Therefore, since it is your task to rule over others, you must triumph over your feelings and curb this appetite of yours, lest such a blemish mar all the splendor of your achievements."°

These words pierced the King to the heart, affecting him all the more profoundly because he knew they were correct. And so, after breathing one or two fervent sighs, he said: "Count, it's certainly true that for the well-trained warrior, all other enemies, however powerful, are actually quite weak and easy to defeat in comparison with his own appetites. Nevertheless, even though I am going to suffer horribly, and even though the strength I will need is incalculable, your words have spurred me on to such an extent that before too many days have passed, I am determined to show you by my actions that just as I know how to conquer others, I am likewise capable of mastering myself."

Just a few days after this exchange, the King returned to Naples, both in order to deprive himself of any opportunity to behave dishonorably and in order to prepare a reward for the knight in recognition of the honorable entertainment he had been given. Even though it was hard for the King to allow someone else to possess what he ardently desired for himself, he nevertheless determined to arrange marriages for the two young girls, not as Messer Neri's daughters, but as his own. Thus, to Messer Neri's delight, after having provided magnificent dowries for the two of them, he gave Ginevra the Fair to Messer Maffeo da Palizzi and Isotta the Blond to Messer Guiglielmo della Magna, both of whom were noble knights and great lords.° After consigning the girls to their husbands, he departed, utterly grief stricken, for Apulia where, by dint of constant effort, he mortified his fierce appetite to such a degree and in such a way that the chains of Love were snapped apart and broken into bits, and for the rest of his life he was never enslaved by that passion again.

Perhaps some will say that it was a trifling matter for a king to arrange the marriages of two young girls, and I will grant their point. Still, if we consider that this was done by a king who was himself in love and who arranged to marry off the person he had fallen for without his ever having taken or plucked a single leaf, flower, or fruit from this love of his, then I would say that this was a very great feat, if not the greatest one of all.

So, that is how this magnanimous King behaved, generously rewarding the noble knight, laudably honoring the girls he loved, and using his strength to triumph over himself.

Story 7

UPON LEARNING THAT A YOUNG WOMAN NAMED LISA HAD
BECOME ILL BECAUSE OF HER FERVENT LOVE FOR HIM,
KING PETER GOES TO COMFORT HER, AFTER WHICH HE
WEDS HER TO A YOUNG NOBLEMAN, AND HAVING KISSED
HER ON THE BROW, FROM THEN ON ALWAYS CALLS
HIMSELF HER KNIGHT.°

When Fiammetta had come to the end of her story, and the manly magnanimity of King Charles had received lavish praise, except from one of the ladies who was a Ghibelline and did not wish to commend him, Pampinea, at the King's command, began speaking:

Distinguished ladies, no sensible person would disagree with what you have said about good King Charles, unless she had some other reason for speaking ill of him, but since his deed reminds me of another one, perhaps no less commendable, that was performed by an adversary of his for the sake of one of our Florentine girls, I would like to tell you about it.

At the time when the French were expelled from Sicily, there was a very rich apothecary from our city living in Palermo named Bernardo Puccini, whose wife had borne him only one child, an exceptionally beautiful daughter, who was then of marriageable age.° King Peter of Aragon, having become the ruler of the island, staged a spectacular celebration in Palermo with all of his noblemen, and it just so happened that while he was jousting in the Catalan fashion, Bernardo's daughter, whose name was Lisa, was viewing the activities from a window along with some other ladies.° Having caught sight of the King riding in the lists, she found him so wonderfully attractive that after watching him perform once or twice more, she fell passionately in love with him.

When the festivities had come to an end, and Lisa was back in her father's house, she could not think of anything except this magnificent, exalted love of hers, and what grieved her the most about it was the knowledge of her own inferior rank, which left her with hardly any hope that it was going to have a happy ending.

Although she could not bring herself to stop loving him, still, for fear of making matters even worse, she did not dare to reveal what she felt.

The King neither knew nor cared about what was going on, which made Lisa's suffering intolerable, worse than anything that can be imagined. And thus it happened that, as her love continued to grow within her, her melancholy was doubled by a yet greater melancholy until the beautiful young girl, incapable of bearing it any longer, became ill and started visibly wasting away day by day, just like snow in sunlight. Heartbroken because of these developments, her father and mother did what they could to help her, continually comforting her, bringing in doctors, and supplying her with various kinds of medicine. It was all to no avail, however, for the girl, despairing of her love, had reached the point where she no longer wanted to go on living.

Now, since the girl's father kept offering to do whatever she wanted, one day the thought occurred to her that if some suitable means could be found, she would like to have the King informed, before she died, about her love as well as her intention to end her life, and she therefore asked Bernardo to arrange for Minuccio d'Arezzo to come and see her.° Minuccio, who was considered a very fine singer and musician in those days, was a welcome guest at King Peter's court, and Bernardo, thinking that Lisa wanted to hear him sing and play for her, sent him an invitation to that effect. An obliging man, Minuccio promptly came to pay her a visit, and after cheering her up a little with words of affection, he played a number of dance tunes sweetly for her on his viol and then sang some songs, although they all only served to stir up the fire and flames of her love rather than providing her with the consolation he intended.°

When he had finished, the girl told him that she would like to have a few words with him in private, and once all the others had withdrawn, she said: "Minuccio, I've chosen you as the most trustworthy guardian of a secret of mine, hoping first that you'll never, ever reveal it to anyone except the person whose name I'm about to tell you, and second that you'll do everything in your power to help me. Indeed, I'm begging you to do this for me.

"What you need to know, my dear Minuccio, is that on the day when our lord King Peter staged the grand festival in honor of his accession, I happened to see him at a fateful moment while he was jousting, and such was the fiery passion he kindled in my heart that it's brought me to the state you see me in here. I know how inappropriate it is for me to love a king, but I've had no success in moderating, let alone expelling, my passion, and since continuing to bear it is sheer agony for me, I've chosen to die as the lesser evil—and that is precisely what I'm going to do.

"Still, the truth is that I'll be utterly inconsolable when I go if he hasn't learned about my love before then, and since I don't know of anyone better than you to inform him about what I intend to do, I wish to entrust you with this task, and I implore you not to refuse it. Then, when you've carried it out, you are to let me know, so that I may thus find release from these torments and die in peace."

Having said all this through her tears, she fell silent. Amazed as much by the loftiness of her spirit as by the fierce nature of her resolve, Minuccio was feeling a terrible sense of distress when, all of a sudden, a thought occurred to him as to how he might honorably be of service to her.

"Lisa," he said, "I pledge you my word, by which you may rest assured you will never be deceived, and as a token of my admiration for your lofty aspiration in having set your heart on so great a king, I shall indeed offer you my assistance. If you'll keep up your courage, my hope is to take such steps as I think will enable me, before three days have passed, to bring you news that will make you exceedingly happy. And to avoid losing time, I intend to go and get started at once."

Lisa promised him that she would take comfort from what he had said, and having repeated her requests all over again, she bade him farewell.

As soon as he left her, Minuccio went off to find a certain Mico

da Siena, an extremely talented writer of verse in those days, and
by dint of many earnest entreaties Minuccio prevailed upon him
to compose the following little song:°

> Bestir thyself, O Love, go to my Lord,
> And tell him of the pains that I endure;
> Tell him I'm close to death,
> Because I hide my longing out of fear.
>   I cry thee mercy, Love, with claspéd hands,
> That thou mayst go where'er my Lord doth dwell.
> Tell him how much I love and long for him,
> So sweetly is my heart enamoréd;
> How by the fire, which hath me all aflame,
> I fear I'll die, and yet I ardently
> Desire to leave behind the pain so fierce
> And fell, which I endure in fear and shame
> Through my desire for him:
> Oh! Let him know, for God's sake, of my woe.
>   Since first I fell in love with him, O Love,
> Thou didst not give me daring, but instead
> Didst make me fear to show him openly
> A single time how desperately I yearn
> For one who keepeth me in grievous pain.
> If thus I die, such death is hard to bear!
> Perhaps he would not be displeased to know
> About the dreadful anguish that I feel—
> If only I'd been giv'n
> The courage to reveal my state to him.
>   Yet since it hath not been thy pleasure, Love,
> To grant such bold self-confidence to me
> As to lay bare my heart unto my Lord
> Through messages, alas, or through my looks,
> I beg thee, sweet my master, of thy grace,
> To go to him and make him call to mind
> The day I saw him bearing lance and shield
> In tourney with the other cavaliers:

On him I fixed my gaze,
So smitten that my heart now perisheth.

Minuccio immediately set these words to music, providing as
sweet and sorrowful a melody as the material required, and on the
third day, he went to the court where King Peter, who was in the
midst of his dinner, asked him to sing something to the accompaniment of his viol. He therefore began singing this song, playing it
so sweetly that every single person present in the royal hall seemed
entranced by it, the King perhaps more than the others, so quiet
and absorbed were they all as they paused to listen to it. When
Minuccio finished his song, the King inquired as to where it had
come from, for he could not recall ever having heard it before.

"My lord," said Minuccio, "the words and the music were
composed less than three days ago." And when the King asked
for whom, Minuccio replied, "I dare not reveal that to anyone
but you."

The King was eager to hear the secret, and as soon as the tables
were cleared away, he took Minuccio with him to his chamber,
where the poet recounted everything he had been told, down to
the last detail. The King was overjoyed by the story, and lavishing
great praise on the girl, he declared that such a worthy young lady
deserved to be treated with compassion. Consequently, he told
Minuccio to go to her on his behalf, to comfort her, and to tell her
that he himself would, without fail, come to visit her that very
same day a little before vespers.

Delighted to be the bearer of such happy news, Minuccio went
directly to the girl, taking his viol along with him, and once he
was alone with her, he told her the entire story, after which he sang
her the song, accompanying himself on his instrument. The girl
felt so happy and contented because of all this that she immediately, visibly, started to show marked signs of improved health,
and without anyone else in the house knowing, or even suspecting, what was going on, she began eagerly waiting for vespers
when she would get to see her lord.

A kind and generous ruler, the King devoted a great deal of

thought to what Minuccio had told him, and recalling the girl and her beauty quite well, he felt even more pity for her than before. Around the hour of vespers, he got on his horse, and pretending he was going out for a jaunt, he rode to the place where the apothecary's house stood. Bernardo had a very fine garden there, and the King, having requested that it be opened for him, went inside and dismounted. After talking with Bernardo awhile, he asked him how his daughter was doing and if he had as yet given her to anyone in marriage.

"My lord," replied Bernardo, "she's not married. As a matter of fact, she's been very sick, and she still is, although the truth is that from nones on she has miraculously improved."

The King immediately understood what this improvement meant and said: "In truth, it would be a shame if the world were to be deprived so soon of such a beautiful creature. Let us go and pay her a visit."

A little while later, accompanied by just two of his retainers, the King went with Bernardo to Lisa's chamber, and once inside, walked right over to the bed, where the girl, sitting up a bit, was waiting for him with eager anticipation.

"What is the meaning of this, my lady?" said the King, taking her by the hand. "You're young and should be comforting other women rather than allowing yourself to become ill. We would ask you to be so kind as to cheer up, for our sake, so that you may make a speedy recovery."

When she felt herself being touched by the hands of the man whom she loved above all else, the girl may have been a little embarrassed, but in her heart she experienced such pleasure that she thought she was in Paradise.

"My lord," she said, doing her best to compose an answer, "my infirmity was caused by my attempt to bear a burden that was far too heavy for my feeble strength, but you'll soon see that I'll be free of it, thanks to your gracious assistance."

Only the King grasped the hidden meaning of the girl's words, and as she thus rose still higher in his esteem, he inwardly cursed Fortune more than once for having made her the daughter of such a man as Bernardo. He stayed there with her for a while longer, comforting her even more, and finally took his leave.

The King's humane gesture was accorded the highest praise, being regarded as a singular honor for the apothecary and his daughter, who was as contented with her lover as any woman has ever been. Within a few days, aided by the revival of her hopes, she not only recovered her health, but became more beautiful than ever.

Now that she was well again, the King, having taken counsel with the Queen about the reward he would bestow on the girl for so grand a passion, mounted his horse one day and rode to the apothecary's house, accompanied by a large group of his lords. Having entered the garden, he sent for the apothecary and his daughter. In the meantime, the Queen arrived with many of her ladies-in-waiting, all of whom received the girl in their midst with such festive cheer that it was a wonder to behold. At length, the King, with the Queen at his side, summoned Lisa to him and said:

"Worthy young lady, the great love you have borne for us has led us to grant you a great honor, with which, for our sake, we trust you will be content. And the honor is this, that since you are as yet unmarried, it is our wish that you should accept as your husband the man we will bestow on you, it being nevertheless our intention always to style ourself your knight, without requiring from you, out of all that love of yours, anything more than a single kiss."

The girl was so embarrassed that her entire face turned scarlet, and in a low voice, adopting the King's pleasure as her own, she replied: "My lord, I'm quite certain that if people knew I'd fallen in love with you, most of them would consider me mad, for they'd think I'd taken leave of my senses and didn't recognize the difference between your rank and my own. But God, who alone sees inside the hearts of mortals, knows that from the hour I was first attracted to you, I knew full well that you were a king, that I was the daughter of Bernardo the apothecary, and that it did not become me to direct my soul's ardent affection toward such lofty heights. But you know far better than I do that when people here below fall in love, they are not making a considered choice but are guided by appetite and sensual attraction. I repeatedly fought against this law with all my might until, no longer able to resist, I fell in love with you—and I continue to love you now and will do so forever.

"The truth is that as soon as I felt myself overcome by my affection for you, I resolved to make your will my own, and for that reason, not only shall I gladly accept and treasure any man it pleases you to bestow on me as my husband, who will bring me honor and dignity, but if you ordered me to walk through fire, I would be happy to do so if I thought it would give you pleasure. With regard to having you, a king, as my knight, you know how appropriate such a thing would be for a person of my condition, and so, on that score I will say nothing more, nor will I grant you the single kiss you request of my love without the permission of my lady, the Queen. Nevertheless, for the great kindness that you and my lady, the Queen, who has accompanied you here, have shown me, may God give you thanks and may He recompense you on my behalf, since I myself have nothing with which to repay you."

At this point she stopped talking, but her answer, which the Queen found very satisfying, convinced her that the girl was every bit as wise as the King had said. King Peter then summoned Lisa's father and mother, and once he knew that they approved of what he was planning to do, he sent for a young man named Perdicone, who was of gentle birth, though poor, placed some rings in his hand, and had him marry the girl, something he was by no means unwilling to do. Then, in addition to the many precious jewels that the King and Queen bestowed on Lisa, the King gave Perdicone Cefalù and Calatabellotta, two excellent, very lucrative fiefs.°

"These we give you as a dowry for your wife," declared the King. "What we have in store for you yourself, that you shall see in the time to come."

Then King Peter turned to the girl and said, "Now we wish to gather the fruit of your love that is our due." And taking her head between his hands, he kissed her on the brow.

Perdicone, along with Lisa's father and mother, and Lisa herself were all quite delighted, and they celebrated the happy marriage with an enormous feast. Furthermore, as many people affirm, the King was most faithful in honoring the compact he had made with the girl, always styling himself her knight for the rest of his life, and whenever he engaged in feats of arms, he never bore any favor other than the one she sent him.

It is by deeds such as these that one captures the hearts of one's subjects, provides occasions for others to do good, and acquires eternal fame. But nowadays, this is a target at which few, if any, rulers have bent the bow of their minds, most of them having become pitiless tyrants.

Story 9

DISGUISED AS A MERCHANT, SALADIN IS HONORABLY
ENTERTAINED BY MESSER TORELLO, WHO, WHEN A CRUSADE
IS LAUNCHED, ESTABLISHES A TIME PERIOD FOR HIS WIFE
TO WAIT BEFORE SHE REMARRIES. HE IS TAKEN PRISONER,
BUT BECAUSE OF HIS SKILL IN TRAINING FALCONS, HE
COMES TO THE ATTENTION OF THE SULTAN, WHO
RECOGNIZES HIM, REVEALS HIMSELF IN TURN, AND
ENTERTAINS HIM LAVISHLY. HAVING FALLEN ILL, MESSER
TORELLO IS TRANSPORTED BY MAGIC IN A SINGLE NIGHT TO
PAVIA, WHERE HIS WIFE'S SECOND MARRIAGE IS ABOUT TO
BE CELEBRATED. SHE RECOGNIZES HIM, AND HE THEN
RETURNS WITH HER TO HIS HOUSE.°

* * *

Pretty ladies, not only is what Filomena says about friendship undoubtedly true, but she was right to complain in her final comments about how little regard people have for it nowadays. If we had come here to correct the errors of the world, or even to criticize them, I would follow up on what she said with a substantial discourse of my own. But since our purpose is different, it occurs to

me to tell you a story, long perhaps but enjoyable from start to finish, that concerns one of the generous deeds performed by Saladin.° Thus, even though our defects may prevent us from winning
the deepest sort of friendship with another person, by imitating
the things you will hear about in my tale, we may at least derive a
certain delight from being courteous to others and hope that
sooner or later we will receive our reward for doing so.

Let me begin by saying, then, that during the reign of Emperor
Frederick I, according to a number of accounts, the Christians
launched a great Crusade to recover the Holy Land. Saladin, a most
worthy lord who was then the Sultan of Babylon, having heard
about what was happening some time in advance, decided to go in
person and see what preparations the Christian leaders were making so that he would be better prepared to protect himself from
them.° Consequently, having settled all his affairs in Egypt, he
pretended he was going on a pilgrimage and set out disguised as a
merchant, taking with him only three servants and two of his wisest senior counselors.° After they had inspected many Christian
kingdoms, one evening close to vespers, as they were riding
through Lombardy on their way to cross the mountains, they happened to come upon a gentleman on the road between Milan and
Pavia. He was named Messer Torello di Stra da Pavia, and he was
going, together with his servants, his dogs, and his falcons, to stay
at a beautiful estate he owned on the banks of the Ticino.°

As soon as Messer Torello caught sight of them, he concluded
that they were foreigners of gentle birth and was eager to offer
them some sort of honorable entertainment. So, when Saladin
asked one of Messer Torello's servants how much farther it was to
Pavia and whether they could still reach it in time to enter the city,
Messer Torello prevented the man from saying a word by replying
himself: "Gentlemen, by the time you reach Pavia, it'll be too late
for you to get in."

"Then," said Saladin, "since we're strangers here, would you be
so kind as to tell us where we can find the best lodging."

"I'll do so gladly," said Messer Torello. "I was thinking just now
that I would send one of these servants of mine on an errand to a

spot not too far from Pavia. I'll have him go with you, and he'll take you to a place where you'll find quite suitable accommodations."

Messer Torello then went up to the most discreet of his servants, told him what to do, and sent him off with Saladin's party. Meanwhile, he himself quickly rode on to his estate where he arranged for the best possible supper to be prepared and for tables to be set up in one of his gardens, after which he went to wait for his guests at the entrance. The servant, conversing with the gentlemen about various subjects, took them on a roundabout route, leading them along various byroads, until he had brought them, without their suspecting it, to his master's estate. As soon as Messer Torello saw them, he went out on foot to meet them and said with a laugh: "Gentlemen, you are very welcome here, indeed."

An extremely astute man, Saladin realized that the knight had not invited them there when they first met, for fear they would have turned him down, and that he had cleverly arranged to have them brought to his house so they could not refuse to spend the evening with him. Thus, after returning Messer Torello's greeting, he said: "Sir, were it possible to lodge a complaint against courteous people, we would lodge one against you, for even leaving aside the fact that you have taken us somewhat out of our way, you have more or less constrained us to accept this noble courtesy of yours when the only thing we did to deserve your goodwill was to exchange a single greeting with you."

"Gentlemen," replied the knight, who was both wise and well-spoken, "if I may judge from your appearance, the courtesy you are going to receive from me is a poor thing in comparison with what you deserve. Truth to tell, however, you could not have found decent lodging outside of Pavia, and that's why I hope you won't be upset to have gone somewhat out of your way in exchange for a little less discomfort here."

While he was speaking, his servants gathered around Saladin's party, and as soon as they had dismounted, took charge of the horses. Messer Torello then led the three gentlemen to the rooms that had been prepared for them. There, after they had been helped off with their boots, he offered them some deliciously cool wine as a refreshment and detained them with pleasant conversation until such time as they might go to supper.

Since Saladin and his companions and servants all knew Italian, they had no difficulty understanding Messer Torello or making themselves understood, and they were all of the opinion that this knight was the most agreeable and well-mannered gentleman and a better conversationalist than anyone they had ever encountered. For his part, Messer Torello concluded that they were all quite eminent men, much more distinguished than he had originally thought, and he regretted deeply that he could not entertain them in company that evening or offer them a more elaborate banquet. He therefore resolved to make amends the next morning, and having told one of his servants what he wanted him to do, he sent the man off to Pavia, which never locked its gates and was not that far away, bearing a message for his wife, a woman of great intelligence and exceptional spirit. This done, he led his guests into the garden and politely asked them who they were, where they had come from, and what their destination was.

"We are Cypriot merchants," replied Saladin. "We've just arrived from our country, and now we're heading to Paris on business."

"Would to God," said Messer Torello, "that this country of ours bred gentlemen comparable to the merchants I see coming from Cyprus."

On these and other matters they chatted for a while until it was time for supper. Messer Torello then asked them if they would do him the honor of being seated at his table, and although it was an impromptu meal, the food was quite good and the service, excellent. Nor had the tables long been cleared away before Messer Torello, seeing how tired his guests were, showed them to the very comfortable beds that had been prepared for them to sleep in, following which, a little while later, he too retired for the night.

Meanwhile, the servant sent to Pavia delivered his message to Messer Torello's wife, who, in a spirit more like a queen's than an ordinary woman's, promptly summoned a large number of his friends and servants, and had all the preparations for a magnificent banquet set in motion. She had invitations delivered by torchlight to many of the most important nobles in the city, saw to it that a supply of fine clothes and silks and furs was at the ready, and took care of everything else, down to the last detail, that her husband had asked her to do.

The next day, after the gentlemen had risen, Messer Torello set out on horseback with them, and having called for his falcons, he led the group to a nearby stretch of shallow water where he showed off how his birds could fly. Then, when Saladin asked if there was someone who could escort them to Pavia and direct them to the best inn in the city, Messer Torello replied, "I'll do it myself, because I'm obliged to go there anyway." They took him at his word and happily set off down the road together, reaching the city just after tierce. Thinking they were being escorted to the finest inn available, they arrived, instead, at Messer Torello's mansion where they found a good fifty of the leading citizens of Pavia who had assembled to receive them and who immediately gathered around them in order to hold their reins and stirrups for them.

When Saladin and his companions saw this, they realized only too well what it all meant. "Messer Torello," they said, "this isn't what we asked you to do for us. You treated us so very well last night, much better than we deserve, which is why it would have been quite proper for you to have just let us go on our way."

"Gentlemen," replied Messer Torello, "with regard to the service that was done for you last night, I am more indebted to Fortune than to you, for it was she who overtook you on the road at an hour when you had no choice but to come to my humble abode. However, with regard to the service that will be done for you this morning, I will be beholden only to you, as will all these gentlemen you see here about you, although if you think it courteous to decline an invitation to dine with them, then you are certainly at liberty to do so."

Acknowledging defeat, Saladin and his companions dismounted and were welcomed by the gentlemen who happily led them to a richly furnished set of rooms that had been prepared for them. After they had removed their traveling clothes and taken a little refreshment, they made their way to the great hall, where every-thing was magnificently arranged. Having washed their hands, they were seated at the table with great pomp and circumstance and were served so many courses in such splendid style that if the Emperor himself had been present, it would have been impossible to honor him more highly. In fact, even though Saladin and his companions were great lords and were accustomed to the grandest displays of opulence, they were nevertheless overcome with wonder at their treatment here, which, considering the position of the knight, whom they knew to be no ruler, but just a private citizen, seemed to them about as fine as anything they had ever experienced.

Once the meal was over and the tables cleared away, they discussed serious affairs for a while until, at Messer Torello's suggestion, the weather being quite hot, the gentlemen from Pavia all went off to take a nap, leaving him alone with his three guests. To make sure they got to see all of his most precious possessions, he escorted them into another room and sent for his good lady. A tall, strikingly beautiful woman, she presented herself before them, decked out in her rich garments and flanked by her two little children, who looked like a pair of angels, and welcomed them cordially to her home. The moment the three men saw her, they rose to their feet, gave her a most respectful greeting in return, and invited her to sit down with them, all the while making a great fuss over her beautiful little children. After starting a pleasant conversation with them, during which Messer Torello left the room for a while, she graciously asked them where they were from and where they were going, to which they gave her the same answer they had given her husband.

"Then I see that my woman's intuition may well be useful," said the lady, with a smile, "for I want to ask you a special favor, namely that you will neither refuse nor look down on the little trifling gift I'm going to have them bring for you. Instead, you should bear in mind that women, with their tiny hearts, give tiny presents, and consequently, you should judge what you are going to get more by the good intentions of the giver than the size of the gift."

She then sent for two pairs of robes for each of the guests, one lined with silk and the other with fur—all of them more suitable for lords than for private citizens or merchants—as well as three doublets of taffeta and a number of undergarments.

"Take these robes," she said. "They're just like the ones I've always dressed my husband in. As far as the other things are concerned, although they're of no great value, you may find they'll come in handy, considering how far away you are from your wives, not to mention the fact that you've come a long way and still have a long way to go, and I know how you merchants always like to be neat and trim."

The gentlemen were astonished, for it had become abundantly clear that Messer Torello was intent upon showing them every conceivable courtesy. Considering how magnificent the robes were and how unlike the ones any merchant would wear, they were afraid that he had recognized who they really were, but one of them nevertheless replied to his wife: "My lady, these things are exquisite and should not be accepted lightly, but we feel compelled to do so because of your prayers, to which we cannot say no."

Thus they took her gifts, and since Messer Torello had now returned, the lady, having said good-bye to them, left the room and went away to see that their servants were supplied with similar gifts according to their rank. In response to Messer Torello's repeated entreaties, the gentlemen agreed to spend the entire day with him, and after they had slept for a while, they got dressed in their robes and rode through the city with him until it was time for supper, at which point they sat down to a magnificent feast in the company of many noble guests.

In due course they went to bed, and when they arose at daybreak, they discovered that they now had three fine, sturdy palfreys in place of their tired old nags and that their servants had likewise been provided with fresh, strong horses. Upon seeing all this, Saladin turned to his companions and said: "I swear to God there's never been a more perfect gentleman than this, or one who is more courteous and considerate. If the kings of Christendom are as good at being kings as this man is at being a knight, the

Sultan of Babylon will be unable to resist even one of them, let alone all those we've seen preparing to descend on him." Knowing there was no way for them to refuse Messer Torello's gifts, they thanked him most politely and mounted their horses.

Messer Torello, together with many of his companions, escorted them quite some distance down the road leading out of the city. Finally, even though it weighed heavily on Saladin that he had to part company from his host, to whom he had formed a deep attachment, he felt he could not delay his departure any longer and begged him to turn back. Messer Torello, who found it just as hard to part from his guests, said:

"Since you want me to go, gentlemen, that's what I'll do. But there's one thing I must tell you: I don't know who you are, nor do I wish to know more than you care to reveal, but whoever you may be, you cannot make me believe you are merchants. Now, that said, I bid you Godspeed."

Saladin, who had already taken leave of Messer Torello's companions, turned to face him. "Sir," he said, "we may yet have the chance to show you some of our merchandise and make a believer out of you. In the meantime, may God be with you."

Saladin then rode off with his companions, utterly determined that, if he managed to survive the war he was facing and avoid defeat, he would show Messer Torello no less hospitality than Messer Torello had shown him. As they went on, he talked to his companions about the gentleman and his wife and about all his gifts and favors and acts of kindness, praising them ever more highly each time he returned to the subject. But finally, when he had with no little labor surveyed all of the West, he put to sea and returned with his companions to Alexandria, where, now that he had all the information he needed, he prepared his defenses. As for Messer Torello, he went back to Pavia, and although he pondered at length who the three men might be, he never arrived at the truth or even came anywhere near it.

When the time came for the Crusade to begin and great preparations for it were under way everywhere, Messer Torello, despite the tears and entreaties of his wife, was fully determined to go. He therefore got everything ready, and just as he was about to ride off on his horse, he said to his wife, whom he loved deeply: "As you can see, my lady, I'm joining this Crusade, both for the sake of my personal honor and for the salvation of my soul. I'm placing our good name and our possessions in your care. And since I feel less assurance about my return than about my departure, considering the thousand accidents that can occur, I would ask this favor of you: no matter what happens to me, even if you don't have any trustworthy news that I'm still alive, I nevertheless want you to wait for a year and a month and a day before you get married again, starting from this, the day of my departure."

"Messer Torello," replied the lady, who was weeping bitterly, "I don't know how I'm going to bear the sorrow you'll be leaving me in after you're gone, but if I'm strong enough to survive it, and if anything should happen to you, you may live and die in the certain knowledge that for the rest of my days, I shall remain wedded to Messer Torello and his memory."

"My lady," said Messer Torello, "I feel confident that you'll do everything in your power to keep your promise, but you're a beautiful young woman who comes from an important family, and everyone knows what a wonderful person you are. Consequently, I haven't the slightest doubt that if there's the least suspicion of my death, many fine gentlemen will come asking your brothers and kinsmen for your hand, and that no matter how much you try to resist, they'll subject you to so much pressure that you'll eventually be forced to comply with their wishes. And that's the reason why I'm not asking you to wait any longer than the time limit I've set for you."

"I'll do whatever I can to keep my promise," said the lady, "and even if I'm forced to act otherwise, I'll certainly follow those instructions you've given me. But I pray to God that neither you nor I ever have to deal with such extremities."

When she finished speaking, the lady wept and embraced Messer Torello. She then removed a ring from her finger and gave it to him, saying: "If I should happen to die before I see you again, remember me whenever you look at it."

Messer Torello took the ring, and having mounted his horse, he said farewell to everyone and went on his way. Upon reaching Genoa with his company, he boarded a galley and set sail, arriving at Acre in short order, where he met up with the rest of the Christian forces.° Almost immediately, however, a deadly epidemic broke out that overwhelmed the army, in the course of which, whether because of his skill or his good fortune, Saladin had no difficulty in capturing almost all the Christians who survived, and whom he divided up and sent away to be incarcerated in various cities. Among those taken was Messer Torello, who was led off to prison in Alexandria. No one recognized him there, and being afraid to reveal his true identity, he had no choice but to apply himself to the training of hawks. Since he was a past master of this art, his abilities soon brought him to the notice of Saladin, who had him released from prison and appointed him his falconer.

Neither man recognized the other, and Messer Torello, whom Saladin referred to simply as "the Christian," thought of nothing except Pavia and tried many times to escape, but always without success. Consequently, when a group of emissaries from Genoa, who had come to Saladin to ransom certain fellow citizens of theirs, were about to depart, Messer Torello decided he would write to his wife, letting her know that he was alive and would return to her as soon as possible, and asking her to wait for him. When he finished the letter, he earnestly begged one of the emissaries, whom he knew, to see that it got into the hands of his uncle, who was the Abbot of San Pietro in Ciel d'Oro.°

This, then, is how things stood with Messer Torello until one morning, as Saladin was speaking with him about his birds, he just so happened to smile, moving his mouth in a way that the Sultan had noted in particular when he was staying at Messer Torello's house in Pavia. It put Saladin in mind of his former host, and after staring intently at him for a while, he felt pretty sure he knew who it was. He thus dropped the subject they had been discussing, and said: "Tell me, Christian, what country do you come from in the West?"

"My lord," answered Messer Torello, "I'm a poor man of humble condition, and I come from a city in Lombardy called Pavia."

When Saladin heard this, he was now almost completely certain that what he suspected was correct, and he happily said to himself, "God has given me a chance to show this man how much I appreciated his hospitality." He did not say another word on the subject, however, but had them put all of his robes on display in another room, and took Messer Torello there to see them.

"Have a look at these clothes, Christian," he said, "and tell me whether you've ever come across any of them before?"

Messer Torello began inspecting them, and albeit he spotted the garments his wife had given to Saladin, it was inconceivable to him that they could possibly be the same ones. Nevertheless, he replied: "My lord, I don't recognize any of them, although it's certainly true that these two look like robes I once wore myself, as did three merchants who happened to come to my house."

Saladin could no longer restrain himself and embraced Messer Torello tenderly. "You are Messer Torello di Stra," he said, "and I am one of the three merchants to whom your wife gave these robes. And the time has now come for me to show you exactly what kind of merchandise I have, something I said, when I left you, might well happen one day."

Upon hearing this, Messer Torello felt both overjoyed and ashamed, overjoyed to have had such a distinguished guest, and ashamed because he thought he had entertained him poorly. But then Saladin went on: "Messer Torello, since God has sent you to me, from now on you should consider yourself, and not me, the master here."

After much mutual rejoicing at their reunion, Saladin had him dressed in regal robes, and having presented him to a gathering of his greatest lords, and spoken at length in praise of him as a most worthy gentleman, he ordered all those who valued his favor to honor Messer Torello's person as they did his own. And from then on, that is what everyone did, and especially the two lords who had accompanied Saladin when he stayed at Messer Torello's house.

For a while Messer Torello's sudden elevation to the heights of glory took his mind off his affairs in Lombardy, all the more so because he had no doubt that his letters had reached his uncle.

On the day that the crusaders had been captured by Saladin, however, there was a Provençal knight of little account named Messer Torello di Dignes who had died and been buried on the battlefield, or rather in the Christian camp itself, and since Messer Torello di Stra was well known for his nobility throughout the army, whenever anyone heard people saying "Messer Torello is dead," it was assumed they were referring to Messer Torello di Stra and not the man from Dignes.° Before those who had been deceived had a chance to be undeceived, however, Messer Torello was taken prisoner, and as a result, many Italians returned home bearing the news of his death with them, including some who were so presumptuous that they did not hesitate to say they had seen his corpse and been present at the burial. When the story finally reached his wife and family, it was the cause of the most intense, inexpressible sorrow not just for them, but for everyone who had known him.

It would take a long time, indeed, to describe the nature and the depth of the lady's grief, the sadness and the woe she experienced. After she had mourned for several months straight in utter misery, however, her sorrow showed signs of abating, and since many of the most influential men in Lombardy were seeking her hand, her brothers and the rest of her relatives began urging her to get married. Although she repeatedly refused to do so, always amid floods of tears, her resistance was overcome in the end, and she agreed to give them what they wanted, but only on the condition that she could refrain from taking a husband until the period of time she had promised to wait for Messer Torello was up.

This, then, was how things stood with the lady in Pavia when, about a week or so before the date when she was supposed to be married, Messer Torello happened to catch sight one day in Alexandria of a man he had seen embarking with the Genoese emissaries on the galley that was taking them home. He therefore sent for him and asked him how their trip had been and when it was that they had reached Genoa.

"My lord," the man replied, "I was left behind in Crete, where I later learned that the galley had had a disastrous voyage. As it was approaching Sicily, a furious northerly gale arose, driving it onto the Barbary reefs, so that no one managed to escape, including two of my brothers who perished along with the rest."

Messer Torello had no reason to doubt the man's account, which was only too true, and when he realized that there were just a few days left until the end of the time period he had asked his wife to wait and that nothing was known in Pavia about his present situation, he was absolutely convinced that she was going to be getting married again. So deep was the despair into which he fell that he lost his appetite, lay down on his bed, and resolved to die.

As soon as Saladin, who loved Messer Torello with great tenderness, heard what had happened, he came to see him. Having discovered, after earnest and repeated entreaties, the reason for his grief and his sickness, he scolded him severely for not having told him about it before. Then, however, the Sultan begged him to take heart, assuring Messer Torello that if he did so, he would arrange for him to be in Pavia on the date prescribed. Saladin then went on to explain how this would be done.

Messer Torello took him at his word, and since he had often heard that such things were possible and had actually happened on numerous occasions, he began to feel more optimistic and urged Saladin to take care of it at once. The Sultan therefore ordered one of his necromancers, a man whose skill he had already tested, to find a way to transport Messer Torello on a bed to Pavia in a single night. The magician replied that it would be done, but that for Messer Torello's own good, he would first put him to sleep.°

When all this was arranged, Saladin returned to Messer Torello, whom he still found fully determined either to be back in Pavia by the date prescribed, if it were possible, or to die, if it were not. "Messer Torello," he said, "God knows I can't blame you in the least for loving your wife so passionately and being so fearful of losing her to another. For I believe that of all the women I've ever seen, she's the one whose way of life, whose manners, and whose demeanor—to say nothing of her beauty, which will fade like a flower—seem to me most precious and commendable. Since

Fortune has brought you here to me, I should have liked nothing better than for the two of us to have spent the rest of our lives together, ruling as equals over this realm of mine. God has not granted me this wish, however, and now that you've made up your mind to die unless you can return to Pavia by the appointed date, I really would have preferred to have known about all this in time for me to have sent you home with all the honor and pomp, as well as the splendid escort, your virtues deserve. But since even this has not been granted to me, and you, moreover, are set upon going there at once, I will do what I can to get you to Pavia in the manner I've described to you."

"My lord," replied Messer Torello, "apart from your words, your actions have given me sufficient proof of your goodwill toward me, which is far, far above anything I've merited, so that even if you'd said nothing, I should have lived and died utterly convinced that what you say is true. But seeing as how my mind's made up, I beg you to act quickly and do what you promised me, because tomorrow is the last day she's still going to be waiting for me."

Saladin assured him that everything had been taken care of, and the next day, it being his intention to send Messer Torello off that same night, he had a very beautiful, luxurious bed set up in one of his great halls. Its mattresses were all covered in the Eastern fashion with velvet and cloth of gold, and on top of them there lay a quilt embroidered with enormous pearls and the rarest of precious stones arranged in oval patterns—the quilt was later considered a priceless treasure in these parts—as well as two pillows selected to match the bedding. When this was ready, he ordered them to dress Messer Torello, who had by now recovered his strength, in a robe of the Saracen fashion, the richest and most beautiful thing anyone had ever seen, while they took one of his longest turbans and wrapped it around his head in their usual style.

It was already late when Saladin, with many of his lords in attendance, went to Messer Torello's room and sat down beside him. "Messer Torello," he began, practically in tears, "the hour is approaching for you to be separated from me, and since I cannot accompany you myself or send anyone with you, because the nature of the journey you have to make won't permit it, I must take my leave of you here in this room to which I've come for that purpose. But before I bid you Godspeed, I beg you, in the name of the love and friendship that exists between us, not to forget me, and if it's possible, before our days have ended, to come and see me at least one more time after you've taken care of your affairs in Lombardy. For not only will I rejoice to see you again, but I'll be able to compensate then for the delight I must now forego because of your hasty departure. Until such time as that should occur, I hope it won't be a burden for you to visit me by means of your letters and to ask me for whatever you please, because there is certainly no man alive I would serve more gladly than you."

Unable to hold back his own tears, Messer Torello only managed to utter a few words, declaring that it would be impossible for him ever to forget Saladin's kind deeds and noble spirit and that he would, without fail, do what Saladin requested if he were given the opportunity. Saladin embraced him and kissed him tenderly. Then, weeping copiously, he said "Godspeed" and left the room, after which the other lords all took their leave of him and accompanied Saladin into the hall where the bed had been set up.

It was getting late, and since the magician was anxious to send him quickly on his way, a doctor arrived with a potion that he got Messer Torello to drink, persuading him that it would enable him to keep up his strength. Soon afterward he fell asleep, and as he slept, he was carried at Saladin's command and laid upon the beautiful bed where the Sultan placed a large, exquisite, and extremely valuable crown, which he marked in such a way that later on everyone saw clearly that it was a present from him to Messer Torello's wife. Then, onto Messer Torello's finger he slipped a ring containing a ruby that gleamed like a lighted torch and whose value could scarcely be assessed. Next, he had him girded with a sword so richly ornamented that its value, too, would be difficult to determine, and in addition, he had them fasten a brooch on his chest that was studded both with pearls, the like of which had never been seen, and with many other precious stones. Finally, Saladin had them fill two enormous golden bowls with doubloons and set them on either side of him, while all around him were strewn numerous strings of pearls, plus rings and belts and other things that would take too long to describe. When they were done, he kissed Messer Torello one more time, and he had hardly finished telling the magician to hurry up when the bed and Messer Torello were suddenly whisked away right before his eyes, leaving Saladin behind still talking with his lords about his departed friend.

As he requested, Messer Torello was set down in the Church of San Pietro in Ciel d'Oro in Pavia, with all the jewels and finery that have been mentioned, and he was still fast asleep when the hour of matins was rung and the sacristan entered the church with a light in his hand. He immediately caught sight of the opulent bed, and after his initial amazement, he was so terrified that he turned on his heels and fled back the way he had come. The Abbot and the other monks were equally amazed to see him running away, and they asked him for an explanation, which he then produced.

"Come on," said the Abbot, "you're not a child anymore, and you're hardly a newcomer to this church, either, so you shouldn't get frightened so easily. Let's all go now and see what gave you such a scare."

After lighting a number of lanterns, the Abbot entered the church with his monks, where they saw this amazing, luxurious bed on which the knight lay sleeping. Then, as they were casting a wary and timorous eye over all the princely jewels, while staying far away from the bed, the effect of the potion just happened to wear off, Messer Torello woke up, and a great sigh escaped his lips. Upon seeing this, the monks were terrified, as was the Abbot, and they all ran away screaming "Lord, help us!"

When he opened his eyes and looked about him, Messer Torello discovered, to his immense satisfaction, that he was in the very place where he had asked to be taken. Although he had been aware of Saladin's generosity in the past, after he sat up and observed, one by one, the treasures around him, he was all the more conscious of it and judged it now to be even greater than he had thought it was before. He could hear the monks running away, however, and divining the reason why, he did not make another move, but began calling the Abbot by name, telling him not to be afraid, as it was only Torello, his nephew.

Hearing these words, the Abbot became even more frightened, because for many months he had thought that Messer Torello was dead. But after a while, reassuring himself with rational arguments, as he continued to hear his name being called, he made the sign of the cross and went up to him.

"O my father," said Messer Torello, "what are you afraid of? I'm alive, by the grace of God, and I've come back here from across the sea."

Although Messer Torello had a full beard and was dressed in Arab clothing, after a little while the Abbot managed to recognize him. Now, feeling thoroughly reassured, he took him by the hand and said, "Welcome home, my son."

"Our fear shouldn't surprise you," he continued, "because there's no one in this city who isn't firmly convinced that you're dead. What's more, I can tell you that your wife, Madonna Adalieta, has been overcome by the threats and the pleading of her relatives, and has been forced to remarry against her will.° In fact, this is the very morning when she's to go to her new husband, and they've made all the necessary preparations there for the nuptials and the wedding feast."

Messer Torello got up off the luxurious bed, and after warmly embracing the Abbot and the monks, he begged them, each and every one, to say nothing about his return to anybody until he had taken care of some business of his. Next, having put all of the rich jewels in a safe place, he gave the Abbot an account of everything that had happened to him up to then. Delighted by his good fortune, the Abbot joined him in giving thanks to God. When they were done, Messer Torello asked him for the name of his wife's new husband, and the Abbot told him what it was.

"Before anyone learns of my return," said Messer Torello, "I intend to see how my wife conducts herself at these nuptials. And so, even though it's not customary for the religious to attend such festivities, I'd ask you, for my sake, to make arrangements for the two of us to go there."

The Abbot said he would be happy to oblige him, and right after daybreak, he sent a message to the new bridegroom, saying that he wished to attend the nuptials with a companion of his. In reply, the gentleman declared he would be quite delighted to see them.

When the hour for the banquet arrived, Messer Torello, still wearing the clothes he had arrived in, went with the Abbot to the bridegroom's house, where everyone who saw him stared at him in amazement, although none of them managed to recognize who he was. The Abbot told them all that Messer Torello was a Saracen who was being sent by the Sultan as his ambassador to the King of France. Accordingly, Messer Torello was seated at a table directly across from his wife, whom he gazed at with the utmost pleasure, thinking that, from the look on her face, she was none too happy about this marriage. From time to time, she, too, glanced over at him, not because she recognized him in any way—for his great beard, his foreign dress, and her own firm belief that he was dead made this impossible—but because of the unusual clothes he had on.

Finally, when Messer Torello felt the time was right to put his wife to the test and see if she remembered him, he took the ring she had given to him at his departure, and holding it in his hand, called over a young man who was waiting on her.

"Tell the new bride on my behalf," he said, "that in my country, whenever a stranger, like me, is attending the wedding feast of a newly married woman, like her, it's customary for the bride to take a cup from which she herself has been drinking, fill it with wine, and send it to him as a token of her appreciation for his coming there to dine with her. Then, when the stranger has drunk his fill, he puts the cover back on, and the bride drinks up what remains."

The young man delivered this message to the lady, who, being both wise and well mannered, and believing that she was dealing with an important dignitary, hastened to show him how pleased she was that he had come. Accordingly, she ordered that a large gold cup, which stood on the table before her, should be washed, filled with wine, and taken over to the gentleman.

They carried it to Messer Torello, who had placed his wife's ring in his mouth, and he drank in such a way as to let it fall into the cup without anyone noticing. Then, when there was only a tiny bit of wine left in it, he replaced the cover and sent it back to the lady. In deference to the custom of his country, she took it, removed the lid, and put it to her lips. At that moment, she caught sight of the ring. After gazing at it for some time without saying a word, she identified it as the one she had given Messer Torello when he left her. She then picked it up and stared intently at the man she had assumed was a stranger. Now that she could see who it really was, she seized the table in front of her and hurled it to the ground, shouting as if she had gone mad:

"This is my lord, this is really Messer Torello."

Then she dashed over to where he was sitting, and without giving a thought to her clothing or any of the things on the table, she flung herself across it as far as she could and hugged him to her in a tight embrace. Nor could she be induced to let go of his neck, for anything the people there could say or do, until Messer Torello himself told her to exercise a little self-control, for she would have plenty of time to embrace him later on.

The lady accordingly stood back up, and although by now the wedding feast was in total disarray, the return of so distinguished a knight actually made it happier than ever. Then, at Messer Torello's request, everyone grew silent, and he told them the story of what had happened to him from the day of his departure up to that very hour. He concluded by saying that the gentleman who, in the belief that he was dead, had married his wife could hardly take offense if he now reclaimed her as his own, since he was alive after all.

Though somewhat embarrassed, the bridegroom freely replied in a friendly manner that Messer Torello was at liberty to dispose of that which belonged to him in whatever way he pleased. The lady accordingly returned the ring and the crown her new bridegroom had given her and put on the ring she had taken from the cup as well as the crown that the Sultan had sent her. They then left the house they were in, and with all the pomp of a wedding procession, they made their way to Messer Torello's estate, where the merrymaking went on for hours, lifting the spirits of his unhappy friends and relations and all the townspeople, who considered his return something verging on a miracle.

After giving away some of his precious jewels to the gentleman who had paid for the wedding feast as well as to the Abbot and to numerous others, Messer Torello sent more than one messenger to Saladin with word of his happy homecoming, declaring himself to be the Sultan's friend and servant. And for many years after that, he lived with his worthy wife, behaving in a more courteous manner than ever.

This, then, was how the tribulations of Messer Torello and his beloved wife came to an end, and how they were rewarded for their prompt and cheerful acts of courtesy. There are many people who strive to do the like, but although they have the wherewithal, they perform such deeds so ineptly that before they are finished, those who receive them wind up paying more for them than they are worth. And so, if such people get no credit for what they do, neither they nor anyone else should be surprised.

Story 10

INDUCED BY THE ENTREATIES OF HIS VASSALS TO TAKE A
WIFE, THE MARQUIS OF SALUZZO, WANTING TO CHOOSE
ONE HIS OWN WAY, SELECTS THE DAUGHTER OF A PEASANT.
AFTER HE HAS HAD TWO CHILDREN WITH HER, HE MAKES
IT LOOK TO HER AS THOUGH THEY HAVE BEEN PUT TO
DEATH. LATER ON, PRETENDING TO HAVE GROWN WEARY OF
HER, HE CLAIMS HE HAS MARRIED ANOTHER WOMAN AND
ARRANGES TO HAVE HIS OWN DAUGHTER BROUGHT HOME
AS THOUGH SHE WERE HIS BRIDE, MEANWHILE HAVING
TURNED HIS WIFE OUT OF DOORS WEARING NOTHING BUT
HER SHIFT. ON FINDING THAT SHE HAS BORNE EVERYTHING

WITH PATIENCE, HOWEVER, HE TAKES HER BACK HOME
AGAIN, DEARER TO HIM THAN EVER, SHOWS HER THEIR
GROWN-UP CHILDREN, AND HONORS HER AS MARCHIONESS
AND CAUSES EVERYONE ELSE TO DO SO AS WELL.°

When the King had finished his long story, which everyone seemed to have really enjoyed, Dioneo laughed and said: "The good man who was looking forward to raising and lowering the bogeyman's tail the next night would have given less than two cents for all the praise you are bestowing on Messer Torello."° But then, knowing that he was the only one left to speak, he began as follows:

My gentle ladies, the way I see it, we have given this entire day over to kings and sultans and people of that ilk, and therefore, lest I stray too far away from the path you are on, I want to tell you about a Marquis whose behavior was not an example of magnanimity, but of senseless brutality.° And even though things turned out well for him in the end, I would not recommend that you follow his lead, because it is a real shame that he derived any benefit from it at all.

A long time ago, there was a young man named Gualtieri who, as the head of the family, had succeeded to the Marquisate of Saluzzo, and being unmarried and childless, spent all of his time out hawking and hunting. He never gave a thought to finding a wife and starting a family, for which he should have been considered very wise, but his vassals were not content with this and repeatedly begged him to get married so that he would not be left without an heir and they without a lord. Moreover, they offered to find him a woman whose character and parents were such that there would be every reason to feel hopeful about the match and he could expect to be quite happy with her. In response Gualtieri said:

"My friends, you are forcing me to do something I had absolutely resolved never to do, considering how hard it is to find a person whose character will be a fit for your own, how very many of the other sort there are out there, and how miserable life will be for a man if he stumbles upon a wife who is not well suited to him. Furthermore, it's foolish of you to believe that you can figure out what daughters will be like by considering how their fathers and mothers behave and on that basis to argue that you are going to find one who will please me. For I don't know how you can get any information about the fathers, let alone find out the secrets of the mothers, and even if you could, daughters are often very different from either one of their parents. But look, since you want to bind me in these chains, I'm willing to do it. Nevertheless, so that I won't have anybody to blame except myself if it turns out badly, I want to be the one who's responsible for finding her. And let me assure you that no matter what woman I choose, if you fail to honor her as your lady, you will learn to your great misfortune just how serious a matter it was for you to have begged me to take a wife against my will."

The gentlemen replied that they were satisfied, as long as he was amenable to taking a wife.

For quite some time Gualtieri had been impressed with the behavior of a poor girl who lived in a village not far from his home, and since she was also very beautiful, he thought that life with her ought to be rather agreeable. Thus, without searching any further, he resolved to marry her, and having summoned her father, who was very poor indeed, he made arrangements with him to take her as his wife.

This done, Gualtieri called all his friends in the area together and said to them: "My friends, since it continues to be your pleasure that I should agree to take a wife, I'm prepared to do it, though more to gratify you than from any interest I have in getting married. You know what you promised me, namely, that you would be content with whatever woman I chose and would honor her as your lady. Now the time has arrived for me to keep my promise to you and for you to keep yours to me. I've located a young woman after my own heart who lives quite close by, and just a few days from now I intend to marry her and lead her home as my bride. So, see to it that the wedding feast is splendid and that you give her an honorable reception. That way I'll be able to pronounce myself satisfied that you've kept your word to me just as you'll be satisfied that I've kept mine to you."

The gentlemen all replied joyfully that they were very pleased with this decision and that no matter whom he chose, they would accept her as their lady and would honor her as such in every way they could. After that, they got everything ready so that the feast would be as grand and lavish and happy as possible, and Gualtieri did likewise, arranging for the most magnificent and beautiful wedding, to which he invited a host of his friends and relations as well as many great noblemen and others from the area round about. In addition, he had them make a fair number of beautiful dresses out of expensive material, all tailored to fit a girl who seemed to him the same size as the one he intended to marry. Finally, he ordered belts and rings, a lovely, costly crown, and everything else a new bride would require.

On the day set for the wedding, halfway between prime and tierce, Gualtieri mounted his horse, as did all those who had come to honor him, and after everything necessary had been seen to, he announced, "Gentlemen, it's time to go and fetch the new bride." Then off he rode with the entire company. Before long they reached the little village, and when they got to the house belonging to the girl's father, they spotted her carrying water back from the spring, hurrying so that she could go with the other women to see Gualtieri's spouse as she arrived. The moment Gualtieri saw her, he called her by her name, which was Griselda, and asked her where her father was, to which she bashfully replied, "He's in the house, my lord."

Gualtieri dismounted and told everyone to wait for him while he went into the hovel by himself. There he found her father, whose name was Giannucole, and said to him: "I've come to marry Griselda, but first, here in your presence, there are certain things I need to find out from her."° Then he asked her whether, if he were to wed her, she would do her best to please him and never get upset at anything he ever said or did, and whether she would be obedient, and many other things of this sort, to all of which she replied that she would.

At this point Gualtieri, taking her by the hand, led her outside and in the presence of his entire company as well as all the other

people living there, he had her stripped naked. Then he called for
the clothing and shoes he had ordered for her and quickly had
them dress her, after which he had them place a crown on her hair,
disheveled though it was. And as everyone looked on in wonder,
he proclaimed: "My lords, this is the woman I intend to take as my
wife, provided that she wants to marry me." Then, turning to her
as she stood there, feeling stunned and quite embarrassed, he
asked her: "Griselda, will you have me as your husband?"

"Yes, my lord," she replied.

"And I," he said, "will take you as my wife." Then, right there, in
the presence of the entire assembly, he married her, after which he
had her seated on a palfrey and led her, honorably attended, to his
house where the wedding was celebrated in as beautiful, festive,
and magnificent a style as if he had married the daughter of the
King of France.

The young bride appeared to change her mind and her manners along with her clothes. As we have already said, she had a fine
figure and lovely features, and in keeping with her beauty, she now
became so charming, so pleasant, and so well mannered that she
did not seem like a shepherdess and the daughter of Giannucole,
but like the child of some noble lord, leading everyone who had
known her earlier to marvel at her transformation. Moreover, she
was so obedient and attentive to her husband that he thought
himself the happiest, most contented man in the world. At the
same time she was so gracious and kind to her husband's subjects
that they all loved her with utter devotion, honored her of their
own free will, and prayed for her well-being, her prosperity, and
her advancement. And whereas they used to say that Gualtieri had
shown some lack of discretion in marrying her, now they declared
him to be the wisest, most discerning man on earth because no
one else could have ever perceived her lofty virtues, which were
hidden under the poor rags of her peasant's clothing. In short, she
comported herself so well that before long she had everyone
talking, not only in her husband's domain, but far and wide, about
how fine her character was and how virtuous her behavior, and

she got people to change their minds if they had ever criticized her husband on her account at the time of his marriage.

She had not lived with Gualtieri very long before she became pregnant and in time, to his great happiness, gave birth to a little girl. But a little while later the strange idea popped into his head to test her patience by subjecting her to constant tribulations and generally making life intolerable for her. Consequently, he started by goading her with words, pretending to be angry and telling her that his vassals were thoroughly disgruntled with her because of her base origin, especially now that they saw her bearing children, and that, furthermore, they were upset about the little girl who had just been born and were doing nothing but grumbling about it.

The lady did not change her expression or show the least resentment when she heard these words. "My lord," she said, "do with me whatever you think best for your honor and your peace of mind, and I will be entirely content with it, for I know that I'm socially inferior to your vassals and that I'm unworthy of the honor that you have so graciously bestowed on me."° This reply was very gratifying to Gualtieri, for he realized that she had not gotten puffed up with pride because of the honors that he or the others had paid her.

Some time later, having already given her to understand in general terms that his subjects could not endure the little girl she had given birth to, he gave certain instructions to one of his servants and sent him to her. "My lady," said the servant, with the most sorrowful expression on his face, "if I don't want to be put to death, I have to do what my lord has commanded, and he has commanded me to take this daughter of yours and to . . ." And at this point he could say no more.

When the lady heard the servant's words and saw his face, and when she recalled what her husband had said to her, she concluded that the man had been ordered to put her child to death. In response, although she was desperately sick at heart, she immediately took her daughter from the cradle, and without ever changing her expression, she kissed her and blessed her and placed her in the servant's arms. "There," she said to him, "do exactly what your lord, who is my lord as well, has ordered, but don't leave her to be devoured by the beasts and the birds unless he's told you to do so."

The servant took the child and reported what the lady had said to Gualtieri, who, marveling at her constancy, sent him away with the baby to one of his relatives in Bologna, asking her to raise and educate the child with some care, but never to reveal whose daughter she was.

Shortly afterward, the lady became pregnant once again, and when she came to term, she gave birth to a baby boy, which made Gualtieri very happy. Nevertheless, not content with what he had already done, he wounded his wife even more deeply. One day, glowering at her with feigned fury, he said: "Woman, ever since you gave birth to this boy, I've found it completely impossible to live with my vassals, so bitterly do they complain that one of Giannucole's grandsons is to succeed me as their lord. So, if I don't want to be deposed by them, I'm afraid that I'll have to do in this case what I did in the other one, and that I'll also eventually have to leave you and find another wife."

The lady listened patiently, and her only reply was: "My lord, you should think about your own happiness and about how to satisfy your desires. Don't waste another thought on me, for nothing is of any value to me unless I see that it gives you pleasure."

Not many days after that, Gualtieri sent for his son the same way he had for his daughter, and having likewise pretended to have him put to death, he sent him to be brought up in Bologna just as he had done with the girl. In response, his wife said nothing more and did not change the expression on her face any more than she had in her daughter's case, all to Gualtieri's great astonishment, who told himself that no other woman could do what she did. And if it were not for the fact that he saw her treat the children with the utmost tenderness as long as he permitted her to do so, he would have concluded that she acted as she did because she had stopped caring for them. He knew, however, that her behavior was the product of her wisdom.

Since Gualtieri's subjects believed he had arranged to have his two children murdered, they condemned him, blaming it all on his cruelty, whereas they felt nothing but the most profound pity for his wife. But to the women who mourned with her for her children because they had suffered such a death, she never said anything except that if such was the pleasure of the man who had conceived them, then it was her pleasure as well.

Finally, many years after the birth of his daughter, Gualtieri decided the time had come to put his wife's patience to the ultimate test. Accordingly, he spoke with a large company of his vassals and told them that under no circumstances could he put up with Griselda as his wife any longer. He said that he had come to realize just how bad and immature a decision he had made when he chose her, and that he would therefore do everything he could to procure a dispensation from the Pope so that he could leave Griselda and take another wife. A large number of the worthy men took him to task over this plan, but his only reply was that it had to be done that way.

Upon learning of her husband's intentions, the lady grieved bitterly inside, for it seemed to her that what she had to look forward to was returning to her father's house and perhaps tending his sheep as she had done before, while being forced to see the man she loved with all her heart in another woman's embrace. But still, just as she had borne all of Fortune's other afflictions, she was determined to keep her countenance unchanged and endure this one as well.

A little later Gualtieri arranged to have counterfeit letters sent to him from Rome and led his subjects to believe that they contained the Pope's dispensation, which allowed him to leave Griselda and take another wife. Hence, he summoned her to appear, and in the presence of a large number of people, he said to her: "Woman, through the concession granted me by the Pope I am now free to leave you and choose another wife. Since my ancestors have always been great noblemen and rulers in these parts, whereas yours have always been peasants, I no longer want you as my wife. You should return to Giannucole's house with the dowry you brought me, and

I will bring home another woman I've found who is a more appropriate match for me."

When she heard these words, the lady managed to hold back her tears only by making an enormous effort that went well beyond the normal capacity of women.

"My lord," she said, "I have always known that my lowly condition and your nobility were in no way suited to one another, just as I have acknowledged that the position I have held with you was a gift from you and from God, nor have I taken what was given to me and treated it as if it were my own rather than as something lent to me. So, if it pleases you to have it back, then it must also please me—and it does—to return it to you. Look, here's the ring with which you married me: take it. As for your ordering me to carry away the dowry I brought here, to do that will not require a paymaster on your part, nor a purse, let alone a packhorse on mine, for I haven't forgotten that I was completely naked when you took me.° And if you think it proper to let everybody see this body that bore the children you sired, I will depart naked as well, but I beg you, in return for the virginity I brought here and cannot take away again, that it may please you to let me take away at least one single shift in addition to my dowry."

Although Gualtieri had a greater desire to weep than anything else, he maintained his stony expression and said: "You may take a shift with you."

The people standing about there begged him to give her a dress so that the woman who had been his wife for thirteen years or longer should not suffer the shame of leaving his house wearing only a shift like a pauper. All their pleading was in vain, however, and thus she left the house in her shift, barefoot, and with nothing to cover her head. After having said good-bye to them all, she returned to her father's home, accompanied by the weeping and wailing of everyone who saw her.

Since Giannucole never really believed it possible for his daughter to last very long as Gualtieri's wife, he had been expecting just such a development every day and had kept the clothes that she had taken off the morning Gualtieri married her. He brought them to her, and after she had put them on, she devoted herself to all the menial chores in her father's house just as she had been accustomed to do, bravely enduring the fierce assault of a hostile Fortune.

As soon as he had sent Griselda away, Gualtieri led his vassals to believe that he had chosen as his wife a daughter of one of the counts of Panago.° And having ordered great preparations to be made for the wedding, he sent for Griselda to come to him. When she appeared, he said to her:

"I'm going to bring home the lady whom I have recently chosen to marry, and I want her to be given an honorable reception the moment she arrives. Since you know that I don't have any women in my house who can prepare the rooms properly and do many of the things that a festive occasion of this sort requires, and since you understand such household matters better than anyone else, I want you to see to it that all the arrangements are taken care of and that you invite as many ladies as you think necessary and receive them as though you were the mistress of the house. Then, when the wedding celebration is over, you can return home."

Gualtieri's words pierced Griselda's heart like so many knives, for she had not been able to put aside the love she bore him in the same way that she had relinquished the good fortune she once had. Nevertheless, she replied: "My lord, I am ready and willing."° And so, clad in homespun garments of coarse wool, she entered the house, which only a little while before she had left in a shift. Then she began sweeping and tidying up the rooms, had bed curtains and bench coverings put in place throughout the great halls, got the kitchen ready to go, and turned her hand to everything just as if she were some little household serving wench, never stopping until it was all as neat and trim as the occasion called for. Finally, after having invitations sent to all the women in those parts on Gualtieri's behalf, she stopped and waited for the celebration to begin. When the wedding day arrived, though the clothes she had on were poor, she displayed the spirit and bearing of a lady, receiving, with a happy smile on her face, all the women who came to the feast.

Gualtieri had seen to it that his children were brought up with care in Bologna by his kinswoman, who had married into the house of the counts of Panago. His daughter, who had now reached the age of twelve, was the most beautiful creature ever seen, and his son was six. Gualtieri sent word to his kinswoman's husband, asking him if he would be so kind as to accompany his daughter and her brother to Saluzzo, to arrange a noble, honorable escort for her, and not to reveal to anyone who she was in reality, but simply to tell them that he was bringing her there as Gualtieri's bride.

The nobleman did everything the Marquis requested, and a few days after he set out on his journey with the girl and her brother and their noble retinue, he reached Saluzzo, arriving around the dinner hour, where he found that all the people there, as well as many others from neighboring communities, were waiting for Gualtieri's new bride. She was received by the ladies, and as soon as she entered the hall where the tables were set up, Griselda, dressed just as she was, happily went to meet her, and said: "You are welcome here, my lady."

The ladies had begged Gualtieri, earnestly but in vain, either to have Griselda remain in another room or to lend her one of the dresses that had once been hers, so that she would not appear in front of the guests looking as she did. But she was nevertheless seated at the tables along with all the rest of them, after which dinner was served. As everyone stared at the girl, they said that Gualtieri had done well by the exchange, and Griselda joined in, praising her warmly, and her little brother, too.

It seemed to Gualtieri that he had now seen as much as he could have ever desired of his wife's patience, for he had observed that no event, however outrageous, had produced any sort of change in her at all. Moreover, he felt sure that her reaction was not the result of obtuseness, since he knew just how wise she was. He therefore decided that it was time to deliver her from the bitter sorrow he guessed she was keeping hidden beneath her impassive exterior, and having summoned her, he smiled and asked her in the presence of all the assembled people: "What do you think of our bride?"

"My lord," replied Griselda, "she seems very fine to me, and if, as I believe, her wisdom matches her beauty, I have no doubt whatsoever that living with her will make you the happiest gentleman in the world. However, I beg you with all my heart not to inflict on her the same wounds you once gave the other spouse you used to have, because I find it hard to believe she'll be able to endure them, considering how much younger she is and also how refined an upbringing she has had, whereas the other one experienced continual hardships from the time she was a little girl."

Seeing that she firmly believed the girl was going to be his wife, and yet had nothing but good things to say, Gualtieri had her sit down beside him.

"Griselda," he said, "the time has finally come both for you to taste the fruit of your long patience, and for those who have thought me cruel, unjust, and brutish to realize that what I've done I've done with a deliberate end in view. For I wanted to teach you how to be a wife, to teach them how to manage one, and at the same time to beget for myself perpetual peace and quiet for the rest of my life with you. When I was at the point of taking a wife, I really feared I'd have no peace, and that's why I decided to choose one by means of a test and have, as you know, inflicted so much pain and suffering on you.

"And since I've never seen you deviate from my wishes in either word or deed, and since it seems to me that you will provide me with all the happiness I've desired, I intend to restore to you in an instant that which I took from you over such a long time, and with the sweetest of cures to heal the wounds I gave you. Receive this girl, then, with a glad heart, the one you believed to be my wife, along with her brother, for they are, in fact, our children, yours as well as mine, the very ones whom you and many others believed for a long time I had cruelly ordered to be put to death. And I am your husband, who loves you more than anything else, since I believe I may boast that there is no one else who could be as content with his wife as I am with you."°

When he finished speaking, he embraced her and kissed her, and while she wept for joy, they both got up and went over to where their daughter sat, listening in amazement to what they were saying. Both of them embraced her and her brother tenderly, thus dispelling any confusion that they, like many others present, were feeling. The ladies were overjoyed, and getting up from the tables, they went with Griselda into a chamber where, with a more auspicious view of her future, they divested her of her old clothes and dressed her in one of her own stately gowns. Then, like the lady of the castle, which she always appeared to be even when clad in rags, they led her back into the hall, where her rejoicing with her children was simply wonderful. Indeed, everyone was so happy about what had happened that the feasting and the celebrating were redoubled and continued unabated for many more days. They all declared that Gualtieri was very wise, although they thought that the tests to which he had subjected his wife were harsh and intolerable, but they considered Griselda to be the wisest of them all.

A few days later the Count of Panago returned to Bologna, and Gualtieri, having taken Giannucole away from his drudgery, set him up in a position befitting the man who was his father-in-law, so that he was treated with honor and lived in great comfort during his last remaining years. As for Gualtieri himself, having arranged a noble match for his daughter, he lived a long, contented life with Griselda, always honoring her in every way he could.

What more is there left to say except that divine spirits may rain down from the heavens even into the houses of the poor, just as there are others in royal palaces who might be better suited to tending pigs than ruling men. Who, aside from Griselda, would have suffered, not merely dry eyed, but with a cheerful countenance, the cruel, unheard-of trials to which Gualtieri subjected her? Perhaps it would have served him right if, instead, he had run into the kind of woman who, upon being thrown out of the house in her shift, would have found some guy to give her fur a good shaking and got a nice new dress in the bargain.

Conclusion

When Dioneo's story was done, the ladies inclined to one side or the other in their responses, some criticizing one detail in it, some praising another. After they had discussed it at length, the King glanced up at the sky, and seeing that the sun was already quite low and the hour of vespers was at hand, he began, without getting up from his seat, to speak to them as follows:

"Elegant ladies, as I believe you know, the wisdom we mortals possess does not merely consist of remembering things past and apprehending the present, but on the basis of these two activities being able to predict the future, which is considered by serious men to be the highest form of human intelligence.° Tomorrow, as you are aware, will be the fifteenth day since we left Florence in pursuit of recreation, seeking both to preserve our health and our lives, and to avoid the melancholy, grief, and anguish that have been inescapable in our city ever since the plague first began. In my estimation, we have managed to achieve this goal without any loss of honor, because as far as I have been able to observe, although the merry stories we have told could have been conducive to arousing carnal desire, and although we have continually enjoyed good food and drink as well as playing music and singing songs—all of which are apt to incite weak minds to less than proper behavior—I have never noted a deed or a word or anything else that is blameworthy, either on your part or on that of us men. Considering what I have seen and heard, it seems to me that our activities have been marked from start to finish by a sense of propriety, harmony, and fraternal friendship, all of which certainly gives me great pleasure and redounds to your honor and credit as well as to my own.

"Accordingly, to keep things from becoming tedious because of an established custom too long observed, and to prevent people from being able to raise frivolous objections to our having stayed here all this time, I think it proper, since all of us have had a day's share of the regal honor I still possess, that with your approval we should go back to the place from which we came. Furthermore, if you examine the matter carefully, there is also the fact that our company has already become known to many people around here, with the result that our numbers could increase to such an extent that it would take away all our pleasure. And so, if my advice meets with your approval, I will keep the crown that was given to me until our departure, which I propose should take place tomorrow morning. But if you should decide otherwise, I already have someone in mind to bestow it on for the next day."

The ladies and the young men debated the matter at great length, but finally, having judged the King's counsel to be both sensible and proper, they decided to do what he had recommended. He therefore summoned the steward and spoke with him about the arrangements for the following morning. Then, after dismissing the company until suppertime, he got to his feet.

The ladies and the other two men rose as well, and just as they always did, they devoted themselves to a variety of different pastimes. When the hour for supper arrived, they attended to it with the greatest pleasure, after which they started singing, playing music, and dancing *carole,* and while Lauretta was leading them in a round, the King called for a song from Fiammetta, which she began singing very pleasantly, as follows:°

> If Love could come unmixed with jealousy,
> There'd be no lady born
> So glad as I, whoever she may be.
>   If youth and gaiety,
> Good looks and virtue, too, could satisfy
> A lady in her love,
> If daring, prowess proved,
> Intelligence, good manners, eloquence,
> Or perfect gracefulness,
> Then I'm the one who's pleased, for I'm in love
> And see those qualities,
> For certain, in the one who is my hope.
>   But since I'm well aware
> That other women's wisdom equals mine,
> I tremble, terrified,
> And always fear the worst,
> Convinced those others want to take the one
> Who stole my soul from me.
> Thus Fortune's greatest gift, bestowed on me,

Makes me disconsolate,
Sigh deeply, and live on in misery.
     Yet if I knew my lord's
Fidelity were equal to his worth,
I'd not be jealous then.
But nowadays one sees
So many women lead men on that I
Hold all men culpable.
This breaks my heart and makes me long to die,
For I suspect each one
Who eyes him, fearful she'll take him away.
     For God's sake, then, I pray
No woman in the world would ever dare
To do me such a wrong,
For should some one of them,
By using words or signs or flattery,
Attempt in this affair
To do me harm, and should I learn of it,
Then mar my looks if I
Don't make her weep her folly bitterly.

As soon as Fiammetta had finished her song, Dioneo, who was right beside her, said with a laugh: "My lady, you would be doing all your companions a great service by revealing who he is, lest they take him from you out of ignorance, considering how angry that is bound to make you."

After Fiammetta's song, the company sang many another until the night was already almost half gone. Then, at the King's command, they all went off to rest.

The next day, they arose at dawn, by which time the steward had already sent all their baggage on ahead, and following the lead of their prudent King, they all walked back to Florence. There, taking their leave of the seven women in Santa Maria Novella, from which they had all set out, the three young men went off to pursue other pleasures of theirs, while the ladies in due course returned to their homes.

The Author's Conclusion

Most noble young ladies, for whose consolation I have undertaken this protracted labor, I believe that with the aid of divine grace, which has been granted to me, I think, more because of your prayers than because of any merits of my own, I have completely fulfilled what I promised to do at the start of the present work. Consequently, after giving thanks first to God and then to you, it is time for me to allow my pen and my weary hand to rest. Before doing so, however, I intend to respond briefly to a few trifling, though unspoken, objections that might have occurred to some of you as well as to others. For what seems absolutely clear to me is that these tales do not enjoy the special privilege of being immune to criticism more than anything else is, a fact I remember actually having noted at the start of the fourth day.

There may be some of you who will perhaps claim that I have employed too much license in writing these stories, because sometimes I had ladies say things, and quite often had them listen to things, that are not very suitable for virtuous women to say or hear. This I deny, for there is no story so unseemly that it may not be told, provided it is couched in seemly language, as I think I have done very well here.°

But supposing you are correct—for I do not want to get into a dispute with you, which you would certainly win—I still say, when asked to explain why I did what I did, that many reasons come quite readily to mind. First, if liberties were taken in a few cases, it was required by the nature of the stories, something that will be abundantly clear to any perceptive individual who examines them with an unprejudiced eye, for unless I had wished to deform them, they could not have been recounted in any other manner. And if perhaps there is some tiny expression in them, some little word, that is freer than might seem appropriate to prudish women who attach more weight to speech than to deeds and make more of an effort to seem good than to be good, then I say that it was no more improper for me to have written them than for men and women generally to go around all day long saying "hole" and "rod" and "mortar" and "pestle" and "sausage" and "mortadella" and lots of other things like that. Besides, my pen should have as much latitude as that which is given to the brush of the painter who, without incurring any, or at least any just, censure not only depicts Saint Michael striking the serpent with either a sword or a lance, and Saint George wounding the dragon wherever he pleases, but also makes Christ male and Eve female, and takes Him who, for the salvation of the human race, was willing to die on the cross, and has his feet fastened to it sometimes with one nail and sometimes with two.°

Moreover, it is perfectly clear that these stories were not told in a church, about whose affairs we should speak with the greatest reverence both in our hearts and in our words, although one can find many things in its sacred stories that go well beyond what you encounter in mine. Nor were they rehearsed either in the schools of philosophy where decency is required no less than anywhere else, or in any locale frequented by clergymen and philosophers. Rather, they were told in gardens, places designed for pleasure, among people who were young, but sufficiently mature so as not to be led astray by stories, and at a time when it was acceptable for even the most virtuous to go about with their breeches on their heads if they thought it would preserve their lives.°

Like everything else, these stories, such as they are, may be harmful or helpful, depending upon the listener. Who does not know that wine is a very fine thing for the healthy, as Cinciglione and Scolaio and many others affirm, but that it is harmful for people suffering from a fever?° Shall we say it is bad because it does harm to those who are feverish? Who does not know that fire is extremely useful, in fact downright necessary, for mankind? Shall we say it is bad because it burns down houses and villages and cities? In the same way, arms are the safeguard of those who wish to live in peace, and yet they also kill men on many occasions, not because of any wickedness inherent in them, but because of the wickedness of those who use them wrongfully.

No single word has ever been wholesomely construed by a corrupt mind. And just as proper language can do nothing for such a mind, that which is improper cannot contaminate one that is well disposed, any more than mud can sully the rays of the sun, or earthly filth, the beauties of the heavens. What books, what words, what letters are holier, worthier, more to be revered than those of the Holy Scriptures? And yet there have been many who, by interpreting them in a perverse manner, have led themselves and others to perdition. All things, in themselves, are good for some purpose, but if they are wrongly used, they will cause a great deal of harm. And I say the same thing about my tales. Anyone who wishes to extract some wicked counsel from them or to come up with some wicked plan will not be prevented from doing so by the tales themselves if by chance they contain such things and can be twisted and distorted to such an end. But anyone seeking profit and utility in them will not be prevented from finding it either, nor will these stories ever be thought of or described as anything other than useful and seemly if they are read at the proper time and by the people for whom they were composed. As for the lady who is forever saying her rosary or baking cakes and pies for her holy confessor, she can just leave them be. These stories will not run after anyone demanding to be read, even though they are no more improper than certain little things pious hypocrites both talk about and actually do, if offered the opportunity.

There will also be those who will say that it would have been better to have omitted some of the stories that are included here. I grant you that, but still, I had to write down—indeed, I had an obligation to write down—what was actually said, which means that the speakers should have made their stories truly beautiful, and then I could have written them down that way. But even if people assumed that I was not just the writer, but the inventor of the stories—which I was not—then I would still reply that I am not ashamed if some of them were less than beautiful, because there is no craftsman other than God who has made everything perfect and complete. Even Charlemagne, who first created the Paladins, did not know how to make a sufficient number to form an army.°

In a multitude of things one will necessarily find many differences in quality. No field was ever so well cultivated that nettles and thistles and brambles were not found mixed in with the better plants. Besides, since I have to speak to unaffected young ladies, as most of you are, it would have been foolish of me to have exhausted myself by looking everywhere for the most exquisite material and to have taken great pains to speak about it in the most carefully measured style. Still, whoever reads through these stories can skip over those that give offense and read only those that promise delight, for lest anyone should be deceived, each story bears a sign on its brow of that which it keeps hidden within its bosom.°

I suppose there are also people who will say that some of the stories are too long. To them I will say, again, that if anyone has something better to do, it would be foolish to read them, even if they were brief. Although a great deal of time has passed from the day I started writing until this present hour, in which I am now approaching the end of my labors, it has not slipped my mind that I offered this effort of mine to ladies living in idleness rather than to anyone else, and nothing will seem long to those who read in order to pass the time, if it serves the purpose for which they chose it. Brevity is much more fitting for students, who undertake their labors not to pass the time, but to put it to good use, than it is for you ladies who have all that spare time left over that you do not spend in the pleasures of love. And besides, since none of you is going to be a student in Athens or Bologna or Paris, I need to speak to you here at greater length than to those whose wits have been sharpened by their studies.

I have no doubt but that there will be yet other women who will say that the matters I have related are overly full of clever quips and jests, and that it is unbecoming for a serious and substantial man to have written such things. To these women I feel obliged to express my gratitude, and I do so, indeed, because, moved by a well-intentioned zeal, they feel so tender a concern for my reputation. But I also want to respond to their objection this way: I confess that I am a man of some substance and that in my day I have been weighed on many occasions, but speaking to those women who have no experience of my weight, let me assure them that I am not heavy—in fact, I am so light that I float on the surface of the water.° Moreover, since the sermons preached by friars nowadays in order to rebuke men for their sins are, for the most part, filled with clever quips and jests and gibes, I concluded that such things would not be out of place in my stories, which were written, after all, to dispel the melancholy with which ladies are afflicted. Still, if they should laugh too hard because of them, the Lamentations of Jeremiah, the Passion of Our Savior, and the Complaint of Mary Magdalene will easily be able to cure them.°

And who can doubt that there are still others who will say that I have an evil and venomous tongue because in certain places I have told the truth about friars? Nevertheless, women who say such things ought to be pardoned, for there is no question but that they are moved by the best of motives, seeing as how friars are truly good men who flee hardship for the love of God, do their grinding when the millpond is full, and never blab about it afterward. And if it were not for the fact that they all give off a faint odor of billy goat, their company would be most agreeable.°

I acknowledge, however, that the things of this world are completely unstable and endlessly changing—which could explain what happened with my tongue. For not so long ago, distrusting my own judgment, which, in matters concerning myself, I avoid as much as possible, I was told by one of the women next door that I had the best and sweetest tongue in the world, and in all honesty, this occurred when only a few of the stories I have been talking about still remained to be written. As for those other ladies who speak of me so spitefully, let what I have just said suffice as my reply to them.

And now I leave it up to every lady to say and think whatever she wishes, for the time has come to bring these remarks to an end and give humble thanks to Him who, after aiding me in my immense labor, has brought me to the goal I pursued. As for you, charming ladies, may His grace and peace be with you always, and may you remember me if perhaps any of you have benefited in any way from having read these stories.

Here ends the Tenth and final Day of the book called Decameron, *also known as* Prince Galeotto

Notes

p. 3 *by seven ladies and three young men*: *Decameron*, the title of Boccaccio's work, derives from Greek and means "ten days." Prince Galeotto (Gallehault, in French) is a character from Aurthurian romance who served as a go-between in the love affair of Lancelot and Guinevere. On both the title and the alternative title, see the Introduction.

p. 3 *I am one of them*: Boccaccio follows the principles of medieval rhetoric and opens his work with a proverb: "misery loves company." He also personalizes the idea, for earlier in his career he had memorialized his suffering for the love of Maria d'Aquino, referring to her by the pseudonym of Fiammetta, in his work of the same name. Fiammetta (Little Flame) will reappear as one of the ten narrators of the *Decameron*. In the next sentences, he acts out one of the conventional tropes of courtly love by stressing his low condition in relationship to the beloved and to love itself (although the experience of loving was also thought in the Middle Ages to be so ennobling that it compensated for whatever degradation the lover might experience).

p. 5 *unless it is removed by new interests*: Melancholy (black humor) meant more than just an unhappy mood, as it does today. In the medical theory of Boccaccio's time, the body contained four "humors" (blood, choler, phlegm, and melancholy) that determined both its physical functions and the mental states accompanying those functions. Good health required that all four humors be in balance, so that to have one, such as melancholy, become dominant was to suffer a serious disease.

p. 5 *or whatever you wish to call them*: Boccaccio's different names for the narratives making up his collection are not synonyms, nor can they be applied individually to distinct subsets of them. Furthermore, all of these names are, to some degree, approximations, since the genres they label were rather fluid in the period. Nevertheless, some distinctions can be made among them. "Story" (*novella* in Italian) was a late medieval descriptive term, fairly new in Boccaccio's lifetime, that defined a story focused on a single incident. "Fable" probably refers less to something like the moralizing tales of Aesop than to what the French called a *fabliau,* a short tale usually concerned with lower-class characters in which the main action involved their tricking one another in pursuit of money or sex. A "parable," by contrast, was a story with an explicit, usually conventional moral, like the parables recounted by Christ in the New Testament or like similar tales told throughout the Middle Ages and typically called *exempla*. Finally, "history" (or "story," *istoria* in Italian) identifies a narrative involving elevated and important historical persons or incidents.

p. 6 *what they should pursue*: In insisting that his stories will offer readers both "pleasure and useful advice," Boccaccio is rephrasing the well-known and widely endorsed dictum of the Roman writer Horace who said that art should be both *dulce* (sweet) and *utile* (useful); see his *Ars poetica* (*The Art of Poetry*) 343.

DAY 1, INTRODUCTION

p. 8 *both their ascent and their descent*: Boccaccio's image of the reading of his work as the making of a journey up a difficult mountain recalls the opening of the *Divine Comedy* in which Dante is trying without success to climb a mountain (Purgatory). In the next sentence, Boccaccio rephrases Proverbs 14.13.

p. 8 *Florence, the most beautiful of any in Italy*: For Florentines in this period, the year began on March 25, the date of the Incarnation or Annunciation, and in fact, the plague did appear for the first time in Florence in April 1348.

p. 8 *from place to place*: The plague started in Asia—to be precise, in the Crimea—from which it was brought by sea to Sicily in 1346. Boccaccio offers two conventional explanations for the disease: the influence of the stars and God's anger at the sins of humans. Boccaccio's description of the plague, although pretending to be an eyewitness account, is generally based on earlier accounts such as that by Paulus Diaconus in his 8th-century *Historia Longobardorum (History of the Lombards)*.

p. 9 *appear at random over the rest of the body*: *Gavocciolo* is a Tuscan word meaning "a swelling" or "protuberance"; it is a diminutive and derives from the late Latin *gaba* (*gozzo* in Italian), meaning "goiter," "crop," "throat," or even "stomach." These swellings are called *bubboni* in modern Italian and buboes in English (from the Greek word for groin or gland), and it is from this term that we get the name of the sickness, the bubonic plague. It was also called the Black Death because of the black spots on the body that were due to internal bleeding (described in the next sentence).

p. 15 *even simple people regard with indifference*: Boccaccio is, of course, being ironic in this sentence. Those "things" that the wise, like the simple, must learn to bear, are the suffering and death that are part of the "natural course of events"—that is, the human condition.

p. 16 *thought it contained so many*: Boccaccio's estimate of the number of deaths due to the plague is somewhat exaggerated, perhaps for the sake of rhetorical effect. Historians, relying on various 14th-century chroniclers, think that about 60 percent of the population, or anywhere from fifty to eighty thousand people, perished in Florence and the surrounding countryside. Boccaccio's interest in rhetorical effect is also evident in the heightened language of the following paragraph.

p. 16 *their ancestors in the next world*: Aesculapius (Asclepios in Greek) was the Greco-Roman god of medicine. Galen (2nd century c.e.) and Hippocrates (5th century b.c.e.) were the two most famous doctors of the ancient Greek world.

p. 21 *rarely does anything we do accord us praise*: Elissa's opening remark alludes to Ephesians 5.23.

p. 22 *decked out in their green foliage*: Although some scholars have attempted to identify this palace with a specific country villa Boccaccio owned, the ensuing description is so general and so idealized—and is so similar to the description of the palace to which the group goes at the start of Day 3—that it makes more sense to see it as being inspired not by Boccaccio's recollection of a specific place but by the literary tradition of the *locus amoenus,* the "pleasant place," that serves as a setting for pastoral poetry. This tradition lies behind similar descriptions in Boccaccio's earlier works and in such medieval classics as *The Romance of the Rose.*

p. 24 *choose his or her successor*: The hour of "vespers" is in the evening.

p. 24 *clear sign of royal sovereignty and authority*: Crowning a victorious athlete or a poet with leaves from the laurel tree, which was sacred to Apollo, was an ancient Greek custom; the Romans awarded such a wreath to a victorious general. The custom of crowning writers and poets with laurel wreaths was revived in 1315 by the citizens of Padua for the humanist scholar Albertino Mussato. More famously, on April 8, 1341, Petrarch was crowned poet laureate by the Roman Senate on the Capitoline Hill.

p. 24 *the service of our dining hall*: The names of all the servants who accompany the group into the countryside have Greek roots, although they are taken by Boccaccio, for the most part, from Roman comedy and satire. They function generically as "names for lower-class servants" rather than pointing, through their etymologies, to specific qualities the individual servants might possess.

p. 25 *unless that news is good*: "News" in this sentence translates Boccaccio's *novelle,* which can also mean "stories."

p. 25 *eat while it is still cool*: "Tierce" is in the midmorning.

p. 25 *could dance a carola*: A "carola" is a dance in which the dancers join hands and move in a clockwise direction, usually accompanied by music and the singing of the dancers themselves.

p. 25 *dancing at a steady pace*: The "viol" (Boccaccio writes *viuola*; the more common French name was *vielle*) was a stringed instrument like the modern violin, but with a longer, deeper body and an indeterminate number of strings. It could be bowed or plucked and was used to accompany singing or dancing.

p. 26 *sleep too much during the day*: "Nones" is in the midafternoon.

DAY 1, STORY 1

p. 27 *and is called Saint Ciappelletto*: There is no specific source for this story, although hypocrisy is frequently a subject of satire in the Middle Ages, and there were occasional cases in various countries of criminals and the like actually being venerated as saints.

p. 28 *had sent for and was encouraging to come*: Musciatto di Messer Guido Franzesi (died 1310) was a merchant from Tuscany who grew rich in France where he served as a counselor to the French King Philip the Fair (Philippe le Bel, born 1268, ruled 1285–1314), who did, in fact, make Musciatto a "gentleman." The latter wickedly advised the king to falsify his coinage and to plunder the Italian merchants living in France. He also had a close business relationship with a certain Cepparello da Prato. King Philip's brother, Charles Sans Terre (Charles "Lackland," 1270–1325), was the third son of Charles III. Although the Count of Valois, Maine, and Anjou, he owed his nickname of "Lackland" to his failure to acquire a kingdom. In 1301 he was invited by Pope Boniface VIII (born c. 1235; pope 1294–1303) to bring an army to Italy to support papal forces fighting the Florentines. Note that "Tuscany," like "Lombardy" (the usurers mentioned later in the story are identified as Lombards), was often used in this period to refer to all of northern Italy.

p. 28 *often a guest in his house in Paris*: Cepparello da Prato (or Ciapperello Dietiaiuti da Prato) was a historical personage whose name appears in documents from the period as a receiver of taxes and tithes for King Philip and Boniface VIII. Although he did have business relations with Musciatto Franzesi, he was not, as Boccaccio says, a notary; moreover, he was married and had children. The "Ser" before his name is short for *Messer* and is an honorific, like calling someone "sir," but without the implication of aristocratic status.

p. 28 *few knew he was really Ser Cepparello*: Cepparello's first name is the diminutive (*-ello*) of Ciapo, short for Jacopo (James), although Boccaccio plays with the fact that *ceppo* meant "log" or "stump." Cepparello could thus be translated as Little Log. The French-speaking Burgundians mistake his name, thinking it sounds like their word for "hat" or "garland," *chapelet*, and transform it into the half-French, half-Italian Ciappelletto, Little Garland. In the course of the 14th century, *chapelet* also acquired the meaning of "rosary," so his name could also mean Little Rosary.

p. 31 *garbage pit like a dog*: Like other Italian cities of the time, Florence had *fossi,* "garbage pits," on its outskirts. However, *fossi* could also refer to pits dug in unconsecrated ground where suicides, heretics, the excommunicated, and even usurers were dumped. According to the chronicler Giovanni Villani (c. 1275–1348), such bodies were thrown into the *fossi,* that is, the *fossati* or (dry) moat, outside the walls of Florence. The specific meaning of Boccaccio's term is thus hard to determine even if the general meaning of what will happen to Ciappelletto is clear enough.

p. 32 *redeemed with His precious blood*: Ciappelletto's last words here echo a line from the *Te Deum*: *quos pretioso sanguine redemisti* ("whom Thou hast redeemed with Thy precious blood").

p. 33 *the sin of lust with a woman*: The friar begins by asking Ciappelletto about sins of incontinence (lust, gluttony, sloth, avarice, and anger).

p. 36 *I had my servant sweep the house*: According to Church law, the celebration of the Sabbath began at vespers on the preceding Saturday, and since nones (midafternoon) was the canonical hour before vespers (sunset), it was not officially part of the Sabbath. Out of feigned religious scrupulousness, however, Ciappelletto extends the observance of the Sabbath back to nones as well.

p. 37 *at least I may die a Christian*: The "body of Christ" is the Host, the bread that is eaten during Communion. "Extreme Unction" is a sacrament of the Catholic Church administered to those who are on their deathbed.

p. 39 *of the promises they had made*: An "ex-voto" is a votive offering (the phrase means "out of or because of a vow" in Latin).

p. 40 *who, as you have heard, became a saint*: Panfilo begins the final paragraph of his story by echoing the formulas used at the ends of medieval saints' lives.

p. 40 *at this point he fell silent*: This is the only case in the *Decameron* in which the narrator of the story is mentioned, albeit briefly, at the end.

DAY 1, STORY 2

p. 40 *returns to Paris and becomes a Christian*: Although there is no specific source for this story, arguments like the one that Abraham makes at the end can be found in a variety of medieval sermons and stories.

p. 41 *man named Giannotto di Civigni*: In French, the last name of Giannotto di Civignì could be Souvigny, Chauvigny, Chevigny, or Chovigny, all typically French names. His first name would be Jehannot or Jeannot in French, and both it and the Italian variant Boccaccio uses are diminutives, meaning Little John. Since Giannotto could be a form of Boccaccio's own first name, and Giovanni is the new name that Abraham will adopt later in the story, Boccaccio may be encouraging readers to see both characters as projections of the author himself.

p. 42 *those of his brothers, the cardinals*: Popes typically address the cardinals as *fratres,* "brothers."

p. 42 *tell you what you want to know*: In the late Middle Ages, the University of Paris was an intellectual center celebrated for the study of philosophy and theology.

p. 43 *Giannotto stopped arguing*: That is, there was nothing to lose because if Abraham stayed home, he would not become a Christian any more than if he went to Rome and saw how decadent it was.

p. 43 *by the names that are given to things*: Boccaccio's Italian for the first of the clergy's euphemisms, "procurement," is *procureria*, which means simply "to obtain the means to live." His second, "daily rations," is *substentazioni*. *Substentatio* (or *susstentatio*) was a late Latin word that referred to a monk's meager daily allowance of food. Both terms are clearly ironic, and the second one in particular deepens Boccaccio's religious satire in the story.

p. 44 *truer and holier than any other*: Abraham's repeated architectural metaphors for the Church recall the biblical notion that Saint Peter, the first bishop of Rome, was the rock on which the Church was built (see Matthew 16.18). His counter-intuitive argument here is not Boccaccio's invention; it exists in many of the sources of the story.

p. 44 *he named him Giovanni*: By lifting Abraham up from the baptismal font and naming him Giovanni, Giannotto is acting as his godfather.

DAY 1, STORY 3

p. 45 *trap set for him by Saladin*: Stories of the wise Jew and the three rings were widespread in the Middle Ages, including a version that appeared in the *Novellino* (73), sometimes leading to the conclusion that Christianity was the true ring and at other times endorsing a notion of skeptical tolerance. Similar stories continued to appear after the *Decameron* as well, and included, most famously, Gotthold Ephraim Lessing's Enlightenment play *Nathan der Weise* (*Nathan the Wise*, 1779). The name Melchisedech (or Melchizedek) means King of Justice and was common among the ancient Hebrews; see, for example, Genesis 14.18 and Psalms 110.4. Saladin (Salah al-Din, 1138–1193) was the Sultan of Cairo, and he was most famous for the reconquest of Jerusalem from the crusaders in 1187. A popular figure in medieval literature, he was celebrated for his knowledge, his chivalry, his military leadership, and his generosity. Dante placed him among the great pagan figures in Limbo (*Inferno* 4.129), Petrarch exalted him in his *Trionfo della Fama* (*Triumph of Fame* 2.148–50), and Boccaccio speaks glowingly of him in his earlier work, the *Amorosa visione* (12.28 ff.) as well as here in this story and in Story 10.9, where his generosity in particular is on display.

p. 45 *and became the Sultan of Babylon*: Babylon is the medieval name for Cairo.

p. 45 *money-lending business in Alexandria*: Lending money at interest (*prestare a usura*, in Boccaccio's Italian) was widely practiced in the Middle Ages by Jews and by many Christians as well. Although it was classified by the Church as a sin—the sin of usury, which is the term (*usura*) Boccaccio employs here—it seems unlikely that he considered it one.

DAY 1, STORY 4

p. 48 *rebuking his Abbot for the same fault*: Versions of this story were widely diffused in the Middle Ages, appearing in French *fabliaux* as well as in the *Novellino* (54), which was one of Boccaccio's models.

p. 48 *saved his body from the gravest punishment*: In his first story, Dioneo lives up to his name by focusing on the body and, in particular, on illicit sexuality, as he will do repeatedly in the stories he tells on the other nine days. In fact, when he is made King on Day 7, he chooses as its topic the (sexual) tricks that women play on their husbands. And, starting on Day 2, he is allowed to tell the last story, thus ending almost every day on a note of sexual license that often parodies what goes on in the preceding stories.

p. 48 *more holiness, than it does today*: Lunigiana is a mountainous region in northwest Tuscany extending from Emilia-Romagna down to the sea. It had two Benedictine monasteries in the 14th century, that of Montelungo near Pontremoli and that of the Priory of Santa Croce del Corvo near Lerici. The latter is the more likely candidate for the one in this story, since it was the scene of an encounter between Dante and a monk named Frate Ilaro whose letter describing their encounter Boccaccio had transcribed in his *Zibaldone* (*Notebook*).

p. 50 *as much as in the young monk*: The narrator calls the Abbot "Messer l'abate" in this sentence. I have retained this Italian title *Messer,* as I have done generally throughout this translation, rather than replace it with something like "Mister" or "Master." In most cases, it is used before a person's name as a sign of his status, but in satirical stories, like this one, it is clearly ironic. An abbot might well deserve such an honorific, but this one clearly does not, especially at this point when he is doing a sexual appraisal of the girl.

p. 50 *'a sin that's hidden is half forgiven'*: This last clause (*peccato celato è mezzo perdonato* in Italian) was a proverbial saying in the 14th century, as was its contrary, "a sin confessed is half forgiven" (*peccato confessato è mezzo perdonato*), a saying still current in Italian.

p. 51 *ordered them to put him in prison*: Monasteries typically had rooms to incarcerate monks who violated the rules.

DAY 1, STORY 5

p. 51 *love of the King of France*: There are various versions of this story in Eastern collections such as *The Book of the Seven Sages* and *The Thousand and One Nights* as well as in popular traditions of storytelling in Europe. Monferrato is a region of Italy to the south of Turin lying along the roads running between France and Genoa.

p. 52 *Christian army on a Crusade*: By referring to specific historical figures, Boccaccio dates his story to the time of the Third Crusade (1189–92), which attempted unsuccessfully to retake Jerusalem from Saladin who had conquered it in 1187. The Crusade was led by the French King Philippe Auguste, known as "le Borgne"

(The One Eyed), together with the Holy Roman Emperor Frederick Barbarossa and the English King Richard the Lion-Hearted. The Marquis of Monferrato, Corrado degli Aleramici, was a successful commander who was named the Defender of Constantinople and of Tyre and then the King of Jerusalem before he was assassinated on April 28, 1192. In the story, he is called a "Gonfalonier (that is, Standard-Bearer) of the Church," an honorific title that popes bestowed on various kings and noblemen between the 13th and the 17th centuries. He had succeeded to the title of Marquis of Monferrato upon the death of his father, Guiglielmo, in 1190, and he had already been in Palestine for several years before he was joined there by the crusaders in 1189. Boccaccio's story is thus set sometime in the months before March 1191, when Philippe signed a treaty of alliance with Richard in Sicily while they were on their way to the Holy Land. However, Boccaccio departs from the historical record in two important details. First, the Marquis did not leave a wife behind him in Monferrato. A widower when he went to the Holy Land, he married Theodora, the sister of the Byzantine emperor in 1187, but then abandoned her and married Isabella, Princess of Jerusalem, in 1192; neither of his wives was ever in Monferrato. Second, Philippe did not stop in Monferrato on his way to Genoa to sail to the Holy Land. This interweaving of history and fiction is typical of Boccaccio's stories.

p. 52 *opportunity to satisfy his desires*: Falling in love with a lady from afar, merely on the basis of her description, was a commonplace in medieval romance. This motif is consistent with other suggestive details in the story that seek to create an idealized portrait of a courtly and chivalric society of the past. The Marchioness's final quip to the king works, of course, to undercut this idealization to some extent.

p. 54 *same way they are everywhere else*: The Marchioness's remark needs interpretation. She may be saying that the King should not expect women in Monferrato, and especially her, to be unlike women elsewhere. In other words, they will be faithful to their husbands. There might also be an implied criticism of the King in her choice of "hens" for the banquet. On the equation of hens with women and cocks with men, see the supposedly deaf-mute Masetto's first words to the Abbess near the end of 3.1.

DAY 1 STORY 7

p. 54 *an unexpected fit of avarice*: There is no source for this story, although some critics see similarities with *Novellino* 44 and Peter Alphonsi, *Disciplina clericalis* (*A School for Clerics*) 4. Filostrato tells this story.

p. 55 *say about himself and his lord*: Messer Can della Scala is said to be a *magnifico signore*, which I have translated as "great lord." However, the adjective really means "grand," "magnificent." It defines the idealized lifestyle of the secular and religious elite as being one of splendor and lavish expenditures and also of generosity and hospitality. Avarice or miserliness is clearly opposed to this set of characteristics. The noun form of *magnifico*—namely *magnificenza*—which is applied to both

Can della Scala and to the Abbot of Cluny in the story, has sometimes been translated as "magnificence" and sometimes as "munificence"—that is, generosity.

p. 55 *time of the Emperor Frederick II*: Messer Can della Scala is also referred to more simply as Messer Cane in the story. He is usually called Cangrande (or Can Grande) della Scala (1291–1329) and was the ruler of Verona. His magnificence and generosity were well known and had been celebrated by Dante (*Paradiso* 17.76–93). The liberality of Frederick II (1197–1250), King of Sicily and Holy Roman Emperor, was also well known. One sign of such lordly munificence was to arrange for elaborate festivals, as Cangrande does in this story. Scholars have not, however, been able to identify the festival in the story with any particular one Cangrande organized.

p. 55 *believe it if you heard him talk*: Nothing is known about Bergamino who was most likely a storyteller by profession. His name may simply mean that he came from the town of Bergamo. Boccaccio groups him with the other *uomini di corte*, a phrase translated as "court entertainers" to avoid suggesting that they were "courtiers"—that is, individuals, often aristocrats, who were more permanent residents in the courts that were attached to powerful rulers and noblemen. In Boccaccio's time, the word *corte* meant such a body of individuals, but it also referred to a festival like the one Cangrande della Scala plans to hold and to which "court entertainers" such as Bergamino would flock from all over the peninsula.

p. 56 *greater facility than anywhere else*: During the first half of the 12th century, Hugh d'Orléans, who was called Primas (The Primate) by his friends at the University of Paris, was a canon in Cologne. He may have been the author of numerous satirical poems and drinking songs in Latin, writing under the name of Golias. He was imitated by many other poets, known consequently as Goliards, whose works were often critical of the Church and eventually provoked it to attempt to suppress them. The *Carmina Burana* is the best-known collection of verse produced by these poets.

p. 56 *Pope, in God's Church*: The Benedictine Abbey of Cluny, located in Burgundy, was founded in 910 by Duke William the Pious of Aquitaine. It controlled a number of abbeys elsewhere, including one in Paris, and by the late Middle Ages its wealth had become legendary. It is not clear which abbot is the one involved in this story. Note that another abbot from Cluny appears in Story 10.2.

p. 57 *something he especially cared for*: A poem in which wine is celebrated as being superior to water is attributed to the historical Primas.

p. 59 *come and go as he pleased*: This last clause rehearses a formula used by rulers welcoming ambassadors to their courts; it is used again at the end of the story, and essentially means something like, "you have the run of the place."

DAY 1, CONCLUSION

p. 60 *provide adequately for the future*: Pampinea is paraphrasing a medieval proverb: *providus est plenus, improvidus extat egenus* ("the provident one will be full, the improvident will wind up needy"). The moment she has chosen to name the next queen is the canonical hour of vespers, which marks the end of one liturgical day and the start of the next. Her decision heightens the ritual-like nature of what they are doing, as does her use of the proverb here and her reference to the deity in the next sentence, which echoes Luke 20.38.

p. 60 *on this, our second day*: Filomena was the one who worried at the start about the women going off into the countryside without any men along to guide them. Hence, Pampinea is pronouncing her "prudent" here.

p. 62 *May come from such desire for loveliness*: Emilia's song invites allegorical interpretation, as Boccaccio's next sentence suggests. Some critics see the "good that makes the mind content" (*ben che fa contento lo 'ntelletto*) as God, who is contained within the beauty she sees in her mirror. Dante speaks of the damned in Hell as having lost *il ben dell'intelletto* (*Inferno* 3.18: "the good of the intellect"; cf. *Purgatorio* 27.103 and *Paradiso* 26.16). Dante took this concept from Aristotle (*Nicomachean Ethics* 6.2), for whom the "good of the intellect" meant the truth that the intellect has as its proper object; Dante then redefined it as the truth that is the proper object of all human striving and knowing—namely, God. Other critics, however, have imagined the good of which Emilia sings as wisdom or one of the liberal arts.

DAY 2, STORY 1

p. 64 *he gets off in the end*: Although there is no literary precedent for this story, its characters appear to be historical. Stecchi and Martellino were lower-class professional entertainers (*buffoni*), whom Sacchetti also mentions in his *Trecentonovelle* (*Three Hundred Stories*) 144. There was a Saint Arrigo who worked as a humble porter (or perhaps a wood carrier) while he was alive. When he died on June 10, 1315, the church bells rang of their own accord, and after a reverent crowd had taken his body into the cathedral, it became the source of miracles, one of the first being the curing of a cripple. The tomb of the Blessed Arrigo can still be seen in the Cathedral of Treviso. Also lying behind the story is the episode in the New Testament in which a man stricken with palsy cannot be brought before Christ because of a crowd and has to be lowered down to him from the roof (see Mark 2.3–12 and Luke 5.18–26). Neifile tells this story.

p. 65 *there to prevent disturbances*: The "Germans" here are probably compatriots of Arrigo rather than mercenaries and most likely hailed from Bolzano in the far north of Italy where German is still spoken.

p. 67 *"Help me, for God's sake"*: In the early 14th century, Treviso was in fact governed by a Ghibelline *podestà* from Gubbio named Manno della Branca. "*Podestà*" was the name given to the chief magistrate, usually functioning as a judge, in the towns of northern and central Italy during the late Middle Ages.

p. 68 *given a thorough shellacking*: Boccaccio's phrase, which I have translated as "a thorough shellacking," is *senza pettine carminato*. It means literally that Martellino was being "carded without a comb." Wool was carded in Boccaccio's time by means of heavy iron carding combs that were drawn through it to straighten out the fibers and remove dirt and debris. Such combs were also used as torture devices to tear off the skin of their victims. Saint Blaise, the governor of Sebastea (Sivas in modern Turkey), was martyred by being carded and then having his head cut off, and in representations he often appears holding such combs in his hands. In Boccaccio's day, "being carded" was slang for being beaten.

p. 68 *series of good, hard jerks*: The "strappado" was an instrument of torture that consisted of a rope running through a pulley affixed to the ceiling. The victim's hands, tied behind his back, were attached to the rope, and he was hauled up into the air by them, then suddenly released, his fall being stopped with a jerk before he hit the ground. Such jerks, which would have dislocated most people's shoulders, were supposed to make the victim confess the truth.

p. 69 *with the ruler of the city*: The Agolanti was a noble Florentine family that was exiled from the city in the 13th century, and some of its members were in Venice and Treviso where they probably worked as bankers. A certain "Bernardus de Agolantis de Florentia" appears in a document concerning a miracle performed by the Blessed Arrigo on June 20, 1315, and at least one critic thinks that this member of the family may have told the tale in Florence that Boccaccio is reworking here.

DAY 2, STORY 2

p. 69 *returns home safe and sound*: There are precedents for Boccaccio's *novella* in Asian story collections such as the *Panchatantra* (4.1) as well as in the *Novellino* (99). However, its true origins can be found in the widely known legend of Saint Julian the Hospitaller, also known as Saint Julian the Poor, the patron saint of travelers. Probably of French origin, the legend is romantic fiction rather than historical fact. It concerns a nobleman who killed his parents unintentionally and then performed various acts of penance, which included building a hospice, taking care of the poor, and offering hospitality to travelers, until an angel, disguised as a traveler, told him he had been forgiven. Well into the Renaissance, travelers did, in fact, offer a variety of prayers to Saint Julian, and it is worth noting that in Boccaccio's time, the "hospitality" of Saint Julian often included the furnishing of one's guest with a bed companion. There is a Castel Guiglielmo in the province of Rovigo not far from Ferrara, and it is possible, considering the accuracy of the details Boccaccio supplies about the setting of the story, that he might have traveled there at some point.

p. 70 *how good his bed may be*: Filostrato's claim that his story will be merely "profitable" echoes the Horatian dictum that poetry should be *dulce*, "sweet," and *utile*, "useful" or "profitable"; see the *Ars poetica* (*The Art of Poetry*), 343. Although he implies that his story may not be particularly "sweet," most readers would disagree.

p. 70 *take care of some business*: Marquis Azzo VIII d'Este da Ferrara (1263–c. 1308) is the most likely candidate for the figure to whom Boccaccio is referring. Dante identifies him as a patricide (*Inferno* 12.109–11).

p. 70 *many prayers on hand*: "*Soldi*" and "*denari*" were coins of the period, each *soldo* being worth twelve *denari* (*denaro* comes from the Latin *denarius*, which is usually translated as "penny"). What Rinaldo means is that he is the sort of man who "says what's what," or "calls them like he sees them."

p. 71 *grandmother used to tell me*: The bandit cites, with some inaccuracy in the second case, the openings of three medieval prayers: *Dirupisti* (from Psalms 116.16: "Thou hast loosed my bonds"), *O intemerata Virgo* ("O intact Virgin"), and *De profundis* (from Psalms 130.1: "Out of the depths have I cried").

p. 76 *heels in the north wind*: At the beginning of the next story, Boccaccio records the group's response to what it has just heard: "The young women and men listened with admiration to the adventures of Rinaldo d'Asti, praising his devotion and thanking God and Saint Julian who had come to his aid in the time of his greatest need. Nor, for that matter, did they think the lady a fool for knowing how to take advantage of the gift that God had sent to her house, although they did not say so openly."

DAY 2, STORY 4

p. 76 *returns home a rich man*: Although this story has no literary source, it generally recalls Greek romances, such as Longus's *Daphnis and Chloe* and Achilles Tatius's *Leucippe and Clitophon,* works whose heroes experience the highs and lows of Fortune as they wander around the Mediterranean world, often over a period of many years.

p. 77 *who was really extraordinarily rich*: There are records of the Rufolo family living in Naples and Ravello in the 13th and 14th centuries. The branch in the latter city was extremely wealthy and cultured, as can be seen today from the palace it possessed there and from the pulpit dedicated to the family in the city's cathedral. A certain Matteo and his son Lorenzo, who managed a lucrative trade with Greece and Egypt, were condemned to prison by the Angevin rulers of Naples in 1283 for having joined in the uprising against their rule called the Sicilian Vespers. Lorenzo was later pardoned, but after becoming a pirate, he was captured and died in a Calabrian stronghold in 1291. In the story, Boccaccio is clearly recollecting the time he himself spent in Naples and the surrounding region as well as the story of Lorenzo, although he has given his version of it a happy ending.

p. 78 *that was blowing head-on*: "Archipelago" is the medieval Greek name for the Aegean Sea.

p. 79 *glass shattered against a wall*: Cephalonia is the largest island in the Ionian Sea off the west coast of Greece. Corfu, to which Landolfo will eventually drift, is a small island to the north close to the southern tip of present-day Albania.

p. 81 *to be fellow townsmen*: Trani is a town on the Adriatic coast of Italy about twenty-five miles west-northwest of Bari.

DAY 2, STORY 5

p. 82 *returns home with a ruby*: There are many literary and folkloric antecedents
for various aspects of this story, although it is difficult to speak here of "sources."
The story contains, however, quite specific references to places in Naples, where
Boccaccio spent a substantial time in his youth, as well as to individuals associated
in different ways with the city. A certain Andreuccio da Perugia appears in a
14th-century document, although he was not a horse trader by profession and
for that reason does not seem a model for Boccaccio's character.

p. 82 *space of a single night*: This story is unique in the *Decameron* in that it begins
quite directly, with scarcely any mention of the reaction of the listeners to the
previous story or anything more than a passing reference to the rules of the
storytelling game they are playing. Nor does the narrator supply a moralizing
framework within which to place the narrative she is about to present.

p. 82 *a horse trader by profession*: Andreuccio's first name is a pet name and means
something like Little Andrew in English, but it also could have the more general,
symbolic meaning of "man" or "little man" since its Greek root means "man."

p. 84 *how honest a place it is*: Malpertugio was a commercial area of Naples near
the port and the arsenal in which many foreign merchants, including those from
Sicily, located their businesses. Not far away was the Bardi bank in which Boccaccio had worked when he was in Naples. Needless to say, the district also
attracted prostitutes, thieves, and all sorts of riffraff. *Malpertugio* means "bad
hole" and refers to a gap in the city's wall.

p. 86 *grandest lady ever on the island*: The houses of Anjou and Aragon were struggling in the later Middle Ages for control of the Kingdoms of Naples and Sicily.
Charles I of Anjou, supported by the papacy—thus making him a Guelf—took
control of the two kingdoms in the 1260s. His harsh rule, however, led to an
uprising against him in 1282 known as the Sicilian Vespers. The French and
their Guelf supporters were expelled from the island, and in 1296, the Guelfs'
opponents there, the Ghibellines, had Frederick II of Aragon proclaimed king
of the island, over which he reigned until 1337. Boccaccio's story is set some time
after the Treaty of Caltabellotta in 1302, by which Charles II of Anjou, then King
of Naples, gave up all claims to Sicily after a series of unsuccessful attempts to
restore the Angevins to power there. The lady's fictitious husband presumably
took part in one of those attempts.

p. 87 *some of it to drink*: "Greco" is the name of a wine grape, originally from Greece,
that is grown in southern Italy. Although there is a red variety, when people
speak of Greco, they usually mean the white wine, which is most likely what
Andreuccio and the lady are drinking here.

p. 89 *Andreuccio to the bottom*: The streets in the oldest part of Naples form a grid
that was laid out by Greek settlers when the city was originally founded (Naples
comes from the Greek *Neapolis*, meaning "New City"). Those streets and the
houses on them were very close together, so it is easy to imagine how the

inhabitants in Boccaccio's time could put beams from one house to the next across a street in order to create something like an elevated outhouse.

p. 89 *Madame Fiordaliso's brother*: Fiordaliso (*fleur-de-lis* in French) means "lily," and may be a fictional name the lady has adopted.

p. 91 *street called Ruga Catalana*: The Ruga Catalana (Catalan Street) was named for the numerous Catalan expatriates living there who were attached to the Angevin court. By turning left and going up this street, Andreuccio is heading away from the sea.

p. 92 *at Boss Buttafuoco's house*: Boccaccio calls this character Scarabone Buttafuoco. His last name was—and is—common in Sicily; it means Throws Fire and hence, perhaps, could be translated as Spitfire or Belchfire. His first name is probably a common noun, not a name. *Scarabuni* meant "thief" in Sicilian and may thus identify him as the leader, the "boss," of one of the gangs of criminals who terrorized Naples in the period (their modern successor is the Camorra, the Neapolitan equivalent of the Mafia). *Scarabone* also suggests *scarafuni,* which means "scrounger" and derives from *scarafaggio,* "cockroach."

p. 92 *Messer Filippo Minutolo had been buried*: There was an archbishop named Filippo Minutolo who had been an important figure in the Kingdom of Naples and who had died, not during the heat of the summer as Boccaccio's story suggests, but on October 24, 1301. His tomb can still be seen in the chapel of the Minutolo family in the Cathedral of Naples.

DAY 2, STORY 7

p. 96 *marry the King of Algarve*: Alatiel, the heroine of the story, actually sleeps with just eight men; the first ship's captain who seizes her is prevented by his wounds from taking her to bed. This story has some general plot similarities to *The Tale of Anthia and Habrocomes,* a romance by the 3rd-century Greek writer Xenophon of Ephesus. There are also parallels to stories in *The Thousand and One Nights,* to various versions of the Tristan story in medieval romances, and at the most general level, to stories of wandering about the Mediterranean, including those of Odysseus and Aeneas. Panfilo tells this story.

p. 96 *they are made of gold*: Boccaccio is quoting a line from Seneca that had become quasi-proverbial: *venenum in auro bibitur* (*Thyestes* 453: "poison is drunk from a golden cup").

p. 97 *went contrary to his wishes*: Babylon is the medieval name for Cairo. The Sultan's name is fictitious, although an Amminadab appears in the Bible as the father of Nahshon, one of the followers of Moses (Numbers 1.7 and 7.12) and as one of the ancestors of Christ (Matthew 1.4). His daughter's name, Alatiel, is likewise fictitious, although it might be an anagram for La Lieta (The Happy One). The different parts of her name are particularly suggestive: *ala* is the word for "wing" and thus evokes the heroine's "flight" around the Mediterranean, while the ending of the word, *tiel,* points to the names of angels, such as Raphael and Michael, which end in *el,* the Hebrew word for "God," thus ironically under-scoring the un-angelic character of Alatiel's earthly experience.

p. 97 *to defeat them decisively*: In Boccaccio's time, the Kingdom of Algarve was an Islamic state that included most of the Mediterranean coast of North Africa as well as a portion of the Iberian Peninsula (the southernmost province of Portugal is still called by that name); *el Gharb* was the Arabic name for "the West."

p. 99 *several of his servants*: Pericone da Visalgo is a purely fictitious character. His first name is a diminutive of the Catalan *Pere* (Peter); his last is the name of a castle in Majorca, a large island off the east coast of Spain almost directly south of Barcelona and east of Valencia.

p. 101 *to have his way with her*: The notion that wine functions as "Venus's assistant" (or minister or companion) has been a commonplace since antiquity and can be found in several of Boccaccio's favorite classical authors, including Horace, *Odes* 3.18.6–7 and 3.21.21, and Apuleius, *Metamorphoses* 2.11 and 2.15.

p. 101 *in the Alexandrian manner*: By "Alexandrian" is meant Egyptian, presumably belly dancing.

p. 102 *for Chiarenza in Romania*: Boccaccio's "Romania" was the name given generally to the Byzantine (that is, Eastern Roman) Empire, although the Pelo-ponnesus, in which the port of Chiarenza (or Klarenza) is located, was more frequently called Morea, the term Byzantine Greeks used for the area.

p. 104 *honor amid great rejoicing*: The Duke of Athens, like the Prince of Morea, is a fictional character. However, Boccaccio had known a real Duke of Athens, Walter of Brienne, who had been made the ruler of Florence in 1342–43. The Duchy of Athens, which included Attica and Boeotia, was created in 1205 during the Fourth Crusade, when the territory was taken from the Byzantine Empire. It was then held by a variety of European rulers until it fell to the Turks in 1456.

p. 105 *passionately in love with her*: The notions of love as a poison and as a snare or trap were commonplaces in the courtly love tradition. For some examples of the former, see Petrarch, *Canzoniere (Song Book)* 152.8 and 207.84; of the latter, see 55.15 and 165.5–8.

p. 107 *head of a fine large force*: There was, in fact, a Constantine who was the son of the Byzantine emperor Andronikos II (1259–1332, ruled 1282–1328) and whom Boccaccio may have known about. However, the name, like Manuel, may simply be generic for Byzantine rulers. Constantinople was the capital of the Byzantine Empire until it fell to the Turks in 1453 and was renamed Istanbul.

p. 109 *before dawn the next day*: Aegina is the name of both a city and the island on which it is located. It is about twenty miles southwest of Athens.

p. 110 *set up any defenses there*: Smyrna, the modern Izmir, is a city on the east coast of Turkey not very far across the Aegean Sea from Chios, a Greek island just off the coast of Turkey.

p. 110 *and get their weapons*: Osbech, or Uzbek (ruled c. 1312–c. 1342), was a Mongol who was the Khan of the Golden Horde in what is now southern Russia. He had good relations with both Christians and Muslims and encouraged the Black Sea trade of the Venetians and the Genoese. Boccaccio turns him into the King of the Turks and has him engage in a fictional struggle against the Byzantine Empire.

p. 110 *assaulted him from the other*: Like Osbech, Basano is a fictional character. By the early 14th century, Cappadocia, a province in Asia Minor, was not an independent state, but was ruled by the Turks. The name of Boccaccio's character may be a reflection of that of Baudon Bassian (Baldon Bassano in Italian) who was the chamberlain of King Robert of Naples (ruled 1309–43). His Italian-sounding name might also be meant to suggest that he is a Christian.

p. 111 *Antioco contracted a fatal illness*: Rhodes is an island strategically located off the southwest coast of Turkey, to the south of both Chios and Smyrna. Now a part of Greece, it was much disputed in the Middle Ages by the Byzantine Empire, the Arabs, the Genoese, and others, until it was captured by the Knights Hospitaller in 1309 who held it until it was taken by the Turks in 1522.

p. 112 *about to sail to Cyprus*: Currently an independent republic, Cyprus is a large island south of Turkey and west of Syria and Lebanon that was part of the Byzantine Empire until it was conquered by crusaders in 1191 and ruled by various Europeans states until it was annexed by Venice in 1489 and eventually fell to the Turks in 1570.

p. 113 *like a regular married couple*: Paphos was a major center on Cyprus for the worship of Aphrodite in classical times. The Greek goddess of love was said to have been engendered in the Mediterranean Sea when the god Chronos cut off Uranus's testicles and threw them into the water. Some versions of the myth have Aphrodite coming ashore at Paphos; others, on the island of Cythera.

p. 113 *always been his enemy*: Antigono's name, like Antioco's, is generic and is meant to evoke the Hellenistic eastern Mediterranean. His full name is Antigono di Famagosto, which means that he is from the town of Famagosto, which, like Paphos, is located on Cyprus. Although the King of Cyprus is not identified by name, the island was, in fact, a kingdom. It had been part of the Byzantine Empire until 1192, when it became an independent state ruled by the crusader Guy de Lusignan. During the period in which Boccaccio sets his story, the early 14th century, the relevant kings would have been Henry II of Jerusalem (ruled 1310–24) and Hugh IV (ruled 1324–59).

p. 116 *a place called Aigues-Mortes*: Aigues-Mortes, a walled city on the coast of Provence to the east of Montpellier, had a flourishing commerce with Florence and Genoa. Its name means literally Dead (that is, stagnant) Waters, referring to the marshes on which the city was built. The name suggests a contrast with the literal and sexual storms of Alatiel's Mediterranean odyssey.

p. 116 *of that country are passionately devoted*: Although Alatiel's saint seems her, or Antigono's, clever invention, there was, in fact, a sanctuary dedicated to San Cresci in Valcava (Saint Grows-in-the-Deep-Valley) that was located in Mugello, a river valley about fifteen miles north of Florence. "Cresci" is short for Crescenzio or, to use his more usual Latin name, Crescentius, an eleven-year-old Christian martyr who was brought to Rome during the persecutions of Diocletian in the early 4th century c.e. and was tortured and beheaded after he refused to deny Christ. The appellation *Valcava,* which I have translated as "Deep Valley," really means something like "the valley of the mine," most likely because a mine of some sort was located in the Mugello Valley.

p. 118 *But just like the moon, it's forever renewed:* Boccaccio's story is the first recorded instance of this Italian saying: *Bocca basciata non perde ventura, anzi rinnova come fa la luna.* It is composed of two clauses, each of which is a perfect hendecasyllabic line (the standard Italian verse line in Petrarchan sonnets and the *Divine Comedy*), and the two clauses are also almost rhymed (*ventura* and *la luna*). What I have translated as "charm" (*ventura*) means, literally, "adventure" or "luck," which is the central theme of the story. The saying has a romantic quality that Verdi famously brings out by means of his wonderful musical setting of the words when they are sung by the young lovers in *Falstaff,* his last opera. Boccaccio's story is, of course, anything but romantic—it is, indeed, a satire of romance—and the saying is, instead, witty and ironic.

DAY 2, STORY 10

p. 119 *becomes Paganino's wife:* This story of a May–December marriage has so many antecedents in world literature that identifying any one of them as its source would be a mistake. There was a quarter in Pisa called Chinzica, but there is no record of a Ricciardo ever having lived there. His wife comes from the Gualandi family, which was well established in the city, but there is, likewise, no record of a Bartolomea among its members. Dioneo tells this story.

p. 120 *as little wormy lizards:* The ugliness of Pisan women was proverbial among Florentines. In the Italian, Dioneo speaks of *lucertole verminare* (wormlike lizards), an expression that is Neapolitan in origin and refers to a small greenish lizard found in the Campagna.

p. 120 *the land of the living:* Vernaccia wine is a white wine made from a varietal of the same name that is grown throughout Italy. The name derives from a word meaning "vernacular"—that is, "local." Nowadays, when people say Vernaccia, they are usually referring to the Tuscan white wine Vernaccia di San Gimignano, but in Boccaccio's time that was not necessarily the case.

p. 120 *once been used at Ravenna:* Ravenna was famous for having almost as many churches as there are days of the year, thus making practically every day a saint's day. Calendars made there would have been attractive to schoolboys because they contained nothing but holidays.

p. 120 *civil cases in the law courts:* "Ember Days" is the English name (*quater tempora* in Latin) for the periods of fasting to be observed in the four seasons of the year, specifically on the Wednesday, Friday, and Saturday following four specific holy days: the first Sunday in Lent, Whitsunday or Pentecost, Holy Cross Day (September 14), and St. Lucia's Day (December 13). They are also referred to as Ember Weeks.

p. 121 *enjoying the fresh country air*: Monte Nero is a promontory located some twenty miles south of Pisa.

p. 121 *suddenly arrived on the scene*: Although the character is called Paganino da Monaco (Paganino of Monaco) in the rubric that serves as the title for the story, here Boccaccio supplies his family name *da Mare*, which was that of a well-known noble family in Genoa. There are no historical records concerning this figure, although there are many instances of members of important Italian families becoming pirates or bandits in the late Middle Ages. Boccaccio features such figures in Stories 2.4 (Landolfo Rufolo), 2.6 (Guasparrino Doria), and 10.2 (Ghino di Tacco). The Monaco from which Paganino hails was a notorious haven for pirates at the time.

p. 121 *feast days and holidays*: Boccaccio writes *essendo a lui il calendaro caduto da cintola*, which I have translated as "he had lost his calendar." More literally, the phrase means that the calendar had fallen off his belt, which is apparently where people would carry it.

p. 125 *good whacking day and night*: After being sheared, raw wool had to be cleaned, a process that involved washing it and then beating it. Boccaccio clearly uses beating, or "whacking," wool as a metaphor for sexual intercourse here.

p. 125 *live with the pestle's-in too*: The lady's sexual wordplay in this sentence is brilliant. First, she replaces Ricciardo's *in peccato mortale* (in mortal sin) with *in peccato mortaio* (in mortar sin). Then, as she looks to her future with Paganino, she transforms the phrase even more cleverly into *imbeccato pestello*, which I have translated as a matter of living "with the *pestle's-in*," a pun on "pestle sin." More literally, the phrase means a "pestle [that has been] put in a [baby bird's] mouth [to feed it]." Boccaccio will later see mortar and pestle in such sexualized terms in his Introduction to Day 4, in Story 8.2, and in the Author's Conclusion.

p. 126 *to make it stand up*: Another untranslatable set of plays on words. The first of the phrases is *di farla in tre pace*. This contains a play on the expression *fare patta*, meaning "to finish a card game in a stalemate," and thus "to accomplish nothing." The entire phrase would mean something like "to accomplish nothing three times in a row." But there's also a play on *patta* and *pace* (peace), suggesting that the matches were not all that energetic. The second phrase, *rizzare a mazzata*, means "to straighten [something] by dint of blows [as with a *mazza*, a mace]." However, the phrase can also refer to lifting up a fishing rod to see if any fish are dangling there. I can see no way to work this second meaning into my translation. Note that in her next sentence the lady will refer mockingly to Ricciardo as a *pro' cavaliere*. I have rendered this as "sturdy rider" to bring out the latent sexual meaning, but it meant something more like "valiant or worthy knight," a phrase suggesting that *rizzare a mazzata* may be less about fishing than about wielding a mace, as knights were wont to do.

p. 126 *whistling in the wind*: Dioneo's phrase here is *non montavano un frullo*, which could be rendered: "[his words] did not amount to anything"—that is, they made no difference. However, a *frullo* is a bone that has been hollowed out and tied to a cord; when whirled in the air, it makes a sound like the sound of the word itself. *Frullo* was also used for the sound certain birds make when they take off in flight.

p. 126 *never takes a holiday*: Boccaccio's original reads: *Il mal furo non vuol festa.* The word I have translated as "hole," *furo*, is a parody of the Pisan pronunciation of *foro*. Although *foro* means "hole," it could also mean "the bar" or "the law courts," a meaning that is ironic in context, since Messer Ricciardo is, after all, a judge. However, the word Boccaccio actually supplies, *furo*, also suggests "thief" (*fur*, in Latin), a meaning that likewise seems to fit the context, since Ricciardo's wife has been stolen from him. In fact, the "evil thief" could be the lady herself as well as Paganino since she prefers to remain "stolen."

p. 127 *complete fool of himself*: Referring to the dispute at the start of Story 2.9 between Bernabò and Ambruogiuolo concerning the chastity of Bernabò's wife, Dioneo uses an Italian saying that is untranslatable in any direct way: *Bernabò . . . cavalcasse la capra inverso il chino* (literally, "Bernabò . . . was riding a she goat down a slope [or toward a precipice]"). The Italian saying *cavalcare la capra* (literally, "to ride a she goat") means to do something stupid, deceive oneself, get things all wrong. Dioneo develops the saying by having the rider go *inverso il chino* ("down the slope" or "toward the precipice"). His having Bernabò ride a she goat rather than a horse is also in keeping with his conception of women (and men) as driven by their sexual appetites, since goats were well known for their randiness.

DAY 2, CONCLUSION

p. 127 *glittered like the morning star*: The younger women in the company—Filomena, Neifile, and Emilia—frequently blush as a sign of their modesty and innocence. Sparkling or glittering eyes were an attribute of Dante's Beatrice (see, for example, *Purgatorio* 12.89–90), but they were also a cliché in courtly love and popular poetry more generally, as was the association of women's faces with roses. The "morning star" is Venus.

p. 127 *the food we normally eat then*: Both Fridays and Saturdays were days for fasting. Note that the Sabbath was celebrated in Florence between noon on Saturday and noon on Sunday.

p. 128 *recover something they had lost*: Neifile's topic focuses on the *industria* displayed by people in getting what they want. I have translated that key word as "resourcefulness," but it actually has a range of meanings from industriousness and hard work at one extreme, through resourcefulness and inventiveness, down to cleverness and trickiness at the other.

p. 128 *led them in a carola*: A "carola" is a dance in which the dancers join hands and move in a clockwise direction, usually accompanied by music and the singing of the dancers themselves.

p. 129 *from His Kingdom up above*: Pampinea's song reflects her general serenity and happiness. Its motifs can be traced back to Petrarch's *Canzoniere* (*Song Book*). For examples, see poems 14, 26, 59, and 70.

DAY 3, INTRODUCTION

p. 131 *plain on a little hill*: This new palace is very much like the first one the company stayed in, the only exception being the walled garden next to it that is accorded an elaborate description that evokes the Garden of Eden. "Halfway to the hour of tierce" would make it in between sunrise and midmorning.

p. 131 *live in the grand style*: Boccaccio's narrator says that the members of the company considered the owner of the palace to be *magnifico*. Although that word started being used as a substantive in the 15th century to mean a great and noble person (Lorenzo de' Medici was known as *il Magnifico*), when Boccaccio was writing it was an adjective that meant someone endowed with greatness, nobility, and especially, generosity or liberality. In the Aristotelian tradition, it was one of the defining features of aristocrats and referred to a liberality of expenditure combined with good taste. That Boccaccio is thinking of just such an aristocratic sense of the word is evident in his use of *signore* (lord) when speaking of the owner of the palace.

DAY 3, STORY 1

p. 134 *get to sleep with him*: There are antecedents for this story in the *Novellino* (62) as well as, more generally, in the *fabliau* tradition.

p. 134 *native village of Lamporecchio*: Lamporecchio is a small village near Pistoia to the north of Florence.

p. 135 *find me sending him there*: Nuto's oath in this sentence ("unless God gives . . .") is *il faccia Idio san delle reni,* which means literally, "May God make him sound in his loins." It may reflect the fact that the Bible frequently connects God with the loins (see Psalms 16.7, 26.2, and 73.21).

DAY 3, STORY 2

p. 141 *thus escapes a terrible fate*: Although there are many antecedents for the groom's cleverness and the King's prudence in tale collections that appeared before the *Decameron,* no particular story can be identified as the source for this one.

p. 142 *the former Lombard ruler*: Agilulf, who had been the Duke of Turin, ruled over the Lombards from 590, the year in which he married Theodolinda, the widow of King Authari, until his death in 616. The Lombards had taken Pavia in 572 and controlled most of Italy north of the Po River. Boccaccio's source for this historical information is the third book of the 8th-century *Historia Longobardorum* (*History of the Lombards*) of Paulus Diaconus. This work was also a source for Boccaccio's description of the plague in the Introduction to the first day.

p. 142 *to such a lofty height*: According to the conventions of courtly love, even though the lover is rejected or ignored by his beloved, the very fact that he loves such a worthy object serves to ennoble him.

DAY 3, STORY 4

p. 147 *with the friar's wife*: There is no source for this story, which was also told by Chaucer, in a very different way, in "The Miller's Tale" and by Giovanni Sercambi in *Il novelliere* (111 and 117). The figure of the gullible religious devotee appears frequently in the *Decameron*; see, for instance, Stories 3.3 and 7.1. "Dom" (from the Latin *dominus*, "lord") was a title given to monks who had earned some sort of distinction, such as, in this case, having completed theological studies at the prestigious University of Paris. Felice means "happy, fortunate." Puccio is a pet name derived from Giacopuccio and means Jimmy. Panfilo tells this story.

p. 147 *the name of Frate Puccio*: San Pancrazio is a church in the center of Florence not far from Santa Maria Novella. Tertiaries (from the Latin *tertius*, "third") were lay members of the "third order" of the Franciscans (after the Friars Minor and the Poor Clares); they did not have to follow all the rules of the order or live in the monastery, but took simple vows and were allowed to wear the habit.

p. 147 *lay brothers were chanting lauds*: "Lauds" is the second canonical hour (after matins) celebrated before daybreak.

p. 147 *was one of the Flagellants*: The Flagellants were organized bands of the devout who whipped themselves in public. They started appearing in the 12th century and became quite numerous after the outbreak of the plague in 1348.

p. 148 *as an apple from Casole*: Casole is a town in the Val d'Elsa some seventeen miles to the west of Siena.

p. 148 *Mary Magdalene, or things of that sort*: Frate Nastagio (Anastasius) here is probably meant as a generic name for preachers, since there is no collection of sermons attributed to such a person. There were many versions of the Lament of Mary Magdalene circulating in late medieval culture.

p. 149 *about the hour of compline*: "Compline" is the last canonical hour, celebrated after dark.

p. 151 *Saint Giovanni Gualberto*: Both Saint Benedict and Saint Giovanni Gualberto were frequently depicted in the Middle Ages as riding on an ass. The image here is, of course, sexual in nature.

DAY 3, STORY 8

p. 152 *his wife had with the Abbot*: This story has, at best, vague antecedents in French *fabliaux* and tales from the East. Lauretta tells this story.

p. 154 *leads to the life eternal*: Penitents typically kneeled at the feet of their confessors; the confessional booth was introduced only after the Council of Trent met to reform the Catholic Church (1545–63).

p. 156 *bring them back from it again*: The Old Man of the Mountain was Rashid ad-Din As-sinan (died 1192), leader of the Syrian branch of a Shiite sect known as the Assassins that was active between the 11th and 13th centuries. He got his name from the fact that his stronghold was a fortress at Masyaf in the mountains of northern Syria. His followers were called Assassins (Hashishim) from the hashish they smoked, which induced visions before they were sent off to murder their enemies. In his *Il milione* (*The Million*; known in English as *The Travels of Marco Polo*), from the late 13th century, Marco Polo described how the Old Man of the Mountain supposedly had a beautiful garden in the mountains that he identified as Paradise. He attracted a following of young people, would put them into a deep sleep, and have them transported there, after which he had them consume a drug before sending them off on their murderous enterprises. Boccaccio actually transcribed this passage from *Il milione* in his notebooks and wrote in the margin *il veglio della montagna* ("The Old Man of the Mountain").

p. 160 *His love for San Benedetto*: That is, Saint Benedict. The Abbot's words here distantly parody those of the angel to Zacharias, the father of John the Baptiste.

p. 162 *devoutly sing the Miserere*: *Miserere* ("Have mercy upon me") is the opening of Psalms 51, which constitutes a prayer asking for God's forgiveness.

p. 162 *before he came back to life*: The "Ark-Ranger Bagriel" (*Ragnolo Braghiello* in Italian) is Ferondo's corruption of either "Archangel" or "Angel Gabriel" (*Arcagnolo* or *Agnolo Gabriele*), revealing a verbal deficiency he shares with other dupes in the *Decameron*. His linguistic confusion is especially funny in the original, since he is conflating the high with the low, the word for archangel or angel with that for spider (*ragno*), and the name Gabriel with the word for breeches (*le brache*) to which a diminutive ending has been added.

DAY 3, STORY 10

p. 163 *becomes the wide of Neerbale*: There are only the vaguest of antecedents for this story. Throughout history there were a number of holy men named Rustico who were known for their continence, including several saints, the most famous of whom was probably Saint Rustico of Narbonne (died 461). Rustico's name was probably meant to recall such figures, but it is clearly ironic in the story and was most likely chosen because of its meaning: Rustico is a "rustic," a rube, who badly overestimates his ability to satisfy Alibech. The latter's name is equally suggestive. It is meant to sound Arabic: the name Ali was well known in western Europe during the Middle Ages as being that of Mohammad's follower who founded the Shiite branch of Islam (see Dante, *Inferno* 31–33). However, "Ali" could also suggest the idea of nourishment (*alimentare* means "to feed"), and "bech" might evoke the idea of eating (*beccare* means "to peck at [like a bird]"). These meanings of Alibech's name may be relevant at the climax of the story when the exhausted Rustico can no longer handle his all-too-willing pupil, and the narrator makes a joke about a bean and a lion's mouth.

p. 163 *little daughter named Alibech*: Barbary is the old name for Tunisia. Capsa was the name for the southern Tunisian town now called Gafsa. The "desert around ebes" mentioned later in the paragraph is the Sahara.

p. 165 *of the flesh took place*: This last phrase also occurs in Apuleius, *Metamorphoses* (2.7), where it has a similar sexual meaning.

DAY 3, CONCLUSION

p. 168 *through your hollow bones*: Neifile's last phrase is, in Italian, *l'ossa senza maestro avrebbono apparato a sufolare*, which could be rendered more literally as: "your bones, without a teacher, would have learned how to whistle." The essence of her gibe is that Filostrato, like Masetto with the nuns, would have been so worn out from having served the "sheep" sexually that he would have been reduced to nothing but hollowed-out bones emptied of their marrow. That they would be making a whistling sound allows for two different interpretations. One is that the men would be reduced to a heap of hollow bones that had been turned into flute- or pipe-like instruments through which the wind could whistle. This meaning derives from the fact that *sufolare* (*zufolare* in modern Italian) means not just to whistle but to play an instrument, such as a pipe or a flute, a *zufolo,* that makes a whistling sound. Another possible interpretation has Neifile compounding her insult by implying that Filostrato would be reduced to a skeleton hanging on a gibbet, the fate usually meted out to lower-class criminals, through which the wind would whistle as it blows.

p. 169 *certainly knew what it meant*: Boccaccio thinks *Filostrato* means "he who is cast down or overcome by love."

p. 169 *to a game of chess*: The song of Messer Guiglielmo and the Lady of Vergiù was evidently an Italian version of the 14th-century French poem *La Chastelaine de Vergi* ("The Mistress of the Garden").

p. 170 *cast down by Love*: Lauretta's phrase here, *lassa innamorata* ("cast down, tired out, or exhausted by Love"), seems intended to echo the meaning of Filostrato's name (cast down, or overcome, by Love). The third line of the song is based on the last line of Dante's *Commedia,* which describes God as *L'amor che move il sole e l'altre stelle* (*Paradiso* 33.145: "The love that moves the sun and the other stars").

p. 171 *my swift return above*: Lauretta's melancholy song anticipates the sad tales that will be told on Day 4. Critics have attempted to link it to Boccaccio's own life and to allegorize it in various ways, but with little success.

p. 171 *rehearsed at present*: To approach things in the "Milanese fashion" is to be very practical and down to earth. The saying about the "good pig" and the "pretty gal" means that it is better to have something like a pig that one can eat than a girl whose attractiveness offers no tangible benefit. In other words, it is better to have a live husband, though bad, than a good one who is up in Heaven.

p. 171 *had begun its descent*: The reference to the setting of the stars indicates that the group has stayed up past midnight.

DAY 4, INTRODUCTION

p. 172 *and the highest treetops*: Boccaccio's image of a fierce wind striking the tops of trees is taken from Dante, *Paradiso* (17.133–34). In what follows, Boccaccio will defend the artistic value of the low genre of vernacular prose. He will also deal with potential critics of the perspectives and themes he adopts in his works, anticipating their objections and responding to them one by one. It is possible that the thirty stories of the first three days of the *Decameron* were already in circulation at this point, but there is no hard evidence that that was the case.

p. 173 *homeliest and lowest style possible*: Boccaccio's reference to his work as being *senza titolo*, "without a title," is clarified by what he wrote in his commentary on Dante, in which he says that Ovid's love lyrics, his *Amores* (*Loves*), were often dubbed *Sine titulo* (*Without Title*), because of the diversity of the work's contents. A similar statement might be made about the *Decameron*, which offers many different kinds of stories. Note that Boccaccio's claim about his humble and low style is an example of false modesty; he is extremely capable of manipulating many different stylistic registers in his work.

p. 173 *in this our present life*: Boccaccio is citing Valerius Maximus, *Factorum et dictorum memorabilium libri IX* (*Nine Books of Memorable Deeds and Sayings*), 4.7.2: *sola miseria caret invidia*.

p. 174 *our city quite some time ago*: The partial tale that Boccaccio recounts here has antecedents in the Indian epic the *Ramayana* as well as in *Barlaam and Josaphat*, a Christianized version of the life of the Buddha that came to the West through a variety of intermediaries. The story was widely diffused thanks to translations of this last work, and it appeared in the *Novellino* (14), among other texts. Note that several members of the Balducci family were employed by the Florentine banking firm of the Bardi, for which Boccaccio's father also worked.

p. 174 *little cell with his son*: "Monte Asinaio" (Mount Donkeyman) is a playful corruption of *Monte Senario*, whose many grottos served as cells for Florentine hermits.

p. 175 *"They're called goslings"*: Filippo calls them *papere*, which means "(female) adolescent geese." In many of the versions of this story recounted before the *Decameron*, women are dubbed "demons" instead.

p. 177 *tail is still green*: This image of the leek also appears in Story 1.10.

p. 177 *beauty was so dear to them*: Guido Cavalcanti (c. 1259–1300), Dante Alighieri (1265–1321), and Cino da Pistoia (c. 1265–1336) were the three greatest practitioners of the *Dolce Stil Novo* (Sweet New Style), a type of courtly love lyric celebrating women's beauty and linking it to philosophical truths. Guido appears in the *Decameron* as the protagonist of Story 6.9, and Dante is a constant, though implicit, presence in Boccaccio's work. Cino was a lawyer as well as a poet, and Boccaccio apparently attended his lectures on law in Naples.

p. 178 *I do about myself*: The Apostle is Paul. See his letter to the Philippians 4.12: *Scio et humiliari et abundare ubique et in omnibus institutus sum et satiari et esurire et abundare et penuriam pati* ("I know both how to be abased, and I know how to abound: everywhere and in all things I am instructed both to be full and to be hungry, both to abound and to suffer need").

p. 179 *any warmth in themselves*: Boccaccio's "warmth" may be referring to the "heat" of love and passion or to some warm feeling of sympathy his critics might have for his work.

p. 180 *drinks it down and thus dies*: Although there is no specific source for this story, one of the most popular in the *Decameron,* a poisoned chalice does appear in a love story in Paulus Diaconus's *Historia Longobardorum* (*History of the Lombards*), 2.28, as well as in the French *Roman du Châtelain de Couci* (*The Romance of the Lord of the Castle of Couci*). The characters in Boccaccio's story are not historical, but their names are those of various Norman princes, who did, in fact, control Salerno, although none of its rulers was named Tancredi in the period before Boccaccio wrote his story.

p. 184 *than either you or I*: Note that this is Guiscardo's only speech in the story. His words may be seen as echoing Virgil's in the tenth eclogue (69: *Omnia vincit Amor*: "Love conquers all") and perhaps those of the tragic lover Francesca in Dante's *Inferno*: *Amor, che a nessun amato amar perdona* (5.103: "Love, that does not pardon someone who is loved for not loving").

p. 189 *guarded so tenderly*: Ghismunda is addressing Guiscardo's heart, and it was a common belief in Boccaccio's time that the soul of an individual was lodged in that organ.

p. 191 *proceed to incarcerate him*: Boccaccio was familiar with several versions of this story that were circulating in the Middle Ages. They are all traceable back to Greek antiquity to such works as Chariton of Aphrodisias's romance *Chaereas and Callirhoe*, the *Romance of Alexander* of the Pseudo-Callisthenes, and the story of Mundus and Paulina in Flavius Josephus's *Antiquities of the Jews* (18.7).

p. 192 *all of their lies*: According to the rule of their order, the lives of the Franciscans were to be modeled on that of their founder, Saint Francis of Assisi. They were to wander from town to town, preaching and aiding the poor and the sick, while living in poverty themselves and avoiding any contact with money. On the basis of topographical references in the story, one may imagine that the protagonist joins the convent of Franciscans that was attached to the Venetian Church of Santa Maria Gloriosa dei Frari, which is located to the south of the Grand Canal and the Rialto bridge.

p. 192 *laugh and enjoy yourselves*: What I have translated as one of the "most authoritative churchmen" in Venice appears in Boccaccio's Italian as one of the greater *cassesi*. This word comes from Arabic and appears in Turkish as well, and in the 16th century it was used to denote a particularly important Christian priest. The fact that Boccaccio employs it here suggests that it had already gained some currency by the 14th century and perhaps especially in Venice, which had substantial communities of Middle Eastern traders. If so, then Boccaccio is using it for the sake of providing something like local color.

p. 192 *lying or telling the truth*: No historical figure has been found with whom Frate

Alberto may be identified. His name, Berto (short for Alberto) della Massa, suggests he may be imagined as having come from Massa Lombarda, a town close to Imola, which lies to the southeast of Bologna in the province of Emilia-Romagna.

p. 193 *anywhere else before then*: Boccaccio gives vent to anti-Venetian sentiments here and throughout this story. He may have been motivated by the fact that Venice was a great political and commercial rival to Florence in the 14th century (as it would continue to be for the next two hundred years).

p. 193 *to Flanders with his galleys*: Madonna Lisetta's name is given in the Venetian fashion: she is Lisetta (short for Elisabetta, or Elizabeth) from the House ("Ca") of the Quirini (or, more usually, Querini), an important family in the city. In the late Middle Ages, there were many women in that family whose first names were variants on Elisabetta. The reference to "lover" in the next sentence is my translation of *amadore,* the variant that Boccaccio uses for *amatore* (lover) and whose spelling is intended to suggest Venetian dialect.

p. 196 *knees in front of her*: Madonna Lisetta is thinking about paintings of the Annunciation in which the Angel Gabriel typically kneels before the Virgin as he tells her she has been chosen by God to bear the Christ child.

p. 198 *how attractive other women are*: Boccaccio's word for "friend" here is *comare.* Technically, this means godmother, but it often simply designated a close female friend, a neighbor, and a gossip, as it does here.

p. 198 *or in the Maremma*: The Maremma was a sparsely populated, marshy, desolate, inhospitable area in the southwestern part of Tuscany. Madonna Lisetta's reference to it as being something on a par with the world suggests, again, the limits of her knowledge and intelligence.

p. 200 *what had become of him*: The Rialto was one of the business centers of Venice where the only bridge spanning the Grand Canal was located. It was on the opposite side of the canal from Lisetta's house.

p. 200 *go wherever he wants*: Although it is not clear which festival is occurring here, the activities associated with it in the story were shared with many festivals throughout the year, and especially with carnival. Among those activities were dressing people up as wild animals or wild men and staging a hunt, which typically involved tying a boar up with a chain and then setting dogs on it, dogs like the two Frate Alberto will be leading. The dogs were normally chained as well. In the story, Frate Alberto himself becomes a version of the chained animal, and he is physically and symbolically punished by the crowd for his mockery of religion and his violation of marriage. Festival times were often used by the populace of towns and cities to visit such unofficial justice on those who broke the largely unwritten rules of the community.

p. 200 *gotten from the slaughterhouse*: Frate Alberto is being dressed as a wild man. In medieval and Renaissance folklore, such figures were believed to dwell in the woods and were usually represented as hairy, naked or semi-naked, and carrying a stick or club. Since they were symbolic of everything opposed to civilization, Frate Alberto's being dressed up like one is certainly suggestive.

p. 201 *all the others like him*: At the beginning of the next story, Boccaccio writes: "After listening to the end of Pampinea's story, Filostrato remained pensive for a while, then looked in her direction and said: 'The conclusion of your tale contained a little something of merit, and I liked that part, but there was far too much to laugh about before then, which I would have preferred to do without.'"

DAY 4, STORY 5

p. 202 *she herself dies of grief*: There is no specific source for this story, although the tragic ghost of a former lover does appear in Apuleius, *Metamorphoses*, 8.8 and 9.31. The beginning of the song cited at the end of the story resembles that of a song in Neapolitan dialect that has been preserved in several different versions, although none recounts the tale that Boccaccio provides to explain why a woman would be weeping over a pot of basil. The sexual innuendo involved in the song, in which a woman complains about a man's having stolen her pot of basil, has been considerably transformed in Boccaccio's story. This story is the source of Keats's poem *Isabella; or, The Pot of Basil*. Filomena tells this story.

p. 202 *there from San Gimignano*: In the 13th and 14th centuries Messina actually had various "colonies" composed of merchants from San Gimignano, the celebrated City of a Thousand Towers in Tuscany, which was an important center of the wool trade in the period. There were also close connections among traders in Messina and Naples, to which the three brothers move at the end of the story.

p. 204 *or her own tears*: Since Salerno is not especially known for its basil, this could be a slip of the pen on Boccaccio's part, who might have been thinking of the basil of Benevento, which was famous for its powerful aroma.

p. 206 *herbs from me, etc.*: At the beginning of the next story, Boccaccio writes: "The ladies were quite taken with the story that Filomena had told, for they had listened to people sing that song on more than one occasion, but had never been able, no matter how often they asked, to ascertain the reason for its composition"

DAY 4, STORY 9

p. 206 *buried with her beloved*: Versions of this story can be found in romances throughout the late medieval period. Boccaccio's narrator indicates that his story is based on some Provençal account of a (fictitious) love triangle involving the troubadour Guilhem de Cabestaing (1162–1212), his lord Raimon de Castel-Rossillon (died 1209), and the latter's wife, Saurimonda de Pietralata, who married Raimon in 1197; was remarried in 1210, a year after Raimon's death; and was still alive as late as 1221. The motif of the eaten heart can also be found in the courtly love tradition immediately preceding Boccaccio. In his *Vita nuova* (*The New Life*), 3, for instance, Dante has a dream in which his heart is eaten by a woman. Filostrato tells this story.

p. 206 *exactly the same device*: "From head to toe" is a translation of *s'armavano assai*. This is the reading in the most important manuscript of Boccaccio's work, the Hamilton codex, although there is a variant in other manuscripts: *s'amavano assai*. In this case, the clause would read: "they loved one another very deeply." A knight's "device" was an emblematic figure or design that he wore on his armor or carried as a banner; it had heraldic significance and enabled him to be recognized on the field of battle.

p. 209 *saddled and rode away*: In the Provençal versions of the story, Rossiglione is in fact punished by King Alfonso II of Aragon (born 1152, ruled 1162–96), who inherited the County of Roussillon in 1172. Note that he died before the events in the story could have taken place.

DAY 5, STORY 1

p. 214 *homes with their wives*: Although this story contains many motifs from Greek romance, there is no single source for it. The theme of its first half—the educational and transformative power of love and beauty—made it quite popular, and it was both imitated by later writers and made the subject of paintings by Botticelli, Veronese, Rubens, and others.

p. 215 *as "stupid ass" in ours*: Cimone's real name, Galeso, comes from a Greek word meaning "milk," but Boccaccio's etymology for "Cimone" is misleading. It could be related to the Greek words for goat or for the muzzle of an animal, but is more likely meant to recall the historical Cimon (510–450 B.C.E.), who was the son of Miltiades, the hero of the battle of Marathon. Cimon himself became a famous political leader and general in Athens who was celebrated for his bravery in the naval battle of Salamis but who was said to have been somewhat simpleminded when he was a young man by both Valerius Maximus, *Factorum et dictorum memorabilium libri IX* (*Nine Books of Memorable Deeds and Sayings*), 6.9.3, and Plutarch in his *Life of Cimon*. The name might also suggest the Italian word *scimmione*, which means "large monkey" or "ape." The name of Cimone's father, Aristippo, is also Greek and may have been chosen simply for that reason, although there was a famous philosopher named Aristippus (c. 435–366 B.C.E.) who was a follower of Socrates and founder of what was known as the Cyrenaic school of hedonism. Efigenia, Cimone's beloved, is Boccaccio's Italianized version of Iphigenia (Wellborn), but it is hard to see much of a connection between her and the tragic Greek heroine. All the other characters likewise have Italianized versions of Greek names, which seem chosen primarily to suit the setting of the story.

p. 217 *"God keep you, Cimone, farewell"*: In Italian, she says, *Cimone, rimanti con Dio*, which means, literally, "Cimone, abide [remain] with God." Although she is essentially saying good-bye, her phrase is a variant of the more usual *va' con Dio* (nowadays: *addio*), and she has no doubt chosen it because she really does want Cimone to *remain* where he is and to let her get away.

p. 226 *returns with her to Lipari*: There are a few antecedents for the advice that Martuccio offers the King and even more for Gostanza's voyage at sea, but there is no specific story on which this one is modeled. Lipari is the largest of the Aeolian Islands off the northern coast of Sicily. During the late Middle Ages it was often used as a base by pirates, which is what the hero of this story becomes.

p. 227 *well mannered and exceptionally handsome*: Although there is no historical record of a Martuccio Gomito, there were many people named Gomito living in the Kingdom of Naples in Boccaccio's day. Martuccio is the diminutive of Martino. Gostanza is a variant of Costanza (Constance).

p. 228 *hundred miles beyond Tunis*: Boccaccio is usually quite accurate about geography, but a light, northerly wind would have driven Gostanza's boat to the shore of Sicily, not to Susa (which does indeed lie about a hundred miles south of Tunis).

p. 229 *fishermen who were Christians*: Carapresa is made up of two words: *cara*, which means "dear," and *presa*, which means "taken" or "acquired." Thus the name means something like "dear (or precious) acquisition," which is why Gostanza will take it as a good omen in the next sentence.

p. 230 *important family in Granada*: Meriabdela may be a mistake for Muliabdela. *Muli* derives from an Arabic word meaning "my lord," and *abdela* is an Italianized version of Abd Allah, which was the actual name of several kings who ruled in Tunis during Boccaccio's lifetime.

p. 233 *returns with her to Rome*: There is no antecedent for this story, although the protagonists of medieval romances typically wander through landscapes filled with surprises and adventures.

p. 234 *by his fellow citizens*: There were two families named Boccamazza living in Rome in the 14th century, one of which had an Angela in it who was still alive in 1394 and may have been a descendant of Agnolella. There were no Pietros, however, in either branch of the family, and nothing is known about the family of Gigliuozzo Saullo. Boccaccio's complaint here is about the decadence of contemporary Rome is not an isolated one in his works and is a sentiment he shared with Petrarch. Both were reacting to the decay of the city during the period known as the Babylonian Captivity, when the papacy was transferred to Avignon between 1305 and 1377 and was under the thumb of the French kings, leaving Rome to be overrun by gangs of bandits. Boccaccio's reference to Rome as being once "the head of the world" is a translation of a common inscription found on Roman coins, *Roma caput mundi*.

p. 234 *whom he trusted implicitly*: Anagni is a town about thirty miles southeast of Rome. To get there, the couple plans to follow the ancient *via Latina* that continued on to Naples. Scholars have suggested that they make a wrong turn at Casale Ciampino, about nine miles outside of the city, and then get lost in the forest of Aglio near Frascati.

p. 235 *on one of these oaks*: The Orsini was a powerful, aristocratic Roman family who, as Guelfs, supported the Church in its struggle with the Holy Roman Empire in the 13th and 14th centuries. Their enemy was the Colonna family, who, as Ghibellines, backed the empire. Presumably, the soldiers who capture Pietro are members of the Colonna faction.

p. 239 *staying there at the time*: One branch of the Orsini family had taken its name from the properties it owned near the Campo dei Fiori in Rome, and one of its members, who was, in fact, named Liello (most likely a diminutive of Raffaello), lived around the end of the 13th century and the start of the 14th. His wife was Banna di Tolomea de' Leoni di Montanea, and she was still alive in 1352. The family actually did have a castle east of Grottaferrata. Note that one of Boccaccio's friends and patrons was Niccolò Orsini who often entertained the writer in his castles.

DAY 5, STORY 4

p. 241 *on good terms with her father*: Although a number of different stories have been proposed as sources for this one, none of them is sufficiently close to merit that label. However, the nightingale, which is central to the story, was frequently associated with sex throughout medieval European literature.

p. 241 *called Messer Lizio da Valbona*: Lizio da Valbona is a historical character, a Guelf lord who was a minor military and political figure in the second half of the 13th century and who was celebrated for his nobility and generosity. Lizio appears as a character in the *Novellino* (47) and is mentioned by Dante in *Purgatorio* 14.97, a line that also contains a reference to Arrigo Mainardi. In Boccaccio's story, the family name appears as Manardi, and there was no Ricciardo among its members.

p. 243 *girls are than older women*: According to ancient and medieval medical theory, women became colder (that is, colder humors such as melancholy became more dominant in them) as they aged.

p. 247 *to his heart's content*: At the beginning of the next story, Boccaccio writes: "In listening to the tale of the nightingale, all the ladies had laughed so much that even after Filostrato stopped, they still could not contain themselves. Finally, however, when their merriment had died down, the Queen said: 'Although you did make us suffer yesterday, Filostrato, you have certainly tickled us so much today that no one has the right to hold it against you any longer.'"

DAY 5, STORY 8

p. 247 *accepts Nastagio as her husband*: Tales of diabolic hunts were widespread in ancient and medieval literature and folklore, and theologians used them to describe the punishments of the damned. For Nastagio's astute use of the scene for his own ends, there are also precedents, such as Peter Alphonsi's *Disciplina clericalis* (*A School for Clerics*) 14, a work with which Boccaccio was certainly familiar. However, the most important influences on Boccaccio's tale were the punishments described in Dante's *Inferno* (for example, those meted out to the profligate in *Inferno* 13 and to the sowers of discord in *Inferno* 28) as well as Boccaccio's various sojourns in Ravenna where his tale is set (he lived there at least four, and possibly five, times between 1346 and his death in 1375). Chiassi, or Classi, to which Nastagio retires, is a forested spot on the shore of the Adriatic outside of Ravenna; the name is recalled in that of the modern town Sant'Apollinare in Classe.

p. 248 *and one of his uncles*: The Onesti was a noble family in Ravenna, although no Anastagio can be found among its members in the 14th century. Boccaccio could have learned about the family from commentators on Dante who, in *Purgatorio* 14.107–10, has Guido del Duca, a member of the family, lament the dying out of other notable families in Ravenna such as the Traversari and the Anastagi. Paolo Traversari, who is mentioned in the next sentence, served as the patron for various poets; he died in 1240, leaving behind a single daughter named Aica. Guido degli Anastagi appears later in the story, but there is no historical record of any Guido in the family.

p. 249 *into the pine forest*: Boccaccio echoes Dante here in his selection of the date (April was traditionally a month associated with visions and with both the Annunciation and the Crucifixion), the location (at the very start of the *Commedia* Dante finds himself in a dark wood), and Nastagio's being transported into the forest (Dante is similarly transported into the forest of the Earthly Paradise; see *Purgatorio* 28.22–23). Note that some medieval commentators identified pine trees as symbols of immortality because they remained green throughout the year.

p. 249 *earsplitting shrieks of a woman*: The "fifth hour" of the day is sext, or noon.

p. 250 *to the pains of Hell*: In many of the sources of this story, the woman is being punished in Purgatory, not Hell.

DAY 5, STORY 9

p. 253 *makes him a rich man*: Although there are several Eastern tales involving birds who sacrifice themselves for people, and several medieval stories vaguely rehearse a similar motif, there really is no precedent for Boccaccio's tale except perhaps for Ovid's story of Baucis and Philemon, who sacrifice their only goose for guests who turn out to be gods and reward them for their generosity (*Metamorphoses* 8.611–724). In the Middle Ages, the falcon was considered a symbol of the triumph over lust and over the passions more generally, and it was, of course, a hunting bird trained and used by the members of the upper classes.

p. 254 *his noble lineage*: Hailing from a prominent family that lived in the Santa Croce quarter of Florence, Coppo (Giacopo, or Jacopo: James) held numerous important civic positions during the first four decades of the 14th century, including that of Gonfaloniere (mayor) in 1315; he died sometime before April 1353. Sacchetti features him in two of his stories in his *Trecentonovelle* (*Three Hundred Stories*), 66 and 137.

p. 254 *any other squire in Tuscany*: The Alberighi, one of the oldest families in Florence, lived in the Porta San Piero quarter near the church bearing their name, the Chiesa di Santa Maria degli Alberighi, and not far from the home in which Dante had grown up. By the early 14th century, they had fallen on hard times, as Dante notes in *Paradiso* 16.88–93.

p. 255 *where his little farm was located*: Campi, or Campi Bisenzio, is a tiny town a few miles to the northwest of Florence not far from Prato.

DAY 5, STORY 10

p. 261 *an understanding with her*: The source of this story is Apuleius's *Metamorphoses* (9.14–28), one of Boccaccio's favorite works, which he was actually making a copy of at the time he wrote the *Decameron*.

p. 261 *he had to take a wife*: The story is set in Perugia, which apparently had a reputation for homosexuality in the period and was otherwise one of Florence's mercantile rivals. The Bardi bank, for which Boccaccio's father worked, had a branch there. There was, in fact, a Pietro from the well-known family of the Vincioli who held various administrative positions in and around the city at the end of the 13th and start of the 14th centuries.

p. 262 *through the rain*: The two expressions in this sentence were proverbial: *andare in zoccoli per l'asciutto* ("go in [his] clogs up [literally, through, along] the dry [path]") for homosexual love; and for heterosexual love, *portare altrui in nave per lo piovoso* ("get others to board my boat and carry them through the rain"). The first saying may involve the idea that since clogs had high soles, there was no need for them when walking on a dry surface—that is, homosexual love is superfluous or irrelevant. But clogs, in and of themselves, generally evoked homosexual love in the period, perhaps through their association with friars. "The dry path" is suggestive in its own right, of course, and the second saying about heterosexual love, involving carrying people on board one's boat when it is raining, should need no comment.

p. 262 *considered her a saint*: According to popular legends recounting the life of Saint Verdiana Attavanti (1182–1242), the most venerated saint in Castelfiorentino, Tuscany, two serpents entered the nun's cell there, and since she thought they were sent by God to tempt her, she fed them and took care of them. The saint's name was thus synonymous with devotion and asceticism.

p. 263 *to light my fire for me*: The old woman's phrase is *mi desse fuoco a cencio*, which means literally "he would give me fire for my rag." She is referring to the fact that in the Tuscan countryside, people would take a rag and go to their neighbors for a light to start their fires with back home, since a rag would burn longer than glowing coals or a lighted brand.

p. 264 *carried out with alacrity*: Ercolano was a common name in Perugia, since Sant'Ercolano (Saint Herculanus) was the patron saint of the city. He had been a bishop there and had been martyred by the Ostrogoths in 549.

p. 269 *as good as you get*: Dioneo's final comment repeats almost exactly a comment made by one of the merchants when they are talking together at the start of Story 2.9. The point of the comment is that when an ass bumps into a wall, he is, in a sense, bumped back by the wall. In short, Dioneo's advice is that it is a game of tit for tat: women should feel free to cheat on their husbands since their husbands feel free to cheat on them.

DAY 6, INTRODUCTION

p. 271 *singing about Troilus and Cressida*: During his youth Boccaccio had himself composed a long romance on the ill-fated love of Troilus for Cressida called *Il Filostrato*, whose title is constantly recalled in the *Decameron* by the name Filostrato, which Boccaccio gives to one of the three young men in the company whose lovelorn condition matches that of Troilus. Since *Il Filostrato* also features an unfaithful heroine, their singing the poem at this point anticipates the dispute between the servants that is about to occur.

p. 271 *serving men in the kitchen*: This is the only time in the *Decameron* when the idyllic retreat of the ten young storytellers is interrupted by any sort of external reality. The servants' argument rehearses one of the main themes of the text, the ubiquity of sexual desire and, in particular, its importance for women, as well as touching on the themes of this day—namely quick retorts and witticisms as well as that of trickery, which will become the chosen topic for the next day. This is also the only place after the start of Boccaccio's work where the servants' names are mentioned (except for when Tindaro is said to play the bagpipes), and it is the only place where they actually speak.

p. 271 *and with much bloodshed*: Although *Sicofante* sounds like the English "sycophant," it is not connected with that word. Rather, it is a Greek-based name, like those of the servants in the *Decameron*, and since the etymology of the word is uncertain, it is impossible to know if Boccaccio means anything by it other than to say that Sicofante belongs to the same class of characters as Licisca and Tindaro.

DAY 6, STORY 1

p. 273 *set her down on foot*: Boccaccio's story has an antecedent in the *Novellino* (89), but can also be counted more generally as one of a host of stories that are told during trips, including those in Sercambi's and Chaucer's collections. Boccaccio is, of course, actually equating horseback riding and storytelling here. The Madonna Oretta of the story was the wife of Geri Spina, who appears in the next story. She was left a widow by him in 1332 and was apparently considered something of a wit. Oretta is short for Lauretta, which is the diminutive of Laura, but it also suggests the meaning "little, or brief, hour" (*ora* means "hour"), thus underscoring one of the faults of the knight's narrative, its long-windedness.

p. 274 *incidents he was describing*: In this story, Boccaccio offers a commentary on the art of storytelling itself. By having the knight make a mess of his narration, Boccaccio implies that his own stories are free of the particular flaws the knight's displays. Coming roughly at the halfway point in the collection, the story thus focuses readers on the issue of proper and improper modes of storytelling as one of the main themes of the collection. In this way, the *Decameron* also parallels the *Divine Comedy,* which devotes its central canto (*Purgatorio* 17) to the poem's chief concern, love.

p. 274 *bogged down in the mire*: Boccaccio's word here is *pecoreccio,* which means "sheepfold," the muddy, mucky place where the sheep sleep at night.

DAY 6, STORY 2

p. 274 *made an inappropriate request*: There is no literary source for this story, which may be a retelling of a well-known anecdote. Cisti (short for Bencivenisti) was a fairly common name in Florence in the 14th century, and a certain *Cisti fornaio* (Cisti the baker) does appear in a document of 1300 from the Chiesa di Santa Maria Ughi next to which Cisti's bakery is located in the story. Geri Spina was Geri (short for Ruggeri) di Manetto Spina (died 1321 or 1322), who was a merchant and a figure of some political importance in Florence. Neifile tells this story.

p. 275 *at Messer Geri's house*: The ambassadors sent by Pope Boniface VIII (born c. 1235, pope 1294–1303) were attempting (unsuccessfully) to negotiate peace between the White and the Black Guelfs. After defeating the (imperial) Ghibellines at the battles of Campaldino and Caprona in 1289, the Guelf (papal) Party had itself split into these two factions, the Blacks continuing to support the papacy, while the Whites allied themselves with the empire. Messer Geri was one of the heads of the Blacks.

p. 277 *"To the Arno," replied Cisti*: Cisti is saying that the flagon is large enough to contain the water of the Arno, the river that flows through Florence.

p. 278 *dispose of it as you please*: Cisti is being extremely polite and deferential, essentially saying that from the time Messer Geri started tasting the wine, it became his, and that since Cisti was now merely its guardian, he wanted to give up that role and hand the wine over to its rightful owner.

DAY 6, STORY 4

p. 278 *had threatened him*: There is no literary source for this story, although Apuleius's *Metamorphoses* contains an episode involving a cook who makes off with a haunch of venison (8.31). Currado di Vanni di Cafaggio Gianfigliazzi, who lived around the turn of the 14th century and was known for his lavish lifestyle, was a member of an important family associated with prominent Florentine bankers, including the Peruzzi. Dante places one of the Gianfigliazzi in the circle of Hell reserved for the usurers (*Inferno* 17.58–60). Boccaccio knew several members of the family in his own day and celebrates at least two of them in his minor works.

p. 279 *roast it for supper*: Chichibio's name is derived from an onomatopoetic Venetian word for the song of the chaffinch: *cicibío*. The implication is, of course, that he is a birdbrain. Peretola is a small town in Tuscany just a short distance from Florence in the direction of Prato. Currado Gianfigliazzi actually owned property in the area.

p. 279 *not a-goin' a get it from me*: Making fun of Chichibio's Venetian dialect, Boccaccio has him "sing" his response and use Venetian forms of Italian words, which must have made the dialect sound somewhat songlike to a Florentine. Chichibio is also satirized for his use of a courtly vocabulary with his ladylove: he uses *donna* for her, meaning "lady," calling her *donna Brunetta*, and addresses her as *voi*, employing the plural and more polite form for "you," rather than the singular, more familiar *tu*.

p. 280 *you gluttonous rogue*: Currado calls Chichibio a *ghiottone*, which meant "glutton" but also had the extended meaning of "rogue, rascal, knave, or scoundrel," all of which fit Chichibio well, since Currado thinks his cook cut off the crane's leg in order to eat it.

DAY 6, STORY 5

p. 281 *another's disreputable appearance*: Although there is no extant source for Boccaccio's story, later Renaissance writers treated it as historical. Forese da Rabatta (died 1348) was a well-known jurist who was a professor at Pisa (1338–39); held various political offices in Florence, including those of prior and Gonfaloniere (mayor) between 1320 and 1340; and served as the city's ambassador to Pisa in 1343. Although it is generally agreed that he died in 1348, he is mentioned in historical records as late as 1359. Giotto di Bondone (1266/67–1337) was, of course, the famous painter whose innovative works have been seen as inaugurating the Renaissance from at least 1549–50, when Vasari's *Le vite de' più eccellenti architettori, pittori, e scultori italiani* (*Lives of the Most Eminent Italian Painters, Sculptors, and Architects*) appeared. He was greatly admired by both Petrarch and Boccaccio who celebrated him in several other works beside the *Decameron*. Mugello is an area northeast of Florence; both Forese and Giotto were born there.

p. 281 *the ugliest of men*: Pampinea's story is that of Cisti the baker (Story 6.2).

p. 281 *encyclopedia of civil law*: The Baronci were proverbial for their ugliness.

p. 283 *gotten as good as he gave*: A more literal rendering of the final clause in the story would be that Messer Forese perceived that "he had been paid in coin equal in value to the merchandise he had sold."

DAY 6, STORY 7

p. 283 *changed at the same time*: There is no precedent for this story. Filostrato tells this story.

p. 284 *loved as much as life itself*: The Pugliesi and Guazzagliotri families were important families in Prato who were also notorious enemies; the latter played a principal role in the expulsion of the former from the town in 1342. Prato is about seventeen miles northwest of Florence.

p. 286 *throw them to the dogs*: The lady's remark echoes Matthew 7.6: *Nolite dare sanctum canibus* ("Give not that which is holy unto the dogs"). In Boccaccio's time, the words *sanctum* and *sacrum* could refer to a woman's body.

p. 286 *to her house in triumph*: At the beginning of the next story Boccaccio writes: "As they listened to Filostrato's story, at first the ladies felt a slight twinge of embarrassment within, which was revealed in the modest blushes that spread over their faces, but soon they started exchanging glances with one another, and barely able to contain their laughter, they snickered as they heard the rest of it."

DAY 6, STORY 9

p. 286 *taken him by surprise*: Guido Cavalcanti (c. 1255–1300) was, along with Dante, the leading poet of the *Dolce Stil Novo* (Sweet New Style) as well as being Dante's close friend. His poetry justifies his being termed a logician and natural philosopher by Boccaccio. In the tenth canto of the *Inferno* Dante places Guido's father in the circle of Hell reserved for those, including the Epicureans, who did not believe in the immortality of the soul. This was the most likely source of the notion that Guido was also an Epicurean. The quip attributed here to Guido had been assigned to other figures earlier in the Middle Ages and first appeared in the *Dialogues* of Pope Gregory the Great (4.3) in which a passage from Psalms 48 in the Bible was cited to condemn the Epicureans for denying the immortality of the soul: *domus suas in saeculo tabernacula sua* (Verse 12: "their sepulchers shall be their houses forever"). (The King James Bible identifies this as Psalms 49.11 and translates it rather differently.)

p. 287 *driven them all away*: Boccaccio denounces avarice and greed throughout the *Decameron*. See, for example, Stories 1.8, 3.5, 6.3, and 8.1.

p. 287 *Messer Cavalcante de' Cavalcanti, to join them*: Betto (short for Brunetto) Brunelleschi came from a Ghibelline family, but was a White Guelf for a short time and a friend of both Guido Cavalcanti and Dante, who dedicated a sonnet (99) to him. However, after the defeat of the White Guelfs in 1301, which led to Dante's exile, Betto became one of the leaders of the Black Guelfs. In 1311, after having caused the death of another leader, Corso Donati, he was himself assassinated by two of Corso's young kinsmen.

p. 288 *located today in Santa Reparata*: The Cavalcanti family lived in Orsanmichele, an area in the center of Florence named after the *orto* (kitchen garden) of the monastery of San Michele. A building designed to be a grain market was built there in 1337, and between 1380 and 1404, it was converted into the church we see today. The Corso degli Adimari, which Guido is taking as he walks from Orsanmichele to the Baptistery of San Giovanni, is now called the Via Calzaiuoli. The baptistery was the second-oldest building in the city and had been rebuilt in its present octagonal form around 1059; it was surrounded by a cemetery containing Roman sarcophaguses that Florentine families had moved there and were using as tombs. The Church of Santa Reparata was located on the site next to the baptistery where the Duomo, or Cathedral of Florence, to be named Santa Maria del Fiore, would be built, starting in 1294. By the middle of the 14th century, when Boccaccio was writing the *Decameron*, the old Church of Santa Reparata had not yet been demolished, although a great deal of work had been done on the new cathedral, which locals would continue to call Santa Reparata for quite some time. The "porphyry columns" mentioned in the next sentence still flank Lorenzo Ghiberti's *Gates of Paradise* on the east side of the baptistery. The columns were given to Florence by the Pisans in 1117 in gratitude for the city's assistance in their fight against Lucca. The Pisans had originally taken them from the island of Majorca.

DAY 6, STORY 10

p. 289 *to roast Saint Lawrence*: There is no direct source for this story, although analogues may be found in Eastern collections, such as the *Panchatantra*, and in the Middle Ages there was an abundant literature concerned with the abuse of relics, such as a swindle involving the "arm" of Saint Reparata that occurred in Florence in 1352.

p. 289 *and pretty well-to-do*: Certaldo, which is about eighteen miles southwest of Florence, was probably Boccaccio's birthplace, and although he often referred to it elsewhere with warmth, here it is viewed more critically. Boccaccio spent the last years of his life there, living in his house in the citadel (the upper part of the town); he was buried there as well. The friars of Saint Anthony, mentioned both earlier and in the next sentence, were members of the oldest monastic order, which was founded by Saint Anthony of Egypt (c. 251–c. 356) around 313. (This Saint Anthony should not be confused with the Franciscan friar Saint Anthony of Padua.) Saint Anthony was venerated for protecting animals from diseases and was often represented with a pig at his feet. By Boccaccio's time, however, friars in the order were condemned for their greed, which Dante denounces in *Paradiso* (29.124) where he identifies them with their own pigs that were allowed to wander freely in the streets.

p. 289 *famous all over Tuscany*: Frate Cipolla's name means Brother Onion, for a vegetable whose many layers with no real "center" and whose particular odor are quite suggestive when one considers what Frate Cipolla does in the story.

p. 290 *himself or maybe Quintilian*: Marcus Tullius Cicero (106–43 B.C.E.) and Marcus Fabius Quintilian (35–96 C.E.) were, of course, the two most important

Roman writers on rhetoric. Although Quintilian did give speeches in the law courts, his greatest fame was as a teacher and writer. By contrast, Cicero was so celebrated for his public oratory that his name (often in the form of Tully, or *Tulio*, as it is in Boccaccio's story) became a byword for eloquence.

p. 290 *Lord and Master Saint Anthony*: Cipolla refers to the saint as the *baron messer Santo Antonio*, which could be translated as the Baron Messer Saint Anthony. *Baron*, though normally a title for men in the secular hierarchy, was also used as an honorific for saints.

p. 290 *the other, Biagio Pizzini*: Both Bragoniera and Pizzini are the names of families that lived in Certaldo in Boccaccio's day. The Pizzini owned property that adjoined Boccaccio's, and a Biagio Pizzini was a close friend of Boccaccio's father.

p. 291 *Guccio the Pig*: Guccio's three nicknames in Italian are, in order: *Balena*, *Imbratta*, and *Porco*. The first one translates directly as Whale and the last as Pig, while *Imbratta* means "he who makes a mess": hence The Slob. Historical records from the years between 1318 and 1335 mention the existence of someone variously referred to as Guccio Aghinetti, Guccio Porcellana, and Frate Porcellana, who lived in the quarter of San Paolo in Florence and worked in the Hospital of San Filippo. There is also a document dating from 1305 that mentions a Guccio Imbratta (a Guccio Imbratta makes an appearance as a gravedigger in the *Decameron* at the end of Story 4.7). Lippo (short for Filippo) the Mouse (*Topo*), who is mentioned in the next sentence, was a proverbial character to whom various eccentricities and jokes have been attributed.

p. 291 *careless and witless and rude*: It is impossible to duplicate Boccaccio's triple rhymes: *tardo, sugliardo e bugiardo; negligente, disubediente e maledicente; trascutato, smemorato e scostumato*. A more literal translation would be: "slothful, filthy, and untruthful; neglectful, disobedient, and foul mouthed; careless, witless, and ill mannered."

p. 292 *covered with soot*: The Baronci were proverbial for their ugliness. Boccaccio refers to them in this way in Stories 6.5 and 6.7.

p. 292 *than his master could*: A possible alternative translation for the last part of this sentence might be: "he knew how to say and do more than God ever could." The serving girl's name, Nuta, is short for Benvenuta. The phrase translated as "gentleman by proxy" is *gentile uomo per procuratore*, which means "gentleman through, or by way of, the procurator (or prosecutor)." In other words, he enjoys a title that does not attach to his person, just as someone delivering a warrant for a prosecutor may possess the title and authority of the prosecutor, though only temporarily. In bragging of his wealth, Guccio says he has *de' fiorini piú di millantanove*, "of florins more than *millanta* and nine" (*millanta* is a fanciful derivative from *mille*, "thousand," and refers to any very large, indeterminate number).

p. 292 *in hope of a better fortune*: The monks of the Abbey of the Hospitallers in Altopascio near Lucca were renowned for the generous portions of soup they prepared for the poor twice a week. The "cloth," most likely silk, of the East was famous for its wealth of colors, as Boccaccio himself noted in his *Esposizioni* on Dante's *Inferno* (17.8). Tartary here is probably China. The Lord of Châtillon is a fictional title meant to suggest great wealth.

p. 293 *and neighbor to neighbor*: The friends referred to here are male; the neighbors are *comari*, technically, a term identifying the godmothers of someone's child, but often used for close female friends from the neighborhood, or gossips, as it is here.

p. 294 *had two large candles lit*: The Confiteor (I Confess) is a prayer recited at the beginning of the Mass.

p. 294 *others than to us*: Frate Cipolla's sermon is a brilliant performance, filled with words designed to impress and mystify the people of Certaldo that have much less exalted meanings a more sophisticated audience would get. He also uses truisms and tautologies and sometimes seems to produce sheer nonsense. "Parts of the world where the sun rises" in this sentence is meant to suggest the East (the direction in which we see the sun rise), but the phrase literally means all countries, because the sun rises everywhere. The "Privileges of the Porcellana" is a nonsense phrase, whose literal meaning is obscure. It may be linked to Frate Cipolla's servant, who was called Guccio Porco and whose real last name may have been Porcellana, or it may refer to the sodomitical practices often associated with the clergy. However, this name and most of the following ones, while suggesting faraway places, also designate streets and quarters in Florence, and they take us on a journey, generally from east to west, through the city. There was thus both a street and a hospital named Porcellana near the Arno to the east of the Ponte Vecchio. In the next sentence, Venice (Vinegia) and Greekburg (Borgo de' Greci, the "burg or suburb of the Greeks") were quarters lying between the Piazza della Signoria and Santa Croce; they were also the names of streets. Algarve (Garbo) was a street of that name (now via Condotta), while Baghdad (Baldacca) was a street near Orsanmichele, although both names are meant to suggest exotic lands (Algarve was the name of a kingdom in the southern part of the Iberian Peninsula). Parione, perhaps meant to suggest "Paris," is the present-day via da Santa Trinità alla Carraia, and Sardinia (Sardigna) was a deserted stretch of shoreline on the Arno. Although Saint George (San Giorgio) was the name of a quarter near the Dogana, or customshouse, as well as one in the Oltrarno (the part of Florence on the left bank of the Arno), the Straits of Saint George (Braccio di San Giorgio) may suggest something like the Bosphorus.

p. 295 *pursue their own advantage*: Conland and Clownland are Truffia and Buffia. Truffia comes from the verb *truffare*, "to deceive, con," whereas Buffia suggests *buffone*, "clown," as well as *beffare*, "to trick, play a practical joke on." Liarland is the *terra di Menzogna* (*menzogna* means "lie"). The denunciation of the clergy in this sentence is focused on abuses generally associated with the Order of Saint Anthony whose members Dante accused not merely of fattening themselves on the offerings they received but also of mystifying others with the empty language of their sermons ("money that has not been minted").

p. 295 *the water flows downhill*: To "clothe pigs in their own guts" is to make sausages, while carrying "bread on sticks" can be done with *ciambelle*, ring-shaped buns, and wine can be put in a sack if the sack is a wineskin. All three expressions have phallic overtones. Abruzzi, an actual region in southern Italy, is sufficiently far away to appear exotic. The Basqueworm Mountains translates *montagne de' bachi*, literally, "Mountains of the Worms," but *bachi* also suggests Basques, another faraway people.

p. 295 *sells their shells retail*: Parsinippia is Partinaca, which means "parsnip," perhaps to suggest the spices and delicacies of the East; it may also mean a "fantastic, unbelievable story," for which modern Italians would say *carota* ("carrot"). "Pruningbills" is my punning translation of *pennati*, the pruning hooks or tools with curved blades that were used to prune vines; the word contains a play on *pennuti*, "feathered ones"—that is, birds. Maso del Saggio was a Florentine, by profession a broker or middleman, who was known in his own time for his tricks and his mocking humor. He makes an appearance as a trickster in Stories 8.3 and 8.5.

p. 295 *relics he had about him*: The Patriarch's name is a translation of the Old French *Nemeblasmez Sevoiplait,* which echoes the kinds of allegorical names one finds in such works as *Le Roman de la Rose* (*The Romance of the Rose*).

p. 295 *of others as well*: Boccaccio is satirizing the cult of holy relics here by assigning material parts to spiritual entities. The "whole and sound" finger of the Holy Spirit is bawdy and blasphemous as well. There is no adequate way to translate *Verbum-caro-fatti-alle-finestre* ("Word-flesh-made/get-you-out-the-windows"), which plays on the biblical *Verbum caro factum est* ("the Word was made flesh," John 1.14).

p. 296 *particularly devoted to the saint*: The two "books" Frate Cipolla gives the Patriarch are part of a complex set of puns. What he says is that *gli fece copia* of them, a phrase that I rendered as "I . . . gave him," and which means both that "I gave him a gift of" and "I gave him plenty of." Moreover, both of the book titles suggest sodomy, a practice with which the cloistered male clergy were frequently associated in Boccaccio's time. The first of the "books" is *le piagge di Monte Morello,* the slopes (or, as I rendered it, the "dingle") of Mount Morello, while the second one is *il Caprezio,* a made-up word that plays on the Italian *capro,* or male goat, and that may also contain a pun on the name of a Latin author such as Lucretius (*Lucrezio* in Italian, although the *-tius* ending in Latin was pronounced as though it started with the letter *z*). The "teeth of the Holy Cross" contains a play on the notion of the "arms" of the cross. Gherardo di Bonsi was an important member of the *Arte della lana*, the Wool-Workers Guild, and was devoted to the saint after whom he was named, Saint Gherardo (1174–1267), who was one of the earliest followers of Saint Francis and was frequently represented wearing *zoccoli*, or "sandals." Note that *zoccoli* had associations with sodomy as well in the period.

p. 296 *just two days away*: The Feast of Saint Lawrence takes place on August 10. Tradition has it that he was martyred by being burned to death on a gridiron, which served as his symbol throughout the Middle Ages.

p. 296 *saint's most sacred body*: "Humors" here are fluids, such as blood or sweat.

DAY 6, CONCLUSION

p. 298 *discovered by them or not*: The word for "tricks" in this sentence is *beffe*, which can also be translated as "practical jokes" or "pranks" or "con games." Moreover, the verb *beffare* not only meant "to play a trick on" but also "to mock or make fun of," thus underscoring the potentially sadistic element in such tricks and the way they "put down" the one who is their victim.

p. 300 *of a lovely little castle*: The Valley of the Ladies is a literary fiction, an idealized description of a natural spot that presents a perfect balance of Nature and Art. It is a version of the *locus amoenus* (pleasant place), a commonplace that goes back to the Garden of Eden in the Bible and to the ancient tradition of pastoral. To some degree, all the settings in which the ten young men and women tell their stories are examples of such an idealized natural spot, although Boccaccio heightens the idealization in this particular case. It is noteworthy that he produces this description just after Dioneo has suggested a topic for storytelling that has met with resistance from the women in the group and that they retreat to a valley that is, as its name would suggest, their natural place.

p. 302 *managed to trick you today*: The word that Pampinea uses here for "tricked" is the slightly less charged *ingannati*, which lacks some of the scornfulness that would have been implied by *beffati*. Dioneo's reply, however, suggests that he sees the two terms, for his purposes, as interchangeable.

p. 303 *flowers red and white*: Elissa's song, like most of the others in the *Decameron*, is a love lament, and it should also be remembered that Elissa is another name for the love-stricken, tragic figure of Dido in Virgil's *Aeneid*. Her reference to red and white flowers at the end of the poem alludes to the marriage ceremony in which women were adorned with orange blossoms, lilies, and roses.

DAY 7, INTRODUCTION

p. 305 *one we call Lucifer*: Lucifer (light bearer) is another name for the morning star Venus. This may be a suggestion that love, or sex, will play a large role in the stories to come.

DAY 7, STORY 1

p. 307 *prayer, the knocking stops*: This tale has no literary antecedent, but seems to be one of many such popular stories current in Florence during Boccaccio's life.

p. 307 *duties of the same sort*: The Laud Singers of Santa Maria Novella was a confraternity officially called the *Società delle Laudi di Santa Maria Novella*, one of whose functions was to sing lauds—that is, hymns of praise, particularly during Lent. A number of men named Lotteringhi worked at different times as agents for the Bardi bank during the 14th century. Some of them were connected to the confraternity of the Laud Singers. There was no Gianni (short for Giovanni) among them, however.

p. 307 *other nonsense like that*: There were many popular religious texts in the vernacular such as the ones named here. Saint Alexis was a Florentine mystic who, with six companions, founded the Order of the Servites, or Servants of Mary, some time after 1233. The text may be referring to the *Ritmo de Sant'Alessio*, one of the earliest examples of Italian verse. There were many laments attributed to Saint Bernard of Clairvaux (1090–1153) who was a key figure in the spread of the austere Cistercian Order during the 12th century. The Laud of the Lady Matilda was one of many hymns of praise for the German mystic Mechtilde of Magdeburg (c. 1210–c. 1285), whose fame was spread in Italy by the Dominicans who also happened to own the monastery at Santa Maria Novella.

p. 308 *daughter of Mannuccio dalla Cuculia*: There was a real Monna Tessa who was a member of the Mannuccio family who lived in the quarter of San Frediano on the far side of the Arno; she was born in 1307 and was married to Neri (short for Rinieri) Pegolotti. The name Tessa, short for Contessa, was common in Tuscany because of the fame of Matilde di Canossa (1046–1115), the Countess (*Contessa*) of Tuscany, who supported the papacy against the Holy Roman Emperor Henry IV, sometimes even donning armor and leading troops into battle. Mannuccio is a nickname used as a family name; it is derived from Alamanno, a name adapted from that of a group of Germanic tribes (the *Alamani*). One of the districts in the San Frediano quarter was called Cuculia (Cuckoo), because it had a chapel containing a painting of the Virgin with a cuckoo in it. Tessa's father's name may thus symbolically foreshadow the cuckolding Gianni is about to receive.

p. 308 *Gianni had in Camerata*: Camerata is a village just north of Florence on the road leading up to Fiesole.

p. 308 *that held up the vines*: Putting the skull of an ass on a stake in order to protect one's crops was a practice going back to Etruscan times.

p. 310 *how powerful he may be*: Gianni names two popular medieval hymns. The first was a prayer to God said at the end of the day: *Te lucis ante terminam* ("To Thee before the light has ended"). The second was to the Virgin: *O intemerata* ("O unspotted [Virgin]"). It was also mentioned by a robber in Story 2.2. In the first of the hymns appear the words *procul recedant . . . noctium phantasmata*: "may the phantoms of the night stay far away." In his *Specchio della vera penitenza* (*The Mirror of True Penitence*), Jacopo Passavanti (1302–c. 1357) defined what Monna Tessa calls a *fantasima* as a kind of satyr or a bogeyman (*gatto mammone*) that went about at night disturbing people. While it is possible to translate the Italian word, which is derived from the Latin *phantasmas,* as "phantom," Passavanti's description makes "bogeyman" a better choice, in that it is an old English word for Satan, who was traditionally imagined as being part animal with cloven hooves and a tail just like a satyr. Moreover, since Boccaccio's tale expresses some skepticism about such creatures, even though the credulous and extremely pious Gianni does not, it seems appropriate to use a word that in modern English has a slightly old-fashioned character and is chiefly employed when talking with children. Finally, Boccaccio's own drawing of the figure in the Hamilton codex is clearly the portrait of (the top half of) the Devil.

p. 310 *spit when I tell you to*: Spitting was a common practice in rites of exorcism.

p. 311 *his breathe, "Your teeth!"*: Federigo actually says *I denti!* meaning "the teeth." There are two explanations for his words. The first is that he wishes Gianni would expel his own teeth when he spits. The second is that Federigo is pretending to be the bogeyman and is saying that his own teeth are being drawn out by the magic spell. In my translation, because Federigo says this "under his breath" (*pianamente*), I selected the first possibility as the more likely.

p. 311 *than Gianni Lotteringhi*: There was a Giovanni di Nello who was a successful apothecary and who was buried in Santa Maria Novella in 1347 where he had had a chapel built at his own expense. He did not live in the quarter around the Porta San Piero, however. Emilia condemns Gianni di Nello as being *non meno sofficiente lavaceci* than Gianni Lotteringhi; her phrase, which I have rendered as "no less a pea brain," literally means he was "just as good at washing chickpeas"—that is, not good for very much at all.

DAY 7, STORY 2

p. 312 *back home for him*: This story, like Story 5.10, derives from a tale told in Apuleius's *Metamorphoses* (9.5–7), one of Boccaccio's favorite authors, occasionally following it word for word.

p. 313 *young girl named Peronella*: Peronella was a common name in Naples at the time. It comes from the French Peronnelle (Little Peter, with a feminine ending).

p. 313 *after just a short absence*: In 1324 the brothers Giovanni (Giannello is a diminutive) and Niccolò Scrignario were living on or near the Piazza Portanova, which is not far from the harbor in the Avorio neighborhood where the story is set. Their family was an important one in the city at that time.

p. 315 *came back home at this hour*: Not far from the neighborhood in which Peronella and her husband live there was a chapel dedicated to Saint Galeone (San Galione in Neapolitan), also known as Saint Eucalione.

p. 315 *five silver ducats for it*: The man who wants to buy the barrel is offering five silver *gigliati*, coins minted in Naples around 1300. They got their name from the *gigli* (lilies) with which they were decorated. I have turned these coins into the more familiar *ducats*.

p. 316 *her husband climbed out*: With the image of the Parthian stallions and mares, Boccaccio is recalling not just Apuleius, but several passages in Ovid's *Ars amatoria* (*The Art of Love*), 1.209–10 and 3.785–86. The Parthians, an Iranian people in central Asia, were famed for turning their backs and feigning retreat on their horses before bringing their enemies down by shooting arrows expertly behind them. Boccaccio may have been thinking of Parthian horses in particular because of this trait.

p. 316 *carry the barrel home for him*: At the beginning of the next story Boccaccio writes: "Filostrato could not veil his reference to the Parthian horses sufficiently to prevent the perceptive ladies from laughing over it, although they pretended they were responding to something else."

DAY 7, STORY 4

p. 317 *screams insults at him*: This story is a reworking of an exemplary tale (14) from the *Disciplina clericalis* (*A School for Clerics*) of Peter Alphonsi. Stories about women's deceptiveness were, however, widespread in medieval literature.

p. 317 *for no particular reason*: Tofano is short for Cristofano (an alternative version of Cristoforo: Christopher). There is a record of a Tofano, the son of a notary, living in Arezzo in the mid-14th century. The town also has a *pozzo di Tofano* (Tofano's well), but it was probably called that because of Boccaccio's story. Tofano's wife is named Ghita, which is short for Margherita.

p. 321 *to Avarice and all his company*: In her next-to-last sentence, Lauretta has recourse to a rhymed proverbial saying: *E così, a modo del villan matto, dopo danno fé patto*. A more literal translation would be: "And so, just like a crazy (or stupid) peasant, after (his) defeat (or harm or damage), he made a pact (or treaty)." Lauretta's last sentence echoes her praise of Love at the start of the story, although why she condemns Avarice (*soldo*: "money, pay") is unclear. The structure of the sentence itself is puzzling, for she first says "long live Love," then "death to Avarice," and then adds *e tutta la brigata*, which I have translated as "and all his company," meaning all those associated with Avarice. But some editors and translators feel that this last phrase is actually the object, like "Love," of "long live." Thus what Lauretta may be saying is: "So, long live Love and all his company, and death to Avarice!" Or even: "So, long live Love, and all our company, and death to Avarice!"

DAY 7, STORY 5

p. 321 *passes the time with him*: Although the theme of this story was widely diffused in medieval literature, no specific source has been found for it.

p. 325 *sat down at his feet*: Penitents typically kneeled at the feet of their confessors; the confessional booth was introduced only after the Council of Trent (1545–63) met to reform the Catholic Church.

p. 326 *young clerks from time to time*: Clerk (*clericus* in Latin) is another word for "clergyman" or "priest," and since the text specifies that he is a *cherichetto*, "a young clerk," the husband is probably referring to a boy who was training to become a priest and who assisted the priest in church services.

p. 326 *and went to hear Mass*: The *Confiteor* (I Confess) was a special prayer that penitents said when they had finished confessing their sins. It was also recited in the Mass.

p. 326 *what he thought he knew*: For "spoiled his holiday," the text says that *ella gli aveva data la mala pasqua*, which literally means, "she had given him a bad Easter." However, *pasqua* in this phrase was used to mean any holiday, and the general sense is that she spoiled things for him.

p. 329 *instead of just a single pair*: What the wife really says here is that she would *porti le corna*, "put horns on his head"—that is, make him a cuckold. The horns metaphor is still actively used by contemporary Italians. To make the sign of the horns by extending the index and fifth fingers, while clenching all the rest, remains the Italian equivalent of "giving someone the finger" in American culture. The mention of "a hundred eyes" may well be an allusion to the mythological figure of Argos, a giant possessing many eyes (his epithet was *Panoptes*, "all seeing"), who was tasked with guarding a sacred white heifer by Hera. The heifer was in actuality the nymph Io, and Zeus sent Hermes to blind and then kill Argos so that he could sleep with her.

DAY 7, STORY 8

p. 330 *a stream of insults at him*: There are many tales in Eastern collections such as *The Thousand and One Nights*, as well as in French *fabliaux*, which involve an unfaithful wife tricking her husband by putting another woman in her place. Neifile tells this story.

p. 330 *by the name of Monna Sismonda*: The Berlinghieri was a merchant family that rose to prominence in the middle of the 14th century; none of them was named Arrigo or Arriguccio, however. This story, like Story 3.3, may be read as an implicit warning to the nouveaux riches, the *gente nuova*, in Boccaccio's world about their excessive social ambition.

p. 337 *stuck in their butts*: The mother's comment alludes to the fact that merchants and notaries used to carry their quill pens and inkwells around in holders that they attached to their belts or put in the back pockets of their pants. Her diatribe against Arriguccio is generally filled with insults that associate him with filth and excrement, and in this particular example, she actually uses the word *culo*, which I have translated as "butt," but could be rendered as "ass." The mother's speech gives voice to the hostility that Florentine aristocrats not only felt to the nouveaux riches, the *gente nuova*, in their society but also to country lords who had once controlled the city and were now associated with lawless violence, as the reference to Arriguccio's having "come up here from some country lord's gang of thugs." The word she uses here for what I have translated as "gang of thugs" is *troiata*, which is defined as the band of men-at-arms who served a feudal lord. It is an unusual word, and there is good reason to think that she chooses it because it echoes *troia*, the word for "sow," which was beginning to acquire in Boccaccio's time its modern slang meaning of "whore."

p. 337 *bread for your dowry*: The Guidi family was a byword for aristocratic status.

DAY 7, STORY 9

p. 338 *what he saw was unreal*: This story is a retelling of the *Comoedia Lydiae* (*The Comedy of Lydia*), a work written by the 12th-century French poet and theorist Matthieu de Vendôme, which Boccaccio had transcribed with his own hand. The two motifs that make up the story—the trickery used by a woman on her husband to prove herself to her lover, and the enchanted pear tree—were widespread in medieval literature.

p. 339 *who was called Lidia*: Nicostrato is the only name that Boccaccio changes from his source, in which the character is called Decius. This change may have been dictated by a desire to make the name fit the Greek setting, but since it means "triumphant warrior," the change can also be seen as ironic. Boccaccio retains the name of Lidia's maid, Lusca, from his source, where it is the Latinized version of the French *louche*, which means "squint eyed" or "disreputable."

p. 343 *against the wall and killed it*: "Jesses" were strips of silk or leather fastened to the legs of a falcon to which a leash could then be attached.

p. 345 *have him extract it for me*: Surgeons were socially placed well beneath doctors in the period, handling minor injuries, setting fractures, pulling teeth, and even cutting hair.

p. 347 *there on top of yours*: Pirro says he saw Nicostrato *in sul vostro*, which means literally "on top of yours." This most likely refers to the notion that a man's wife was considered his belonging or property; ironically, Nicostrato is sitting in his garden and in that sense is thus quite literally *on* his property.

p. 347 *to make love together*: Chaucer's *The Merchant's Tale*, which generally follows Boccaccio's story quite closely, but may not be directly derived from it, has Pirro and Lidia, somewhat improbably, making love together in the tree rather than on the ground.

DAY 7, CONCLUSION

p. 349 *Queen of our company*: Lauretta, whose name means "little laurel tree," is being crowned with a wreath of laurel.

p. 350 *together with Fiammetta*: Arcite and Palamon are characters who appear in Boccaccio's long narrative poem *Teseida* (1340–41), which Chaucer reworked as *The Knight's Tale*.

p. 350 *that of other instruments*: "Carole" are dances in which the dancers join hands and move in a clockwise direction, usually accompanied by music and the singing of the dancers themselves.

DAY 8, STORY 3

p. 353 *better than he does*: This story, set in a working-class milieu, has no specific literary antecedent. The heliotrope was a name for a sandstone, green with blood-red streaks, that some medieval thinkers believed could render its bearer invisible; such a power was mentioned by Pliny, *Istoria naturalis* (*Natural History*), 37.60.165. The Mugnone is a stream that flows into the Arno near Florence; in the hot months of summer, it is usually just a dry bed. The protagonist of the story will be featured again in Stories 8.6, 9.3, and 9.5, and by the 16th century his name had become a byword in Italy for someone who was a pathetic simpleton and dupe. Elissa tells this story.

p. 354 *with some strange habits*: Calandrino was the nickname of the painter Nozzo (short for Giannozzo) di Perino who lived in Florence in the early part of the 14th century. He was probably a pupil of Andrea Tafi and thus a member of a school that resisted the new realism associated with Giotto. There are some frescoes of no great importance that he painted in a villa at Camerata, but his real claim to fame is his simplemindedness and gullibility. His nickname may refer to a square with hinged arms used by stonecutters and painters to measure angles or, more likely, to a kind of lark, since birds in general were frequently seen as being gullible, as the verb *uccellare* (to catch birds, to make a fool of) suggests. The word is also a diminutive of Calandro (Lark), a fairly widespread name in the period. Note that in this sentence Florence is said to be full of *nuove genti,* which I have translated as "bizarre characters." Although the phrase could be rendered more literally as "new people," the word *nuovo* had a range of meanings from the more positive, such as unfamiliar, strange, or unusual, to the more negative, such as bizarre or weird. The same adjective is applied later in the sentence to Calandrino himself, who is said to be a man *di nuovi costumi,* a phrase that I have rendered as "strange habits." At the end of the paragraph, Maso del Saggio is said to be planning to make Calandrino believe *alcuna nuova cosa,* "some far-fetched (that is, novel) notion." Finally, near the end of the story, Bruno and Buffalmacco ask Calandrino, *che novelle son queste?*, which I have translated as "What's the story here?" It would have been more accurate, though less idiomatic, to have said, "What are all these strange goings-on about?"

p. 354 *and his simplicity really funny*: Bruno was Bruno di Giovanni d'Olivieri, a minor painter who was active in the first decades of the 14th century and who worked along with Buffalmacco, an acknowledged master artist. Buffalmacco's real name was Bonamico (c. 1262–1340), and like Calandrino, he was a pupil of Andrea Tafi. He was a more accomplished artist, however, and the remains of his paintings can still be seen in the Badia in Florence, the Cathedral of Arezzo, and, perhaps, the Camposanto in Pisa (*The Triumph of Death*). He was reputed to be quite a prankster, and writers after Boccaccio, including Sacchetti and Vasari, told stories about him. The nickname Buffalmacco comes from a combination of *buffo,* an alternate for *beffa,* meaning "trick" or "prank," and *macco,* the name of a soup made from shelled fava beans, thus suggesting the character's pleasure in eating but also his relatively slender income, since bean soup was the food of the poor.

p. 354 *believe some far-fetched notion*: Maso del Saggio is also remembered as a prankster by later writers. Although he was, by profession, a broker or middleman, he was known in his own time for his tricks and his mocking humor. He was mentioned by Frate Cipolla in Story 6.10 and will appear again as a trickster in Story 8.5.

p. 354 *placed above the altar*: The Church of San Giovanni is the baptistery in Florence, which stands opposite the Duomo, or cathedral. A contract was signed for the decoration of the canopy in 1313 with Lippo di Benivieni, a Tuscan painter (active 1296–1327).

p. 354 *thrown in for good measure*: Maso's discourse conjures up a magical land of plenty for Calandrino. This was a fantasy place that appears in various kinds of popular literature throughout the Middle Ages (and after). Maso calls it *Berlinzone*, which I have translated as "Gluttonia," since Florentines at the time referred to someone who stuffed food into his mouth as a *berlingaio*. He places it in the land of the Basques, which was "beyond beyond" for 14th-century Italians, and he also says it is in the *contrada che si chiamava Bengodi*. *Bengodi* is made up of *godi* (enjoy) and *bene* (well) and thus means something like the "land of real enjoyment, or pleasure," but since food is the central feature of Maso's fantasy country, I have turned *Bengodi* into "Gourmandistan."

p. 355 *single drop of water in it*: "Vernaccia wine" is a white wine made from a varietal of the same name that is grown throughout Italy. The name derives from a word meaning "vernacular"—that is, "local." Nowadays, when people say Vernaccia, they are usually referring to the Tuscan white wine Vernaccia di San Gimignano, but in Boccaccio's time that was not necessarily the case.

p. 355 *are told," replied Maso*: Not only does Maso fool Calandrino by talking of fantastic places and using equivocal expressions but, like Frate Cipolla, he sometimes comes close to talking nonsense, although he uses an impressive style as he does so in order to dupe his listener. In this sentence he says, *Haccene più di millanta, che tutta notte canta*, which means, literally, "There are more than a thousand (miles) to there, which sing all night long." Maso renders his statement impressive by using the variant *millanta* for *mille* (it means "a thousand" but also refers to any very large number) and by rhyming that word with *canta* (sings). *Millanta* also suggests *millantare*, a verb meaning "to boast or brag." That Calandrino is appropriately impressed is indicated by his response that the place is "farther away than Abruzzi," the name for a province in Italy that at the time belonged to the Kingdom of the Two Sicilies and that was used proverbially, like the country of the Basques, to mean a land at the other end of the earth.

p. 355 *"but it's really nothing"*: Maso is punning here when he says *Sì é cavelle*. It can be translated as "It's really nothing" in the sense that the extra distance to Gluttonia is nothing at all but also that Gluttonia itself is nothing at all—that is, a complete fiction.

p. 355 *millstones from Montisci*: Settignano and Montisci (more correctly, Montici) are hills (and towns) near Florence, just as Monte Morello is.

p. 355 *well, good night to you*: This is another bit of linguistic foolery on Maso's part. Speaking of the emeralds, he says *rilucon di mezzanotte vatti con Dio*. The first part of this clause speaks of how the stones shine in the middle of the night, but the word *mezzanotte* (middle of the night) is followed by a standard locution for good-bye, *vatti con Dio* ("God go—or be—with you"), which I have rendered as "good night to you," perhaps because Maso's clause is structured by a process of association: speaking about the middle of the night leads him to say good-bye, since it is long past bedtime.

p. 356 *all the way there to find them*: Faenza is a reference to the old Faenza Gate that was located less than half a mile to the west of the present-day train station of Santa Maria Novella in Florence. There was a convent just outside it in Boccaccio's day.

p. 357 *wasted all our efforts*: Boccaccio's Italian here reads: *noi avremmo perduto il trotto per l'ambiadura*. Literally, this means, "we would have lost the trot for the sake of the amble." The proverb involves two different gaits of horses. The amble is a leisurely pace that is more comfortable for the rider, whereas the trot is faster, but less comfortable. Also, the trot is a natural gait for horses, whereas they must learn to amble, and they may lose the ability to trot if they do. Thus Buffalmacco's proverb means essentially that they will potentially be losing a sure thing (the natural gait of the trot that is sure to lead them to the prize of the heliotrope) by doing something that promises to be easier (ambling, or going to the Mugnone right away) but is less sure (because ambling has to be learned and may keep them from getting to their goal as they could by trotting there).

p. 358 *with stones in no time*: Hainault is a city in present-day Belgium, which was an important center for making cloth and clothing in the late Middle Ages. Shirts cut in the "style of Hainault" would have been short and tight fitting, thus not having a skirt that hung down below the belt.

p. 359 *near the Canto alla Macina*: Canto alla Macina means "Millstone Corner" and actually exists at the intersection of Via Ginori and Via Guelfa. Having Calandrino live at a place associated with another stone (probably because there was a mill there once) makes sense in terms of the imagery in the story.

p. 360 *woman named Monna Tessa*: The name Tessa, short for Contessa, was common in Tuscany because of the fame of Matilde di Canossa (1046–1115), the Countess (*Contessa*) of Tuscany who supported the papacy against the Holy Roman Emperor Henry IV, sometimes even donning armor and leading troops into battle.

DAY 8, STORY 5

p. 362 *administering justice in Florence*: There is no specific antecedent for this story, although Florentines were well known for playing practical jokes on outsiders. The judge in this story is named Niccola da San Lepidio, which means he comes from the town of San Lepidio, now known as Sant'Elpidio a Mare, which is located in the southern part of the province known as *Le Marche* (The Marches). Florence frequently found its *podestà* and the magistrates who worked with them in that region, which is west and slightly south of Tuscany. Filostrato tells this story.

p. 363 *completely blackened by smoke*: The ceremonial caps and gowns of physicians and lawyers in the Middle Ages were normally lined with "vair," the fur of a gray and white squirrel.

p. 363 *as much as Maso did*: Although Matteuzzo has not been identified, Ribi was a well-known professional entertainer, according to the writer Sacchetti, who recounts several of the clever quips he was supposedly responsible for making; see his *Trecentonovelle* (*Three Hundred Stories*), 49 and 50. Matteuzzo is a pet name for Matteo (Matthew); Ribi, a nickname for Garibaldo, Ribaldo, or Riberto.

p. 364 *back from the country*: Santa Maria a Verzaia was a church near the Porta San Frediana, a gate in the walls of Florence on the south side of the Arno.

p. 365 *appeal this to the superior court*: Ribi actually says he will appeal the matter to the *sindacato*, which is really short for *il momento del sindacato*. The "moment of the *sindacato*" was the moment when all the magistrates in Florence ended their tenure in office and delivered a report (the *sindacato*) about their activities. At that moment, citizens could appeal their cases to the magistrates, known as *sindacatori*.

DAY 8, STORY 6

p. 366 *tell his wife about it*: There is no specific antecedent for this story, although it has some general points of contact with a number of medieval tales involving trickery where the prize pursued is bacon, which is precisely what Calandrino would turn his pig into.

p. 369 *it's just flown away*: There is an untranslatable pun here: Calandrino has been complaining that his pig has been "stolen" (*imbolato*), to which Bruno replies that he cannot believe it has "flown away" (*volato*).

p. 369 *see right away who took it*: The "bread and cheese test" was a widespread magical rite in the Middle Ages in which people suspected of theft were given a portion of bread and cheese to eat over which a magical formula had been recited. Their inability to swallow it was assumed to be proof of their guilt.

p. 370 *come here for a drink*: "Vernaccia wine" is a white wine made from a varietal of the same name that is grown throughout Italy. The name derives from a word meaning "vernacular"—that is, "local." Nowadays, when people say Vernaccia, they are usually referring to the Tuscan white wine Vernaccia di San Gimignano, but in Boccaccio's time that was not necessarily the case.

p. 370 *with fresh hepatic aloes*: "Forty *soldi*" were worth about half a florin, which was a reasonably valuable coin at the time. There is a debate about what exactly "dog ginger" (*zenzero canino*, in the original) is. Some scholars think the phrase refers to an inferior type of ginger, while others argue that it is a name for water pepper (*Persicaria hydropiper*), a marsh weed with an acrid juice. Yet another school of thought believes that "dog ginger" was a euphemism for "dog excrement," which was, in fact, occasionally used in medieval medicine. "Hepatic aloes" (*Liliacea amarissima*) was a bitter, nauseating drug used as a purgative. "Hepatic" (pertaining to the liver) refers to its dark red color.

p. 372 *amount to six florins*: Since the florin was a fairly valuable coin, and "six" was used in the period to mean something like "a large, indefinite sum," Buffalmacco is suggesting that Calandrino made a killing when he sold the pig.

p. 373 *his losses and his humiliation*: A more literal translation of the last words of the story—*col danno e con le beffe*—would be that Calandrino is left "with the loss and with the tricks (that had been played on him)," or "with the loss and the ridicule (he had been subjected to)."

DAY 9, STORY 7

p. 373 *gadflies and the sun*: There is no specific literary antecedent for this story, although it is clearly related to a long tradition of misogynistic writing throughout the Middle Ages. Many scholars also see it as being autobiographical, the reworking of an unhappy episode in Boccaccio's life, which he also wrote about in his *Corbaccio* (1354–55), a virulently misogynistic work about a widow who had jilted him.

p. 373 *with the goods of Fortune*: Elena is Helen, a name that cannot help but evoke that of Helen of Troy. The scholar's name, Rinieri, is less suggestive.

p. 374 *toward the nether regions*: My translation "nether regions" is a compromise. Boccaccio writes *in inferno*, "in the direction of Hell." Most translators see this as an emphatic way of saying that she did not stare down at the ground and translate the phrase accordingly. But in the context of a story filled with allusions to devils, serpents, Hell, and Dante's *Inferno*, Boccaccio's phrase is quite suggestive.

p. 382 *with diabolical cunning*: What Boccaccio actually says here is: *che di mal pelo avea taccata la coda*. A literal translation would be: "who had attached to him a tail with (tufts of) bad hair." The clause connects the scholar to traditional images of the devils, such as the ones who appear in Cantos 21–22 of Dante's *Inferno*, one of whom is named *Malacoda* (Bad Tail). The devils were traditionally supposed to be cunning and malicious, as Dante's are, and as the scholar is.

p. 387 *from this folly of mine*: This may be a slip on Boccaccio's part in that the scholar could not have known about the question the lady had asked her lover. Or perhaps she may have revealed this in some way when she was asking Rinieri for his assistance.

p. 388 *if you were our oldest enemy*: The "oldest enemy" is Satan.

p. 389 *caught in one of them*: The scholar's "snares" (*lacciuoli*) here may be an ironic reference to the snares that courtly love poetry said women used with men and that were frequently identified, metaphorically, with their hair. The word also looks forward to the end of the story where the lady is said, in a phrase alluding to Dante's *Inferno*, to have a plentiful supply of snares or tricks.

p. 393 *ugliest thing in the world*: "Madder" (*Rubia tinctorum*) is a plant whose root was used to make a range of red dyes up through the 19th century.

p. 398 *result of diabolical spells*: The lady's "plentiful supply of tricks" (*a gran divizia lacciuoli*) echoes the scholar's boast about having many snares or tricks (*lacciuoli*) earlier in the story and also constitutes an allusion to the anonymous Navarese, a con man appearing in Dante's *Inferno*, who *avea lacciuoli a gran divizia* (22.109: "had snares [or tricks] in abundance") and uses one of them to escape the clutches of the devils who are about to punish him.

p. 398 *are dealing with scholars*: At the beginning of the next story, Boccaccio writes: "Grievous and painful though Elena's misfortunes were for the ladies to hear, they felt only a moderate degree of compassion as the story unfolded because they thought she had partly deserved them, although they did judge the scholar to be inflexible and uncompromisingly fierce, if not downright cruel."

DAY 8, STORY 9

p. 398 *to wallow in filth*: There is no specific literary antecedent for this story, although it reflects a belief in magic that is a staple of many classical and medieval stories. Neifile tells this story.

p. 399 *from head to toe*: The ceremonial caps and gowns of physicians and lawyers in the Middle Ages were normally lined with "vair," the fur of a gray and white squirrel. During this period, the University of Bologna was celebrated for its medical school throughout Europe.

p. 399 *now call Via del Cocomero*: There was, in fact, a da Villa family: a Messer Simone da Villa is mentioned in a history of Pistoia as living between 1315 and 1326, and a Messer Simone Medico (Doctor) was buried in Santa Croce in Florence around the middle of the 14th century. The doctor's family name means, essentially, that he is from the country, reinforcing the notion that he is simpleminded, something of a bumpkin. Via del Cocomero corresponds to a section of the present-day Via Ricasoli near the Mercato Vecchio, which is where the house of Boccaccio's two trickster painters, Bruno and Buffalmacco, is located (compare Story 9.3). *Cocomero* means "watermelon" and thus, like the earlier reference to the sheep, constitutes a comment on Messer Simone's intelligence: his head is as (relatively) empty as a melon.

p. 400 *of the Lucifer at San Gallo*: The hospital of San Gallo had a devil's head painted on its facade with multiple mouths, each devouring a sinner. This iconography was widespread in the late Middle Ages. Dante's *Inferno*, for example, features a three-headed Satan, whose three mouths are devouring those whom Dante saw as the most sinful traitors in the history of the world: Judas, Brutus, and Cassius.

p. 400 *grant your every wish*: Bruno refers to Simone as *vostra qualitativa mellonaggine da Legnaia*, which I have rendered as "your qualitative melonosity of Legnaia." *Qualitativo* was an adjective used in contemporary philosophical writing; it has no precise meaning here, but is designed to make what Bruno is saying sound impressive. The reference to *mellonaggine*, "melonosity," like later ones to pumpkins and cucumbers, is a comment on Simone's lack of intelligence, his empty-melon-headedness. Legnaia is a village not far from Florence that was famous for its watermelons. Montesone (or Montisoni) in the next sentence is a hill near Florence with a famous cross on its summit.

p. 401 *so-called because he came from Scotland*: Bruno addresses Simone as *maestro mio dolciato*, "my sweet (or, more accurately, sweetened) Master." *Sweet* here is an antonym for *salty*, meaning witty or clever; hence my "dull-cified"—that is, sweet means dull or stupid. Bruno will repeatedly use this opposition between sweet and salty—that is, between stupid and witty—in addressing Simone. Michael Scot (c. 1175–c. 1235) was a scholar and mathematician whose translations of Aristotle from Arabic and Hebrew initiated the late medieval vogue for the Greek philosopher. Scot wrote works on philosophy, astrology, and alchemy, and served as the court astrologer for Holy Roman Emperor Frederick II. Although he has been praised for his learning, Dante placed him in Hell with the magicians and soothsayers (see *Inferno* 20.116–18). Commentaries on the *Divina commedia* speak of the magical banquets Scot supposedly held for his followers.

p. 402 *to the Skinkimurra of Prester John*: Bruno's list of famous women veers between real people and places, on the one hand, such as the Basques, the Sultan, Osbech, and Norwega (*Norrueca* is, perhaps, a corruption of Norvegia, or Norway), and pure fantasy, on the other. *Barbanicchi,* which has been left as it is in Italian, may suggest "barbarians." "Chitterchatterer" is *ciancianfera,* the "bearer of *ciancia,*" which means "chitchat." *Semistante,* which I have rendered as "Semistanding" (*semi*-means "half," and *stante* is the present participle of *stare,* "to stay, stand, or be"), also distantly suggests *almirante* (admiral) or *amorante* (lover). *Scalpedra di Narsia* suggests both *scalpitare* (to claw) and *puledra* (female colt) to Italian scholars. However, Bruno's *Narsia* may be a reference to the Umbrian town of Norcia (*Nursia* in Latin), which was the birthplace of Saint Benedict, the founder of Western monasticism, who was known in the Middle Ages as Saint Benedict of Narsia (as well as of Nursia, Norsia, and Norcia). If so, then *Scalpedra* may be a play on words on both *scapolare* (scapular), the hooded cloak worn by monks over their shoulders (*scapula* in Latin), and *cattedra* (*cathedra* in Latin), the name for a bishop's seat in a church that was accordingly called a cathedral. Hence my decision to make her the Scapulathedral of Narsia. Legends concerning Prester John were brought back to Europe by crusaders after about 1200, identifying him as the legendary Christian ruler of an empire in Asia or Africa, sometimes specified as Ethiopia, who was going to retake Jerusalem for Christendom. He supposedly signed himself simply as Prester John—that is, John the Priest. Florentines called him Presto Giovanni (Quick John). His wife, Skinkimurra (Schinchimurra in Italian), is, of course, a pure fabrication; her name is possibly intended to suggest the exotic language Prester John was imagined as speaking.

p. 402 *you're grinding the cumin*: Cumin seeds are very aromatic and were used not only to flavor dishes but also in medicines, including those to control flatulence.

p. 402 *make your fabric nice and tight*: Bruno is making a bawdy play on the actions involved in weaving.

p. 403 *beautiful beyond description*: The "figure of Lent" would have been that of an emaciated woman. An *"Agnus Dei,"* the "Lamb of God," was the figure of a lamb bearing a cross or having a small cross above it; it was a symbol of Christ. Since doctors diagnosed diseases by examining patients' urine, it would make sense for Master Simone to have a urine flask painted over his front door. Cats and mice were frequently represented in medieval painting and sculpture, although there are few examples of actual battles between groups of them. Cats were usually associated with the Devil; mice sometimes had similar associations but were also linked to weakness and hence to frail humanity.

p. 404 *of the Great Khan of Altarisi*: Gumedra seems sheer nonsense, but Marco Polo had spoken of the Genghis Khan who lived in a region called Altai. "Altarisi" could thus be seen as a conflation of that place-name with the word for "altar," *altare*, although it could also be a comical corruption of *Tartary*.

p. 404 *don't say anything about it*: Bruno is caricaturing the names of two medical authorities in the Middle Ages, the Greek physician Hippocrates, and the Arabic philosopher Avicenna. Bruno's *Porcograsso* (for Hippocrates) means Fat Hog; his *Vannaccena* (for Avicenna) means Vain (or Empty) Supper.

p. 404 *much to get me to do it*: Peretola is only a few miles from Florence.

p. 405 *me, but she didn't want to*: Cacavincigli is the name of a street or alley in Florence associated with lowlifes. The first part of the word, *caca*, means "crap" and thus anticipates the end of the story. Simone offered the woman ten Bolognese *grossi*, the early modern equivalent of which was the Dutch or English groat, a silver coin of relatively modest worth.

p. 405 *whistles to shame," replied Bruno*: Bruno's nonsense, which sounds impressive and which he is counting on Simone not to understand, can be only approximated in translation. Bruno first tells the doctor that his singing would beat *le cetere de' sagginali*—literally, "the lyres (or harps or whistles) made from sorghum stalks." The word *cetere* can also refer to the mumbo jumbo of doctors and lawyers who were given to saying *etcetera* a great deal. Then Bruno says to the doctor: *sí artagoticamente stracantate*—literally, "you sing beyond the limits [*stra-*] in so super [*arta-*, or *arci-* in modern Italian] Gothic a manner." *Gothic* was clearly already a pejorative term for the art and architecture of the late Middle Ages. However, since the word begins with *arta-*, Simone is meant to hear it as praise for his *artfulness*.

p. 405 *born into a family from Vallecchio*: Vallecchio is a small town in Tuscany near Castelfiorentino about eighteen miles southwest of Florence.

p. 406 *make me change my mind*: When Bruno says that Simone's wise words would "draw pious old ladies right out of their boots," his term for them is *pinzochere*, which meant the pious laywomen who associated themselves with various religious orders but who did not take vows, did not live in convents, and could choose to marry. Many went around barefoot—hence the humor of Bruno's comment, which is another bit of the deliberate obscurity that he uses to make fun of the linguistically challenged Simone. Boccaccio seems to have thought such women were generally hypocrites.

p. 406 *I feel certain you'll succeed*: Bruno refers to his *grande e calterita fede*, his "great and *calterita* faith (or word)." *Calterita* is the past participle of *calterire*, which means "to bruise" or "to damage," and thus really means *bad* faith. It is another bit of verbal mumbo jumbo on Bruno's part.

p. 406 *such a good secretary*: There was a professor of medicine named Guiglielmo da

Saliceto who was active in the late 13th and early 14th centuries, although it cannot be certain that Boccaccio is thinking of him here. Forlimpopoli is a town located between Forlí and Cesena; the name has farcical overtones. Simone calls himself a good *segretaro*, using a word that could mean in the late Middle Ages both a "keeper of secrets" and the person who was entrusted with his master's secrets as well as with correspondence and the like—that is, a secretary. *La Bergamina* (the Woman from Bergamo), who is mentioned in the next sentence, has not been identified.

p. 407 *like a thousand years to him*: The narrator refers to Simone as *maestro sapa*, which I have translated as "Master Sappyhead." Since *sapa* is actually concentrated grape juice, once again Simone's lack of wit, his lack of "salt," is the point of the joke.

p. 408 *revealed these things to the Master*: High up on the facade of the church at Passignano there is a painting of God the Father. Buffalmacco's playing on the word *high* (*alto* in Italian) works on the assumption that the parochial Simone has never seen the image.

p. 408 *you were baptized on a Sunday*: Boys were sometimes taught the alphabet by having letters carved on apples. The reference to Simone's "great big, long melon" is, of course, a satirical remark about his stupidity, his empty "melon" or "pumpkin" of a head. The remark that he was baptized on a Sunday has the same function, since salt was not available for sale on that day, meaning that there was no salt, no "wit," available for Simone on the day of his christening.

p. 409 *a member of our company*: Buffalmacco uses a word Boccaccio appears to have made up here: *frastagliatamente*. The verb *frastagliare* means "to cut an intricate design" or "cut something into pieces" and, by extension, "to confuse or deceive by talking in a grandiose and extravagant manner." Simone is supposed to hear, perhaps, the idea of "intricate detail" as a form of sincere praise. Hence I have translated it as "frankastically," conflating *frankly, fantastically,* and *sarcastically.*

p. 409 *ass-sembly of the human race*: Here begins a series of scatological puns inspired by the countess's name. In Italian she is the *contessa di Civillari,* the name of a spot in Florence near the monastery of San Jacopo a Ripoli that was used as an open sewer and an outhouse of sorts. Buffalmacco says the Countess is the most beautiful thing in *tutto il culattario dell'umana generazione.* The key word here is *culattario,* an Italianized play on a late Latin word such as *collectarium* (*collecta,* or "assembly," plus *-arium,* "place of"). The initial part of the word has been replaced with *cul-,* from *culo,* meaning "butt." Hence "ass-sembly."

p. 409 *get a whiff of fresh air*: The Countess's trip to the Arno refers to the practice of taking household waste to be dumped into the river at night. There actually is a town near Arezzo called Laterino that had existed since Roman times and had been the source of jokes as early as the *Curculio* (*The Weevil,* 4.4) of Plautus (254?–184 B.C.E.).

p. 410 *recall them at the present moment*: "Her staff and pail," *la verga e 'l piombino,* is an untranslatable pair of puns. *Verga* means both the staff or rod a ruler held and a cleaning instrument, while *piombino* (from *piombo:* "lead") could mean a (lead) seal or a pail or bucket. The Countess's retainers all refer to different sizes and forms of human excrement. They are called *il Tamagnin dalla Porta, don Meta, Manico di Scopa, lo Squacchera,* which mean, respectively: the little old man who keeps, or stays by, the door; don turd; broomhandle; and the loose one (*Squacchera* comes from a verb meaning "to squirt")—that is, diarrhea.

p. 410 *weren't actually there at the time*: The tombs outside of Santa Maria Novella were erected around 1314, thus suggesting a possible date for the story. Although the word *bath* will have a special meaning in the story, there was an actual "ceremony of the bath" in which knights-to-be were washed of their imperfections.

p. 412 *a devil and horns on top*: The festival they no longer celebrate is probably the *Gioco del Veglio* (Game of the Old Man) in which someone would impersonate the Devil. It was banned in 1325.

p. 413 *as the nunnery at Ripoli*: Buffalmacco is going along the present-day Via della Scala. His route takes him by the hospital of Santa Maria della Scala (founded 1316; later the monastery of San Martino) toward the nunnery of San Jacopo di Ripoli, which had been founded in 1300–01 and contained paintings by Bruno and Buffalmacco, according to Vasari.

DAY 9, INTRODUCTION

p. 416 *young men summoned to her*: In the Ptolemaic universe, the "eighth heaven" is the heaven of the fixed stars; it is surrounded by the ninth heaven, or *Primum mobile*, and the *Empyrean*, neither of which is visible to us on earth.

p. 417 *permission to go and do so*: "Carole" are dances in which the dancers join hands and move in a clockwise direction, usually accompanied by music and the singing of the dancers themselves.

DAY 9, STORY 1

p. 417 *rids herself of both of them*: There are many stories in medieval literature in which women impose virtually impossible tasks on would-be lovers in order to keep them at bay, but there is no particular tale that is the source for this one.

p. 418 *to win her affection*: The Palermini was a noteworthy Ghibelline family from the quarter of San Pancrazio in Florence who had been exiled in 1267; another member of the family appears in Story 3.7. The Chiarmontesi was an important Florentine family living near the Orsanmichele that had originally been Ghibelline and had likewise been exiled in 1267; the family later switched political allegiance and turned Guelf.

p. 418 *from importuning her*: The Lazzari was a powerful Guelf family in Pistoia and included among its members Dante's Vanni Fucci, who is punished among the thieves in Hell (see *Inferno* 24.122–51), as well as a famous lawyer named Filippo de' Lazzari. There is no record of any Francesca de' Lazzari.

p. 419 *bravest men in this town*: The name Scannadio means literally He Slits the Throat of God.

DAY 9, STORY 2

p. 424 *her lover at her leisure*: Versions of this story can be found in devotional works, such as Jacobus de Voragine's *Legenda aurea* (*The Golden Legend*), 146, as well as in several French *fabliaux*.

p. 425 *everyone else who knew her*: The Abbess's name is unusual, but the family name Usimbardi did exist at the time.

p. 425 *in place of her veils*: A "psalter" (*saltero* in Italian) is an arrangement of veils worn by nuns on their heads that had a triangular shape like the musical instrument of the same name (also called a psaltery).

DAY 9, STORY 3

p. 427 *without having to give birth*: The theme of the pregnant man is very ancient and was widespread in classical and medieval literature, from the Greek geographer Strabo's *Geography* (3.4) through Marie de France's fable *Du vilain et de l'escarbot* (*The Peasant and the Beetle*) to the *Legenda aurea* (*The Golden Legend*), 89.

p. 428 *was going to buy himself a farm*: The joke here is that Calandrino's "two hundred *lire* in small change" (*dugento lire di piccioli contanti*) are not worth all that much, although he fantasizes about buying a farm with them.

p. 428 *to make mud pies out of it*: The original speaks of Calandrino going about *comperando terra come se egli avesse avuto a far pallottole*: "buying earth (or land) as if he had to make pellets." The pellets in question were clay projectiles shot out of crossbows. The point here is that the only "farm" Calandrino has enough money to buy would be a tiny plot just large enough to obtain clay for making pellets; there would not be not enough land, in other words, for a proper farm, which was what anyone with social ambitions would have wanted to purchase in Boccaccio's time.

p. 428 *at Calandrino's expense*: Nello di Dino (or Bandino) is mentioned in several documents at the start of the 14th century, and like Bruno and Buffalmacco, he may have been a disciple of Andrea Tafi, a painter who is best known for his work on the mosaics in the Florentine Baptistery. Nello is said to be a relative of Calandrino's wife in Story 9.5. Nello is short for Antonello or another name ending in *nello*.

p. 429 *tell you what you have to do*: Master Simone da Villa appeared in Story 8.9, where he was identified as a particularly stupid doctor from Bologna and was the object of a complex practical joke that Bruno and Buffalmacco played on him.

p. 429 *at the sign of the Melon*: In Story 8.9, Master Simone is said to live on the Via del Cocomero (the present via Ricasoli), which was near the Mercato Vecchio where Bruno and Buffalmacco also lived. Note that Cocomero means "watermelon," and that here Master Simone lives "at the sign of the Melon"—that is, he advertises his practice by means of a sign with a melon painted on it. Both watermelon and melon are, of course, images of his (empty) head.

p. **430** *every one of his teeth*: Here Boccaccio replaces Simone with Scimmione, deforming the name only slightly (in pronunciation), while turning it into the word for monkey or ape.

p. **431** *as healthy as a horse*: In the original, Simone assures Calandrino he will be *piú sano che pesce* ("healthier than a fish").

p. **431** *he sent around to Calandrino*: Master Simone sends Calandrino a little bit of *chiarea*, which critics have glossed in various ways. The word may derive from the French *clarée*, meaning "liquor." Since Calandrino finds it inoffensive, "spiced wine" seems a reasonable translation, since it was often used as a cure itself or as a base for other medicines.

DAY 9, STORY 5

p. **432** *serious and unpleasant predicament*: This story has no literary antecedents. Filostrato tells this story.

p. **433** *stately mansion built for himself*: The Cornacchini was an important family of merchants in Florence in the 14th and 15th centuries and owned a house in Via del Cocomero, which is close to where Bruno, Buffalmacco, and the others lived. Camerata, a hill just below Fiesole where many suburban estates were located, was mentioned in Story 7.1.

p. **433** *to let her out for hire*: Niccolosa was a common name in Tuscany at that time. Her pimp is referred to as *il Mangione*. *Mangione* may possibly be his last name, which is how I have translated it, even though it is preceded by the definite article, since such a procedure was—and still is—common enough in the Tuscan dialect of Italian. It is also possible, however, that *il Mangione* may be a sobriquet, so that his name is The Glutton. Camaldoli was a lower-class quarter in Florence.

p. **434** *it would astonish you*: Calandrino called Niccolosa a *lammia*. The word had been used since classical antiquity for a female monster with the body of a snake and the head of a woman who supposedly came out at night to kill children and drink their blood. The word could also have the less threatening meaning of an enchanting nymph or fairy or siren. Calandrino intends it in this second sense, but the other meaning may resonate in context.

p. **434** *and he'd ruin everything*: Tessa is Calandrino's wife.

p. **435** *you get my meaning*: Calandrino is mangling the conventional language of courtly love here.

p. **436** *in order to get you*: The "rebeck," a relative of the viola, was a three-stringed, pear shaped instrument played with a bow.

p. **436** *mad mother doting on her son*: This last comparison is simpler in Boccaccio's Italian: *come va la pazza al figliuolo*. Literally, it means "as the madwoman goes for her child (or son)." It was a proverbial expression for anyone who pursued without restraint the person whom he or she loved passionately.

p. **440** *that wasn't Tessa*: See Story 9.3.

DAY 9, STORY 6

p. 441 *words restores the peace*: There are several *fabliaux* that narrate versions of this story, including Jean de Boves's *De Gombert et des deux clers* (*Gombert and the Two Clerks*) and the anonymous *Le meunier et les deux clers* (*The Miller and the Two Clerks*). Chaucer's "The Reeve's Tale" does so as well and may have been influenced by Boccaccio's version of the story. Note that the valley of the Mugnone, which provides the setting for the story, also appears in Story 8.3. The Mugnone flows from Fiesole south to Florence and at one time entered the Arno near the Ponte Vecchio.

p. 444 *to the wife's great satisfaction*: In this sentence, Boccaccio writes simply that Adriano *caricò l'orza* ("yanked his rope"). The *orza* was the rope or cable attached to the yardarm of a sailing ship. The expression *caricare l'orza* meant to make or keep the line taut (so that the sail attached to the yardarm would swell out in the prevailing breeze). I have had to fill out Boccaccio's phrase in order to bring out the obscene double entendre it contains.

p. 444 *nothing could be sweeter, in any way*: Pinuccio's enthusiasm expresses itself as a rhyming couplet in the Italian original.

DAY 9, STORY 10

p. 446 *completely ruins the spell*: There are many stories in which human beings are turned into animals in both antiquity and the Middle Ages, including one of Boccaccio's favorites, Apuleius's *Metamorphoses*.

p. 447 *by buying and selling things*: Barletta was a coastal city northwest of Bari in the southern Italian province of Apulia (Puglia) where the Bardi bank, for which Boccaccio's father worked, had a branch. This is the only story in the *Decameron* set in this region of Italy. Gianni di Barolo, who is introduced here, means Gianni from Barletta, Barolo deriving from the Italianized version of the Latin name of the town. *Donno* is the southern Italian version of *don*, which derives from the Latin *dominus*, an honorific meaning "lord" or "master" and used for religious as well as secular figures. Pietro da Tresanti (in the next sentence) means Pietro from the town of Tresanti.

p. 447 *to the best of his ability*: "Compar" (or *compare*) technically meant "godfather," but it often simply designated a close male friend, a gossip, as it does here. The female equivalent is *comare* (*comar*) and is applied to *compar* Pietro's wife in the story.

p. 447 *in the bed with her husband*: Zita (which means Little Girl in the Tuscan dialect) was a common name in southern Italy, and there was a Saint Zita (c. 1212–1272) from Tuscany who was the patron saint of maids and domestic servants. Carapresa (Dear—or Precious—Acquisition) is the name of the woman from the island of Trapani off the northern coast of Sicily who appears in Story 5.2. Giudice (Judge) was also a common southern Italian name, and an actual Giudice Leo appears in chancellery records from the town of Bitonto. The wife's name, which appears a little later in the story, is Gemmata, which means One Adorned with Gems.

p. 450 *asked him for such a favor again*: Bitonto was a market town ten miles west of Bari and held a famous fair on All Saints' Day, just eleven days before a similar fair at Barletta. Boccaccio chooses the name, however, for its suggestiveness, since it could be read as *bi-* (or *bis*) + *tonto*, "twice stupid." Pietro is twice stupid, first for being tricked by the priest and then, according to his wife, for having to return to his ordinary life. That we are repeatedly told he uses an *ass* to carry his goods is also suggestive.

DAY 10, STORY 3

p. 453 *and becomes Nathan's friend*: There are some antecedents for this story in Persian and Arabic literature, and especially in Arab legends concerning Hatim Tai, a heroic character from the pre-Islamic period who was celebrated for his courage, wisdom, and unmatched generosity. A story in Arabic about this figure may have shaped elements in the life of Saint John the Merciful (also known as Saint John the Almsgiver), which is included in Jacobus de Voragine's *Legenda aurea* (*The Golden Legend*), 27; Saint John, who was the Patriarch of Alexandria from 606 to 616, was famous for his liberality, especially toward the poor. In Hebrew, the name Nathan means He Who Has Given. The name Mithridanes (Boccaccio writes Mitridanes) seems to be Boccaccio's invention. It may have been meant to echo Mithra or Mithras, a Persian god who was the center of a mystery religion practiced in the Roman Empire from the 1st to the 4th century C.E., but since the character in the story has little or nothing in common with the Persian god and the religious practices he inspired, Boccaccio may simply intend to evoke the exotic by means of his name, just as he does by situating the story in faraway China. Filostrato tells this story.

p. 454 *was rich beyond compare*: Both Nathan and the palace he has built (which is referred to in the next sentence) seem to echo what the Venetian Marco Polo reported about Kublai Khan and his residences in Cathay (that is, northern China), but Boccaccio has deliberately named the Genoese, not the Venetians, as the source of his story, perhaps because of a typical Florentine sense of rivalry with Venice. That rivalry may also be seen in the story of Frate Alberto (4.2).

p. 457 *soon change for the better*: Nathan says that the world is *miserissimo*, which I have translated as "quite a miserly place," but the word could also mean that the world is "quite a wretched place."

DAY 10, STORY 4

p. 461 *to Niccoluccio Caccianemico, her husband*: Various antecedents for this story can be found in Eastern tale collections as well as in classical and medieval literature in the West. Boccaccio had already told a version of this story in his early prose work, *Il Filocolo*.

p. 461 *and the nobility of his blood*: Bologna is not in what is now identified as the province of Lombardy, but in Boccaccio's time the entire region north of the Apennines was referred to as Lombardy. The Carisendi, like the Caccianemico mentioned in the next sentence, was actually a noble family in the city, and there is still a leaning tower there named after them. Catalina (in the next sentence) is the Bolognese form of Caterina (Catherine).

p. 462 *where the lady was buried*: Modena and Bologna are about twenty-four miles apart.

p. 467 *"Stand up, compare," he said*: Gentile identifies Niccoluccio as his *compare* and later calls Catalina his *comare*. These terms mean "godfather" and "godmother," but could also designate something like a close friend or what was once called a gossip, which is how Gentile uses them here.

p. 467 *baptism and named Gentile*: Gentile's name means "noble" or "gentle," and the word designates both a class position and a set of ethical attributes. In some ways, the story identifies its protagonist's magnanimous behavior as the epitome of gentility or gentle behavior, but there are moments, such as this one, in which Gentile makes himself into the godfather of Niccoluccio's child and names the child after himself, which may give one pause.

DAY 10, STORY 5

p. 469 *any sort of payment from him*: As with the preceding story, Boccaccio had told a version of this one in *Il Filocolo*. It has Eastern antecedents in Chinese, Indian, Persian, and other literatures as well as in that of medieval France. Chaucer's "The Franklin's Tale" resembles it, although scholars are not sure that Chaucer knew the *Decameron* the way he knew (and translated or adapted) many of Boccaccio's earlier works. It is more likely that both writers were working from a common, probably French, source.

p. 469 *exceptionally pleasant and amiable*: Friuli, a province located in the northeastern part of Italy, was—and is—known for its severe winters. Udine is its main city. Neither Dianora nor her husband has a last name in the story, and thus their identities cannot be determined. Nor can that of Ansaldo Gradense, who is mentioned in the next sentence, although his last name means his family probably came from the town of Grado, which was also located in Friuli.

p. 471 *trees and fruit of every kind*: The "calends" is the first of the month.

p. 471 *almost nothing they can't accomplish*: Boccaccio is echoing a classical notion, formulated by Cicero as *Nil difficile amanti* (*Orator* 10: "Nothing is difficult for a lover").

p. 474 *could be compared to this one*: In her conclusion, Emilia is referring, of course, to the previous story.

DAY 10, STORY 6

p. 474 *marriages for her and her sister*: There is no literary source for this story. Its principal figure, Charles the Old, usually referred to as Charles I (1226–1285), was Charles of Anjou who ruled as the King of Sicily from 1266 to 1282, when he was expelled from the island; he was known thereafter as the King of Naples, which he controlled until his death. Charles, who also appears in the tale of Madama Beritola (Story 2.6), is generally treated sympathetically by Boccaccio. He was actually a notorious womanizer, and since the story is set just after 1266, he can hardly be called "the Old."

p. 474 *the Guelfs allowed to return*: Manfred (1232–1266), a Hohenstaufen and son of the Holy Roman Emperor Frederick II, had usurped the throne of Sicily from his nephew Conradin (1252–1268) in 1258. The papacy wished to detach the Kingdom of Sicily (which included Naples and southern Italy) from the Holy Roman Empire, and enlisted Charles of Anjou to conquer it, which he did by winning the battle of Benevento on February 26, 1266, at which Manfred was killed. This led to the expulsion from Florence of the Ghibellines, who supported the empire, and the reinstatement of the Guelfs, who supported the papacy.

p. 475 *under the protection of King Charles*: Messer Neri degli Uberti cannot be identified with any specific historical figure, although the Uberti was a powerful Ghibelline family in Florence. Its most famous member was Farinata degli Uberti, immortalized by Dante in *Inferno* 10, who had served with Manfred in his victory over the Florentine Guelfs at the battle of Montaperti in 1260. Farinata died in 1264, but after defeating Manfred in 1266, Charles had Farinata's children hunted down, imprisoned, and murdered. Boccaccio's Charles is a very different ruler. Note that some critics have found it strange for Boccaccio to have Messer Neri, a Ghibelline, elect to live anywhere in Charles's realm.

p. 475 *with an abundant supply of fish*: Castellammare di Stabia is a resort on the southeast side of the Bay of Naples. The Angevin rulers of the city had a summer palace built there in 1310.

p. 475 *according to Messer Neri's instructions*: Guy de Montfort, one of Charles's most loyal followers, was appointed his vice regent in Tuscany in 1270. During that same year, in revenge for the killing of his father, he murdered Prince Henry, the nephew of Henry III of England, in the Cathedral of Viterbo during High Mass. Dante places him in the part of Hell reserved for those who committed acts of violence against their neighbors (see *Inferno* 12.119–20).

p. 477 *the other, Isotta the Blond*: Ginevra and Isotta (or Isolde) were common names in courtly romances.

p. 478 *had come down there to sing*: Medieval theologians believed there were nine (in some cases, seven) orders of angels arranged in a hierarchy. The most influential classification was that of Pseudo-Dionysius the Areopagite from the 5th century, whose hierarchy included (ranging from the lowest to the highest): Angels, Archangels, Principalities, Powers, Virtues, Dominions, Thrones, Cherubim, and Seraphim.

p. 479 *more glorious to conquer oneself*: Conradin I, Manfred's nephew, led an army to Italy in an attempt to retake Sicily from Charles in 1267. He was defeated at the battle of Tagliacozzo in August 1268, and after he fled, he was captured and turned over to Charles, who had him tried and beheaded in Naples on October 29. With Conradin's death, the legitimate branch of the Hohenstaufens became extinct.

p. 479 *splendor of your achievements*: In the preceding sentence, Count Guy rehearses a well-known saying of Publilius Syrus: *Bis vincit qui se vincit in victoria* ("he conquers twice who, when victorious, conquers himself"). In this sentence, he echoes the argument, though not the exact words, that the Roman general Scipio Africanus used to persuade Massinissa, a Roman ally, to give Sophonisba, the beautiful wife of the defeated African king Syphax, up to the Romans rather than to ravish her; see Livy, *Ab urbe condita* (*From the Founding of the City*), 30.14.

p. 480 *were noble knights and great lords*: The Palizzi family was one of the most powerful in Messina and had ties to the Uberti; Matteo was a common name among its male members. There was a Guiglielmo d'Alemagna (William of Germany) in the retinue of Charles's son in 1306, and the family was still flourishing in Boccaccio's time.

DAY 10, STORY 7

p. 481 *always calls himself her knight*: Several chronicles recount the story of a certain Macalda di Scaletta who fell in love with King Peter of Aragon after he entered her town as a conqueror. There was also a now-lost poem on the subject, from which the poetical material in the center of this story may derive. Boccaccio's story thus seems an unfolding of the kind of biographical scenario that courtly love lyrics often seem to be alluding to. Since Peter of Aragon was a Ghibelline (and thus a supporter of the Holy Roman Empire's claims in Italy), while the protagonist of the previous story was a Guelf (and thus a supporter of the papacy), the two stories balance one another nicely.

p. 481 *was then of marriageable age*: There were seven distinct families named Puccini living in Florence during this period, but none of them had a Bernardo among its members. The King Peter mentioned in the next sentence was Peter III of Aragon (born 1239, ruled 1276–85). Famed for his great stature and physical strength, he became ruler of Sicily in September of 1282, after the French, who had held the island since 1266, were expelled during the revolt known as the Sicilian Vespers, which began on March 31, 1282.

p. 481 *with some other ladies*: To joust "in the Catalan fashion" meant to follow the rules established in Catalonia, which had been united with the Kingdom of Aragon in the 12th century.

p. 482 *for Minuccio d'Arezzo to come and see her*: There was a Mino d'Arezzo (Minuccio is a diminutive) who was a minor 13th-century poet active in Sicily during this period. King Peter was also a poet and welcomed poets and musicians in his court.

p. 482 *the consolation he intended*: The "viol" (Boccaccio writes *viuola;* the more common French name was *vielle*) was a stringed instrument like the modern violin, but with a longer, deeper body and an indeterminate number of strings; it could be bowed or plucked and was used to accompany singing or dancing. "Dance tunes" is my translation of *stampita,* a rhythmic instrumental composition accompanying a poem.

p. 484 *to compose the following little song*: A Mico da Siena is named by Dante in his *De vulgari eloquentia* (*On Vernacular Eloquence*), 1.13, and a song directly attributed to him is preserved in a Vatican codex. The name Mico was short for either Michele or Amico ("Friend") and was quite common in Sicily in the period. It is most likely, however, that the poem is Boccaccio's and represents his attempt to compose verse in the then somewhat archaic style of the so-called Sicilian School, a group of poets who were attached to the courts of Frederick II and his son Manfred. These poets wrote during the middle third of the 13th century and included Tuscans and Sicilians as well as King Frederick himself. In keeping with the archaic flavor of Boccaccio's poem, I have elected to translate it using at times slightly older forms of English.

p. 488 *two excellent, very lucrative fiefs*: Cefalú is located in the province of Palermo; Calatabellotta, in that of Agrigento. I have translated Boccaccio's *terre* (literally, "lands") as "fiefs" in order to reflect the emphatically medieval character of this story. Even though fiefs and the feudal system are usually thought of as being typical of northern rather than southern Europe, Sicily had been conquered by the Normans in the 11th century and was later ruled by the Hohenstaufens, the Angevins, and the Aragonese, all of whom maintained versions of the feudal system on the island.

DAY 10, STORY 9

p. 489 *then returns with her to his house*: The first part of this tale has antecedents in stories concerning Saladin that spread his legend throughout Europe, including some that had him going about among Christians in disguise. One such story appears in the *Novellino* (23), for example. There are even more antecedents in the literature of the Middle Ages for elements in the second half of Boccaccio's tale (Messer Torello's magical voyage and his appearance at the wedding of his wife). Panfilo tells this story.

p. 490 *generous deeds performed by Saladin*: Saladin (Salah al-Din, 1138–1193) was the Sultan of Cairo and was most famous for the reconquest of Jerusalem from the crusaders in 1187. A popular figure in medieval literature, he was celebrated for his knowledge, his chivalry, his military leadership, and his generosity. The Frederick I (1122–1190) who is mentioned in the next paragraph—also known as Frederick Barbarossa ("of the Red Beard")—was a German king and Holy Roman emperor (from 1152 on). One of the leaders of the Third Crusade, with Richard the Lion-Hearted of England and Philip II of France, which began in 1189, he drowned in the Saleph River, which is in modern-day Turkey, the following year.

p. 490 *protect himself from them*: Babylon is the medieval name for Cairo.

p. 490 *and two of his wisest senior counselors*: Since both Muslims and Christians made pilgrimages in the Middle Ages, Saladin's doing so would not have been perceived as unusual.

p. 490 *on the banks of the Ticino*: There are records of a Torello who was Frederick II's *podestà* in various cities during the early 13th century; he may also have been a poet who wrote works in Provençal. Torello was a popular name in Tuscany in the late Middle Ages and is a nickname (with a diminutive ending) probably derived from Salvatore; *torello* in Italian means "little bull," although how that could apply to Boccaccio's character is uncertain. The last part of his name means that he comes from Strà (or Strada, Street) in the province of Pavia, which is about twenty miles south of Milan and lies on the east bank of the Ticino River.

p. 498 *with the rest of the Christian forces*: Boccaccio is following inaccurate contemporary accounts of the battle of Acre. The city, called Saint John of Acre, had been captured by crusaders in 1104 but was taken back by Saladin's army in 1187, only to be attacked two years later by members of the Third Crusade. Saladin attempted to lift the siege unsuccessfully, and the crusaders eventually captured the city in 1191. During the siege, disease ravaged the camps of both the armies. Acre was finally recaptured by the Muslims in 1291.

p. 498 *who was the Abbot of San Pietro in Ciel d'Oro*: The Church of San Pietro in Ciel d'Oro (Saint Peter in the Sky of Gold) stands in the center of Pavia.

p. 500 *and not the man from Dignes*: Dignes (more accurately, Digne) is a town in the French Alps at one time controlled by the Angevin rulers of Naples.

p. 501 *would first put him to sleep*: Although magic has a significant presence in medieval literature, Boccaccio is skeptical about it, as he clearly is in Story 8.7, and he rarely accords it much of a place in the *Decameron*. On this day, however, which is devoted to examples of magnanimity, his narrators sometimes include magical elements, thus giving their stories an increasingly exalted—if implausible—character.

p. 505 *remarry against her will*: Adalieta is a diminutive of Adelaide, a popular name among noble families.

DAY 10, STORY 10

p. 509 *everyone else to do so as well*: Although there are many examples of faithful wives put to harsh tests in medieval literature, the clearest source for this story is that of Job in the Bible. No scholar has been able to find anyone in the historical record who resembles Griselda. Indeed, her name seems to have been invented by Boccaccio, possibly as an ironic variation of Criseida, the notably unfaithful lover of Troilo (Troilus) in his romance *Il Filostrato*. Saluzzo is a town south of Turin lying in the foothills of the Alps. It was ruled by a series of marquises between 1142 and 1548, one of whom named Gualtieri was mentioned in a document dating from 1174 to 1175.

p. 509 *bestowing on Messer Torello*: Dioneo is alluding to the language used by the heroine in Story 7.1.

p. 509 *but of senseless brutality*: Dioneo's phrase here, *matta bestialità* (literally, "insane bestiality"), echoes Dante, who uses it to sum up the two types of sins in the lowest regions of Hell (see *Inferno* 11.82–83). The concept was developed by Saint Thomas Aquinas in his commentary on Aristotle's *Nicomachean Ethics*, 7.1.1.

p. 511 *need to find out from her*: Giannucole is a diminutive of Giovanni and means Johnny or Little John.

p. 513 *graciously bestowed on me*: Griselda's response here echoes what Mary says to the Angel Gabriel: *Fiat mihi secundum verbum tuum* (Luke 1.38: "be it unto me according to thy word").

p. 516 *completely naked when you took me*: Compare Job's words: *nudus egressus sum de utero matris meae et nudus revertar illuc Dominus dedit Dominus abstulit sit nomen Domini benedictum* (Job 1.21: "Naked came I out of my mother's womb, and naked shall I return thither: the Lord gave, and the Lord hath taken away; blessed be the name of the Lord").

p. 517 *one of the counts of Panago*: Panago (or, more correctly, Panico) was located near Bologna and was ruled by counts of the Alberti family.

p. 517 *I am ready and willing*: Another biblical allusion, this time to Mary's *Ecce ancilla Dei* (Luke 1.38: "Behold the handmaiden of the Lord").

p. 519 *his wife as I am with you*: Gualtieri's "I believe I may boast" (*credendomi poter dar vanto*) is a formula used by medieval knights who would boast, often at the dinner table, of some heroic deed they had done or some extraordinary possession they had, challenging the others present to match their claim.

DAY 10, CONCLUSION

p. 521 *the highest form of human intelligence*: Boccaccio is here paraphrasing Dante's *Convivio* (*The Banquet*): *Conviene adunque essere prudente, cioè savio: e a ciò essere si richiede buona memoria de le vedute cose, buona conoscenza de le presenti e buona provedenza de le future* (4.27.5: "Thus one must be prudent, that is, wise, for which it is necessary for one to have a good memory of things seen in the past, good knowledge of those in the present, and good foresight with regard to those in the future").

p. 522 *very pleasantly, as follows*: "Carole" were dances in which the dancers joined hands and moved in a clockwise direction, usually accompanied by music and the singing of the dancers themselves.

THE AUTHOR'S CONCLUSION

p. 524 *I have done very well here*: Boccaccio's self-defense here was a commonplace in medieval poetics.

p. 525 *one nail and sometimes with two*: In the early Middle Ages, Christ was depicted on the cross with four nails hammered into his two hands and feet. A new tradition arose in the late 12th century of their being just three nails (one for the two feet together), because of the symbolic significance of the number three. Boccaccio's references to Christ as male and Eve as female, like his reference to Christ on the cross, may also evoke the image of the naked body, which has particular resonance at this point in his text.

p. 525 *it would preserve their lives*: Boccaccio's last comment here refers to a common saying about how topsy-turvy the world is, but it also recalls an earlier story (9.2) in which the crime of an adulterous Abbess is discovered because she has mistakenly placed her lover's breeches on her head.

p. 525 *people suffering from a fever*: Both Cinciglione and Scolaio were proverbial drunkards (the former is also mentioned in Story 1.6).

p. 526 *sufficient number to form an army*: In medieval literature concerned with Charlemagne (the so-called Matter of France), the Paladins were his twelve peers; the term was later extended to mean all knights. It originally designated the Roman emperor's chamberlain and personal guards who lived with him in his palace in Rome on the Palatine Hill (from which the word is derived). The term was later used for high officials in the Catholic Church, the Holy Roman Empire, and various countries throughout Europe.

p. 527 *hidden within its bosom*: The "sign on its brow" is the summary of each story, the "rubric," that Boccaccio has placed at its beginning.

p. 528 *the surface of the water*: Aside from the sexual banter in this passage, Boccaccio is doubtless joking about the fact that he was actually quite corpulent.

p. 528 *easily be able to cure them*: The "Lamentations of Jeremiah" were sung during Holy Week. There were several medieval poems on the Passion of Christ, and there were several other poems called The Complaint (or Lament) of Mary Magdalene to which Boccaccio may be alluding, although his reference in this case may simply be generic. (The Lament is also mentioned in Story 3.4.)

p. 528 *would be most agreeable*: Boccaccio is, of course, being ironic in praising friars for avoiding hard work. His image of their "grinding when the millpond is full" is a reference to their sexual behavior, suggesting that they have sex, but only at infrequent intervals (that is, "when the millpond is full"). That they smell like billy goats may refer both to their filthiness and to their randiness, since goats have been credited with excessive sexual appetites since antiquity. Note that all of these statements about friars have appeared before, sometimes verbatim, in the *Decameron* (see Cipolla's comments in his sermon in Story 6.10 for the references to friars avoiding hard work and the allusion to goats, and a comment about the priest of Varlungo in Story 8.2 for the millpond image.

ABOUT THE NORTON LIBRARY

Exciting texts you can't get anywhere else

The Norton Library is the only series that offers an inexpensive, student-friendly edition of Emily Wilson's groundbreaking version of Homer's *Odyssey*, or Carole Satyamurti's thrilling, prize-winning rendition of the *Mahabharata*, or Michael Palma's virtuoso *terza rima* translation of Dante's *Inferno*—to name just three of its unique offerings. Distinctive translations like these, exclusive to the Norton Library, are the cornerstone of the list, but even texts originally written in English offer unique distinctions. Where else, for instance, will you find an edition of John Stuart Mill's *Utilitarianism* edited and introduced by Peter Singer? Only in the Norton Library.

The Norton touch

For more than 75 years, W. W. Norton has published texts that are edited with the needs of students in mind. Volumes in the Norton Library all offer editorial features that help students read with more understanding and pleasure—to encounter the world of the work on its own terms, but also to have a trusted travel guide navigate them through that world's unfamiliar territory.

Easy to afford, a pleasure to own

Volumes in the Norton Library are inexpensive—among the most affordable texts available—but they are designed and produced with great care to be easy on the eyes, comfortable in the hand, and a pleasure to read and re-read over a lifetime.

W. W. NORTON & COMPANY
Independent Publishers Since 1923